QUIET BRAVERY

A NOVEL

by

P. A. Varley

QUIET BRAVERY is a work of fiction. Names, characters, places, and incidents either are the product of the author's imagination or are used fictitiously. Any resemblance to actual persons, living or dead, events, or locales is entirely coincidental.

Dedication

To my amazing husband who suffered deprivation and hardship but remained a complete and compassionate human being.

Hungary
Szeged
Pécs
Arad
Alba Iulia
Zagreb
Subotica
Deva
Sibiu
Timishoara
Croatia
Romania
Karlovac
Osijek
Novi Sad
Zrenjanin
Petroshani
Slavonski Brod
Reshita
Ramnicu Valcea
Panchevo
Belgrade
Banja Luka
Brčko
Drobeta-Turnu Severin
Bosnia-Herzegovina
Tuzla
Smederevska Palanka
Craiova
Zenica
Zadar
Serbia
Bor
Sarajevo
Požega
Vidin
Split
Montana
Pleven
Mostar
Niš
Vratsa
Novi Pazar
Bijelo Polje
Leskovac
Bulgaria
Montenegro
Sofia
Priština
Pernik
Dubrovnik
Kosovo
Podgorica
Kyustendil
Adriatic Sea
Shkodër
Skopje
Bar
Tetovo
Blagoevgrad
Veles
Manfredonia
Gostivar
Foggia
Barletta
Macedonia
Tirana
F.Y.R.O.M
Durrës
Serres
Bari
Ohrid
Bitola
Kavala
Italy
Albania
Matera
Brindisi
Thessaloniki
Potenza
Taranto
Korçë
Lecce
Vlorë
Kastoria
Greece

Significant Characters

The Berisha Family

Babush [*m* Nona]	**Midge Arif [*m* Teze]**	**Midge Hasan**
Skender (eldest son)	Jakup (eldest son)	Aslan (son)
m Gillian	Emin (son)	Besim (son)
Drita (daughter)	Hava (daughter)	Nurije (daughter)
	Ilyria (daughter)	

The Mali Family

Migje Mali [*m* Mrs. Mali]
Sabri (eldest son)
Luan (son)
Vehpi (son)
Jusuf (son)

UDBA – Yugoslavian Secret Police

Colonel-Director Victor Popovich	Head of Udba
Colonel Stefan Mihajlovich	Udba Director, Kosovo Province
Colonel Bora Vucsich	Udba Director, Rep. of Croatia
Captain Alex Kulich	Udba Director, Rep. of Bosnia
Anna	Secretary to Colonel Mihajlovich
Sergeant Dragonovitch	Sergeant, City of Pristina Police

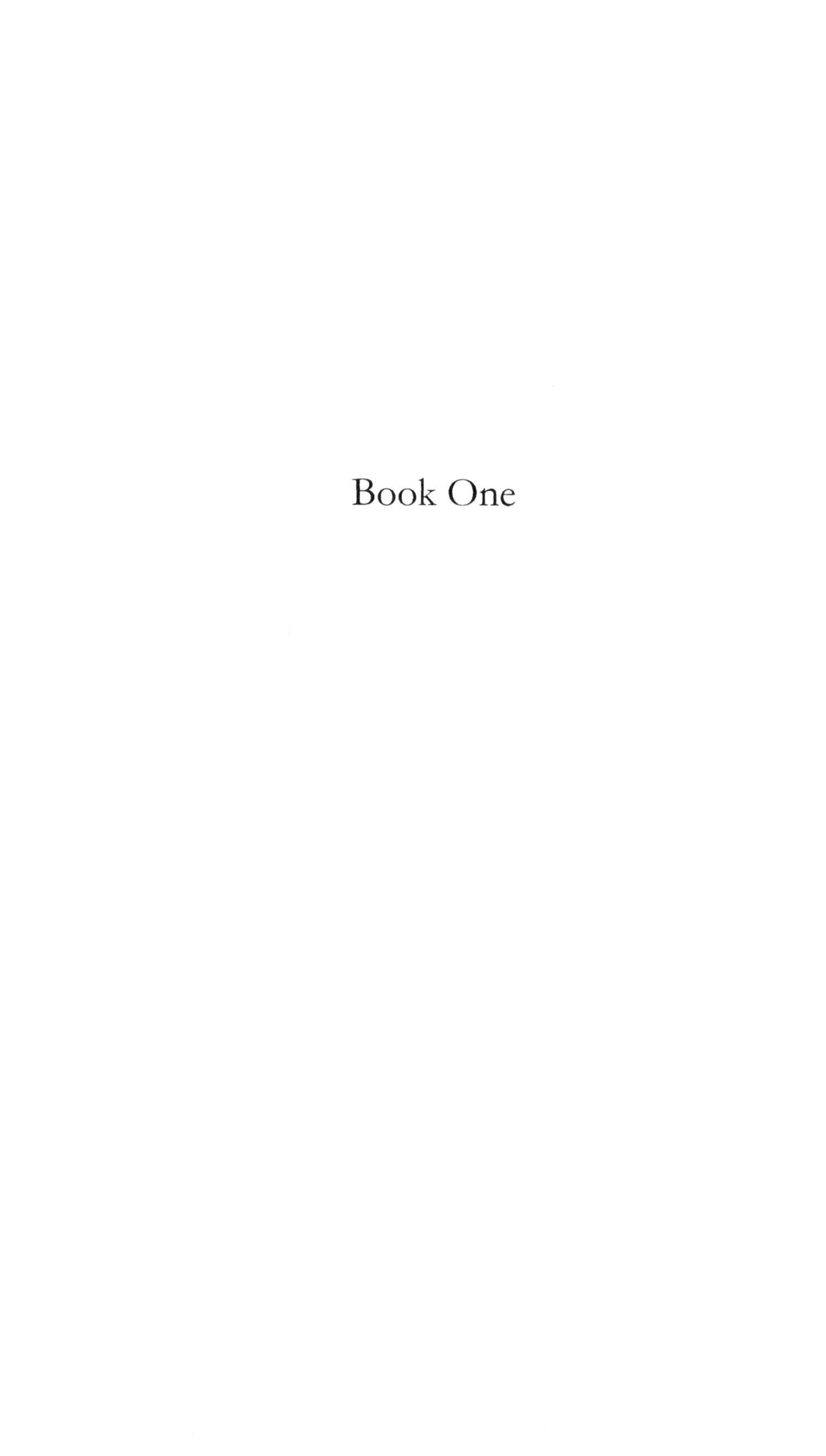

Book One

Chapter 1

Prishtine, Kosov (... late 1960s)

The taxi driver picked his way carefully between the icy patches on the deeply rutted street and halted outside 1764 Ruga Lapit. The passenger, a man in his thirties of medium height and with thick dark brown hair, pulled the heavy suitcase from the taxi, included a generous tip with the fare requested, and watched as the taxi slithered and slid down the street and out of sight. He pulled his coat tightly about him as he turned.

The big wooden gate was before him. With a shaking hand he felt its rough, unfinished surface. How often he had stood here, reached for this moment of touch and found soft sheets usu+0rping that rough wood. He breathed deeply, a long, steadying breath and pushed against the only barrier between him and those he loved and longed to see. The gate opened with a protesting groan. *Still needs oiling … after seventeen years the damn thing still needs oiling.*

He closed the gate behind him and turned toward the house, dark, save for the one softly lit window. Tall brick walls on each side of the path obscured everything but the full pale moon which lit his way. He walked carefully on the frosty surface, passed beneath the lighted window and climbed the stairs to the front door which yielded to his touch.

The small room was glass enclosed. A bench-style seat, approximately twelve inches deep, ran around three sides of the room and the well-worn floorboards were bare. Three pairs of shoes were placed side by side on the left of the door. Old memories stirred as he bent, undid his laces, and removed his shoes, as was their custom. He placed them beside the others, neatly, as he had been taught as a child.

The family were alone tonight, the shoes told him that, and he was glad that there were no visitors. Soft voices flowed through the door on the right and, careful not to make a sound, he went toward it. The handle turned effortlessly, and he stood in silence, letting the scene soak into the very core of his being.

It's hardly changed. I could have stepped back in time; the room is the same.

The older woman sat nearest to the stove, warming first one hand and then the other. The young one sat beside her with the old man on her right. Both women wore the traditional Kosov dress, long-sleeved blouse with high neck and long harem-style pants, very full and gathered in at the ankles. The young one's hair wound around her head in a thick rope and was uncovered, indicating that she was unmarried. A dark brown scarf covered her mother's hair and came down to within an inch of her eyebrows, knotted in a complicated fashion behind and underneath, giving the effect of a nun's wimple. Her blouse was dark brown too, and her dimi was of a somber hue and not as full as the young girl's.

The old man was splendid! The heavy woolen trousers of dark brown with contrasting trim of black fitted tightly below the knee to the ankles and his waist was encircled with a black and white striped cummerbund. His long, drooping mustache was snow white and he puffed constantly on an unlit pipe, his head nodding rhythmically with his puffing. A soft, white felt hat, round like a basin, was pushed to the back of his head, a true Kosovar!

The young girl was talking animatedly to the old man who had been listening with a slight smile, but he interrupted the flow of words with a gesture toward the stove.

Immediately, the girl stopped her chatter, raised herself to her knees and, taking a pot from the side of the stove, poured tea into small crystal glasses, each delicately laced with gold filigree. Carefully she added a spoon of sugar and stirred. With her left hand she picked up one of the full glasses, held out her right hand with the first three fingers extended and sat the brimming glass of amber tea on them. With a slight bow of her head, she offered the tea to her father. "Babush." She sat quietly awaiting his nod of approval, and then picked up a second glass. Again, using the three fingers of her right hand as a tray. She offered the tea to her mother. "Nona," she murmured with a slight bow of her head.

The older woman leaned forward to accept the tea and, in doing so, the doorway came into view. For a second, and eternity, they stared at each other. "Djali?" Her trembling lips could hardly form the word.

He wanted to speak the beloved name, but no sound came. How many times he had cried out for his mother and now, when she was within hearing, touching distance, his tongue would not obey. He gave a slow nod.

All four watched the dark, swiftly spreading stain of the tea on the brilliant rugs and then the old woman half rose. "Djali? Djali?" Disbelief, hope, joy, tears, were in her voice as she pushed herself to her feet, never taking her eyes from him. "Is it you, Djali? Has God returned my son to me?"

"Yes Nona, it's me." Skender moved as she held out her arms to him. She almost fell when she heard his voice, but he caught her. "Hush, hush, I am here." He soothed her as they clung together, tears mingling as cheeks touched.

"I knew one day I would hold you again," she said between sobs. "Even in the darkest days, the longest nights, I knew…."

"Hush, you have me in your arms." He started to lower her to the rugs, whispering, "I must greet my father." He felt her take a long, deep breath, deliberately calming herself. He kissed her cheek, then stood, turned to the old man and bowed.

His father was already standing. Slowly he took his pipe from his mouth. "Welcome home, Skender." But the rigid self-control he sought eluded him, and for the first time he cried in front of womenfolk as he arms closed around his son.

"Babush, I have dreamed … so many years … longed … prayed for…."

"I know, Djali, I know. As have we." They held tight to each other, until each knew that the other had control. Babush gripped his son's shoulders as they drew apart. "My prayers have been answered, Skender. My son is home." He half turned, roughly smoothing his mustache as he felt tears welling again. "Drita, this is your brother."

Skender turned to face the young girl who stood shyly, eyes downcast, smiling through teeth-clenched lips. "Do you remember me, Drita? No! Of course not! That would be impossible, you were only a baby, three, I think, when I was taken…" he stopped, wondering how much she knew, "…when I left here. Come greet your brother, little sister."

She came to him then, took his right hand in her right hand, bowed over it, raised it to touch her forehead, lowered it, raised it to her lips, lowered it, and again raised it to her forehead. She released his hand, took one step back and stood before him with head bowed, awaiting his instructions.

He had watched closely, all his instincts wanted to stop this subservience, but custom and tradition demanded it so he allowed her, knowing that for her it was only right to greet him thus. Gently he took her to him and kissed her on each cheek. "Thank you, little sister, you honor me. Please, sit down." With a slight gesture of her hands she indicated that she would after he and her father were sitting.

His mother was calmer now and they sat close together, his father opposite and Drita slightly behind him. He wished she would come closer to the fire, but he knew she would not. And, while he wished she would sit beside him, he was glad and proud too that she would not and that she behaved and conducted herself in the accepted way of this land.

Drita rose, bowed to Babush. "I will bring some food for my brother," she murmured.

Skender watched her as she left the room. "I would not have known her," he sighed.

"Naturally, Djali, there is much growth from three to twenty." Babush threw a log into the fire. "The years have affected all of us."

"Yes," Skender said. "You, especially, have aged more than I expected, Nona."

"You remember your mother as you last saw her, Skender. That was the way we remembered you. You do not see the change in yourself, as we do not see the change in each other." Babush's smile was sad and a little forced as he added, "It is, perhaps, the only blessing of separation, memory gives constant youth."

"So many years, Skender," Nona sighed. "So long … seventeen years. So much fear, so much sadness and terror…." She stopped, her eyes frightened, "Is he safe here? Is it safe for him to be here?" she demanded urgently of her husband.

"Yes, yes," Babush spoke soothingly, "He is safe. There is no need for you to fear. Let your worries rest, put them from you. Ah, good, here is Drita."

Skender stood as his sister came toward him. In her right hand she carried a jug of warm water, her left hand held a bowl. Across her left arm a clean towel hung. She was nervous and he wanted to comfort her, to tell her not to worry, and that he loved her.

The water poured in a thin, continuous stream over his hands, and she caught it in the bowl held beneath them. She waited, eyes downcast never looking directly at him, until he had dried his hands and returned the towel to her arm. He took a step toward her as she carried in a table, but stopped himself, realizing he must not offer his help.

The table was round, the wood almost white from much scrubbing, and stood about ten inches off the ground on three legs. She smoothed a bright red cloth over the table, leaving a good twelve inches of extra cloth to drape to the floor.

Skender sat down, cross-legged, and picked up the overhanging cloth and laid it across his lap. Babush and Nona joined him at the table although they did not eat. Soft, sour-tasting goat cheese, pickled tomatoes and bread were placed before him. He picked up the bread. "In God's name," he murmured as he broke a piece. Memories flooded him as he tasted the coarse-ground flour of the bread. *This is the first meal in my home since….* He pushed the thought away as he felt his throat constrict. *No, you cannot permit yourself that indulgence, it would place too great a strain on them….*

He ate hungrily, appreciatively of the simple meal. Drita stood slightly behind him, waiting, watching to make sure he had all he needed. He finished and, again, she brought the water and bowl for him to wash. The table and cloth were removed and she brought his coffee, serving him as she had her parents with their tea, and standing three paces back until he had drunk the thick, rich Turkish coffee. He looked up to thank her and caught her off guard, staring at him. Their eyes met and he smiled at her, but she dropped her eyes immediately and blushed furiously embarrassed to have been caught staring at a man, even though he was her brother.

"It is late," Babush said, with a glance at his wife and daughter. "You two must go to bed. A soon as it is known that Skender is home there will be many visitors and you will both have much work. Djali, come, we will go to the kitchen and have one more pipe before we, too, go to bed. Tonight, I sleep with my son," he added as he turned to Nona to bid her goodnight.

To reach the kitchen it was necessary to go outside the house. The two men, so much alike in bone structure one would not have to ask if they were father and son, slipped into their shoes, walked down the flight of steps to the garden, took a right-angled turn and went down three more steps to the kitchen. They left their shoes just outside the door.

The window on their right let in no light from the moon. Beneath the window a large wooden box with a table-top held various cooking pans, their dark outlines mixing and blending into a whole. A squat black wood-fired stove with two ovens occupied the opposite wall. The glow from the still-hot ashes lit the room with a softness that pleased both men and, as one, they discarded the use of electricity. Skender's toes curled into the thick rug which covered the kitchen floor, the wool still full of life and warmth although its colors were faded, its patterns indistinct. A pile of sheepskin rugs was placed near the stove.

"Let us sit, Djali." Babush's hand gave gracious permission for his son to sit down.

Skender waited until his father had settled himself, then pulled one of the sheepskin rugs closer to the fire. The cold seemed to penetrate even to his bones, and he was grateful for the warmth exuding from the hot ashes. He took out his packet of cigarettes and shook one free.

"What I said to your mother…" Babush painstakingly pushed a strand of tobacco into the bowl of his pipe, nodded his thanks to Skender as he took the lighted match and pulled deeply on his pipe. He waited until the tobacco was well-lit and then continued, "What I said to your mother was to comfort her, she has suffered much and has aged more than her years. I do not know if it is safe for you here, Skender. There have been changes since … things are a little better now, but…" Babush's shoulders lifted. "The authorities' power is absolute, unquestionable, we still live with fear." Babush's voice was low, pitched for Skender's ear alone.

"I burn to hear your story, I ache to know what happened to you since they snatched you from the bosom of this family; but, for now the most important thing is that you know what is expected of you, Skender Berisha, while you are in Kosov. Tomorrow morning you must go to Police Headquarters to register." He saw the start, the sudden pallor. "It is the law, and you, Skender, must obey every law that exists, while you are here. You must do nothing, nothing, to bring their eyes in your direction. Do you understand?"

"Yes, sir," Skender licked his dry lips, "What do you mean, register?"

"The law is explicit; any visitor must register with the Police. Anyone, visitor or resident of Kosov, must obtain permission if they wish to leave this city."

"But what if you wish to visit a relative, or a friend, in another part of Kosov?"

"You must obtain a permit. Anyone spending three nights or more in a bed other than his own must register with the police of that town or city." Babush pulled on his pipe, "Do you understand, Djali?"

"Yes," Skender's face was grim, "I understand, they know where you are at all times."

Babush nodded. "Exactly. Where you are, where you will be, how long you will be there." He blew out a long puff of smoke, "And when you will return."

"Such control … I had almost forgotten how closely they watch." Skender's voice was a whisper.

"And in America…?"

"Nothing. You can go and come as you please … when you please. See, speak, stay with whomever you wish."

Babush nodded. "You must be careful, Skender. While you are in Kosov, you must forget this sweetness. It will not be easy."

They puffed quietly on their smokes, watching the changing patterns in the fire. "Seventeen years … so long ago, another lifetime. And yet, sometimes, yesterday. I was always so proud of you; you were such a good boy. A boy … they took a boy from me, and now look at you … a man, full-grown, married…." His clenched fist struck at his forehead. "Your wife! Forgive me, Skender, but I had forgotten … where is your nusé?"

"In England, with her own family. I wanted to come by myself, to make sure that … I did not know how you would … if you would…." He stopped, searching for the right words.

"Skender, she is your wife, your nusé. We have accepted that. Our anger, our dismay, has passed. Surely you wished to bring her, to let us meet her?"

"Yes. I wanted you to know her, and to … and to love her. But I had to be sure. I will not subject her to any … embarrassment."

"I think the word you want is rejection. We have accepted your marriage, Djali. And we will accept your nusé. Bring her home, we will open our hearts to her."

"It will not be easy, Babush. For you or for her."

"We know she is of the West, that her customs and traditions will not be as ours, but until we meet her, begin to know her, we cannot learn to love her."

Skender smiled, "She will be here in three weeks. I want you to know her. I want her to see my birthplace, walk the same streets I walked." He shivered; fatigue was overtaking him.

Babush saw and understood his tiredness. He stood. "Skender, my years demand rest. We will sleep now, tomorrow we will talk until our throats are dry." The old man was slightly taller than his son, and he laid his arm around the younger's shoulders.

Silently he said a prayer of thankfulness that this was possible once more in his lifetime, and together they climbed the stairs to the main house.

Chapter 2

Sleep left him slowly as the tantalizing smell of baking bread teased his nostrils. He let himself lay contentedly still. The dream had become reality, he was home. He half turned toward the side of the bed where Babush had been, but only the impression of his head remained on the pillow, and Skender let himself ease back into his waking position, seeking the warmth where his body had lain as his hand crept out of the covers and reached to touch his nose.

"You still do that, eh, Djali?" Nona laughed gently as surprise brought Skender to a sitting position and the cold encouraged him back under the covers. "Well? Is it too cold to get up today?" She went to him, sat close as he held out his hand to her, then bent and kissed his cheek, murmuring softly, "Mirëmëngjes, Djali-eim."

"Mirëmëngjes, Nona." Skender continued to hold her hand and they stayed, filling their eyes with each other, quenching the thirst that had raged for so long in their hearts.

"Up! Up!" Nona turned, taking unnecessary pains at smoothing the already crease-free apron. She blinked away her tears before facing Skender. "I can never get you from your bed when it is cold. Do you wish your sister to find you here? Up. And right now, or do I still have to pull the covers from you?"

He smiled at her, letting her treat him as a child, reveling in the half-remembered, loving impatience of her voice. "Two minutes, Nona, two minutes," he promised as he had so many times before, so long ago. He permitted himself a luxurious stretch and a long sigh of contentment as the door closed on her. He lay, body stretched taut, shivered, and groaned as he anticipated the icy air, then threw back the covers.

The kitchen was fragrant with the warm, yeasty smell of baking bread. The glow of the hot ashes pulled him into the room as he stopped at the door to kick off his shoes. Drita stood as he opened the door, and Nona turned from her work at the flour box to smile a welcome.

"Mirëmëngjes, Babush."

"Mirëmëngjes, Skender." Babush interrupted his breakfast with a warm smile, dipped the hunk of rich, dark bread into his bowl of milk and asked, "Did you sleep well?"

"Thank you, sir, very well." Skender realized how hungry he was as he heard the soft sound of Babush drawing the milk from the bread, then gave a slight bow to this mother. "Nona, Mirëmëngjes again." He smiled at Drita. "Drita." She bowed to him, her eyes never raising higher than his chest.

Babush glanced at Skender. "Your sister needs to continue with her work, Djali," he murmured as he sensed Skender did not realize why she was still standing.

"I'm sorry … of course." Skender's hand moved, motioned Drita his permission as he moved to join Babush beside the fire. He pulled one of the black and white sheepskin rugs forward and prepared to sit. He stopped, barely in time, swore to himself as he realized that he had almost sat without his father's permission, indeed had even forgotten that it was needed. His eyes lifted and found Babush's on him even as the old hand moved in a gracious invitation. Skender inclined his head, lowered himself to the soft wool.

"Brother…" Drita's voice was low, nervous, as she addressed him for the first time, "would you prefer tea or coffee?"

"Coffee, please." Skender watched as Babush's head dipped to catch the milk-laden bread, hat and hair blending together. *His hair is white now, but otherwise….* The steady rhythm of Nona kneading the dough brought his attention to her. *With her back to me, now that I cannot see the lines of worry, this could be seventeen years ago. Drita … she is the one that has the greatest change. She was a child, a baby even, and now….* Drita's profile was strongly etched as she rose and stood, half turned toward the window. *She is a beautiful young woman.* He watched as she picked up the smallest of the low, round tables stacked against the wall, selected a cloth from those hung on a line above and tucked both under her arm. He stiffened as she took plate, knife, and spoon from a drawer. "Where are you going with those things?"

Babush's hand stopped halfway to his mouth at Skender's sharpness.

Drita's lips moved, but there was no sound, and she took a breath before she managed, "To … to prepare the room for your meal, brother."

"Prepare?"

Nona's and Babush's eyes met, questioned, as they heard Skender's anger.

Her tongue passed over her dry lips. "I am sorry, brother, if I had realized that you were waiting to eat…." Her eyes flicked to Babush, to Nona, "I will be quick, will be but a moment." She moved toward the door.

"Stay!" He moved with speed, stood between Drita and the door. "Where are you going with that?"

Her eyes followed his to the table, then raised to his chin. "I … upstairs, brother, to the guest…."

"The guestroom! Am I a guest?" The table clattered, rolled, and landed; three legs turned to the ceiling as he knocked it from her hands. "Am I a guest?" She stood stiff, hands clasped in front of her, eyes glued to the floor, and he took her chin and forced her to look at him as there was no response. "I am your brother. I am of this family, and as such I eat here." He forced her eyes to his. "Do you understand me?" He released her at her half-nod.

She stood in frozen immobility as he stood, watching her. He moved away from the door and, with a half-sob, she fled.

Skender lowered himself to the rug in the still room. Slowly Babush dipped the bread into his milk while Nona, too carefully, continued with her work. "I am not a guest. How dare she treat me as a stranger? I am her brother…."

"Are you, Djali?" Shocked out of anger, Skender stared at Babush. "Are you her brother, Djali?"

"What on earth do you mean?" Skender's startled eyes flew from Babush to Nona, but she did not turn, only continued with the steady movement of her hands to work the dough.

Babush continued to watch Skender as he bent his head and took a bite of the milk-laden bread, he chewed slowly before swallowing. "You arrived here last night, grown, already a man, her brother, yes, but also a stranger." He put down his bowl of milk.

"You two have never played and fought as all brothers and sisters do and should. She has never had you here to advise her, to share her confidences and listen to her dreams. How can you expect her to think of you as her brother? You are a stranger to her. And … you are a man." Babush's smile held a trace of sadness as Skender's eyes questioned him. "Have you forgotten, Skender, how our girls are raised? We took Drita from school when she was sixteen, the way all good families do, and since that time, four years, no man outside of our own family has looked at her. Remember that. Remember, too, that she has seen no man. Into her sheltered life you drop, her brother, but a stranger, and a man … a man who has not only the right to look at her, but to put his hand on her."

Skender's eyes closed as he remembered the wild flush when he had held his sister's chin. Babush had to lean forward to catch his words. "I had forgotten." He started to push himself to his feet. "I will go to her, explain…."

"You will not. Sit down!" Babush's command returned Skender to his seat. "You will not embarrass your sister further by witnessing her distress, she needs time to gain control."

Skender sat, head bent, his words ragged as he asked, "She has no recollection of me at all?"

Babush laid his hand on Skender's arm. "If she remembers you at all it was as a young boy, laughing, full of fun, with your white hat pushed so far forward only your eyebrows held it in place! You must give her time, Skender, time to combine this memory with the stranger who sits here dressed in Western clothes." He smiled as Skender started. "Of course! This style of clothing has become commonplace to you, but for us, for her especially … I see you begin to understand her confusion."

"Yes."

"Skender, listen to me. You have been gone from us for many years, and in those years you have had to learn, and accept, customs from other lands. This is only right, and to be expected. But remember ours. Remember our ways, our traditions, our rules, and honor them." He laid his hand on Skender's shoulder to stop him from standing as he rose. "It is important that you do not forget." He smiled. "Come, wife, feed this son of ours. I will see you later, Skender," he added as Nona pushed the pan of milk over the hottest part of the stove.

"Yes, sir." He caught the affectionate smile as his parents said their good-byes.

"I will be back within the hour; I am just going to walk the cow."

Skender's startled expression brought a smile from Nona. "He is going to do what, Nona?"

"We have a cow…" Nona checked the milk, "…it is forbidden but nearly everyone has one, your father is going to take ours for some exercise." She laughed as she cut a slice of the rich bread, dark and moist inside, with a crisp crust that crumbled under the knife. She poured a full bowl of the hot milk and passed it to Skender. "Eat, Djali, and then, if you hurry, you will be able to go to the river and see the men walking the cows which we are forbidden to have!"

Chapter 3

It was bitterly cold. He was glad of the heavy coat, and he pulled the collar up around his neck as he picked his way down the icy street to the river. He turned the corner and stood, staring in astonishment. The riverbanks were busy with old men walking up and down, each leading a milk cow, stopping to exchange words with a friend now and then. The crisp air was rent with the noise of cows greeting each other, their breath sending spirals of steam into the atmosphere. "It looks more like market day in a country village than a busy city," Skender marveled. "And from among all those old heads, each covered with the same white hat, I have to find my father! Good heavens, I don't even know what our cow looks like, so there's no help there," he laughed to himself. He started to walk the left bank, feeling the stares of many as he moved slowly forward.

"Ho, Skender, ho." The call came clearly and Skender turned to search the opposite bank for his father. "Wait there, Djali, and I will join you."

Skender watched as his father made his way through the throngs of men and animals then crossed the rickety wooden bridge which joined the two banks. "She is a fine cow, sir," he said as his father came toward him.

Babush glowed with pride. "Yes, she is. Come, let us go home, both she and I have visited enough with our friends for today." They picked their way carefully through the mud and puddles of the riverbank, the cow plodding beside them until they turned onto Ruga Lapit.

"Nona said you were not permitted to have a cow, and yet…" Skender's arm waved in the general direction of the river behind them, "…can you explain?"

"Yes, Djali, at home."

I had forgotten, forgotten that only generalities are spoken once you leave the safety of your house. Even this, the owning of a cow, cannot be discussed in a public place. Skender opened the gate and allowed his father and the cow to precede him.

"Welcome home, Babush." Drita came toward them. She gave a furtive glance at Skender before she murmured, "Welcome home, brother."

"Take the cow, Drita, and settle her and then I would like some tea, please." Babush passed the rope to Drita and started up the stairs toward the main part of the house. "Come, Skender. Your sister will bring us some tea."

The room was warm and pleasant after the cold dampness of the riverbank. Babush stood warming first one hand and then the other at the fire, then turned and stood with his back to the blaze. "Sit down, Djali, do not wait for me." He smiled. "Strange places get cold when you get older!"

"Babush … please, about the cows?" Skender sat close to the fire.

"Well, Skender, milk is very expensive and not always available. A few families decided to get a cow and when other families saw what a good thing this was, plenty of milk, always fresh, they, too, got a cow. The authorities were furious, and so a new law was written: no family is permitted to keep a cow in the garden."

"But sir, there is a cow in our garden. And in most neighbors' gardens, too, from what I saw at the river!"

"No, Skender, you are wrong. The cow is in a shed." The old eyes twinkled mischievously. "That, my son, was the mistake made by the authorities, too. They specifically said 'garden,' and so … instead of getting rid of our cows, we each built a shed!"

"But…."

"There is no 'but', Skender. The official paper says 'garden', it makes no mention of a shed. Ah, here is Drita with the tea." The old man sat down, accepted the tea from Drita. "Thank you, child, this will be most welcome." He watched Skender carefully as Drita placed the second glass of tea on her fingers, then turn toward her brother. He took it from the trembling hand and sipped appreciatively at it as he gave a nod to her. The old man gave an approving smile and waited until the door had closed on Drita. "You learn fast, Djali."

Skender placed the tea on the rug beside him. "It was not easy. I wanted to take her hand, explain, and beg her forgiveness…." He trailed off as he saw his father's shock. *I have changed, changed more than I realized.*

"Besim will be here before noon to escort you to…" Babush smoothed his mustache, "…to escort you to Police Headquarters." Skender's head jerked up. "You do remember who Besim is?"

"One of Migje Hasan's sons, I cannot remember which cousin he is…."

"Your brother, Skender. Remember that if any brother of mine has a son, then you, too, are brothers. There is a closer relationship than just cousin." Babush had spoken sharply, angry that Skender had apparently forgotten one of their strongest customs. Skender bowed his apology. "Besim is the fourth son … a good boy. I am glad Hasan is sending him."

"How old is he?"

"Seventeen, eighteen, nineteen … who knows? They grow too fast." He yawned as he took out his pipe and put it, unfilled, into his mouth and pushed his white hat to the back of his head. "The fire feels good." He held up a finger as Skender started to speak. "Later. Let us be quiet and appreciate this moment."

The crackle and hiss of burning wood was the only sound in the room. Soon the old man's eyelids began to droop. Silently, Skender left the room and went down to the kitchen. He heard his sister's laughter as he approached the door and a young, male voice telling some tall tale. He entered and the young boy leaped to his feet. Drita was busy at a low table helping her mother, but she stood when he entered, wiping her hands on the long apron, first the palms and then the backs, leaving white splashes of flour on the dark red material. He indicated with his hand that she should continue her work. With a half-bow and a smiled, "Nona," he acknowledged his mother, then turned to his cousin. He was tall, skinny, more than a boy, but not yet a man. He bowed to Skender. "Skender, I am Besim, Hasan's fourth son." Excitement lit his face, his voice, as he extended his hand. "Welcome to Kosov."

"Thank you. I am more than happy to be here." Skender was glad that the young man's grip was firm and sure. "Now, let us sit down while you finish your tea." He glanced up as Drita came and stood in front of him. "No, no tea for me, thank you."

"With your permission, brother…." Drita indicated she wished to leave the room and Skender gave a brief nod.

"I cannot express how glad, how proud, I am, we are, all of us, at having you again in your home, Skender. When my father told me…."

"Drink your tea," Skender interrupted, "we can talk as we go. Nona, what are you making?" he asked, suddenly curious.

She turned with a smile, "Can't you guess, Djali? Laknor." She turned back to her work, rolling the paper-thin dough with a rolling pin as long as her arm, as slim as a pencil.

Skender salivated in anticipation as he watched her mix the cheeses, eggs, and spinach together. "My favorite meal, it was always my favorite."

"I know." Mother's and son's eyes met, held, and they smiled at each other. "That is why I am making it." She picked up the bowl, turned the mixture onto the pastry, then started to roll more of the dough into thin, thin sheets.

Skender stood, placing his hand on Besim's shoulder as he did so, so that the young man would not have to rise. "Wait here for me, I am going to get my coat."

He opened the living room door quietly, not wishing to awaken his father. He was surprised to see Drita there. She had put a pillow beneath Babush's head, had removed the pipe and with great care was covering him with a blanket. She turned as she heard the door, looking anxiously to see who was coming to disturb her father's rest.

Skender put his finger to his lips as he moved to pick up his coat. He turned as he reached the door again, gave Drita an approving nod and a smile, then closed the door with as much care as he could. He felt in his coat pocket, yes, his passport was there. He would say goodbye to Nona and be on his way. The sooner it was accomplished, put behind him, the better.

"Brother…" the door was opened just a little, "would it be possible …just a little tobacco, for his pipe tonight?"

"Of course. I will get some on the way home. Anything else? Something for you?"

Hot color flooded her cheeks. "No, nothing, thank you. I should not have asked but … he enjoys his pipe so."

He pushed the door open a little wider, bent and kissed the smooth cheek. "He shall have it; I am glad that you asked."

Skender shrugged into his coat as he went down to the kitchen and, at the door, he bent to tie his shoes. "Nona, I am going now."

She came to him, hugged him close and hard, then whispered, "God be with you, Djali."

He held her from him, searching her face. His finger traced her cheek, wiping some flour from her face. A single tear joined the flour on his finger. He stood looking down at it, then put it to his mouth. "Too salty, Nona," he said softly. He turned, joined Besim, and together they walked the path toward the gate.

Chapter 4

The three-story building of gray stone was near the town center, three blocks off Main Square.

Fear became a living, clawing thing in Skender's stomach as they approached it. Instinct told him to turn, run, and he was hard put to continue walking quietly beside Besim toward the building where he had been detained so often in his youth.

Two policemen, talking noisily to each other, stood near the heavy doors and the sight of the blue-gray uniforms increased Skender's panic. *Don't go in there.... Don't go in there....* He took a long breath, deliberately relaxed his shoulders, and forced the screaming inner voice to silence. But it was the thick rubber that edged the doors that was almost his undoing, their soft sigh as they met each other told him that the door had closed behind him. He swallowed the collected saliva as he followed Besim toward the long counter that separated the large waiting room and the general office area.

There were two policemen at the counter. One perched on a high stool, filling out forms, he gave a glance in their direction without disturbing his work. The other came and stood opposite Skender and Besim, his arms stretched out, thumbs supporting his weight against the counter. There was no greeting, just a grunt and a jerk of his head, giving them permission to speak.

"My name is Berisha, Besim Berisha...."

Skender started, he had forgotten that Serbo-Croat would have to be spoken.

"...and here is my identity card."

I am going to have to speak it, no, not just speak it, I must think in it. If they question me, they will not give me time to listen, translate into my own language, and then answer. He watched as the guard studied Besim's identity card. *It has been seventeen years ... how much have I forgotten...?*

"What about him?" The guard's head nodded toward Skender.

"He is my cousin. He has come to visit his family."

"So why are you here?"

Besim shrugged, "Just to show him the way, keep him company."

"How long will he be staying?"

Skender realized he should answer himself, not allow the policeman to speak as if he were not there, or as if he were a child. He could not.

"Three, perhaps four, weeks."

The guard turned, addressed Skender directly for the first time, "Papers."

Skender took the soft gray-green passport from his coat pocket and silently handed it to the guard. He saw the surprise, the quick sizing up of him by the man at the sight of the American passport.

He stood, uncertainly tapping the passport against the wooden counter, then turned to his colleague and whispered to him, all the while watching Skender. The other guard slowly raised his head, his eyes were watchful, suspicious as he looked at Skender, then, without moving, said, "Dragonovich."

"You sure?" the first policeman demanded suspiciously. He received a slow nod. Still, he hesitated, tapping the passport against the wood. "Watch 'em."

Skender and Besim glanced at each other as the guard made his way across the room. "Must be outside of their jurisdiction," Besim whispered.

"Silence! You…" the blue-coated arm extended, finger pointing at Besim, "…out."

Skender saw Besim's hesitation, laid his hand on his cousin's shoulder and gave a slight nod. He felt vulnerable, isolated as the door closed on Besim. He caught the mocking grin of the guard and knew that he realized how he felt. He turned away.

"You were right…" the first policeman addressed his colleague as he returned, "…Dragonovich has to see him. Follow me," he instructed Skender as he lifted a section of the counter.

They turned left from the waiting room, Skender a pace or two behind the policeman as they walked the long corridor. A musty smell permeated the air, a strange combination of mildew, dust, and age. And despair. *Can you smell despair?* Skender wondered, and with a silent sigh answered, *Yes, you can smell it, touch it, feel it creep into your bones….*

The walls pressed in on him, the nondescript biscuit color stretching up, across the high, narrow ceiling and down again to touch the worn brown linoleum on which they strode.

They stopped. The door was brown, pitted in parts to show more brown paint beneath. There was no number, no name, nothing on the door. Skender wished he'd listened, remembered the name the policeman at the entry hall had spoken. The guard knocked, opened the door, his thumb jerked as he spoke the one word, "In."

An officer sprawled behind a desk which stood centrally in the room. There was one wooden upright chair opposite his, and another against the wall beside two filing cabinets. The desk was littered with papers; files – buff-colored – fat and thin, were piled on top of the two cabinets.

Skender was aware of the officer's swift but thorough appraisal as he took the chair indicated, opposite the man.

"Name?"

"Skender Berisha." His passport lay atop the mess, directly in front of the officer.

"Skender Berisha…." it was repeated slowly, the pronunciation correct, "well, Skender Berisha, why are you here?"

Skender sat stiffly on the edge of his chair. "I was told that I had to register with the police," he replied, thankful that his voice came firm and steady.

"No, you misunderstand. I do not ask why you are here in my police station…" the voice was lazy, unhurried, "…I ask why you are here, in this city."

"My mother and father live here. I have come to visit them."

"How nice, how very nice." The officer smiled. "And for how long do you plan to, er, visit your family?"

"Three weeks, maybe a month."

"A month? Well, well…." The tobacco-stained fingers reached for the passport, opened it, reading it with apparent carelessness.

The room was hot, stuffy. A single fly buzzed constantly around a naked bulb that seemed to be deliberately hung at eye level. Skender closed his eyes to relieve them from the brilliance for a moment.

"You are an American citizen?" The demand was harsh, quick.

"Yes." Skender cursed himself for letting this man see his weakness.

The officer sat back, stretched, lazily asked, "Why?"

"Why?" The question caught Skender off guard. "I live there, work there."

"Yes … maybe…." The officer put his hands behind his head, locking the fingers together. "But where were you born?" He rocked steadily in his chair, he smiled at Skender as the silence stretched. "Where were you born, Skender Berisha?" he asked in an amused, mocking voice. The chair snapped upright; the passport was pushed in front of Skender. A nicotine-stained finger tapped the appropriate column in the passport. "Here. You were born here." He let himself lay back in the chair again, slowly rocking. "Why did you become an American?"

The passport tantalized him with its nearness. "I live there now." His mind searched for a reason that would satisfy this man. "It was more convenient…." The silence stretched. Skender dug his nails into the palms of his hands, forcing himself to be quiet, not babble further information to his tormentor.

"Tell me, did you know that our government does not recognize this, er, 'change' of citizenship?" Dragonovich stood, sauntered to the opposite side of the desk, and sat on the edge. He leaned close to Skender and, in a confidential manner, asked again, "Did you know that?"

"No."

"You belong to us, do you understand?"

Skender swallowed. "Yes."

"Any children you have belong to us. You are ours, Berisha, ours. Remember that." He stood, walked back to the opposite side of the desk, and sat down. "Let him go."

Skender started, turned immediately toward the door. He had been unaware that the guard was still there. He stood, licked at his dry lips. "May I have my passport, please?"

"I will keep it for you."

"But … what if I am stopped? I have no papers, no identif…."

"You may tell them that I have your passport. Comrade Officer Dragonovich." He smiled, "I am very well known, the name will suffice."

Skender took a long breath. "I would prefer to have the passport with me." He was furious to hear his voice trembling as he held out his hand for the valuable green book.

"You are dismissed, Berisha." It was an order to leave. Skender let his hand fall and turned toward the door and the guard. "Enjoy your … visit."

Was there really a slight emphasis on that last word? Skender was not sure as he followed the guard. His only protection was laying on a desk littered with papers, without a passport he could not move, could not even leave Prishtine, let alone the country. His hand reached toward the heavy entry door.

"Wait!" The command came as his fingers brushed the door. The warm, sweet taste of blood was in his mouth before he realized that he had bit hard on his inside cheek. He wanted to flee, bolt through the door to imagined freedom. "Perhaps, after all, it would be better if you kept this."

He turned to find Dragonovich behind him, holding his lifeline out to him.

"Thank you." He took the passport, thrust it deep into his coat pocket.

"Goodbye, Skender Berisha."

He ignored the mocking salute, turned, and left.

Chapter 5

He could feel the nausea rising in him. Besim stood against the wall, huddled into his coat against the biting wind, but he could not stop to speak to him, he only knew that he must turn the corner, out of sight of the hated building. He felt embarrassed, ashamed, as he retched and vomited into the gutter. Besim stood close, shielding him as much as possible from the curiosity of passersby. "I'm sorry." Skender took the proffered handkerchief and wiped his mouth.

"Come, brother." Besim took hold of Skender's arm and hurried him down a side street. Dimly, Skender realized they had entered Old Town. "In here." An overhead bell tinkled their arrival.

"Besim! What brings you here?" The young man, about mid-twenties, was tall, slim, the Kosovar outfit suited him to perfection.

"This is my brother. He has just left the 'hotel', I think they did not deal too kindly with him."

"Welcome." The young man gave a brief bow to Skender. "This way, please." They were led into the back of the shop, past a curtain of dark blue material that concealed a small stockroom before entering through another door. The room was not large, but was furnished for comfort, a black stove warmed the room and several sheepskins lay in front of the fire. A bed was pushed against one wall, and it was covered with a quilt and many pillows. A blanket lay at the foot of it. "Sit here." The young man indicated the rug closest to the fire, reached and pulled the blanket from the bed and placed it around Skender wrapping it close about him.

Skender watched as the young man moved away, but as the violent shivering caught at him again, he turned back to the fire. "I am sorry to disturb you…."

"Drink this." A small glass of clear liquid was held to his lips. Skender looked up questioningly. "Slivovitz, plum brandy," the young man answered. "Drink, it will warm you quickly and help your stomach." Skender gulped it down, felt it searing down his throat, coursing through his body. He handed the glass back to the young man, received a quick smile and nod of encouragement. "Good, now

… rest." He guided Besim to the bed and they both sat down, chatting quietly together.

The shivering had passed. His stomach had stopped its erratic behavior. Skender eased the blanket off of him.

"Ah, you are feeling better, that is good." The young man took the blanket.

"I must apologize…." Skender stopped as the young man raised his hand.

"It is not necessary, I recognize your feeling, understood your need. Once one has been the, er, 'guest' of the authorities…." His shoulders lifted. The sound of the shop bell froze them. The young man placed his finger in warning to his lips, then left the room, closing the door firmly behind him.

"Who is he?" Skender demanded in an urgent whisper.

Besim gave a curious look at Skender, then asked, "He doesn't remind you of anyone?"

"No. Now, who is this man?"

"Luan Mali." Besim watched the incredulity, the shock. "Sabri's brother, the youngest."

"Sabri's brother?" Skender repeated as he stared at the closed door.

"Yes. Sabri was your closest friend, wasn't he, brother?"

"More than a friend, much more." Besim had to lean forward to catch the words. "Then … we can trust him?"

"Luan Mali is as honorable as Sabri, I would trust him with my life."

They both started as the door opened, but it was Luan who entered. "A customer, that was all," he assured them, then crossed to Skender. "Did they hurt you?"

"No. No." Skender gave a brief smile. "Just frightened the guts out of me."

Luan nodded. "They are experts. Somehow they know and probe your greatest weakness." He hesitated, bowed. "We have not formally met; I am Luan Mali." He held out his hand.

They shook hands. "You know who I am, don't you?" Skender asked.

"Yes, I know." They embraced then, as brothers. "Sabri … in your letter to my parents you said that he was dead. Were you with him … at the end?"

Skender swallowed. "Not now, Luan, when I am calmer, more in control, I will tell you everything. Suffice now that it was quick, he did not suffer."

Besim felt the tension, felt it prudent to bring the conversation to a more general topic. "Luan runs this shop for his father. Did you remember, Skender, that the Mali family had this store? They sell scarves, gloves, hats…." his voice trailed off.

Skender traced the outline of the rug, wondering out loud, "Why did they act that way? The officer deliberately baited me, threatened to keep my passport…." He glanced up at the two young men. "It was lying there, within reach, he did not take it from me, let it lie there. And then, just as I was leaving … he stopped me, my hand was on the door when he called me … I almost ran. Thank God, I did not. And then he gave me my passport. It is beyond me; I cannot fathom it."

"May I offer a possible explanation?" Luan waited until he had a nod from Skender, then sat down beside him. "If the officer … by the way, was it Dragonovich?"

"Yes."

Luan smiled. "You received top billing! He is in complete charge, only Udba surpasses him." He glanced under his lashes at Skender. "You do remember Udba?"

Skender gave a grim smile. "Does anyone ever forget the Secret Police? But go on."

"If Dragonovich could have provoked you into committing some act … for example, if you had snatched the passport or tried to run.… Do you see, Skender? Then he would have a legal reason to hold you … or question you."

"Does he need a legal reason?" Skender demanded ironically, "As I remember, they took you, reason or not."

"Not for us, we are under his control, but you? You are an American citizen now. Does that alter anything for him? Can he deal with you as a Kosovar, or must he handle you more diplomatically now? Do you understand my reasoning? It could be that he must seek direction from a higher authority."

Skender gave a bitter laugh. "Are you trying to comfort me, or scare me, Luan?"

Luan sighed, "We can only try to out-guess them. Dragonovich likes power, likes to feel it, use it. It is my opinion that he will not mention your arrival to any higher authority because he will not want to be told what he must do."

"I pray you're right." Skender stood. "Not a word at home, Besim, let us keep this to ourselves. Luan, thank you, there are no words…."

"None are needed. I thank God that it was possible for me to be of service to you, Skender." Luan walked with them toward the shop.

Skender stopped. "A hat! I need a hat!" he exclaimed as he saw the Kosovar hats piled one atop the other. "There." He selected his size, put it on his head, tipping it forward until it reached halfway to his eyebrows. "How's that?"

"Very daring!" Luan laughed.

"Too daring," Besim replied firmly.

"It is at the same angle as yours," Skender retorted with a sly wink at Luan.

"Yes, but I am young…." Besim stopped in horror, gave a slight bow as he started to apologize to Skender.

Skender laughed, slapped him on the back and adjusted the hat. "I agree. Luan, again my thanks. We will talk soon." They shook hands and Skender and Besim left, waving goodbye as they did so. They climbed the narrow winding street that led away from Old Town toward the main center of the city. The aroma of tobacco reminded Skender of his promise to Drita.

"I want some tobacco for my father," Skender told Besim.

"This way, brother." Besim led the way to one of the small stores that crowded the narrow, winding streets of Old Town. "This is the best place in Prishtine."

A wizened old man sat cross-legged on a pillow. He glanced up from his game of checkers as they entered his store. "One moment," he murmured as he studied the board in front of him. He made his move. "Can I help you?"

"Good morning." Skender included both the old men, then pointed to the glass jars lined up behind the counter. "Some of your finest tobacco, please."

The watery old eyes glanced toward Besim, "For your father?"

"No, sir, my uncle."

The old man looked Skender over, then stood, picked up one of the glass jars and shook some tobacco out into a piece of paper laying on a brass scale. "It is good you are here, Skender Berisha, your father has missed you…." He looked up, put the jar down and started to wrap the tobacco. "This is his favorite."

"Thank you," Skender paid the man, bowed to each of the two men. "Goodbye." He pushed the tobacco into his coat pocket. "I do not remember them."

"Your father always bought tobacco from here, as does my father and Migje Arif too." Besim glanced at Skender. "You do not remember being sent here as a boy?"

"No," Skender sighed, "I do not remember. Besim, do you know of a good pastry shop? I want to get something for Nona and Drita … do you know of one?"

"Of course!" Besim grinned. "Is there a young man alive who does not know where to find the best pastries in town? Come, this way."

The aromatic smell of honey drew them forward into the sweet-smelling shop. An array of pastries stretched from one end of the store to the other, chewy, nutty baklava, dripping with honey, kadaif, their round bodies swollen with almonds. In another tray, Skender's favorite, a diamond shaped sponge cake swimming in a sea of honeyed syrup. Besim pointed to an egg custard, deep cream colored. "Drita's favorite."

"And yours, Besim, which is yours?" Skender asked after he had ordered one of the custards from the young man attending them.

The young lad gave a sheepish grin as he pointed to a delicate shortcrust pastry, round, with a center hole, "This."

"Lady's Navel!" Skender hooted with laughter, "Shame on you, young man!" He dug deep into his pocket. "How much do I owe you?"

The effusive thanks of the proprietor followed them into the chill air. Their spirits were high as they wended their way back toward Main Square, each carrying one of the boxes of pastries.

"What a feast we shall have tonight," Besim said happily. He put his arm across Skender's shoulder. "I am inviting myself for dinner." He made a face of disgust. "My mother was preparing cornbread and beans…."

Their eyes met and they both laughed, enjoying the warmth between them. "I will be glad of your company, Besim." Skender gave a contented sigh. It was good to be home, to be with family.

Chapter 6

"Nona, we are home," Skender called as he took the steps to the kitchen in one leap and opened the door. "Besim and I are home … and we are starving!" He bent to take off his shoes. "How long before we can eat? Here, Drita, a treat for all of us. Babush, we will enjoy a pipe together this evening." He handed the package of tobacco to Babush and the box of pastries to Drita.

Babush opened the small packet, breathed the rich smell of good tobacco and nodded his approval. "Mmmm, smells good, Djali. We will try some after dinner."

Drita carefully opened the box as Nona came forward and peered over her shoulder. She pulled in a breath of excitement and, shining-eyed, turned to Skender. "Oh, thank you. Besim, you must have told … this one is my favorite," she added, pointing to the shimmering custard.

"Oh, no," Skender cried in mock dismay. "I chose that for myself."

But before he could tease his sister further, Nona winked at Drita. "Then you had better have this one, Drita … it looks very good," she said, pointing to the sponge.

"You remember too well, Nona," Skender retorted as he gave her a quick hug, adding, "Besim wishes to eat with us."

"If it is possible?" Besim asked, turning to Nona.

"Of course, Besim, and welcome."

"I wonder if my brother's family is having cornbread and beans tonight," Babush mused, staring at the ceiling and stroking down his white mustache. "It seems to me we always have an extra guest when cornbread and beans are served next door." He waited until the laughter had died, then added, "Come, Besim, give me a hand up. Are you coming to the house, Skender?"

"Skender, there is a pair of nalle for you by the door. They will be easier for you to slip on and off than your shoes." Nona pointed to a pair of clog-like shoes as the men prepared to leave the kitchen.

The three men settled themselves comfortably on the rugs by the fire. Babush turned to Skender. "At the Police Station … was there any trouble? Your mother was getting very nervous, you were gone a long time."

"Not so long, really, Babush. You know how they are. It makes them feel important to keep you waiting. No. No trouble. Just routine registration."

Drita entered, carrying a low table large enough for five people to sit comfortably. She smoothed the bright red cloth, leaving an even amount on all sides, then opened the door to retrieve the bowl, jug of warm water and towel which she had put there before entering. She laid the towel over her left arm, picked up the bowl and jug and reentered the room.

Besim stood. "May I help?" he asked.

The shrug of 'If you want to' was canceled by the grin she gave him as she held out her arm for him to take the towel.

Babush rose as the two young people came and stood beside him, holding out his hands. Drita held the bowl with her left hand, pouring the warm water over her father's hands from the jug, catching it in the bowl. Besim stood on her left, holding the towel ready for Babush to dry himself.

"I took Skender to see Luan Mali."

Drita started slightly at Besim's words and water splashed over her father's coat. "Pardon, Babush," she said, pulling the jug back too quickly and, again, splashing water on him.

"What is the matter, child?" Babush asked sharply as he grabbed the towel from the grinning Besim and tried to dry his coat.

With an angry glare at Besim, Drita apologized to the old man and went to Skender. As she carefully poured water over his hands, he looked at the two young people, Drita upset and angry, Besim amused, idly wondering what joke Besim had played on his sister. Had he bumped her elbow as she poured the water? If so, he had not noticed. He took the towel from Besim, slowly drying his hands, remembering how he had played this trick on his older sister, Lula, when they were young. He smiled to himself … how angry she would be. He felt the towel being taken from him, looked up from his reverie to see Besim's lips moving. "Yes, thank you, I am finished." He said with a sigh. *I suppose that's what he was asking.* He sat down on the rugs close to the table and slid the cloth over this lap.

Nona carried in a large round pan, the bottom and sides burned black from long use. She held the two handles carefully with folded towels to protect her hands from the heat and placed the huge pan centrally on the low table. Drita, who had followed her, took one of the towels from her mother and laid it beside Babush, setting the two plates she carried onto it.

Babush waited patiently until Drita sat down, then picked up the round, dark, crusty bread from one of the plates beside him and, as he tore the first piece, said quietly, "In your name, O God." He passed a piece of the still warm bread to each, picked up the other plate. "Spatz?" he asked.

"Yes, for me." Skender and Besim spoke together, they turned and laughed at each other.

Babush smiled and passed the plate to Skender. He took one of the pale-yellow peppers, divided it in half and started to hand it to Besim. "A little djathë?" he asked as he broke off a piece of the white, sour cheese and placed it on the pepper half.

"Yes, and a little of the pickled tomato." Besim pointed to the plate beside Skender. Skender cut the tomato, the full, ripe fruit spurting as the knife pierced the skin. Babush reached and ripped open the top layers of pastry in the huge pan of laknor, releasing the fragrant steam into the room.

Skender leaned forward, breathing in the aroma. "Mmmm," he grinned at Nona, "no one can make laknor like you, Nona … no one!"

Babush finished tearing the top layers of dough into bite-sized pieces, turned to Skender, and with his right hand offered Skender the first piece, "Djali."

Slowly, Skender looked at Nona, Babush, Drita and Besim, all quietly watching him. He took a deep breath. "In God's name," he said, his voice choked with emotion. He leaned forward and picked up the top flaky pastry in his right hand, scooped up some of the soft filling and put it in his mouth. They all sat, silently watching him and, with full mouth, he nodded at them, pointing to the laknor. "Hurry, or I shall eat the whole pie myself."

The tension-fraught moment passed and, laughing, they all reached, took up a piece of pastry and scooped up the spinach glistening with cheese and eggs.

"It is delicious, Nona, better than I remembered," Skender said between chewing. "And these spatz … just right. You could always make better pickles than anyone."

"I didn't do any pickling this year," Nona replied, adding proudly, "Drita did it all this time."

Skender leaned over, pinched his sister's cheek. "Then you, little sister, are the best maker of spatz in Kosov." He took another bite of the pepper. "Mmmm … I change my mind! The best in the world!"

"No," Drita denied shyly, her eyes sparkling with joy at the praise.

The top flaky crust was finished, along with the creamy spinach filling. Babush leaned forward and divided the bottom crusty dough with the firmer topping of spinach and cheese.

"I never know which is my favorite part." Besim reached forward and took a good-sized piece. "The top, all soft and melty, or the crispy bottom part."

"You seem to be doing a pretty good job with both," Skender laughed back at him.

"I am still trying to make a decision," Besim retorted.

Skender picked up a really golden, crusty piece. "Drita, here," he said, laying it in front of her.

She bit her lower lip and laughed shyly at him. "This is my favorite part," she admitted as she sank her teeth into the golden pastry.

They ate until the pan was empty. Skender took a piece of bread and wiped the pan clean with it, popped it into his mouth and licked his fingers. He closed his eyes, put his finger and thumb together. "That was a meal! Thank you, ladies."

Nona sat smiling contentedly. *How good it was to cook for her son, to see him at her table. All I have to do is stretch out my hand and I can touch him. I can cook for him again. And I can touch him again.*

Besim stood, stretched. "Drita, may I fetch the pastries for you?" he asked.

"It is not your place to go, Besim. I will fetch them," she answered as she made to rise.

"Agreed." He put his hand on her shoulder. "But I think I owe you." Besim gave her a conspiratorial grin.

She looked down with a tiny smile, then nodded agreement with him.

"Look, Drita, the pan is so clean you won't have to wash it." Besim picked up the empty pan.

Skender waited until Besim had left the room, then turned to Drita. "Did he bump your elbow? When you were pouring the water?" he asked. She shook her head. "Then why does he 'owe you'?" he asked teasingly.

Drita gave a quick, nervous glance at Babush, then answered quietly, "It is nothing, brother. Just a joke."

"A good one, too, to make your cheeks like two rosy apples." Skender was surprised when Drita did not answer him but kept her eyes fixed firmly on the table, except for another sideways glance at Babush.

Babush reached for his pipe. "Babush, wait," Drita urged, "We are to have some sweet, don't you remember Skender bought some for us?"

"Not for me, daughter. Sweets are for the women and the young. I'll stick to my pipe."

Skender stretched, "Well, I must still be young for I intend to have some."

Besim entered and, with a flourish, put the plate of pastries on the table and handed Drita a spoon. She hesitated, then offered the spoon to Skender.

"Go ahead, you are the youngest," he smiled, letting her know that he remembered their custom. "The only time the youngest female is allowed to eat first is the sweets … correct?"

She nodded, bit her lower lip in anticipation and then pushed her spoon into the custard. Skender passed the plate to Nona who chose one of the kadaif. "Besim?" Skender offered the pastries. "Take care, Besim, where you put your teeth!" he teased as Besim picked up his pastry.

Babush leaned forward to see what the youth had, laughed loudly, about to say something, but remembered the ladies and changed his mind.

With a puzzled look Drita asked, "Why? Why must he be careful where he bites?" But this brought even louder chortles from Skender and Babush and a sheepish grin from Besim.

Skender bit into the dripping sponge, some honey escaping and running down his chin. He caught it with his finger, helping it travel back to his mouth.

"Ho. Anyone home?" The call came with a rap of a stick on the window.

"Arif," Babush answered the questioning look from Skender as he went to the door. "Here, brother, here. Come in, come in."

Skender rose to his feet, hurriedly wiping his sticky fingers and mouth on the cloth so as to be ready in time when his uncle entered. He bowed. "Migje Arif."

Arif stood looking at Skender, his lips pushed tightly together, making his mustache reach his chin. "Skender!" He held out his arms and they held each other close, the old man, shaking a little with emotion. "It is good to have you again in Kosov." He released his nephew and took off his coat. He turned to shake hands with Babush and acknowledged Nona and Drita. "Hello, Besim, what are you doing here? Your mother must be having beans for dinner," he said laughingly as he greeted his other nephew.

Besim bowed to his uncle. "Migje."

"Where is the rest of the family?" Nona asked.

"Coming later. Emin had to complete his studies." He leaned on his stick, staring at Skender.

Drita picked up the remaining pastries, table, and cloth. "Migje, will Ilyria be coming?"

Arif nodded. "Later. With her mother and brothers, but I could not wait longer … I had to see Skender." He gripped his nephew's shoulders and studied him closely. "You look good, son. I am proud to see you a man." He pulled him close, hugged him, slapping him on the back. "You were always my favorite nephew," he whispered.

"Besim, go down to Drita. Tell her to make coffee for us." Babush turned to Arif. "Come, let us sit."

"May I take your walking stick, Migje?" Skender asked as he took it from his uncle and laid it against the pile of firewood. Arif groaned, "Don't put it there. Emin will be here soon." Babush and Arif laughed.

Babush turned to explain to Skender, "About two or three months ago, Arif had laid his walking stick against the wood … he has done it for years. Emin burned it."

Arif interrupted, "Can you imagine someone to stir the fire with a walking stick? Emin! His professors tell me how smart, how brainy, he is." He sighed heavily as he laughed. "But he surely isn't very bright at home. He plans to be an engineer … it will be many a day before I cross his first bridge! Please, put the stick somewhere safe." He waited until Skender returned to the fire and, with a gracious movement of his hand, gave him permission to sit, "Do you remember your cousins?"

"Not clearly, but a little," Skender admitted.

"My son, Emin, is twenty-three now and, as I told you, is studying to be an engineer. Jakup is a tailor. He is twenty-four. Ilyria is twenty-one."

"And Ilyria, what does she do?" The question was asked before he could recall it.

"Nothing, of course. Nothing." Arif looked at Skender in amazement, annoyance in his voice.

"Yes, Migje Arif. I'm sorry. That was a stupid question."

"Yes, it was," Arif promptly agreed.

"I have been in the West a long time. All the girls work there, and for a moment, I forgot…."

"Even those from good families?" Arif demanded in disbelief.

"Yes. There is no disgrace in a girl working." Arif pursed his lips and shrugged, conveying without a word that he strongly disapproved. "And Hava? How is she?" Skender asked.

Arif smiled, "Ah! You remember that I have one more daughter." Skender inclined his head, glad to have sailed back into smooth waters so easily. "She is well, married. She has two sons and, God willing, another will be born next month." He half-turned toward the door.

Drita entered, carrying a tray. She placed it on the floor and knelt beside it. On the tray there were three demi-tasse sized cups and saucers and a jesva, a brass container with a long handle, especially made for serving Turkish coffee.

Arif watched as she half-filled each of the three cups then, holding the long handle she carefully swung the jesva in a small circle until the coffee was swirling gently. She quickly poured the remaining coffee, filling the three cups and ensuring that each had some of the foamy liquid. She stood, picked up one of the cups and put it on a matching saucer, then placed it on the first three fingers of her right hand. With a small bow she offered the brimming cup to her uncle. "Migje Arif?"

Arif took the coffee with a fond smile. "Thank you, my child. You are looking as fresh as a spring flower tonight."

Skender turned and looked at his sister. Yes, she certainly did. She had changed her dimi for a pale yellow one, the delicate material falling in soft folds from her waist. The firelight caught the shining brown hair, sending back flashes of chestnut hue.

She blushed as she thanked Arif, then bent and picked up a second cup of coffee, placing this on her fingers too and went to her father. "Babush?" She bowed to him and offered the coffee. He took the cup from her. She took one step back and stood, waiting. Babush sipped the coffee and nodded his approval.

The last cup was delivered in the same way to Skender and, as she bent to hand him his coffee, he whispered, "Migje Arif is right, you look lovely … as lovely as a nusé."

Her eyes flashed to Babush. "Thank you, brother." Her voice was low, nervous. She took three steps backwards, picked up the tray and jesva and backed out of the room.

Skender sipped on the strong, sweet coffee. He was puzzled. He had given his sister the highest compliment and she had reacted so strangely. Had he imagined it, or had panic shown in her eyes? Reflectively he looked at Babush…. *No, Babush would never force her, he knew that. She would be consulted before a marriage was arranged. Perhaps she was not ready to leave home yet.* He put the problem from him and listened to the two old men comparing notes on the day's activities.

Babush proudly took the package of tobacco from his pocket and offered it to his brother. Arif filled the bowl of his pipe, packing the tobacco with his finger and carefully catching any stray pieces before they dropped. Babush filled his just as painstakingly while Arif sat watching, patiently waiting so that they could light their pipes together.

"Not now, Babush. Perhaps later," Skender refused as Babush proffered the tobacco. He watched as the two brothers sat, contentedly puffing on their pipes. *How alike they are. If Babush did not have white hair it would be hard to tell them apart.*

"Kosovar. Ho, Kosovar." A quick roll on a drum preceded the call. Skender slowly stood and walked to the window. Babush and Arif exchanged glances, put their pipes down on the stove and followed Skender. Babush pushed forward, opened the window and all three peered out.

Migje Hasan stood beneath the window, grinning from ear to ear, hands on his hips. A drum rested on his slightly round stomach, supported by a string slung across his shoulder. The round, clean-shaven face beamed when he saw Skender. "Nephew! Skender!" he boomed. "It is your own Migje come to welcome you home." He turned and yelled up the pathway toward the gate. "Make ready! He is here, at the window." He started another roll on the drum.

The sound of giggling and laughter came in soft waves as Skender stood at the window, grinning down at his uncle. "Migje Hasan, you haven't changed at all."

Hasan looked anxiously up the pathway, then turned back to Skender. "Wait! Wait there," he urged, holding up his finger before hurrying out of sight. Smothered voices, more giggling and laughter floated up to the window.

"What is he up to?" Babush asked in exasperation.

"I don't know, brother, but whatever it is, it will go wrong, mark my words," Arif replied, returning to the fire and sitting down.

A roll from the drum came again, this time joined by the tinny sound of a gypsy tambourine. Young voices lifted, "Oy, Kosov, oy Kosov, mother of mine…."

Skender's nails dug into his palms, his lips moving as, silently, he joined the young voices singing of their love for their homeland. He sensed Babush watching him and turned. Their eyes met, held the old man's full. Skender took a deep, steadying breath, then moved to Babush who placed his arm across his son's shoulders, pulling him close.

A movement down the path drew their eyes and slowly the line of singing, dancing cousins came into view, led by Migje Hasan beating time. The first young man looked up, his dark eyes sparkling in the light which streamed from the open window above him. He grinned, flicked the handkerchief he carried in his right hand across his chest and gave a bow to the watchers. There had been no pause in his singing, his dancing and the slow-moving line pushed on down the path, past the window. Skender watched him, captivated by his skill and enthusiasm, the young man glanced back, and up, at the window, then cheerfully raised his hat in a salute as he was pushed out of the line of vision. The cousins were joined in a long chain held together by scarlet handkerchiefs carried shoulder high. They dipped and twirled to the music as they wound their way down the path and up the stairs.

Babush moved quickly to the door, opening it as they arrived. The beat was faster now, and they joined hands, letting the handkerchiefs float from one corner. The young men, all in traditional Kosov dress, their white hats sitting dangerously forward on their heads, and the girls in colorful dimis moved in a joyous line toward Skender, and as each passed, they turned their heads, smiled, and introduced themselves.

"Emin." "Ilyria." "Jakup." "Aslan." The young people smiled and gave their name until the last young man laughed at Skender. "Besim," he shouted, offering his hand. Skender grinned back at him, nodded an acceptance, and took the proffered hand. He bent, snatched up his hat from the rug near the stove as he was pulled into the dance. He tipped it forward to the same daring angle as his cousins'. His feet fell into the pattern of the dance without hesitation, and he extended his free hand to the leader so that the circle could close.

"La-lala-lala-la, la-lala-lala-la…." The men crossed their hands behind the girls' backs, supporting them as the tempo increased, rising to fever pitch, feet seemed barely to touch the ground. Skender's head spun, he was hard pressed to keep his balance as faces, walls, carpets whirled faster and faster. "La-lala-lala-la, oy KOSOV!" The joyous shout released them and they fell, exhausted, panting to the ground.

The leader pushed himself to a sitting position, resting on his elbow as he extended his hand to Skender. "Welcome to Kosov, brother, I am Emin, youngest son of Arif."

Skender wiped his left hand across his sweating forehead as he extended his right. "Thank you…." He looked long at his cousin. A sadness filling him as he realized that if they had met on the street he would not have known him. "That was quite a welcome, brother, thank you." The grip was firm, hard, each knowing intuitively that they liked each other.

Hasan took off the drum, letting it slide to the rug as he watched his two nephews greet each other. He moved forward toward Skender.

"The welcome … it was his idea." Emin spoke quietly to Skender as he saw Migje approaching them.

Skender, turned, rose immediately toward Hasan. "Migje…."

"Never mind that." Hasan stopped the customary bow, emotion shaking his voice. He swallowed, then held his arms wide. They held each other close, with silent sobs. Hasan took a slight step back, looked Skender over, then looked deep into his eyes. "Do you remember the last time we saw each other?" Skender nodded, and the older man took a long, shuddering breath. "Did they let you keep the bread?"

"Yes, Migje."

Hasan nodded, licked his dry lips. "Good." He took hold of his nephew and held him in a long, hard embrace. "I was afraid they they…."

"Enough, Hasan," Arif warned. "We will talk later. For now, join us … have a pipe of this good tobacco."

"Yes, we will talk," Hasan promised quietly to Skender before turning him toward the door. "Greet your aunt, and then I will sort out all of these cousins for you…." He turned toward the young people as Skender moved toward the door to greet Hasan's wife. "I have them in my house all the time and even I don't know which one belongs to who!" Derisive grunts, groans and laughter came from the young people scattered on the floor. He grinned down at them affectionately. "Every night, when it is time for bed, I take a tally, When I reach the right number for my house … I throw the rest out!"

Skender glanced back, grinning at the hoots of laughter from the cousins. Hasan was the favorite uncle, the more tolerant father. He moved toward Migje Hasan and put his hand on his shoulder. "Yes, Migje, I can see you throwing one of your own out," he mocked gently.

Hasan gripped Skender's arm. "I have carried a weight in my heart all these years. Seeing you again, here in your own home, has lifted that weight. You cannot know…." He drew in a long breath, "Skender, you cannot know how much happiness…." He stopped, fighting for control, tried to speak again. He slapped Skender across the shoulders, then turned and joined his brothers beside the fire.

Skender appeared to be waiting for his uncle to settle himself, but most knew that he needed the time to compose himself. His smile as he turned to face his cousins was fragile. "May I thank all of you, especially you, Migje Hasan, for the wonderful welcome. Now I know I am home!" The ripple of laughter eased the tension. "Sometimes, when you are lonely and homesick, your imagination wings you home. For a second, a moment, you feel the warmth of family … maybe taste a favorite meal. Or touch the roughness of a special door. Tonight you have given me something very special. I know that in memory I shall return to this welcome many times. You have given me a small piece of Kosov to carry with me for the rest of my life. Thank you." The air was pregnant with emotion. He forced a smile. "And now, if one of you young ladies would fetch Nona and Drita, we can continue our celebration."

One of the youngest stood immediately. "I will go," she said shyly.

He smiled. "Thank you. And what is your name?" he asked as she stopped in front of him.

"Nurije, brother." She waited, but Skender did not offer his hand.

"No, wait, please…." He hesitated, wondering how to explain that he didn't want such subservience. He glanced around. All the cousins were staring at him in shocked dismay. Babush deliberately turned away as Skender glanced toward him. He looked down at all the young people. "Please, I do not want any of you to make obeisance to me…." He could feel their shock, "I know that it is our custom, but…." He stopped, realizing that he had no words to explain that the act embarrassed him instead of honoring him as was intended.

There was uncomfortable silence. Skender felt their shock, their anger, and did not know how to cope. Nurije stood, head bowed, in front of him and he could see that she was shaking with nervousness. Her dark eyes stole a quick look at him through her thick lashes before she sent a long, pleading look to her father. Migje Hasan, not knowing himself how to resolve the problem, ignored her. The moment grew, expanded. And none knew how to deal with it.

Emin hesitated, then, in one quick movement, came to his feet. He held out his hand to the girl beside him and pulled her, reluctantly, to her feet. Slowly he walked toward Skender, leading the girl. He looked directly at Skender, then bowed, "With your permission, brother…? This is Nurije, Migje Hasan's youngest daughter…." His hand moved graciously toward the girl standing in front of Skender. "And this is my sister Ilyria, Arif's youngest daughter. They are ready, brother, to greet you and welcome you." His hand dropped behind Ilyria's back and urged her forward. "Ilyria…" it was a command, in spite of the polite smile, "…greet your brother Skender and welcome him back to Kosov."

She glanced nervously at Emin, then at Skender, then snatched for Skender's hand, made quick but complete obeisance, released him, bowed, and took two steps backward.

"Thank you, Ilyria," Skender's voice was a hoarse whisper.

"And now you, Nurije." Skender saw that Emin had to give Nurije a hard push as he spoke. Emin looked directly at Skender. "Brother, your sister is waiting to greet you," he said firmly.

Slowly Skender extended his hand toward the terrified girl. She took it, bowed over it, and he could feel her trembling, as she raised it to touch her chin, then to her forehead and again to her chin. She released his hand. "Thank you,

Nurije." She bowed, took two steps backward and then, with an agonized glance around, fled from the room. Ilyria received permission from her father and then she, too, followed Nurije.

"I made a mistake," Skender said quietly to Emin. Emin bowed his head in acknowledgment. "I should not have interfered, should have let them greet me in the accepted way…." He sighed, "What a mess I made of it."

"You have been gone from here a long time, Skender, it cannot be easy."

"No, it is not." Skender sighed, "What shall I do now?"

Emin shrugged. "Let them greet you in our way, it is your right," he replied simply, then he turned and led the way toward the waiting cousins.

Chapter 7

"Have your aunts and cousins gone, Djali?"

"Yes, Babush. I escorted them as far as our gate."

"You look cold, Skender, come close to the fire." Arif's hand gave gracious permission for him to sit down.

"Thank you. I think it has turned even colder." Skender sat close to the fire, held out his hand to the blaze as a flurry of rain beat against the window, giving emphasis to his words.

Hasan took a log from the depleted pile. "We shall have snow before morning," he said as he pushed the wood into the fire. He glanced at Babush. "The wood is getting low, brother…."

"Emin is fetching some from the storeroom," Babush replied.

Skender sat quietly. There was an air of expectancy, anticipation, in the room that touched his nerves. Preparations were being made, the aunts, cousins, had been told to return to their homes. Emin had been ordered to remain and he would be expected to be on call for the night, bringing tea, coffee, or whatever refreshments might be required by the men … even now he had been sent to replenish the pile of wood. His father and both his uncles were ready. Skender shied away from the conclusion, he did not want to relive that anguish, that pain….

"Come in, Emin." Babush's voice broke in on Skender, and he watched as his cousin stacked wood beside the fire, and Drita placed piles of blankets against one wall. "Drita, you are to go to sleep." Babush's finger stopped her protest. "There have been many guests today, there will be even more tomorrow, and I can see that you need rest. Emin is here and will attend to us. Natën e mirë, daughter, sleep well."

She smiled her thanks as she bent and kissed his cheek, "Natën e mirë, Babush." She gave a slight bow to each of her uncles as she murmured her goodnights to them, too.

"Emin, take one of the blankets, and keep the kitchen fire going then you will stay warm. If we need you, we will let you know." Emin picked up a blanket, gave a slight bow to the men and followed Drita toward the door. "And now, Skender," Babush continued, turning toward his son, "we have waited many years so, please, begin."

Babush's words reached Emin as he was half-way through the door. He hesitated, looked back at the group around the fire, then turned to Drita, silently laid his finger to his lips, as he indicated that he intended to stay.

Drita's eyes widened. "No," she mouthed to him, her quick glance at the men called forth a more vehement denial. "No, Emin, you will get into trouble."

Emin cautioned her to silence. "I must know … I must," he whispered into her ear. He urged her on her way, and with extreme care closed the door on her, without a sound he laid the blanket at his feet, leaned back against the wall. His heart thumped against his ribs as his mind searched for an excuse if his father should happen to glance up and see him there. He licked at his lips, there was no excuse. If he was caught, punishment would be swift, and it would be justified. He decided to stay.

"When you are ready, Djali," Babush's words were soft, encouraging.

Skender looked at him, then sat staring into the fire. His sigh was long, ragged, seeming to come from deep inside him. "I have tried so desperately to put this behind me, to wipe it from my mind…." He held up his hand as Arif was about to speak. "Please, let me say this. I intend to tell the story; you must know what happened. But the telling will not be easy. Please remember that and make allowances for my…." He took a deep breath, his hands clenched and unclenched in his lap. "Make allowances for my emotions and, possibly, my lack of control sometimes." He paused, forcing himself to calmness. "Now, where shall I begin? When they took me from Prishtine?"

The three brothers looked from one to the other. Babush and Hasan nodded agreement. "No. I would like to hear all of it, from the time they first began to take an interest in you," Arif turned to Babush, "I think we should know what happened right from the beginning. Do you both agree?"

"The beginning, Migje Arif? That was in your youth, not mine." Anger sparked Skender's voice, "I can tell you what happened to me, to my generation, my friends. I can tell you how they beat us, starved us, and slaughtered us with less consideration than you kill a sheep. But…" he was trembling with rage as he leaned close to Arif, "I cannot tell you why, in your youth, our freedom, our nationality, was snatched from us. I cannot explain why strong nations can play with small, weak ones. Tell me, Migje Arif, tell me, why someone, someone who had probably never set foot on this land, was allowed in your youth, to take a pencil, draw a line on a map and announce to the world that we were no longer a free and independent province of Albania; that we could no longer speak our own language or stand proud and say, 'I am an Albanian'? Why was this land given to the Serbians? What right, what claim, have they to it?"

"Steady, son, steady," Hasan said quietly as he laid his hand on Skender's arm.

The pause was long, fraught with tension, before Arif asked, "Do you hold us responsible in some way?" He took a long, steadying breath as Skender sat in silence, not even looking at them. "It was not for ourselves that we were careful, it was for our families. It was a time of great danger; one careless word would bring disaster. Whole families vanished, disappeared without trace. Sons and fathers were snatched from the bosom of their families for speaking just one word of greeting in our own language. Wives and daughters were abused, often in front of their husbands, their fathers, for no reason other than to give amusement to the guards." Arif's hand shook as he picked up his pipe and started packing it with tobacco. "My own wife's sister, already heavy with her first child, was slit from one end to the other by a Yugoslav bayonet and the unborn child ripped from its resting place … and her husband, bound to a chair, was forced to watch." He reached for a spill and lit his pipe, took several deep pulls. "And to this day we know of no reason…."

"Forgive me, I did not know…."

"All of us carry pain of some kind, Skender." Arif saw Skender's agitation, reached and poured a glass of water from the jug beside him and passed it to his nephew. "I doubt there is a family in Prishtine who does not have some memory similar to mine, to yours. Probably not in the whole of Kosov." He took the glass from Skender, returned it to the tray beside him. "But we are not here to listen to this, it is finished, history." He leaned back, took another long pull on his pipe. "When you are ready, Skender…."

Sadness pressed on Skender. What he had to tell them would increase the burden these men carried, not relieve it.

A log fell, sending sparks flying and, as if a signal had been given, Skender started to speak:

> The whole school had assembled together. We were buzzing with curiosity. What could be so important to stop class, assemble all students at one time? There were two men. They spoke for a long time, the gist of it was that there were to be no more borders, no more conflicts between nations. We were to be united, comrades, marching forward, shoulder to shoulder, towards peace and a better life. From the Yugoslav border to Moscow, we were one family.
>
> But what was it he said that caught our attention? Made our hearts leap with joy? Kosov was to be a free, self-governing, and independent state. In future we would be permitted to say we were Albanian. We would be allowed to fly our own flag, use our own language, and read our own books. Never again

> would we have to step into the gutter to let a Serb pass by … we were to be equal.

Skender looked from his uncles to his father, gave a sad little laugh. "They knew what to offer, didn't they? We believed it. Of course, we believed it, we wanted to. We were young … idealists still. Dreams could come true."

> There were some who voiced doubts … not many. We soon shouted them down, pointed out that Serbs and Albanians had fought against the Germans, shoulder-to-shoulder. Had died together … that all this would create an understanding, an acceptance of each other. Strangely enough, not one of us seemed to pick up on the 'Brotherhood' of Communism. We were concerned with freedom from Communism and Yugoslavia: we looked no farther than that.
>
> Meetings were held regularly, we were fed the same diet, week after week. I don't remember when things began to change … some of us started getting individual attention. Then they started to demand information about our parents and relatives. Several of us began to feel uncomfortable, we stopped going to the meetings. We were picked up by the Police, taken to Headquarters. I refused to join the Party. They told me that in future I was to register at Headquarters every night at six o'clock. I asked why. "We have to be sure that you have no reactionary inclinations," they replied. "Be here. Six o'clock. Every evening."
>
> I thought I would be there for five or ten minutes … just to sign in … then leave. The first night I arrived just before six o'clock, they kept me until ten. By the time I got home, Nona was frantic with worry.
>
> For several nights it was the same pattern, I sat on a bench in the hall waiting for permission to go home, permission usually came about ten o'clock and I would leave. It was irritating and a nuisance, but nothing more … not then. A week, maybe ten days later, I checked in, signed the form, and started toward the bench as was my custom. 'No sitting'. The order startled me, and I turned to look at the guard. "Stand!" From six until ten I had to stand there, I was not permitted to lean against the wall, or against the counter, and I was forbidden to speak.
>
> One night, probably two weeks later, as I took up my customary position, the guard smiled. "Not tonight. Tonight,

> you come with me." I felt a trembling fear as I followed him down some stairs and then we stopped beside a door: number four … it was always number four.

Skender pushed his hands against his legs to stop their trembling.

> There was another guard already there, and an officer … it wasn't bad that first time, they slapped me around a bit, but….

He took a gulp of the water that Arif passed to him.

> That was the end of standing around. Every evening I was taken down those stairs and ordered into that room. There was always an officer, if there was only one guard, you sighed with relief, there would be questioning, some slapping….

He swallowed.

> Two guards meant a beating: the officer would question you; one guard would hold you, and the other would….

He closed his eyes, hearing the leather cutting the air.

> A curfew had been imposed on Prishtine, which meant that a guard had to escort me home if I was held later than ten o'clock. He was young, not much older than I….

He smiled as remembrance came.

> It had been raining all day and I do not need to remind you what our street is like after the rain! He slipped, fell into the mud and the rifle clattered to my feet. I remember standing there, staring at it, knowing that I could pick it up, shove it in his belly before he could even stand. As I bent, picked it up, my thoughts raced, 'I can shoot him, get away, hide in the mountains or even join the guerillas….' By some miracle I remembered all of you. He was still down in the mud as I handed him the rifle.

He gave a soft laugh.

> I will never forget the look on his face, he thought I was quite mad, and I wondered if maybe he was right.

The men exchanged grim looks, each realizing that the lives of every Berisha had rested in a sixteen-year-old boy's hand.

> As the days passed, the questioning was stepped up. The beatings got worse, and it became harder and harder to present myself to them every night. Sometimes, if I had trouble walking, the young guard would help me a little, one night he asked gruffly, 'Is it worth taking this punishment? Join the damn party and be over with it'.

Skender sighed, gave a sad smile. "That was the closest I ever came to receiving kindness from any communist."

> We all knew by now that the promises of self-government and freedom were empty words.

Skender's voice, full of anger, tinged with sadness, continued,

> The Socialist Republic of Serbia had, once again, been given the Autonomous Province of Kosov. The iron-hand was closing on us again.
>
> They left me alone for about a month, I did not even have to report to Headquarters. At first, I was wary, suspicious … and then after a while I decided that they had given up on me and would leave me alone.

He laughed. "Such innocence! They never give up, never!"

> It was afternoon and I was on my way to Sabri's house when they stopped me, told me I was needed for 'questioning'. I was taken straight off the street to Headquarters: there was no way of letting my family know where I was. It was a different room this time, larger, and with a lot more guards. Within an hour, six others, all from my class, were added to the room. We were not permitted to speak, not allowed to sit. They lined us against one wall, then one of the guards pointed … we were made to watch while two of them beat him. Then they asked, 'Does anyone wish to join the Party?' Then they would take another. Then another…."

Skender's teeth clenched.

> They worked their way through all of us. But we fooled them … even there in their own stinking cell we fooled them.

He looked up at his father and uncles. "We were forbidden to speak, so we 'talked' to the one being beaten and told him to stay quiet."

"How, Djali?"

"The way our old farmers tell their women to hold their chatter!" Skender put his thumb to his mouth, nail against lower lip, top teeth against the nail, then gently pulled, making a small 'click'. He gave a broad grin, "God, did that help. To hear your friends talking to you when you were being beaten. To hear their encouragement. And the best part was that the guards did not even know."

"The guards were not from Prishtine, then?" Hasan asked.

Skender shrugged, "Even if they were, they would not know our customs, especially one that old, that outdated." He stretched.

> They kept us for five days … a little bread, a little soup, and plenty of beatings.

"I was worried to death. I had come to Headquarters and asked for you. They told me you were not with them, that they had no idea where you might be." Babush shook his head, "I did not believe it, I knew, I felt your presence…."

"And so Babush stood outside, from sun-up to sunset, watching. Did you know that Skender?"

Skender's hand reached for Babush's, and they held tight to each other for a moment. "No, I did not. And yet … perhaps so … something helped me, gave me strength."

Emin was shaking and he put his arms around himself trying to bring control. He was not sure whether anger gripped him or fear.

> They didn't bother me again for quite a while, that was what was so….

He stopped, not being able to find the word. "You never knew, just as you began to relax, think that maybe it was over … then, they'd come for you again. I think that was their greatest weapon, you could be at school, walking with a friend, sitting in the comfort of your own home … there was nowhere, nowhere, where you were safe, they could reach for you at any time, any place."

He sat staring into the fire completely absorbed with his memories.

> Sixteen is such a bitter-sweet year, soon the girls would be gone, you would never see them again.

His voice was low, dreamy.

> Ariana Deva had sat on my left, one desk forward, for three years. My only interest in her was to ask her for help with mathematics … until that spring. I couldn't keep my eyes off her. The Professor's lecture was unheard, the blackboard unseen. I would sit and stare at the white nape of her neck, at the wisps of dark, curling hair, I would dream, wonder what it would feel like to run my fingers up that neck, release all that thick curly mass….

Babush grunted noisily.

Skender turned, grinned. "Sorry, Babush, but in spite of everything life's juices were stirring!" He eased himself down, laid his head on his father's lap, as he smiled up at his father. "I used to lay here, just like this, and you thought I was studying … but my mind was on other things, sir."

Babush returned the smile, cuffed gently at his son.

> I think she must have felt me watching her. Sometimes she'd glance back at me, she'd bite her pencil … just that would send my blood racing.

The three men exchanged amused glances and then Hasan said, "If one of her brothers had even suspected your feelings, it would have been your legs racing, not your blood!"

Skender laughed with the men as he nodded his agreement.

> Her brother, Morat, was a classmate and close friend of Sabri's, and the three of them walked to and from the school together. Sabri was a little surprised that I was, suddenly, prepared to take the long route home so that I could accompany 'him'.

Skender laughed, said softly, "I had to take a lot of teasing once Sabri realized that Ariana was the real reason. We always walked together she and I, so that we could discuss the lectures given that day, he explained with undue seriousness to the men." He waited until their chuckling had quieted.

> Sometimes we would drop back a little and then, when I knew that Morat was out of sight, I would take her hand, hold, just for a moment. She would not permit more than a moment. And my daring was content with that, I knew better than to let Morat catch us! He lay still, a smile curving his mouth as remembrance came. "How little it took to make life sweet, a few words, a smile, fingers touching….

Carefully Emin flexed his back, wondering if he dare to sit down. He was not used to standing for such a long time and his body ached with fatigue.

Skender leaned up onto one elbow, picked up a log and threw it into the fire. Quickly, shadow-silent, Emin took advantage of the crackle and hiss from the fire to lower himself to the rugs. A sigh of relief blew through his lips as he eased himself down and rested his back against the wall, using the blanket to pillow his head.

> In another few weeks, school would close for the summer."

Skender continued.

> Final examinations were under way, the only sound in the classroom the scratching of pen against paper. The classroom door was thrown open. I remember we all jumped, looked up wondering who dared to make so much noise during Exam time. In the doorway there were three men, two guards and one agent from the Secret Police. They arrested the Professor, took him from the class right then. We were all nervous, upset … some of the girls were crying.
>
> It was mid-afternoon, two days later, when the door was opened again. The same three stood there. All eyes went from them to the Professor and there was a nervous murmur as we anticipated his arrest. But it was not the Professor they were after this time. All the boys in the class were ordered to the school grounds.

Skender's voice carried the fright of a sixteen-year-old boy to the listening men.

> The older boys were already assembled, some on the right and some on the left as we reached the top of the steps. There were guards everywhere, guns drawn and at the ready; there were two agents at the top of the steps and they ordered us all

to their left, then one announced that if our name was called we would move to the opposite side.

Sabri was already on the right, and Chenan.

He glanced at Hasan. "Your neighbor's son, Migje, and several other friends of mine."

I knew my name would be called, and yet … my feet did not want to obey, but thank God, I did not have to make him repeat it. I deliberately took a devious path through my colleagues so that when I crossed the grounds I could walk directly to where Sabri was standing.

As the names went on, I took the opportunity of whispering to Sabri, "What's going on?"

"I don't know, but I don't like it." He saw my silent questioning. "Look at those they are assembling on this side … be careful!" he warned, "do not let them see your interest. All of us on this side are from old-established families, like ours, sons of wealthy families even a few from the city officials, and teachers' and intellectuals' sons. Now, look over there … mostly farming families, some new arrivals, a few tradesmens' sons."

Fewer and fewer were being sent to the right as the younger boys filed out of the school, and those that were directed to our side were usually the elder son of one of the better-known families.

The agent folded his papers and ordered our group to form a column, four deep. Tension was high, and the guards were nervous as no move was made to obey. My glance went upwards, past the agent to the school, every window on every floor was open and crowded with girls. The order was barked at us again, and the guards backed away lifting their rifles as we still stood in silent disobedience.

The sweet, soft sound of a girl's voice trembled on the air, she faltered as a rifle was swung and pointed at her and then, from another window, another level, a second voice came, and then another, and another, and another, until the whole building, the grounds, rang with their voices, singing, 'Oy, Kosov, Mother of Mine' and then without a pause they went into another of our national songs.

The guards still surrounded us, rifles pointed, but now there was a doubt in the way they held them, watched us. The agent yelled, ordered the girls to silence: if anything, the singing swelled. One of the guards swung round from facing us and fired. As he did so, the boys on the left of the grounds joined in the singing, anger in their voices. And then our group, with deliberate insolence, added our voices to theirs. There was pandemonium among the guards, somehow, we had become the ones in control.

One of the boys nearest to the school swept off his hat, gave a deep bow toward the girls, the whole column of boys picked up on it and we all removed our hats and bowed to the girls. The boys on each side of the school ground turned, bowed to each other. We were intoxicated, singing our heads off and laughing.

I suppose the agent had managed to convey his orders to his men for we were pushed, prodded, and manhandled into line.

"March!"

We came smartly to attention, replaced our hats at their most daring angle.

"March!"

We marched! Soldiers! In time to the music! Out of the grounds, wheeled in formation round the corner and down the street, and still our fellow students' voices carried us along. Then, we had to listen carefully to hear them … as their voices faded, so did our bravado, our steps faltered, the left-right-left-right march broke into a walk, and the song died on our lips.

We felt very alone, very vulnerable. Each of us realized that there were too many to be taken in for questioning, apprehension grew as we passed Headquarters and pulled away from it, nervous, questioning looks were exchanged, as we all tried to push away our fright.

"Sabri." I called his attention to our neighbors who was standing staring at the long column of boys. When we were almost abreast of him, Sabri gave a nod and I pushed at him.

Skender laughed.

I was too enthusiastic, he almost tripped! He turned, grabbed at me and threw me out of the column, his aim was better than mine and I landed right at our neighbor's feet. There was not much time, a guard had already seen me and was running toward me. I gave a sharp tug on the old man's jacket as I said, 'Sir, it's me, Skender Berisha. Please tell my father

> what is happening'. And then, 'he pushed me, he pushed me,' I whined to the guard waving at no one in particular.
>
> "Silence! Get into line!"
>
> Sabri was almost helpless with laughter as I took my place beside him. I glanced back, wondering if the old fellow had enough time to realize … he was already making his way from the front of the crowd.

Skender turned to Hasan, "He must have really moved. We hadn't reached the outskirts of Prishtine when you caught up with us."

Hasan nodded, "Yes, he was a good neighbor and a good friend. He came straight to your house. Babush was at work, so he came to me. I could not believe what he was saying … students being marched through town under armed guard! I asked him how many there were. 'I'm not sure, sixty or seventy, possibly. It was the older students they had with them, none of the younger boys.'"

"When he said that I knew I had to go to see for myself. There was some bread cooling on the kitchen table. I looked at it, on impulse picked it up as I left."

"I ran for as long as I could. My heart was pounding, I had to slow to a trot. The big mill had come into sight when I spotted the column. I pushed myself to one last effort. I ran alongside the boys, my eyes searching each line, hoping you weren't there. I suppose I got about half-way up the column when one boy looked up. 'Sir, he's about four lines ahead,' he said. It must have been a friend of yours, but I didn't know him," Hasan said, turning to Skender.

"And then I saw you, recognized your walk, called you. You didn't hear me. I gave another push and caught up with you." Hasan looked at Babush, "I asked him, 'What's happened? Where are they taking you?' All he answered was, 'I don't know. I don't know'."

"The guard in their section was an older man. 'Better go home,' he told me."

"'Please, where are you taking them?' I asked."

"'Go home', he repeated."

"They were still walking along the road. I was out of breath, panting, half-walking half-running beside them. I remember the bread, held it out. 'Here, Skender, take this.' Then, blackness."

"When I came to, they were gone. My head was bleeding. I tried to stand, everything started to swim. I felt awful. I sat still for a while, stood up, started back towards the mill." He looked up at Skender. "You know where the bend in the road is? Near the mill?"

Skender sat up. "Yes?"

"I had almost reached that spot when I saw a column coming towards me … at first I thought it was you and your group. I felt confused, shook my head trying to clear my thoughts. These people were coming from Prishtine, from the north, but you had already passed this spot going south … it couldn't be you."

"Once they had rounded the bend, I could see that this column was much larger, three times as many, and they weren't just students, their ages went from 15 to 50. I stood watching them pass, many were in bad shape and looked near exhaustion. They were under heavy guard. Most of the guards on horseback and some marching beside the column."

"I called to them, 'Where are you from?'"

"No one answered, so I called again."

"'Kosovars! Where are you from?'"

"A man in a line near me turned, called back, 'Podiev'."

"One of the guards on horseback rode up to that man, kicked him on the side of his head, growled at him. 'Silence.' Then he turned his horse, came back to me. 'Go about your business or I'll take you with us.'"

"He was young, only about 20 … but his eyes…." Hasan shook his head in sorrow.

"I walked on sad that I had caused that man to be hurt, watching, aware, now, of a difference in these guards. They were all young, very sure of themselves, you could see it in the way they carried themselves, the way they behaved. And smart, too. Their uniforms were well pressed, all buttons buttoned, boots blacked till they gleamed. Just the sight of them instilled a great fear in me."

"I reached the mill. They helped me, bandaged me up. The manager offered me a ride to town in one of their wagons if I was prepared to wait. I still did not feel well, so I accepted gladly."

"We were almost at the main square when three trucks passed us, full of guards. They looked the same as those I had passed earlier, very smart, very … evil, somehow. We stopped. I turned to the driver, he, too, was watching the trucks."

"'What are they doing here, I wonder?' he asked."

"I don't know. Why? Do you know anything about them?"

"He nodded, spat. 'From Nis, the cream of the Yugoslav army. God help anyone they get their hands on'. He pointed to a shop. 'This is where I deliver my flour.'"

"We both got down, I thanked him, and started toward home. Tears were running down my face, people were turning, staring at me, but I could not stop. I knew that you, Skender, were destined to come under the jurisdiction of those guards. And there was nothing I could do to stop it … or help you." Hasan dashed away the tears that crept down his face. "That was the last time I saw you, the last memory I had of you. I thank God that now I can wipe it from my mind."

"And my last memory of you, Migje. Pray God this next parting will be with health and happiness," Skender's voice shook, and he reached for a cigarette from the pack close to him. Permission came even before he asked his father, and he drew deep on the cigarette.

Arif sat smoothing his mustache, "Skender, we assumed a guard hit Hasan, was that what happened?" he asked.

Skender nodded, "Yes. One of the younger guards, a brash, ugly type, had come up behind Migje. He used the butt of his rifle, hit Migje on the side of the head. I started to go to you, Migje," Skender said turning to his uncle, "but he stuck his gun into your stomach: 'Come on, boy,' he said, grinning at me all the time, 'come on, just one more step and this dog will die, nice and slowly'."

I had never felt hatred as I did at that moment. I wanted to kill him. God forgive me, if I could have got to him before he could shoot you, I would have choked him. Choked him till his eyes popped."

There was a pause, then Skender continued:

> Sabri had stopped when I did. He put his arm around my shoulders. 'Come, Skender,' he said, 'better for your uncle if you leave immediately.' I knew he was right, let him turn me around. Another boy took hold of my other arm and they started to lead me back into the column.
>
> "Hey! You!"
>
> I turned back. It was the older guard.
>
> "Here!" He bent, picked up the bread you had dropped and threw it to me. I held it close.

"For three days I carried that bread!" He said, turning to Hasan with a slight smile, "I had some insane idea that all the time I had the bread you'd be alright. I had to leave you, lying there, I kept looking back, wanted so desperately to see you move, get up."

> I felt Sabri's concern, knew he was watching me. I wanted to tell him that I was alright, in control, but I couldn't. I couldn't speak to anyone, not even Sabri.

Skender sighed, rubbed his face with his hands.

> We kept walking until we came to the crossroads outside of the city. We turned right, towards Prizren and the south. We only went a few yards though, then they turned us into a field.
>
> There were about one-hundred fifty or two hundred men already there, all from Prishtine. Many tearful reunions

> occurred, fathers found sons, sons found fathers, brothers were reunited, friends clasped hands again. Most of the men had been rounded up and held at various places in Prishtine for three or four days. Some had been snatched from the street that very afternoon. And there were some....

Skender paused a long moment, head in his hands. "It was the first time they'd seen daylight, sunshine, for months, they were not men anymore ... just shadows."

He rubbed at his eyes as he sighed, then continued.

> I suppose we'd been there ten minutes. Someone called, pointed towards the crossroads. From the west a really huge group was approaching. We all crowded to the fence, watching.
>
> They were being marched towards us at a pretty-fast pace, I wondered how far they'd come, how long they'd had to keep up that pace. Most of their guards were on horseback, they were smart devils, much smarter than the guards from Prishtine. They halted them at the field and ordered them in with us.
>
> "Where are you from?" we asked.
>
> "Mitrovice."
>
> He was a big fellow. He forced a smile. "Thank you for inviting us. We left Mitrovice four hours ago and, as you see, hurried ... didn't want to be late for your party!" He sobered. "Have you any idea what's going on?"
>
> We shook our heads, just as another call came, more pointing. Again we crowded to the fence.
>
> A small group, probably 50 to 70 this time, approached from the north-west. The guards with them were on foot, looked more like those from Prishtine, and they were coming at a walking pace. The front guard opened the gate, lazily waving them in. After seeing the guards with the Mitrovice group it looked sloppy, unprofessional, yet more humane.
>
> The same question was asked. "Where are you from?"
>
> "Vuciteren. And you?"
>
> Sabri and I sat down. "What do you think they are doing?" Sabri asked.
>
> I shook my head. "I don't know, the big group was from Mitrovice, the small one from Vuciteren, both within a twenty-kilometer radius of Prishtine. Are they rounding us up for some reason?"

My words were cut short by a roar from the fence. We pushed ourselves forward, straining to see.

A long column approached from the north, down the very road we had come from Prishtine, and they were coming at a slow run. We could see, even that far away, that they were being pushed hard. When they halted them outside the gate they were heaving, sucking in great mouthfuls of air. Some fell to their knees. The guard opened the gate, "Get up. March."

We cleared the path. As they got past the gate, we took hold of them, helped them. And, of course, as soon as they got their breath, the inevitable question. "Where are you from?"

"Podiev. And you?"

Sabri turned to me. "Podiev! That's about 16 kilometers from us. It looks like you were right. But why?"

I stood up, shaking my head, and went to the fence, stood, watching the guards. Sabri came to me, pulled me down and back a little.

"Watch, but don't be obvious," he whispered, "never bring yourself to their attention. Anonymity is your armor, the only protection you have."

"These guards are like those with the Mitrovice group," I said quietly. Sabri nodded.

I closed my eyes, a sick dread in my stomach. The noise of trucks rumbling, grinding to a halt jerked me back to attention. I watched, my panic increasing, as the three trucks emptied, these guards, too, were from Nis. Their smartness, their cold contempt of us was reflected in the stance, the attitude, of their officer as he stood on one of the tailgates, his riding crop tapping unhurriedly at his high polished boots. He did not even have to call for quiet, he had our attention.

"Listen carefully to me. I give an order once. I never repeat myself."

But it was not his words that held us all in silent amazement, it was the language. He spoke in Albanian. Not the dialect that we use in Kosov, but that spoken in the south of Albania.

"A Serbian?" Arif questioned in disbelief.
"Yes, a Serbian Officer. Wait Migje, the explanation comes:

"Some food is being prepared for you. Each man will take one bowl of soup and two pieces of bread, one piece of bread is for tomorrow morning. You will be ready to march at six a.m.

prompt. You will march for two hours, rest for ten minutes. All orders are done by whistle, and the first six lines of the column will be men from Podiev. They already know the meaning of the whistle blasts." He looked around with a small smile, added softly, "We practiced them today. Ask them. They will tell you." There was a low angry murmur from the Podiev group, and his smile deepened, and he straightened himself before continuing. "Follow their lead, memorize the order blasts, and obey. You may converse quietly with each other. You may not sing, or shout. You may not speak to anyone we meet on the road. Anyone attempting to escape will be shot. That is all. Are there any questions?"

Someone stood. "Where are you taking us, and why?"

"If you address me, or my men, you say 'Comrade.' All you need to know is that you are in our care, have our protection…." The roar silenced him for a moment, but he stayed cool and unperturbed until it died. "Are there any more questions?"

Another stood up. "You are an officer in the Yugoslav army, yet you speak to us in Albanian, the language we are forbidden to use. I would like to know why." He started to sit, straightened, "Comrade", he added.

It was a deliberate insult, we all knew it, so did the officer. His stiffness, the constant tapping of his boot with his riding crop told us that.

"I chose to learn Albanian, and I speak it perfectly … better than any of you. It pleases me to know that I speak what you consider your language more correctly that any of you. It amuses me that my native tongue, the one you despise, comes more readily, more correctly, from your lips than the one you claim as your own." He smiled as his eyes swept the men at his feet. "I am superior to you in everything, even your own language." He had effectively silenced us. There was no sound, not a movement as he jumped from the truck and marched toward his tent.

We seemed to have had the will sucked from us. If we spoke, it was in a whisper, but mostly we sat in silence, waiting for our meal, watching the preparations, our minds scurrying from one terrifying explanation to another, ending always with the most important, 'What do they intend to do with this many…?'"

Chapter 8

The black tarmac was endless, stretching, shimmering to a narrow ribbon, reaching for the sky, my legs jarred as they pounded the unyielding surface.

"Four blasts, four blasts," I pleaded silently, the throbbing blood pulsating the cry throughout my whole body. Automatically I counted the shrill scream of the whistle, One. Two. Three. "Please," I prayed, "one more, one more." Four. I sat, not looking for a patch of grass, not caring where I sat as long as I could rest. My mind tormented my throat with thoughts of cool water, my aching body longed for the soft comfort of my home.

The whistle called us. "No," I cried silently, "not yet … not yet." I didn't move, men started shuffling past, one of the guards saw me, started towards me, I forced myself to stand. A thud hit between my shoulder blades.

"Move," the guard snarled. I staggered, a second blow came, pushing me into the slow-moving column. I swore softly, watching as he walked forward, encouraging the tired and exhausted to greater effort with a blow from his rifle.

"Skender?" Using as little effort as possible, I turned. It was Jakup, pushing forward to reach me. "Have you seen Morat or Sabri?"

I shook my head, "No, no one from Prishtine. Oh God, how much farther?"

He ignored my question. "Tomorrow we must keep together, we must."

I sighed my agreement, not wanting to think of tomorrow. A shot, followed by a second before the echo of the first had died, reminded me of those I'd heard throughout the day. "What are they shooting at?" I asked wearily. We walked on as I waited for an answer. "What are they shooting at?" I asked impatiently.

Jakup stared straight ahead, then after a moment, "If someone can't go on, or refuses...."

"Yes?" I demanded.

"They're shot."

I stared at him stupefied. "I don't believe you," I whispered. He didn't answer, walked on looking straight ahead. I waited until the guard passed us. "I don't believe you," I repeated, knowing it was true.

The truck moved slowly, the guards were changing ... those going off duty still fresh ... climbing effortlessly into the truck, laughing and joking with their colleagues as they anticipated rest and food.

My legs moved to a run as the whistle ordered, my weakened body trembling as I demanded more from it: there had been no food, no water for us, and only two rest periods. Six brutal hours of run, march, run, march, sparsely broken with brief walking periods, had converted us to machines, mechanically switching to the pace demanded, our senses, feelings, dulled to listening, waiting, for the one thing which gave us blessed relief.

Unexpectedly soon, a single blast called us back to a walk, our numb minds relayed the message to our shaking limbs, and we eased into our slow, shuffling, pace.

The shrill order "Run" came from the whistle's mouth, we shuffled on, "A mistake, a mistake," our nerves cried, "You brought us from a run, now five, six, walking steps, then run again? No, no ... it must be a mistake." The demand came again, "Run." Our legs trembling, objecting, we pushed to a run.

"Walk," the single blast ordered.

Dazed, uncomprehending, I looked at the guard, his back was to us, he was calling to the guards in the truck, whistle swinging from his hand, pointing to us, and they were laughing, enjoying our confused misery.

Jakup touched my arm. "Prizren," he said, pointing ahead.

"How far?"

"A kilometer probably, maybe two."

"Do you think we will stop there?"

He sighed, "Possibly, I hope so," he said as, again, the whistle ordered a change of pace.

"Halt!" We came to a grinding stop, my heart a wild thing, leaping, seeking escape, my parched throat fought the air needed by my bursting lungs, my legs threatened to let down the shuddering body they so feebly supported. I could feel the weakness claiming me, pulling me down into blackness, I fought back, pushed the ugly thing away, forced myself to remain standing. "Why didn't they open the gate?" Men crowded the fence, staring, gaping, as we had done yesterday. Guards came sharply to attention. Their officer climbed onto the tailgate of a truck parked near the fence. He stood there, waiting for silence from the heaving sea of humanity at his feet.

"We will stay here, in Prizren, tonight, be ready to march at six tomorrow morning. Are there any questions?" He straightened, "Comrades," he added, softly sarcastic.

The silent minutes dragged as he stood there smiling. "Three hours without rest is much harder than two, isn't it?" His hand moved, the riding crop tapping his boot. Tap. Tap. Tap. Tap-tap-tappity-tap-tappity-tap, tap-tap-tap. He stopped smiling, stopped tapping. "It is hard to constantly break into a different rhythm, a different timing." His riding crop tapped a slow, even, beat on his boot. "This, you see, is much easier, smooth, even." The stick hit his boot again, tap-tap-tap, tappity-tap-tappity-tap, tap-tap-tap. "It is the uneven, the erratic, which tires."

He stood there, watching us, then nodded to the guard, we filed slowly past him into the field. He had made us pay dearly for one man's insult, one man's stupidity.

I sank down, spread-eagled on the ground. Cool grasses fanned my burning face, I pressed close to the damp earth, letting her suck the shuddering heat from my body, I opened my mouth, pulling on the sweet grass, seeking, finding, moisture. A long trembling breath escaped as I gave myself up to the welcome blackness.

Nona was gently bathing my face. Cool water was dropped onto my burning lips, I licked it in, felt her hands pushing the damp hair from my forehead, dropping more water onto my lips. I tried to open my eyes, heaviness held the lids shut.

"Nona," I whispered, "Nona." I felt her arm under my head, raising me, something hard touched my lips, water trickled slowly into my mouth. Gently she laid me down again, her hands rubbed my legs, firmly easing the jumping tension from them. I lay peacefully still, content that she was with me, caring for me.

I shivered, suddenly cold, reached to pull covers, my hand touched the cold, damp ground. I opened my eyes, slowly, sat up.

His hands didn't stop their firm rubbing of my legs. "Do you feel better, boy?" he asked as he looked up at me.

I stared at him. "Who are you?" I asked in bewilderment, "Where's Nona?" He continued rubbing my legs with long, smooth strokes. "Where's Nona?" I repeated.

"Son, the love a mother gives to her child is very special, it is the purest, most unselfish love you will ever know. When great pressure, great stress, is put on us, we instinctively reach out for that love, it is always there." His hands stopped. "You are going to have to stand, walk around."

I shook my head.

"Yes," he said holding out his hand, standing over me.

I stayed where I was, looking up at him. "I was so sure Nona was here, was so certain."

"Perhaps she was," he said simply, as he pulled me to my feet.

I stared at him.

"There are many things we do not understand, son, many things that cannot be explained by logic. If you needed her, needed her badly enough, Almighty God would make sure she came to you. Now … move around."

I groaned, but he insisted, made me move, slowly at first, and then, as my muscles warmed, a little faster.

He was a tough, wiry, little man, about sixty I would say. He was a farmer, had been one all his life.

His was a typical Kosovar story, his grandfather had started a farm when he married as a young man, his father had been born there, he had been born there, and his sons, too. The grandparents, his father, mother and two of his own sons were buried there. The authorities had given him twenty-four hours to get out. He refused. So, he found himself with us. Two days later he died … pushed from a mountain path by one of the guards.

I have never forgotten him.

The three men sat silent, each with his own thoughts. Babush turned his head, wiping his eyes on the back of his hand when he knew his face was out of sight of his brothers, his son. The window rattled as the wind blew blasts of snow, Skender shuddered.

Arif looked up, took a breath, about to ask something. Babush raised his finger, warning him not to interrupt.

> Next morning, we were ready to leave at six o'clock, the column stretching to eternity. I don't know how many men had been added from Prizren, but it seemed to be a large number.
>
> By some good fortune, the four of us had found each other as we were getting into line. Chenan was six or seven lines ahead, chatting with a friend of his.
>
> Thanks to the old man's attentions I was in pretty good shape, so was Jakup, he had always been athletic, so the physical drain had not been too great for him. Sabri was so-so, the cold night had been hard on him, he had no jacket, just a shirt, but he was alright.
>
> Morat was the one we worried about. How he had managed to keep up with the column the day before I will never know. At the beginning of the march we had all taken turns at helping him, but somehow we got separated. Sabri was the only one from our little group who had managed to stay with Morat for the whole day. Fortunately, the big fellow from Mitrovice had seen Morat's need and offered assistance; between him and Sabri they had managed to keep Morat on his feet.
>
> Jakup was determined that in the future we would stay together, "Now we are as one family," he said, "each of us responsible for the other, we are brothers, do not forget.'"
>
> His words stayed with us…."

Skender looked up at his father, "If one started to lag behind, two would take his arms and urge him forward. Let despair take hold, you would be encouraged, ridiculed sometimes, into further effort. When your strength was at its height, you shared it, and when our spirit sank to its lowest ebb…. No one, not even blood brothers could have been as close as we, as caring for each other…."

His hands clamped to his mouth, stifling his sobs.

"Djali, Djali…." There was no comfort Babush could give, except to hold his son.

"None left. All gone. Taken. Snuffed out like candles … just me left. Why? Why me? That's what I asked the Grey Lady … she didn't answer…." Great sobs shook him and Babush held him closer.

Babush looked from one brother to the other, perplexed. Arif shook his head, unable to offer any explanation of Skender's words.

Hasan shivered, said soflty, "Zona."

"Don't be absurd!" Arif's voice was low and angry as he turned on Hasan, "A folk tale, nothing more." His hand moved in disgust as Hasan shrugged. Arif waited until Skender had put down the glass of water that Babush had offered him, gave a nod of approval as he saw that Skender was again in control of himself. "Why didn't Morat tell you that he had been beaten? It is obvious that you had guessed it, but why didn't he tell you himself?"

Skender sighed, "We never discussed what happened to us at Headquarters."

"Why not?" Arif asked, "I would have thought it would be better for you to know what was happening to each other?"

"I thought so too, once." Skender gave a sad smile. "I will digress for a moment, Migje, and tell you what happened, I don't think any further explanation will be necessary once you have heard this:

> I was with Sabri, we were down by the river studying, but my mind was not on my work, it was occupied with the beating I had been given a few days before. I remember I kept looking at Sabri, wondering if he or any of the others, were given the same kind of treatment. I had to find out, had to know, so I worked the conversation round and round until I had an opening.
>
> "Why do you talk about being at the 'hotel', being their 'guest'? I think it is stupid to joke about something so serious."
>
> He didn't answer, just went on with his reading. I leaned over, put my hand on the book, "Why do you do it?" I asked.
>
> He removed my hand. "Because it is the only way to handle the situation."
>
> I was furious. "It is not. It is infantile."
>
> He looked up from the book. "Is it? What would you do then?"
>
> "I think that we should be honest and open with our friends, tell them what happens." He had gone back to his book but I continued, "Tell them exactly what they do to you."
>
> "It wouldn't help," he said, without looking up.
>
> "It might. It would," I insisted.
>
> He sighed, closed the book, and said, "Alright, tell me."
>
> But that wasn't what I wanted! I wanted him to tell me. I hesitated, "You were at Headquarters last."

It was obvious he didn't want to talk about it. "Skender, this is not going to do any good, let us stop now," he said, opening his book.

I leaned over, snapped the book shut, "How the hell can we stop when you haven't even started?"

"All right then, let's start." I had never seen him so angry. "A guard comes for you. He takes you from the entry hall, down a corridor to a room, it is quite small. An officer is seated at a desk, and there is another chair beside his desk. Out of the corner of your eye you see a second guard, and as you sit down they stand, one on each side of you. You are questioned about your father, who does he see, what does he talk about with his friends, how long do guests stay, what discussions does he have with his brothers? The questions go on and on. Your answers become more and more feeble."

"You are told to stand. One of the guards holds your arms. The other stands, waiting ... usually smiling."

I was shaking, but still I had to know, had to be sure....

"The officer asks one of his questions again. You don't answer, or your answer does not satisfy his and he looks at the guard. The guard lifts his hand, smashes it down and across your face. The officer asks again, but this time the guard does not wait for an answer ... peowww. Your ears are ringing as the short, sharp slaps come ... slap, slap, slap."

"Another question, a pause for the right answer. This time the force of his hand almost knocks you down. But his friend is doing his part, holding you nice and still, so you are still on your feet. Your head is ringing, your lips bleeding, but you are still on your feet. Somewhere from a great distance you hear the officer speak, and you wonder if he is speaking to you, but the guard who was hitting you turns his back on you. Relief starts to flood you. And then you see his direction, he is beside the belts carefully choosing one."

"That's enough. I'm sorry, I was wrong."

"No. You wanted this, so now you'll listen to it," Sabri said coldly. "He usually turns and looks at you as he fingers the belts, trying to decide which one to use on you. Cold trickles of sweat run down your back. He takes down the one he thinks will work the best, walks back and stands in front of you, flicking the damn thing. He orders you to remove your shirt, you do so as fingers of fear claw at your insides."

"For God's sake, stop, I was wrong."

"The officer gives a nod. The other guard doubles his fist, punches you … hard … in the stomach, you gasp, automatically bend over…."

"Sabri, please?"

"…so that now you are in the correct position for him to drop that strap on your back, your shoulders. The number of times he lays the leather across you depends…."

"I'm leaving." I jumped up.

"No. No you're not," Sabri said icily, as he held on to me, "…depends on the officer, but they always finish the same way. The guard who had held you straightens you up, the other one gives you another hard punch in the stomach, and then they let you slide to the floor. One of them grinds his heel deep into your stomach…."

He grabbed me, held on, as I tried to leave.

"You think all your insides are coming out of your mouth, but it is only your own vomit. And so you lay there in the stinking stuff, thanking God that you did not cry out, praying that when they start again you will have the strength to take it."

He let go of me. Neither of us spoke for a long time.

"It doesn't help, Skender. It doesn't help me to talk about it and it won't help you the next time they come for you."

We lay there awhile then, just before we were leaving to go home, he turned to me.

"Skender, listen, only recently have they started on you and given time, you would come to this knowledge by yourself, but I am going to tell you now. You will always be afraid of them, but don't let fear latch on to you, don't let it make you its prisoner. When you walk out of that door, leave it there. Don't let your mind dwell on what they did, or what they might do next time. The only way we can handle their terror, and our fear, is to fight it, push it away, then try to laugh at it, and at them."

Skender looked at Arif. "He was right, Migje. It had been hard on him to tell it, and it was harder to listen, and it didn't help. Do you understand now?"

Arif sat staring at the rug, then looked up, tears in his eyes. "You had to do a lot of growing up in a very short time, son. All of you did."

"Yes, I suppose we did," Skender agreed quietly.

We had been marching about an hour, the pace easy and even….

Skender's voice was steady as he took up the story of the march.

> The humid heat we had suffered the previous day on the vast plains between Prishtine and Prizren had been left behind, the air that came down from the great alps was exhilarating and fresh. Under different circumstances we would have felt gloriously alive, happy, and grateful to be experiencing such a morning.
>
> Morat's weakness was worrying. He kept pace with us but the strain was obvious and we knew that if they should push us hard as on the previous day….

Skender reached, took a cigarette from the pack beside him, his eyes lifted to Babush for permission.

"Of course, Djali, it is not necessary to ask."

He took a long steadying draw.

> We entered Prizren, more beautiful than I had ever imagined. No postcard, no photograph had ever done it justice. Ochre and white houses clung to the cliffs, their red tile roofs gleaming as the pale morning sun sparked their dampness. The river gurgled its way through the town, walls of grey stone silent sentinels to ensure that this happy child from the mountain kept to her assigned path. Our guards, too, were watchful, determined that not one of us should stray from the path dictated by them … but their vigil was cruel and far more violent….
>
> Prizren fell behind. Ahead lay Mount Shari, awesome, terrifying, yet full of majesty. The column fell silent, even the guards felt her power and their whistles swung from their hands, holding their voice, their discordant jarring of our bodies held in abeyance. The order to fall out was a surprise. We were apprehensive, nervous, as we lowered ourselves to the grassy verge edging the black tarmac, it was too soon for a rest, the guards' attitude increased our fear, they were alert, watchful…."

Skender threw the remainder of his cigarette into the fire.

> Sabri saw my appraisal of the tall grasses and his hand rested lightly on my arm. I shook it off, eyes measuring the distance, body tense, ready. "You would not reach its safety before…."

> The gunshot stopped him. Even as our eyes swiveled toward the sound it fired again, and then once more, our eyes followed the direction of the pointing rifle, witnessed the three figures drop; drop as casually as the guard dropped his rifle. We sat in silent horror. A moan, so low, so soft, it could have been the wind, passed by our ears before the rifle roared again. The slight movement of the grass was stilled. No movement. No sound.
>
> "Thank God for His mercy in giving him a quick death." We murmured a few words after Morat's prayer, he gave a sudden shudder, beads of perspiration formed along his lip … I wondered, later, if he had a premonition, a sense … his own end was agonizingly slow, lonely…."

Babush and his brothers looked from one to the other in helpless sorrow. "How did Morat die, Djali?"

Skender's eyes raised, "Later, Babush, later, let it come in sequence."

> Trucks ground slow and heavy toward us.
>
> "From Prizren," Jakup murmured, "more guards, by the look of it."
>
> "Perhaps they intend to kill us all, here and now," Chenan said, voice low and angry.
>
> ""Shut your mouth!" Sabri wheeled on him, eyes narrowed. "If you have such thoughts, keep them to yourself."
>
> Chenan had voiced the thought of all of us. His mumbled apology was ignored as our attention fixed on the trucks which ground to a halt, the guards jumping out even before they were completely stopped.
>
> "You. You. And you…." One of them walked by pointing indiscriminately as he went. Fear jellied my stomach as his finger pointed in my direction. As I stood, I saw him point at Morat, "You … and you…." As the guard passed, Sabri pushed Morat back to the grassy verge and took his place.
>
> We did not look at each other but kept our gaze riveted on the uniformed back, neither wanting to see the fear mirrored in the other's eyes.
>
> "Five to this truck, five to the next…." The guard assigned us to the first truck, waved the others on. "Got those out and onto the road…." Sabri and I exchanged a quick grin of relief as we were put to work. The containers were iron, heavy, and huge. God knows what they were intended for originally, but now they contained a meal for us. We strained, struggled, and

got them to the ground, the lukewarm liquid slopping, spilling.... "One bowl, one piece of bread, to each. And make it quick."

I dipped the ladle, filled it to capacity for each one as they filed past. Grease floated in congealing pools. At any other time I would have turned from it with distaste, but now panic clawed at me as I saw the level drop lower and lower as I dipped and filled, dipped and filled. Would there be enough? Would there be some left for us, for me? I pushed the ladle down, lifted. Give less, give less, make sure there is some left for you. I pushed the ugly thought away, filled the waiting bowl to the rim.

Everyone had been served. I picked up one of the wooden bowls, filled it, and handed it to Sabri, then filled my own. There was only one piece of bread, Sabri broke it in half and handed me my piece. I let the bread lay on the soup, turning it to soak and soften as I sipped slowly, reverently, at the watery slop, it was nectar. I used my finger to scoop every crumb, every morsel of bread. My tongue searched, found, every droplet....

Hunger is a strange companion, give a little nourishment and your body demands more, rears up and searches. The gnawing ache which should be vindicated by the food swallowed increases instead of diminishing. So it was with us.

There was a little left in the iron pots. The guards kicked them over, let that precious liquid run across the smooth tarmac. I could have cried with frustration over the waste ... I hated them for wasting food when we wanted it, needed it, so desperately. It was just as well, had I eaten, taken just one more sip than the others, I do not think I could have faced myself. All eyes followed the loading of the pots, all eyes showed the tormented wish for more.

"Skender, why did you not eat the bread?"

Skender looked long at Hasan. "I could not. That bread was my link with home, family. To break it would break that tie. My stomach growled for it, the eyes of my friends lingered on it, but I could not break that precious bond. At least not then."

"How many did you number?"

"I cannot be sure, Babush..." there was a ghost of a smile, "they did not let us take roll call, but the column stretched farther than the eye could see. As the trucks departed another group was added, they came from the direction of Gjakov. At a guess I would say four thousand."

"Four thousand!" The gasp of disbelief came from all three men.

"Yes. Four thousand. Mostly young men, from sixteen to twenty-six, there were a few younger, some older, but mostly it was the youth…."

"The hope. That is what they took," Hasan interrupted quietly.

"Take our young men and they take away our will, resistance is minimal," Arif glanced around, adding bitterly, "they know their trade." The brothers nodded agreement then Babush signaled to Skender to continue.

> We were closely guarded, carefully watched as we assembled, the guards did not intend to let anyone escape. And then…" Skender stopped, eyes half closed, his voice low, as if he spoke to himself, "it was a fluke, an accident … an accident that brought tragedy. Morat stopped, bent to tie his shoe … one of the guards was laughing and calling to one of his colleagues, his back to Morat. Had he turned a second earlier, had Morat looked up a moment sooner, tragedy might have been averted. As it was, he collided with the stooping Morat, flipped over him, and landed, sprawled on his back, in the spilled soup.
>
> There was a moment of silence as we watched him, legs and arms flailing and then … the ripple of laughter grew, spread even to his own comrades. They stood at the same moment … he and Morat … and Morat gave a slight bow and apologized, then turned to move back into line. The guard, full of anger, grabbed his rifle and there was a sickening thud as he hit Morat with all his force. Morat stumbled, was caught before he fell…."

Skender took a long, shuddering breath.

> "The wounds from his beating at Headquarters had not healed enough, they opened, blood oozed and stained the white shirt, and of course the guard saw it immediately.
>
> "Been questioned lately, Kosovar dog?" Morat stood stiff and silent as the man shoved his face close. Then he laughed. "Or perhaps your mother scratched your back as you were doing it to her, eh?"

Skender heard the shocked gasps from the men, looked up at them and said, "There was no holding him, he leapt at the man, had him by the throat … he would have killed him if his comrades had not intervened."

Their officer came running when he heard the commotion and demanded an explanation.

He was sharp with his guard. He turned to Morat. "This time I'll let it pass, I know your rules. Get back into line." And then he faced the group of guards, "Speak against a Kosovar's mother and he will kill you for it. Remember that. Now get this column assembled and move."

The guard took his time to dust himself off, waiting until his officer was out of earshot. "I'll find you," he threatened, then turned and walked away.

We marched south toward Albania. Morat, silent and full of anger, seemed to feel no pain from his back.

Jakup glanced at the shirt. "Those stains are like a flag, the guard will find him in an instant," he murmured to Sabri. "Dammit, I've begged him to take my jacket … he will not…."

"His honor, his name, have been smeared," Sabri soothed. "Wait, he will accept later." Jakup's worry was still obvious. "The support he needs now is our ignoring of the incident. It did not happen, we heard nothing … agreed?"

The land was no longer flat. Mount Shari pushed her way from the mists, seeming to grow taller, more majestic, as we moved ever closer to her, while we felt smaller, more insignificant, as she towered over us, our marching even and steady.

Sabri touched my arm and I followed the direction of his finger. Three caravans lumbered toward us, gawdy and gay in their brilliant paints. The Romanies were flagged to a stop, their coal-dark eyes flicked, in the same nervous fashion as their horses' ears, from the polished smartness of the guards to our dusty, dirty column. The screaming voice called its order and we obeyed. We had learned our lesson, now we obeyed immediately.

Before the whistle dropped from the guard's hand we were at a halt. Sabri, Morat, Jakup, and I were still together. Chenan, still a little ashamed at his outburst, had dropped back although I noticed that Jakup kept a sharp watch on him. The four of us stopped opposite the last caravan.

Sabri half turned and checked the position of the guards then called in a low whisper, "Romany".

The driver, middle-aged, moustache thick and clipped to just below his upper lip asked through barely moving lips, "Who are you? Where are they taking you?"

"We do not know their plans. We are Kosovars." Sabri carefully checked for the guards, body hardly moving, then his hand dug, pulled money from his pocket. "Have you a jacket? We can pay…."

"No!" Anger flashed in the man's eyes as he, too, checked the guards.

"We need a jacket desperately," Sabri insisted as he looked around.

"Why should I take such a risk? What are you to me?"

Sabri's answer was soft, but carried, "A true Romany never denies one that is in great need…." His eyes remained front, not looking at the driver. "Only a gypsy would do that."

Skender gave a soft laugh.

His oath was explicit. Then he turned, reached into the caravan, and threw an old, dirty jacket toward us.

He watched as Sabri caught the jacket and started to help Morat into it, demanded, "Why for him?", and then as Morat turned he saw. "Beaten, eh?"

We stood in silence as a guard passed by. As soon as it was safe Sabri rounded the money into a ball, his aim sure and accurate. "You have our thanks, Romany."

"When you get there…" his eyes flicked toward the Albanian Alps, "…your need will be almost as great as his; you should have kept the coat."

Sabri looked up at the man, smiled.

"Do you remember his smile, Babush? It lit his whole face … I used to tease him about it…." Skender was smiling himself as he continued.

"My friend needs it more than I." It was simply said. There was no self-suffering, no gesture of heroics…."

"That was Sabri, it was his way," Babush said quietly.
"Yes," Skender nodded. "That was Sabri.

The Romany looked long at Sabri and then said, "I thought only my people understood true friendship…." And then the

> caravan ahead started to creak and prepare to move. "Good luck to you, Kosovars," he said, as he let his reins tap the horse's rump. The scarlet and yellow wheels crunched the gravel as he started forward. "Kosovar…" the call was low, urgent, and we turned toward him, he reached into his caravan, "…for you." We gasped as Sabri caught the coat, it was new, a pale coffee, heavily embroidered in every hue imaginable. He gave a grin as he saw Sabri's astonishment.
>
> "Thank you. You are a true Romany."
>
> "'Romanies know and honor friendship more than any race on this earth." He gave a wicked laugh as he encouraged his horse again. "Are you sure, Kosovar, there is no trace of Romany blood in you?" His laugh floated back to us as he pulled away.
>
> We waited until we were at a steady march and then helped Sabri put on the handsome thing. We chuckled at the sight of our quiet, conservative Sabri wearing such a colorful jacket!
>
> He gave a sheepish grin as he looked down at himself. "I feel like a peacock!"
>
> Morat looked him over, managing a smile. "It is an interesting combination."
>
> Sabri looked at him, "At least mine does not smell like a horse!" They both looked at each other and laughter caught them.

Skender sat staring into the fire, smiling. "If you could have seen the pair of them…" he shook his head, and laughed gently, "Morat, the fastidious, correct Morat, sporting a jacket so dirty, so old … and it did smell of horse! And Sabri…" he chuckled, "…can you imagine? A Kosovar outfit, white hat, white shirt, black and white cummerbund, dark trousers … topped by a Romany jacket!"

Emin slipped silently from the room, being careful to close the door softly. He stretched, easing his tired muscles to life, he was filled with a cold, sad anger. The pale grey of dawn lit his way down the steps, slippery with ice and snow.

A soft red glow enveloped the sleeping girl near the stove, and he was careful not to let the kitchen door bang as was its want. He was glad it was warm and that she slept soundly. He checked his watch, decided to let her sleep a while longer and pushed wood into the opening before moving the copper kettle onto the crackling logs.

He pulled one of the sheepskins close and sat warming his hands, thoughts in turmoil. He sighed and admitted that he would not have had the courage to return to Kosov had it been he in Skender's shoes. His eyes lifted toward the room he had just left, he had wanted to stay, longed to hear the rest but knew that he dared not, soon the men would want coffee, hot milk, and bread and once their thoughts turned to these things their eyes, too, would have turned toward the door.

He reached for the red jesva, hanging beside the stove. It held a little more than the brass ones, and he poured the now warm water into and pushed it deep into the hot ashes, frowning at his thoughts. Thoughts and feelings tumbled over each other in his brain, each screaming for his full attention.

He gingerly pulled the hot handle of the jesva toward him and put in the soft, fine, coffee, added sugar, stirred, and pushed it back into the fire. He looked down at Drita, said softly, "Be proud of him. I do not think I could have lived through that horror and come out unscathed, a whole man as he." The coffee rose and he pulled the jesva from the fire and stirred down the coffee, allowing it to sit on the edge and rise again slowly so that the creamy froth could form. "What shall I do? My brothers should know of this, it is their right, their heritage. Do I have the right to tell them when I was not permitted to hear it? And if I intend to repeat it, to whom shall I go for permission? Skender? My father?"

He poured the coffee, sipped on it as he sighed at the thought of admitting his action to his father. He checked his watch, reached, and shook Drita gently.

Her eyes were puzzled as she awoke and saw him. Her gaze traveled to the kitchen and, as remembrance came, she smiled, "I fell asleep," she apologized.

"I know, I regret waking you, but it is dawn."

"The bread!" she exclaimed, as she scrambled to her feet.

"There is not time to bake, today I will fetch it from the bakery…."

"Babush does not care for bakery bread," she interrupted urgently, "he likes me to…."

"Today he will not notice," Emin assured her. He stood, shrugged into his coat, "I will fetch the bread, put it in the oven to warm." She stared as his eyes filled with tears and he held her tight to his chest. "I swear to you, Drita, he will not notice."

He let her go, turned as he reached the door and faced her. "I am proud to call Skender my brother. Remember, Drita, always hold him in high regard."

Chapter 9

Skender put down the empty bowl, the hot milk had been soothing, but now the men sat waiting for him to begin.

> That night we camped in the frosty embrace of Shari. If the Romany had not given us the coats Sabri and Morat could not have survived. The guards crowded their fires, the lick of flame, the crack of burning wood intensifying our freezing misery, while the aroma of their cooking drove our stomachs to torment. I took the bread from my coat, held it in my lap, cradling it in my arms. I felt the eyes of my friends on me, but they said nothing. After a while I took it, asked a blessing, and broke a piece of it for me, then passed the remainder to Sabri.

Skender's eyes lifted to Hasan. "Many benefited from it, Migje. I do not know how many, but it was passed from one to the other, it gave us hope as well as nourishment."

Hasan wiped at his face, smearing the tears, "Thank God you had something, Djali."

"Yes. Thank God we did," Skender answered on a sigh. He pushed closer to the fire, reveling in the luxury of warmth.

> The hour before dawn is the coldest, longest, in the world. To generate heat from each other we stayed close. If one shivered violently, we crowded him, making our cold bodies warm him. I pressed close to the frost-bitten ground trying to escape the cruel wind. My eyes fastened to the east and I prayed for break of day. The night was endless.
>
> Day broke, bringing kicks from the guards, a blow from a rifle butt, and the order to move. We climbed higher, the thin air, the steep path slippery from the night's frost, took many

> lives, their cries, long and frightened, as they slipped into nothingness haunt my dreams even now. The path narrowed, became deep with snow, which was churned to muddy slush, treacherous ice hid beneath it waiting to suck your balance and send you plunging into blackness.
>
> Breath came in short hard rasps, heart hammered, head throbbed but do not stop, do not rest, otherwise a guard would raise his rifle….
>
> The mountains caught the shots and sent them back threefold, the sound shattered us, disturbed us and eventually passed unnoticed. Death became commonplace, survival a miracle. I watched the guards. Some killed without feeling, I accepted that. It was the others … those that killed with pleasure, anticipated it, salivated over it, that shook me to my depths. What had brought about such monstrosity? What breast had fed, what milk nurtured, such hatred of his own kind? To call him animal was an injustice to that species for none in that kingdom kills for pleasure, the lowest of their form has more dignity, more control, than these we called men.
>
> Darkness came early, welcomed for the relief from walking, dreaded because of the damp cold, the thought of the long night. We pushed close to the rocks, ate a little snow as hunger clawed again….

Skender was shivering.

Arif looked at Babush, his silent question 'Shall we put a stop to this?' was answered in silence. He frowned at the rug, not agreeing with his brother's decision.

> I felt someone watching. Fear bathed me in a cold sweat as I looked up and saw one of the guards swagger toward us. But it was not me he watched. His interest was in the one sitting next to me.
>
> He stood there, not saying a word, just looking down at Morat. "Get up." Morat was slow as he stood. "Undo the jacket…." He waited until all the buttons were undone. "Take it off. Turn around." His slow smile was terrifyingly evil as he stood looking at the stained shirt. "Turn around." He waited until Morat faced him, said softly, "I told you I'd find you. Now I'm going to beat the shit out of you. Move!" His thumb jerked over his shoulder. Morat's hesitation amused him. "You can have it here, right in front of your friends, or…." His head

> jerked, and he stood hands on hips, waiting. "Yes … I thought you'd prefer privacy." He looked down at us before he started to move away. "Listen well, you'll hear him whimper."
>
> We sat in silent anger. Fear for Morat filled us, choked us, and we could do nothing. We watched as they moved into the circle of light cast by the fire. The guard called out and three of his friends joined him, enclosing Morat, then they moved into darkness.
>
> "Four of them…." Chenan was shaking, his horror echoed in his voice.
>
> "I prayed he would not find him," Jakup whispered, as a sob caught him.
>
> Tears ran unchecked down Sabri's face, "May God help him."
>
> Despair and anger had me too tight in their grip. I sat silent and still.
>
> Red pierced the sky, turned the granite giant to rose and diamonded the snow, but we had no eyes for the dazzling beauty. The night had passed in such slowness as not to move. Our straining ears wanting, not wanting, to hear a sound, a cry … it was the howl of the wind that we heard. We moved our frozen limbs with care as our eyes searched for Morat….

Babush watched Skender carefully, the woodenness of his son's face, the cold, unfeeling voice, worried him far more than the emotional Skender.

> We did not speak, did not voice our fear as we were pushed and prodded into line. We shuffled forward, past the now dead fire, and then … then we saw him. His face was barely recognizable, a purplish mush, congealed blood crusted his lips, filled his half open mouth … there was no sign of life, no movement … we thought him dead. I wish to God he had been.
>
> A guard kicked at him, the moan came low and deep. The guard turned, even he surprised that life still flickered in one so beaten, then he moved on.
>
> But another had heard that moan, he came, calling for a friend…."

Skender's hands clenched, his eyes blazed with fury, and Babush's concern grew.

> They picked-up Morat … it was then that we saw both legs had been broken … then they swung him, as one would a sack of grain, out and over the ravine. His scream started even before they released him. I prayed it would be a long fall, that he would be killed on impact. The thump came too soon. And then … that long blood-chilling cry of pure agony…. And they laughed.

Skender picked up the cigarettes laying beside him, shook one out, then looked up at Babush. "Do I have your permission?"

Babush inclined his head, deeply hurt at the insolence of the question.

> Chenan broke from the column, ran to the edge, and looked down….

Skender let the spill light, then lifted it to the cigarette, took one short inhale, then continued.

> He must have been able to see Morat. His eyes showed horror as he turned away, then he ran to the guards. "You cannot leave him. Not like that." He realized that that was their intention. "For God's sake … one bullet is all that is needed," he begged.
>
> The two looked at each other and chuckled … I suppose that should have clued us … and then one of them lifted his rifle, pointed it and said, "Then, for God's sake, here it is." The snow took Chenan's blood, drank it greedily. They kicked at him, made sure he was dead, then moved away.

Skender took a long drag at the cigarette, then another.

> We were beyond feeling.

His voice, flat, not even a hint of emotion continued,

> Our minds were as frozen as the landscape through which we moved. Mechanically our limbs did their bidding. Hatred thawed us, and then when the numbness wore off, pain and anger tingled us to life and we made wild plans for revenge, even as we knew the uselessness, the futility….

"Enough, Djali, let it rest." Babush laid the blanket around Skender's shoulders.

"No!" Skender's violent denial, his angry throwing off of the blanket shocked the men. "How dare you ask me that? How dare you not listen, not want to hear…."

"It is you we worry for, not…."

"Do not worry for me, Arif," anger sparked Skender's eyes, "I have lived it, re-lived it, and will again and again until my death. You must know of it. You and every Kosovar who draws breath, from the youngest to the oldest, male or female." He took a long steadying breath, continued more quietly, "Kosov must know; the world should know." His eyes lifted. "One thousand eight hundred youths is the 'Government's 'official' figure of those killed. Double that, almost triple it, and the true number starts to appear. No crime had been committed, no sin. They were beaten, tortured, starved, then murdered for one reason, and one reason only: we, the Albanians, are the legitimate and rightful heirs to this land … and Serbia knows it, and hates us because of it."

The men sat in grave silence. Hasan bent, picked up the blanket, and offered it to Skender. A long moment passed and then he took it, wrapped it around himself. "Forgive me." His voice was subdued and low. "I warned you at the beginning, it is not easy to keep control…." He picked up the cigarettes and his hand stilled as he started to take one from the pack. His voice was choked, eyes full as he looked up at his father. "Babush, I did not mean to…."

Babush's hand laid gently along his shoulder.

Skender sat smoking, deep in thought. "Babush, I want you to know that I am proud to have you as my father. If I can bring half of the dignity and tenderness that you have given to this family to my own, I will be content." He threw the remainder of the cigarette into the fire. "Shall I go on, sir?'

Babush's head lifted and he looked straight at Skender. "When you are ready, Djali, continue."

Chapter 10

Skender closed the gate, turned left down Ruga Lapit. As he turned again onto the River Road he pulled his coat close about him for the wind was biting and cold. It had been his decision to use this route to the Mali house, he was not able, not yet, to pass the gymnasium.

He picked his way carefully over the muddy ground, circling the larger patches, jumping the smaller. The visit was not one he looked forward to, but he had delayed longer than he should. The Malis had a right to know how Sabri had passed the remainder of his days, and how he had died and he, Skender Berisha, was the only one who could tell them that.

The road was unchanged. He stood at the corner for a moment, then moved forward. Two boys, twelve, or thereabouts, shouted at him and he retrieved the football for them and headed it toward them. They applauded him and called their thanks. He smiled, remembering Sabri and himself at their age. A frown replaced that smile as he wondered how he should approach the old man, he had always called him Migje-Mali, had said it in a sing-song way as a small child, and it had stuck, even when he was sixteen. Sabri's father had always gravely greeted Skender in the same manner. 'Hail Skanderbeg, how is the King of Albania today?' A thrill of pride for bearing that great name had always seared Skender.

How shall I greet him? How to greet Sabri's mother? His hand lifted the latch on the gate. The heaviness was taken from his hand.

"Welcome, Skender," Luan gave a slight bow, "my father awaits you. He wished me to tell you that you must feel free in this house, that it is yours now as it was before. Please, come in." Luan closed the gate behind Skender. "My brothers' wives are not here; they have gone to visit friends…."

So, Migje-Mali was unchanged. He had made sure that Skender was free to wander this house as he pleased, had even arranged for the nusas of his sons' to be away so that he, Skender, should be unhindered, could pass in and out of any room without hesitation. Skender gave a shaky smile to Luan, Luan bowed and left him.

> 'Come on Skender! Race you! My mother is making laknor.' Sabri faced him, 'Sometimes I think she cares more for you than me!' he laughed as he washed at their fountain.

Skender sighed, returned to the present as the cold water touched his fingers. His steps were slow, dragging, as he went to the kitchen, the door squeaked, the dimness blinded him.

> He and Sabri sat close, heads touching as they planned some prank, stuffing their mouths with the hot savoury pie of spinach and cheese.

"Oh God, help me. How can I tell them?" he cried as he sank to his knees. "How can I put them through such hell, bring them such misery?"

"Your being here is a joy to us, a comfort." Skender's eyes lifted at the quiet voice. "We have accepted Sabri's death, now you must."

"I did not know you were here, Teza, did not see you." Skender came slowly to his feet and bowed. "Forgive me." He moved to take her hand and kiss it, but she held out her arms to him.

"Welcome home, Skender," she smiled through her tears. "My son and you were such friends…" she bit at her lip, "…I knew this was where you would come first, Sabri and you were always hungry…." She turned away as sobs caught her.

Skender held her close. "I would give much to not bring this news to you," he whispered, "I pray for your forgiveness…."

"Sshh. If I cannot hold my own flesh, I thank God I can hold you in my arms. You were as a son to me, Skender. I feel only joy in having you here." She wiped her tears, forced a smile, "Go to him, he has waited seventeen years." Her eyes closed as she held him close to her once more, then released him and smiled encouragement. "Go."

His feet faltered as he climbed the steps, slowly he eased off his shoes and stepped onto the thick rugs in the hall. Memories raced toward him, battering him as he took the few steps to the living room. His hand moved toward the handle, hesitated and he half turned toward the guest room, *Will he be here, where I always found him, or…. No, not the guest room. I am family.* The handle turned effortlessly, without sound, as it always had. Sabri's father was alone, sitting beside the fire. He laid down the book, stood. There was a moment, an eternity, as they stood looking at each other and then his hand raised in salute, "Hail, Skanderbeg, how is the King of Albania today?"

Skender's voice trembled as he made the expected reply, "He is well, thank you. And you, sir…" the old name would not come, "…how are you?"

The old man stood gravely watching Skender. "Migje-Mali is well, thank you." He held his arms wide. "Now I know and believe that you are home again, Skender," he said as his arms closed about him. "Come, sit down, close to me but so that I can see and feast my eyes on you." He smiled, then nodded. "Yes, it is you. There are changes but … our Skender has returned to us. Tell me, Djali, are you well?" Skender nodded, not trusting his voice. "And Babush, Nona?"

"Well."

"And your sister? Arif, Hasan, their wives?"

Skender realized that Migje-Mali was giving him time. He took a deep breath, "Well, I saw Teza. She is well." Mali smiled, nodding. "And your sons, their wives?"

Mr. Mali smiled, "Does any other nation go through this ritual? Everyone is well. Let us dispense with our formalities and go to the heart of the matter, you. Are you truly well? I am glad to hear it. Your wife?"

"Well, she will be here later."

"In Prishtine?"

"Yes, I will bring her here. I wish for you to meet her." The old man nodded, glanced up as the door opened and Skender turned, leapt to his feet. "Vehpi, Jusuf…" he exclaimed as the two sons entered with Luan and their mother.

Mrs. Mali served the tea, some sweetmeats, and they visited, laughing at old memories, then saddened. "Was it quick? Did he suffer?" Sabri's mother's question brought strained silence. "I have to know, Skender," she insisted, voice quiet but controlled. "Imagination runs uncontrolled, knowing will be easier."

"I am sorry, Skender." The old man looked toward his wife. "That was wrong of you," he told her gently.

"No, sir, you have a right to know and I am prepared to tell you." Skender hesitated, not sure if Mr. Mali wished him to speak in front of Luan, the youngest son.

Mali saw it and understood. "He is old enough. Sabri gave his life at seventeen; Luan, at twenty-six, is old enough to hear it." He gave a slight bow to Skender. "If you agree…?"

"Of course. Teza, this will be hard on you." Skender's voice was wistful. She settled herself, straightening her shoulders. "I will begin at the beginning…."

> …and so I prayed for Morat's death … begged that I would not be put to such a test. I think my mind preyed on his lonely end and sucked my willpower: the cold, hunger, and fatigue pushed down on me and I knew I was finished. My legs trembled as I dragged one to push it ahead of the other, the effort needed to continue was insurmountable. And so I sat down in the snow and mud. I believe that I had a fleeting thought of heroically giving up my life, but mainly I did not care

anymore. I had seen what happened to others who sat, it would be simple, an easy solution to the cold misery, the constant hunger.

'Get up.' It was Sabri's voice, listless from the thin air. I shook my head, too exhausted even to answer. He bent, tried to haul me to my feet. 'Get up!'

Strength flowed through me and I pushed him away. "No, I can't. I have had enough. I am prepared to die."

His eyes flashed with scorn. 'Coward.' Anger brought me to my feet. 'You are prepared to die, you are ready to admit defeat, let them win their game, have their way with us.'

My laugh mocked him. "They have already won! They do as they please with us. Look around you…." I made a grandiose gesture.

'No.' He pushed me forward, back into the column as a guard saw us and started toward us. 'They cannot win as long as we hold our pride, maintain our dignity….'

Anger was still strong in me. "I see little dignity in this hell hole." My eyes swept the exhausted and bedraggled line.

'Look closer, it is there. Each one who refuses to give up eats at them and undermines them. They can push your body into the dirt, can tread you into the mud, but they cannot touch your soul. Only you can do that, only you can dim that light, or put it out. Do not seek death, Skender, but accept it if it finds you.' The wind tore at us as we stood facing each other.

"God, I wish I had your strength."

He laughed, pushed me lightly. 'Since I could speak I have told you to follow me, let me lead….' Our old teasing continued, it was difficult to breath and took more effort to talk, but we needed to speak, to underline each other's effort.

Skender looked directly at Sabri's father. "He saved my life. He used the one thing, the only weapon, that would bring me back to my feet."

The old hands trembled as he passed cigarettes, they smoked in silence.

I had dreamed, longed, to step on my homeland's soil. The dream had become a nightmare of reality. Many froze that night; dawn's pale greyness did not reveal their death and we thought they slept. There was nothing to be done and so we left them, some sitting with head bent as if dozing, some smiling.

We lost Jakup at Lake Shkodra, the raft he was on sunk, deliberately, as it reached the center of the lake. It was a quick

> death; the icy waters took his life in minutes. The raft we were on was punted across … I can still see that blueness, the white hats bobbing … mushroom caps bobbing in a bowl of water.

He sighed, "Now I feel shocked that we saw and accepted death so easily. It had become commonplace, a natural happening. I felt a deep sadness at Jakup's death, he had become a dear friend, as my knowledge of him had increased so had my respect and liking. Sabri's sadness was stronger than my own, Jakup and Morat were his age, had been his friends and classmates."

Skender looked up at Mr. Mali. "What shall I do, sir? I know neither family and yet…."

"Both are known to me, Skender. I will carry their story for you. But why open such a wound for Morat's family? Suffice to say he died, let them not know the details." Skender nodded. "I feel sorrow that we put you through this…."

Skender brushed aside the old man's apology.

> "That night we slept in warmth, that night we lay without the harsh breath of frost upon us. We had dropped steadily from the mountains into green valleys, the sun was warm on us and we found new strength. As we passed some bushes others ahead of us pulled leaves and pointed out the right bushes to us, their warning, "Chew very well before swallowing," was passed back along the column.
>
> The mill was large and very clean, we could not believe our luck as we were ordered inside. Others were shut into various sheds and shacks, but we were in the main building. It was warm and smelt of flour. We had carried chunks of ice when we realized that we were leaving the mountains, ensuring that we could quench our thirst. Now we sat, in pairs, letting the ice melt in our hands and then dribbling flour into it, smoothing it with our fingers into a paste … a feast, a banquet! Our bodies cried out in agony as warmth penetrated them and muscles stretched instead of being held tight against the cold. But we slept, oh, dear God, how we slept. The wooden floor was a feather bed after the granite rocks.
>
> Our numbers were depleted but there were still many, yet the miller gave us each a swallow of milk, a piece of bread before we left….

"May God bless him and his family for that."

"May God bless him…." The voices of the Mali family unified in an earnest whisper as the old man finished speaking.

Skender waited, then his voice slow, hesitating, he began again.

> The air was warm, the sun pale but encouraging as we tramped the road edged with grassy fields. The warmth and color after the bleakness we had passed through brought hope creeping from dark recesses, even the black tarmac felt soft beneath our feet, our hearts lifted, we began to think of life and living.
>
> It was agreed between us that if Sabri or I found an opportunity to escape each must snatch at it and not depend upon the other, it tore me apart to think of separating, even as I saw the sense of it and acknowledged the logic of it.
>
> That afternoon I saw the sea for the first time. I was breathless with the wonder, the beauty of it. My imagination had never given such depth of color to the sea, and nature conspired to give me a never-to-be-forgotten picture, the sun, a fiery ball, sitting on cool green … I watched as the sea took the fierceness, cooling it, taking it deep within herself.
>
> A finger pointed, 'Tivari.' I did not know then that the name would be burned into my mind. Did the sun burn the sea…?"

He shook his head and sighed as he pulled himself back to Prishtine, then let his eyes meet Mr. Mali's. "It was at Tivari that Sabri's life ended, as did more than a thousand others." His hand shook as the match neared his cigarette, he saw it and glanced quickly at the others even as he realized that they had noticed. And so he took his time and smoked.

> Mostly Sabri and I were together, but there were times when one dropped back or pushed forward … perhaps to chat with a friend or help one we saw had need. Did Sabri move ahead? Had he pushed forward, or had I dropped back? The question still runs in my brain, torments me … there is no way of knowing. But we were separated, by five, maybe six lines. Five, six paces separated us, five, six paces gave me life and brought him death…."

Mali leaned forward, gently eased Skender's hands from his face. "Better for one to have life than for both to die, my son."

"But why…?"

"That is not for you to question, only One has that power." Mali gave a slow nod as Skender's agonized eyes searched his. "Only One, my son. You were meant to live; your time had not come." He was unprepared for the violent start his words brought, the intense shaking and he asked as he leaned forward. "What is it, Skender? What troubles you?"

"That's what she said..." Skender's voice was barely above a murmur, "...the Grey Lady spoke those very words."

"The Grey Lady?" Mali too was shaking. Oblivious of his sons' curious stares he slid closer to Skender. "She came to you too?"

"Too?" Skender's eyes bore into the old man's. "Then..." he licked at his lips, "then you have ... have seen her?"

The old man's head slowly denied. "Not seen ... felt ... her presence. I was climbing as a youth and fell. I broke my leg. I was alone. None knew where I was. When night came bringing her freezing mists, I thought I was finished, but...."

"She came. And she laid her grey cloak over you, warming you...." Skender looked hard at Migje-Mali and then as he received the slow nod of agreement, his eyes closed and he let out a long breath of relief. "I thought ... I have never mentioned it to another living soul." He sat rocking slowly back and forth and then asked, "What were her words to you?"

"She never spoke. Not to me."

"She did to me, Migje-Mali, she did to me." They were sitting very close, voices low. "The last night we spent on Shari ... She spoke to me." He looked long at Migje-Mali and knew that he had to continue.

"She said ... she said, 'You will live, your time has not come.' And then she smiled, that long, sad smile...."

> I slept well that night and was refreshed and ready for the next day's journey, but, as we started to leave the mountain she spoke, 'Remember me, we will meet again.' It was day. It was not cold and damp, there was no freezing mist dropping over me, and we were headed toward the valley ... and yet, I knew, knew, that she was near.

There was a long silence as Skender sat, head in his hands. "I have tried to tell myself it was the foolish dreamings of a young boy ... even as I tired to persuade myself I knew it to be untrue." He looked up at Migje-Mali. "Something, someone, was on that mountain."

"She is called Zona." Skender's attention was all his. Mali felt the intense concentration. "And sometimes we call her 'the Grey Lady'. She is buried deep in the mists of time...."

"She was young, beautiful...."

Migje-Mali's hand stopped Skender's protest. "She dwells in the bosom of Shari, she is revered and held in awe by all mountain people. There are poems, stories, all manner of folk lore about her...." He glanced around as he saw the amused smiles of his sons. "And I, too, laughed. Until she came. I, too, dismissed her. It was the ignorant, uneducated people that believed such superstitious nonsense." He pulled in a long, slow breath and released it slowly. "It is easy to dismiss the Grey Lady when you are on the valley floor, warmed by your own fire, or the sun. But … enter her domain … then you believe." The silence was a cementing of something between him and Skender that only they could share. After a while they smiled at each other and each moved a little apart from the other. The moment had passed. Skender could continue with his story.

The silver sand was crimsoned by the setting sun as we came ever closer to Tivari, the sudden blast grated against the peaceful scene. The pace had been the same all day and the sudden 'halt' order was a surprise. The rifles of two guards came across, in front of me, even as the order to proceed sounded and the first section of the column was waved ahead. Panic surged upward in me as I saw Sabri and the other friends move away and I started to push forward, the weight of the barrel was across my chest…. He licked at his dry lips. "Sabri turned … instinct? Perhaps a sudden realization that I was not with his group? I don't know. The metal was no longer weighting me, holding me back and I took a step….'

'One more step and you move into the next kingdom.' My eyes wavered from the big Mitrovice man who spoke, then to the guard. The rifle was pointed directly at my chest. His eyes bore into mine without a flicker as his finger waited…."

'Until tomorrow,' Sabri's warning was conveyed.

"I stepped back into line, raised my hand and answered him. "Until tomorrow." His steps faltered as he moved to keep up, glancing over his shoulder toward me. And then, when he saw that all was well, he grinned and shouted, 'Natën e mirë.'

I grinned back at him, "Sleep well!"

The rifle moved, waving us towards a large barn. That was my last sight of him."

Later … was it an hour? Two, even three? … we heard sporadic gunshots. We barely glanced up for it was a sound we had become accustomed to. The sudden constant and sharp rat-atat-tat turned us to marbled silence, then brought us in terrified fear to our feet. No one moved or spoke as the chatter continued, and continued … our eyes questioned, our heads answered. Perhaps we knew but did not want to know….

Skender paused. Tears ran unchecked, unnoticed, hands moved and gripped to give strength from brother to brother, father to mother. He sat in silent anguish and then continued.

> Next morning, early, before dawn, we were marched toward the beach. The guard was heavy, more than double. We swallowed, tried to push our panic down into us as we saw the pier.... Machine guns, manned by guards, nervous and eager, lined each side, leaving a path for only two to walk. On the right lay silver smooth sand, cool and quiet, on the left ... cold death.

Skender's shudder was violent, uncontrollable. "All of them. All dead." He rose sharply, went to the window.

"Why?" Mali asked after a long silence. "Why did they kill them?"

Reluctantly Skender turned to face them. "I can only repeat what I was told later." He moved with slow care toward the family, resumed his seat near Sabri's father.

> We were driven forward onto the pier, past the death onto a ship. I have no clear memory of boarding her. As I was pushed forward my eyes searched for a coat, pale coffee, heavily embroidered....
>
> 'I'm sorry, he was a good friend to you.' It was the big man from Mitrovice who spoke.
>
> I was numbed and stared at him, then managed, "Are you sure?"
>
> He nodded. I started to turn toward the rail, sobs ripping through me, and he held me. 'Do not grieve too harshly. Death has its own reward; he is free of their terror.'
>
> I stayed with him, needed him, as we moved across the Adriatic toward Dubrovnik. The story was passed in whispers, the first section of the column, mostly from Prishtine, had been assembled on the beach. A guard slapped a Kosovar, the man rounded on him, hit back and grabbed the guard's rifle....

Skender sighed.

> We had been through so much; we had kept control ... what made that control slip? Why turn for a slap when a beating had been accepted? He shot the guard, as the other Kosovars saw they moved swift as lightening toward their guards. They

> managed to disarm, kill some, but the warning had been given and machine-gunned guards came running.
>
> It did not take long to control the Kosovars. But the guards' own control had gone. Snapped. They killed them all. Their guns chattered their death chants until not one from that whole group survived, well over a thousand young men … in less time than it takes to tell.

Sabri's mother sobbed in silence. Jusuf stood ram-rod stiff at the window. Vehbi and Luan comforted each other and hid their tears from Skender. The old man remained as he had throughout the telling, cross-legged, straight-backed, hands quiet in his lap, the quiver of his white mustache his only movement.

Mali's voice was quiet as he broke the long silence, "The last time my eyes saw my son he was happy, smiling, that was when he left this house for the gymnasium. The last time your eyes saw him, Skender, he was smiling. Let us remember him this way. Let us pray that he will greet us with a smile when we meet him again in God's garden." He signaled to his wife and sons. "And now I want a moment with Skender."

The door closed quietly on them. Skender's voice came, barely audible. "Forgive me, Migje-Mali, for bringing such news." There was no reply and his eyes lifted to the old man.

"There is nothing to forgive, Skender, at least not from me. You carry a burden of guilt when there is none. We have accepted Sabri's death and now you must. Put the weight from your shoulders. Leave it here. When you think of him remember the light, the memories filled with sunshine."

"I do not think I can."

"It is much easier to hold old hatreds tight to you than to forgive."

Skender raised angry eyes to the old man, "I do not want to forget; our suffering was too great for that."

"I do not ask you to forget. I ask that you forgive." His hand stopped Skender. "Hope lies in the future; we cannot progress if we linger in the shadows of yesterday." His hand was gentle on Skender's arm. "You were given your life, live it to the fullest. Do not forget this tragedy, but let it enrich you. Let it fester and it will consume you, Skender." He lit his pipe, his hand encouraged Skender to have a cigarette. "Let me hear the rest, then close it, have done with it."

"I am not sure I can," Skender spoke slowly, and his eyes raised to meet the wise ones watching him.

"I am. Please…?" His hand urged Skender to continue.

There was silence for a while then, quietly, Skender started to speak.

> The townspeople of Dubrovnik are, as you know, Croatian. When they saw us, realized how near we were to collapse there

> was an outcry. The guards were surprised, bewildered, and there was a moment of confusion. In that space of time my eyes met and were held by a young man's. He lifted the tarpaulin of his wagon and I slipped beneath it. Darkness smothered me as he dropped the cloth, I could see nothing, hear nothing. I pressed back into the sweet-smelling hay as I waited for a bayonet to rip through me. After an eternity I felt a jerk of movement, the steady rhythm of iron-clad wheels on cobblestones.
>
> I must have slept. The brilliance of noon hurt my eyes as I was beckoned from the cart.
>
> 'Follow me.' He took me to a river, 'Wash, I will return soon.'
>
> I stripped myself of the foul-smelling rags, let my body slide with joy into the cold cleanliness. He was waiting on the riverbank when I climbed out. The clothes he offered were old, patched, but gloriously clean and smelt of the outdoors. He handed me bread, cheese and meat and waited as I wolfed it down. 'You must go, you cannot stay here.' He handed me a red neckerchief containing another meal, then anxiously asked, 'You understand? If they discover you, found out that I had helped you….' I stopped him. I already knew what his fate – and his family's – would be if the authorities knew of his assistance. I thanked him, stuffed the bundle into my coat and started away from the farm, away from warmth and people….

A grim smile crossed Skender's face. "It was two years before I could sit in peace and speak to someone without wondering if I endangered their life. Two years before it was safe to stay for more than a week in one place. The years pass slow and long when they are spent in fear … always hiding, always running."

"It was two years, then, before you crossed into Italy?"

"Yes."

"It took much courage to make that journey, to cross a border illegally. One day, when you feel you can, I would like to hear it."

Skender's smile was sad, wistful. "One day, Migje-Mali. But not now." He glanced up as the light tap came.

"Yes, Luan?"

"Skender's brothers are here, sir, Jakup and Emin. They wish to know if Skender is ready to leave."

"Stay and eat with us, Skender."

"Thank you, Migje, but no. Not today." He saw the disappointment. "This is my second home, now I need my first. But before the week is out, we will break bread together."

"As you will. Skender. Thank you for coming. My joy is beyond words at seeing you."

"And mine at seeing you, sir." He looked at the old man. "Thank you, I know, deep in my heart, that your words are true, I will try to accept."

"That is all I ask of you, my son. And now goodbye." His hands gripped Skender's.

"Goodbye, Migje-Mali."

The old man's hand lifted in the familiar salute. "Take care, Skanderbeg, last King of Albania."

BOOK TWO

Chapter 11

Skender smiled at his father as he entered the room. "Emin and Luan have arrived. We will be leaving shortly to pick up my wife."

Babush nodded, "I will be waiting to welcome her, Djali."

"May I sit for a moment, sir?"

"Of course." Babush waited until Skender was seated. "Something troubling you?"

"Yes, a little. Our customs and traditions are strictly adhered to, there is a rigid code which we follow. You do realize that she will know nothing of these customs? That they will be new to her?"

"I am expecting her to make mistakes, how could she do other? Have you told her anything of our ways?"

"No. Time slips by so fast, there is always so much to do." He laughed, "There is always a rush in America."

The old man nodded, "Then I am glad to be here where I can take my time." Their eyes met and they smiled together.

"But there is something I must ask you before she enters this house."

"What is that?"

Babush smoothed his moustache, watching his son, then slowly asked, "If you had married this girl here; if, as your Nusé, she had been brought to you in the traditional way, when Nona came to your room the morning after your wedding night would she have found what she sought?"

Skender stared at his father in angry amazement. "Are you serious? Are you expecting me to answer you?"

"Of course. Why are you surprised at the question?"

"Surprised! I can't believe my ears!"

"Believe them!" Babush's tone was firm, "Now, I ask again, Would Nona have found what she sought?"

Angrily, Skender stood up, "No, she would not. And now?"

Babush leaned back, folding his arms. "Now, you had better explain." He watched Skender closely as he paced the room, his lips tightening as the time stretched.

Skender turned to Babush, still visibly angry, "Because you are my father, because of my respect for you, I will. But in future remember this, she is my wife, and I will allow no one, no one, to question me about her." He sat, looked straight at his father. "Strangely enough, Babush, it was something you did that triggered the whole thing. I had gone to the post office to pick up a package, yes, the one you sent. It was raining hard. I decided as I was near, and it was time for Gillian to leave work, I would give her a ride home. She offered to make some coffee while I opened the package.

"Can you imagine my feelings when I opened it? When I realized that it was from you? Our wedding day was less than three weeks away and suddenly I had not only your approval, but your blessing. All those months of cold, angry, bitter letters had cut deep, had hurt me more than you will ever know. I pulled away the last wrapping. The Kosovar outfit was on top. I picked up the slacks, felt again, after so many years, that rough, heavy wool in my hand. I traced the black embroidery with my finger. Who had done that work? Nona? Drita? Can you imagine how I felt, after all those years of missing, to hold something that had been worked by them for me? The shirt was next, the soft, open weave … the unbleached whiteness … calling memories from deep inside me. I slid it aside, picked up the cummerbund. 'Pull it tight, Skender, show off that small waist for the girls,' Sabri laughed at me.

"I took the jacket, but I did not stop to examine all that wonderful, intricate work … my eye was caught by what lay beneath. I could hardly breath. Slowly I took the heavy silk brocade in my hands, lifted it, let the shimmering whiteness fall … a dimi. A dimi for a nusé. A dimi for my nusé."

"Your approval, your blessing, given to me with unbelievable generosity … your love, spanning an ocean, a continent, forgiving me for refusing to obey you. I held them close to me, holding you, and cried."

"At that moment Gillian came in with the coffee. She stood for a moment, shocked to see my tears. 'What is it?' she asked. I pointed to the clothes. 'From Babush.' She came to me, held me close. 'I'm so glad, so happy for you' … she was almost crying herself."

"I can't tell you why I needed her so desperately at that moment. She didn't object, didn't resist, gave herself willingly to my need of her."

"She slept for a while. When she awoke, I asked her, 'Why? You have never let me before, why now?' She was embarrassed, pushed her head close to my chest, her words muffled. 'This was different … you needed me, needed my love.'"

"And then, Babush, I made love to her as if she were already my wife. This time there was no despair, no desperate need, only a great tenderness, a great love for her, for her understanding and love of me. We became man and wife, Babush, three weeks before the announcement said we would. We belonged to each other as surely then as three weeks later when the judge signed the legal paper."

Babush was stiff with anger, "She should have kept her dignity."

"She did! Our customs, traditions, keep you easily on your path. How can you pass sentence when you do not know, cannot possibly understand, the circumstances, the way of life in the New World?"

Fury shook Babush's voice, "The girl was at fault!"

"Was she? Would she have been correct to turn her back when I needed her most? Would it have been more virtuous to hold me away, say, 'wait three more weeks and then I'll comfort you?'"

He knelt beside the old man. "Which one exercised control during our engagement? Which one pulled gently away? Which one, when there was too much insistence from the other, said, 'No, please, let us wait'?"

Babush did not answer.

"We are not known for our patience in these matters. Do you really think it was me?"

"Were you the first for her?"

"Why should that concern you? That is my business, no one else's."

"Were you the first?" Babush demanded again.

"Yes," Skender's answer was quietly firm.

"Are you sure?"

"Absolutely. But why does that concern you, Babush? How can it affect you?"

"It affects me. You are my son. What touches you touches me."

"And," Skender demanded proudly, "do you really believe that I, your son, would permit another man's leavings to carry our name?"

The old man was silent.

Skender sighed, checked his watch. "It is time for me to go. I do not want to be late … for the train to arrive before me." He stood up. "Before I go, before I bring her here, be very sure that you are prepared to welcome her."

"Djali, we will never reach agreement on this matter. I wish you had waited, but it is done and nothing can change it. The most important question has been answered." He stood up, took hold of Skender's shoulders. "But I will tell you now, had the answer been no, not a foot, not even a toe, would she have put past my gate." He pulled Skender to him, hugged him. "As it is, I am waiting to welcome her."

Skender closed his eyes, returning his father's hug. "Thank you, Babush."

Babush let him go, put his arm around his son's shoulders and walked him to the door. "Go now, Djali, bring your Nusé home."

Emin and Luan lounged on the hood of the car, lazily watching Skender pace up and down. "My cousin seems anxious," Emin grinned to Luan.

Luan shrugged. "I told him the train would not arrive for another hour, but he wanted to be here." He lay back on the car, letting the pale wintry sunshine on his face.

Emin looked at him. "Sleepy?"

Luan smiled, "No. Getting an early tan!"

Emin looked down at his friend. "Are you eager to see her?"

"Not as eager as you!" Luan laughed.

Emin grinned back. "Yes, I admit it! I am very curious." Idly he watched Skender. "I wonder why he didn't wait, marry one of our girls?" When no answer came he looked down at Luan, poked him. "Did you hear me?"

"Uh-huh," Luan nodded.

"What do you think?"

Luan opened his eyes, shielding them with his hand. "It is not my place to venture an opinion on a member of your family."

"This is between us. You have met some Western girls; did you like them?"

Luan fought hard to swallow his laugh. "Yes, I liked all of them!"

"Would you marry one?"

"No." The answer was definite, decisive.

"So sure?"

"Yes."

"Why?"

Luan sat up, "I would never permit one of them to carry my name." He saw Emin stiffen. "Emin, we are on dangerous ground, your family's honor closely involved. Let us walk away from this?" Emin nodded. "I intended no slight on Skender, you understand that?" Emin nodded. "One can hardly judge the rest of the world's women by the ones I met in Dubrovnik. I am sure…."

"Stop! It's alright." Emin punched him on the shoulder, "You're giving me a headache with your babbling!" he said, laughing, "how much longer before the train comes?"

"Half an hour, if we're lucky."

"I hope everything will be alright for him," Emin frowned, "that our family will accept his Nusé." He looked at Luan, "Babush refused, you know, when he asked for permission to marry."

Luan was startled, "Then he married without…?"

"No, but he would have. The date was firm and very close before Babush agreed. When Babush got the first letter asking for his permission, he went up like Vesuvius! Letters whizzed back and forth." Emin shook his head, laughed, "No plane was needed for the ones from Babush! They were so fiery they just zipped across the Atlantic by themselves! Skender dropped the subject for a month or so, if I remember rightly. Babush acted immediately, started to look for a Nusé for him."

"From here? Are you serious?"

"Yes. And, by heaven, so was he! He sent feelers everywhere." Emin jumped down from the car and peered towards the station. "I have not seen Skender for a while, but he's there, sitting down." He eased himself back onto the car.

"Did Skender know about his father's search for a Nusé?"

"Yes, Babush wrote and told him. The next letter was very clear, 'Do not search for a Nusé in Kosov. I have found my own and intend to marry her with or without your permission.' Boom! Skender must have heard the old boy all the way to California!"

"But he went ahead with his plans?"

"Yes. They became engaged. Letters were still exchanged, but there was a coolness. It was a sad time."

"What happened to make Babush change his mind?"

"We never knew … not even my father knows. Suddenly Babush ordered a Kosovar outfit, and a wedding outfit for a Nusé … everything, from top to bottom. When they were ready, he sent them to Skender."

"Did she wear it?"

Emin looked surprised, "Yes, we have pictures."

"I thought she might have refused, even laughed at the idea."

"How could she? It had come from her father-in-law," Luan shrugged. "Are you saying that she could?"

"A girl from the West? Yes!"

"Are they so different from our girls?" Emin asked curiously.

"As chalk and cheese." Luan laughed at the expression on Emin's face and nodded, "They're different, believe me!"

"How?"

"Everything. They're very bold, very sure of themselves, very … free with their affections."

Emin's eyes danced. "Ah-ha! Did you, er … take any of them out?" Luan laid back on the car, grinning. Emin leaned over him. "Did you?"

"Move! You're ruining my tan!" Luan was grinning broadly.

"Not till you answer!"

"Well, Emin, I'll tell you. My father insists that I behave myself in an acceptable way at all times. So I did … the acceptable way of Dubrovnik, of course!"

Emin punched him and they laughed together.

"I have to go!" Emin said, banging his fist on the car. "This spring. Come with me?"

Luan shook his head.

"Why not?"

"I have lost interest in variety. Someone special holds me here." He sat up. "I have told no one else, but my father has promised to ask for a Nusé for me this spring."

Emin stared in happy amazement, then held out his hand. "And has he started to search?"

"He does not need to. I know who I want. She is here, in Prishtine."

Emin laughed. "Sly one! And you never told me, never breathed a word."

"I care for her, Emin." Luan was suddenly very serious. "More than I thought possible. If the family refuses…."

"Why should they? Your family's reputation, your own, are beyond question!"

"Thank you. I pray you're right."

"Of course I am! I will be there to escort her, right to your property. A year from this spring…." He started to dance, hands held above his head, winking and raising his eyebrows at Luan, who sat grinning at his friend's excitement. He stopped, listening. "At last!" he said as the whistle of a train called in the distance.

Emin studied the people stepping down to the platform. "That must be her. Yes, I'm right, Skender has seen her too." He took a step forward, stretching eagerly to get a better view. "I did not expect her to come in men's trousers."

Luan's smile deepened at the expression on Emin's face. "You can expect a few more surprises in the next day or two, my friend! What did you expect her to wear … a dimi?" he laughed.

"I don't know." Emin was excited. He glanced back to Luan, grinning, "I am anxious to see how she greets her husband."

"She will … never mind. Watch! You will see for yourself." Luan was enjoying himself. He watched the smile fade, a look of disbelief come over his friend's face.

"Thank God Babush did not come," Emin said in a shocked voice. Quickly he glanced around. "I hope nobody is here who knows us. Did you see? Right here in a public place! He kissed her! And on the mouth!" He grinned back at the smiling Luan.

Luan winked, tipped his hat well forward. "Wait till you see what goes on at the beach at Dubrovnik." He bit his lip, narrowed his eyes, leaned toward Emin. "That'll make you dance!" He laughed as Emin did a few quick dancing steps. "Why don't you go and help with the bags? I'll wait here." Emin adjusted his hat, smoothed his moustache. "Go on! She will not notice you! She will have eyes only for him," he said, giving him a shove.

Emin winked. "She may have a friend!" He pulled his cummerbund tighter and started in the direction of the station.

Luan smilingly watched him. *We have been wondering about our reaction to her … I wonder what her reaction will be to us.* He stretched, checked that the car seats were clear and clean. *I hope Skender's prepared her.* He opened the trunk, ready to receive the bags.

Chapter 12

"What did you say?" Emin asked Luan.

"I am swearing about your street! Why don't they do something?" He felt despair as he saw his hours of polishing ruined by the splattering mud.

"I am sure they will, as soon as a non-Kosovar family moves here," Emin answered smoothly.

"Better keep the mud!" Luan grinned.

Skender turned to Gillian with a smile, "They are making jokes about our street. When it is wet, we skid down … when dry, bump, and when frozen, slide. There is never a time when we can travel in a normal way." She nodded, not turning, continuing to stare out of the window, "Why so quiet?"

She glanced quickly at him, then turned back to the window, "I'm … scared."

"Don't be silly … it is my family you are meeting."

Her smile was shaky, "That's why."

The young man beside the driver half-turned to talk to Skender. She watched his mouth forming words she could not follow, laughing … at what? She wished desperately that she knew the language, knew something of their ways. *What was it that Skender asked me to do when I meet his father, his mother? Oh, I wish I was back in London, or San Francisco, or anywhere. No, I don't … I wish it was next week and the first meetings, the first problems were behind me. I think I'm going to be sick. Why can't I just shake hands with his parents instead of going through all that rigmarole? What if they don't like me? What if I do everything wrong? They'll think he's married an idiot. I am going to be sick!* She felt the three pairs of eyes on her for a moment, the one driving seemed to be arguing. *Have I already put my foot in it?* Skender's hand touched her hair and she tried not to stiffen, not to pull away. *Smile at him, stupid. He'll think you already regret coming.* Shakily she returned the encouraging smile given her by Skender. She sighed with relief as he removed his hand from her head and leaned forward to talk to the two in front.

"Skender," Emin half-turned to talk to Skender on the back seat, "I have a wonderful idea! When we get to the house, you go ahead. I will wait for five minutes, then I will bring her to you … in my arms, the way she should have been given to your family."

Skender hesitated, tempted by the idea of receiving his Nusé in the accustomed way. He caught the angry glare that Luan gave to Emin. "You do not approve, Luan?"

Luan concentrated unnecessarily on the road.

"What is your reason?"

"I feel she has enough to cope with, without adding to it," Luan replied quietly.

"I still think it is a good idea … we will proceed," Emin insisted. "Do you agree, Skender?"

"It is not a good idea!" Luan glared angrily at Emin. "Try to understand her position. She is nervous, does not know our language, and she has had a long journey." He looked in the rear-view mirror at Skender. "You have already asked one difficult thing of her … is it right to ask another?"

"King Arthur's knight … to the rescue!" Emin's voice was cool, sarcastic.

Luan inclined his head, "I apologize. It was not my place to voice an opinion."

"Correct at last," Emin agreed icily.

"I think Luan is right, it would probably embarrass her." Skender put his hand on Gillian's hair. "She is already nervous, as you say. Thank you for your offer, Emin, but I will take her in with me." He leaned forward, removing his hand from Gillian's head. "Please do not put a cloud over this moment … it is a small matter and not worth argument."

Luan applied gentle pressure to the brake. The car skidded slightly and then stopped outside of 1764 Ruga Lapit. Both young men softened, anger evaporating, as they realized the significance of this moment to Skender.

"Luan…" Emin stopped Luan as he started to open the car door, "I was at fault. I will make it up to you in some way."

Luan punched his friend's shoulder, "Yes, you can help clean this car." He laughed as he opened the door nearest Gillian. "No, wait," Luan's hand told her to stay where she was as she started to move, "Skender or Emin will help you." He smiled at her, then shook his head, "Not me, I am not family."

Gillian did not understand all of it, but, warmed by the young man's kindness, smiled back at him as she remained seated. Emin leaned in, offering his hand with a murmured word. *How friendly they are … why am I still so worried?* She took his hand. The pull, the support was enough to help her without throwing her off balance. She thought fleetingly of her friend Maggie. *She'd go nuts over these men. They're so good-looking, so … gallant!* She smiled, "Thank you." Emin gave a slight bow, turned to Skender. *Not one of them would be safe from Maggie's roving eye!*

There was some exchange between the three, the taller, the driver, came to her, held out his hand and gave a slight bow.

"He is saying good-bye, that it was an honor for him to meet you, and that he hopes you will find pleasure in his town, and happiness with your family," Skender translated.

"Thank you." She felt suddenly shy. She shook hands. "Please thank him for picking me up at the station … and I hope I will see him again." She was awkward, embarrassed, and angry at her lack of words after he had made such a charming speech. She took a long, steadying breath and looked at the big wooden gate while they said their good-byes.

"I … er … dressed it up a little." Skender waved to Luan as he started the car, then took Gillian's arm. "Here you cannot tell a strange young man that you hope see him again. Emin, I will let you see to the bags. Now I am going to give Babush and Nona their new daughter." He pushed open the heavy gate, let it close behind them. "I have dreamed of this moment, Jill, but now that the time has come … I don't know what to say. I had all kinds of speeches prepared, but now…."

"Please don't say anything. I am so nervous you'll make me cry."

"Alright." He bent his head, kissed her gently. His fingers reached, pushed an escaping curl into place. "Give me your hand. Careful, it is very slippery." He guided her along the path up the steps. "Five steps…." Emotions could be controlled if he concentrated on the unimportant. He closed the entry room door against the biting wind. "Take off your shoes. Never go past this room with shoes on."

"I know. We do this ourselves, remember?"

He smiled, "Yes, but sometimes you cheat. That was only half a smile." His finger traced the outline of her cheek. "Are you still nervous? Don't be. They are anxious to meet you. Ready?" He paused as he reached the first door on the right. "Do you remember what I told you? How it's done?"

"I think so," her smile was tremulous, "I hope I don't goof it up."

"You'll do fine," he assured her as he gave a light tap on the door. They waited until a voice answered, then Skender gave Gillian's hand an encouraging squeeze and opened the door.

Babush and Nona sat beside the fire. The air crackled with excitement, anticipation, as the door opened and Skender led Gillian forward.

Skender gave a slight bow as he released Gillian's hand. "Babush, Nona, may I present my Nusé, Gillian. Gillian, this is Babush."

Both old people rose, smiling a welcome. Babush moved forward, "Welcome home, daughter."

Tears stung Skender's eyes at his father's words. "Thank you, Babush." The old man gave a nod of encouragement. "Go ahead, my love," Skender said as he passed the encouragement to Gillian.

With slow hesitation she stepped forward, took hold of both of Babush's hands in hers. Embarrassed, awkward, she bent her head and raised his hands to her chin, toward her forehead….

Babush stilled with anger. Without interrupting Gillian he glanced toward Skender. "How dare you demand this of her?"

Surprise fitted across Skender's face at his father's reaction. "I did not demand! I asked!" he retorted.

"She is your wife … demand or ask is the same for her."

"No! Not for her … for her there is a difference." Skender's anger matched his father's.

Gillian had completed the ritual. Babush smiled, bent and kissed her on each cheek, then guided her toward his wife. "Go to Nona," he encouraged gently. He waited until she had turned toward Nona before again addressing Skender. "Make sure it goes no further than this room, your mother and myself." His finger pointed at Skender, emphasizing the rest, "And I demand that!"

Skender's hands lifted, fell, as he sighed, "I sought only to please you, Babush."

"You will please me by not embarrassing guests in my home."

"She is not a guest." Anger was subsiding. Skender continued more quietly, "She is your daughter."

Babush inclined his head. "Agreed. She enters this house as your Nusé and my daughter," his tone was very firm as he added, "make sure she is treated as she should be."

Gillian's nervousness had increased as she sensed trouble between Skender and his father, "Have I done something wrong, Skender?"

Skender's answer was sharp and he did not even glance in her direction, "No."

"Skender, do not be short with her because of your anger at me. I do not know the language but I recognize the tone. Watch yourself." He turned his back on Skender. "Wife, take the child to meet Drita … let her freshen herself and then we will eat."

Skender waited until the door had closed on them. "I am sorry if my wife's greeting offended you," he said, voice tight.

Babush lowered himself to the rug, made himself comfortable. "Your wife did not offend, you did." His hand gave gracious permission for Skender to sit. "Bring your head together, Skender … you are at odds with yourself. You distress Nurije by demanding a stop to our customs and then, within days, you turn about and ask this girl … who does not know our customs … to follow it. Make sure she is not embarrassed further by your own confusion." He glanced up at the stiff figure of his son. "I gave you permission to sit."

"I do not wish to."

Babush inclined his head. "As you will." He took his pipe from his coat pocket. "When did you ask this of her?"

"On the way from the station … does it matter?

"No. But I would like to know why."

Skender sighed as he joined his father on the rug by the fire. "I wanted to please you, wanted you to…." His hands gripped tight in his lap.

"Wanted me to love her?" Babush leaned toward Skender. "How would you have had her greet me if I had come to your home?"

"I would not have interfered. She would have hugged you, perhaps kissed your cheek."

"With respect? Happiness?"

"Yes, of course." Skender's voice was low.

"And do you think that I can be happy with a greeting given in embarrassment, humiliation? Or would one given willingly, with happiness and respect have pleased me more?" Skender did not answer. "When our girls wanted to greet you in our way it was from happiness at having you here, respect for my son. Was that so hard for you to accept? For myself, I would rather your Nusé had greeted me in her way, giving freely of herself, allowing me to accept freely, than to be greeted in our way with embarrassment. By taking her dignity, you took mine." He finished packing his pipe. "My love cannot be given to her because you want it … nor because you ask certain things of her. That she must seek out and win for herself."

"I was wrong. I see that now. I thought … if she conducted herself as if she were from here, if she would follow some of our ways … you might accept her more quickly."

"Skender, I accepted her when she walked through the door. What were my words to her?"

"'Welcome home, daughter' … I was deeply moved when I heard them."

"Djali, listen to me. My objections to your marrying this girl may have seemed harsh, but they were done for love of you. I was afraid for this marriage, afraid for you. The girls from the West do not enjoy a pleasant reputation. Loyalty to their husbands, their families, does not seem to be one of their strong points.

"You were alone, no one from your family near you … how was I to know that it was not loneliness that drove you to your decision? What kind of girl had caught your heart? You said she had no family near … what was she doing by herself so far from guidance? Is it so strange that I objected? That I begged you to wait, let me find a girl for you? One that I could trust. One that I knew would serve you, honor you." He lit his pipe, pulled deeply on it. "In my place, what would you have done?"

"The same, the very same," Skender had his head in his hands. "But…."

"No, let me finish. I struggled many hours over my decision. And then I knew that I had acted wrongly. Since sixteen you had had to grow straight and strong without my guiding hand, and you had done just that. My seed had blossomed and grown to manhood … no one ever mentioned you name without respect. If you had conquered all obstacles and achieved that respect, that dignity, without my help, now was not the time for me to interfere. You wanted to choose your own wife … so be it." He leaned forward, "And if you were making a mistake you, not me, were the one who would have to live with it … and suffer with it.

"Now she is here … I can do no more than I have. If she is prepared to search for my love, she will find it. But the move must come from her, you cannot reach for it on her behalf … the effort must come from her, and her alone." He took a deep pull on his pipe laid it down and softly continued, "If she desires more than acceptance from me, let her seek more … and this I would expect from any girl who was your wife, whether she came from Kosov, or the other side of the world."

Skender moved closer to his father, laid his head in the old man's lap, "Babush, forgive me, I was confused."

"There is nothing to forgive, Djali," Babush laid his hand on his son's hair, "your confusion comes when you try to merge two cultures that cannot mix. We can touch, understand, but the two can never blend to make a new."

"Where shall I draw the line with her? When shall I ask her to step to our side? When to stay where she is?"

"Ask only on essential things, important things … anything that affects our name, our honor. Let her be herself in everything else. The most important thing is that she understands our position when men come to visit. Make sure she realizes that she must not be seen by them.

"If she wants to hug me, to kiss my cheek instead of my hand in greeting, why not?" A smile curved his lips. "She is a pretty thing, so I will not object!" Skender raised his head, smiled back at his father and they laughed gently together. "Don't you think you had better find her? Perhaps Nona has treated her like one of the girls and put her to work!"

"If ever I have a son, Babush, I hope I can be as understanding as you."

"Enough. Go find your Nusé. And tell Drita to hurry with our meal." Skender stood, went to the door. "Skender, do you realize there is no one here who knows her name yet? We have seen it often on paper, but…" he shrugged.

Skender nodded, smiled back. "While we eat, Babush … I will give you all a lesson!" He closed the door quietly.

Babush sighed, put his chin in his hand, frowning at the fire. *I pray she's right for him.*

Chapter 13

Gillian sat on the bench by the window, casually watching as an old man left the house and walked down the path to the gate.

"Don't let him see you," Skender said quietly, slipping his arms around her waist.

She jumped, startled, "I didn't hear you come in."

"The benefit of thick rugs and no shoes." He kissed the top of her head, laid his cheek against hers. "Be careful when you look out of the window, don't let any of the men see you."

She lay back against him. "Why not?"

"They would be embarrassed for you and themselves." He laughed at her look of incredulity. "You have entered another world, my love, as far removed from your world as the stars. Did you rest this afternoon?"

She nodded, pointing to a pile of cushions near the fire. "There. Nobody came in … I dozed and read all afternoon. I feel fine now."

"Good. I am sorry that I had to leave you alone as soon as you arrived in my home, but Babush was anxious for me to see our guest and, of course, Rashid wished to see me." He sat down beside her. "I think I'd better tell you some of the things expected of you. First of all, and this is most important, when we have guests you must stay out of sight, let no man who visits here see you."

"Why not?" She was defensive, head tilted high. "Because I'm not from here?"

"No, that has nothing to do with it. It is our custom. The women stay out of sight when any men are around."

"Then why did those two young men come with you to pick me up at the station?"

"Emin, the one who did not drive, is family. He is my cousin; but here, because he is a blood relation on my father's side, he is more than a cousin, he is a … second brother, shall we say."

"What if he was a cousin on your mother's side?"

"Then he would be just a cousin. Why so sad about that?"

She sighed, asked wistfully, "The woman doesn't seem too important here, does she?"

"Very wrong! She is very important. Not to the outsider, not to the stranger, but to her husband, her family, she is the pivot, the cornerstone. We have a saying … 'A good woman can build a house overnight; a weak one can destroy a castle in an hour.' Do not be deceived into thinking that we are hiding our women away, that we are ashamed of them. On the contrary, our wives and daughters are more treasured than our own lives. Let me give you an example: how long have you known Emin?"

She shrugged, "Five minutes."

"Do you realize that if it was necessary he would give his life to protect you? To protect your honor, your dignity? For him you are family … there is nothing on this earth more important than that. It is not easy to understand … for someone raised as you were, almost impossible. But watch, see how Nona is treated, how carefully Drita is shielded from any unpleasantness."

"And the other one, the driver, who is he?"

"A close friend of Emin's … the youngest son of my father's oldest friend, the youngest brother of my dearest friend."

She smiled, "Now it is my turn to ask, 'Why so sad?'"

"His brother, my friend, is dead, Jill. One day I will tell you all about it."

"I'm sorry," she leaned forward, laid her cheek against his, "I would not have teased you if I'd known."

"I know that. The young man's name is Luan. Because of his close ties with us, and because his family have a car, he offered his services today."

"That was nice of him."

Skender laughed, shook his head, "No, for him it was an honor that I accepted."

"Why didn't he help me out of the car? Why did he tell me to stay put until you or your cousin came? After all, he was on the side nearest to me."

"He is not family. It would not have been right for him to touch you. Don't make that face! It is the truth! Had you been from here he would never have met you, never have seen you. But enough of this. There is one more thing to remember, when my father or mother … or I," he grinned at her, "enter the room, stand up immediately. Do not sit until they are seated, and they give you permission. Sometimes, when they come in and you are already seated, they will tell you, with their hand like this…" he showed her, "…to stay where you are. They are being polite … you return the courtesy by half standing, then sitting down again. These rules also apply to my uncles and their wives."

"Why do I have to stand up for you?" she teased.

"Because I am your husband, your lord and master." He pulled her close, sighed. "It's not going to be easy for you being here." They held each other, he, worried, wondering if he had done the right thing in bringing her here … she, hoping that she would fit in, not make any mistakes.

"Who was that man who visited you?" she asked idly.

"A very old friend of the family. Someone is interested in Drita." He spoke slowly, with a slight frown.

"Interested? What do you mean?" There was no answer, she looked up questioningly.

Reluctantly, Skender answered, "He had come to see if Babush would give her in marriage. There is a family, a very good family, who is interested."

She moved from the circle of his arms, staring at him, "I don't think I understand."

He nodded, "Yes, I think you do." He leaned forward, took both her hands. "Things are done differently here, my love, the marriage is arranged by the parents."

Slowly she withdrew her hands, "But your sister does know this boy, doesn't she?"

"No. None of us do, this was just a preliminary inquiry."

"A preliminary inquiry! Skender, you are talking of your sister, not some new product that has come out on the market," she retorted angrily.

Skender sat very still, watching her, "Don't you think you had better listen before you get so excited?"

"You're worried about me getting excited! Worry about yourself! How can you sit there calmly talking about … 'preliminary enquiries'? You are talking about your sister, Skender! Not some stray kitten that needs a home."

"That's enough!" His voice was cold, angry.

She jumped up, walked over to the stove and kicked at it. "Oh, boy, we've really got off to a good start for my first day in your home, haven't we?" she said in a wobbly voice.

Skender walked over to her, put his hands on her shoulders and turned her to face him, "I have never told you of this custom because everyone in the West reacts so violently to arranged marriages, but now that you are here, now that you are with the people, don't you think you could listen? Try to understand?"

She didn't answer for a while, then, "I'm going to make a hash of this visit, Skender, I know I am, and it scares me." She slipped her arms around him, laid her head on his chest. "I'm sorry," she sighed, "why do I always see everything in black and white, why can't I accept grays?"

Skender relaxed a little, "I don't understand you. What are you trying to say?"

"Oh, you know, everything is 'right' or 'wrong' for me, nothing in between, no 'alrights' or 'maybes' … just 'yes' or 'no', 'right' or 'wrong.'"

He laughed and let his arms circle her, "I've noticed! Can we sit down now? Talk? Without you getting excited and nervous?"

"I'll try," she flashed a quick smile at him, "but I'm not giving any guarantees."

He sat down, waited until she was comfortable. "I want you to listen and not interrupt. I am not asking you to accept, or approve, just to listen and try to understand." She nodded. "When a girl is old enough to marry … no, wait. I'll start earlier than that. When a girl passes her sixteenth birthday she is taken from school and the preparation for her married life starts to take place. She is 'apprenticed', for want of a better word, to her mother. Gradually she takes over the household. She is taught everything there is to know about the running of a home … how to clean, how to wash clothes, iron. Her mother passes on to her daughter all the knowledge and experience that her mother passed on to her, plus that which she has accumulated during her own lifetime.

"She is shown how to serve people correctly, how to behave with her elders. She is taught a little first aid, how to sew, how to cook … there is nothing missed. By the time she is at an age to marry she will be armed with all the knowledge she will ever need during her life to run a home, look after children, and serve her family.

"If her mother has done a good job, there will be no shocks or surprises for the girl when she enters her husband's home. She will know exactly what is expected of her. Her mother-in-law will expect her to be armed with that knowledge. She will be ready to show the girl how to run the home in their style, to 'polish' her, but the wood must be ready."

He paused, saw that he had Gillian's attention. "The man who left here is an old and trusted friend. He and Babush have been friends ever since I can remember. He does not live here in Prishtine anymore, he lives in … Prizren." '*You are going to have to stand, walk around.*'" Skender put his hand over his eyes.

"What is it?"

Skender heard her concern, forced a smile, "Nothing important … just a ghost. Prizren is about 70 kilometers from here. Rashid, that is the name of the man who was here, has some close friends in Prizren who have a son. The son is 26 years old and is ready for marriage. When Rashid was visiting this family, he told them about us. 'I have a friend,' he probably said, 'who lives in Prishtine. The family is very honorable, much respected … their roots go deep, and they are well-known for their hospitality.' Then the boy's father might have responded, 'I am happy for you to know such a family.' Rashid would continue, 'Thank you. This friend of mine has a daughter who follows in the footsteps of her mother. She holds to our traditions, our ways and serves her father with love and devotion. Whoever has her in their family will indeed be fortunate.'" Skender smiled at Gillian. "The stage was set! The boy's father was interested, so he asked, 'What is the name of this family?' Our family is well known, so he knew immediately with whom he would be dealing, he knew of our honor and our dignity. Then he would have said to Rashid, 'It sounds well, but let me think about it.' As soon as Rashid left, he would have called his son and told him what had happened."

"Go on, what happened then?" Gillian, excited, eyes shining, demanded.

"Well, the boy was willing, so the work started!"

"What if he wasn't? What would happen then?"

"Then he would tell his father, 'Father, I am not ready for marriage … I would like to wait a year or two.'"

"His father would not insist?"

"No. Of course not. He would say, 'Agreed. We will leave this matter until you are ready, then you can come to me and we will talk.'"

"What if the boy…" Skender shook his head in despair, "I'm sorry! Surely you don't expect me to sit still and say nothing!"

"I'm amazed you've been quiet this long," he smiled. "What is it you want to know?"

"What if the boy was in love with someone else?"

"Then it is easy. He will say, 'Father, I appreciate your asking but…'" Skender put his hand on his heart, looked up at the ceiling then, with great drama, said, "'my heart is held captive by another.'" He stopped, looked down at Gillian and then smiled.

Tentatively her hand slid along the rug to his, her smile was shaky as he took it. "Sorry," she whispered. He gave her hand a reassuring squeeze, "please go on."

"The boy will then tell his father the girl's name. If the family is acceptable, wedding arrangements will begin. But, if the family in not honorable, not acceptable, the son will never be allowed to marry that girl … never."

"What if the family is honorable and all that jazz, but there is some … you know, rumors about the girl?"

"That cannot happen here. The girl must be spotless, otherwise no family will accept her."

"So, the girl must be a virgin when she marries?"

"Exactly. But more than that even. Once our girls leave school they have no social life with men. Apart from immediate family, they do not meet or talk socially with a man."

"Not even her brother's friends?"

"Definitely not! When his friends come to visit, she stays out of sight. And she is very careful about that … if she is around when those young men visit the house and her father finds out…" he shook his head, "she's in big trouble."

"Wow!"

Skender laughed, "Wow is right! I told you, this is a different world."

"What happened next? Did they come and ask for Drita's hand?"

"Heavens no! Not yet! There was still a lot of work to be done. The boy's father would ask his friends if they knew of our family … he will have sent all over Kosov to find someone who knew us. He probably came to Prishtine himself and quietly made inquiries. In the meantime, the mother and sisters of the boy will go to work too." He laughed at the look on his wife's face. "This is a very serious matter … it is not undertaken lightly. The mother would search for an acquaintance of hers who also knew us. Then, somehow, she would get herself invited here. That way she would be able to see Drita for herself, how she behaves to her mother, how she receives guests, how she conducts herself … what she looks like." He leaned forward, winked and gave Gillian a brief kiss. "After all, that is important to her son too! Of course, we knew nothing of their interest in us, so when they came they were not treated in a special way … we would have received them as we would anyone. And that is exactly what they wanted, of course."

Jill shook her head in disbelief, "What a complicated procedure!"

"Yes, I agree, and yet … well, let's leave my feelings out of it. I'll just tell you what happens. When the boy's father had enough information on our family to know that he wanted Drita for his son, he went to Rashid and said, 'We are interested in this family.' Watch now … it is always the family, not the girl. Then Rashid came to visit Babush, and that is what happened today, and so now I will tell you exactly what transpired this afternoon."

"While Babush and Rashid were talking together, very carefully, and very casually, Rashid said, 'Your daughter is approaching an age to marry.' Now, if Babush had reacted in a negative way, the subject would have been dropped immediately and that would have been an end to the whole business. But I think Rashid caught Babush off guard … perhaps the excitement of me being here, your arrival…."

"What did Babush say?"

"He hesitated, then said, 'You know how much we love our daughter; I hate to lose her yet.' Then Rashid started, 'I have a friend….' He told us about them, just as he told them about us! He told Babush what a good match it would be, what good foundations the family had, what a fine son, etc., etc. Babush nodded, didn't say anything and then Rashid…" Skender grinned, made a clicking sound, "…turned the key a little more, the family's name is Drini." He looked at Gillian. "This family is very well-known, very dignified, it is an honor to our house that they have asked for Drita."

"Did Babush agree?" she asked slowly.

"No! Oh no. The girl's family would never do that. Babush said, 'I'll think about it.'"

"Do you think he will agree?"

Skender shook his head, "I don't know. After Rashid had left, he kept saying, 'Prizren is too far away … I do not want her that far from me.' It is a good family, would be a good match. But before he does anything he, and my uncles and cousins, will search for information on the family and the boy. Of course, our main concern is Drita, to be sure that she will be happy. Babush would have to be very sure that the family, and the boy, treat their women correctly and with respect before he would agree."

"Can you go on?" Jill asked eagerly. "Will you tell me what would happen if Babush agreed?"

Skender smiled, happy that she was interested. "Alright, if you wish. Let us assume, then, that Babush is interested. He will talk to Nona, tell her everything that has happened."

"And will Nona tell Drita?" Skender nodded. "What would happen," she asked slowly, "if Drita refuses?"

"I don't think that could happen. She would have to have a very valid reason."

"But … what if she was in love with someone else?"

He shrugged. "How could she be? She has seen no man, had no association with any male since she was sixteen."

"But you said if a boy was interested in someone else…."

"Ah yes, but that is a little different! A boy might have seen a girl and become interested in her, but the girl would not have seen him. Once our girls leave school they do not socialize with young men." Gillian's bewildered look brought a laugh. "There is always a way for a young man to see a girl if he's interested. Believe me! You can always find a way!"

Gillian's eyes narrowed suspiciously. "Ha-ha, and I suppose you had found a way, even at sixteen?"

"You bet your life!" He dodged the pillow she threw at him. "You do realize, don't you, that here you are not allowed to strike your husband? That I could beat you for that?"

She leaned toward him, kissed him. "Try it!" she dared.

He let his hand smooth her hair. "I missed you." He was suddenly serious.

"I missed you, too … looks like we're stuck with each other, doesn't it?"

"Looks like it," he said softly, lips seeking hers.

"Tell me the rest," she said after a moment.

"Sshh." His kiss was long, lingering; muffled voices in the hall disturbed her. She glanced nervously at the door, pulled away. Skender watched her, a slight smile on his lips, his disappointment tempered by approval of her modesty.

She smoothed her hair. "What happens next?"

He smiled. "You'd have found out if you had not jumped from me!" he teased.

Gillian smiled back, "In the story … what happens next in the story?"

Skender sighed dramatically, forlornly, "You are not a bit romantic!"

"Is there anything more romantic than a wedding?" Gillian asked mischievously.

"Oh yes!" He leaned toward her, eyes narrowing, "A Kosovar whose nusé has been away from him too long, and I promise you will find that out very soon." He kissed her nose before he laid on his back and put his head in her lap, wriggling to get comfortable. "You are not as well-padded as my father. Where were we in the story?"

"Babush was searching for information on the boy."

"Yes. While Babush is doing that, the boy's family will get in touch with Rashid. 'We will be very honored to have the Berishas for in-laws,' they will tell him. 'We will be forever grateful if you would speak to them for us, to see if they are willing to give their daughter to this house.'

"Rashid will come again to Babush, have coffee, visit, and then he will casually ask, 'Have you thought about the matter we discussed?'"

"And Babush will say, 'Yes, go ahead' or 'No, I am not agreeable' … right?"

"Wrong!" he laughed. "Babush will say 'I have not decided … why don't you come back in three months?' In three months, maybe two if the boy's family is anxious, Rashid comes again. More coffee, more visiting and then, again, casually, 'Have you thought about the matter we discussed?' And then Babush will give him his answer. If it is no, he will say, 'I have decided to keep my daughter home, she is too young, but we are honored that the Drini family asked for her.' If it is yes, he will say, 'It is meant, it is God's will, and so be it.' Rashid will make an appointment with Babush to meet the boy's father … there will be a big dinner…."

"And then he will meet Drita," Gillian interrupted happily.

"No! He will not see Drita until she enters his house as his son's bride. He will see none of our women … not one."

"Then … who will serve the dinner?"

"The young men in the family … Emin, his brother, cousins … any or all of them. Now the men watch each other … how do we receive guests, how do they behave as guests." He shook his head, grinning at the picture. "After the meal, the young men are dismissed. If all has gone well, the boy's father will tell Babush that he is here to ask for his daughter's hand for his son.

"Babush will say, 'We are honored that you ask', The boy's father will reply, 'It will be our honor to receive your daughter.' When they have finished talking, they stand, shake hands, embrace cheek-to-cheek, and then the marriage is bound. That action is more binding, more tight, than any of your legal forms in the West." Skender's finger tapped the rug. "Up till that moment, either family could have walked away but, after that, if either family changes their mind, there could be bloodshed."

"Why?"

"Because until that time it was still private, between the two families. Now it is common knowledge for anyone, and the family's honor is at stake, and that you never touch.

"After the guests leave Babush will tell Nona that their daughter is engaged … there may even be a tentative wedding date. Nona will go to Drita and tell her that it is settled and Drita will start work on her … dowry?" he questioned Gillian.

"No," she grinned, "trousseau. Your English is getting worse!"

"That is a French word that you English-speaking people have stolen! But never mind that, I'll go on. Drita, her cousins, her friends, will start to sew. Everything is made by hand … clothes for her, at least one garment for every member of the boy's family, rugs, anything that she will need she makes."

"When does she meet the boy?" Gillian demanded in exasperation.

Skender shook his head. "She doesn't." He gave a light laugh. "At least not until her wedding night!"

"You are joking, aren't you?"

He shook his head and very seriously answered, "No."

Gillian bent down to look at him, still in her lap. "Before I get all upset and excited, perhaps you'd better tell me the rest."

"Good! You're learning. It's taken me two years to teach you patience … there is hope for you yet." He sat up. "There is a big celebration, the bride wears her wedding outfit … exactly like the one Babush and Nona sent to you, except that hers will have a heavy veil. She is completely covered, from the top of her head to the tip of her toes … you cannot see an inch of her.

"She stands in a corner of the room, not moving, not speaking and, I'm sure, scared stiff. The celebration can go on for three days before the actual wedding day."

Gillian gasped, "Three days? Impossible! I don't believe it!"

Skender laughed, "It is true! Of course, when the guests leave and only her family or close friends remain, she will sit down, visit, relax, but as soon as another guest arrives…." His hands lifted, indicating that the Nusé would rise to her feet. His lips twitched, "What a pity I didn't bring you here, let you go through this ceremony before we married."

"I don't think we'd have made it. I can't stand still…."

"Or keep quiet," he interrupted her.

She ignored him. "…for five minutes without wriggling. Go on, please. I'm dying to know what happens next."

"On the wedding day, the boy's brothers, his cousins, his closest friends, come to the bride's home. Behind the men comes a small party of women … his sisters, an aunt or two." Skender sat, hugging his knees, a dreamy look on his face. "The men go into the guest room and a huge dinner is served. We will have to ask Nona what goes on in the women's room as, of course, I don't know. Sometime after the dinner, the girl's father will go to a separate room … they will bring his daughter to him…." He paused, then sadly and quietly continued,

"He will take his leave of her. When that time comes for us, Babush will no longer have a daughter."

Gillian stared, "What? Why not?"

Skender did not answer right away but sat, staring into the fire. His head lifted, "He will have given her to their house … when she steps past our gate he no longer has any claim on her. She is theirs … for the rest of her life."

Tears filled Gillian's eyes.

"That is why it is so carefully done." He took out his handkerchief and wiped her eyes. "Do you think you understand a little better now? Can you see why I got so angry when you compared our way of giving a daughter to the giving away of a miserable kitten?"

"I feel … so badly. It was such a horrible thing to say."

"Yes, it was, but sometimes we speak without thinking. Do you want me to tell you the rest, or shall we drop it?"

"I'd like to hear."

"When the father and daughter are saying good-bye it is a very emotional time for both of them. He is heartbroken at the thought of losing her. And she? Who knows what is in her heart at the thought of leaving her father, the one she has received love and guidance from all of her life? I have often wondered how either can bear the pain of that moment." Skender paused, took a breath, "While the father is saying good-bye to his daughter, the men start to leave…."

"Can I interrupt for a minute?" Gillian asked, still wiping her eyes. He nodded. "Is the bridegroom there, with the men?"

Skender smiled. "No, he still hasn't entered the picture. But wait, he will be along soon enough. The men crowd around our gate, take out their pistols." He stopped. "They wear them here," pointing to his waist, "stuck into their cummerbunds. Usually they are made of silver, beautifully worked in intricate filigree. The Nusé comes out, completely surrounded by the women from the boy's house … she is right in the middle, all of their women close about her … you can hardly see her.

"They usher her out, down the path … she steps past the gate, into the car … sometimes it is a horse-drawn wagon. Whichever it is, it is beautifully decorated with flowers and rugs. It is completely covered … no one can see in.

"They start to move … crack-crack-crack-crack-crack-crack. All the men fire their pistols at once. It is a sign of joy and happiness … the Nusé is in their protection." Skender took Gillian's hands. "Can you imagine her mother's feelings, her father's, when they hear those pistols? To know that your daughter is gone, forever? Can you imagine the heartbreak of losing her, sweetened by the joy of giving her?"

Tears spilled down Gillian's cheeks.

"When they arrive at the boy's home, the pistols go again, crack-crack-crack-crack-crack-crack. His brothers come to the bride's car. The oldest picks her up in his arms, carries her, just like a baby, into their home. As he enters their door, the pistols go wild … she is theirs!

"He carries her to the guest room, stands her in a corner…." He smiled. "The poor thing has exchanged one corner for another! The boy's mother and sisters come in, lift the veil and look at their Nusé. They drop the veil, open the door and admit the boy's father and brothers. She is still standing in the corner, hands clasped in front of her at waist level, eyes turned down, the veil covering her, not an inch showing. The mother-in-law will lift the veil and show her husband and sons the Nusé … the poor girl must be terrified. She cannot speak, cannot raise her eyes, cannot move.

"The men will leave, the mother-in-law will open the door, and all the relatives, friends, neighbors … women only, mind … come in to see the Nusé." Gillian was hanging on his every word. He couldn't resist teasing, "Are you sure you want me to go on?"

She gave a quick, eager nod.

"In the evening one of the aunts will take the Nusé to the wedding room. It has been beautifully decorated. She will help her to wash and freshen herself, and then she will fetch the mother-in-law who will make sure that the girl's dress is just so, that the veil covers her properly. Then she will go to the door, open it…" he paused, smiling, "…and admit the bridegroom."

Gillian's attention was all his.

"Still the Nusé cannot raise her eyes, cannot look at him. She stands, waiting, the boy's mother and sisters behind her. The boy comes in … goes to his bride … for the first time, he is going to see her. He lifts the veil…." Gillian, hardly breathing, mouth slightly open, eyes sparkling, was too much for him. "Aaahhh," he yelled, shielding his face with his arms, "what a shock!"

She jumped, startled out of her dreamlike state. Skender laid back on the rugs, laughing at the look on her face.

"Why did you do that? I thought you were going to say she was so beautiful. Go on! Don't leave me up in the air," she begged in exasperation, "what happens next?"

He rolled onto his side, face close to hers. "Can't you guess? Do you really want me to tell you?" he asked, smiling. "Or, better yet," he added softly, reaching for her, "show you?"

Gillian dodged him, "Don't be smart! The mother and sisters are still there!"

"He'll throw them out as soon as possible, if he has any sense!" he laughed.

Gillian sat dreamily hugging a pillow. "I feel so sorry for her. To have left her home, her family, go to strangers. All that emotional upheaval in one day," she sighed. "Do you really think he will make love to her straight away?"

Skender sat up, shrugged. "I don't know. I have never been a bridegroom here, but I will find out if you like. For your sake I am willing to sacrifice myself. I will have Babush find me a beautiful girl…." He ducked as she hit out at him.

"I will be very good and…." He dodged her flailing arms, laughing. "Take notes, and I promise I'll tell you everything, everything, that happens." He caught her hands, pulled her down across his knees. "I warned you, didn't I, about hitting your husband?"

"Beast! Let go of me!" she laughed.

Neither heard the door open to admit Babush. He stood in the doorway, a smile curving his lips.

"Why should I? Give me one good reason…." Skender bent his head to look at her. "Babush!" He let her go immediately, jumped to his feet.

"I'm sorry, Djali, next time I'll knock," Babush smiled. "I didn't know these festivities started so early. I see there are some good customs in the West, eh?" He walked over to the stove, smoothed Gillian's hair, noting with approval the hot flush of embarrassment before he sat down.

"We were just … we were not … I was trying to explain one of our customs, sir."

Babush opened his newspaper. "Yes, Skender. I explained some to your mother a long time ago," he remarked as he disappeared behind it.

Gillian gave a nervous glance at the newspaper. "What on earth must he think?" she asked quietly.

"He's a very wise old man. He certainly doesn't think we've been talking all afternoon," Skender teased, smiling as he saw the flush deepen.

"Tell him then, explain," she pleaded in a whisper.

"Do you think he will believe me?" he whispered back. Still whispering, he asked, "What shall I say?" Then, in a normal voice, "Father, I did not make love to my wife this…."

"Skender!"

"What? He doesn't speak any English … or not much anyway," he lied, enjoying his wife's embarrassment.

Gillian glanced nervously at the newspaper. "You said he didn't speak any. I remember you telling me that." She was trying to convince herself.

"Well then! Why so worried? I will tell him again, perhaps he didn't hear. Babush…."

"No!" It was louder than she meant it to be.

Babush lowered his paper a little, peering over the top at them, wondering what brought about that quick, loud denial, so clear in any language.

"You see, I told you he understands a little. Ask him yourself if you don't believe me."

Gillian's fingers plucked constantly at the rug as she looked from Skender to Babush, then back to Skender before she took a deep breath and turned to Babush. "Babush, do you speak any English?"

Babush sensed her nervousness, he smiled, nodded encouragingly at her, trying to put her at her ease. He was startled to see a look of horror come over her face, and even more startled to see Skender rolling around on the floor.

"Is there something wrong, Djali?" he asked mildly. Skender, unable to speak, shook his head. "I thought the child seemed nervous; I was trying to help...." Babush's confusion increased as this brought another bout of uncontrollable laughter from Skender while his daughter-in-law continued to stare at him in horrified disbelief.

"You don't speak any English, do you, Babush?" Gillian spoke slowly and distinctly. Babush smiled, gave an encouraging nod. "Oh my God!" Color flamed her face; her hands covered the heat and she turned away.

Babush looked down at his son. He was shaking with laughter, holding his stomach as tears ran unchecked down his face. Babush smiled, retired behind his newspaper. *I do not know what this was all about, but I have never seen my son laugh like that before. If she can do that for him, I am happy with her.*

Skender's laughter subsided. He sat up, saw Jill sitting disconsolately beside the stove. "Jill, I was teasing," he sought to reassure her, "he doesn't know a word."

Still she did not face him, whispered, "I asked him, and he nodded."

"It was coincidence, my love. I promise, not a word."

She turned to face him. His lips twitched, "I'll get you for that!" she promised, starting to laugh herself.

Skender slid across the rug to Gillian, checked that his father was occupied, then kissed her. Both kept one eye on the paper. "They will expect you to put on something a little more feminine for dinner. Can you do that?"

"Yes, but I wish you'd told me how they dress here; I would have brought floor-length dresses. I think I'm going to feel all legs in the ones I have." She stacked the pillows together, gathered up the magazines and books as she went to the door. "I'm going to change now." She blew him a kiss as she was closing the door.

"Jill." She poked her head back around the door. "I didn't tell you what he said to you when you arrived, did I?" She shook her head. "Welcome home, daughter."

She bit her lip, eyes suddenly wet as she glanced at Babush. "I hope I don't disappoint him."

Skender shook his head. "You won't," he said softly.

Chapter 14

Gillian slipped he dress over her head, zipped herself up and smoothed it to its full length, sighed. *Too long for London, now too short for here.* Carefully she cleaned up the mess she had made in the bathroom, gave a despairing glance at the dim light overhead, gathered up her things and left.

She opened the door of the room where Skender still sat with Babush. "Hi," she said with a grin. "Can I put my war paint on in here? That light in the bathroom is useless."

He smiled back, "He's still deep in his newspaper so you won't disturb him."

"Did you know that there's no mirror in this whole house?" She prattled on as she organized her makeup on the window seat. "That I had to get this far with just this little thing from my bag?" Skender watched her, smiling, as carefully she smoothed the makeup over her face.

Babush lowered his paper to see what was going on, stared in shocked horror. She picked up the eyebrow pencil, carefully following the lines, sitting back, checking that both were the same color and evenly finished. She hesitated a moment, frowning. Dark or light blue shadow? She grinned. Dark! I fell kind of dashing tonight! She bent forward, smoothing and blending the blue shadow across her lids, picked up the mirror, leaning back to get into a better light and caught the reflection of Babush watching her, she turned and smiled at him.

"What does your Nusé think she is doing, Djali?"

"Putting makeup on, Babush."

"Does she think she can improve on God's work?"

Skender swallowed his grin, "I'll ask her."

Gillian smiled, "Guess I have to. He must have run out of colors by the time he got to me."

Skender laughed, turned to Babush. "I don't think I should repeat it, Babush," he said before telling his father her reply.

The old man smiled slowly, "We are not having any guests tonight. I hope you can talk her out of all that … paint … before tomorrow night." Skender inclined his head. Babush watched as she applied mascara. "She is not finished yet?"

"Almost," Skender murmured. Babush sighed, shook his head and returned to his paper. "Don't I get a kiss before you put that stuff on your mouth?" Skender asked.

She shook her head, grinned at him. "You know, you are always quoting 'old sayings' to me … now here's one for you, a kiss without lipstick is like fish and chips without vinegar!"

"Oh no," he groaned, "only the English would bring romance down to that level."

"Oh, I don't know." She packed her stuff away. "Fish and chips is one of our national dishes and also one of my very favorite meals." She turned, pursed her mouth. "Come here and let me put my seal on you!"

He laughed. "Hurry, they will bring the meal at any time now."

"I'm finished. This is the longest dress I have. Is it alright? She asked anxiously. He nodded. "I'm starving! What's for dinner?"

"I don't know. You should have eaten lunch with us instead of escaping."

"I couldn't. I was too nervous. What I needed then was a place to rest, be by myself for a while. I hope they've got something I like … which cuisine do you follow here?"

"Our own! What did you expect? Spaghetti because we're opposite Italy?" he teased.

"Right now I'd settle for a T-bone steak, a huge salad, and some sourdough bread with lashings of butter."

"I can guarantee you won't get it."

Drita came in carrying a table and cloth, set it down in the middle of the room and smoothed the cloth into position.

Gillian stared at the low table, "Do we eat off that?" Skender nodded. "What do we sit on?"

"The God-given thing you're sitting on now," he replied with a broad wink.

She turned to him in dismay. "I'll never be able to sit through a whole meal! You know I can't sit cross-legged like you do."

"Then kneel."

"For a whole meal? I couldn't possibly."

"Well then, my love, I think you are going to be very hungry, and a lot thinner, before we leave here."

Gillian, about to make a face at Skender, caught Drita watching her. They smiled at each other before Drita left the room. "She's lovely, Skender … have you noticed?"

"Of course. I am very proud of her in every way, in all senses."

Drita returned, carrying a bowl and jug, a towel over her arm. She walked over to Babush. Gillian watched, fascinated. "Why doesn't he go into the bathroom to wash?"

"It will be your turn after me." Skender stood. "Be ready so that she doesn't have to wait for you."

"But I've just had a bath!"

Drita came toward Skender. "We are going to eat … you have to wash your hands before you sit at the table." He nodded, smiled his thanks to Drita who moved to Gillian. "Make sure your hands don't touch the floor as you sit down after you've washed. We often use our fingers when we eat so it is important that your hands are spotlessly clean. Take the towel from her. When you have finished drying your hands, lay the towel over her arm, then come and sit next to me."

"The bathroom's right next to this room. Why go through all this rigmarole when you could go there to wash? This just makes more work for your sister."

"She has nothing better to do! No, I was teasing," he laughed as he saw her glare at him. "It is custom. I don't know how or why it started, but this way people are not inconvenienced by having to leave the room, the water is the correct temperature." he said on a shrug.

Nona entered carrying a large round pan. She set it down on the table.

Gillian peered in. "Looks good," she smiled at Skender as she knelt beside him. "Chicken, rice. What's the red color? Paprika?"

"Yes, and possibly pepper … our pepper is red, not black or white. Take the cloth, lay it across your knees as I have. That's right."

Nona carried in more bowls, followed by Drita with the rest of the meal.

"Bread, tomatoes. What is that white, wet stuff?"

"Kos … yogurt." She made a face. "You'll like this. Nona makes it. It is not as sour as the commercial kind you've tried."

"What's that plate of yellow things? They look like bell peppers that have been sat on."

He laughed. "They are called spatz, and they are bell peppers. We have three kinds here … red, green, and yellow. These have been pickled in brine and a heavy weight put on them. The tomatoes are pickled too, but in a different manner." He glanced at Babush. "Quiet, now, they are ready. Babush will ask a blessing."

Babush broke and handed each a piece of bread. Gillian watched, waiting to see how the others ate.

Skender leaned toward her. "Eat from the section of the dish in front of you, use your spoon for the rice. If you wish, you can use your bread to soak up the juices as we do." He accepted the dish of spatz from Nona. "Would you like to try some of these?"

Gillian nodded, "Just a small piece, though, in case I don't like it."

He cut a small piece, placed a little cheese on top and passed it to her. "Tomato?"

"No, thank you." She tried a piece of the spatz as he smilingly watched her. "This is super." She pointed to the cheese. "That is feta, right?"

"Djath … use the Albanian word. If you speak Greek here they'll throw you out," he laughed.

"It says feta on the package in Safeway," she smiled back at him, then whispered, "My legs are killing me!"

"Which is our nusé's favorite part of the chicken?" Babush asked.

"White meat, Babush."

Babush looked around, found what he sought, picked it up and placed it in front of Gillian. She smiled at him as she shyly tried out her limited Albanian. "Te faleminderit."

Babush beamed. "Good! A word from her at last! Nusé, ma nape pake uje te lutem." He stopped Drita from rising with a slight movement of his hand. "Sit down, Drita, I am asking your sister."

"She knows it, Babush. Take it slower, let her catch the main word," Skender said as Gillian glanced questioningly toward him.

The old man nodded, repeated his request slowly, emphasizing the words.

Gillian turned to Skender. "He wants some water, right?"

"Yes. It's beside you, on the tray."

She picked up a glass, filled it and handed it to Babush. There was a moment's hesitation before he took it. Drita, horrified at the casual way the water had been given to her father, stood up. "Sit down, child, we will do it her way tonight. You can show her our way another time."

Babush smiled, offered the empty glass back to Gillian. Assuming that he wanted more, she picked up the jug and refilled the glass. Babush hesitated, nodded his thanks and drank again, almost emptying the glass. He again offered the glass to Gillian. Looking slightly surprised, she picked up the jug. "Skender! Your Nusé is trying to drown me. How do I stop her?" Babush laughed as his glass was filled again.

"He has had enough, Jill. Take the glass and put it on the tray." Skender turned to Babush. "Perhaps you should have let Drita show her our way, or had me show you her way."

Babush looked at his son for a long moment, then smiled, "Our way, Skender. I am too old to learn new tricks. Is she happy with this meal?"

Skender turned to Gillian, "How do you like this meal?"

"I do. It is good, really good." How do I get the chicken to my mouth? Do I pick it up in my fingers, or do I try to pry the meat off the bone with the spoon?"

"Pick it up in your fingers, just as you would at a picnic. That's right."

He turned to Nona, "My cup is full, Nona. To be together, the four of us, and have her here beside me. I ask nothing more from life."

"One thing more, Djali … that I could talk to her."

Skender nodded, "I am at fault … I should have tried to teach her," he smiled. "But wait! Next time we come she will speak fluently and then you can talk until your throats are dry." He saw that Gillian had stopped eating. "Have you had enough? Are you sure?"

"I'll pop if I eat another bite. Who does the cooking … Nona or Drita?"

"They share the work. Why?"

"I was going to ask you to thank whoever had cooked, say that I enjoyed the meal."

"Tell them yourself. You have enough words if you think about it."

"I don't. All I know is 'thank you', not the rest."

"What about 'very good'?"

She smiled at him as she turned to Nona and Drita. "I hadn't thought of that."

Drita started to gather the things together, picked up the pan. "Can I help her?" Gillian asked, starting to get up.

"No," Skender stopped her, "not on your first night." He laughed. "Be thankful that they are treating you as a guest … if you were from here, tomorrow most of the work would be yours."

"You're kidding?" Gillian's eyes were round with shock at the idea.

Skender shook his head. "You would be the first one up in the morning and the last one to bed at night. Close your mouth!" he laughed, putting his finger under her chin. "And remember, all I have to say to Nona is, 'Here, take her, put her to work' and your fate is sealed."

Gillian smiled sweetly at him, "Remember, we are here for only a visit. Once I am back on familiar ground it will be your fate that is sealed." They smiled together. "Want to call a truce?"

"I will think about it. Somehow the idea of seeing you slaving away is very appealing to me. Why do you keep wriggling like a worm?"

"My legs are dead. I am in agony, you unfeeling brute."

Nona passed a small bowl of yogurt to Babush, another to Skender. "Only a little for our Nusé, Nona … I am not sure she will care for it." He handed a bowl to Gillian. "We usually finish with yogurt; it settles the stomach and cleanses the whole system. Try it, see if you like it, if not, leave it. Well?"

"It's okay. I think I'd prefer it with some brown sugar on it."

He sighed, shook his head, "I give up on you … you are beyond hope." Everyone had finished. Babush held out his hands, palms facing up. "Hold your hands as we do. Babush is giving thanks for the meal," he whispered. Then, "After Babush leaves the table, you can get up."

"I'll never be able to move again," she moaned. "I will stay in this position for the rest of my life. Do we sit like this for every meal?" she asked as he helped her up, then smiled at him. "In the biggest case there are some gifts for your family, do you want me to give them to them now?"

He stared at her in surprised pleasure, "How did you know?"

"Know what?"

"To bring gifts for the family. It is a custom here."

Gillian shrugged. "I think it is the same in every country. I didn't know the sizes, so I had to guess from photographs. I hope I got them right."

"I am sure you did. I will get them right now. I could hug you for thinking of this."

She smiled at him, "Who's stopping you?"

"He is." He glanced toward Babush who had settled himself in front of the fire with Nona. "We never touch our wives in front of others, especially our fathers. But you could come with me if you wish," he winked as he went toward the door. She smilingly shook her head and stayed on the window bench.

Skender returned almost immediately, carrying the case. "Is this the one?" Gillian nodded.

Skender hesitated as he saw that his father and mother were in deep conversation. "Babush and Nona would not want to be disturbed just at this moment, and, in any case, I think we should wait for Drita to join us. Tell me about your journey. Did everything go smoothly?" He joined Gillian on the window bench.

"Yes. My cousin took me to London Airport," she grinned. "He's like you. We had to be there an hour earlier than necessary. The plane ride was smooth, we arrived in Belgrade fifteen minutes late."

"And then?"

"Then I went to the British Embassy."

Skender stared at her, puzzled, "What on earth did you do there?"

"Told them I was coming here, to Kosov."

"Why? What interest was that to them?"

She stood up, went and picked up her handbag from the other end of the seat, opened it and took out her passport. "Look toward the back," she said as she handed it to him.

He opened it, flicked through and found the page. A large, impressive stamp with a rampaging lion and unicorn holding a crown informed him that Mrs. Gillian Berisha was known by the British Embassy of Belgrade to be visiting the Kosov area for a month. Her Britannic Majesty's Government charged and requested that full assistance be extended by the leaders and governing bodies of said area to Her Britannic Majesty's Subject.

She wrinkled her nose at him, "Makes me sound kind of important, huh? After we leave here, as soon as we are out of all Communist countries, I have to send a letter or postcard to advise them that I am safely out of the area."

"And what happens if they do not receive this letter or card?" Skender asked reflectively.

"They instigate a search, make 'official inquiries' as to my whereabouts." She hesitated. "I don't know if it would do any good if the authorities here decided to … detain … us. But at least it looks impressive, might make someone think twice before…." She bit her lip, shrugged, "It's better than nothing."

Skender smiled, shook his head at her. "You constantly amaze me; it was a very good idea. But what made you think of it?"

"I don't know, probably trying to get my money's worth of service for all the taxes I had to pay." She dropped her eyes, slid her hand along to his. "You've never told me anything … you know, about your leaving here … just that you left home at sixteen and later on escaped to Italy. I felt … a little bit unsure, in need of some 'insurance'." She looked up, forced a smile, "Can you guess what I did next?"

He watched her for a while then, accepting her lighter mood, smiled. "Went to rest?"

She laughed, "Me? When I had a whole capital at my feet?" She shook her head, "Found a super pastry shop…"

He laughed loudly, "I should have guessed."

"…had some Turkish coffee and a pastry…"

"One? Truth, now!"

"Well, two … but they were small. Then I went exploring."

"By yourself?" he asked, shocked.

"Of course. Belgrade is beautiful…." Skender glanced quickly toward Babush, put his finger warningly to his lips. Gillian looked puzzled, but continued quietly, "Such wide streets, and so clean. The shops are magnificent. I almost wished we lived in a cold climate so that I could buy some of those gorgeous things … boots soft as butter, leather and suede coats lined with real lamb's wool … I just drooled. Do you think we could stop over on the way home to do some shopping?"

He didn't answer for a moment. "We'll see. Did you eat dinner?"

She laughed, "Can a duck swim? Of course I ate dinner." She sat grinning at him for a little while. "The hotel had a restaurant and I ate there, so now you can stop worrying. I did not go out after dark by myself."

"I cannot help worrying about you," he smiled.

"I am quite self-sufficient, you know. I existed without any undue problems for quite a few years until you came along," she teased.

"I know. But now you're mine. What would I do if anything happened to you?"

She shook her head, "Nothing will. I do not take unnecessary risks, but you can't wrap me in cotton wool and pack me away in a box."

"I wish I could. I would keep you in my pocket, take you out whenever I wanted."

"How boring! No more pastry shops, no theaters." She flashed a smile at him. "On the other hand, no more fighting for a streetcar, no more yelling boss to contend with … oh, good, here's Drita."

"Brother, I am making coffee for you and Babush … does our Nusé prefer coffee or tea?"

Skender checked with Gillian. "Whatever you are having she will have. Do not take too long, Drita. Gillian has something special here for you."

She smiled at Gillian, turned to leave, hesitated, "I will ask the water to boil quickly, brother!"

Skender smiled with delight as the door closed on his sister. *She is beginning to relax with me.* He looked over to Babush, about to tell him, but stopped himself as he realized that his father was deep in conversation with his mother. "Just a moment, Jill," he stopped her as she started to speak to him. "Babush is telling Nona about Rashid's visit, his purpose in coming here," he explained quietly.

"Would he like us to leave?"

Skender smiled, shook his head. "If he had wanted that he would have told us."

Gillian watched, saw the old man take his wife's hand in both of his, saw his gentleness with her, the warm smile. They love each other, she thought, surprised. Care deeply about each other. How wonderful. She whispered to Skender, "Unless it is private family business, will you tell me what he is saying?"

"He is telling her about the family who have asked for Drita. He is saying that he does not want her that far away, does not want her to leave him at all, but that it is not right to tie her to two old people, that she must be allowed to make a life of happiness and fulfillment for herself," he smiled as he passed his handkerchief to Gillian. "You'd better start to carry one of these for yourself," he said as she wiped her eyes.

"Now he is telling Nona that the boy is the third son, that there is one more son after him. This pleases him because she would be one of the middle Nusés, that the workload would be less for her, especially after the youngest son takes a wife." Skender frowned. "He is saying that he would never give her to the eldest son, especially if there was a large family. He is asking my mother…" he swallowed, blinked rapidly, "he is asking my mother's forgiveness for the heavy load she had to carry as a young bride in this house."

He turned to Gillian. "There was a large family, my grandfather, my father, and three more brothers, and there were no women when Nona came as Babush's Nusé. The whole load fell on her shoulders. There was no help, not even a mother-in-law, and she was very young.

"He is telling her how it hurt his heart to see her hands rough, bleeding sometimes, from too much work. She had to rise at dawn to make bread, prepare their morning meal, and often did not get to bed till after midnight, where a young and eager husband waited for her, preventing her from sleeping even then. Now he is telling her how happy and grateful he was when his brother took a wife, relieving his Nusé of some of the heavy load." Skender's voice was gentle, soft. "Nona's reply was not meant for our ears. They have forgotten we are here. Let us not eavesdrop on them."

Gillian dragged her eyes from the two by the fire, "Let us be like them, Skender. There is so much caring, so much tenderness between them."

"That is up to us, isn't it? Love must be protected, nurtured to grow strong and be able to withstand the stress of daily life." He glanced toward his parents. "We have a good example to follow. We will never be put through the physical hardships, the mental anguish they have, it should be easier for us."

"I wonder if that's true," Gillian's voice was low, "I don't know what problems they have had, don't know what ours will be. But here they have time for each other … time to listen to the other, time to love each other. Will we? The speed and turmoil of life in the States will make it harder for us. We are going to have to jump off the roundabout instead of calling to each other as we pass by."

"That is what I am saying, it is up to us," he smiled, took both her hands in his. "What a deep and serious discussion on your first night here! Let us go to a lighter topic, shall we?" The door opened. "The decision has been removed from our shoulders … here is Drita. Let us join Nona and Babush by the fire." He stood up, bent, whispered in her ear, "Don't look so worried. Even when you are a hundred, I will care for you."

Gillian's smile was a little shaky as he pulled her to her feet. "I'll settle for ninety-nine."

Chapter 15

The lid of the case snapped open as Skender released the locks. Gillian knelt beside him, "Stay here, if I've chosen the wrong thing for someone, stop me from giving it to them, okay?"

He threw the lid of the case back. "I thought this for Babush," she continued, taking out the top garment and handing it to Skender. He took the silver-gray sweater from her. "It is from the Shetland Isles, way up off the north coast of Scotland, and is the warmest wool spun."

Skender gave the sweater to Babush, explaining its origin as Babush stood up and tried it on.

"It seems to fit fine," she said with a quick smile to Skender. "This is for Babush, too." Skender took the small rectangular box from Gillian.

"It is a handsome sweater and very warm … thank you, daughter. What is in here?" Babush asked as Skender passed the box to him.

"Open it, Babush. We are all dying of curiosity," Drita urged.

Babush sat down, took off the lid, pulled away the soft tissue paper and slowly took out the pipe of polished rosewood, the glorious red color gleaming in the firelight as he lovingly let his fingers feel the bowl.

"You will need this, too, Babush." Gillian handed him a large tin of pipe tobacco, shyness in her voice, her action.

"I am lost for words, do not know what to say. A good pipe is something I have always wanted for myself, thank you, Nusé.

Gillian smiled back at him, feeling a great relief that she had pleased him. "These are for Nona." She passed a soft, rose-colored sweater, with matching blouse, to Skender. "And this goes with it, too," she added, passing a darker rose shade of woolen material to him. "It is woven in Cumberland, one of the northernmost areas of England." She frowned. "I hope there's enough material for a dimi. I didn't realize they wore them all the time, I bought enough for a jacket and skirt…."

"These are for you, Nona. Gillian is concerned that there may not be enough material for a dimi. The color is beautiful for her," he said smilingly to Gillian who sat anxiously waiting to see her mother-in-law's reaction.

Nona gently fingered the blouse. "I have never seen such fine wool as this, and what a wonderful idea to have a sweater to match." She laid down the blouse and picked up the sweater. "The color is beautiful; don't you think so?" she asked Babush. "Does she know what it is called, Skender?"

He checked with Gillian. "Old rose, Nona."

Babush laughed, "You should not have asked!" Nona shook her head, wagged her finger at him.

"I will be peacemaker!" Skender laughed, "Is there enough material for a dimi?"

"Let me see." Nona stood up, spreading the material. "I cannot get over how soft these wools are."

"England is famous for their woolen materials. If there is not enough material for a dimi, you will have to have a skirt like Gillian's," Skender said, voice serious.

Nona laughed, "Not me! My knees are too old to show. Perhaps Drita…."

"Yes. How about it?" Skender teased his blushing sister.

"Well, Drita, why don't you answer your brother?" Babush stroked down his moustache, eyes sparkling mischievously, as Drita shyly shook her head.

"There is enough if we cut carefully. Thank you, child." Nona kissed Gillian's cheek, "I will take it to the seamstress tomorrow. Perhaps you would like to come with me?"

"Yes, I would, that would be interesting," Gillian smiled. "Now, Drita's…" She held out some colorful material. "I hope she likes tartan. This is one of my favorites and is called Dress Gordon. Gordon is the name of the Clan. Dress Gordon means that this tartan is the one the Gordons wear for special occasions."

Drita's eyes lit as she took the tartan. "Look at the colors!" she exclaimed. "Why, there are at least two shades of blue, two of green, plus yellow and white. Oh, these too?" she asked joyfully as Skender passed her two blouses. She was careful as she unfolded the yellow one, a soft wool with a lacy collar and drawstring neck. She opened the long, full sleeves, also with drawstrings with the lace work repeated at the cuffs. She bit her lip as she looked at Gillian, "It is beautiful, so very beautiful."

"I'm glad you like it," Gillian smiled back, not needing any translation from Skender.

"The other one is warmer, more of an everyday style," Gillian added as Drita carefully folded the yellow one, then turned to the royal blue. "Both of them match the tartan so you can interchange them, depending on your mood or where you are go … er, what the weather is like."

"Why not where you are going?" Skender demanded.

"I … thought, perhaps she doesn't go anywhere."

"Of course she does! To visit her friends, her cousins. She is just as anxious to dress up, look nice, as you when you go out." He laughed, covering his face with his hand.

"What are you laughing at?" Gillian asked suspiciously.

"You! You have convinced yourself that our women are mistreated."

"Not mistreated, exactly … not appreciated is a better word, taken for granted."

"I will ask you this question in about two weeks' time." He smiled. "I will be very interested to hear your answer."

"They are all lovely." Drita hugged Gillian. "Thank you, thank you."

"You are taking my mind off what we are doing," Gillian complained to Skender as she turned back to the case. "There is one more for Drita. This does not go with the tartan, though. Ah, here it is. It is cashmere. Please tell her that I will show her how to wash it, as it must be done very carefully." She passed the sweater to Skender.

"How light and soft." Skender passed it to Drita.

Drita gasped as she took the sweater. "It is as soft as down, softer." She smiled at Gillian; her eyes alight with pleasure. "I have no words … nothing can tell you how much I like it."

"The color is heather, the shade of the Scottish Highlands in late summer. When you walk through the Highlands they are that same soft, bluey-misty-lavendery color." Gillian's voice was dreamy, she smiled at Skender. "I hope we can see them together one day, Skender."

"I hope so. I have never seen this … cashmere?" She nodded. "You do not have any sweaters like this, do you?" She gave a little laugh as she shook her head. "Why not?"

"It is not something that you buy yourself, cashmere is more of a 'special' thing." She turned back to the case.

Expensive, then. You will not treat yourself to one, but you willingly buy one for my sister. Jill. Jill. How precious you are to me.

She turned back to him with a smile and held out a box, "And this is for you."

"Me? Why me?"

"Why not?" she asked softly. He smiled at her, opened the box and stared in amazement.

"I didn't know if we could buy these here, so I made sure you had a good supply," Gillian added as she passed a small package of tapes to him.

"What is it, brother? Aren't you going to show us?" Drita excitedly leaned forward.

"It is a tape recorder," he answered, his eyes on Gillian. He passed the box to Drita. "You may take it out to look at, then show it to Nona and Babush." His eyes were still on Gillian. "It was a long time ago, Jill, what made you remember?"

She flushed, dropped her eyes, "Oh, I just saw it in the shop … thought you might like to have one." She busied herself with things in the case.

Skender watched her closely, "That is not true, is it?" Gillian didn't answer. "Is it?" he insisted. She shook her head. "You remembered my saying that if ever I had an opportunity I would like to have tapes of my mother's voice, my father's. You did remember, didn't you?"

"Yes." He had to bend his head to catch her answer.

"We weren't even married when that conversation took place, and yet you remembered?" he asked wonderingly. His eyes didn't leave her, he reached, took her hand in his and slowly raised it to his cheek, then turned his face and kissed her palm, closing her fingers over his kiss. "Do you know how much I wish we were alone right now?" he asked softly. "I love you, and I want to be alone with you…."

"Don't, Skender, please," Gillian's voice was ragged, "not here in front of your family. It is hard enough for me…."

"Nusé, come here to me," Babush cut in, beckoning to Gillian. She turned from Skender, slowly stood up. "Skender, much thought went into the choosing of these gifts, it was not done in haste." He tapped the rug beside him. "Ulu afar meje," he smiled up at Gillian. "Tell her how much she has gladdened our hearts by her thoughtfulness for us, how much she has pleased us." He glanced up at Skender. "I see she has pleased you too, Djali."

"Yes, Babush, she has pleased me." *You have no idea how much.*

Babush leaned toward his son, "Skender come close … these words are meant for your ears only. You have missed her haven't you, Djali?" he asked quietly as Skender moved close to him.

"Yes, sir, I have."

Babush nodded. "I understand your feelings, your emotions. I am happy beyond words that you feel this way for her. I sensed immediately that she had touched a special place in your heart with her gift to you but remember who is here…" he gave a quick glance to Drita, "you will be alone with your Nusé soon enough." He smiled. "For now, you must share her with us. Now, tell her my words. Let her know how much she has pleased us … be explicit. Let her know that it is the care with which she has chosen for each, as much as the gifts, that I value."

"Babush…."

The old man smiled. "Do not apologize for loving her, Djali. Now, tell her my words."

Skender gave Gillian Babush's message, making sure she understood. Then, in an attempt to help her, turned to the case, and, in a businesslike manner, asked, "What else is there in here?" Gillian stayed stiffly beside Babush. Skender took out a pile of scarves.

Gillian took a deep breath. "The heavier ones are for your uncles, the pastels for your aunts."

"These are like gossamer." He held up a pale blue.

"Yes, but very warm … they are handmade from mohair and wool."

"In England?"

She nodded.

"Which part?"

"The West Country, Cornwall. They have the best cream cakes down there." Her voice shook, quickly she turned from him.

Easy, Jill … I won't embarrass you again. He pulled out a pile of records, spilling them onto the rug. "Pop music! For here?" He laughed at her. "Everything else was fine, but these…?" He shook his head. "I think not! 'West Side Story', 'Elvis the Pelvis'?" He raised his eyebrows at her, relaxed as he saw the quick grin. "'Tommy Steele and the Steelmen!' Who are they?"

"Top pop group in England. He lived about ten blocks from my home before he became famous."

"Jill!" he exclaimed in mock horror, as he held up one of the records.

"I love it! I loved the movie and I like her," she said defensively.

"You don't understand the words! Here they probably will, and the life of a Greek prostitute is hardly suitable!" He tossed the 'Never on Sunday' record back into the case.

"Well, I love the music and it was a marvelous movie."

"You didn't understand most of it…."

"Yes I did!" she insisted indignantly as he looked skeptically at her.

"This is better … Frank Sinatra. I personally don't care for him but at least he is an improvement over Melina Mercouri."

Drita leaned over, looking at the records. "American?" she asked Gillian, who nodded. "Oh good! We all like American music here … well, not the older ones." She smiled at Skender.

"Do you? I am surprised." He glanced at Gillian. "I was wrong, it seems, the young ones enjoy American music. What else do we have in here?" He sorted through the things in the case. "Nylons … dozens of them … hair spray, hair brushes. Gum? Good heavens! What are you doing? Organizing an American colony here?" He laughed. "I thought you despised the stuff?"

"I do, but when I first went to America I wanted to try it so I thought they might, too. I wish I could have brought doughnuts and milk shakes," she added wistfully.

Skender raised his eyes to the ceiling. "Thank God you didn't try. What's in here?" He zipped open a small plastic bag, Drita leaned over his shoulder, watching. "Lipsticks, eye shadow, perfume…" he grinned, "are you trying to give your immediate neighbor a heart attack?"

"I didn't know it was not used here."

Drita leaned over, took one of the lipsticks and pulled off the top. Skender took it from her, showed her how to twist the bottom to raise it, ready to use. She took it from him, eyes shining, licked her lips and looked expectantly, hopefully, at Babush. He gave a brief shake of his head. Slowly she wound it back into its case, put the cover on, pushed until it snapped. Her shoulders drooped as, reluctantly, she handed it to Skender.

"You may have one … to keep as a memento."

Drita's eyes shone. "Thank you, Babush."

"Wait!" Skender stopped her. "There are many colors to choose from. Jill, this is your department. Babush says she may have one. Which color for her?"

"Something soft, delicate but clear, to show off her lovely complexion." Gillian was down beside Drita in a moment, embarrassment forgotten, as she read labels, opened, checked colors, discarded some, stood others in a line so that Drita could choose.

Skender moved to join Nona and she smiled at him as he sat beside her. "They are like sisters, only the coloring is different." He nodded, then watched with his mother and father as the girls enjoyed themselves.

Gillian looked over her shoulder at Skender. "Drita likes this dark red but it is wrong for her. Can you tell her? The rose colors would suit her better."

"You had better listen to her, Drita … she is an expert. We have an army of lipsticks marching across the bathroom cupboard." He looked over at Babush. "Thank heavens they are not expensive in the States."

"Why does she need so many?" Nona asked.

"It is her way of treating, or rewarding, herself. If there has been some trouble or upset at work, or if we…." He stopped.

"Skender, this gray-green shadow would be super with her hazel eyes, and she likes this perfume, which is good for her, light and fresh."

"Babush said one lipstick. He didn't mention eye shadow or perfume."

"Oh. Not even one of each?" Skender shook his head. Drita and Gillian sat looking disconsolately at each other.

"One of each then," Babush said quickly, "but that is all. Hmmm! I think I am getting soft with you, daughter. Make sure I never see it on your face!" He smiled. "Until your wedding day!"

Drita blushed furiously. Skender laughed, pinched her cheek, then explained to Gillian the reason for the merriment. "When the girl is a Nusé she uses makeup."

"Is that the first time?"

"Yes."

She wrinkled her nose. "Bet they make a hash of it … it takes quite a time to know how to put it on correctly." She hesitated. "Hmmm…."

"What now?"

"Perhaps I could show Drita how to use it, practice, will he let us?"

"Don't press your luck!" He smiled. "Another time we might broach the subject, but not now, he could very well change his mind, take them from her…."

"Ho. Anyone home?"

Babush sighed, frowned. "Arif," he said as he stood up and went toward the door.

"Why did he come tonight?" Skender asked in a tight, angry whisper.

Babush stopped, turned back to face Skender. "He is family, this house is open to him at all times."

"Yes, but he knew Gillian was coming today. Couldn't he have allowed our family one evening together? He has been here every evening since I arrived…."

"There are not 'buts', no 'ifs' … he is family. Be prepared to greet him." Babush opened the door. "Here brother, here. Come in, come in."

Skender stood up, held out his hand to Gillian. "Stand up, my uncle is coming."

"How do I have to greet him?" she asked nervously.

Skender, recalling his father's words, smiled, and gently answered, "However is comfortable for you." He gave her hand an extra squeeze, then let it go.

Gillian swallowed as she felt Arif's eyes run over her when he entered the room and was acutely aware of the appraisal of the lady standing slightly behind him, whom she assumed was his wife. She watched as Arif shook hands with Babush and greeted Nona. She saw that Skender gave a slight bow before shaking hands with his uncle. Her eyes moved back to Arif and she caught the affectionate look given to Drita as she smiled, also giving a slight bow to her uncle.

I cannot, I just cannot bow to him. Skender said whatever is comfortable for me, so I will shake hands, nothing more…. She stood stiffly, trying to control her nervousness.

"Migje Arif, may I present my wife, Gillian. Jill, this is my uncle Arif. The word for uncle is *migje* so you will call him Migje Arif."

She held out her hand. "How do you do?"

Arif frowned, sent a quick, questioning look toward Babush. Babush looked steadily back at him. Slowly Arif took hold of Gillian's hand. "Welcome to Kosov, child." He turned to Skender, let go of her hand, "What is her name again?"

"Gillian."

"I will never remember that … we will give her another."

"No, her name is Gillian. I want no other for her."

Arif watched Skender for a moment, inclined his head. "Then I shall call her 'Nusé'."

Skender inclined his head to Arif, "If you wish." There was a slight edge as he continued, "Of course I expect her to learn yours." He turned from Arif to Gillian. "And this is my aunt, we call her Teza."

Gillian forced a smile, held out her hand. "How do…?"

She was enveloped in a smothering hug. "Skender, we have waited too long to welcome your Nusé." She held Gillian away, looked her over from top to bottom. "She is not as I imagined for you." She pulled her back into another hug, smiled at Skender over Gillian's head. "But she is delightful, I am going to love her, I know."

Skender was grinning at his aunt, his grin broadening as he guessed at his wife's reaction to the effusive greeting. He laughed as he saw the look on her face. "Are you shocked? Tut-tut, a stranger to touch you! Hold you! Hug you! How very un-British!"

Gillian gave a nervous laugh, smoothed her hair. "Why are you implying that we are a cold, unfeeling people?"

"Because you are!" He glanced over at his family, missed the hurt look, the quick blinking away of tears. "They have sat down now, so we may."

"Let our Nusé sit next to me," Babush said with a slight frown at Skender.

"Babush wishes us to sit next to him," Skender said as he and Gillian moved back to the fire.

Babush stopped Skender as he started to sit, pointing his finger. "Over there, next to Arif." He then turned to Gillian, added gently, "Here, child, next to me." *What did he say to upset you so?*

Gillian sat down, felt Arif's eyes on her, nervously she dragged at the hem of her dress, watching Skender talking to his uncle. *'Because you are … because you are.' How could you say such a horrible thing to me? You have never set foot in my country. Never met any of my family, never been in my home. How dare you?* She felt Babush watching her, returned his smile. *I admit it takes a little time to know us. We do not wear our hearts on our sleeve, but once our friendship, our love, is given, it is given forever. We do not give it lightly but once it is yours nothing will shake it. You can lean on it, depend on it….* She jumped, startled. "I'm sorry, what did you say?" Why is Skender frowning at me like that?

"I have asked you twice."

Even his voice is angry. "I'm sorry, I didn't hear."

"Migje Arif is inquiring after your parents' health."

She looked at him, startled. "He doesn't know them."

"I know that!" Skender said sharply. "Pull yourself together … stop dreaming. Now, are your parents well?"

"Yes, thank you. Should I ask after his?"

Skender glared at her. "His father was my grandfather, and he died when I was a child. You know that."

"Yes, I'm sorry, I'd forgotten."

He sighed. "Keep your mind here," he said wearily before turning again to Arif. Gillian glanced nervously at Babush, then at the women, deep in conversation. Relief flooded through her as she realized that they had not witnessed the scene with Skender. *Why was he so angry? Such a little thing to cause that much anger. Unless it was something else, something I've done, or not done. I can't think of anything…. 'Because you are … because…' He doesn't know any English people. I have very few English friends in San Francisco, meet most of them at lunch time so he doesn't mix. Who does he know to enable him to make a judgment like that?* She searched her mind. *No, there is no one, no … one … except me. It's me, there is no one else.* Her hand flew to her lips, she took a deep, shuddering breath, willing herself to stay calm.

"Drita, will you make some tea for us?" Drita stood immediately at Babush's words.

"Take our Nusé with you." He smiled at Gillian. *You need some time away from Skender, child, from all of us.* "Skender, please ask her to go with Drita, help her with the tea."

"Jill, Babush would like you to go with Drita to make some tea." He turned to her, smiling, the smile fading as he saw her set face, "Is something wrong?"

"No."

"Are you sure?"

"What could possibly be wrong?" she asked coldly. He watched her as she followed Drita to the door, started to stand. "I think there is something bothering…."

"Sit down!" The command from Babush came immediately, firmly.

Skender hesitated. "Babush, Gillian seemed…."

Babush looked steadily at him, then turned to Arif, "Our Nusé brought a little sunshine with her today, brother … it was pleasant after the cold weather we have had."

Slowly Skender sank back to the rug, only half-listening to the conversation of Babush and Arif. He turned to Nona, asked quietly, "Nona, would you mind going to the kitchen? Gillian seemed upset; I am a little worried…."

She smiled, "Of course," started to rise. Babush reached out his hand, laid it on Nona's arm, gently detaining her without interrupting his conversation with Arif. Surprised, Nona glanced at her husband, then smiled at Skender, "Drita is with her, Djali."

Skender nodded as he glanced at Babush. "Yes, I suppose so, yes, of course." He took out a cigarette, lit it. *What is the old boy up to? First, he won't let me sit next to her, now….* He felt Arif slap him across the shoulders and raised his eyes to the laughing face. "I'm sorry, what did you just say?"

"I asked if you were happy to have her here, but you were too busy dreaming to answer me."

"I'm sorry, yes, of course, I am very happy."

Arif grunted. "You could have deceived me; you are like a thundercloud tonight."

Then why the hell don't you go home?

Teza laughed, poked Skender in the ribs, "He is worried that we will tell his Nusé how he chased the girls, eh, Skender?"

"Yes, something like that," he answered absently.

Arif raised his eyebrows at Babush, shrugged.

"Ahh, the tea," Babush said gratefully as the girls arrived. He waited until the trays were set down onto the rug. "Nusé, ulu këtu." He patted the rug beside him. "Drita, you will serve." Gillian smiled back at him as she sat down. *Good, you have calmed yourself.* He turned to Arif. "After our tea, Drita will show you the gifts we were given by our Nusé. But I cannot resist showing you this now." He held the pipe out to Arif.

Arif took the pipe, examined it. "It is a beauty." Babush nodded, smiling proudly. "I will keep it, break it in for you." Arif started to put it in his pocket.

Babush nodded, eyes narrowing. "Go ahead … if you think you can get past me." They laughed together as the pipe was returned to Babush.

Arif turned to Skender, pointing to the pipe. "Does she have a sister? For Jakup?" Skender laughed. Babush held up the tin of pipe tobacco. Arif nodded. "Two sisters? Another for Emin?" he asked, his eyes on the tobacco.

"No," Skender laughed, "but if we stop in London on the way home and it is possible to send a pipe to you, and some tobacco, I will."

"Good! If you cannot send them, find a Nusé … let her bring them."

Skender turned to Gillian. "Babush is showing off his pipe to Migje. Migje is joking, has asked if you have a sister to marry his oldest son so that she could bring a pipe for him. Then Babush showed him the tobacco so he asked for another Nusé for his second son so that she could bring the tobacco."

"We can send him one from London," she smiled, "…a pipe, I mean."

"Yes, that is what I have told him." Skender sat, watching her, smiling gently. "Are you alright? Happy?" She nodded, smiling at him. "He won't let me sit next to you, damn it."

"I guessed," she laughed up at him, "they must think we're nuts, sitting here grinning at each other."

He laughed with her, "Probably. I wish they'd all go, leave us…." He stopped himself. "You remember Emin? The one who came with me to pick you up at the station? This is his father and mother."

"Really?"

"Yes. Why so surprised?"

"Oh, Emin was friendly, kind. Your uncle seems so … fierce!"

"He is, but always fair. His house is run with an iron hand. Emin is very like his father, very strict. His sister was supposed to have come tonight but at the last moment Emin forbade her, made her stay home."

"Was there a reason?"

He shrugged. "Some small indiscretion on her part. But he is like that … everything must be correct, precise. Watch Drita and the other girls when he is near … they are very careful around him, make no mistakes." He laughed, "They hear about it very quickly if they do. Ahh, Babush has asked Drita to show them the gifts. Let us watch this."

"Jill, they have admired all the things brought for my family. Why don't you give Migje and Teza their gifts?"

"I'd rather you did, or let them choose their own if you agree," Gillian answered, not wanting to move now that she had managed to pull the hem of her dress low enough to cover her knees. Skender smiled his agreement, showed the selection of colors to Teza, asked her to choose.

"All of these are lovely … which is your favorite?" she asked Gillian.

"This," Gillian pointed to a lime-green, "but the pink would be my choice for your aunt."

Teza took the pink. "Then this is the one I shall have." She leaned forward, kissed Gillian's cheek.

"Migje Arif?"

Arif chose a soft camel color. He gave Gillian a warm smile, "Thank you, Nusé, this will help to keep the cold out."

He turned to Skender, talking. Gillian watched his moustache moving up and down, felt the laugh bubbling in her throat. *He looks a little bit like an angry walrus.*

"Jill, Migje Arif thinks you are very brave to come by yourself on such a long journey. He wants to know if you were frightened of traveling alone." He smiled as he saw her eyes sparkling. *What has amused you now?*

"No, not at all."

Arif said something else. Skender turned to Gillian. "Not even a little?"

"No, I love traveling, seeing new things."

"He wants to know if you were worried about getting on the wrong train, going in the wrong direction?" She shook her head, smiled. Skender laughed at the next question. "What would you have done if you had gone east instead of south? Arrived in Romania instead of Prishtine?"

Arif was smiling at her, she smiled back. Perhaps he's not as fearsome as I thought! "Stayed a couple of days, had a look around and then caught a train back."

Skender smiled. "I will leave out the first part. I don't think he would approve or believe you."

"It is true. I wouldn't miss out on an opportunity to see another country, another city, just because I'd been stupid enough to go the wrong way."

"I know. But then I know you very well." It was said softly, the tone conveying more than the words. Gillian glanced nervously at Babush. Skender laughed. "You wouldn't have seen much, just the inside of a cell, probably. You have no visa for Romania," he answered her questioning look before turning back to Arif.

Gillian's mind wandered as the talking went on. *So far everything has gone smoothly, at least it seems that way.* She glanced at Babush. *I'm not sure about Babush, I think I like him but feel nervous around him. Thank God it is he who is Skender's father and not the other one….* Her eyes traveled only as high as Arif's knees. *Drita is so sweet. I really … like her … wish I … could … talk … to her, and … Nona … so….*

Teza tapped Skender's arm. "Don't you think you had better let your Nusé go to bed, Skender? She is almost asleep here." Skender did not answer. Teza turned to Drita. "Drita, take our Nusé and let her rest."

"She will wait for me, Teza," Skender said sharply as he indicated to Drita to stay where she was.

Teza shrugged, "If you wish, but she is tired and we are prepared to excuse her if you are." Drita started to stand, Skender didn't answer. Slowly Drita sat down again, deciding she had better wait for more explicit instructions from Babush or Skender. "Well, Skender, are you going to excuse her?" Teza persisted.

Drita looked quickly at Babush. He ignored her, studied the logs piled beside the fireplace. She turned to Nona but she was busily smoothing the rug.

Skender turned to Gillian, saw her lids drooping. "Are you sleepy, Jill?"

She jumped, shaking her head. "No, I'm fine," she said, forcing her eyes wide.

Skender continued to watch Gillian. "Teza, she is not tired."

Arif laughed, "If you had yelled at me like that I would have woken too. Even the dead would wake!"

Skender wiped his mouth on the back of his hand, frowning into the fire.

Drita's eyes flew to Babush, to Arif, and then back to Babush. She looked at Nona, received a slight shake of her head so stayed where she was.

Teza pointed to Gillian, "Skender! She is asleep, I tell you. Let her go to bed." Skender didn't move, didn't answer, stared solidly at the fire. "Do you see…?"

"Drita, take that girl and put her to bed," Arif commanded. He waited until Drita had bowed to him, then turned to Teza and softly added, "And you, wife, had better go and make us some more tea."

There was a moment of embarrassed silence and then, face flushed, Teza rose and hurried toward the door.

"I will help you as soon as my new daughter has bid us goodnight," Nona tried to reassure her. Teza nodded, then closed the door behind her. The silence was heavy. Arif sat expectantly, watching the dozing Gillian. Babush concentrated on the pile of logs. Drita moved nervously from foot to foot as she stood slightly behind Gillian. "Skender, please? Our Nusé has no idea what is expected of her…." She saw Arif's frown deepen as Skender folded his arms and continued his perusal of the fire. Nona glanced at Babush, realized that she could expect no help from him. "Djali? Please?"

Skender turned his head slowly, gave a long, deliberate look at Arif. Babush sat silent, not moving, wondering for one long second if his son was going to challenge Arif's order. "Jill, you are very tired. Go with Drita. She will show you to our room."

Babush pushed his hat to the back of his head, let out a long sigh of relief, the relief short-lived as he saw that Gillian had not moved. *What now? Did he tell her to go to bed? If so, why hasn't she gone? Or, could it be, has he told her to stay where she is?*

Nona closed her eyes, said a silent prayer. Drita's fingers folded and unfolded into her dimi.

"Jill. Get up. Go with Drita. I will join you shortly."

With a sigh she stood up, smiled at him, "I'm sorry, I was dozing. Wish them all goodnight for me. Don't be long."

Nona and Babush's eyes met, held for a moment. Drita's panic subsided as she saw the frown on Arif's face clear.

"Gillian wishes you all goodnight," Skender said quietly.

Nona rose, came to Gillian, kissed her cheek. "Noten a mire, daughter."

"Noten a mire, Nona, noten a mire, Babush." Gillian smiled her goodnight to Arif.

"Sleep well, child," Babush answered gently as the two girls started toward the door.

"I will help Teza with the tea," Nona murmured as she followed the girls.

The room was quiet after the women had left, only the fire disturbing the silence. Arif sat, chin in hand, watching Skender.

Babush glanced at his son, then at his brother. He took the tin of tobacco and offered it to Arif. "One more pipe, brother?" He returned the tobacco to its place beside the logs at Arif's refusal.

Arif smoothed the left-hand side of his moustache, "You are very quiet, Skender."

"Yes, Migje."

"Why do I have to drag every word from your mouth tonight?"

"I'm sorry." He stood. "If you will excuse me…." Arif watched him leave, turned back to Babush.

"What's wrong with him tonight?" Babush gave a half smile, looked steadily at his brother. "Well? What is wrong with him?"

"Better ask what is wrong with you, brother!" Arif's puzzled look brought a laugh. "You are getting old! Your blood runs thin."

Arif's puzzlement turned to bewilderment. "I'm sorry, but you have lost me."

Babush grinned broadly. He looked at his brother, laughed at his bewildered expression, then leaned toward him and asked softly, "How long has he been away from her?" His grin broadened as he saw enlightenment come. "And you, brother … old man … have sent her to sleep!"

Arif swore silently, turned his eyes to the ceiling, then banged his clenched fist onto the rug. "I did not think…." His eyes met Babush's, they both started to laugh. He wiped his tears. "I would have killed my uncle for such a trick!"

"Take care! Skender may do that yet," Babush said with laughter.

"Why didn't you give me some warning, a clue?"

Babush grinned wickedly, "You are younger than I, at least in years, I did not know it was necessary." Arif shook his finger at him, swore softly but thoroughly. Babush laughed, gave a slight bow. "Thank you. May you, too, brother."

Arif rubbed his chin. "What shall I do now?" he laughed, "tell him he is tired? Send him to bed?" He sobered suddenly, frowned. "Brother, I am sorry. I almost put my nephew in a corner a moment ago. My concern, really, was not whether his Nusé went to bed or not, but to shut my wife's mouth." He sighed deeply, shook his head. "I should have addressed myself to her and not interfered with Skender's business."

"It is past … no harm came of it."

"Only because of the caliber of the son you have. I am very proud of him, and you must be even prouder. To be able to keep his dignity, accept our customs after all these years…." He shook his head. "It could not have been easy for him to give me that obedience. But he did it! He remembered our ways and honored them. Congratulations to him, and to you too."

Babush inclined his head slightly. "Now I will break one of our customs, for I do not intend to deny anything you've said. I am proud of him, prouder as each day passes and I see his strength, his character. Sometimes it is hard not to grab him, hug him…." He sighed deeply, "He is my only living son, brother … there have been too many years of missing … and soon I shall lose him again." He smoothed his moustache, lips tight together, adjusted his hat as Arif leaned toward him.

"Better one good apple than a full barrel of bruised."

Babush gave another deep sigh. "Yes, but you don't know how hard … you are fortunate, all your flock surrounds you, while I? Only two left out of five … Skender and Drita. How much longer will I have him here? Two, three weeks? And Drita? How long before I have to part with her? Give her into another's care?"

Arif crossed to his brother, sat close, put his arm along Babush's shoulders. "I have no comfort for you, unless perhaps to pray that Skender will stay, make his home here where he belongs."

Babush raised his eyes to Arif's, "And have him live in fear? No. I would rather he left, rather I never saw him again, than that."

Arif glanced quickly at the door, "He is coming." His eyes searched Babush's. "Are you alright?" Babush's nod was brief. Arif stood up, gave one firm, hard, grip to his brother's shoulder, then quickly returned to the other side of the fire. "Are you ready for him, brother?" Babush gave another brief nod. "Good. A general topic then. Make sure you appear to enjoy this tale; it is easy to follow…."

Chapter 16

"I hope you will be comfortable." Drita smiled to Gillian as she bent and turned back the bedcovers. Gillian held out her hands to the fire, smiled back at Drita. "Put more wood on the fire if you are cold." She pointed to the pile of logs, shivered. Both girls stood smiling at each other, wondering what the next move should be. Drita turned as Skender opened the door. "The room is ready, brother. I have told your Nusé to put more wood on the fire if she is cold."

Skender nodded, turned to Gillian. "This is the women's guest room. They have given it to us because they think we will be more comfortable." He leaned back against the door. "Are you warm enough? Would you like me to put more wood on the fire?" he asked politely.

"No, thank you, I am fine."

Skender smiled. "Well, then…." He smiled at Drita, turned back to Gillian. "It gets cold at night here … much colder than in California."

"Yes, I imagine it does." Gillian took a breath, "It was colder in London too." Skender nodded. "We had frost at night," she smiled, "it froze … a couple of times." Drita stepped closer to Gillian, gave a small bow, said something. "She said goodnight, didn't she? Sleep well?"

"Yes."

"Noten a mire, Drita, sleep well." They both hesitated for a moment, then, as one, moved and gave each other a quick hug.

Skender continued to lean against the door as Drita approached. "Excuse me, brother."

Gillian watched, saw the surprised look on Drita's face at Skender's answer before she moved to one side of him.

"Get to bed, Jill. Try to sleep."

"Aren't you coming?" she asked in surprise.

"No, not yet. Our guests are still here."

Gillian's eyes flew briefly to Drita, back to Skender. "She has said goodnight. Why didn't she leave?"

"We are leaving now. Sleep well."

"I asked why your sister hadn't left, not you."

"She is waiting for me. Goodnight, Jill." He turned, "Ready, Drita?"

"Skender?"

"Yes?"

"Let her leave. Stay, just for a minute. Please?"

"No. I have to go. Goodnight, Jill." He opened the door, leaned back against it. "Yes, yes, go," he said irritably as Drita looked questioningly at him. *Blast! Blast Arif and his damn interference, and Teza too.* He glared at the door of the room where Arif sat with Babush. *Jill, she must be confused, wondering why I didn't let Drita leave, kiss her goodnight, hold her … that much control I don't have. If I had let myself be alone with her….* He took a deep breath. *I'd better get back to them. Arif asked for tea to be brought … if the women come back, find me standing here….*

The cold water felt good, refreshing, calming. Skender turned the tap, letting it run a little faster, splashing his face quickly and often. He glanced up at the light as he dried his hands. *I've been here two, almost three weeks and never noticed how dim it is….*

He walked across the hall, reached for the doorknob, stood still, frowning. *If Babush has said anything to Arif, if Arif teases, makes a joke….* He sighed, took a deep breath, ran his hand over his hair, and opened the door.

Slowly, still watching the door, Gillian sank down to the mattress.

Skender stopped Drita from leaving, but why? She said goodnight to me, walked directly to the door but then Skender said something that stopped her. Why? So he wouldn't be alone with me? Why would he do that? Even if he had to go back to his uncle he could have stayed for five minutes with me, kissed me goodnight…. Unless, is it possible? Has he … could there be someone else? She put her hand to her lips, stopping their trembling.

"'I love you and want to be alone with you.' Would he have said that to me if there was someone else? Babush was so anxious for him to marry one of the girls from here … wouldn't it be an opportunity not to be missed?" She stood up, walked over to her case, slowly took out her nightdress, continued musing, "Skender here, alone … would his father miss out on such a golden opportunity? Wouldn't he jump at such a chance, make sure he met someone? No … wait … the boy doesn't see the girl until their wedding night." She came back to the fire, sat close to it. But this is a different situation." Her voice was barely a whisper, "What if Babush talked to the girl's father, convinced him, made him agree to letting Skender and the girl meet? No, Skender would never … 'Because you are' … he must have meant me, there is no one else … was I ever like that? Not that I know of, especially with him, but … if he found me that way? Then perhaps…."

Her thoughts flew to Drita, *so anxious to please, so feminine … all the girls here must be that way. They treat the men like kings. Could any man resist that? Resist their natural instinct to dominate, especially when the girl is so willing? Could Skender? Would he want to? He was raised to expect that service, demand it even. If he thought of me at all, where would I stand? How would I measure up beside these girls? I have never given that service, couldn't be that way.*

She walked around the room biting at her clenched fists, "Don't cry! Don't cry! You don't want to have red, swollen eyes if he comes." She put her arms around herself trying to stop the shaking. She stopped beside the fire, staring into it, then bent, picked up a log and pushed it into the flames. *What good will that do! That isn't the kind of warmth you need.*

She sat down on the mattress, holding her hands to the fire. "I have always felt insecure about him, always wondered why he chose me, especially when there were so many of those long-legged American beauties available … and not only Americans. What about when he lived in Italy, Germany? He must have known girls there.

"All those snapshots I found when I was cleaning out his closet. We had only been married a week, two at the most … and then when I asked him about them, he laughed. 'Of course there've been girls in my life, dozens of them! Why so upset, Jill? I asked none of them to share my life. You are the only one I ever offered my name to.' And then that stupid, naive question 'Did you sleep with any of them?' She dropped her face into her hands, tears running through her fingers as she remembered. He didn't answer, but you had to insist, didn't you? 'Let it go, Jill, it is past, finished.'"

"Would you have accepted that answer if it had been me? If I'd hopped in and out of bed with…." She took a deep, steadying breath, remembering how angry he had been, how he'd grabbed her, shook her till her head spun. 'Don't ever speak that way, think that way even. Now, take the damn pictures, burn them do what the hell you like with them, but don't you ever, ever, say such a thing again.'

She saw the jug and glasses beside the stove, shakily poured herself a glass of water. "What happens if he comes, tells me there is someone special here … what will I do?" She gave a short, bitter laugh. *What will you do? It won't be your decision … he will ask you to leave. I won't, I can't … not feeling the way I do about him.* She sipped at the water, dragged in a long breath, "If he doesn't care about me anymore, how could I stay? I'd have to leave, go. Go? Where? Back home? Tell my mother she was right after all, that the marriage didn't last? No … never! Back to San Francisco?" Tears spilled again. "I couldn't, not there … every corner, every street, reminding me of him, of us. Damn! I don't have a handkerchief … 'You'd better start to carry one of these for yourself.' Oh, Skender, you've become so important to me, pushed out everyone, everything from my life. What am I going to do now? Where shall I start? What should I do first?" She walked around, sat down on the window bench, lifted a corner of the drape and laid her forehead gratefully against the cold pane, staring out into the night. "Not a light to be seen anywhere, just cold, dark emptiness."

She stirred, shivered, went quickly back to the fire. She undressed, hurrying as the chill air struck at her skin, muttered, "I should have brought warm granny gowns." She slipped into the filmy nightdress, undid her watch, automatically checked the time. *I must have dozed, almost an hour's gone by.... So he isn't coming ... he isn't coming....*

She ignored the insistent voice, walked to the door and switched off the light. Slowly, feeling the way with her feet, she made her way to the mattress. She shivered violently, picked up a log and put it on the fire. *It was almost two years ago when we slept beside a log fire. I wonder if he will remember? If he will care anymore?*

The sheets struck chill as she slid between them. She lay stiffly, trying to stop her shivering, staring up at the ceiling, watching the dancing firelight making strange shapes. *There was no fuss ... just the two of us. Did he miss all that ceremony, that celebration? Would he have liked to come, find his Nusé waiting, veil covering her?* She turned with a sigh. *Would he have liked to have a shy, terrified girl to cajole and woo on his wedding night?* She turned restlessly. *Up till now I had always worried, wondered ... all those other girls he went with ... they must have know other men, known how to please, how to ... while I?* Her lids, heavy with tears and fatigue, began to droop. "What does he want? He could have gone in either direction, had ... any girl. Ended ... me ... stuck, somewhere ... middle...." Wearily she pulled the covers up to her chin, turned on her side, traced an outline on the other pillow. "Noten a mire, my darling ... wish...."

"Noten a mire, Skender."

"Noten a mire, Babush." Skender turned, opened the door to their room. The light from the hall stabbed the dark room as he slipped inside. He closed the door quickly against the brilliance, stood, waiting for his eyes to become accustomed to the darkness. The fire gave more light than he expected and he made his way easily to the mattress on the floor. He looked down at her, so soundly asleep, covers pulled tight to her chin, the fair curls rosy from the glowing embers. He smiled. As usual, she had taken the whole bed, her body stretched across rather than up and down.

Carefully he eased himself down onto the mattress, sat, watching the flickering firelight sending shadows over her face. *I did not know that I could become so deeply involved with one person, never realized until this, our first separation, how important you are to me, how much I have grown to love you.* He took out a cigarette, reached for a piece of wood from the fire. *The smell of burning wood always reminds me....* Slowly he pushed one of the curls from her face. *Always so soft and shiny.* He smiled to himself, remembering her arrival at his home, how he had pushed one of those curls back into its proper place then. *I would not have believed anyone could become more important to me than my own family, but you have. If Babush had refused to accept you, I would have left here immediately. If, by a look, a word, he had made you feel unwelcome, I would have taken you from here.* He tossed the unfinished cigarette into the fire, traced the outline of her cheek with his finger. *But you have been accepted, haven't you? Nona cares for you already … Drita too….*

He pushed the covers closer about her shoulders. *Even Babush feels that special warmth of yours, is already melting. And your husband? He has missed you more than he thought possible….* He bent, gently put his lips to hers. She stirred restlessly, a long deep sigh escaping as she settled herself again. He hesitated, sighed. *I should not wake you….* He reached, picked up a log, sat staring into the fire.

"Skender?"

He turned quickly. "I thought you were deeply asleep." Her eyes didn't leave his face. "I wanted so desperately to waken you. Now I have mixed feelings … sad that you have broken that sleep … happy…." He smiled at her, "So serious? Not a smile or a word for me?"

She lay still, watching him. "I thought … was I dreaming? Or … did you … kiss me?"

"Yes. I should have let you sleep, shouldn't I?" He realized he was still holding the log, gave a half-smile and turned, pushed it into the fire, added another.

He watched as the logs began to catch and burn. "It was so right for us, wasn't it, my love? Quiet, peaceful, just the two of us…." He pulled her close as she came and sat beside him, laid his cheek to hers. "At the time we both wished our families were with us, but now, looking back, I would not change it."

He was still, arms close about her, remembering the sound of the ocean crashing against the rocks, emphasizing their warmth and coziness, the feeling of isolation, of the two of them being completely, utterly alone. He pulled her in closer, sighed deeply, contentedly. "It feels so good to have you here, to be able to hold you." He felt her tremble, misunderstood, and reached for a blanket from the bed, wrapping it around the two of them. "There, that better?" He smiled down at her. "Comfortable? Happy?"

She wriggled in closer, smiled up at him then put her arms tightly around him.

Chapter 17

"Skender, Skender." Nona shook him gently.

His lids lifted heavily; sleep-glazed eyes looked at her uncomprehendingly for a moment. "Nona? Is something wrong?"

"No, Djali, but you must get up … there will be guests here within the hour."

He groaned, gently eased his arm from under Gillian's head. "What time is it?"

She bent down, picked up the nightdress from the floor, carefully folded it. "Almost six." She walked over to the bench, laid the nightdress down, lifted the drape and looked out. "It is trying to snow."

Skender groaned. "Why so early? Can't they come later?"

"They started very early, have come a long way and they are making this trip to see you, greet you." She gave him another shake. "Up, now, you must be ready to welcome them."

He sighed. "Give me five minutes to wake up. Nona…." He stopped her as she was opening the door. "I shall need hot water for a bath."

She beamed at him. "Yes, Djali." She gave a quick, fond smile at the sleeping Gillian, beamed again at her son, and left the room. Carefully she made her way down the slush-covered steps to the kitchen.

Babush looked up from his bread and milk as the kitchen door opened. "You are smiling like an overripe cherry, wife … did you waken our son?"

"Yes." She beamed at him. Babush turned back to his bowl, moustache quivering as he fought his laughter. "Do you want to hear or are you too busy eating?" she asked, hardly able to contain herself.

"News will keep, this will not." Babush said, knowing that she would tell him anyway.

"They were sleeping like two doves, as close as … as close as…." No simile came to her. "Not even a breath of air could have come between them. Are you listening to me?" she demanded in exasperation as Babush continued his meal.

"Yes, I am listening. It is not necessary to stop eating to hear." He looked up at her, bread suspended in mid-air. "Well, what else? Before you burst a seam."

She smiled, waited, so that her news would have full impact. "He has asked for hot water." Babush looked steadily at her. "For a bath!" She beamed at him expectantly.

"That is it? That is why you are so excited? So full of importance?"

She shook her head at him, excitement still in her voice. "Isn't that enough?"

Babush laughed. "Woman, I could have told you that last night, yesterday afternoon." He leaned toward her, softly added, "I could have told you that he would need hot water even before she set foot in this house." He laughed. "I could have told you last week."

She walked over to the water heater, turned a knob and made some adjustments. "Impossible! Even you could not know that." She turned, saw him smiling at her. "How could you know?" she asked suspiciously.

"Because…."

"Because what?"

"Because he is my son, my seed," he said, watching Nona with a devilish grin. "Because his Nusé is almost as pretty as…." He winked. "Because I remember how I was at his age. Why are you blushing, wife? Old memories stirring?" he asked softly, his smile broadening.

She laughed at him, looked away. "Eat, it must be cold."

Babush put the bowl down, stood up, stretched. "I am finished, it was not cold." He walked over to her, put his arms round her waist, made a low growl in his throat. "And neither am I!" They laughed as they hugged each other. "I suppose I must go and put on a tie," he sighed. She nodded, jumped and tut-tutted at him as he gave her a sharp whack across the buttocks. He slipped on his shoes, leaning against the door-jamb, saw her watching him, winked, pointed upstairs. "That is my seed up there, he will ask again tomorrow. Do you want to bet on it?"

"You are impossible." Nona shook her head, smiled. "Hurry, go and get ready for our guests."

Babush opened the door. "Drita! Mirëmëngjes."

"Mirëmëngjes, Babush. Mirëmëngjes, Nona." She was out of breath. "I am sorry … I overslept."

Babush frowned, nodded. "I see that. Don't let it happen again."

"Why didn't you waken me, Nona?" Drita asked as she closed the door behind her father. She walked to her mother, kissed her cheek, started to roll up her sleeves.

"Your father said I was to let you sleep. He is sending Besim for bread … you do not have to bake today."

Drita glanced at the door, back to her mother. "I thought he was angry…."

"No, he was teasing. Get some food for yourself, the milk is hot. Put some more on to warm for your brother." Nona pulled up one of the sheepskin rugs to the fire and sat down.

"Have you eaten, Nona?" Drita sat opposite her mother, poured some honey into the bowl of hot milk. Carefully, she dipped the bread into it, letting the bread stir the honey and milk together. "How many for dinner tonight, Nona, and what time?"

"Our own family, plus Arif and Jakup. Babush has to speak with Arif, so they are coming to eat with us, the rest of Arif's family will come later, as will Migje Hasan and his family." She smiled as she saw her daughter's quick look of relief. "Not too many for dinner, daughter, but six or more are due within the hour."

Drita jumped up, putting the bowl from her. "The guest room…?"

"It has been taken care of … finish your meal."

"The fire?"

"Already lit and burning well." She saw Drita glance around. "The cups are there, ready … the water is heating for coffee."

"Nona, you should not have done all this! You should have called me."

"Do not be distressed, Drita, there will be plenty for you to do." She smiled. "You do your share and more. I was already awake, so it was no hardship. Mirëmëngjes again, Skender."

He bent, kissed his mother's cheek. "Mirëmëngjes, Nona, Mirëmëngjes, Drita. Please sit and finish your meal." He put his hand on Drita's shoulder, stopping her from getting up.

"After I have prepared yours, brother."

"Then coffee, please. I will eat later." Skender sat down next to Nona.

"Did you sleep well, Djali? Did our Nusé sleep well? Is she awake yet?"

"Yes, yes, and no."

"I will go and light the fire so that it will be warm for her when she wakes. I will be very quiet, not waken her." Drita smiled at Skender as she carefully swirled the jesva of coffee.

"There is no need, the fire is fine." Skender accepted the coffee. He breathed deeply. "I'm not sure which satisfies me most, the aroma or taste."

Drita stood, staring at him, then, "Brother, did you light the fire?"

Skender sipped appreciatively at his coffee. "No, I did not let it go out."

"You kept it going all night?" Drita asked in disbelief and astonishment.

Skender saw Nona's warning look, swore silently. "The coffee was good, sister. Let me eat before these guests arrive."

Drita handed him a bowl, poured in the hot milk, passed a piece of the dark, crusty bread. "Honey, brother?" she asked, her tone still puzzled.

Skender shook his head, dipped the bread into the milk, waiting until it was soaked full, then bent his head to catch the bread before it fell. He glanced at Nona. "Do you remember nagging at me when I was a boy for waiting, leaving the bread in the milk too long?"

"Yes, you always let it take too much milk, then it could not carry itself to your mouth, would fall, splashing milk … Skender!"

"Don't worry, Nona, I caught it," he laughed.

She shook her head at him. "And then you would have that wet bread swimming around in your bowl. You'd tip the bowl, making an awful slurping noise as you tried to catch…."

"Like this?" he asked, tipping the bowl to his mouth. He laughed at his mother's horrified expression, winked at Drita as he saw her laughing behind her hand.

Nona turned as the door opened. "Ah, I am glad you are here … your son needs a spanking."

Babush gravely nodded. "Go ahead. I give you permission. Let me know when this spanking is to take place, I will be interested in seeing you put him across your knee!" He turned to Skender. "Our guests should be here soon. Are you ready, Djali?"

"Yes, sir. Drita, a glass of tea, please." Surprised at the request for tea, she stood staring at him. Skender raised his eyebrows. "Drita?"

"Did you hear your brother?" Babush's tone was sharp. Quickly she moved, poured the tea and handed it to Skender.

"Thank you. Babush, I will be in the guest room in five minutes."

"Where are you going now, Djali?" Babush asked, puzzled.

"I am taking this tea to Gillian. I will see you upstairs in five minutes."

All three stared silently as the door closed on him.

Slowly Babush turned to Nona. "Did he say he was taking tea to his wife?" Her head moved once. Babush sat down heavily. "I would not have believed if I had not seen … a man to carry to a woman! My son to carry to his wife?" He sighed and blew out a long breath. "Not a word of this to anyone," he said threateningly to his wife, his daughter. "If this got out … we would be the laughing stock of Prishtine! Of the whole of Kosov!" He sighed, shook his head in sorrow. "My own son … to carry tea to his wife? And she? Where is she? In bed yet! He is up and she is still in bed!"

He frowned, pushing his lips tightly together. Slowly his eyes twisted to Drita, he shook his finger at her. "Don't ever let me hear … don't ever let me hear that you were still in bed when your husband was up. Don't ever let me hear that you allowed him to carry to you. Do you hear me, girl?"

"Yes, Babush."

He grunted, glared angrily at her, banged his fist on the floor.

"Drita! Drita!"

"Babush, Skender is calling me. May I go?"

"Go."

Quickly she opened the kitchen door, slipped on some nalle and climbed the three stairs.

"Don't come any farther, Drita. I just wanted to tell you that Gillian is still sleeping. Let her sleep, do not disturb her." Drita nodded. "And tell Babush I await him in the guest room."

"I know, I know, I heard it all." Babush angrily stopped Drita from relaying Skender's message. He turned to Nona. "What next? What next in this house?" Still muttering, he made his way to the door, slammed it shut behind him.

Nona and Drita stood still, looking at each other. The door opened.

"If our Nusé should decide to get up at all today, make sure you keep her out of sight. Make sure … or answer to me." The window rattled protestingly as the door slammed.

"Ulu, ulu, Nusé." Babush motioned with his hand that Gillian should remain seated but nodded approvingly as she stood when he entered the room. He sat down, with a brief smile gave his permission for her to sit, then took out his pipe, watching as she returned to her book. He reconsidered the pipe and put it back in his pocket, still watching Gillian. He frowned, slightly annoyed that she did not stand as Skender came in. "Have our guests gone, Djali?"

"Yes, Babush, I took them right to our gate." Skender flashed a quick smile to Gillian, "Hi, sleepy-head."

"Hi yourself," she replied softly as a slow smile curved her lips.

Skender winked, turned back to Babush, expecting the customary permission to sit.

"Our guests stayed longer than necessary. Too long," Babush said with a sigh.

"Yes, sir." *Is something wrong? He has never kept me standing before.*

Babush pushed his hat back, smoothed his moustache, "Ask her to leave us."

"There is no need. She doesn't understand…." He stopped as he saw his father close his eyes. "Jill, would you leave us for a moment?"

She looked from him to Babush in surprise, "You've only just got here."

"I know, but he has asked you to leave." She got up. "I won't be long, five minutes probably."

Babush waited until the door closed, took out his pipe, slowly packed it, pushing the tobacco tight. Skender stood watching him, wondering what could have happened in the short time elapsed since the guests' departure. Babush looked up, watching him for a moment, "Don't let me see you carry to your wife again." Completely bewildered, Skender shook his head. "This morning, before our guests came, did you or did you not carry tea to your wife?"

"Yes, I did. Ahh. I think I understand now. I thought nothing of it, it was an automatic thing, I'm sorry, it will not happen again."

Babush frowningly lit his pipe, "You said 'automatic' … do I understand that you do this in your own home?"

"Yes. Whichever one of us is up first makes coffee. Sometimes it is Gillian, sometimes me." He watched his father, saw the frown deepen. "Do not forget, Babush, that we both work. If she were at home all day it would be a different matter. As it is, we help each other as much as possible, share the work."

"God forgive me! Don't tell me you work in the house?"

"Yes. I do."

"Are you mad? Have you lost all your senses?"

Skender sighed, "Babush, she works as many days, as many hours, as I. Would it be right to leave all the housework to her too?" Babush did not answer, pulled on his pipe. "By sharing the work, we have time to be together, do things together, enjoy each other's company…." His voice trailed off as he realized the futility of trying to explain to his father.

Babush motioned with his hand, giving Skender permission to sit. "There is something here that really worries me, Skender, why don't you keep her home? Can't you make enough money to support a wife?"

"Yes. But only if she continued to work could we afford to make this trip. We discussed whether we should come here first or have a child…."

"What?" Babush stopped him angrily. "You discussed that? With her?"

"Of course with her; who else but her?"

"Enough! No more of this!"

"Babush, it is important to me that you understand…."

"No! I don't want to understand, don't want to know." His hand shook as he put his pipe back in his mouth.

"Babush, please? You must let me explain…."

"Take care, Skender … you are pushing me too far." He pulled deeply on his pipe. "What kind of world do you live in if you think it normal to discuss such a thing with your wife?" He banged his fist angrily on the rug. "What is she thinking of to allow you to mention such a thing to her?"

"Mention? Of course I mentioned it! She is the one who will have to carry the child…."

"Enough! How dare you!" Babush, shaking with anger, was halfway to his feet. Slowly he sank back to the rug, took a steadying breath. "How long have you been married to her?"

"Two years," Skender said wearily.

"Two years … two! She is still wet behind the ears and you discuss such a thing with her. Even now I would not dream of bringing up such a topic to your mother. I cannot understand you, Skender."

Skender stared at the rug, lips tight together. He sighed, looked up at his father, "I must handle this matter as I see it, Babush. I cannot be governed by your traditions when I do not live here. And I cannot treat my wife the way I would treat a girl from here."

"Perhaps it would be better if you did," Babush said sharply.

"Perhaps. I cannot say. Some of the ways, the customs of our girls I miss, always will, but I have changed, Babush, want more than our girls are able to give. What Gillian can offer is more important to me."

"Make sure she offers and does not lead."

"What do you mean?" Skender asked quietly.

Babush frowningly pulled at his moustache, "Make sure it is you holding the reins. Take my advice and keep a tight grip on this filly."

"I will," Skender nodded.

"I hope so. For your own sake I hope you heed my words. You see her gentleness, her softness, but she is stronger than you think. Let her run free and you will lose her respect. Without respect everything is lost." Skender frowned, slowly nodded. "Ah, I see our Nusé has already tried to get the bit between her teeth, eh, Djali?"

Skender gave a brief smile, "Once or twice."

Babush nodded, "I am not surprised. Be careful with her, make her strength work for you, not against you." He stood up. "Gentle, but firm, Skender. Make sure she knows you are the one in control. I am going to rest for a while. Arif is eating with us and then I will discuss the offer of the Drini family with him." He put his arm across his son's shoulders. "It will not be easy for your wife tonight, Skender. There will be many people here."

"It will not be so difficult. The biggest hurdle was taken last night." He smiled at his father's puzzled look, "Hassan is softer, easier than Arif."

Babush glanced sideways at him, "Mmm, you think so, eh?"

"And Gillian is well rested…."

"And Teza will have been told to shut her mouth," Babush intervened, eyes twinkling. They laughed, walked to the door together. "Rest, Djali, you look tired. I will see you in an hour."

Skender watched his father walk across the hall towards his room. *Almost a battle between us … and over what?* He glanced around as he heard the door of the guest room open. "Hello, Nona."

"Djali." She laid down her broom, smiled at him. "Everything is clean again. Now we are ready for the next onslaught."

"Yes." His smile was sad, "Do you need to get into this room, Nona? Good, then I am going to rest before Arif arrives. I am suddenly exhausted."

He watched as she placed pillows in front of the fire for him. "You are spoiling me, Nona."

She turned, stood looking at him for a moment. "I thank God I can, Djali. Come now, lay down and rest. I will send your Nusé to you." She kissed him, picked up the broom and quietly closed the door.

Chapter 18

"Stop staring! I am getting jealous," Skender whispered with a grin.

"I can't help it … it's like meeting Omar Sharif! Better!" Gillian laughed back as she broke off a piece of bread.

"Now you can see why I made sure you were tightly tied to me before I brought you here," Skender said with a wink.

She glanced under her lashes at Arif, "I wonder if he looked like that when he was young."

"Like Jakup? No, I would imagine Arif looked more like Emin than Jakup." He glanced at Nona, "I'm sorry, Nona, what did you say?"

"Has our Nusé had enough to eat?"

"I will not allow her to have more … she will get heavy." He laughed at Nona's startled look, pinched her cheek. "She has had enough."

Jakup stretched, smiled at Drita as she started to help Nona clear the dishes. "Delicious, Drita, as always."

"One day I will burn something and you will still say that."

"Just don't put too much salt," Jakup said softly, almost to himself.

"Be careful, Jakup, I heard and do not find it amusing," Arif snapped. Jakup inclined his head to his father, whispered to Skender, "I will tell you later, it is a wonder my dear sister is still in one piece."

Skender grinned, "I am anxious to hear. Jill, do you want some kos … yogurt?"

She shook her head. "No, thank you. Drita makes these, doesn't she?" she asked, examining the tablecloth.

Skender shrugged, "I suppose so."

"She's very proud of her country."

Skender shrugged again, "The girls are not concerned, not as we are."

"Wrong. I don't know about the other girls, but Drita cares. She is also very proud of her family." She glanced up, saw Babush watching her and dropped the cloth back over her knees.

"What was she saying, Djali?"

"That Drita is very proud to be an Albanian. And a Berisha."

"And you?" What did you answer?"

"I told her that the girls are not overly concerned with nationality. I made no comment about the family."

Babush laughed, turned to Arif. "She must be the Kosovar, not him."

Arif nodded agreement, smiling at Gillian, "Well done, daughter. Your husband has been here three weeks and not noticed." Arif, still smiling at Gillian, glanced at Skender, "Nephew, I see you are still in the dark … ask your Nusé to explain."

Skender smiled, "They are very pleased with you. What is going on?"

Her eyes slid sideways to Babush. She received an encouraging nod and picked up the cloth. "Haven't you noticed? All the tablecloths are red and they all have this black embroidery along the edges."

"So?"

"The Albanian flag … red and black. But she has also made the stitches look like the spread wings of an eagle. In the center of this one…" she moved the basket of bread, "…she has worked a 'B' for Berisha, but if you look carefully you can see that it could also be a double-headed eagle at the top of the letter. See?"

"Does she know anything of our problems here, Skender?" Arif asked. Skender shook his head, studying the cloth. "Then, she has no idea that we are not allowed to use our flag, that we have to disguise our emblem?"

"Correct, Migje."

Arif glanced at Babush, "It is not easy to catch those eagle-heads, you have to look carefully. She is sharp."

Babush nodded. "Skender, are you sure that she did not know that we are forbidden to use our flag?"

"Certain." He looked at his father, looked back at the cloth, feeling the stitches with his finger. "I am ashamed to say I did not see it." He looked directly at Babush, "She had no reason to search for something. She knows nothing of the problems here, and nothing of my story. The only thing I told her was that I left home at sixteen and that later I escaped from Yugoslavia to Italy."

"How does she know our flag?" Jakup asked.

"One of her friends sent one from the U.N. in New York. It is in our apartment. There is a small stand with two flags mounted on it … the Albanian and hers. We drilled another hole and put the American one in the center. She always jokes, says that once we have a child…" he glanced quickly at Babush, "…we will be an All-American family." He saw the questioning looks, went on to explain, "Three different nationalities making one family, that is America … a glorious mixture of nationalities and faiths making a whole, one reason why I love the country so much."

"I am glad, Djali, glad that you have found a place where you can be happy. Now, let us ask a blessing for this meal." Babush waited until everyone was ready, noted that this time Gillian did not have to be told how to hold her hands.

Skender and Jakup stood as their fathers did. Jakup held out his hand to help Gillian.

"Tell your mother that we will wait for Hassan before we have coffee. Come, Arif, we will use the guest room, then we will not be disturbed." The two walked across the hall. Babush opened the door. "Good. It is nice and warm. Sit down brother, sit down."

Arif settled himself to one side of the brightly burning fire, "Your Nusé surprised me, brother."

"Yes, I was pleased with her."

"She seems a nice girl." He glanced quickly at Babush. "No comment? Are you unhappy with her?"

"It is too soon to tell. How can I judge in one day? She is quieter, shyer than I expected, and that pleases me, but … do not misunderstand, she has done nothing to cause my concern, but I wish Skender was firmer in his handling of her."

"She has only just got here; he will come to earth in a day or two."

"Yes, you're right. Let us leave Skender and his problems. There is something else for us to discuss, Rashid came yesterday."

"I remember you told me he was coming. Did you enjoy your visit?"

"Yes. The news he carried is why I have to talk to you."

"Nothing wrong?" Arif asked anxiously.

"No. Nothing wrong. Rashid has asked for Drita for the son of one of his friends."

"If it is meant, may it be with happiness for this house and theirs. Yesterday was an exciting day for you, brother … a Nusé arrived and an inquiry for your daughter. Your happiness must know no bounds." Babush smilingly nodded. "Do you know the family?"

"No, but Rashid spoke well and highly of them."

Arif nodded, "I have great faith in Rashid, but we will find out for ourselves. The name?"

"Drini."

Arif's eyes widened, "They are one of the leading families in Prizren." He smiled warmly at Babush. "I could not be happier for you; it is an honor to your house and our name that they have asked for her."

Babush sighed, "Prizren is so far … even if everything about the family is right, if everything checks out, I do not think I want her that far from me." He looked steadily at Arif, "I must be sure, very sure, that they are right for my daughter, that she will be happy with them, that they will treat her kindly, correctly…."

"It is hard to give a daughter," Arif broke in gently, "I was heart-broken. But now, when I see how happy Hava is, how complete her life is with her husband, her child, my cup is full. You, too, will taste the bitterness of giving your daughter to another house, but when you see her as a wife, and later as a mother, your happiness will be unbounded, limitless as the sky."

Babush nodded, his face worried, "How will I know if this family is right for her? Even if everything checks out, how will I know that I should give her to them, that it will be right for her? How can I be sure?"

"You will know. You will know as surely as the sun rises and sets … it is a feeling deep, deep inside. I cannot explain, but, believe me, you will know." Babush sighed, frowningly stroked his moustache. "I will start making some inquiries, see what this family is like, what kind of son they have."

"No, not yet Arif. Let me think about it for a few days." He looked up at his brother. "Of course, Nona and Skender already know of this offer, and now you. No one else has been told. I want it kept that way until I have had time to weigh this, to see if I want to go further with it."

"Then Drita does not know? Has not been told?"

"No."

Arif nodded, "I will do nothing until you speak to me again. Some advice, tell your wife not to mention this to Teza … she could not hold news of this kind to herself."

Babush nodded, gave a slow, sad smile. "Drita is too young…."

"Your daughter will always be too young to give. To you she will always be your little girl, your baby, but look at her … she is a young woman, beautiful in all senses. She is ripe for marriage and motherhood." He leaned toward Babush, "How old was her mother when she came to this house as your Nusé? Look at your daughter, you will see your own bride standing there. She is her mother's daughter, brother. Wherever she goes, she will bring joy to that family and honor to you. The Drinis already know this … that is why they want her. Watch, Rashid will be back sooner than a month. I'll stake my life on it."

"Yes, you are right. She is ready. I have seen it myself, would not admit it." He sighed. "How easy to become selfish, to tell yourself, 'She is too young' or 'She is not ready,' when what you really mean is 'I do not want to lose her, I want to keep her close to me.'" He sighed again deeply, put his hand over his eyes for a moment. "How did you stand not seeing Hava for weeks, months? How will I feel, brother, when there is no quick foot on the stairs, no bright smile to light a dark day?"

"It was hard. It will be harder for you than me. I still have Ilyria , the boys."

"I cannot give her, and yet I must. If not to the Drini family, to another."

"There is no hurry … she is still young."

"Young, yes, but ready. What are your thoughts? Should I explore this family?"

"It would do no harm. An inquiry into their background, their character, does not commit you to anything. One thing is certain … their reputation is beyond question. What we must know and be sure of is the son. Give me the word, I will find out everything. When I am finished, I will be able to tell you everything, even what he eats and when." Babush smiled at him. "Drita is as dear to me as if she were my own. I will leave no stone unturned; you can rest assured on that."

"Good. Then I will sleep on it and let you know in, say, two or three days. I am glad I talked to you. This has been eating at my heart since yesterday." He turned toward the door, "Yes, Skender?"

"Migje Hasan is coming, Babush."

"Bring him in here." He turned to Arif. "Tea or coffee? Tell Drita to bring coffee to us here and have your mother and aunts join us as soon as they can." He turned back to Arif as the door closed. "Our wives have a lot to gossip about. A pack of tobacco that it will be an hour before we see them?"

"Hmmm, let me see, there is a new Nusé here…" Arif mused, eyes half-closed, "done!" I say two hours!" He laughed, "You will lose. First your wife will have her say, then my wife will boast that she was the first aunt to see Skender's Nusé … then Hasan's wife will have to get even so will praise Aslan's Nusé! Two hours at least before we see a hair of them!"

Babush laughed, stood up as he heard Hasan's voice. "I almost hope you're right! What a quiet and peaceful evening we would have."

"Aslan!" Gillian heard the pleasure in Skender's voice as she turned to see who had come in. She watched with a smile as she saw the two give each other a quick, warm hug. "Come here, Jill, I want you to meet Aslan. He is the eldest son of the uncle and aunt you have just met. When we were children we were inseparable and fought occasionally."

Aslan laughed as he was told. "Correct. But heaven forbid anyone else to touch the other!" He looked over at Jakup, "Please sit down, Jakup. There is no need to stand on ceremony when we are by ourselves."

The three walked back to the fire and joined Jakup. Skender caught Jill's hand, stopped her from sitting down. She watched, noticed that Aslan let Skender sit a second before he did, that Jakup did the same with Aslan, then felt a gentle tug on her little finger as Skender let her know it was alright for her to sit down.

"Well, Nusé, how do you like Kosov?"

"I have not seen much yet," Gillian smiled to Aslan as she settled herself next to Skender.

Aslan watched her while the translation came, then smilingly turned to Skender. "What happened, Skender? You were always after the brunettes, the exotic ones…" He winked at Jakup. "I always thought he would end with a gypsy, and look…" he laughed, "look at those eyes … like a summer sky. Can you deny her anything, brother?"

Skender laughed with them, "It is hard. Sometimes impossible. But be careful before you give away my secrets. You can do no damage here…" he glanced at Gillian, "she does not know the language, but your Nusé…?"

"A truce then," Aslan cried in mock dismay, warding off an imaginary blow, "and you, Jakup, how was your day?"

Skender turned to Gillian, "Aslan was married just a few months before us."

"Is his wife coming tonight?"

"No, she will come tomorrow. They have a child, so she is staying at home tonight. Tomorrow Aslan's mother or his sister, Nurije, will stay home and then his Nusé will come to visit you."

"How neat! A built-in baby-sitting service."

He laughed, "Yes, and a most reliable one too."

"Girls, do come in and close the door … we are losing all our heat," Aslan called as Drita, Ilyria and Nurije stood giggling together at the open door.

Skender turned around to look at the doorway, "Good evening, Ilyria, Nurije, how lovely you all look tonight … there must be some special occasion." He turned back to Aslan, winked, dropped his voice so that the girls could not hear. "The 'special occasion' will soon be beside you. Jill, go over to meet the girls, Drita will introduce you."

Drita smiled excitedly at the other two girls as Gillian came near, "This is our Nusé and this is Migje Arif's daughter, Ilyria, and this is Migje Hasan's daughter, Nurije … Nurije," she repeated as she saw that Gillian had not caught the name.

Ilyria stepped forward with a quick, welcoming smile, took hold of Gillian's hand and raised it to her chin, her forehead, back to her chin, chattering all the time to Drita. Gillian watched with confusion, wondering what to do as Ilyria let go of her hand and stepped back with a small bow. Almost immediately, her hand was taken by the younger girl and she was greeted in the same way. As Nurije released her hand, stepped back and bowed, Gillian turned, about to ask Skender what she was supposed to do.

She sighed as she saw that he was deep in conversation with his back to her. She smiled nervously at the three girls, sucked in a long breath, muttered, "When in Rome…" and took hold of Nurije's hand.

Nurije looked from Drita to Ilyria as she guessed at Gillian's intention. She giggled, "Remember now, I want this service from both of you in future," as Gillian started to raise her hand to her chin.

Gillian flashed a quick grin at Nurije. *What's up? Aren't I doing this rigmarole correctly?*

Aslan smilingly glanced over at the girls as he heard his sister's infectious giggle, the smile fading as he saw what was happening. Quickly he crossed the room. "No, Nusé, no," he smiled at Gillian, shaking his finger. "You do not do that, not you." He turned to his sister, his face serious. "Nurije, I did not know that you were important enough to have our Nusé kiss your hand. How is it that I was unaware of this change in your position in our family?"

Nurije's face flamed, she dropped her eyes from him. "I meant no harm, brother."

Gillian looked from one to the other. *Now what?*

"No?"

"It was … it was just a little joke…."

"At Skender's expense? How would you feel if he had seen you allowing this? How would you feel if it was he reprimanding you now instead of me?"

Skender? What is he saying to her? Have I put my foot in it again?

"I'm sorry," Nurije whispered, "I didn't think…."

Aslan stood watching her for a moment then turned and returned to the fire, joining into their conversation.

Gillian looked from one to the other, wondering why the giggling and laughter had ceased so abruptly, what Aslan had said, why Skender's name had been mentioned.

Drita and Ilyria watched as Aslan returned to the fire, waited until he had sat down. Ilyria whispered to Nurije, "He has sat down, is not looking at you." Nurije didn't look up, chewed on her lip in embarrassment.

"Let us go downstairs … we can be by ourselves, have some tea," Drita whispered.

"Yes," Ilyria put her arm around Nurije, "don't worry, all brothers are bears sometimes."

Nurije shook her head, "Not Aslan. He was right … I was at fault." Her eyes glazed with tears, "If Skender had seen … I would never have been able to face him again."

"Sshh, he didn't see, didn't even turn around." Ilyria started out the door, leading Nurije.

Drita pointed downstairs. "Would you like to come with us? We are going to have some tea … tea."

Gillian, understanding her, nodded, glanced over at Skender, then moved slightly so that she was in his line of vision. Without turning his head, he looked toward her. Her eyes signaled that she was going with the girls, he smiled, closed his eyes briefly. She turned to Drita, "Okay, let's go."

"Be careful," Drita warned as Gillian put on her shoes, "the steps are very slippery."

Ilyria was squatting in front of the fire, blowing into it to make the wood catch. "The water is not hot enough yet but I have added some wood," she called to Drita as they opened the kitchen door. She watched in surprise as Drita picked up a stool. "What are you doing?"

Drita put the stool close to the fire, smiled her invitation for Gillian to sit. "She has trouble sitting on the floor, prefers to sit on this."

"Thank you, Drita." Gillian moved the three-legged stool slightly so that she could rest her back against one of the wooden support posts.

"Why? Has she been sick?" Ilyria asked, eying Gillian with curiosity.

"Not that I know of," Drita dismissed the subject, turned with a smile to Nurije. "Do you feel calmer now?"

"Then why does she have trouble sitting?" Ilyria persisted. Drita shrugged. Ilyria studied Gillian as she leaned back, eyes half-closed, against the wooden post. Her gaze rested deliberately on Gillian's stomach. "My sister sat on a chair when…."

"Ssshh," Drita cautioned in shocked awe.

"Do you think she…?"

"Ssshh, be careful. If Skender hears you he'll have your skin."

"He can't hear me," Ilyria whispered. Her gaze riveted on Gillian's stomach. "Perhaps that is why she cannot sit on the floor." Excitement lit her face, her voice. "Do you think she…?"

"Please, please, don't," Nurije begged. "If Skender or Aslan came, heard…." She glanced fearfully toward the door. "I don't want any more unpleasantness."

Gillian stirred slightly as she heard Skender's name mentioned. She smiled as she saw Ilyria and Drita watching her, then let her lids droop closed. *How good to relax. With them I don't have to worry about my dress riding up … don't have to worry about when to stand, when to sit down….*

'Stop being so nervous, Nurije! You are such a baby sometimes." Ilyria sighed with exasperation, then turned to Drita, "Do you like her?"

"Yes. There is so much I want to ask her. It is so frustrating not to be able to talk to her. Can you imagine all the things she could tell us? What it is like in her country? What kind of life the girls have there? How they dress … ooh, I must show you the things she brought for me." She jumped up, ran from the room.

Gillian's eyes opened as she felt the cold draft. She watched idly as Ilyria started to prepare the glasses for tea, humming as she did so. Nurije's wistful sadness caught at her. "Is something wrong? Was it something I did? You were so happy and now…." She sighed as she saw Nurije's puzzlement.

"I'm sorry…" Nurije came and knelt beside Gillian, "I meant no harm, I was wrong, and I see that now, but…." She sighed, turned as Drita came in carrying a box. "Drita, how can I make her understand?"

Drita put the box down. "I would forget it, Nurije. I don't think she knew there was a problem. How could you possibly make her understand that you are sorry for something when she doesn't realize there is something to be sorry about?"

Gillian leaned back, gratefully closed her eyes. *Let them chatter, I can rest. Why do I feel so tired? Perhaps it's the newness, the tension of meeting Babush, Nona....* She smiled. *The excitement of seeing Skender again....*

"Are you sure?" Nurije asked, anxious for reassurance.

Drita nodded. They looked reflectively at the resting Gillian. She hesitated a moment then started to explain, "I do not think she realizes Skender's position in the family. If she does not know his, how can she know hers?" She glanced around the room, beckoned her cousins close, leaned toward them and confidentially told them, "She treats my brother very casually, and he accepts it, never questions it." She looked meaningfully from one to the other.

"What do you mean?" Ilyria questioned with a sidelong glance at Gillian.

"Well, she does not stand when he enters or leaves a room." Drita's announcement brought a gasp from Nurije who turned, stared at the sleeping Gillian before she nodded at Drita to continue. "I have never seen her ask his permission to leave the room ... she did not ask when we left just now..." her cousins' open-mouthed astonishment encouraged her, "and I have never seen her bow to him."

Ilyria stared in disbelief, "And he permits it? Has not called her on it?"

Drita shook her head, "Not once. She treats him..." she glanced around, dropped her voice, "...as if she were his friend, as if she were his equal." Her lips curved in a smile as she saw their horror. "Don't you wish we could find out more about her customs, her ways?"

"Yes!" fervently burst from Ilyria. Drita's finger flew to her lips in warning as Gillian stirred. Ilyria 's voice dropped as she continued. "Perhaps we could put some of them into practice here!" She dug Nurije in the ribs, "Stop staring at her! She is not from some other planet," she gave a wistful sigh, "or is she? Can you imagine," she continued dreamily, "to be able to behave in her way ... one week, one day ... that is all I ask."

"For what?" Drita demanded.

"To see my brother's face if I could do that to him ... an hour! Even that would be enough. I could live happily forever if I could see Emin's horror, his shock."

Drita laughed at her, "He stopped you from coming last night, didn't he? Why?"

Ilyria wrinkled her nose. "He caught me." Drita's hand flew to her mouth, her eyes wide and round. Ilyria turned to Nurije, "You do not know this ... our neighbor is having some repair work done on his house. There were several young men there. I put an old box beside the wall and have been climbing up and peeking." The three girls giggled together. "One of them..." she flicked her eyes to the ceiling, smiling, "...oh, so good looking, so handsome!" They all giggled again. "Yesterday this particular young man was there all day and I was watching him as often as I dared. I think I got a little careless ... I did not hear

Emin, did not even know he was home, until I felt myself grabbed and pulled down."

"What did he do?" Nurije's eyes were wide, her voice nervous.

"He just stood there looking at me for a while … I was terrified. Then he said, 'If one of them had seen you, even a hair of you, I would have beaten you black and blue.'"

"What did you do?" Nurije gasped.

"Nothing. I was too scared. I just stood there waiting for his next move."

"Go on," Nurije urged.

"Then he said, 'Your choice … will you answer to me or to our father?'"

"W-w-what did you say?"

"Nurije! Do you need to ask? If it were you in my place, what would have been your choice? Ahh, I see your answer … better to face two Emins than one Arif, eh?"

Drita's smile was nervous, "If it had been Nurije instead of you, she would have melted with fright. I think I would have too. What happened?"

Ilyria wiped her palms against her dimi. "He … he told me that if I ever … if he ever caught me doing anything like that again … I'd, er … I'd remember that day, and him, for the rest of my life." She bit her lip, looked from one to the other. "And he meant it. And then he kept me home last night."

All three girls sat silently, looking at each other. Drita sighed, shook her head, "You were lucky, you escaped lightly. I am surprised that Emin…." She stopped as she saw her cousin's expression. "You … didn't … argue? Make him angry again?"

"N-n-o. Not him." Ilyria sighed. "I might as well tell you. This morning I was over my fright, but I was so mad, so angry at Emin for keeping me home, was so disappointed at not seeing…" she glanced at the sleeping Gillian.

Drita groaned, "What did you do this time?"

"This morning Emin said to me, 'Make sure I have a rice pudding this evening.' He was teasing me, but serious. I was still mad at him, madder because I knew I'd have to obey him … so, I made him one, a special one." Her eyes danced; a smile started to curve her lips upward. "Only instead of sugar…" she laughed, looked from Drita to Nurije, "…I put salt!" She gazed with satisfaction at the two horrified faces, added mischievously, "I wish I could tell her", with a toss of her head toward Gillian.

"What did Emin do when he found out?" Nurije whispered.

Ilyria sobered, bit her lip, dropped her eyes to the floor, then quietly answered, "My father got the rice, not Emin." The two girls gasped, stared at her in horror.

"But he never eats rice pudding, never eats sweets," Drita exclaimed.

Ilyria smiled wryly, "He did today."

"How? Why?"

"We had an unexpected visitor who stayed for lunch. Emin was at the University, so Jakup had to serve. When he brought the meat dishes back to the kitchen he saw the rice pudding, thought it would be nice to offer … I was not there, so…." She shrugged.

"The visitor, did he…?" Drita held her breath.

"No, luckily for me he refused, but my father…." She bit her lip, then started to giggle. "Jakup said it was the funniest thing to see. My father took a spoonful, put it in his mouth … sat there almost spluttering…." She could hardly speak, laughter bubbled from her. "He had to swallow it, could do nothing else with a guest…." She couldn't continue. Drita and Nurije were laughing too, tears ran down Ilyria 's face as she fought to stop her laughter. "So much salt … he must still be thirsty! Jakup came rushing down to the kitchen. 'What did you do to the rice?' he asked me. I glared at him, but he insisted again. 'Put salt instead of sugar,' I mumbled. He threw my coat at me. 'Was it intended for Emin?' I nodded. 'Well, our father did not enjoy it.' Well, when I heard that, I almost died. Jakup hurried me up and took me to visit a friend. I did not need to be told more than once when I realized … I shook all over until we were out of our street, expecting my father's hand to fall on my shoulder any minute, his voice to tell me, once again … 'Ilyria, to my room, please.'"

Nurije swallowed. "What happened? When you came home?"

Ilyria looked nervously from Drita to Nurije, "My father had left, come here before … I have not seen him yet."

"Oh, Ilyria," Drita sighed, "I dread to think … how lucky that it was Jakup at home and not Emin. At least Jakup protected you when Arif's rage was hot."

"Yes. But Emin would have done the same. He jumps all over me, but always shields me from my father's anger."

"Emin?" Nurije questioned in disbelief. Ilyria nodded. "I did not think he would, especially when he knew it was intended for him."

Ilyria stared, aghast, "I had not thought of that! Of course Emin will realize it was meant for him." She groaned, shoulders drooping, "What can I do? What can I say to him? He will know for sure. As soon as my father gets me home…."

"I would think he already knows. Surely Jakup would have told him?" Nurije asked.

Ilyria groaned louder, "Yes, of course! I had forgotten about Jakup. Drita, what shall I do?"

"You are always up to some mischief. Why do you do such things, get yourself into so much trouble?" Drita asked angrily, worried for her cousin.

"I don't know," Ilyria answered miserably, "I just can't help myself…." She looked at the two worried and concerned faces. "Don't worry! It gave us a laugh this evening and it was fun to peek at the boys."

The exuberance of her voice, the soft giggling, reached Gillian and she stirred, opened her eyes and stretched.

"Come, Drita, show us your gifts and let us not dwell on what might happen. Perhaps my father will forget...." Drita's withering look canceled Ilyria 's momentary hope. "Perhaps he ... oh perhaps, perhaps ... are you going to show us these gifts or not?"

Gillian sat up as Drita removed the lid of the box and started to take out the gifts. She watched as they admired the things she had given to Drita, glad that she had chosen gifts that Drita was proud and happy with.

Ilyria held up the yellow blouse, smiled at Gillian. "This is lovely." She stood up, held it against her. "Can you imagine wearing this for someone special?" She twirled around their room. "When I am a Nusé, I hope my husband is as handsome as the young man working next door. You should have seen him, Drita...." She came to an abrupt halt, grinned wickedly, bent closer to Drita and said softly, "But perhaps there is someone else you'd rather see?"

Drita blushed furiously, gave her an angry warning glare, then turned away.

Gillian saw the exchange, glanced lazily at Nurije and saw that she was not included. Idly she wondered what secret the two girls shared.

"Look at this! Now you will be envious!" Drita held up the lipstick, determinedly changing the subject. "And here, for the eyes. She has not got much color on tonight, but last night ... I wish you had seen, she looked gorgeous. And here, smell this, isn't it lovely?"

Gillian stood up. "There are some for them, I'll get them." The three girls watched her as she left the room, wondering briefly where she was going before they turned back to examine the rest of the gifts.

Gillian knelt beside them when she returned, handed each some hair spray and a hairbrush and a bundle of nylons, grinning at the 'oohs' and 'aahs'. She unzipped the plastic case, tipped the makeup onto the rug and sat back on her heels, smiling happily as she saw their excitement, and watched Drita mildly showing off her knowledge of how the lipsticks worked.

"I'm going to try! Drita, quick, a mirror." Ilyria 's eyes shone with excitement.

Drita jumped up, ran to the cupboard beside the door. "Here."

"Let me be first, please?" Nurije begged. She took the mirror, picked up one of the lipsticks.

"No," Gillian stopped Nurije. "You put lipstick on last, this first." She hesitated as she started to hand the makeup to Nurije, suddenly recalling Babush's objection the evening before. "Are you sure it's alright?" she asked Drita. All three heads bobbed eagerly. Gillian laughed, "Alright, we can always wash it off before we go upstairs."

All watched as Nurije smoothed the cream over her face. She bent forward, chose a soft, blue eye-shadow and dipped her finger into it and drew it over her eyelid.

"No! You look like a clown! Here, let me show you ... there." Gillian sat back and surveyed Nurije. "Now some mascara. You don't really need it. I wish I had those lashes … just a touch. Now for some lipstick. Here, this one. Careful, not too much." The three girls sat admiring the new Nurije as she studied herself in the mirror. "Perfume?" Gillian pushed the bottles toward her.

Nurije grinned, opened one bottle and drew in a deep breath, then applied it where Gillian indicated, raising her eyes to the ceiling and preening herself as she did so. "This is fun!"

Ilyria reached for one for herself and another for Drita.

"Here, let us use some too," she urged her cousin. Excitement lit her whole being as she asked Gillian, "Which color for me?" and pointed to the eye shadows and then her own face. She watched as Gillian chose. "And now one for Drita." She had observed well and took only a dab of the eye shadow. "Give me the mirror, Nurije." She grinned at Drita waiting patiently for her turn. "Tomorrow night I will bring our mirror from home. You bring one, too, Nurije, and then we can all do this together. That will be even more fun!"

Approaching footsteps froze them. Ilyria sent an inquiring glance to Drita who shook her head at the unspoken question.

"Who can it be? Besim?" Ilyria asked in a whisper.

"Perhaps. Perhaps the men have sent him for more coffee." Drita reached and plucked the towel from above her head, letting it drop over the makeup on the floor. Hastily she pushed a few stray lipsticks under the towel as the door opened.

"Mire mbrama, girls. How are you all?" Emin kicked off the nalle he was wearing as he stepped through the door.

Ilyria swallowed hard as the three of them stood. "Mire mbrama, Emin," she murmured a second or two after Drita and Nurije. She rubbed her hands over her eyelids, then turned to face him with a forced smile. "Do you wish coffee, brother? Please, go upstairs, I will be happy to serve you there."

Suspicion was born as soon as the offer was made. "Why so anxious to please me, Ilyria? What have you been up to now?"

"Nothing, brother." Confidence returned as Ilyria realized that Emin did not know about the rice. Chance took her eyes to Gillian, still kneeling on the floor and she sighed dramatically, "How fortunate to be born elsewhere."

"What is that supposed to mean?"

She gave another long, dramatic sigh, "I wish that I enjoyed her privileges."

"Explain yourself, Ilyria."

Ilyria ignored the frantic signals from Drita. "If our Nusé were from here, you would have given her hell for not being on her feet by now. you would have been after her for not greeting you correctly, would have her skin for not bowing to you, not kissing…." She stopped as Emin folded his arms and she saw a grin spreading across his face.

"Go on, sister, you were saying…?" He looked deliberately past her to Gillian. Slowly Ilyria turned her head, closed her eyes with a sigh as she saw that

Gillian had finally understood what was expected of her and had risen to her feet. "Well, I am waiting. What was it you wished to say?" Ilyria shook her head, eyes fixed firmly on the ground while Emin thoughtfully rubbed at his chin. "Forgive me, Ilyria, but I thought I heard you mention something about our Nusé not standing…." He laughed, started toward the door.

"Well, she did not bow to you, did not kiss your hand," Ilyria muttered. Emin turned back to his sister.

"What did you say?"

Drita's pleading glance stopped Ilyria and she shook her head.

"Nothing, brother."

Emin started again toward the door, suddenly became aware of Nurije. "Why are you standing with your back to me, Nurije?" He couldn't catch the mumbled words and was surprised that she did not turn toward him. "Nurije, I was speaking to you."

"I am attending our Nusé, Emin."

"She does not need you to stand staring at her feet. Come here!" He waited. Nurije did not move, did not turn around. "Did you hear me?" His voice was sharp. He waited, impatience surging as she edged toward him, until she stood in front of him, eyes cast down. "What is so important on the floor tonight?" He took a long breath as there was no response. "Look at me!" Her beauty was breathtaking … the lips wet and moist as she licked nervously at them. "Well, what have we here, then. A Nusé! I thought we had only one in this family but now, it seems, there are two! When did this happen, Nurije? I did not even know you were engaged!" He reached, took hold of her chin, tipping her head up. "How dare you put that stuff on your face! Wash yourself immediately."

"It is my fault." Gillian pushed herself between Emin and the trembling Nurije as she guessed the problem. "I put the makeup on…." Frantically, she searched for Nurije's name. "Her," she finished with a gesture toward Nurije. Emin's startled stare made her think he had not understood. She picked up a lipstick, pointed to herself, then to Nurije. "Me … this … on her. I did not know that you would object. I thought it was just the older men." She felt herself tremble under his obvious displeasure, straightened her shoulders and continued firmly, "It will wash off…."

"Be quiet!" Emin's tone conveyed his meaning.

Ilyria winked at Drita, a small grin quirking the corners of her mouth as she saw that Gillian had no intention of backing down to Emin, "Well, brother, what are you going to do now?"

Emin still watched Gillian. "She is Skender's Nusé, and she is not from here. There is nothing to be done by me." He forced himself to turn away from Gillian. "Open the window … this room stinks of perfume."

"Yes, brother."

Emin's eyes went briefly, angrily, to Ilyria. "Nurije, I told you to wash your face. All of you wash that smell from yourselves and then you had better join us so that I can keep an eye on you. And bring coffee with you." He turned toward the door.

"Yes, brother. How many, brother?"

Emin stopped, came slowly back to Ilyria. "Be careful. Remember you are from here, and you will still be here tomorrow, and I will still be here with you." He waited until she looked away, then started to count on his fingers, "Jakup, Shamsi, Adnan, Besim…."

He returned again to the door, opened it. "And don't forget one other … me! That is five of us, and in five minutes I want you up there with us … all of you … including her. Five minutes, not a second later."

Four pairs of eyes watched as he left.

He closed the door, leaned back against it, chuckling silently as he slipped on his shoes. *Nurije, what a beauty she is, and with that color on her face … like some lovely doll.* He checked his watch by the light from the window. "I said five minutes…." He took the stairs two at a time. "I must hurry, let Jakup and the others enjoy this tale before the girls come…."

Chapter 19

"…sat there, his mouth full, eyes popping from their socket." A surge of laughter stopped Jakup. "He had to swallow the miserable stuff, could not spit it out with a guest there. It must have been like brine." Laughter drowned his last words.

Adnan grasped his stomach, "I have a pain from laughing! To do that to Arif, of all people! I'd have given a month's wages to have seen."

Shamsi winked broadly at his brothers and Jakup, "Your sister had great plans for you, Emin."

Emin grinned back, smoothing his moustache, "Yes, I have great plans for her, too."

"Tell me," Shamsi leaned forward confidentially, "what are you going to do to this wild sister of yours?"

"I am not sure…" Emin said thoughtfully, gave a wicked grin, "but she does not know that. For the present she is very careful, very obedient and I am enjoying the change." He waited for the laughter to subside. "While she is anxiously wondering what I am going to do to her she will behave, and I will enjoy the peacefulness and her immediate response to my wishes." He bowed as they all laughed, each knowing that Ilyria 's quiet acceptance would be short-lived.

Shamsi reached, poured himself another glass of tea, "What happened when Arif got her home last night? I guessed there was something wrong, she was so reluctant to leave here."

Jakup stopped Emin. "Let me. She was first in the house, made a beeline to her room, but my father was too quick for her. 'Ilyria, to my room, please.' She wilted. Before our very eyes she shrank two inches." The room rocked with laughter as Jakup stood and mimicked his sister's despondent sagging. He turned, shook his finger at Emin. "You should have left her to our father, let her feel Arif's tongue, but…." He shrugged.

"How could I leave her to face him alone? A kitten to stand against a tiger? Come, Jakup you would have done the same, admit it. In fact, you did help her

… Ilyria said you rushed her from the house. Ha, ha, I see it's true, eh?" He laughed, shook his head and swore softly at his brother.

"What happened?" Adnan demanded impatiently.

Emin ducked out of reach as Jakup cuffed at him. "After Jakup told me the story, explained why she had to go to my father's room I went straight there. My welcome was not too warm…." He laughed with them, frowned as remembrance came to him. "She had refused to answer, refused to offer any explanation." He pursed his lips, looked from one to the other their suddenly sober faces telling him that they, too, knew what the outcome would have been had he not intervened with his father. "I told him that the rice had been intended for me, that Ilyria was getting back at me for punishing her…." He stopped, added reflectively, "If I did not know better, I'd swear he was amused."

"Nothing amuses Arif," Adnan said grimly, adding quickly, "I'm sorry," as he saw Emin's eyes narrow.

Emin leaned to him, "No one speaks against my father, no one, not even you, brother." He sat back as Adnan inclined his head, "He lectured us for almost an hour, with us standing all the time, of course." He joined in their laughter, gave a short, quick nod at Adnan to let him know that all was well between them. "Then, with that beautiful, graceful movement of his hand that we all know so well…." He waited until the chortles had died down, "…he told my sister, 'I will let it go this time. I give you to your brother … you are in his hands."

Shamsi sighed dramatically, "Poor girl! Out of the frying pan into the fire. Poor girl." Emin joined in the laughter, nodding agreement. "Why did she try to poison you in the first place, Emin?"

He hesitated, acknowledged Jakup's warning look. "It was a minor thing, between my sister and me, it concerns no one else." He turned as he heard the kitchen door open, beckoned as he saw Gillian hesitate. "Come in, Mirëmëngjes, Nusé." He stretched, coming to his feet in one long, graceful movement. "I have to go. I promised Luan I would help him with stock-taking this morning." He beckoned to Gillian. "Move, Besim, let her sit near the fire. Get her some tea." He watched as Gillian sat down, pulled his cummerbund tighter, "Are we meeting here tonight?"

"Of course," Shamsi answered, surprised at the question. "We may have an opportunity to talk to Skender." He smiled gently as he caught Gillian's eye.

"Put another log on, Besim, she is shivering." Jakup glanced up at Emin, "Where is Drita's shawl? We could put it around her until she warms herself."

"I do not know." Impatience flitted across Emin's face before he turned to Shamsi. "Your hopes of catching Skender are slim, Shamsi … our fathers catch him every night and now…." He pointed his chin at Gillian, "…even more competition for his time. I have to go … until tonight then." He smiled his goodbyes, gave a brief nod to Gillian, called out as he closed the door, "It is freezing out here."

Shamsi watched as he passed the window, looked at Gillian, then at Jakup. "Why is he so stiff with her?" Jakup shrugged. "Has she offended him already?"

"I do not know."

"He was that way last night when the girls joined us. Why?" Adnan insisted.

"I said I do not know," Jakup said, sharply looking from one to the other. "Question my brother directly if you want more information."

Besim glanced over at them as he finished pouring the tea, held out the brimming glass. "Mirëmëngjes, Nusé."

Gillian accepted the tea, carefully holding it to avoid a spill. "Mirëmëngjes," she smiled as she nodded her thanks, sipped at the tea. She glanced around a little apprehensively at the suddenly quiet young men watching her, then dropped her eyes to the tea, wondering if she should be there, if she should get up and leave.

"Do you wish to eat?" Shamsi asked. Gillian continued to sip at the tea, unaware that he was addressing himself to her.

Besim hesitated as he was about to sit down, "Shall I get her something, brother?"

Shamsi shook his head, "Sit down. Let Drita worry about it when she has finished upstairs."

Gillian kept her eyes riveted on the tea, desperately wishing that she had not come to the kitchen, as she felt the four pair of eyes on her.

"How difficult it must be for her," Jakup watched her with concern. "Last night we were all enjoying ourselves, laughing ... I wonder what she was thinking, what her feelings must have been? I wonder if she thought we were laughing at her? She was so quiet, not a sound from her. She was not that way at dinner...." He smiled, added softly, "But then she had her husband by her side."

Shamsi winked at the others, "Our romantic!"

Jakup gave him a quick smile, turned back to look at Gillian. "Dammit, I'm going to teach her." He pointed to the tea. "Caj, Nusé, caj." He put his fingers up near her mouth and beckoned, "Caj."

"Caj," Gillian repeated, a little self-consciously, smiled, and relaxed as she saw the quick, pleased grins.

"Good. Now what else? Something simple." Jakup looked around.

Hesitantly, Gillian pointed to the kettle and little apprehensively said, "Uje." Jakup shook his head.

"Yes!" Adnan exclaimed, "water, that's what she said." He picked up the kettle, shook it. "Water, in the kettle." He looked triumphantly at the others, came and knelt in front of Gillian, asked excitedly, "What else do you know?"

Shamsi watched carefully. "You've lost her, brother, she must know just a few odd words. Point to something else."

Besim pointed to the sugar, "I will."

Gillian fought to remember, couldn't and shook her head sadly at Adnan's look of disappointment.

Jakup leaned forward. "She knew that, has forgotten it. Try something else." Besim pointed to the small dish of salt.

Gillian didn't hesitate, "Kryp."

Shamsi laughed, dug Jakup in the ribs, "So there is another girl in the family who knows about salt! Besim, try something else."

"Buke," Gillian said immediately as Besim turned from the flour box and held up a piece of bread. Adnan jumped up, picked up a potato from the basket on the floor. She hesitated, frowningly trying to remember, then questioningly asked, "Kepuce?"

There was a roar of laughter. "No, this is a kepuce." Adnan opened the door, picked up one of the shoes, offered it to Gillian with a fork. "Would you like to eat it?" She laughed with them, shaking her head.

"She has a sense of humor anyway," Jakup smiled to Shamsi.

Shamsi nodded. "What's her name? Has anyone found out yet? Well, then, it is time we did. You name, Nusé … name?"

"She doesn't understand. We will have to try a different way." Jakup reached into his pocket, took out a notebook and pen, started to write.

BABUSH	ARIF	HASSAN
Skender******	Jakup****	Aslan*****
Drita	Emin***	Shamsi**
	Hava	Adnan*
	Ilyria	Besim*
		Nurije

Gillian watched him. As he finished he looked up and smiled at her, pointed to each in turn, then to the name. "Shamsi, Adnan, Besim … Migje Hasan's sons. And I…."

"Jakup," she said quickly with a smile.

"Yes." He smiled back at her.

She pointed to the spelling of his name. "Then the 'J' is pronounced as a 'Y' … I must remember that," she murmured almost to herself.

"Emin, my brother, is the one who just left." He looked at her until she smiled her understanding to him. "The stars," he continued, pointing, "show our position in the family so now you will know who you should stand for." He glanced over at his cousins. "I wish I could caricature each of us beside our name, then she would know immediately who was who … would learn quickly."

"Emin could," Adnan volunteered.

"Yes, but Emin would not," Shamsi said grimly. "Give her the book, tell her to write her name. That was the object of all this, wasn't it?"

"I don't think it will help us if she writes her name. The pronunciation of it is what we are after. Then we can use the phonetic spelling so that we will remember, agreed?" Jakup tapped her arm. "Your name, Nusé?" He pointed to the list and then to themselves.

"Gillian." She repeated it slowly as he indicated with his head.

"We have that sound." Jakup picked up his pen and, beneath Drita's name, started to write X-h-i-l-i-a-n. He glanced up, caught her quickly hidden laugh as she saw the spelling, grinned at her. "You do not like that? Well, there is one other way. Do you prefer this … G-j-i-l-i-a-n?"

She gasped, "Why that is almost correct. May I?" She took the pen and notebook, printed the correct spelling, then pointed to his, "You have to use the 'Gj' to get the soft sound of J?"

He nodded, surprised himself at the similarity of the spelling. Gillian hesitated, wondering if she should try to explain that normally G would be a hard sound, but that in the pronunciation of her name it took the softer J sound, but decided it was beyond her capabilities, that it would probably cause confusion.

"Attend now! The name is not hard, listen and let us learn it. Shamsi, you first…" Jakup went from one to the other.

How pretty it sounds. They emphasize the middle of the name, not the beginning … I almost prefer their way. How nice he is … all of them. Last night I felt so left out, so … alone, wondered if I was welcome … but it's the language barrier, that's all.

"GiLLian." Shamsi saw the hastily swallowed grin. "Did I say it correctly? GiLLian?" She nodded, he laughed, "I think you are being polite, but it is close enough, I believe. Where do you come from in America?" He frowned as he saw she didn't understand. "America." She nodded expectantly. He sighed, looked at the others. "Now how do I ask her which part she comes from?"

Adnan took the pen and notebook from Gillian, carefully ripped out the page with their names and handed it to her, then on a clean page drew an outline of America. He pointed to her. "You … where?" Gillian pointed to the west, wrote in San Francisco. "That's where Skender lives now so they must have stayed in her home town. I wonder if she knows anything…." He stopped. "Besim, make sure the windows are tight, the door firmly closed." He waited until Besim nodded that everything was secure, then continued quietly, "If she knows anything of their political situation."

"A girl?" Shamsi gave a derisive laugh, "Are you serious?"

"Why not?" Jakup asked quickly. "It is possible. She has been raised differently to our girls … that is obvious to all of us. Let's try. What have we got to lose?"

"Our necks!" Shamsi laughed grimly, "But go ahead if you wish."

"Besim, stand guard!" Adnan waited until Besim was beside the window, positioned so that he had a clear view up the pathway. "Go ahead, Jakup, let us see what she knows, if she knows anything."

Jakup held out his hand for the pen and notebook, sat frowning at it, wondering how to ask so that she would understand. "Does anyone have some colored pencils, crayons, something like that?"

"In the cupboard," Besim answered, not moving from his position by the window. "Adnan, on the top shelf."

Jakup wrote "Kosov" and a large figure "1", took the packet of crayons from Adnan and colored a large red circle underneath. He looked at Gillian, pointed to the red patch. "Communist, one party," held up one finger. "In Kosov, one party." Gillian nodded. "I think so far she has understood," he said, glancing at the others clustered around. Next to the word "Kosov" he wrote "America," passed the book and crayons to Gillian and pointed for her to write.

Gillian took the notebook, sat staring at it, biting the pen as she tried to remember what colors, if any, the American political parties used. "I don't know, I think there are only two main parties … I don't want to tell you something like that when I'm not sure though." She shook her head, crossed out "America" and wrote "England." Better to talk about my own country … I know about that."

Jakup pulled at his moustache, puzzled. "Why is she telling us about England?" He saw her watching him, smiled encouragement at her, pointed to the crayons. "Go ahead."

"We're wasting our time … she doesn't know what we are after. You've lost her, Jakup."

"I do not think so, Shamsi … watch what she's doing here."

Underneath England, Gillian wrote the figure "4", picked up a blue crayon, hesitated and looked at Jakup. "You do understand that his information is about two years out of date. If you are interested in politics, you must know that the political situation changes almost daily…." She stopped, wondering if he understood. "I'll just go on anyway." She colored a large blue patch, another, slightly smaller, green … a third of half-yellow and half- black about the same size as the blue, and a small red one slightly off to one side, then turned the book so Jakup could see.

"Four?" He held up four fingers. "Four political parties in England?" She nodded. He took out his wallet, opened it and pulled out a handful of money. "Which?" he asked, holding up the money and handing her back the notebook.

Gillian pointed to the blue patch. "Conservative party." Jakup took away three or four of the bills, held up the money again. "Liberal," she said, pointing to the green and then moved her finger to the red patch. "And a few Communists." Jakup shook his head, took more money away, leaving only a couple of bills, then pointed to the red patch. "No, the poorer, working class are usually Labor," Gillian said firmly, pointing to the yellow-black patch.

Jakup glanced at his cousins, puzzled. "According to her the poor people belong to this group, not the Communist party. That's contrary to everything we've been told." He stood up, picked up an imaginary shovel and pretended to dig, sweating and puffing. Adnan handed him two bills. Jakup bowed, thanked him and pretended to leave. He turned to Gillian. "Communist?" he asked, pointing to the red patch.

"No. Labour." She took his finger and moved it to the yellow-black patch. "Communists," Jakup insisted, moving his finger back to the red patch.

"No." It was sure, emphatic. Gillian moved his finger again to the yellow-black patch, pushing it against it hard. "In Britain only a few workers are Communists ... most of them are with this party, the Labor party." She let go of his finger, looked up at him. "Most of the Communists are teachers, intellectuals." She stood up, pretending to read a book, put on glasses. She looked hopefully at them, they shook their heads. She chewed on the pen, wondering how to tell them, make them understand ... suddenly she smiled, started to write, A-B-C-D, 2+2=4, 3+3=6, turned the book to them.

"Students," Shamsi exclaimed, turning with a smile to Gillian. "Students?" He watched her carefully. "A few ... but that isn't what she was after. Can you get it, Jakup?

"What is she writing now?" The three crowded around her. "Two plus two equals ... no answer, three plus three equals ... no answer."

Gillian lined them in front of her, stood very erect. "Two plus two equals ... you, give me the answer." She pointed, but her voice, her bearing, her manner had already given them the answer they really wanted.

"Teachers, dammit, teachers," Jakup said through clenched teeth. "And they tell us it is the poor, the under-privileged ... damn them. Wait, there's more ... what else is the girl trying to tell us?" He read over her shoulder, "Bach, Chaucer, Shakespeare, Beethoven, Gainsborough, Raphael ... I don't understand." He shook his head, moved so that Shamsi and Adnan could read easier.

Gillian continued to write as Shamsi read, "Chopin, Fonteyn, Benjamin Britten...." He shook his head as she glanced at him. She frowned, then started again.

"Nurieyev, Gorky ... got it! The arts, people connected with the arts!" He turned to her. "They are Communists?" he questioned her in disbelief, smiled as she nodded, grabbed hold of her and gave her a quick, hard squeeze. "My God, you're good! To make us understand...." He smiled at her, turned to Jakup, "I'm sorry, you were right. To think we might have missed all this because of me and my set ideas. Why won't she tell us about America? We are told constantly that they are forbidden to speak on political issues. I never believed it, but now ... do you think it's true, and that is why she won't tell us?"

"I don't know … I cannot believe that there is a police state there. Let's have her try once more." Jakup turned to a clean page in the notebook and wrote "America" and handed it to Gillian, watching her closely.

She sighed, hesitantly wrote a figure "2" underneath, hesitated again and then put a question mark. "I'm sorry, I just don't know. I think there are only two main political parties in the States." She looked up at them, slowly told them, "I was actively involved at home, but since I've been in the States I haven't bothered … especially since I met Skender."

The three young men clustered about her, perplexed, wondering what she had said, while Besim continued his vigil at the window.

"I couldn't follow that at all, could you?" Jakup asked.

"There was something said about Skender," Shamsi said slowly. "Perhaps he won't allow her to speak about American politics, perhaps he feels it is safer if…."

"Someone coming," Besim warned.

Quickly Jakup pushed Gillian down to the rug, put a half-filled glass of tea into her hands while Adnan ripped off the pages of the notebook and stuffed them deep into the fire, making sure they were burning well before leaning casually against the wall.

Gillian watched in amazement as Shamsi hid the crayons under the rug, sat down, yawned, letting a sleepy, half-bored look come over his face. Her eyes slid to Jakup. She watched him, puzzled, as he carefully checked the room before sitting down and starting a casual conversation with the others.

"Shamsi?" Djali?" They all grinned, relaxed and stood up as Hasan opened the door. Adnan turned to Gillian and offered his hand, pulling her to her feet.

"Sir?" Shamsi listened, nodded. "Yes, father, immediately." He turned, smiled his goodbyes, giving a special nod to Gillian, murmured to Jakup as he passed him, "Meet here tonight, early. Make sure we get her with us," then turned and followed his father out the door.

Jakup nodded to Besim who took up his position by the window. "Now, let us start again. Gillian, tell us…."

"The guests are leaving," Besim called. Jakup sat watching him, notebook poised. Gillian sat very still, feeling the tension. "It's alright…" Besim turned with a smile, "they have started down the path … Skender is taking them to the gate."

Jakup smiled, putting the notebook away in his pocket. "Then he will be here shortly looking for his wife. We must leave this until another time." He pulled back the rug, picked up the crayons and tossed them to Adnan. "Put them away, we will need them again." He caught Gillian's concerned look. "We must be careful … it is forbidden to talk politics, especially with someone from the outside."

"Skender is coming," Besim said, stretching his arms and walking from the window.

"Get up, quickly, your husband is coming." Jakup smiled. "You do not know that word? Husband? It is important, you should. Skender is coming, get up." He raised his hands, smiled his approval. "Good, you must always be ready to greet him correctly." He turned as the kitchen door opened. "Mirëmëngjes, brother ... you are cold?"

Skender kicked the nalle off outside the door. "Mirëmëngjes, Jakup. Yes, it is bitter today. Mirëmëngjes, Adnan, Besim. Some tea, please." He turned with a smile to Gillian. "Hi, darling, did you eat breakfast?"

"No, but that doesn't matter, we have...."

"I'm taking my wife to see the town," Skender said, turning back to his cousins. "If any of you are free I would be happy to have you accompany us. Thank you, Besim." Gillian glared, angry and hurt, at Skender's back as he sipped at the tea, warming his hands on the glass at the same time.

Adnan picked up his coat, "I am due at work in less than an hour ... another time, perhaps. Besim, you are behind in your work so must study," he added quickly as he saw his young brother about to accept the invitation. He grinned at Skender. "He finds it easier to take pleasure than work." He gave a small bow to Gillian. "Enjoy our town. Jakup, until tonight..." then added softly, "be sure we have her with us." He smiled, waved, and was gone, calling, "Besim!" as he left. There was a sharp rap on the window, he peered in at them. "Skender, there is a new department store at the north end of town. They have a lot of nylon goods there ... she might like to see."

Skender nodded, waved to him, then grinned at the downcast Besim. "Too much play, eh? Off you go, catch up with your studies. There will be plenty of time for us to go to town together." He slapped him on the back, pushed him toward the door. "Jakup? How about you?"

"I am free today but have promised to take Drita to the store for her house shopping. We could walk that far together, perhaps? After that my father has made plans for my free day," he laughed softly, "and he knows how much work can be completed in how much time."

Skender laughed, "You cannot cheat him, eh? Tell Drita to hurry. Let us get out of here before more guests stop me." He put the glass down as the door closed on Jakup, pulled Gillian to him. "What have you been up to all morning? What's the matter?" he asked as he felt her rigidity.

"Nothing."

He frowned, "Obviously there is something bothering you. Did one of my cousins say something to upset you?"

"No." She fiddled with the button on his jacket.

He smiled down at the blond head. "What is that strange thing you ask me? Something about the bed and getting off on the wrong side?" He waited in vain for the quick grin, the correct saying.

He put his hand under her chin, bent his head and kissed her. "My, my, we are as frosty as the weather! It is colder in here than outside. Still no smile? Hurry, get ready and I will take you to see the town." He started to smile. "Ahh, I see the sun is trying to come out…." He laughed as she glanced quickly at the window, "Not out there! In here! Hurry now, before more guests come and we have to stay here."

She turned just as she got to the door. "Skender…."

"Not now, later, Jill. Hurry," he urged, "and bring my coat and gloves with you," he called as she slipped on her shoes. "And my hat," he yelled a little louder as she passed the window.

"Are we ready now?" Skender looked from Jakup, to Drita, to Gillian. "Jill, ready?"

Gillian nodded, watching as Jakup laughingly wound a scarf around Drita's neck. "He's so nice to her … even my own brother wouldn't bother with me like that."

"Yes, they are all very fond of her, have gone out of their way to give her the love and attention she would naturally have got from me had I been here." Skender held open the gate, waiting until they had passed through. "Turn right, Jakup … let us avoid the River Road with this wind." The gate squeaked closed. "Look at this street, it is a disgrace."

"Only a little way and we will be on the paved surface," Jakup consoled him. "How can she walk in those silly things?" he asked with a quick grin at Gillian's shoes.

"She runs all over the hills of San Francisco in them … frankly, I will be glad when the fashion changes to something more sensible." He saw Drita looking at him. "Yes, Drita?"

"For dinner, do you think it will be alright if we have beans?"

"The hell we will! I lived off cornbread and beans for years from necessity. I don't intend to eat them again … ever!" He caught Gillian as she slipped. "Are you alright?"

Jakup squeezed Drita's hand, whispering, "He did not mean it, has forgotten that we do not use such language in front of our sisters. Be careful here, it is slippery." He helped her negotiate the icy patch that Gillian had slipped on.

She stopped for a moment and looked up at Jakup, "It is not my place to criticize what he says, Jakup."

He inclined his head with a slight smile, "You said nothing, but the implication is clear … I'm sorry."

They turned the corner onto the paved street, fanning out into a line, girls between the two men.

"Is that your old school, Skender?"

"Yes."

Gillian stopped to stare at the stone building, letting her eyes travel up the three floors, the gray dullness of the windows reflecting the heavy sky. She shivered, pulled her coat tighter about her. "I can't imagine you going to school … were you a pest?" She turned to him with a smile, "Did you give the teachers a hard time?"

"No. They gave us a hard time. Especially one." He took hold of her hand, putting the gloved tips together. "He used to make you put your fingers together like this, hold your arm straight, then would cane your fingertips until they bled."

She shrank back from his harshness, pulled her hand away, "How old were you then?"

"Nine or ten," he sighed as he looked at the school. "We start here, this is our first school and then, when we are eleven or twelve we go to the Gymnasium where we stay until we are eighteen." He turned away.

"That was very young for such a harsh punishment. What had you done to deserve it?"

He laughed bitterly. "Done? Nothing. We were here … that was enough." He saw Jakup watching him closely. "She is asking about the school. I was telling her how kind our communist teachers were." He sensed Drita's nervousness, patted her cheek. "Let's go."

Jakup laid his hand on Skender's arm, "You have passed this building many times since you've been home, almost every day, in fact. Why are you letting it upset you now?"

Skender sighed, shook his head, "I don't know, Jakup … could it be because she is with me?"

"Wait," Jakup stopped him again as he started to move, his face worried, "you realize that by taking this road we will also pass the Gymnasium?"

"Yes, but I am prepared now. Even if she stops, asks about it, I will be able to answer her…." There was almost a smile, "Quietly and with control." He slapped Jakup on the back. "Let us go. Jill, come along, we are wasting time and getting cold hanging about."

She allowed herself to be pulled along, her eyes looking back at the school. "It is a nice enough building … why do I feel…." She grinned at him. "I'm glad I didn't go there."

"So am I, my love, so am I." She glanced quickly at him wondering at his intenseness.

"Nusé, look." Drita pointed down the street. Gillian's eyes followed the pointing finger. "An Albanian hansom cab!" she exclaimed, smiling as the horse clip-clopped past, the driver flicking his whip lazily.

"These are the old taxis, only a few remain, unfortunately. Cars are used mostly now. More comfortable, much more convenient, but not as colorful." Skender smiled down at her, but her eye had been caught by another means of transportation.

Two oxen pulled a long, flat, wooden cart, the sides two boards nailed together to slope gently inwards. The wood was rough, bleached gray by the sun and snow. The animals plodded peacefully down the street, passing them. Small pieces of straw drifted from the back of the cart.

Hansel and Gretel with straw instead of bread. Her eyes lifted to the two on the front seat. The old man's white hat, placed firmly central on his head, blended perfectly with his white hair … *an extra cap of snow to top an already white mountain.* Her lips curved into a gentle smile as she watched the white moustache move up and down as he encouraged his beasts. *He is almost blowing kisses to them!*

Hardly an inch of the woman showed. A rug of strange, brown-gray color covered her from waist to feet and a long, triangular shawl of the same shade covered her head, falling and blending with the rug at her waist. The ends were wound up and around her mouth and almost reached the bridge of her nose. She looked straight ahead, turning neither to right nor left … a flash of darker, richer brown showed for an instant as she moved her arm to wrap the shawl tighter. *Hello, Mother Earth, are you sixteen or sixty?*

Gillian turned slowly to Skender, her smile deepening as she saw him smilingly watching her. She tucked her arm in his, sighed deeply, pleasurably, "Weren't they wonderful? I have never seen cows pulling a wagon before."

"Oxen, not cows."

"Is there a difference? I mean, I know there's a difference, but I thought the ox was a boy and the cow was a girl."

Disbelief mingled with amazement on his face before laughter caught him.

"Was she joking?" Jakup asked as Skender told them.

Skender laughingly shook his head, "You know the size and weight of a watermelon? The first time we had one she said to me, 'It must be heck of a big tree to hold these.' I thought she was joking then too, but…." He shrugged, joined in their laughter, his eyes soft as he watched her eyes darting from one excitement to the next. "Jill!" He pulled her tight to the wall, letting some people pass.

"That wasn't very polite," she whispered as the group walked straight past without breaking their line or even glancing in their direction. "They are wearing western dress … are their families more modern in their outlook or what?"

He waited until they were well past. "They are Serbians," he whispered, "don't stare, don't look at them even."

"Why?" Her eyes followed them.

"I will explain at home." He shook her arm urgently. "Keep your eyes to the front. If anyone in western dress wishes to pass, stand well out of their way, give them free access. I mean that," he added firmly. He pointed, "That is the bakery we use if Drita does not bake."

Gillian cupped her hands around her eyes so she could see in. "They sell only bread? No pastries or cakes?"

"Correct. Aren't I fortunate?" He laughed, took hold of her hand, "Look, another cart with cows!"

"Does Babush or any of your uncles have one?"

"Of course not! We are not farmers. Why?"

"I wanted to have a ride before we left...." She stopped, staring in amazed horror at a man carrying an oil heater on his back. "It is impossible for a man carry that weight. How can he do it?"

"When we get to the old part of town you will see many of these men They have a special strap, made from linen ... there is a pad filled with straw which fits into the small of their back. The way it is made enables them to carry almost three times their own weight."

She held her breath as he passed by them, biting her lip as she saw the strain and difficulty he had. "Why?" she demanded angrily, "why load someone like an animal...?" She was close to tears.

Skender took hold of her arm. "They are very poor, have no schooling, and this is the only way they can make their bread."

"But I thought in a Communist cou...."

Quickly he slapped his hand over her mouth, looked around, "Be careful, don't say that word," he whispered, slowly taking his hand from her mouth.

She took a long breath, continued quietly, "I thought they were supposed to take care of everyone, that nobody went hungry."

"You earn your bread or go without, as my family did for years ... there is no Unemployment Department or Welfare to run to under this regime." His eyes searched ahead, "Come along, they are getting ahead of us."

"You said your family went without ... do you mean they went hungry?"

"Yes." He held up his finger to stop her. "No more questions, no more talk about this until we are home."

Jakup and Drita were waiting for them to catch up. "Skender, around the next curve...." Jakup left the warning hanging. Skender gave a brief nod.

The brown, dirt-streaked face broke into an enchanting smile, henna-tipped fingers held out the pegs to Gillian. She smiled, shook her head. The enchanting smile vanished and a pained, hurt look appeared as she scratched at her matted hair. "Pay her, Skender. I know I shouldn't encourage her...." She caught his annoyed look. "But Gypsy children are always so sad and appealing."

"They rehearse well," he said bluntly as he handed the child some change. "Take the pegs, Jill."

"No, let her keep them. Buy yourself a chocolate bar," she called softly as the child ran gleefully off, her brilliant clothes flashing as she darted in and out of the people. "Don't be cross … I haven't seen any Gypsies since I left Europe."

He smiled at her, "I am not cross, but give to one and you will soon have a dozen here."

"Oh, look, another school. This must be the … what did you call it? It's bigger, much nicer than the other one." She tilted her head. "It reminds me a little bit of mine, only mine was red brick, not yellow, and we had four floors, not three. We had steps just like that going down on each side. 'Up on the right, down on the left, girls … no running, it isn't lady-like.'" Her voice mimicked one of her teachers. "The girls used the front of the building and the boys the back…." She turned and laughed at him. "You would have approved. We weren't allowed to speak to each other. One of my friends was kept in every day for a week during break period because she spoke to a boy…." She laughed softly, "It was her own brother, but she'd broken a rule so was punished."

Skender acknowledged Jakup's signal that he and Drita would walk on to the shops. "Why weren't you allowed to speak to the boys?" he asked in bewilderment.

"Originally there were two buildings but during the war the one the boys had was bombed. There was nowhere to put them so they 'borrowed' half of the girls' building until they could rebuild. When I went back to visit this year there was still no sign of a new school building, and it was still being run as two separate schools with a headmaster and masters for the boys and a headmistress and mistresses for the girls." She laughed, "The British are amazing. They can pretend for years that something doesn't exist if that's the way they want it. Can you imagine if the building requisition has been lost or misplaced? In a hundred years they'll still be pretending that there are no boys in the building!" She turned to look at the school again. "What was your last memory of school, Skender? Mine was my headmistress shaking hands with me, telling me to sit up straight, not slouch, and to treat life more seriously." She gave a nervous laugh, bit her lip, "Her advice went unheeded, I'm afraid." She turned back to him, "What was yours?"

He pointed. "All those windows were filled with our girls and they were singing our national songs."

"Where were you?"

"In the courtyard." He took hold of her hand, walked her across the road, in through the big, wrought iron gates. "I was here with a lot of other boys and we all joined in the singing." He swallowed hard as he felt his stomach quake. *This is the first time I've set foot here since that day.*

She smiled, "Was it a national holiday, something like that?"

He thought a moment, wondering what to tell her. "It was a day that all of Kosov remembers." He pulled her behind the tall brick wall, out of sight of the road, took hold of her face between his gloved hands, looked into her eyes. "I love you, Jill. Whatever happens, always remember that." Slowly, deliberately, he kissed her. Emotion surged in her as his mouth moved on hers. When he let her go she clung to him, fighting for calmness, her throat dry.

She blinked rapidly, licked at her lips. "What do you mean … whatever happens? There is some danger for you here, isn't there? Let's go, Skender. Leave. Now. Today," she urged, looking up at him. He shook his head. "If something happened to you…." Tears choked the rest.

"Hush now." He held her close. "Don't cry. Nothing will happen. I shouldn't have frightened you like that. I did not mean to. Look at me, Jill." He took her face in his hands again. "I have been here three weeks and there has been no trouble with the authorities." He took out his handkerchief and wiped her face. "We have to catch up with Jakup and Drita … you mustn't let them see you crying. A smile now … throw away the advice of your head lady. Just be my own Jill."

"Headmistress," she blew her nose, scrubbed at her eyes.

"Mistress?" He winked, determined to help her, "I thought that is what I will have later when I am tired of you."

She laughed shakily as she returned his handkerchief. "When I'm ninety-nine you may." She turned the sob into a sigh, "Let's go … you are deliberately keeping me away from the shops." She took hold of his arm, holding tight, comforting herself with his closeness.

As they reached the gates, he glanced up at the empty windows. *Be proud of her, she would have stood with you, even though she's not from here.*

She looked up at him, "Penny for them?"

He smiled. "They are worth more. A dollar?" She shook her head. "Seventy-five cents?" She shook her head. "A kiss and a hug?"

"Sold." She bit her lip, turned her head away. He gave her arm a quick squeeze, laughed softly. "I will accept payment at home." They walked close together down the street, turned the corner. She stopped abruptly.

"How beautiful." Her eyes followed the graceful curve of the street as it ran gently downhill to join the main thoroughfare. She looked to the right at the mosque, its squat, round building emphasizing the delicate spiraling minaret, at the park with its benches, empty and coldly frosted, the trees' stiff fingers bare, stretching to touch the leaden sky. "In the summer, the spring, it must be lovely, green and full of life…." Her smile was soft as she glanced at Skender. "I bet the benches are full of Babushes playing chess with each other, puffing their pipes and nodding…." Her eyes traveled over the white grass. "Jack Frost had a time for himself last night. It's beautiful, even its cold emptiness…."

She let her eyes continue to the other side of the park, to another mosque, its round dome blue, showing clearly and brightly against the gray skies, the tall gracefulness of its minaret etched against the sky, with others showing in the distance, pricking the horizon with their delicate beauty. "So many mosques … can we go inside? I have never been, would like to see." She grinned as she looked again at the white-domed one her right. "It looks like the hats you wear! Let's go in, please?" Skender shook his head, smiling at her. "Why not?"

"It is locked, all of them. You are not allowed to go in any more. The government will not allow it. That one over there, the blue one…" he pointed, "…has been turned into a stable … the one a little way beyond is now a warehouse."

"But…" her eyes turned to the blue dome, "how could they? It is so lovely."

He took hold of her arm, leading her forward. "It was very beautiful at one time. The inside had colored tiles from the floor to the ceiling and thick rugs all over the floor. The old men would come, wash themselves at the fountain, leave their shoes outside and spend half the day in there during the heat of summer. It was always cool, always pleasant. I know, it saddens me too. What kind of mentality would take a place of beauty and worship and turn it into dirt? That is the main square … the big monument has been added since I left. Do you like it?"

She shook her head. "I'm sorry, but no. It is too big, too harsh for the space, does not blend with this." Her hand swept the area.

"I agree. Let's hurry, they are waiting for us," he added as he saw Jakup and Drita standing outside one of the shops. They quickened their steps, swinging down to the main thoroughfare. He noticed Gillian's quick glance to the side. "Jakup," he called beckoning to them. "Sujuk." He pointed to the shop at the side of them. "Wait here, Jill."

She salivated realizing how hungry she was, as she looked at the sausages sizzling goldenly on the charcoal grill in the window, sending out small spurts of moisture to the glass. Her eyes lifted to the young boy who was nodding his head as Skender gave his order. She watched as he picked up a piece of flat, round bread, carefully turned one of the sausages to make sure it was browned on all sides, then placed it on the bread, folding it over before handing it to Skender. She caught her breath as the stacked pyramid swayed when Skender dug for his money but the boy foresaw the problem and steadied the four-high pyramid with his finger.

"Here, Jill, your first Albanian hot dog." Skender handed one to each of them. "Watch this, it will be amusing when she bites into the sujuk."

"Don't they have these in America?" Drita asked as she unfolded hers and re-rolled it.

"Something like it, but not as hot as ours. Be careful, Jill, it is a little spicy."

Gillian grinned happily at him as she raised it towards her mouth. "Smells yummy." She bit, chewed, smiling as the others did the same, watching each other. She stopped, opening her mouth, sucking in air, tears pricked at her eyes as the spicy hotness and the cold crispness of the air fought together. Skender winked at the others. She swallowed, fanning at her mouth. "A little spicy? My mouth is on fire!"

"Come, I will get you something to drink." Jakup took hold of her arm, first shaking his fist at Skender. "You are cruel," he laughed as he propelled Gillian toward a small shop.

"Not in there," Skender called after him. "We will never get her out! Or you either." He smiled as he took Drita's hand.

"Tea. Four, please.

Gillian frowned at the sujuk, took a deep, determined breath and took another bite, making sure that this time she had more bread with it. Jakup pinched her cheek. "Good! Never give up straight away." He touched his sandwich to hers, raised it in a salute and took a good bite. "Drita, choose a table … we will be there directly."

"What are those big bottles of brightly-colored water, Skender?"

He glanced at the huge bottles, similar in shape to apothecary jars. "Soft drinks. The red is cherry, I think … the yellow is lemon…."

"That violent blue-green color, what's that? I've never seen such vivid, violent colors for drinks," she marveled, wandering slowly along the counter. "Look at all these goodies … it would take a month to sample all of them." Her eyes studied and traveled along the rows of sweetmeats. She put her finger against the glass, pointing. "What's that one? The one that looks like a Life Saver with some jelly in it." Skender winked at Jakup who grinned and winked back. "And look at these, you can almost blow that pastry away, it's so thin. What's that one, rolled round and round with green stuff on top?"

"Well, brother, will you tell her the name of Besim's favorite?" Jakup teased as he accepted the tea.

"Sit down and stop making trouble for me," Skender laughed, then turned to Gillian. "That one is called kadaif and has honey and pistachio nuts rolled inside. Do you want a pastry?" he grinned. "What a stupid question! Of course you do! Chose which you would like. Drita, would you like custard?" He turned to the man behind the counter who had already handed Gillian her choice. "And a custard." Gillian stood beside him, pastry in one hand, sujuk in the other. He laughed as he saw her contemplating the sausage. "You do not have to eat it if it is too hot for you."

"I think I quite like it; it just took a little getting used to." She glanced under her lashes at him, "Just as I had to get used to you!"

"Have you got used to me?" he asked softly, letting his lips brush her hair. He accepted his change and together they joined Jakup and Drita at one of the small marble tables.

Gillian sat down next to Drita, picked up her tea, glancing at the huge bottles. *I should have had something cold.*

Jakup guessed at her thoughts, shook his finger. "No, never take something cold after something hot, always fight fire with fire."

"Fight fire with fire, mmm?" she murmured as Skender translated. Her eyes flirted with him. "I'll remember that."

He smiled at her. "Yes, do. Drita, how is your custard? Good?" He took the spoon from her and took a little for himself.

"Have more," she urged him as he returned the spoon. "Does our Nusé wish to try?" Skender shook his head after he had checked with Gillian. "What is her favorite meal? What can I make to please her?"

"Her? Do not bother with her! What about your brother?"

"Do not rise to his bait, Drita," Jakup warned, laughing.

She shook her head, smiling. "I have filled him full of laknor for three weeks. Now it is her turn."

"Let me think…." Skender's eye fell on the pastry Gillian was eating. "I know! Manti … she will love it." He saw Jakup's face and laughed. "So do you, eh? Good! Eat with us tonight."

"I will not have time to prepare it today, it takes a long time … perhaps tomorrow?" Drita asked diffidently.

"Anytime. Jill, Drita has offered to make something special for you. It is the same paper-thin dough as your pastry but it's filled with meat and rolled into bite-sized balls. They place them side by side in a large round pan until it is completely filled, then bake them. They come out golden brown and crispy with the meat juicy and tender inside. You will go crazy about it."

"It sounds like a lot of work, Skender. Please don't ask her to go to all that trouble."

He shook his head in despair. "When will you learn? That is her joy, her happiness. If she pleases you, makes something special that you enjoy, she will be in the clouds, walking on air." He saw Jakup glance at his watch. "Yes, we had better go."

The air seemed colder, more biting, after the warm, sweet-smelling shop. They hurried along, the wind turning their cheeks white before whipping them to a rosy glow.

"Jakup!" They stopped as they heard him being hailed The young man ran across the street. "Jakup, what luck! I thought I would have to come all the way to your home."

Drita caught hold of Gillian's hand, urging her to hurry as the young man came up to them. He inclined his head to Skender, held out his hand, deliberately turning his back on the girls.

Gillian allowed herself to be pulled along by Drita, turned to look in the shop window when they stopped. "A tool shop," she exclaimed in disgust. "Why were we rushing to this?" Drita tapped her arm, pointed back to the men. Gillian looked at them, uncertainly back to Drita, then pointed to the shop window and wrinkled her nose.

Drita's eyes lit, she smiled excitedly and beckoned Gillian to a shop a little further along. Together they pasted their noses to the window. "That one is gorgeous," Gillian said, pointing to a bracelet of intricate silver filigree, set with dark red stones. Drita nodded, pointed to a matching necklace. Their breath fogged the window and as one they lifted their gloved hands and cleaned a peephole. Eyes met and they grinned at each other before pushing their noses again to the window. "The earrings are too big...." She turned, laughed as she saw Drita's hands telling her the same thing.

Drita pointed to a pair at the back, smaller, much more delicate. "Those are better for us." Eyes met, heads turned back and solemnly nodded silent agreement.

"Girls, are you planning on buying the whole store?" Jakup pushed his head between them, peering in at the jewelry, an arm around each of their shoulders.

"Tell her they make them here in Prishtine." Drita smiled up at him, turned. "Tell her, Skender."

"Great! Let's go in and see." Gillian started toward the door at his translation

"Later. First we have to let Drita complete her shopping so she can get home and cook, and we have to go to the Post Office. You have not sent word to your parents," he reminded her as they followed Jakup and Drita.

"Golly, I'd forgotten. If my mother doesn't hear soon, she'll organize the whole Grenadier Guards to invade you!" She pulled Skender near. "What was all that commotion with that young man? Drita almost pulled my arm off dragging me away."

"Drita must not stop. She probably assumed the same applied to you."

"Why couldn't she stop?" She did a skip to catch up with his longer stride.

"I've told you, she must not socialize with strangers."

"Talking on a public street is hardly socializing."

He laughed. "It is here. The young man is a friend of Jakup's ... they were friends in school and have remained that way. He often walked partway home with Jakup and Drita before they left school, but did you notice that he did not acknowledge her in any way, pretended that he had not seen her? Or you?"

"Yes, of course I noticed ... I thought he was somewhat rude."

"He was being extremely correct," he laughed. "I could tell he was itching to turn around and look at you ... probably did as soon as our backs were turned ... but he was too polite, has too much respect for us, to let me see his interest." He slipped his arm around her waist, gave her a quick hug. "It makes me feel very strong, very possessive."

"It makes me feel like something that's been bought and paid for."

"I did buy you ... two-and-a-half US dollars you cost me."

She laughed. "The best bargain you ever got in your life, mate. Was that all the marriage license cost?"

Jakup stopped and turned. "We go in here, brother, and then home. Until tonight."

He held out his hand to Skender, gave a quick smile to Gillian. "Enjoy our town. Drita … " He held the door open for her as she smiled her good-byes.

"Where are we going now?" Gillian asked as they continued in the same direction.

"Up those steps … that is the Post Office at the top. After we have sent a telegram to your family we are free, but I don't want your family worrying about you."

"Which flag is that? Yugoslavia's?"

He glanced quickly at the flag on top of the white building as they crossed the road. "Yes."

"I haven't seen any Albanian flags around. In fact, I think that's the first flag I've seen. We don't fly our flags in Europe as much as they do in the States, do we?" She glanced up. "I like the idea of flags on public buildings, do you?" He opened the door for her. "If there's a flag on top of Buckingham Palace it means the Queen's at home … did I ever tell you that?" She stopped. "Why don't I just call my mother instead of sending a telegram? I hadn't thought of that. Seeing the phones reminded me … what do you think?"

"Yes, why not? I will go and find out the procedure." He started to walk away, came back rubbing at his forehead.

"What's up?"

He grinned. "I can't remember the words! Wait a minute…." He closed his eyes, trying to concentrate.

Gillian stared, started to laugh. "You've forgotten your own language!"

"No. I will have to speak Serbo-Croat. Dammit, I just can't recall…."

"Why? Don't they know Albanian in here?"

"We are not allowed to use our language. This is a government office. Wait here, I'll try to muddle my way through."

She leaned back against the wall, watching the long lines of people waiting, covered a yawn. *The clerks don't give a hoot, just take their time, same as in England, the States … as soon as government gets its finger on the pulse, things slow down.* She stifled another yawn. *Stuffy in here.* Her eyes wandered to the telephone booths. *Why did Skender go over there to the counter? Why didn't he just dial?* She smiled as she saw him making his way back to her. "Well?"

"You will have to wait between forty-eight and seventy-two hours to place the call."

"What! That's crazy. It only takes an hour or so to call England from San Francisco and this is only a stone's throw away." He shrugged. "Are you sure he understood you?"

"He understood."

She eyed the telephones. "Let's just go in and call the operator and see what happens."

"If you want to try, go ahead, but I think you will come up against a blank wall."

"But Skender, I called my mother from Belgrade, and got through in just a short time."

He looked down at the floor, then back up at her. "But you are not in Belgrade. If you were there, or at the coast, there would be no problem. Why don't you try? You aren't going to be happy until you do." He propelled her toward the wooden boxes.

They squeezed in together, she laughing at him. "Did you choose the smallest one?" She waited impatiently as he talked. "Ask for the international operator," she hissed. He signaled for her to be quiet. "Tell her it's an emergency...." She giggled as he tried to push her away. "Tell her the country will be invaded if we don't get through to my mother." She started to laugh, pretending to ride a horse. "The British are coming; the British are coming.'"

"No, operator, I am not laughing at you..." he covered the mouthpiece for a moment, "I assure you, believe me, I am not laughing at you...." He glared, still laughing at Gillian. "Yes, I understand. Thank you. You are quite mad..." he said, pushing her out of the telephone booth. "Forty-eight hours at the earliest. What are you going to do? Wait, or send a telegram?

"Send a telegram ... it will be there tomorrow."

He handed her a form. "I got this while I was over there. Fill it in and I will take it back to the very official-looking man in blue.'"

She started to write the name and address. "How strange ... they are using green ink."

"What's so strange about that?"

"It's an untrue color, not a primary. I never use it." She flashed him a quick grin, then added solemnly. "Never trust someone who uses green ink! Now..." she sat, pen suspended in mid-air, "what shall I say?"

"It is a telegram, not a letter, 'Arrived safely', Love, Gillian."

"No, that doesn't sound like me ... I know!" She started to write "Found me ball and chain. T.T.F.N. Gillian." Skender read it, frowning. She pointed. "It's Cockney, see, this is you. 'Found my husband, Ta-Tar-For-Now ... good-bye, Gillian.' Why are you shaking your head? Skender!" Indignantly she watched as he ripped it into little pieces.

"I'll get you another form, and this time you will say, 'Arrived safely, Love, Gillian.'" She followed him to the counter.

"My mother will know you sent it. I never send stuffy things like that." She stood on tiptoe, leaning her chin on his shoulder. "Is it because you object to being my ball and chain?" He didn't answer. "Do you know what you'd call me? Your trouble and strife … it's rhyming slang, trouble and strife … wife."

He laughed. "That one is correct, it is right for you…." He nodded his thanks to the man as he handed him another form. "You are a trouble to me. What is the other word? What does it mean?"

"It means…" she glanced up at him, "…it means you are a very fortunate and lucky person to have me."

"Sit down and write." He dipped the pen in the ink, handed it to her. "Arrived safely, Love, Gillian. That is all. And I don't believe you," he whispered with a grin.

She shook as she laughed silently. "Now I've made a blob. I'm not used to writing with ink any more … can you get me another form?"

"No. Write around the mess." He watched her carefully. "Stop, that's all."

"I was going to add 'and Skender.'"

"No, leave it. Wait here and I will hand it in." She sat, watching the comings and goings. "Ready? Where are your gloves?"

"You were quick."

"I told him someone important was waiting." He opened the door. "He served me quickly. I think he was afraid I was going to ask for another form!" Carefully they made their way down the icy steps. "This is the beginning of Old Town … we can go there or go straight along the main street to the modern section. Adnan said there is a big new department store with a lot of nylon goods out there. Well, which would you prefer to see?"

"Do you need to ask me that?"

"No, I don't." He led her down the winding, cobbled street, the small shops made of stone with terra cotta tiled roofs huddling together companionably, sometimes leaning in towards each other, imparting secret thoughts, or maybe just supporting each other in their old age.

"Madame…" his hand offered her the square, "what is your pleasure? Leather? Hand-tooled bags, wallets, belts. Or, maybe, blouses, scarves dresses … hand-embroidered in glorious technicolor!" He laughed with her, picked up a huge, round pan. "Copper? You can instruct him how to beat it into any shape your heart desires … a bowl perhaps, a kettle? Anything you wish he will do." He smiled, nodded his thanks to the young boy as he returned the pan. He took her hand, leading her past the small shops, each window laden with the owner's special craft.

"Aha! Silver! A necklace, perhaps, delicately worked in filigree? Earrings, then, a pair that swing and gently caress your face?" His face fell. "Oh, I am sorry! There is nothing here to your liking … just ask, he will make it for you…."

Her eyes danced for him. He smiled down at her, took both her hands. "If I can, I want to take you to Prizren. Prizren is the mother of filigree. There you will see things you've never dreamed of, mostly in silver, but gold too. It is a beautiful town, one of the most lovely I have seen, with a great river running through it, and a snow-capped mountain standing guard … you will like it. I am going to buy you something there, Jill … sshh!" His finger stopped her protest. "Yes. We have economized and saved long enough. I have not bought you any jewelry, only a wedding ring, and I want you to have something from here. Don't cry." He laughed as she flung herself at him. "I wanted to make you happy, not sad."

Her muffled voice reached him. "I don't need jewelry to make me happy."

"I know, my love. If you demanded material goods you would not be mine." He made her look at him. "This gift to you will be my pleasure, my joy … you must not deny me that." He saw the curious stares of the passers-by. "We are stealing the trade from the shopkeepers … their customers are more interested in us than the goods they offer."

They walked slowly, pausing to admire and stare when the fancy caught them. They left the square, taking one of the small, winding streets that climbed slowly up to another that climbed just as slowly down again.

Gillian paused as she saw the window crammed with wooden plates, bowls, jugs. "Whatever could be carved, they're carved," she marveled, grimacing back at one of the donkeys showing its teeth, then laughed self-consciously as she saw the owner watching her.

"I have to get a pair of these," she said as she saw the nalle in the shoe shop.

Skender laughed. "You had better try one of the pairs at home first. They are not easy to walk in unless you are used to them. See, underneath the wooden sole? There are only two wooden supports, about one inch wide, running across the shoe. One at the front and one at the instep, and the only thing that keeps it on the foot is this leather strap. You have to learn to balance in them."

"Drita runs all over the place in them."

"Drita was born in them, you were not. But try … only promise me one thing."

"What?"

"That when you try, I am there to watch."

"Why?" she asked suspiciously, grinning at him.

"I want to see you fall on your face! Or…." He laughed, gave her a quick hug. "At the bottom of this street is Luan's shop … shall we go see him?" She nodded. "Good, he will be delighted to have us call on him. Perhaps he will have time to have coffee with us."

Chapter 20

"There are seventy-eight scarves on display. Do you want the ones on the shelves included in this figure or separate?" Emin turned, "Luan, are you stock-taking or window-gazing?"

Luan glanced around at him with a quick smile, "Look, there's your brother at the top of the street."

Emin, following the pointing finger, asked brusquely, "Are you ready for these figures?"

Luan laid his pencil on the counter. "What has she done?" Emin looked quickly at him before returning to the scarves on the counter. "Well?"

"Why should it be her?"

"I know you too well, Emin. It is not Skender, so that leaves his Nusé."

Emin sighed, stood up, and joined Luan at the window, his eyes on Gillian. "She just irritates me. I would like to shake her, shake her until her teeth rattle. And I don't know why." He gave a sudden exclamation of disgust.

Luan laughed at him, "Don't be so sticky! It was just a hug, an involuntary act on his part. Something pleased him, perhaps the way she looked at him, something she said…."

"And she allowed it. What is she thinking of? A little more reticence would not go amiss with her." He turned angrily away.

"Emin, calm yourself. So he hugged his wife…."

Emin wheeled on him, "In a public place? Doesn't he see where he is? That the streets are full?"

Luan shrugged, smiled, "Love is blind…."

"Love may be. The neighbors aren't." Emin glared angrily as Luan laughed. He watched Gillian and Skender for a moment. "I wish my father, or his, would see. He'd hear about it soon enough, and then it would stop immediately."

Luan smoothed his moustache, hiding his grin, "If you feel this strongly why don't you speak to Skender yourself?"

"Are you mad?" Emin looked up startled, "He remembers our customs too well. I'd have his hand across my mouth before I could draw breath," he grinned back at Luan, "As you well know! Now if she were from here…." he sighed meaningfully.

"You'd speak to her?"

Emin nodded grimly, "Indeed I would. Her skin would burn from my words. But…" he frowned, rubbing at his lip, "I don't know how to handle her. Last night I was after Nurije about some misdemeanor and Gillian stopped me." He looked directly at Luan. "She actually came and stood between my cousin and me."

"What did she say?"

Emin shrugged, raised his hands, "I don't know! It put me in a difficult position though. I did not know what to do. There was no precedent." He laughed shortly. "Of course there wasn't! Can you imagine one of our girls challenging me, standing between me and the girl I was chastising? No. Never! In a million years they would not dare." Luan sat silent, watching Emin. "Strange … I admired her courage. I wanted to shake her like a rag doll, and at the same time…." He was staring into space, lost in thought, then suddenly he turned to Luan. "For the rest of the evening she was like a mouse … not a word, not a sound from her. If he would give her to me, put her completely in my hands for two, maybe three, days…."

"You are dreaming, Emin. If Skender had wanted that he would have handed her directly to his mother."

"Three days, Luan. I guarantee you'd swear she was born here."

"Don't even think it," Luan said firmly, turning back to the window. He sat watching Skender. "He is so happy now, so relaxed, a different person." Luan looked back at Emin. "Do you recall how he was? How tense? Older than his years? When he came to our house my father was shocked at the change in him."

"Of course there was a change in him. He left a boy, came back a man."

Luan shook his head, "My father expected that, knew that the years would bring a change in appearance, manners. It was the sadness that shocked him. There was no light in him, just a deep sadness." He watched Skender. "I wish my father and mother could see him today. I think, now, he is as they remembered him."

Emin's frown deepened as he listened, "You give her credit for this change?" Luan looked long and seriously at him. "One of our girls could have done the same for him," Emin added obstinately.

Luan turned back to the window, smiling as he saw Skender's sudden laugh. "Maybe, but I think he needed someone to make him laugh. Could our girls do that?" He waited. "They would serve him better than she. Before his mind could crystallize a thought it would be done. He would hardly have to raise his voice and she'd be there. But could one of ours walk down a street with him like that, and make him laugh? I doubt it." He half turned as Emin came and stood beside him. "Each one of us has our own need from life, Emin. She would be as wrong for you, or me, as she is right for him."

Emin did not comment for a while, then, "Perhaps. I hope you're right."

They both stiffened as they saw two policemen stop a boy and a woman, watched as they insisted that the woman remove her scarf from around her mouth. "Damn their eyes," Luan muttered through clenched teeth. He turned sharply as he heard Emin's sudden indrawn breath.

"Skender does not know of this law. My God, if he interferes...." He went quickly to the door, running up the street. He threw his arms around both, pulling them into a hug. "Say nothing. It is the law," he whispered, "Be happy to see me and walk casually to the shop."

Statue-still, knuckles showing whitely, Luan watched. Slowly the woman unwound the scarf. Tears ran down the riverbeds of her cheeks to drop unchecked from lips and chin, staining the offending scarf. Old eyes begged for compassion from her tormentors as she prayed silently that no one would witness her shame. People passed them by, eyes firmly on the ground, all deliberately giving her the privacy she sought, except the two policemen who stood, hands on hips, watching her with cruel pleasure.

"Old woman! Wrinkled like a prune! Who would want to see you anyway?" one taunted her. They both laughed, turned, and went on their way.

The young boy, about thirteen, put his arm about her shaking shoulders, took the scarf and wrapped in around her neck, talking to her, comforting her.

Angrily Luan watched the retreating blue-grey uniforms. *What did it profit you to humiliate an old woman? Or did you hope to bait the boy? Spark his manhood too soon? An old woman and a boy ... did it make you feel your power? One day you will feel ours, I swear it.* He stood up, went to the door, and held it open for the three coming toward him.

Skender waited until the door closed then turned to Emin. "What was that all about? What law?"

"The women are forbidden to cover their faces."

"Why?" Skender sighed as Emin shrugged. "Surely they gave some explanation when the law was passed?"

"You have been away too long, brother. The government does not have to explain anything. However, this time a reason was given. 'The government is acting for the oppressed women of Kosov and Sarajevo.'" He laughed angrily as he saw Skender mouth, "Oppressed?" and added, "Amusing, isn't it?"

"No. Not amusing. Just another excuse to hit at our culture and traditions."

"Exactly." Angrily Luan banged his fist on the counter. "But this time it was almost a waste of time. None of the girls or young wives kept that tradition." He sighed, "Unfortunately it is the old women like her," he glanced toward the window, "our mothers and grandmothers who have been hurt. My mother never leaves the house now unless it is dark. My father, my brothers and I have used every persuasion, but she refuses."

Emin leaned closer to Skender. "You have never wondered why Nona stays home, never leaves the house, Skender?"

"No, I had not thought of it until now." He gave a sad laugh. "My ego, probably, assuming that as I was home…." He sighed and looked over at Emin. "Your mother?"

"Stays home until dark. Hasan's wife, too."

Skender nodded sadly. "Aslan's wife?"

"She is not affected, has never used the veil. It is as Luan said. Only the older women felt the need."

Luan noticed Gillian watching them closely, her eyes darting from one to the other as she tried to guess at the problem. "Do not frighten her," he warned the others.

Skender looked over at her. "She is not frightened … just curious."

"Skender, what's going on?" Gillian asked quickly as she saw she had his attention for a moment.

"The old woman who was outside?" She nodded. "The police made her remove the scarf from her face."

"Why?"

"It is forbidden for the women to cover their faces. It is the law now."

"Oh, what a strange law." She smiled her thanks as Luan pulled up a stool for her to sit on.

"She is not concerned, is she?" Emin asked Skender in surprise. "You were explaining the problem to her, were you not?"

"Yes, I explained, and you are right. She is not concerned."

"You do not find that strange, brother?"

"No." Skender's tone closed the subject.

"Come to the back room. I will make some tea," Luan offered.

"No, Luan. We came here to invite you to have coffee with us. We have a bonus in finding you here too, Emin. Can you both join us?"

"We are in the middle of stock-taking," Emin said uncertainly, glancing at Luan.

"Leave it." Luan looked ruefully at the neat piles on the counter. "Unhappily it will still be here when we return. Let's join Skender."

Emin grinned. "I was hoping you'd say that. I'll get our coats from the back room."

Luan nodded his thanks. "Have you shown your Nusé our town, Skender?"

"Yes, we have seen most of the Old Town. I want her to see the bridge though."

"Good. We will go that way. There is a nice coffee house quite near."

Skender saw Luan's eyes lingering on Gillian's scarf. "The wool is different from ours. Feel it." He noted Luan's hesitation and smiled to himself. "Jill, could you take off your scarf and let Luan see? He sells them here and is interested." He turned back to Luan as Gillian started to unwind her scarf. "I think of you as a brother, Luan. It would honor me if you would feel the same toward me and mine." He took the scarf from Gillian, holding it out to Luan.

"Thank you." Luan looked directly at him as he accepted it. Skender inclined his head, knowing it was not the scarf Luan was thanking him for. "This is softer, more closely woven than ours. From America?"

"No, England."

"Scotland," Gillian corrected him.

Luan laughed. "I see you speak our language, Nusé!"

"Only if you use the words she knows!" Skender smiled back at him as Emin came in and threw Luan's coat at him.

"Where are we going? To the hotel?"

"Skender wanted to show his nusé the bridge, so I thought the old coffee house? The distance is about the same."

"Fine." Emin finished buttoning his coat and took Gillian's scarf from Luan. "Nusé, your scarf." He stepped up to her and wound it about her neck.

Gillian's eyes flew to Skender. He smiled at her. "You see? Now you do have a brother who worries about you. Thank you, Emin."

Luan opened the door. "Be careful," he warned, "Three steps down and they are slippery." Skender repeated the warning to Gillian.

"Wait, one moment please." Luan left for the back room, returning almost immediately, stuffing a book into his coat pocket.

Skender waited beside the door of the shop while Luan changed the sign and locked the door. "How are your parents? Your family?"

"Well, thank you. And yours?"

Skender nodded, "Well, thank you." they turned the corner, and the full force of the wind whipped at them, tearing at their coats.

"Are you sure you want to go to the bridge, brother?" Emin asked hanging onto his hat.

Skender hesitated, "No, there will be other days. Let us go somewhere close."

Emin took hold of Gillian's arm, guiding her toward a small shop. He leaned forward to open the door. "Damn." He bit his tongue, eyes going quickly to Gillian, then turned with an apologetic smile to Skender. "Sorry, brother … I forgot for a moment…." He glanced again at Gillian.

"There is no harm. She does not understand. What is the matter?"

"They are closed so it is the old coffee house by the bridge after all. Come, Nusé." He took hold of Gillian's arm again, and started up the cobbled street, bending his head against the wind. "What on Earth … how does she walk in those ridiculous things?"

Skender laughed. "She could outrun you."

"Never … not in those."

Skender nodded, remembering Gillian racing to catch a cable car. "Yes. Do you want to try?"

Emin turned, his face shocked. "Here? In the street?"

Skender shrugged. "Why not?" laughing as he saw Emin turn away, shaking his head.

Luan smiled at Skender. "You have shocked my friend."

"He is as tight as his father, sometimes tighter!"

Gillian slowed her steps, then stopped. Skender followed the direction of her eyes. "It is not right," she muttered angrily, watching as one of the carriers was loaded with a heavy chest. She turned sharply to Skender. "Why doesn't the shop use a horse and cart to deliver?"

"It is not the shop owner's responsibility to deliver. It is the buyer who must transport the goods."

Her eyes flashed to the man who was organizing the loading of the chest. "Then why doesn't he hire a horse and cart?"

"The man is cheaper." He saw her face crumple as she half turned from him. "I'm sorry, that was a cruel thing to say, but it is the truth." He sighed. "Life is cheap here, my love."

She turned her back on Skender, on the carrier struggling to stand. "Can we go? I don't want to see this." Skender, taking hold of her other arm, started to walk forward.

"What has upset her?" Emin asked.

"Seeing the carriers … seeing them load that one…."

"That upset her?"

Skender nodded.

"But she wasn't upset, wasn't concerned, about the old woman … why?"

Skender stopped, looking perplexedly at him. "I don't know. I hadn't thought about it." He turned Gillian to him. "Jill, why didn't it upset you when the policeman made the woman remove her scarf?"

She shrugged. "I don't know. It didn't seem all that important to me. Frankly, I couldn't understand why she was crying."

Slowly Skender turned and repeated it to Emin and Luan, adding, "Western culture. They are unable to understand why that is so valuable to us, particularly to our women. At the same time, it is impossible for us to comprehend that they cannot understand its importance for us. This…" he gestured back toward the carrier, "has shaken her, she is trembling…."

"But we accept this, do not like, but can accept it. Whereas with the woman…?" Emin stopped.

"Exactly," Skender nodded, "A completely different outlook and value from ours." He looked reflectively at Gillian. "Now, if she could perceive why for us the one is more important than the other, she would have the key, would understand all of our customs and the reasons for them." His eyes shone with excitement as he looked from Luan to Emin.

Emin had watched him closely. "Your hope, then, is that she will understand our customs and accept them?"

"Yes."

Emin flashed a triumphant glance at Luan. "Do you not want her to embrace them?"

Skender smiled. "Impossible, Emin. Wish for a star instead of that!"

"We are here." Luan held open a heavy wooden door, set with large brass knobs and stood waiting for Gillian and Skender to enter. He put his hand gently on Emin's shoulder. "Let it go, my friend. If she were yours you could do with her as you pleased. That is his privilege, too."

Emin gave a sad smile, then sighed dramatically, "Perchance to dream...."

Luan laughed at him. "Such drama! You have missed your vocation!"

Emin grinned back at him. "I know! But I'd still like to have her in my hands..." he whispered, his eyes on Gillian.

They stood in the hallway for a moment, letting their eyes become accustomed to the dimmer light. "I knew you'd like this place, Jill. It is very old. Be careful, the floor is uneven. The tiles that cover the lower part of the wall are Moorish."

Gillian let her eyes travel past the blues and yellows of the tiles to the wood, dark and richly oiled, that covered the top part of the walls, then on to the heavy beams that supported the wooden ceiling. The slate entry hall gave way to thick carpet as they went down three steps, the wooden balustrade ending in a carved rose of such delicate beauty she almost stooped to inhale it perfume.

Luan led the way toward the back of the room. "Let us sit here, then your Nusé can see everything." He pulled the low table forward, gestured with his hand inviting Gillian to sit. She sat down on the fat pillow, a little surprised that Luan had asked her to sit first. Luan waited until Skender sat down, then pushed the table back into position.

Skender turned to help Gillian off with her coat, as a young boy appeared at the table, dressed in the usual Kosov style, but with a white apron tied around his middle. "I expected a hubble-bubble dancer at least," she whispered, bringing a quick smile to Skender's mouth as Luan placed the order. "What's that thing over there?"

He followed the direction of her eyes to a group of old men. "A water pipe," he whispered back, suddenly laughing, "Don't tell me you want to try that too?"

She shook her head, letting her eyes roam, slowly appreciatively, coming back to the charcoal brazier in the center of the room. She watched the men playing chess, clustered around the fire, with others watching, their moustaches pursing or spreading depending on their approval of the move made, the fire sending flashes of color from the mother-of-pearl inlay on the chess board tables.

"The chess pieces are ivory and hand carved," Skender told her as he saw her interest.

The young waiter returned, his hand held high, balancing a huge brass tray. He set it down with a flourish, waited a moment until he received a nod from Luan that all was well, then left with a slight bow. There were four glasses of water, four demitasse cups and saucers, the china so fine it was almost transparent, and a brass jezve full to the brim with coffee, its rich aroma giving anticipation of the pleasure to come. In the center of the tray was a glass dish full of locum, its delicate pastels veiled with powdered sugar.

"This is locum, a sweet. It is Turkish in origin. Take a piece, dip it into your water and enjoy. Watch me." Skender took a drink of water first, picked up a square of locum, dipped into his water, then put it into his mouth, nodded at her. "This is a particularly good one. Try." She picked up a pale pink piece, dipped it in her water and took a small bite. Skender laughed gently at her, "It is not sujuk. You will not get burned!"

"Mmmm." She closed her eyes, breathing in deeply. "It tastes of roses. I can even smell them in my stomach."

"That is what some of it is made from. We have a jam made from roses, too, which I must let you try."

"She does not know this sweet?" Luan asked as he helped himself to a piece. Skender shook his head. Luan snapped his fingers, "Another locum, with nutmeats." He started to take off his coat. "It is warm in here … ahh! I almost forgot. I have something for you, Nusé." He felt into his coat pocket, took out the book, walked around and sat on a pillow next to Gillian. "Here. I hope it will make your stay a little more pleasant." He held the book out to her with a smile.

Gillian's eyes lit. "An English-Albanian dictionary. Thank you. I ran all over San Francisco and London and couldn't find one. Thank you so much."

Luan smiled and nodded, pleased that his gift had made her happy.

"How do you happen to have such a thing?" Emin asked. A slow smile came as he felt the swift kick under the table. He raised his eyebrows and mouthed, "Dubrovnik?"

Luan grinned, giving him a broad wink. "Skender, tell your Nusé to try this locum with nuts," he said as the young waiter came back and set another glass dish of locum on the tray. "Do you have this in America?"

"I have never seen it," Skender offered some to Gillian. "Jill, do they have locum in America?"

"I don't think so. We have something similar in England and call it Turkish Delight, but it's awful compared to this."

Emin pushed the jezve toward her. "Nusé?" She picked it up, about to pour.

"Wait. Let me show you." Luan took the jezve from her. "You have to make it swirl before you pour, see? Then you only half fill each cup, then swirl again," he glanced quickly at her to make sure she was watching him, "…then fill each cup to the brim. That way everyone will get some of the thick part and some of the foamy part." He handed her the jezve, gave her an encouraging smile, and pointed to the cups.

Gillian started to move the jezve, awkwardly trying to copy Luan's easy swinging movement. It spilled, splashing onto the tray. Luan laughed softly as he saw color flood her face. "Do not worry. Here. let me help you." He hesitated a moment, gave a quick glance to Skender, then put his hand over hers on the handle and helped her to make the coffee swirl gently round. "Good. Confidence is all you need."

Skender felt Emin's stiffness, saw him watching Luan closely, lips tight together. "Emin, I have told Luan that I think of him as a brother … that I would be honored if he would feel the same way toward me and mine."

Luan laughed as he looked over at Skender. "Thank you for telling him. I could almost feel his hand across my mouth."

Emin laughed with them, doubling his fist at Luan. "This, not my hand, my friend. If you had touched her without permission."

Luan grinned at him as he helped Gillian fill the last cup of coffee. She picked up one of the brimming cups. "Emin?" She held it out to him.

Emin shook his head. "Skender first, Nusé, not me."

Gillian hesitated, not sure that she had understood.

Skender reached and took the cup from her. "Luan next, Jill, then Emin," he told her quietly as he set the cup down in front of him.

"Sorry. I can't sort out who gets served first."

"Yes, it must be confusing. We have too many rules."

She smiled as she passed Luan his coffee. "There are always rules. Wait until you get to England. It will be just as difficult for you." She passed a cup to Emin.

"Isn't it the same as America?"

"Good heavens, no. Much more rigid." She gave a quick mischievous grin. "You will have to stand every time a lady enters the room. I thought that would shock you!" Her eyes sparkled at him as she picked up her cup.

"Mmmm, excellent," Luan said appreciatively as he took his first sip, "just as coffee should be, as hot as hell, as dark as night," he winked, adding softly, "as sweet as love."

Gillian settled herself comfortably on the pillow and opened the dictionary, as they laughed and started to chat. *This is going to be a tremendous help. Now I won't have to guess what they're saying. If I'd had this with me this morning, we could really have got into politics….* She noticed that it wanted to open at one section and allowed it to do so. She took out the piece of paper and looked curiously at the neat handwriting. She studied it, puzzled at first, then started to laugh silently to herself. *So, this young man has had a time for himself somewhere! And I thought they were all so stiff and proper! I wonder …* She glanced at Luan, her eyes full of mischief. *Yes, I'll try … see what reaction I get.* She raised the book high enough to hide the sheet of paper. "Luan?"

He turned immediately. "Nusé?"

"Je t'aime." She looked up into his puzzled eyes. "Have you forgotten your French?" She grinned. "Perhaps you didn't get an opportunity to use it! Let's try something else." She glanced at the list. "Jag alskar dig … shame on you! The Swedish girls are gorgeous … well worth remembering their language! Let me see. Ich liebe Dich." He shook his head, completely puzzled. "No? Then how about…" she looked straight at him and with great feeling uttered the Italian, "Ti amo. Oh! I've struck a bell!" She laughed softly at the horrified look on his face.

He glanced quickly at Skender and saw with relief that he was deep in conversation with Emin. He let out a long sigh and held out his hand. "Please. May I have that?" Her eyes laughed into his concerned ones as she shook her head and held the book closer to her. "Please?" His hand extended a little nearer to her.

"What will you do if I refuse?" she asked softly as she shook her head. "You are so very sure of yourselves, so supremely self-confident. Now what?" She half-expected him to demand it, perhaps to snatch it from her but was surprised as he graciously inclined his head and turned back to the others. She felt a stab of guilt. *I shouldn't have teased him … he has been so nice.* "Luan?" He turned to her. She held out the dictionary. "I'm sorry." She stopped as she was about to hand it to him, turned quickly to the correct page and pointed to the word.

He smiled kindly. "Do not be. I was at fault. I should have been more careful." Their eyes met. Gillian felt her lips twitching. Suddenly laughter caught them. Gillian raised her eyebrows at him, shook her head and tut-tutted softly at him, and they both laughed louder. Emin stopped in the middle of a sentence to give them a curious glance.

She leaned forward, opened the dictionary and asked, "Where?" He laughed, shaking his head at her. She ran her finger the length of the list. "You were very busy, I see, or at least had plans to be!"

He put his finger to his lips, smilingly asking her silence, then took the paper, folded it and put it away in his pocket.

"What has amused you two?" Skender asked turning to Gillian as Emin turned and asked Luan the same thing.

As one they both answered, "Nothing." Eyes met. Each guessed at the other's response. They laughed softly together, while Skender smilingly watched.

"What has she to say that can be so amusing?" Emin demanded, frowning.

Luan shook his head, still laughing quietly to himself and picked up his cup and finished the last swallow of coffee. "I must go." He turned his cup upside down onto his saucer and slapped his friend on the back. "Emin, read my fortune." He stood up, shook hands with Skender and grinned. "I know what my fortune will be if I'm away from my father's shop for too long!" He turned with a special smile to Gillian. "Nusé, good-bye and thank you. Emin, stock-taking tomorrow … early!" He shook hands and stopped as he saw that Skender was talking to Gillian. "Get to know her, my friend. I think you will be surprised, and pleasantly so." Astonished, Emin glanced up at him. Luan cuffed at him and laughed, "See you tomorrow."

They watched as he made his way from the coffee house, stopping on his way to the door to talk to some people at the tables. "He knows quite a few people," Gillian said as she smilingly watched him leave.

"His family is very prominent here, plus, he is well-liked for himself." Skender turned over his cup. "Do you want Emin to read your fortune? If so, turn your cup upside down like mine."

Wide-eyed she turned over her cup. "Can he really?"

"Of course. Emin, your cup."

"Clean." He showed them the empty cup. "I prefer to eat mine!"

Gillian shuddered. "Did he eat the grounds?"

"Yes, many do. I, too, sometimes. You should try it one day, you may like it." He smiled as she wrinkled her nose and shook her head. "Emin, can you read these for us?"

Emin picked up Gillian's cup, studying it carefully as he watched. "I see a horse. That means you will be lucky today." Her eyes didn't leave him as he turned the cup this way and that. "There is a river with a man beside it." He held the cup closer, studying it intently and gave Skender a gentle kick under the table. "Give me some clues, then."

"She has a brother, recently married. The family has a large dog. Enough?"

"Yes, you can make up the rest in the translation anyway." He moved the cup. "There is a large dog, Nusé, looking for you…."

"That would be Ruffles," Gillian confided excitedly to Skender. "Ask him to go on." She stared in amazement as Skender told her of a man, closely related to her, who was recently married. "My brother! He's fantastic," she gasped.

Emin put down the cup. "That is all," he said seriously.

She picked it up, studying it closely. "I can't see anything, no man or…."

Emin's hand came over the cup. "Do not doubt me or a terrible curse will fall upon you," he said in a deep and ominous voice. He covered his face, shaking with laughter. "I'm sorry," he looked at Skender, "But her eyes … does she really believe in all this nonsense?"

Skender laughed with him. "Not normally, but she has convinced herself that we are 'different.'"

"We are…." Emin looked over at Gillian, his laughter stopping. *Of course … what a fool I've been … was so concerned with her behavior, I never thought …*

Gillian looked from one to the other and gave a wry grin. "I've been taken, haven't I?"

"Yes, my love. Well and truly taken."

She smiled at Emin. "Well done. I am not usually caught so easily."

He listened to Skender, smiled and nodded at Gillian. "I will not charge you this time, lady!" He stood up and signaled the waiter. "I must go. Black magic will not help with my studies, unfortunately."

"It has been paid, sir."

Emin stopped Skender as he started to leave some money for the boy. "No tipping permitted." He dropped his voice, "You slip it to him on the way out, but Luan will already have taken care of that."

Gillian took a last look around before they left. "It's lovely. I enjoyed it here."

"We will come again, then," Skender assured her.

The three started toward the bridge, Emin holding one arm and Skender the other with Gillian in the middle. "I will come as far as the River Road with you and then my books will claim me for the rest of the day."

"Good. Do you find it hard to study?"

"No, I enjoy my work, but it is difficult to close your eyes when preferential treatment is given to certain others."

Skender nodded, then pointed. "Jill, this is the bridge I wanted you to see." It was small, built from stone. She nodded, not quite sure what to say about the inconsequential bridge. "Well, what do you think of it?"

She glanced quickly at Skender. "It is very nice." She searched her mind as she saw he expected more. "The stones are so nice and … square," she finished lamely. He watched her with smiling anticipation. "It is a very nice bridge … with a river, too," she pressed gamely on as she saw its importance to Skender.

"Yes." He stood admiring it. "I've always liked it." Gillian studied it, at a loss to understand his pride and interest and sighed with relief as the explanation came. "My grandfather and his brothers built most of it." They started to walk across. "She is fascinated with these." Skender pointed his chin at one of the long wooden carts that started to pass them, "Was hoping our family had one."

"What for? We are not farmers!"

"She wished to have a ride."

Emin laughed. "That is easily accomplished." He let out a long whistle, ran up to the driver and spoke to him, explaining the situation. "Nusé, your chariot awaits!"

Skender hurried Gillian forward. "Emin has begged a ride for you," he said as he swung her onto the back and jumped up beside her. "You see … your every wish must be granted!"

Emin walked back to them and held out his hand to Skender. "Brother, until tonight."

"Tonight, Emin," Skender confirmed shaking hands. Emin signaled the driver forward.

"Emin, thank you for asking him to let us ride," Gillian said shyly.

The cart lurched forward. Emin put out his hand to steady her. "Albanian, Nusé. Speak Albanian," he said pointing to the dictionary, as the cart pulled away.

"I hope he likes me." She bit her lip. "That sounds silly after he's been so nice, but I can't help feeling that he doesn't approve of me."

"He has to get used to you, that is all."

"I suppose so," she sighed. "Anyway, if he disliked me, he wouldn't have bothered with me, helping me across the street, holding my arm," she gave a brief smile, "putting on my scarf."

"Even if he despised you he would look out for you." Skender saw the surprised look. "I have told you before, family is everything to us. You are ours now. When you stepped past our gate you became his sister and nobody, nothing, can touch you when he is near, not even a cobweb. He would forfeit his life in a moment for you, to protect you, your honor." He laughed. "And he would jump all over you if he thought you deserved it!"

She smiled nervously. "My stomach has the jelly wobbles. I'm not sure if I want to be that important, protected to that extent."

"The decision is not yours to make."

"I know." She looked straight at him. "Perhaps that's why it makes me nervous. I am not used to…." She stopped, biting her lip.

"Used to … what?"

"Having decisions made for me." She smiled nervously at him. "You and I have already had a few run-ins about that, haven't we? Now you expect me to let Emin…."

"Not only Emin … any of my cousins. Make sure you understand that." He leaned back again. "While we are here, you abide by our rules, accept my decisions, or theirs, without question."

She watched the road running like a ribbon beneath them.

His voice was sharp, "Did you hear me, Gillian?"

Gillian? Gillian? What happened to Jill?

"Did you hear me?"

She nodded. *Let's hope they stick to putting on my scarf, helping me across the road….*

The ribbon continued to unfold beneath her, smoothly, without bumps.

The oxen plodded steadily on.

Chapter 21

Drita stopped for a moment, a dish half in and half out of the hot, soapy water beside her on the floor. The cheerful whistling came closer. *Jakup. I have time to finish this dish and perhaps one more before he gets here….*

"Drita! Still working?" She was already on her feet when he opened the door and greeted her. She smiled as she bowed to him. "Where is our Nusé?"

"Upstairs, in the sitting room."

He closed the door. She glanced down at the dishwater at her feet, looking hopefully at her cousin as he walked over toward the stove. She watched him as he poked at the fire and added a log, glancing down again at the soapy water rapidly cooling at her feet. She coughed.

Jakup turned. "Yes, Drita?" She gestured to the water and the dirty dishes. His smile was apologetic. "I'm sorry, of course you may." He watched her for a moment as she washed a large round plate. "Shamsi and Adnan are not here yet?"

"No. Their father is, and Aslan. Is Ilyria coming tonight?"

"Yes, but later. Emin had not eaten when I left. Are my father and mother upstairs?"

"Of course."

He smiled. "Of course … he is here more than in his own home lately." Drita looked up and smiled back at him, he bent down beside her. "It is hard on you, Drita, all these guests coming and going, the extra meals … are you tired?" She shook her head. "You are, I can see it." *I will speak to Ilyria … perhaps she could come to help her.* He stood up. "I had better present myself to your father." He stopped her from rising. "Hurry so you can sit with us."

He took the stairs two at a time, straightened his hat and pulled his cummerbund tight before opening the door. He walked forward toward the group of men sitting on one side of the fire. *She is with Skender.* "Mire mbrama," he greeted them with a smile and a bow. He turned and bowed to the three women sitting on the other side of the room. "Aunts, mother."

"You are early, Jakup." Arif halted his game of chess and looked up at his son.

"Yes, sir." He declined with a quick smile Babush's offer to sit. "With your permission…." He gestured toward the door. Babush nodded approval.

"How was your day, Jakup?" Aslan asked.

"Thank you, Aslan." He flashed a glance at his father, grinned. "Busy!" Aslan laughed quietly. "Skender, did you enjoy the rest of your morning? Emin said you had coffee with him and Luan."

"Yes, we did, thank you."

"May we borrow your Nusé?" He held out his hand to Gillian. "We will be in the kitchen." He took hold of her hand, started to pull her to her feet, noticed the dictionary beside her, "Bring that with you."

Skender stopped him. "Thank you, Jakup, but I want her here. Sit down, Jill."

"Why can't I go?" Gillian demanded, half-sitting, half-standing.

Skender smiled and nodded to Jakup who gave a slight bow, glanced again at Gillian, then left, closing the door quietly behind him. He waited a moment, frowning at the closed door. *Why did he stop her, she wished to come….* He sighed, went back to the kitchen, signaling Drita not to stand, to continue with her work, as he sat down. He glanced quickly around as the door opened. "Oh, it's you, Shamsi."

Shamsi laughed as he took off his coat, passing it to Drita and acknowledging her greeting with a smile. "What a welcome! 'Oh, it's you, Shamsi!' Well, where is she?"

"Upstairs. I went and presented myself, thought to bring her here with us, but Skender stopped her from coming." He grinned at his cousin. "When the door opened, I thought…." He shrugged.

"Why did he stop her?" He turned as he saw Drita fidgeting, asked irritably, "What is it?"

She waved her hand at the dishes. "The dishes…."

"Do them then," he snapped.

"I was waiting on you, Shamsi." He turned to her, surprised at her sharpness. She dropped her eyes from him, murmuring, "I'm sorry," as she knelt beside the bowl.

Shamsi sat down beside Jakup, asking silently, "What's wrong with Drita?"

"Tired," Jakup mouthed back at him.

Shamsi frowningly drummed his fingers on the rug. "We have to get her here."

"There is no way without Skender's say-so." Jakup looked up expectantly as the door opened again. "Mire mbrama, Adnan, Nurije." Drita sighed quietly, stood up and bowed to Adnan.

Shamsi glanced over at his brother and sister, turned to Jakup. "I have waited, planned for this evening all day."

"As I have."

Adnan threw his coat to Nurije, walked over and held his hands to the fire. "Mire mbrama. It is freezing again. Where is she?" He glanced quickly around the kitchen.

"Please may I continue with my work?" Drita bit her lip as she realized how sharply she had asked. Her face flushed as she saw Jakup and Shamsi turn and stare at her in surprise.

Adnan silently watched her for a moment. Her eyes filled. "You may continue, Drita," he said quietly, beckoning to Nurije. "Help her."

Nurije knelt beside Drita. "What is the matter?" she whispered.

Drita shook her head, tears dropping into the bowl of water. "Now I have angered both of them."

Shamsi stood up, signaling for the girls to continue. "I have to go upstairs to greet my uncles. I will see if I can bring her back with me." He glanced down as he passed the girls. "Hurry with that work, I am tired of seeing it. Be sure it's finished before my return." He slipped on a pair of nalle, ran up the steps and stopped outside of the sitting room, making sure that his cummerbund was straight and smooth before entering. "Mire mbrama," he greeted the men with a bow.

Skender put his head closer to Gillian. "This one is Shamsi … it is his Nusé I want you to see. They have only been married two or three months, so she will still wear her wedding gown, just as she did on her wedding day, except for the veil."

She watched as Shamsi greeted the women. "I didn't know he was married. Didn't you say it was Aslan's wife coming tonight?"

"Yes, she was, but the child is fretful so she decided to stay home. Migje Hasan, the father of Aslan and this one, has invited us for dinner at their home tomorrow. It will be a big affair … you will meet her then."

"Come, Nusé," Shamsi beckoned to her, giving a smile to Skender. "I will return her in an hour."

Skender winked as he caught Aslan's eye, putting his hand on Gillian's arm. "No, Shamsi, I want her here with me."

Shamsi hesitated, "Then, perhaps later?"

"Perhaps."

Arif watched, hand suspended over the chessboard, as he waited for the door to close. "There have been two of our sons asking for her within five minutes of each other. How come she is this popular so suddenly, Skender?" he asked with a smile.

Aslan laughed and turned to his uncle. "We were just discussing that, migje, wondering which one would be here next to ask for her." He leaned forward and picked-up the dictionary lying beside Gillian. "Luan Mali freed her to talk with them," he said as he held it up.

Hasan laughed at his son. "They had better start early in the evening … it will take them ten minutes to make a sentence!" His eyes moved back to the chessboard. "Guardi."

Arif frowned at the move, rubbing at his moustache in concentration.

"You have him, Hasan!" Babush smiled at his younger brother. "Congratulations." His eyes moved to the door, "I think another deputation…?" he smiled at Skender, "Will you sit with us, Adnan?" he asked after he had greeted them.

"Thank you, sir, but I thought we might visit in the kitchen first." He smiled as he received a nod of permission. "If you are agreeable, sir…" he gestured to Gillian, "Perhaps we could have Skender's Nusé join us for a short while?"

Aslan looked at Skender and whispered, "A new tactic is being employed. Now they are going to the fountainhead."

Skender turned his laugh into a cough as Babush graciously inclined his head. "Of course, if Skender is agreeable."

Adnan hesitated, then turned with a bright smile. "Skender?"

"Thank you, Adnan, but no." He almost laughed as he saw the disappointment on his cousin's face. "As you are all so anxious to visit with my wife, why don't you join us? Please ask the others to join us." Adnan almost sighed, bowed. The door closed quietly.

The women stopped their chattering, glanced up as laughter rocked the room.

Arif wiped his eyes. "How many more delegations will there be? Let her go with them. I have lost this game through her!"

"My superior knowledge of chess lost you this game and a pouch of tobacco, not her nor the interruptions," Hasan retorted with a quick wink at Skender and Aslan.

"Why didn't you let her go with them, Djali? If I remember, you were worried that she would find no common ground with them. Are you still concerned after all this interest?"

Skender smilingly shook his head at his father. "I have no worry now, but I want her here when Shamsi's Nusé comes." Babush nodded smiling his approval.

"Neither of our Nusés generated so much excitement, Skender. What is the secret?" Hasan turned to his wife. "You had better listen, bear in mind his answer. We still have two sons left. Shall we ask him to be intermediary for us?"

She laughed. "It is a good idea. I must admit I would enjoy all the excitement."

Skender sighed dramatically. "I will be busy when I leave here. Migje Arif wishes me to send Nusés for Jakup and Emin, each carrying pipes and tobacco, of course." He laughed at Arif. "Now, two for you…."

"They can bring pipes and tobacco, I have no objection," Hasan laughed.

Skender turned to speak to Gillian. "What are you doing?" he asked as he saw her studying the rug.

"Counting how many yellow squiggles there are to how many blue squares." He stared at the rug, looked up, puzzled.

"Why?"

"To occupy myself, stop myself from screaming with boredom. Why won't you let me read a book? It wouldn't bother anyone."

"It would bother me."

She pouted, muttered, "Tough."

"What was that?"

She heard the warning, shook her head. "Nothing."

"Good." He turned to his uncles. "You had better be sure before you order all these Western brides … there will be some storms for you to ride out."

"We will give them all to my brother here." Hasan laughed and slapped Arif across the back. "He will break them in a day, two at the most." He held up his finger. "Listen, Skender … they have accepted your invitation."

The three young men, followed by Drita and Nurije, came in and settled themselves on the opposite side of the room.

Babush smiled back at Hasan as they both witnessed Adnan's urgent beckoning to Gillian. "Your son is determined to have her with them," he murmured. "Nusé, would you like to sit with them?" She gave a quick grin as she guessed at what Babush had asked her, nodded and stood up.

"Gillian." She glanced at Jakup, Skender looked, too, surprised that he knew her name. Jakup pointed, "The dictionary." She picked it up and went toward them. "Ulu ketu." Jakup patted the rug beside him.

"My son has beaten me … he already knows her name," Arif confided to his brothers.

"She will learn quickly with Jakup … my son has a lot of patience." Teza's voice carried to Arif.

He glanced at her, turned to Skender. "A week, Skender, and she would speak if you allow her to be treated as a girl from here."

"What do you mean, Migje?"

"Treat her as you would if she were from Kosov … speak only Albanian to her, let her work with Drita, do the work of a Nusé." Skender smilingly shook his head. "Why not?"

"She has never done heavy work, would have no idea how to light a fire. And as for bread … I doubt she would know where to start."

Babush closed his eyes as the next question came.

"Then who does the work in your home?"

"She does, of course," Babush answered rapidly with a straight, direct look at Skender.

Skender smiled to himself, realizing his father's concern. "It is much easier in the West, many machines are available … one to wash clothes, one to sweep. Push a button for heat to cook, move a lever for warmth … it is not hard work as here."

"Skender, you have all these machines? Even to wash clothes?" Aslan asked.

He hesitated, wondering how he could explain a laundromat, if they would approve. "We do not have them all, but they are available to us."

"Then leave the work, let her learn our ways and customs. Give her to me for a day … make it two … you will be surprised when I return her to you."

I'm sure I would! Skender smilingly shook his head at Arif.

Hasan leaned close to him. "Throw her to the lions, Skender," he growled in a whisper, bringing a broader smile.

Aslan leaned toward him on the other side, not having heard what his father had said. "Between Arif and Emin they'd eat her alive," he whispered with a grin. Skender laughed softly in agreement.

A sudden burst of laughter from the young men made them all turn. The group had already split with Drita and Nurije chatting together, and Gillian surrounded by Jakup, Shamsi, and Adnan.

"She is used to being with young men." Hasan turned to Skender with a smile. "She must have many brothers."

"Just one, but she is the only girl in the family. All her cousins are boys."

There was a light tap on the door and Besim entered, followed immediately by Shamsi's Nusé. Hasan's wife looked the girl over quickly but thoroughly before turning to see Gillian's reaction to her new daughter. Besim's murmured greeting reached Gillian, she glanced up from the dictionary and stared in open admiration at the Nusé before her.

She was young, probably twenty, almost a head taller than Gillian. Her hair was light brown and hung in natural waves to her shoulders. Her dimi was a heavy silk brocade, white with a silver thread running through. Her blouse, sheer silk, cut deliberately to emphasize the swell of her breasts, the sleeves long and very full, was topped by a sleeveless bolero of the same heavy brocade as her dimi. A belt, three inches wide, made of silver and intricately worked in a leaf and flower pattern, encircled her waist, fastening at the center with one huge silver rose.

She stood quietly, hands clasped at waist level, eyes on the ground, waiting until Besim had finished greeting the assembly. Her necklace was magnificent, a rope of gold held a coin the size of an American silver dollar, but hers was gold, it rested just above the line of her blouse, flashing and sparkling in the light. Two more coins, smaller but of the same design, were on each side of the large one. Her lips carried a deep rose lipstick and that, together with her dark eyebrows and lashes, emphasized her creamy complexion. Gillian wished desperately that she would look up so that she could see her eyes, but they were anchored firmly to the rug at her feet.

Hasan tapped Babush's arm, pointed the stem of his pipe toward Gillian. "She is enthralled with our Nusé."

Babush nodded and smiled. "I have seen it."

Hasan leaned toward him. "Brother, I would have given much to see her given to Skender in that way."

"I, too, brother."

"My son, Aslan, would have carried her with pride to your house." He studied Gillian. "She would have been a beauty."

Babush turned his head. "It is past." He wiped his mouth on the back of his hand, then turned back to Hasan. "The most important thing is that we have her now."

"Agreed." Hasan slapped his brother on the back, cursing himself for upsetting him.

Gillian let her eyes slide to Shamsi, anxious to see his admiration of his wife. She was shocked to see that he had his back to her, had not moved, and seemed to be completely unaware of her presence. Her eyes met Jakup's, he smiled, having witnessed her inspection and obvious admiration of his cousin's wife.

Besim left the women, gave a slight bow to Jakup and sat with them as he was given permission. Gillian's eyes went again to the young bride.

The Nusé moved as soon as Besim sat, walking smoothly and evenly to Babush. She took his hand in hers, bowed her head and raised his hand to her chin, to her forehead, back to her chin. She released his hand, took one small step back and stood, head still bowed, before him.

"Welcome, Nusé, you are as fresh as a spring flower tonight." Color flooded her face at Babush's greeting. She moved to Arif.

Gillian watched closely as she took his hand. Arif smiled as the ritual was completed and she stood before him. "How are you tonight, Nusé?"

"Thank you, migje, well." He could hardly hear her, it was so softly said.

Hasan's smile was gently proud as his newest daughter approached him. He extended his hand. When she stepped back from him he said nothing but gave a small nod of approval.

She moved to Skender. Gillian leaned forward, her eyes watching every movement. He stopped talking immediately the Nusé came toward him, held out his hand to accept her greeting. *How natural it seems to him. If he were wearing the Kosov outfit that Babush sent to him you would never know he'd left … No!* Her eyes flew to his white hat for a moment. *I don't want him to be too much from here.*

As Skender spoke to the Nusé, she blushed furiously, then moved to Aslan. Slowly Gillian opened the dictionary, looked quickly at the paper Jakup had written for her, Aslan is her brother-in-law, the eldest son in their house, next in importance to Skender in the family. She watched closely, wondering if he would speak to her. He accepted her greeting with a smile and she moved on.

Panic clawed at Gillian for a moment as she saw the Nusé coming toward them. *Not me, surely, not me?* Jakup extended his hand and she sighed with relief! *Her husband!* Her eyes flew to Shamsi sitting next to her. *He must acknowledge her now.* Shock and disappointment fought together when she saw that he was not looking at his wife, appeared to be unaware that she was only a few feet from him.

It was Shamsi she continued to watch covertly under her lashes as the bride walked over to Nona. *Since she walked in the door he has ignored her. Why?* She glanced over at the women as the girl stepped back from Teza, exchanged a few words with her, then she moved to her mother-in-law. Gillian caught the small smile, the almost imperceptible nod of acknowledgment before she started the hand-kissing ceremony for her mother.

Gillian sighed, turned to Jakup as she picked up the dictionary. He took it from her and laid it on the rug between them. "Be ready, you will be next," he warned as he pointed to the Nusé and then to Gillian. She shook her head, he nodded, "Yes, Gillian."

"Skender?" He heard her panic, turned quickly. "Not me. Tell her to shake hands with me or something, but I don't want…."

"You must, Jill," his voice cut firmly in on her. "It will be very embarrassing for her, for me, for all of us, if you refuse." He glanced quickly toward the Nusé. "She is almost finished with her mother … be ready." He saw that she was about to argue. "Listen to me. I cannot get up and come there to you. If I stand, they must all stand and that will throw this girl into panic, she will not know what to do. Please, Jill? For me?" She nodded unhappily.

Jakup's hand gave her arm a reassuring squeeze as the Nusé approached her. "No, do not stand." The pressure was firm, telling her not to move. "Now, give her your hand." Her arm was given a slight push as the young girl stood in front of her.

Gillian bit at her tongue as nervous laughter threatened. She forced herself to be calm. The hands of both shook as they touched for the first time. Gillian licked nervously at her lips. "Skender, what is her name?"

Skender looked startled, turned to Aslan. "What's her name?"

He laughed softly. "You haven't changed, brother. You still cannot hold a name! It is Adile."

"Jill, it is Adile."

"Hello, Adile," Gillian said as the Nusé stepped back from her. She smiled as she saw the quick peak stolen at her under lowered lashes, too involved with the Nusé to realize that it was she the room watched. She smiled at Skender, gave a nervous laugh as the bride moved to Drita. "She is just as curious about me as I am about her."

"Of course." His smile was warm, meant for her. "You did very well."

"I felt embarrassed."

He remembered his own earlier reaction. "I know. But for us this is as natural as shaking hands. Thank you, my love." He nodded his thanks to Jakup for his help. Gillian looked again at Shamsi. His Nusé was almost touching him as she greeted Adnan and Besim and still he made no acknowledgement of her, completely ignored her. She watched, puzzled. "Skender, can I come there for a bit? I have to ask you something." He nodded. She stood up. As she did so, Drita, Nurije and Besim stood. She looked uncertainly at them, then at Skender. "Are they going somewhere?"

"No, you have stood up so they must."

"Oh, God!" She sat down quickly, her face flushing scarlet. The others sat, exchanging puzzled looks.

He laughed at her, "I thought you wished to come here?"

"No, you come to me." She didn't look at him.

"If I stand, the whole room must, except for the older ones." He smiled, "Well, are you coming or not?"

She grinned at him, glanced at the girls. "What will they do if I crawl over?"

His laugh brought the attention of the whole room to him. "I don't know, why don't you try?" He shook his head at her. "Get up, Jill, what difference if they stand or not?" She shook her head. He sat watching her with a smile, then turned to Drita and Nurije. "My Nusé wishes to come here, but will not for fear of disturbing you and Besim. Please, do not get up when she joins me." He beckoned to Gillian. "Come on, it's alright … I have told them to remain seated." He waited until she sat beside him. "Well, what is it you wish to…." He stopped as he saw his mother start to stand. Everyone in the room stood, except for the three older men, as the women rose to leave.

"We are going to Hasan's to visit with Aslan's Nusé and check the child," Nona said to Babush. He nodded. The Nusé opened the door and bowed as they left. Gillian noticed that everyone in the room waited until Skender had sat before they started to sit and settle themselves.

"Now, what is it you wish to ask me?"

Her eyes turned to the Nusé, standing near the group of young people. "Why didn't Shamsi speak to her? He ignored her completely. Doesn't he care anything for her?"

"I am sure he does, but he will not acknowledge her, or her him, while they are in the company of others."

"But this is all his family, Skender!"

"It makes no difference. He will pay no attention to her at all while someone else is present." He bent closer to her. "But if you watch carefully, I can almost guarantee he will steal a look at her when he thinks no one is watching."

"I don't know how he can help himself … she's gorgeous." She looked at him when there was no response. "Well, don't you think so?"

"No. She is a sweet girl, nice-looking, but no beauty. Now had you asked about my cousin…." His eyes went to Nurije. "She is a beauty, no doubt of that."

"Yes, she is … I thought that as soon as I saw her."

"Did you notice the Nusé's necklace?"

"How could I help it?" she asked with admiration.

"All our brides had them at one time, but now … this government stripped us to the bone. Sometimes there were two or three chains and the coins went all the way around, starting at the back of the neck with the smallest and getting larger toward the front, ending with one huge one at the center."

"They must have been magnificent."

He nodded. "They were … it is rare to see any today thought. Do you like her belt?"

Her eyes lingered on it. "Beautiful, such workmanship. It's silver, isn't it?"

"Yes. Some were made of gold." She gasped and he smiled at her. "I wish you could have seen, but I am happy that you had an opportunity to see how our brides look. I think they are quite beautiful. Do you?"

"They're stunning. Why doesn't she sit down?"

"It is our custom to have the youngest Nusé stand so that she is ready to serve if someone should wish something. Watch, now," he said quickly. "Arif wants something … " The Nusé moved over to him, bowed. "He has asked for a glass of water. Watch, now, how she serves him."

The Nusé came back into the room, carrying a glass of water on her right hand, the first three fingers extended to make a tray, the thumb supporting and balancing the glass. She walked smoothly to Arif, her eyes on the rug, stopped one pace from him, bowed from the waist, eyes still down and extended her hand with the water. He took it, she straightened, took one step back and waited. He finished, she stepped forward, held out her hand as a tray again. As the glass touched her fingers, she stepped back, bowed, took three more steps backward before she turned.

Gillian turned, wide-eyed, to Skender. "Is that how Babush expected me to serve him when he asked for water?" He nodded, she grinned wickedly, "What a shock he got!" He laughed softly and nodded agreement. She glanced over at her father-in-law. All three were concentrating on the chessboard. As Babush picked up one of the pieces, she asked, "Is he good at it?"

"Yes, but Hasan is better."

"Skender." She shook his arm, caught her breath as Shamsi turned and spoke to his wife. "He spoke to her."

"Yes, he has asked for water."

"When she brings it, he will speak to her," she said with satisfaction.

"No."

She turned her head up to him in surprise "He will thank her, at least."

"No." He smiled at her disappointment. She watched closely as the water was served. The Nusé stepped forward to receive the empty glass.

Gillian turned, eyes shining. "Did you see? Just for a moment, he deliberately let his fingers touch hers."

He nodded, smiling at her excitement. "Be careful, don't let anyone know you saw … they would both die of embarrassment."

She glanced over at Aslan watching the chess game. "Does he behave the same with his wife?"

"The same way … or tries to," he laughed. "But he steals a glance at her too often … he is in love with his wife, is very proud of her and his son."

"I'm glad … he seems so nice."

"He is. I am happy that it was he who took my place in the family."

"They've been married two years…" she said slowly, "and he still cannot speak to her?"

"Let us say he will not, rather than cannot … he is head of this family when I am not here … after the old ones, of course. He honors our customs and keeps them." He watched the concerned look on her face, laughed at her. "Yes, I am sure they all find both you and me very strange!" He stopped her reply as Adnan addressed Babush. "Adnan has asked permission, and it has been given, for the young people to listen to some music … do you wish to stay here with me or go with them?"

"Go with them."

He laughed.

"Do you mind?"

"Of course not, I expected that answer. Don't forget to give them the records you brought for them. Besim," he beckoned to him. "My nusé will come with you. If she needs me, fetch me." Besim bowed helped Gillian to her feet.

Jakup picked up the dictionary, winked at Shamsi who murmured, "At last!"

Adnan grinned. "You have to know who to ask, and when," he boasted softly. "Come, Nusé."

Hasan watched. "I knew he'd get her! He always manages to have his way."

Arif glanced up. "He is like his father. You were the spoiled child … still are," he added softly, with a wink at Babush.

Babush smiled back, turned to Skender. "Your Nusé has deserted you, Djali … why don't you and Aslan join the young people? You have had little time with them since you've been home."

Skender looked inquiringly at Aslan, who nodded. "For a while, then I must go. I have to be at work early tomorrow."

"I enjoy all of them, but…" Babush sighed as they closed the door, "I find them wearing. How do you cope, Hasan? They are always at your home."

Hasan shrugged. "I do not notice the noise and confusion … my house is always full of young people. For you, it is different … you are used to peace and quiet here."

"Hasan, your Nusé fascinated Skender's Nusé." Arif tossed some tobacco towards Hasan.

Hasan caught it, opened it and filled his pipe. "Brother, I understand she was in town today with Skender?" He turned and offered the tobacco to Babush.

"Yes," Babush said slowly, reaching for the tobacco. "But not to Police Headquarters."

Hasan stopped filling his pipe, looked quickly at him. "He has not taken her yet?" Babush shook his head. "They will come for her. You realize that?" Babush nodded, smoothing his moustache. "Why haven't you insisted that he take her then?"

"Because I do not want him to." He saw their startled looks. "When he went to register, himself, he told me everything was fine, routine. It seems that it was not, that he was quite upset when he left there."

"My son, Besim, was with him, said nothing," Hasan interjected quickly.

"He was told to hold his tongue. What Skender forgot was that Luan Mali would tell his father that he had seen him … naturally his father asked how Skender was…." He lifted his arms, shrugged. "My dearest friend would not keep something like that to himself." He sighed, looked from brother to brother. "I have known of this since he arrived here … it is a relief to have told you of it."

Arif sighed and pushed his hat to the back of his head. "If he takes her, and they are a little harsh with her…." He sighed again, rubbing at this chin.

"Exactly. You see how he is with her … a breath of air must not touch her." Babush put his head in his hand.

Hasan put his arm across his brother's shoulder, asked softly, "Would you ask less of him? It is our way to protect our greatest treasure … with our lives, if necessary. He has not forgotten … be proud of that."

"I am, but also worried."

"Let our sons take her!" Arif leaned forward. "Aslan, with Jakup or Emin."

"He would never permit it.

"Insist!" Arif banged the rug with his fist.

Babush looked long at him. "He has been out of my hands for seventeen years. I am amazed that he bows to my orders as he does. But when it comes to her…" he sighed and shook his head, "no, he would refuse. That would lead to a direct confrontation with him, and I will not knowingly bring that about."

They sat, staring into the fire, frowning. "It is easily solved." Arif looked from one to the other, smiled. "We will not let him know until it is accomplished! I will ask him to accompany me tomorrow morning to visit…." He shrugged, "We will think of someone. As soon as he leaves this house, Aslan and Jakup will pick her up and take her to Headquarters. She will register, come home." He lifted his hands, shrugged. "He comes home, and you tell him ... there is nothing he can do. He can rant and rave as much as he likes ... it has been done, finished."

Babush looked skeptical. "He will not like it. And if he returns before her?"

"How can he? How long will they keep her? Ten minutes? Fifteen? Half-an-hour at the outside."

Hasan nodded, "It is a good plan."

"What on Earth is that noise?" Arif looked up, startled.

"American music ... she brought some records for them," Hasan laughed.

"It sounds like wailing cats chasing a female in heat! ... I am glad it is your home they meet in, brother," Arif laughed, pointing toward the sound. "Learn to live with it! I donate all of the records to you ... none shall enter my house." He turned to Babush, asked him seriously, "Are we agreed, then? Tomorrow, at ten?"

Babush nodded. "Tomorrow, about ten. I will make sure he has gone from here."

"Natën e mirë, Babush." Skender closed the door, walked over and took the hairbrush from Gillian's hand.

"Feels good," she smiled up at him as he brushed her hair with strong, vigorous strokes.

He smiled back. "I am spoiling you! Did you enjoy yourself tonight?"

"Yes. The dictionary is a tremendous help."

He laughed softly. "My cousins would have managed without it. They were so anxious to have you with them. What were you talking about?"

"The Cuba situation, President Kennedy and how popular he is in the States, Marilyn Monroe...." She grinned at his raised eyebrows when she mentioned the last name. "Adnan and Besim were fans of hers. Besim says he is 'destitute' over her death." She sat quietly, smiling to herself. "They were all so nice ... even Emin was quite friendly tonight." Skender continued with the brushing of her hair. "Jakup is my favorite, then Aslan, I think. Ilyria is nice ... I bet she is a lot of fun."

"She is, she is always into some mischief."

"How odd. Her father is so strict..." she grinned. "And then there's always Emin."

He nodded, smiling. "Yes, but that happens sometimes."

She half-turned to look up at him. "Drita and Ilyria have some big secret going. Do you know what it is?"

"No. Nothing important, I'm sure. Listen, I have to go with Migje Arif tomorrow to visit one of his friends. I should be home before lunch. Can you occupy yourself?"

She nodded absently, thinking about the girls still. "Perhaps I'll go downtown."

"No. You will get lost."

"No, I won't. Once you hit the main square, you just…."

"No." He bent his head to look at her, deliberately gave the brush a small jerk. "Stop pouting." She grinned as she realized he'd seen her make a grimace, caught the brush as he dropped it into her lap. He threw himself on the mattress with a deep sigh, closed his eyes.

"Skender." He half-opened his eyes and looked lazily at her. She hesitated a moment. "What happened here, what danger is there for you?"

"Not now, Jill." She fiddled with the brush. "It is a long and unhappy story and now I am much too tired. Accept the fact that there was trouble, that we have to be careful while we are here and one day, when I am in the right mood, I will tell you everything. Agreed?" She gave a brief nod. "Remember this … when you are out of this house, don't complain of anything, don't mention the government, and always give way to anyone wearing western clothes."

"Because they will be Serbians, right?"

"Quite possibly. Some of our own wear western clothing, but we know them, or they are wearing our hats, or we can tell from their manner that they are Albanians. The Serbs are very arrogant, very sure of themselves, but you might not pick up on that, so always play safe and give way." He smiled as he saw her face. "That is hard for you, isn't it? You are so used to having your rights guaranteed … I am glad you are that way, that you have never had to step aside … promise me that you will do as I ask?"

She grinned at him, gave a scout salute. "I promise."

Chapter 22

Shamsi stood as Emin entered the kitchen. "Shamsi?" What are you doing here? My father said I was to meet Aslan." Emin signaled Shamsi to sit as he spoke.

Shamsi grinned, "My father told me I was to meet Jakup!"

Emin laughed, gave a deep bow, "We have both been promoted! Jakup had to work."

Shamsi nodded, "Aslan too. Do you want some tea?" Emin shook his head. "Then let us go to our uncle and get on with this, shall we?"

They slipped into some nalle, carrying their shoes in their hands as they climbed the stairs to the main house.

Emin glanced at Shamsi. "Skender is not going to like this."

"I know! If my Nusé were put into another's hands, I'd raise hell." Both kicked off their nalle, Shamsi held open the door for Emin, letting it close softly behind them. He hesitated. "She will be in the women's room, I suppose … shall we get her first or see Migje?"

"Him first." Emin led the way to the sitting room, knocked and entered. "Mirëmëngjes, Migje." He bowed to Babush, Shamsi following suit. "You asked for Aslan and Jakup at ten o'clock … they are both working. May we offer our services?" His eyes flicked quickly to Gillian on the opposite side of the fire.

"Mirëmëngjes, Emin, Shamsi. Thank you for coming. I accept your offer." Babush smiled as he saw the slight frown on Emin's face. "She is not sure when she is supposed to stand or for whom … I am certain it is not an intentional slight on either of you." Emin inclined his head, Babush stood up, beckoned to Gillian, "Come, Nusé."

She stood, hesitated, not sure if she was supposed to speak to the young man before they spoke to her or not, "Good morning, Emin, Shamsi."

"Speak Albanian, Nusé … Mirëmëngjes."

She smiled. "Yes, Emin, you are right. I'm sorry. Mirëmëngjes, Emin … Mirëmëngjes, Shamsi."

"Good." Emin turned from her to Babush as Shamsi gave her a brief nod. "As I understand, sir, you wish us to take her to Police Headquarters, then straight back here."

"Yes, that is correct."

"Does she know where she is going, Migje?" Shamsi asked.

"Not yet, Shamsi. You young people can explain to her, you have more success with talking to her than I. Let us get her coat." Babush led the way to the women's guest room. "Make sure she has whatever papers she needs. I will meet you downstairs and walk you to the gate."

Emin bowed as Babush left, turned to Gillian, pointed to her, then to himself and Shamsi. "You are coming with us." He waited to see if she had understood, received her quick nod, turned to Shamsi. "I hope to God she isn't frightened out of her wits when I tell her where we are going." He turned back to Gillian, picked up the dictionary from the window bench and looked up the word 'register'. He smiled encouragingly at her as he pointed to the word. "We are going to the police to register."

Gillian nodded. "OK, I'll get my coat." She went and took her coat from the cupboard.

Emin stared in amazement before turning to Shamsi. "Do you think she understood me?"

"No, but as she is prepared to come with us, I would be happy and leave things alone. There will be time enough for fear and nervousness when we get her there."

Emin nodded, put the dictionary down on the window bench and stood waiting quietly while Gillian put on her coat. "Nusé, do you have your passport?" She nodded as she put on her scarf.

"Make sure, Emin. We do not want to get all the way there and have to come back."

Gillian picked up her handbag. "I'm ready."

Emin pointed to her bag. "Show me your passport." Gillian took it out, showed it to him and started to return it to her bag. "Wait!' Frowningly he took it from her. "A British passport?" He glanced quickly, uncertainly at Shamsi before flicking to her picture and reading the pertinent information. "You are British?" he asked in amazement.

Gillian looked at him puzzled. "Yes."

He smiled as he handed her back the passport. "We thought you were American." She shook her head. "But you met and married Skender in America?" He took her hand, pointed to her ring.

"Yes." *I thought they knew all this … Skender wrote Babush….*

"That explains why she wouldn't tell us about American politics," Shamsi said quietly, "She probably doesn't know much about their system."

"Unfortunately, I missed all that … Jakup told me a little of it." Emin stood looking reflectively at Gillian as she put on her scarf and gloves. "What was she doing in America? How did Skender get together with her? Who arranged things for them?"

Shamsi shrugged as he shook his head. "We had better go, talk about that later. Migje wants us back as soon as possible." He looked Gillian over. "Scarf, gloves … does she use a hat?" Emin shook his head. "Good … she is ready, let's go."

Babush joined them at the foot of the stairs, walked them to his gate. "I want her back here sooner than Skender." He looked seriously at both young men. "She is in your hands, your care. Do not leave her, take your eyes from her for a second."

"Rest easy, Migje … no harm shall come to her, I swear."

Babush nodded as Emin finished speaking. "God be with you."

Shamsi took hold of Gillian's arm. "Which way, Emin?"

"River Road, it's quicker." Emin took her other arm. "Shamsi, when you took your Nusé to register, did it take long?"

"Twenty minutes." He grinned. "Eighteen waiting and two to register."

Emin laughed. "Good … I may be in time for class." The air was crisply cold, but the wind had dropped. "Are you cold, Nusé?" He shivered so she would understand.

Gillian smiled at him. "No, I'm fine."

The three-story building of grey stone loomed ahead of them, Shamsi watched Gillian carefully as they approached it. "When I brought my nusé and we were this close she was as a leaf in a gale … this one is not even trembling." He opened the door, exchanged a surprised look with Emin as Gillian walked in without any encouragement from them.

The stale, hot air closed around her like a blanket, she loosened her scarf as she looked around. A long counter ran along one wall, separating an open office area where three policemen were sitting at desks, filling in and pushing papers around. Another, his uniform straining uncomfortably across his belly, sauntered over to the counter as they walked in.

Shamsi pointed to a bench, the brown paint peeling and pitted. "Ulu, Nusé." Gillian sat down, suppressing a sigh at the dismalness of it all.

Emin and Shamsi approached the counter, Gillian watched, curious about the procedure and what 'registration' actually meant. Each handed over an identity card, they were casually checked and handed back. The policeman's eyes moved to her as Emin spoke to him.

Emin beckoned. "Nusé, come here." She stood up and joined them. "Passport." Emin took it from her, handed it to the policeman who sighed heavily. "Is something wrong?"

"This must be handled by an officer." He glared at Gillian. "She is the second foreigner to come here." Emin and Shamsi exchanged quick amused looks as he walked away, Emin took Gillian's arm and pointed towards the bench.

"It is unbearably hot in here," Emin said, taking off his coat. "Nusé?" He invited her to take off her coat before sitting down. Gillian nodded gratefully, folded her coat and placed it beside her on the bench.

"This is going to take longer than twenty minutes, I fear," Shamsi sighed as he sat down. Emin yawned as he started to sit down, stopped as the policeman opened a door on the far side of the open office space and walked towards the counter.

He signaled them to stay where they were. "Wait there … she will have to be questioned."

Shamsi and Gillian watched as Emin walked to the counter. "What is there to question her? She is here with her husband to visit his family … that is all." The policeman shrugged. "How long will we have to wait?"

He pointed his thumb towards a closed door at the back of the office. "When he's ready you will be seen, not before." He jerked his head towards the bench. "Sit down or out."

Emin raised his eyes to the ceiling in frustration as he walked back to the others, both grinned at him and he grinned back. He sat down next to Shamsi, looked at Gillian. "I can't fathom her … she walked in here without a blink of an eyelid, and yet when that cow came near her she almost wet her pants."

"Emin! Such language!" Shamsi laughed, not sure whether he was shocked or amused.

Emin grinned at him. "Well! It's true!" He leaned forward, resting his elbows on his knees as he watched Gillian, she sat quietly, looking at the action behind the counter. Emin turned to Shamsi, talking softly. "It doesn't make sense … she's out of balance somewhere … she's not at all nervous. I expected hysteria when she realized where we were coming … nothing, not a peep out of her. On the other hand…" he laughed silently, covering his mouth with his hand, "I have never seen anyone so terrified of a domesticated animal! You'd have thought it was a lion at least!" He smothered a sudden burst of laughter, wiped at his eyes. "And then, when the damn thing stretched its neck towards her and mooed…." He shook silently, "I wondered if I'd ever catch her!"

"So did I!" Shamsi grinned, shook his head as he recollected the scene at the river, Gillian racing away with Emin in hot pursuit. He turned casually toward the counter, stiffened immediately, gritting his teeth. Emin sobered as he saw his cousin's anger, turned, too, to see what had upset him. The policeman's eyes were on Gillian, a slight smirk on his face as he let his eyes travel over her, finally resting on her knees, carefully he adjusted his sitting position, eyes never leaving her. Shamsi's hands clenched. "I'd like to beat hell out of him," he muttered angrily.

"Steady." Emin laid his hand on Shamsi's arm. "We can do nothing." Angrily they watched him watching her.

Gillian sighed, stretched a little, her eyes happening to move forward to the policeman at the counter, her face colored slightly, she picked up her coat and dropped it casually across her knees and legs, looked steadily back at the policeman as he leered at her before returning to his papers.

Shamsi turned towards Gillian, wondering why the man had lost interest so suddenly, sat back and relaxed when he saw her coat covering her, he moved his arm slightly to attract Emin's attention.

Emin nodded, almost smiled. "Good … let the bastard look at his own girls," he murmured.

A buzzer called. The policeman lifted a section of the counter. "Get up … he is ready." They all stood as he came towards them. "Come with me." He moved to take hold of Gillian's arm.

"Do not touch her … she is ours." Emin pulled Gillian firmly away, putting himself between her and the policeman.

He gave a derisive snort. "She's not from here … you have only to look at her to see that."

"Do not be deceived by her dress … I tell you she is ours." Emin put his arm firmly across Gillian.

He laughed sarcastically. "She's not like your girls … she's had a man's hand on her … arm … before today." He smirked, pleased at his deliberate hesitation.

Shamsi swore softly, stepped forward, but with a movement of his hand Emin stopped him. "She carries our name … is ours as surely as if she were born here." Steadily he watched the policeman, he gave a final warning as the policeman again started to move his hand towards Gillian. "She is married to my brother … you know our rules." The policeman hesitated, glanced at Shamsi standing silently ready, the buzzer called, insistently.

"Bring her." He turned abruptly.

Emin let out a long sigh of relief as he took Gillian's arm, Shamsi took the other, gave a wry grin to Emin. "Close," he whispered. Emin nodded; they followed the policeman down the corridor.

Gillian tried not to breathe the foul air, fought the sick churning of her stomach and her fear of small places.

'Be calm,' the voice of the man at the Embassy came to her, 'Answer their questions, but volunteer no additional information. Above all, don't argue with them'.

She caught Emin watching her, made herself smile at him. She deliberately recalled her passport number, somehow feeling more secure in its knowledge.

The straining uniform stopped, a door was thrown open and he waved them inside.

An officer half-sat, half-lay in a swivel chair behind a desk in the center of the room. Hardly an inch of space showed through the mound of papers covering the desk, there was one chair opposite him, and another placed against the right-hand wall beside a large filing cabinet. Another door was on the left, Gillian glanced at it, assuming correctly that it opened into the large open office space near the entry hall. The officer rocked lazily back and forth as they entered, he waited until the door closed and the policeman had walked over to stand slightly behind him. He looked directly at Gillian. "Are you the one with the British passport?"

"She is."

His eyes went lazily to Emin. "Let her speak for herself."

"She has no Serbo-Croat." The squeaky rocking went on as he watched Emin, he leaned forward, picked up the passport, slowly opened it, turning the pages unhurriedly. He studied the photograph, looked at Gillian, then back at the photograph. He leaned back in his chair, gave a half- wave at the chair opposite him. "Sit down."

Gillian forced herself to sit all the way back, to appear comfortable and relaxed. "Thank you." She felt someone watching her, looked up and met the fat one's eyes, very deliberately he let his eyes move to her legs before looking back at her with an oily smile. Carefully, she laid the coat across her legs.

The officer pointed for Shamsi to sit on the chair by the cabinet, pulled a long form towards him and studied it. He sighed, looked up at Emin. "There are a lot of questions. I will ask you, then you can ask her. Make sure you tell me her answer exactly."

"Impossible, Comrade."

Gillian's eyes flashed to Emin. *That's the first time I've ever heard anyone use that word … how strange, to hear it from him….*

'Why?"

Emin shrugged. "We are forbidden to use our language, is that not so?"

The officer half stood, leaned across the desk towards him. "Do not play games with me … you will find I have the better hand." Slowly he sat down, never taking his eyes from Emin. "Now, her name."

"Berisha."

Gillian's eyes flashed again to Emin.

"Spell it."

Emin spelled out the name.

"Go on." Emin looked helplessly at Shamsi, Shamsi shook his head to let him know he couldn't help. The officer looked up, pen suspended over the form, "Go on."

"I'm sorry, I do not know … it must be on the passport."

"Yes, I am sure it is, but I want it from her. Ask her." He moved the form into a more convenient position, waiting, slowly he raised his head, as there was no response. Gillian stretched as much as she could, trying to see over the mound of papers between her and the form. "Ask her."

Nervously she licked at her lips, tasting salt, as she heard the threatening tone.

"She has no Albanian, Comrade."

That word again! She looked up at Emin.

"You are lying." He was standing, hands on hips, as he accused Emin, slowly, he walked round to stand opposite him, leaned towards him, repeated softly, "You are lying."

Oh, God what is happening?

'No, she has only her own language."

Shamsi stood. "Pardon me, but what is there to question her? She is here for a week … two at the most … has joined her husband to visit his family … that is all."

The officer looked over at him, a long steady look, his nicotine-stained fingers tapped the form behind him. "This must be filled in, all of it." He walked back to the other side of his desk, stood frowning at the form. "I will be back in a moment." He called to the policeman as he left the room by the side door.

Shamsi shook his head in disgust. "When I brought my Nusé here she handed her card in and it was over in minutes. I didn't expect all this."

"No talking." The policeman took a pace forward, feeling his importance. "So, she is British, eh?" Gillian glanced quickly at him as she heard the word. He leaned forward; stomach supported by the desk. "How did she get involved with your people? What happened?" He smiled knowingly. "You always marry your own … outsiders aren't good enough for you. At least, not to marry."

He laughed nastily as he saw Shamsi's anger. "Well…?" He let his eyes slide slowly over Gillian. "It is easy to see why he was interested … she has good legs, too … pity she covered them."

Emin grabbed Shamsi as he lunged at the policeman. "Be still," his voice softly angry. "He is deliberately baiting us … she cannot understand so there is no harm done."

"Speak Serbo-Croatian!" The command came loudly.

Gillian stood, nervously wondering what was wrong. Emin let go of Shamsi as he felt him relax, turned quickly to Gillian. "Ulu, Nusé, ulu", he motioned for her to sit.

The policeman laughed shortly, "You should have let him try it … I would have enjoyed making sport with him downstairs." He turned with a sneer toward Shamsi." You'd have paid dearly for it."

The door opened. "Hurry," the officer yelled over his shoulder, he stopped, looked from Shamsi to his subordinate, asked suspiciously, "What's the problem here?"

"Nothing, Comrade." The policeman returned to his previous position.

Shamsi shook his head as the officer's eyes moved to him, stepped back and leaned against the filing cabinet. The officer's eyes moved from the policeman to Shamsi, then to Emin. Emin looked steadily back at him. "I have sent for someone who can speak her language. You two may leave … I will give her an escort home when I am finished with her."

"With your permission we will wait," Emin replied firmly. The officer shrugged, pointed to the chair near the filing cabinet. "Thank you."

Gillian watched uneasily as Emin sat down. *What is going on? There was almost trouble just then. Why are they keeping us here? At the Embassy they told me it was routine, should only take about ten minutes. So hot….* She could feel the beads of dampness on her forehead as she licked at her salty lips. *If I could just take this heavy coat off me, get some water … feel so thirsty….* The hot color flooded her face as she glanced up and found his eyes on her again. *If only he would stop staring at me….* Her color deepened as he deliberately let her know his thoughts. She turned her head quickly, fixed her eyes on the barred window, studying the building opposite, willing herself to stop shaking. She glanced at Emin as she saw him bend to speak to Shamsi, he gave her a quick smile of encouragement and she forced a smile back, suppressing a shudder as the policeman sucked at his teeth.

Cigarette smoke drifted past her nostrils, she edged to the side, letting her eyes roam the desk. *What a mess … how can he find anything…?* Her eyes riveted. She eased herself into a better viewing position. *My telegram. It must be … the ink blob is exactly….* She leaned forward a little, trying to see, the officer glanced up, eyes sharply suspicious. Gillian forced a smile, wriggled around a little and leaned back in the chair, he watched her carefully before returning again to his papers. She closed her eyes, sighed with relief, slowly she opened her eyes, let them return to the telegram. *Why would he have my telegram?* She swallowed nervously, trying to ease her dry throat as she sat watching him. The officer's hat moved up and down as he looked from one paper to another, the top of his hat stared back at her, the one large grease spot irregular, spreading … *so hot, so stuffy, no air … like the ink blob, irregular, no shape.* She stared at the hat. *His hat, my ink blob….* the grease spot got closer … closer … larger … larger, started to recede, drifting away from her, getting smaller….

She gripped the arm of her chair, letting the wood eat into her hands. "Emin." She fought against the swimmy feeling, frantically searching her mind for the word she needed.

He stood. "Nusé?" He watched her worriedly.

She licked at her lips, swallowed, "Uje, please."

Slowly the officer raised his head, fixed his eyes on Emin. "You said she had no Albanian."

Emin dragged his eyes from Gillian. "Half a dozen words, that is all. She wants some water."

Permission came after a quick glance at Gillian's pale face. "Get it."

Shamsi gave a brief nod to Emin to let him know he would go, handed Gillian his handkerchief on the way out.

"Do you think we shall be here much longer, Comrade?" Emin asked with concern as he saw Gillian wipe her forehead.

"I have already told you to leave … I will send her home."

"No … thank you, but I will stay."

"Then sit down and stay silent. Or I'll put you out." Emin sat down, glanced often at Gillian as the officer continued with his work.

The tap on the door was sharp before it opened to admit a man about sixty. The officer glanced up, dismissed the policeman with him and the door closed. Nervously the man looked around. "You speak English?"

He twisted his hat in his hands. "I did at one time, sir … I mean Comrade," he corrected himself hastily as he saw the glare, smoothed his thin grey hair. "But it has been many years and I doubt…."

"If you spoke it once you can still speak it. I want to question this woman … you will translate."

"I doubt that I have the ability … it has been many years since I used…." He stopped as the officer slowly but noisily tapped his pen against the edge of his desk. "I will do my best." He turned to Gillian, speaking in heavy broken English, "My name is Boro Petrovich. I here translate very good to you."

She took a long steadying breath, held out her hand. "How do you do. My name is Gillian Berisha." She forced a smile, feeling sorry for the nervous man in the rusty black suit.

Warmed by her, he smiled back, held out his hand. "How do you do."

"What did she say?" Dragonovich's chair squeaked forward.

"It was nothing."

He pushed back his chair, walked round his desk, leaning close to Petrovich and repeated softly and slowly, "I … asked … you … what … she … said."

Nervously he passed his hat from one hand to the other. "She said 'how do you do'."

"How do you do?" he asked, puzzled.

"Yes."

Dragonovich looked quickly at Gillian, demanded suspiciously, "How do you do what?"

"Nothing, Comrade. It is their form of greeting … it means hello, nothing more."

Emin put his head down to hide his grin.

The officer glared at Petrovich, pulled the form towards him as he returned to his seat. "Now tell her to spell her first name … we already have the last." His fingers drummed noisily, impatiently, on the desk as Shamsi came back with the water and handed it to Gillian. She took it gratefully, taking a long drink, it was insipidly warm, but helped. "May we proceed?" Dragonovich asked sarcastically. "Tell her to spell her name."

"Permanent address?"

"Address in this area?"

"Names and addresses of all relatives in this area?"

Emin stood, before the translator could speak. "May I help? She does not know." He received a brief nod, listed the names and addresses of all the Berishas.

"Names and addresses of all relatives in this country?"

Emin stood again. "There are dozens of us … you already know that. You will need two more forms at least to take all that information. The closest, blood brothers, are here in Prishtine…."

"Pristina."

Emin inclined his head. "Pristina," he repeated the hated Serbian name. "Do you really wish me to list all of us?" He paused, slowly asked, "Or can we say she does not know?"

The pen scratched the paper. "Sit down. Father's name?"

"Mother's maiden name?"

"Place of birth?"

Gillian sighed as she answered.

"Date of birth?"

"Husband's full name?"

"Husband's date of birth?"

"You know all this!" The exclamation came angrily from Shamsi.

The officer glared at him, repeated, "Husband's date of birth?" He looked directly at Emin as he asked and answered the next question himself.

"Place of birth? Pristina. Now, where married?" He questioned her answer. "California?"

Petrovich nodded.

The officer glanced at the British passport, looked at Gillian, shrugged and wrote 'California.' How long married?"

"Two years." He repeated. "How many children?" He looked up, surprised. "None?" His eyes turned to Emin as his lips parted in a wide smile, he raised his eyebrows, said softly, directly to Emin, "No children?" He turned back to the form, writing, saying as if to himself but loud enough for all to hear, "Two years … two. And no children."

The policeman stepped forward, bent and whispered into his officer's ear, his eyes on Gillian, the officer laughed, glanced quickly at Gillian, nodded, and laughed again.

Emin gripped Shamsi's arm. "Hold your temper … it is of no consequence. She does not understand … by not understanding, they do not insult her. Their intention is to bait us … do not rise to them."

"No talking. If you speak, use Serbo-Croatian. Now…" the officer turned over the form. "ask her if she was ever arrested."

Petrovich's face blanched, he shook his head in panic. "I do not have the ability…."

Shamsi stepped forward. "Of course she has never been arrested. Is this necessary? She is here for a visit, that is all. She will be gone in a week, two at the most."

The nicotine finger tapped the form. "The instructions are quite clear … all foreigners to this area must be interrogated."

"Her husband did not fill out all this."

The officer's eyes remained coldly fixed on Shamsi, his mouth smiled and his voice came softly. "Of course not … we already have a file on him. All we had to do was bring it up to date." The smile vanished. "And he is not a foreigner. He is ours … born here." There was a long silence, before he asked, "Now, may we proceed?" Shamsi turned away, lips tight together. "Ask her if she was ever arrested."

Nervously Petrovich turned to Gillian. "I am sorry, madam I do not have the words, but he wish to know did a policeman ever held you tight?"

Laughter burst from her, she shook her head, "No." Unless you're talking about one of the bobbies at the local dance!

The officer stared at her, puzzled. "If not in her country, any other?" Petrovich hesitated. "Ask her then, fool."

"Madam, please, perhaps in different land you had policeman hold you tight?"

Helplessly Gillian shook her head.

"Why is she laughing?"

"I do not know, comrade, but her answer is 'no'."

The officer watched her, turned to Emin and demanded, "Why is she laughing?" Emin shrugged, shook his head, as puzzled as the officer. He held the pen over the form, watching her as she wiped her eyes, he looked at the form, dipped the pen in the ink, muttered angrily, "Stupid foreigners." His pen scratched the answer.

"Has she ever been a member of any political organization?"

Emin sighed, raised his eyes to the ceiling as the old man translated.

"Yes."

Shocked disbelief brought Emin to his feet; he sat as he saw the officer glare at him.

"Did she say yes?" Petrovich nodded confirmation. "Which party? When? Where?"

Petrovich licked nervously at his lips. "Where, madam?"

"England."

"Her own country, England, comrade."

"Damn you! Which party? Which party?" He banged his fist angrily on the desk.

"Madam, the name please of political party you belong to one day?"

Gillian glanced nervously at the angry officer, then at Emin sitting on the edge of his chair, spoke quicker than she should, "Labor party. Actually, the section I was with was for the young people and was called the Labor League of Youth … it was as much a social club as a political…." She saw Petrovich's confusion, stopped and was about to start again but was interrupted.

"Old fool, what did she say?" The papers jumped as his hand banged the desk. "Stay where you are or I'll put you out." The order was snapped at Emin as he started to move towards Gillian.

Petrovich turned to Gillian. "Madam, please…."

"Which party, old man?" The tone was enough for Petrovich to know he had better answer immediately.

"A youth group. For workers. Laborers. Workers' Youth Party." He answered quickly, wanting to placate the officer.

He frowned. "Workers' Party?" Petrovich hesitated. "Damn you, are you sure she said Workers" Party?" He was half-way to his feet, leaning across the desk. Emin, too, was on his feet staring at the old man.

"Yes … I am sure." He looked nervously from the officer to the two young men, back to Gillian. "She said Workers' Party for Youth."

Emin sat down heavily, staring at the floor, slowly he turned to Shamsi.

The officer laughed triumphantly as he looked at them. "Workers' Party! Workers' Party! You know what that is! You have been told how we cannot use our proper title in other countries where there is no freedom for the masses." He laughed heartily as he saw the stunned look on Emin's face. "Congratulations! At last your family shows some sense. Perhaps now that you have of ours in your midst you, too, will join our party." He pulled the form towards him wrote Communist Party in the appropriate space. His smile was friendly as he looked up at Gillian, saw her wiping her damp forehead and pushed the glass towards her. "Have some water." He waited until she put the glass down. "Ask her how many years she has been a member."

Petrovich had no trouble with those words. "How many years for a member, madam?"

"Let me think … I joined when I was nearly seventeen … two years, perhaps two and a half."

The officer smiled, nodded as he wrote the answer. "Was she ever active in…?" He stopped as the side door opened, came immediately to attention as did the policeman. Gillian looked over, curious to see who had caused the sudden smartness.

He was quite tall, his dark brown hair neatly combed, and was impeccably dressed in a grey business suit, his snowy shirt cuffs, fastened with oval gold cuff links, extended below his jacket the exact amount dictated by current fashion. His tie was a dark burgundy red, absolutely plain, except for a gold pin showing flames enclosed by laurel leaves reaching for a star.

"Who are all these people? What are they doing here?" His voice was controlled, quiet, his manner sure and unflurried.

"Comrade, we are interrogating this woman. She is a foreigner visiting this area."

He held out his hand for the form as he glanced at Emin and Shamsi. "Who are they?" he asked as he let his eyes run down the form.

"Relatives, Comrade."

"And the other one?" He turned the form over to study the opposite side.

"He is here to translate. She has no Serbo-Croatian."

"Get rid of him." The policeman saluted, hurried the man out. Gillian sighed with relief as the fat one left. "Neither of you are her husband then?" He glanced up at Emin and Shamsi.

Emin stood up. "No, Comrade."

He glanced again at the form, saw the mark indicating that they had a file on her husband. He looked up at Emin. "Why didn't her husband bring her himself?"

Emin hesitated, "He was … busy."

"Yes," he smiled, his voice softly sarcastic. "I am sure he was." He went back to studying the form, held out his hand for her passport. The officer picked it up quickly and handed it to him.

Gillian eased the heavy coat from her legs, not feeling the need now that the leering eyes were gone. She watched as the man flicked through her passport.

Carefully he checked the information on the passport against the form, place of birth, where issued, married name, turned to the photograph, glanced briefly at Gillian and then back to the photograph before flicking the pages, stopped, suddenly, as he saw the large rubber stamp mark. He studied it briefly but thoroughly, gave Gillian a piercing look, then walked to the far corner of the room, beckoning the officer to follow.

"I hope you were careful with her," he said quietly so that no other could hear. "Did you see this?" He showed him the page. "Her Embassy has requested full assistance from us on her behalf." He tapped the passport against his hand as he studied Gillian. "Why?" he murmured. "Who is she? What importance does she have to them?" He turned to the officer. "Did you give her cause to … er … complain at all of her treatment?"

"No, Comrade."

His eyes turned full on the officer. "Are you sure?

"Yes, Comrade. It was routine questioning. She had to wait for a short time for me, and then she had to wait for the translator…" he knew he was talking too fast, too much, but couldn't stop, "…but I let her sit down, I gave her water when she asked and I let her relatives stay…."

"Alright, alright," he was stopped impatiently.

"Comrade, excuse me … did you see? She is one of us." He turned the form over, pointed to the appropriate box.

"Impossible. This family would never have accepted her."

"It is true. From her own lips." He leaned closer. "I don't think they knew … they were shocked when she told me." Their eyes moved to Emin and Shamsi as he spoke.

"Good … let us use that to our advantage." He walked back to the desk, pushed the papers away and sat on the edge. "Good morning, Mrs. Berisha … I see that you are from England, London. Which part?"

She stared at him in amazement, there was barely a trace of accent. "South. Do you know London?"

He smiled, "Yes, it is one of my favorite cities. I studied there for two years." His smile was warmly friendly as he held out his hand. "How do you do. My name is Stefan Mihajlovich."

"What the hell is he talking to her about?" Shamsi whispered.

Emin worriedly shook his head. "I don't know … he's a Party man, must be. Listen, try to catch something…."

"How do you do. Mine is Gillian Berisha." She smiled up at him as she held out her hand, "But you already know that." Her eyes went quickly, briefly, to her passport.

He smiled down at her. "Yes. Do you call yourself Jill?" She hesitated, only a moment, then shook her head.

Emin leaned close to Shamsi, whispered, "He used the name Skender uses for her."

Mihajlovich laughed softly, "I think you mean 'yes', but to be used only by special friends, is that not so?" She bit her lip, feeling a little embarrassed at her rudeness. He smiled. "Does Big Ben still keep good time?"

"Yes, and Bow Bells still chime." She smiled up at him, grateful for his understanding.

He glanced at his watch. "If we were in London now I would invite you for morning coffee. Would you accept?"

"Yes, why not?" She grinned. "I think I'd go anywhere to get away…." She stopped, horrified at her own stupidity, dropped her eyes to her lap, mumbled, "I'm sorry, I shouldn't have said…."

"I agree!" he laughed softly. "It is most depressing in here and far too hot." He glanced down at the form. "When were you last in London, Mrs. Berisha?"

"She made a mistake, said something she shouldn't," Emin whispered to Shamsi.

The officer glared at them, signaled for them to be silent.

"I came from there just a few days ago."

"So you have not had an opportunity to see any of my country?"

"Only Belgrade and Prishtine." The cousins eyes met.

Mihajlovich's eyes narrowed, "Pristina." He repeated it again, as she glanced up at him in surprise. "The correct pronunciation is 'Pristina.' Did you like Belgrade?"

Shamsi looked at Emin, sighed angrily, but did not speak when he saw he was being watched.

"Oh, yes … it is a lovely city, so clean and such exciting shops … I want to go back and spend a few days before we leave."

Casually he marked the form as he answered her, "I am glad … Belgrade is my home and it pleases me that you enjoyed it." He glanced at the two young men, noted with satisfaction their anger and discomfort. "Do not judge the rest of my country by this area … we have many beautiful parts. The mountains are my favorite, I enjoy winter sports. And you?"

"No, I prefer the coast … swimming, laying around in the sun."

"Perhaps your husband will take you to our coast … it is very lovely. Maybe he has offered already?"

"He did say we might visit … I'm sorry … I can't remember the name, but it can't be the coast." She continued as she saw his questioning look. "He mentioned a mountain and a river."

He nodded, smiling easily, glanced at the form. "I see you are interested in politics."

A warning bell sounded for her. She hesitated a moment. "Yes, at one time … not any more."

He caught the hesitation immediately, determined to put her at her ease again, he laughed, "Yes, I know what you mean … other, more interesting, things come along sometimes. What was it for you? A young man perhaps?" he teased gently. She shook her head, smiling back at him. "Which party did you belong to?"

You already know that … why question me again? "Isn't it there? Your policeman here has already questioned me about it."

He dropped the form uninterestedly onto the table as he heard the suspicion in her voice. "I suppose so. I was just curious. When I lived in London I discovered that the English political groups had many social functions…" he smiled down at her, "…at very reasonable prices! It was my greatest discovery … I could always count on being able to enjoy myself with friendly people and not have to spend all of my pitiful student allowance."

She grinned back at him, "I know how that is. When I was seventeen I joined the Labor League of Youth. I like to think it was because I wanted to help put the world to rights, but…" she laughed, shrugged, "…the fringe benefits were also a great attraction." She saw Emin glaring angrily at her. "I had better go." She glanced at the form on the desk. "Have I finished answering all those questions?"

He handed her passport to her, picked up the form. "No, but I will initial the rest and then you will not be troubled further."

"Why, thank you."

"Not at all. Let me walk you to the door." He picked up her coat, pulled the chair out of her way. "Mrs. Berisha?" His hand offered her the right of way, as the officer hurried to open the door for them, he glanced amusedly at the two angry young men following them, beckoned to the officer to come behind them. "What a pity we could not take coffee together," he said as he helped her on with her coat at the entry hall. "We could have had a pleasant half hour reminiscing of London, and then I would have driven you home, but…" he sighed heavily as he glanced at Emin and Shamsi standing near the door, their eyes watching his every move, "I am afraid they would object … they are a hundred years behind the times and still uncivilized."

"They are not! They have been very kind to me," she retorted hotly.

"I'm sorry. I am sure they have." He smiled. "But their customs are … shall we say, a trifle 'quaint'?" He reached into the small card pocket of his jacket. "Let me give you my card, Mrs. Berisha. Please feel free to call on me if you need any assistance … or perhaps just a friendly ear?" He smiled warmly as he handed her the card.

"Thank you." Gillian glanced at it, put it into her bag, she held out her hand. "Good-bye."

"Good-bye." Deliberately he raised her hand to his lips as he saw how closely they watched. Gillian flushed, a little embarrassed. She gave him a quick smile, turned and walked towards Emin and Shamsi.

Mihajlovich moved to the window when they'd left, his eyes coolly, calculatingly, watching as they crossed the street. He turned dropped the form onto the counter and took a slim gold pen from his pocket, he glanced up at the officer standing beside him and with a single stroke deleted "Communist Party" as he coldly said, "She is not with us." He initialed the deletion, printed "Labor Party" underneath it.

"But, she said…."

"A mistake. Be more careful with your translator in future." He moved to the window again, watching them as he returned his pen to his inside pocket. "They plan to visit Belgrade before they leave, there was one other city … my guess would be Prizren from her description. Keep me informed of their whereabouts."

"Yes, Comrade."

Slowly he picked up his coat from the counter. "Pull her husband's file, have it on my desk within the hour."

"Immediately, Comrade." The officer came smartly to attention as Mihajlovich passed him.

As his fingers touched the door, he turned. "And make a file on her … send that to me, too. Good day."

"Good day, Colonel Mihajlovich."

Shamsi held the door open, allowing Gillian and Emin to precede him to the street. "Emin, we have to talk." His voice was coldly angry as he glared at Gillian.

"Not now, Shamsi … let us get out of sight and hearing of this place. You can be certain that we are being watched." He took hold of Gillian's arm, glanced over his shoulder at Shamsi. "Keep abreast of us."

"How can you bear to touch her, be near her even, after what we have just heard?" Emin didn't answer, continued to walk at a steady but brisk pace. Gillian drank in the crisp coldness of the air, gratefully felt it drying the dampness of her forehead, the fast-walking pace did not bother her. She too wished to be far away from the depressing building.

They turned the corner out of sight of Police Headquarters onto the Main Square. Gillian glanced up at the tall granite obelisk in the center of the square.

"Yes, Nusé, look at it," Shamsi gave her an angry push towards the monument. Emin caught her, jerked her back on her feet as she almost tripped. "It was given to us by your friends," he laughed bitterly, "Given is the wrong word … they robbed and plundered enough to provide a dozen of these monstrosities." He grabbed her arm, pulled her around to face him, putting his face close to hers. "Well, do you like it, the gift from our 'liberators'? They freed us from the Fascist regime only to impose one just as harsh.

Angrily Gillian pulled free of him. "Don't yell at me … I don't know what has upset you but I assume because I was talking to whatever his name is." He caught again at her arm, furiously she put both hands against his chest and pushed, hard, away from him.

"You dare to raise your hand against me?" Shamsi angrily took hold of her shoulders, shook her, almost lifting her from the ground.

"Stop it! Enough!" Emin pried them apart, pushing Shamsi away from her. "Have you forgotten where we are, who she is?" He looked carefully around, Gillian tried to pull away from his detaining hold.

"I haven't forgotten what she is … I would prefer to forget who she is."

Emin's grip tightened as Gillian tried again to pull free. He turned to her, looked her straight in the eyes. "Be still." His voice was firm, calm and quieted her. She took a deep steadying breath, smoothed her hair, nodded and he loosed his grip on her. She walked slowly to the low wall surrounding the monument and sat down, tidying her hair and scarf. Emin turned back to Shamsi as soon as he saw that she was calm. "Have you lost all sense? How dare you lay hands on her, especially in a public place?" He sighed. "Come, let us get her home.

"No, not me, you take her if you wish, but I want nothing to do with her."

"I said we will take her home," Emin said, coldly angry.

"No. Not me."

"Yes. I gave my word and you, by implication, gave yours."

"That was before we…."

"Nothing changes that fact, nothing. Once your word is given, it's given and binding. Besides…" he took a deep breath as he smoothed his moustache, "she is Skender's wife, Migje's daughter, our duty is clear. She must be delivered to them unharmed."

Shamsi's voice was disgusted. "Skender's wife! How could he permit himself to become involved with…?" He gestured with distaste towards Gillian.

"He does not know, can have no idea … he would never have become involved with her if he had, not after all they put him through." He turned worriedly to Shamsi. "That man is someone important … confidence and authority oozed from him."

"Do you think you were right, that he is a Party man?"

"He must be, that officer was too anxious to please…" he glared at Gillian, still sitting on the wall. "and she and he sat chatting like old friends."

Shamsi laughed shortly, "Why not? She is a friend of theirs. I wonder what she told him? Skender must be told that she is a Communist, Emin."

"Must he? Do you want to be the one to carry that to him?"

Shamsi frowningly studied the ground, then looked at Emin. "No, but it is dangerous to leave him without that knowledge." His eyes went to Gillian, just for a moment he softened. "He'll beat hell out of her," he whispered.

Emin nodded grimly. "Good. I'd like to beat hell out of her myself right now." His fists clenched. "I'd like to wring her neck like a chicken." He sighed, "Skender's going to be deeply hurt, there have been too many wounds in his life for him to accept this last one. Come, we had better get her home. You and I must talk later, come to some decision, but our duty now is to deliver her safely to Migje."

His face was grim as they both started to walk towards Gillian. "Life plays cruel and strange tricks, brother … did you ever dream you would offer your protection to one of them? Would take hold of one and lead them into the bosom of your family?" He bent down, took hold of Gillian's arm. "Come."

Chapter 23

"Migje, she is here." Babush smiled up at Emin as he bowed, he nodded at Gillian standing beside him. "With your permission I will leave immediately … I am late for class."

"Thank you, Emin. There was no trouble? She is safely registered?"

"Yes, Migje."

"You were gone a long time."

"We had to wait for an interpreter. I hope you were not worried, sir?"

Babush smilingly shook his head, "Not unnecessarily. How could I worry knowing she was in your hands, Djali? Where is Shamsi?"

Emin gave a brief bow. "Thank you, Migje. Shamsi came as far as your gate … he asked your indulgence. He had business…."

"As you have. And I am keeping you. Go. And thank you for your assistance." Emin bowed to Babush, gave a brief cool nod to Gillian and left. "Ulu, Nusé." Babush patted the rug beside him.

Gillian shook her head. "Thank you, Babush, but no. May I go, please?" She pointed towards the bathroom. "I want to wash and clean up."

Babush nodded as he smiled at her. "Headquarters affected you the same way it does us, daughter. You cannot wait to wash the feel of it from your skin. Go." He waved her on her way, watched until the door closed on her. *Thank God she is back safely.* He pulled a pillow near to the fire and laid down. *Arif's plan worked, Skender is still not home.*

"Guess who?" Skender's hands covered her eyes. Gillian jumped violently. He looked at her surprised. "I'm sorry, I did not mean to frighten you." He turned her to him, smiled down at her. "Put your coat on and we will take a short walk, it will do you good, put some color in your cheeks."

"No." She shook her head.

"Why not? It is not too cold … the wind has dropped today."

"I know. I've just got home, about fifteen minutes ago. I don't want to go out again. Did you have a good time?"

He sat down near her. "Just got home? From where?"

"Police Headquarters." She pulled back as he grabbed her shoulders. "What's the matter?"

He gave her a quick shake, demanded angrily, "Who took you?"

Her eyes filled. "Don't. Don't shake me or yell at me." She took a deep steadying breath, "Emin and Shamsi."

"Emin and Shamsi?"

"Yes." She looked up at him. "I assumed you had asked them to take me, had forgotten to tell me about it…."

"No, damn it, I didn't." He let go of her, angrily stood up. "But I think I know who did."

She bit at her lip, trying not to let the tears spill as the door slammed. *I mustn't let Skender know how upset I am. First that awful policeman staring at me, then Shamsi yelling and shaking me … I must be calm, I must.*

"Come in, Djali. I was expecting you." Babush moved his hand, giving Skender permission to sit down.

Angrily he declined his invitation. "Yes, I'm sure you were. How dare you send my wife from this house without my approval? Who thought up this careful plan? Whose idea was it to get me safely out of this house and then send my wife to Headquarters? Was it you or Arif?"

"Does it matter? It is accomplished, she is registered and is home, safely, without any problems."

"No thanks to you." Babush looked up at him. "Do you realize what could have happened without me by her side? She has no fear of the police, could very easily have got angry at them if she thought they were not being polite to her." He laughed bitterly as he saw his father's astonishment. "Yes! It is true! I have seen her do it." Babush watched him as he paced the room. "She was raised to respect the police, not fear them … for her they are there to help and assist her." He bent close to his father. "Do you know one of the first things they teach a child in her country? 'Your best friend is a policeman'. Can you believe that? No, of course not! I still find it hard to believe and I have lived with freedom." He sat down. "You took a grave risk, Babush."

"Maybe. Would the risk have been less if you had taken her?"

"Of course it would."

"Be honest with yourself, Djali … let your mind carry you back to when you yourself registered." He lit his pipe, watching Skender. "Your cousins have not been subjected to beatings … have never been put through the torment you were. They are automatically calmer, more in control, than you could ever be when you are in that awful place." He pulled deeply on his pipe. "If the police had been a little … harsh? … with her, could you have sat quietly? Had you been there with her, do you not realize that they would have taken advantage of the opportunity and baited you? And then what? Even if you held yourself, kept control, inside you would have been tearing apart. What if that control had slipped? What if you had spoken, or acted hastily? You say she is not afraid of them, what would she have done, Djali, if she had been made to witness the beating of you? Could you have taken that? Could she?" He sat watching Skender. "Now tell me that I acted wrongly and I will apologize."

Skender sat silent, head bowed.

Babush put his arm around his son's shoulders. "Djali, would you have given me your permission if I had asked?" Skender shook his head briefly. "I knew I had to act against your wishes in order to protect the very person you cherish most. And to protect you. For myself."

"You were right, Babush … but you should have told me, insisted." He stopped, gave a quick brief smile. "Your insistence would have been for naught. I would have refused and then you and I…" He looked up at his father.

"Exactly, Djali. Now, no more on this. It is past, finished. Go to your wife … make sure all is well with her. She was not as calm as she would have had me believe. Skender…" he stopped him as he reached the door, "I told you she was stronger than you think. She is … but she has used that strength, now needs yours. Be careful what you say. Follow her lead this time."

You wise old man. "I will. I'm sorry I interrupted your rest, Babush. Sleep now."

"Hi!"

"Hi yourself." Gillian closed the book she was reading, smiled up at him. He was watching her closely. "Don't stare … please."

Babush is right, she is not herself. "I'm sorry, I didn't mean to." He smiled as he sat down beside her. "Well, did you register, my love?"

"Yes."

"Emin and Shamsi were kind, considerate to you?" She nodded. "Had I known, I would have arranged for Jakup to take you. You are more at ease with him than Emin." He watched as she sat quietly looking at the fire. *Normally there would have been some comment, a joke about Emin … and she is so pale….* "Are you going to tell me about Headquarters?"

Gillian nodded, smiled brightly. "There was the funniest old man who was the interpreter, he couldn't have spoken English in years. He called me 'Madam'. I am still not sure whether it made me feel very regal or rather old."

Skender smiled back at her. *You are trying too hard, my love.*

"Then, when they wanted to know if I had ever been arrested, he got really confused…." She tried to mimic Petrovich's voice. "Did a policeman ever hold you tight, Madam?"

Skender laughed, "What!" She repeated it, nodding her head up and down as Petrovich had as Skender laughed. "Well, did a policeman ever hold you tight? Be careful how you answer! It is your husband asking now!" He pulled her to him, holding her. *Damn their eyes, they frightened you, didn't they?*

"Skender?"

"Yes?"

She pulled a little away from him, looked up into his face. "When someone uses the word 'comrade', does it mean that they … well, do they approve of the government?"

"Not necessarily. The authorities frown on the old 'sir', comrade is the correct form of address." He saw her relief. "Why do you ask?"

"I was just curious."

"No, that is not it." He was amused. "I assume one of my cousins addressed an officer? Surely you did not suspect them of being…" he laughed, "how shocked they would be if they knew!"

She smiled back at him, reached and pulled her bag towards her. "I admit that I was a little concerned. By the way, what is Udba?" She was busily looking in her bag as she asked, missed the draining of color from Skender's face, his sudden stillness. "Some man gave me his card and now I can't find it…."

Panic clawed at him; he made his voice calm. "What man?"

"I don't know, can't remember his name … he came into the office at Headquarters." She glanced up with a quick smile. "He was very nice, had studied in London and spoke perfect English. When we were leaving, he gave me his card … here it is." She handed the business card to Skender. "He told me to call upon him any time if we needed assistance. Put it somewhere safe … he might be able to help us if we have any problems. He seemed to have some influence with the police."

Skender nodded grimly. "He does. Jill, this is very important, what did you talk to him about?"

"Nothing much … just generalities. Who is he, Skender?"

"Think very carefully. I must know what you discussed, everything you said."

Gillian's stomach somersaulted. "Who is he?"

He heard her fear. "I will explain later … just tell me what you and he talked of," he said soothingly.

"He asked when I was last in London, if I had seen any of his country…."

"What did you say?"

"Belgrade and Prishtine. He corrected me on the pronunciation … is he right or you on that?

"It doesn't matter. Go on."

"He asked if I liked Belgrade. I said yes. That I was impressed with the shops and wanted to spend a few days there on the way home. He was pleased because that is where his home is … " She looked up, shock on her face, "So he's Serbian, right?"

Skender nodded. "Yes, but that isn't important right now. Please…?"

"He asked if I liked winter sports…."

"Winter sports?" Skender asked wonderingly. Gillian nodded. "Why winter sports? Never mind, continue."

"I told him I preferred the coast and then he asked if we planned…."

"Aahh! Now I see what he was after. Did you tell him we may go to Prizren?"

She shook her head. "I couldn't remember the name, but I did tell him we hoped to visit a city with a river … I shouldn't have said anything, should I?"

"It doesn't matter. He hopes to catch me leaving here without permission … at least that is my guess."

She bit at her lip. "Skender, please, who is he? Why are you so concerned about what he said to me and what I said to him? You must tell me who he is."

He looked down at the card with a deep sigh. "He is very important … Deputy Director of Udba. Udba is the Secret Police."

Secret Police. Secret Police. Circles of fear radiated through her body, her mind repeated the words, vibrating as a gong hit too hard in too tiny a space. His lips moved but no sound reached her, only the throbbing, 'Secret Police, Secret Police' pumped in her head.

"Jill! Jill!" He shook her. Fear-glazed eyes stared at him unseeingly. He lifted his hand, brought it stingingly across her cheek, gathered her close as the tears came. "It was the only way, my love, the only way." He let her cry. "Yes, my love, cry, let the hurt out, the fear, whatever it was that you tried so hard to bottle inside yourself." He held her in his arms, rocking her back and forth as he comforted her. They stayed close, holding each other long after the tears had stopped. "Jill." He put her from him a little. "I have to talk to Babush. Immediately. Are you alright?" She nodded. His smile was sad as he let his hand touch her cheek. "I never thought to see the mark of my hand on your face." He bent forward, let his lips brush the white outline, pulled a pillow close to the fire. "Lay down and rest. As soon as I have spoken with Babush I will join you." He stood, went to the window bench and reached for a blanket. "Rest now." He covered her before he left, closing the door softly.

Gillian lay still, staring into the fire. Emotional exhaustion claimed her quickly, her eyelids dropped, she slept.

"…and that is all of it, sir," Babush worriedly smoothed his moustache. "I thought you should know immediately."

"Yes, Skender, you are right in telling me. What I cannot understand is why Emin did not mention this man, I asked if there was any trouble … he assured me not any."

Skender shrugged. "Perhaps he didn't realize…."

Babush raised his eyebrows. "Impossible! They carry their authority like a banner." He sighed, "I will get to the bottom of that later. What do you expect from them?"

"It is almost certain that they will pull me in for questioning within the next forty-eight hours." Babush nodded. "Should I tell my wife? I have to. I cannot let her remain in ignorance until they come for me."

"Yes, Djali, she must be told. But not now … she has enough to digest without adding to it. I suggest you wait, she has only a few hours before she must conduct herself as a guest in your uncle's house. If you tell her now I doubt that she could carry that burden graciously. Tell her tonight when you have her in your bed with no barriers between you. She will need you to comfort her, give her strength to face what must come." He sighed deeply, looked up at his son. "And you, Djali? Are you strong enough?"

Skender's smile was grim. "I must be, there is no way out." He looked steadily at his father, seeking to reassure him. "They will question me, Babush, nothing more. Do not worry. Remember, I am an American citizen now."

"Yes, Djali, that is good. I had forgotten that." He pulled on his pipe, watching Skender. *Do you really believe it will help you to say you are an American? What do they care what papers you carry? If they want you, they will take you.* He smiled at Skender. "Yes, that is good, Djali … I had forgotten about your citizenship."

"Nona must be told, sir."

"Leave your mother to me … but there is another who has my concern."

"Drita?"

Babush nodded slowly. "Old, buried fears will surface." He sighed. "And she has no one to cling to for comfort as you and I … must dry her own tears, find her own strength." Worriedly he smoothed his moustache.

"My poor sister, her life has not been the easiest, has it, Babush?"

"No. No, it has not. I pray she will find her happiness. I pray that she will find it with her husband, that the rest of her life will be free of fear and worry, and that she will know the joy and contentment of a happy marriage. That was my prayer for you, too, Djali. I think it has been answered, has it not?"

"Yes, sir, it has. Have you decided if you will pursue the Drini offer?"

"I have. The answer is yes. I have already told Arif to search … tonight I planned to tell Hasan."

"If it is meant, may it be with happiness."

Babush nodded. "She is in God's hands, as are we all. May He watch upon my children."

Skender swallowed his sigh, murmured, “May He watch upon all in this house, this family.”

Chapter 24

Gillian sighed, glanced around the crowded room, noisy with laughter and talk. *Jakup isn't here, neither Emin.* Her eyes met Shamsi's for a moment, the cold rejection of her half-smile shocked her and she dropped her eyes to her lap. *Why is he still so angry with me? I was prepared to forget the whole unhappy incident.* She glanced under her lashes at Adnan sitting beside Shamsi. *He was the one so full of fun last night, so determined to have me sit next to him … tonight he cut me cold until he noticed Skender watching … even then his greeting was perfunctory.*

Skender turned to her with a quick smile "I wish you could understand. They are reminiscing about the antics Aslan and I used to get into as children."

Gillian nodded; he turned as he heard his mother start another story. She watched with a slight smile as she saw Skender and Aslan hotly denying some part of it, arguing happily with Drita, who was nodding her head, supporting her mother's version. *Drita is enjoying herself tonight … it must be a relief to be the guest instead of the hostess. She likes Aslan's wife, so do I.* Gillian watched as Drita exchanged a quick smile with the young woman sitting beside her. *She is expecting another baby, and soon, too.* Gillian smiled to herself. *Their son is delightful … a chubby edition of Aslan … Aslan is so proud of him he is ready to pop!* She glanced round as all the young people stood except Skender and Aslan. She, too, pushed herself to her feet as Jakup and Emin entered the room.

There was much laughter and merriment as Jakup greeted his father and uncles, then the ladies. Emin, grinning broadly, waited his turn to greet the elders. Gillian watched as Jakup turned and gave a quick bow to Skender and Aslan before sitting down and calling "hellos" to the rest of his cousins and sister.

He turned to Gillian. "Nusé, how was your day?" His smile was warm as he reached and took the dictionary from the floor, she glanced down at it in his hands. It had not been opened since she had arrived in Hasan's house.

Emin bowed, exchanged a few words with his uncles and aunts before greeting Skender and Aslan, he stood listening to something Nona said, his smile deepening as he watched Skender. His short, quick comment brought a wave of laughter as he sat down next to Jakup and greeted the other cousins and Ilyria. He saw Skender watching him, turned to Gillian and inclined his head. "Nusé," his eyes and voice as ice.

"Mirëmbrëma, Emin," Gillian murmured, wishing she was anywhere in the room but that close to him.

"Boys, you must be hungry … are you ready to eat?" Hasan's wife asked.

"If it is no trouble to you, aunt."

"No, of course not, Jakup." She stopped her daughter-in-law from standing. "Stay, I will prepare for them … it will give us ladies an opportunity to chat for a while."

"We must talk too, brother," Babush said quietly to Hasan as the young people stood.

Hasan nodded, stopped his wife as she passed him. "Ask Nurije to bring coffee … we will be in the guest room. Skender? Aslan?" Hasan's hand moved graciously as he invited his oldest son and Skender to join them, he turned with a smile to Jakup. "Feel free to join us after your meal, Jakup."

"Thank you, Migje, I will." Jakup waited until the door closed before he sat down, smiled up at Gillian and, as soon as Emin had sat, patted the rug beside him. "Ulu ketu, Nusé." Gillian sat, swallowing a sigh as she once again coped with the problem of getting back down to the floor in a short skirt. Jakup opened the dictionary. "What did you do today, Gillian?"

"Shamsi and I took her to Police Headquarters," Emin answered with a cold glare at Gillian before Jakup had time to refer to the dictionary.

"Ahh yes, I had forgotten … did all go well?" He looked expectantly from Emin to Shamsi, raised his eyebrows, as there was no reply.

"Yes." Shamsi snapped, saw Jakup frown, and added in a softer tone, "We had no trouble."

Jakup flicked the pages of the dictionary, leaned toward Gillian. "I think it was warmer today, Nusé."

"Yes, it was," Adnan said angrily.

Jakup's eyes moved to him. "I know that, as do all in this room. I wished to speak to her, to let her know that she is not being ignored." Adnan's eyes dropped from Jakup's steady gaze, there was an uncomfortable silence as the door opened and Meliha came in with a small table. She set it down, covered it with a cloth, carefully smoothing all wrinkles from it, she left, returning almost immediately carrying a bowl, a jug of water and a towel. Jakup stood as she approached him. "Mirëmbrëma, Nusé."

"Mirëmbrëma, Jakup." Nervousness made her clumsy.

"May I help?" Gillian asked, rising quickly and taking the shaking jug before any water spilt.

Jakup smiled his approval. "Well done, Gillian." He received a quick smile back as she poured the water over his hands, Meliha handed him the towel, bowed as he handed it back to her after drying his hands, and they both moved on toward Emin. Gillian took a firmer grip on the jug as she felt his eyes coldly watching her. Jakup sat down at the small table, smilingly watching as Emin washed his hands. "How do you like this service, brother?" He turned with a quick grin to the others. "We are being spoiled … two Nusés attending us … she does well, does she not?" He frowned a little as the girls smilingly nodded, but there was no response from the young men, he caught Gillian's eye, nodded, "Soon you will be a real Kosovar."

"Never." Emin almost threw the towel to Meliha.

"Why did you deny so emphatically?" Jakup asked as soon as Meliha left the room. "She did very well, was sharp enough to see Meliha's difficulty and act accordingly."

"I apologize for my wife's clumsiness," Shamsi said tightly.

Jakup's eyes were angry, his voice clipped. "Accepted." He turned back to Emin. "You did not answer me."

Emin adjusted the cloth over his knees, muttered, "She has too much to learn." He glanced at Nurije and Meliha as they entered carrying their meal. "Let us eat."

"She learns fast … if she had the words, would learn even faster."

"I prefer not to discuss it." Emin's eyes dropped from his brother's. "Let us eat."

Jakup watched him for a moment before asking a blessing on the meal, picked up the bread, broke it and passed a piece to Emin, he ate in puzzled silence. *How has she managed to upset my brother again so soon? Not only Emin, Shamsi and Adnan are acting strangely with her.* He glanced around the room, Aslan's wife, Ilyria and Drita sat in a half circle chatting together, Adnan and Shamsi sat close, talking quietly, their faces serious. Nurije had sat near Gillian, but was intent on her immediate responsibility of making sure that Jakup and Emin had all they wanted, Meliha stood nearby, attending them. His eyes went to Gillian. *There is no life in her tonight.* She smiled back as she saw him watching her. *She must have noticed my brothers' attitude and is saddened. Before I leave this house, I will know the reason.*

He shook his head as Meliha offered him yogurt, stood up, putting his hand on Emin's shoulder to stop him from rising. "Stay, finish your meal. If you will excuse me, I will join the men." He rinsed his hands as Nurije came quickly to him with the bowl and jug, took the towel from Meliha. "Thank you." He inclined his head to the others, gave an encouraging smile to Gillian, and crossed the hall to the guest room. He checked that his cummerbund was smooth and tight, adjusted his hat and entered.

"Jakup, welcome, come in. Please…." Hasan offered him a seat, his voice and face concerned.

"Something is wrong, I fear." Jakup sat down opposite Skender, looked around at the serious faces.

"Yes, Djali." Arif turned from his son to Babush. "Brother, do you wish Jakup to bring the boys now? I agree with you, it is the only way to clear this matter." Babush nodded briefly. "Jakup, ask Emin and Shamsi to join us, please."

Jakup stood immediately, gave a quick bow and left, he returned in minutes, followed by Emin and Shamsi. Hasan waited until Jakup was settled before giving his permission for the two young men to sit down, he turned to Skender. "Skender, they are here … please feel free in my house…."

"Thank you, Migje. This morning you took Gillian to Police Headquarters." Emin and Shamsi glanced quickly at each other. "I wish you to tell me everything that happened from the moment you entered the door." Emin and Shamsi glanced at each other again, Skender frowned, said firmly after a few more minutes pause, "I am waiting." Still neither spoke. Aslan's and Jakup's eyes met, Jakup raised his eyebrows as the silence stretched.

"Did you hear your brother?" Babush asked softly, leaning toward them.

"Yes, sir." Emin gave another quick glance at Shamsi, then went on. "It was routine, our identity cards were checked, then I explained about your … wife." He almost choked on the word. "She handed in her passport … as she is a foreigner, we had to wait for an officer to interrogate her, so we sat down. While we were waiting…" Jakup frowned as his brother stopped speaking. Arif cleared his throat. Emin's eyes flew to his father … it was a command. He turned to face Skender, "One of the policemen … I'm sorry, Skender, but he was … he was looking at your wife."

Babush carefully smoothed his moustache as Hasan and Arif exchanged worried looks.

"What exactly do you mean?" Skender asked through clenched teeth.

"It was unbearably hot in there … we had removed our coats, she at my invitation. He was behind the counter, he…." Emin took a long breath, Aslan and Jakup looked with concern at Skender. "He didn't take his eyes off her. As soon as your Nusé was aware of his attention, she took her coat and covered her legs." Babush caught the quick nod of approval between his brothers, felt a stab of pride in his new daughter.

Controlled anger could be heard as Skender instructed Emin, "Go on."

"When the officer sent for us, the same policeman came to escort us … he reached to take hold of her arm…." Emin's eyes went for a moment to Aslan as he heard him swear softly. He turned to Skender, added quickly, "It is alright, brother, not even a finger of his touched her." Skender signaled for him to continue. "We followed him to his officer; he stayed as well. There was a long form to be completed … there was no way to make her understand all the questions, so the officer left for a moment to send for an interpreter…." Emin stopped, his eyes flicked to Shamsi, then he sat silently frowning at the floor.

"The policeman made some remarks that I objected to…" Shamsi's eyes went from Skender to his father, "…I'm sorry, I lost my temper."

Hasan banged his fist on the rug. "How many times do I need to tell you to hold your anger?" He turned to Skender. "I am sorry, please continue." He turned back to his son. "We shall talk later, you and I."

"These … remarks, they were about Gillian?"

Shamsi's eyes dropped. "Yes, brother."

"What were they?" Babush's voice was tightly angry.

"Wait." Aslan stopped Shamsi as he was about to answer, turned to Skender. "This is not easy for you to hear, perhaps it would prove less difficult if Jakup and I left."

"No, Aslan, stay. But I am grateful to you for your thoughtfulness of my feelings. Continue."

"He implied…."

"Word for word, Shamsi, word for word." Skender listened in silence, white with anger as Shamsi related the scene. Arif swore softly. Hasan's fist banged the rug.

Babush turned away, unable to watch the hurt to his son, murmured as Shamsi finished speaking, "Thank God you were not there, Djali."

Skender felt Aslan's hand on his shoulder. "I am so sorry, brother, so sorry. I can imagine your feelings, your anger…."

Skender stopped Jakup as he started to speak. "Gillian's reaction?" he demanded of Emin.

"Of course she did not understand, but when she saw Shamsi start towards the policeman … it was the only time I saw her nervous. She stood. I told her to sit down and she did my bidding. The officer returned at that moment … shortly after, she became very pale, she must have felt…." Emin stopped as he saw Skender close his eyes.

"Go on."

Hasan held up his hand, stopping Emin. "Skender, do not put yourself through this … let it rest."

"No, Migje. My wife is involved in this and I insist on knowing."

Emin waited until he received a nod from Hasan, then continued. "She asked for water … while Shamsi was fetching it, the translator arrived and the interrogation began."

"Was he Serbian, this translator?"

"Of course." Skender nodded for him to continue. "The first questions were what one would expect … place and date of birth, mother's maiden name, and so on and so forth … then they asked for the names and addresses of all relatives in Prishtine and in this country. I answered for her on both questions. Their next questions concerned you, brother … they asked for your place and date of birth…." After a short pause, Emin slowly continued, "In their eyes you belong to them … they do not consider you a foreigner."

Babush sighed, whispered to his brothers, "That has been my fear."

"How did that particular subject come up?" Jakup asked.

"I wondered why she had to fill out such a long form, told them that when Skender went to register…." Shamsi stopped, looked directly at Skender. "He said that he already had a file on you, that all he had to do was bring it up to date." Skender's fist banged the rug. "I'm sorry to be the one to tell you, brother."

"Go on."

Emin hesitated. "They asked your wife if she had ever been arrested…." He looked round the half-circle of faces as he saw Skender's fleeting smile, continued on in a puzzled voice. "The question amused your wife…."

"Amused her, you say?" Arif interrupted in disbelief.

"There was no control on her laughter, her whole body shook, tears came to her eyes…." He stared in open amazement as he saw Skender give an amused shake of his head. Emin turned, bewildered, to Aslan and Jakup, both shrugged. His eyes moved to the men who were sitting watching Skender in astonished bewilderment. "It did not amuse the officer, brother," Emin said sharply. Skender offered no explanation and waved his hand for him to continue.

"They asked her if she had ever been a member of any political organization…" Emin watched Skender closely. "Her answer was yes, brother." Babush stared at Emin, turned quickly to his son, waiting for an explanation, exchanged quick surprised looks with his brothers as Skender nodded and again waved his hand for Emin to continue.

"Do you think he understood?" Jakup whispered to Aslan, Aslan silenced him as Emin started to speak.

"Their next question, brother, was which party…" he stopped, turned to Shamsi, "…I cannot…" he said quietly, "…I cannot inflict that wound on him."

"Her answer, Emin," Arif demanded. Emin lifted his eyes to his father, shook his head, lips tight together as he smoothed his moustache and pushed back his hat. Arif's eyes narrowed. "I demand an answer."

"She is a Communist." It burst from Shamsi, loud and clear, the word radiating out from him until it reached every corner of the room, hanging in the air. In a quieter voice, he repeated it. "She is a Communist, a party member." The still silence of the room was broken suddenly by Skender's chuckle, brother looked from brother to brother in shocked horror, then all eyes turned to Skender.

He wiped his eyes on the back of his hand, nodded at Shamsi, and with amusement still in his voice, instructed him, "Go on."

Babush stared at him. "You find this news of your Nusé amusing, Djali?" he demanded angrily, turning in complete bewilderment to his brothers as his son nodded.

Shamsi half-stood, demanded angrily, "Did you understand what I said? Your wife is a Communist." He stared uncomprehendingly as this brought another amused smile, then asked icily, "Have you lost your senses, brother?"

Aslan jumped to his feet. "Watch your tongue … remember whom you address." Slowly he sat down again as he received a quick apology from Shamsi, felt Skender's hand on his arm.

"It is alright, Aslan." Skender leaned toward Emin and Shamsi. "Listen to my question and think very carefully before you answer, did that statement come from Gillian's own lips? Did you hear her say, 'I am a Communist'?"

"Yes." Shamsi's answer was emphatic.

"Be very sure … be very sure of what you are saying."

"I am."

"Emin?"

Emin frowningly concentrated. "Yes, brother, she told the old man who trans…."

"Did you hear the word communist? It is the same in any language, needs no translation."

"No. In the western world they are forbidden…" Emin hesitated as he saw Skender's quizzical expression, "…forbidden to say they are Communists, must use Workers' Party…."

"Workers' Party is the acceptable way of saying Communist in the west," Shamsi interrupted hotly, "And that is what she said … 'I am a member of the Workers' Party.'"

Skender nodded. "I see. Who gave you this information about the Western world?"

"We have been told many times."

Skender's eyes never left Shamsi's face as he demanded, "By whom?" There was no answer, his eyes flashed to Emin and still there was no answer. "May I guess? Could it possibly be from your teachers? And am I also right in my guess that these same teachers are themselves Communists?" He waited, letting their embarrassment eat at them. "Propaganda! In the west you can be, and say, what you like … can shout it from the rooftops if you wish. There are Communists, and Communist parties operating freely and openly in all western countries."

"Enough! I am not concerned with western politics or western countries." Angrily Babush's fist hit the rug. "My concern is what happened this morning with my own family … and that, Djali, should be your concern too."

"It is, sir … but before we go on, I want this charge against Gillian cleared." Babush lifted his hands in despair, sighed and waved Skender to continue. His voice was quietly firm as he looked directly at Emin and Shamsi. "You are convinced that my wife is a Communist, therefore, you must think I am a very big fool." He stopped their quick, hot denials. "Hear me out before you say another word. These very people whom you think my wife is allied to robbed me of my home, my family, and my country … they have beaten me until I could hardly walk, have terrorized my brother and sisters, my mother and father. These same people murdered my friends in front of my eyes, took me by force from school without warning and walked me through hell and back again. Now, what kind of person would take into his heart and his home someone who has any sympathy with these animals? You have pointed the finger. Answer! Did you at any time hear from Gillian's lips the word Communist? Emin?"

"No."

"Thank you. Shamsi?" Shamsi shook his head. "Answer me!"

"No."

Skender turned to his father. "This will be cleared soon, Babush. I intend to bring Gillian here and ask her what she said. I would imagine that she told them the truth, that she was a member of the Labor Party, which is…" he stopped as he heard Shamsi's quick indrawn breath, "…you have remembered something?"

"We were in your kitchen, were talking to her about politics…."

"Yes," Jakup interrupted excitedly, "she told us the Labor Party is one of the largest political parties in England." He turned to Shamsi, "…the yellow and black circle? Am I correct?" Shamsi gave a brief nod. "The Communist party was a small circle, red…." He smiled with relief as he looked at Skender. "She said there was no connection between the two."

"Exactly … they are opposed to each other, have even voted against each other in her government."

"There is obviously doubt about her reply. My son is convinced she is not a party member, so let us proceed." Babush stopped Skender's objection. "You may call her and speak with her as much as you wish after we are through. Emin."

"Sir?"

"You saw fit to withhold certain information from me when you returned my daughter. I demand that information now, what happened when Mihajlovich entered that room?"

Both young men gasped, exchanged quick surprised looks. "How did you know of him, Migje?" Shamsi asked wonderingly.

"That is not your damned business." Hasan pointed his finger at his son. "Now answer my brother immediately … that is my demand."

"Sir, may I?" Emin received a nod as Hasan dragged angry eyes from Shamsi. "We were probably half-way through the questions when he entered the office. He took the form and scanned it … he asked who we were, who the old man was … he threw him out." He looked directly at Skender. "He asked why you had not brought your wife yourself, was sarcastic when we told him you were busy."

Aslan sighed, "Will they ever leave you alone?"

Skender signaled for him to be quiet, nodded at Emin. "All of it, every word, Emin."

"He studied the passport and form, obviously checked that they agreed, then called the officer into a far corner and spoke with him."

"The subject?" Arif demanded quickly.

"I do not know, sir … they spoke too quietly. He returned to the desk, sat on the corner and…." He stopped, gritting his teeth.

"And?" Skender prompted.

"Skender, how can we doubt that she is a Communist? She confirmed it. She sat and chatted with him, they even laughed together … one only had to look at him to know he is a Party man and she…."

"Not Party," Skender stopped him, took Mihajlovich's card from his pocket and handed it to Emin. "Unfortunately, not from Party Headquarters."

"Udba," Emin whispered in disbelief as he stared at the card, his face drained of color, his eyes lifted slowly to Skender's. "God in heaven, not them."

"Yes, Udba! Now explain to my satisfaction why you saw fit to withhold such a thing from my brother," his father demanded grimly.

"I had no idea…. But she knew … she read his card when he gave it to her. Skender, how did you make her tell you?"

"You still do not believe that she is not with them, do you, Emin?"

Emin's eyes dropped to the card. "Deputy Director of Udba … he sat talking to her brother, laughed with her, gave her this card…." He glared angrily at Skender. "It is you who should have doubts … your wife knew who he was yet put his card in her bag without batting an eyelid." He laughed bitterly. "Who else but one of their own could be so calm when so close to anyone connected with Udba?"

"How the hell did she know? What is Udba to her?"

Emin's eyes sparked, "What did she speak with him of for so long? How dare she speak to a stranger without permission?"

"She does not need permission to speak to anyone … not in her culture." Skender took a long steadying breath before turning to the men. "Babush, Migje Arif, Migje Hasan, there is one person who can tell us what happened once Mihajlovich entered that room. I want her here … now. Do I have your permission? Thank you. Jakup, please, ask Gillian to come here."

There was a silence as they waited for Jakup to return.

"Skender?" Skender looked over at Hasan. "Will she be able to answer your questions? To bring her here, into a room full of men … she will be nervous … it will drive all thoughts from her head."

Skender smiled. "She will not be nervous, Migje." He looked round as he heard the door open. "Jill, come here and sit beside me. We are talking about your visit to Police Headquarters this morning. You are the only one who can tell us what was talked about when Mihajlovich spoke to you."

Gillian nodded asked calmly, "What is it you want to know?"

"Everything. I shall translate for Babush and my uncles as you speak, so go slowly." She nodded. He turned to his father. "I have told her what we want and that I shall translate as she speaks." He turned back to Gillian. "Go ahead, my love."

"I'll try to remember everything, but don't forget that this conversation held no importance for me, so it might not be word for word."

"That's alright … just do the best you can." He translated quickly what she had said and his reply.

"His accent was what surprised me … I knew immediately that he had learned from a Londoner … the inflections, everything…" Skender's voice as a soft background to hers as he translated to his family, who sat silent, concentrating on every word, "…then he asked if I was from London and which part." Jakup and Aslan silently questioned each other.

Aslan whispered, "I thought her an American!"

Jakup nodded. "I, too." His attention returned to Gillian.

"I told him, asked if he knew London … he had studied there for two years. Then he introduced himself, we shook hands, and naturally I told him my name although I knew that he already had that information from my passport. He asked if I called myself Jill…." She looked up into Skender's eyes. He smiled, a slow soft smile, and she smiled back at him.

Jakup leaned to Aslan and whispered softly, "Even at a time like this, they snatch a moment for each other."

"I said no, but he caught me, 'Only for special friends, is that not so?'"

"Wait a moment," Skender stopped her, turned to Emin. "You reacted to something. What was it?"

"We heard him use the name you have for her, thought that she…." He stopped, dropped his eyes from Skender's withering look.

"It seems you have jumped to many conclusions, Emin … most of them wrong. Go on, Jill.

She rubbed at her forehead, concentrating. "I think that was when … yes, he said, 'If we were in London now I would invite you for morning coffee … would you accept?'" She grinned ruefully. "That was when I made a mistake because instead of just saying yes…." She stopped abruptly as she saw the horrified faces staring at her.

"Do not be shocked … in her country it is quite acceptable to take coffee with a man not related to you."

"Even allowing for that, this man is your enemy … you do not find it strange that your wife was prepared to sit and sip coffee with him, Djali?"

Gillian's eyes flew from Babush to Skender as he answered his father. "She did not know who or what he was then, Babush. Let me ask her what she would have answered if she had known." He turned back to Gillian. "Would you have accepted his offer if you had known that he is my enemy, is watching my every move?"

"I'd have scratched his bloody eyes out."

Babush turned his laugh into a cough, his eyes twinkled back at Hasan, while Arif kept his head down and busily poked at the fire with his stick while clearing his throat, Jakup and Aslan laughed silently together. Emin and Shamsi dropped embarrassed eyes from Skender.

"What was said next?"

"I can't remember … I think it was that business about winter sports, but perhaps that came after he'd asked me about the Labor Party."

Skender looked quickly around the room as he translated. "It doesn't matter in which order, just tell us all of it."

"Well, he asked which party I belonged to. I found that strange because he had the form in his hand and I'd already told the police that I had been in the Labor League of Youth … he had written it down, so I asked this … whatever his name is … wasn't it already on the form. He said it wasn't important and then we started to talk about London and the various political functions … do you want all of this, Skender? It's nothing important, just idle chatter."

"Yes, Jill. All of it, please."

"I told him I wasn't interested in politics any more … he asked why not, what had happened to cause me to lose interest…." She looked nervously at Babush before she continued. "He asked me if it was a young man who had come along and made me lose interest in politics…." She bit her lip and whispered to Skender. "He's furious."

"Yes, but not at you, at him for daring to ask such a thing. Go on."

"When he was in London he discovered that our political parties give very good social functions at very reasonable prices, which enabled him to stretch his student allowance. That is true, and I told him that was one reason why I, too, first joined the Labor Party, although I did have dreams of bigger things…."

"What dreams?"

"Oh, you know, the usual teenager ideals of helping to make a better world."

Babush coughed … Skender glanced quickly at him. "Let's get back to Mihajlovich." His eyes traveled round the serious faces, concentrating so earnestly. *So many watching her so carefully … I am amazed that she isn't nervous.*

"He asked when I was last in London, where I had been since arriving in this country and where we hoped to visit. I told him the only places I'd seen were Belgrade and Prishtine … he corrected my pronunciation, but I've forgotten…."

"Good!" Skender gave her a quick grin. "Go on."

"He was pleased that I liked Belgrade, because…" she stopped as she saw the quick, angry look of Babush and the two uncles, took a steadying breath and then continued, "…because it was his home."

"Don't worry, my love. I will clear this problem later, will explain that to you this was just another city, that you had no way of knowing that Belgrade could hold dangers for me. Continue, let us get finished with this."

"That was all. He walked me to the door, helped me on with my coat…." Skender's finger stopped her.

Emin shook his head as Skender's eyes questioned him. "He didn't touch her, brother … obviously knew our rules and was careful not to put his hands on her."

Skender gave her a smile of encouragement and she started again. "He gave me his card and told me to call upon him if I needed any assistance, or just a friendly ear … wait, just before that, he again mentioned the coffee bit, but said that Emin and Shamsi would object, that … don't translate this next part, Skender … your family will be hurt."

"There has been too much hurt and misunderstanding already, Jill. I want this matter cleared forever. What was it that he said?"

Her voice was barely audible. "That your people are a hundred years behind the times and still uncivilized."

He turned to his father, explained Gillian's request and his insistence that it must be translated.

"Nusé." Babush's smile was gentle as he saw her full eyes when she raised her face to his. "They were not your words, daughter, so why should I be offended at you? Is there more?" Shamsi glanced quickly, nervously, at Emin.

Gillian gave Babush a shaky smile as Skender translated. "Not really … we said good-bye…" her face flushed scarlet, "he took my hand and kissed it…."

"No communist would do that, let alone someone from Udba," Aslan interrupted quickly.

"Agreed … unless it was done deliberately … to irritate and offend," Jakup said slowly as he looked from Gillian to his brother and Shamsi.

Skender nodded grimly. "And to underscore a relationship that did not in fact exist, but one that he wished to imply was strong and firm." He sighed, turned back to Gillian. "Anything more, Jill?"

She shook her head. "No, we left. Emin and Shamsi brought me home." Jakup caught the quick exchange of looks between Emin and Shamsi. "I washed, changed clothes and you arrived shortly after that."

Jakup frowned as he saw Shamsi's relief. *There is something more, but what? She has been so open. What is it that she is not telling us? My brother knows, Shamsi too.* He turned to Skender as he heard his name. "Yes, brother?"

"Will you take Gillian to the others, let her be with Drita and the girls?"

"Of course." Jakup smiled, offering his hand, and helped Gillian to her feet.

"We are almost finished here, Jill, and soon I will join you." He turned to the three men. "I think all is clear now. Gillian has told us everything about her conversation with Mihajlovich and in doing that has cleared herself politically. It must have been an error in translation … deliberate or accidental, I have no way of knowing."

He smiled his thanks as Jakup rejoined them, then turned to Shamsi. "After you have been married a little longer, you will know why I had no doubts about Gillian. The person most close to you on this earth is your wife … no other can know her as well as you and none can know you as well as she. Even before her lips form the words, you will know the thought … is that not so, Aslan?"

"He is right, brother," Aslan smilingly agreed. He saw his brother's doubt, added softly, "Not yet … for you it is too soon, but wait … it will come. It is worth the wait, Shamsi. It is something unique, delicate, fragile … beyond explaining and infinitely precious. When that happened for me, I knew that my married life had really begun … until then, we had lived as man and wife, two separate beings, bodies fused, minds separate. Now we are truly one. I am grateful that I have lived to experience it."

Hasan nodded his approval, "Is there anything more you wish to ask the boys?"

"No, Migje, thank you … they may go." He turned to Aslan and Jakup. "Shall we join the others?"

Shamsi leaned close to Emin, whispered, "I cannot let it rest here … he must be told."

"Wait," Emin advised with compassion as he saw Shamsi's white face. "Talk to Skender when he is alone."

Shamsi shook his head. "I cannot … my father, uncles have a right to the rest." He stood just as Aslan and Jakup rose, preparing to leave. "Skender, there is more." All three young men turned to him, staring in amazement. "I have more to tell you." He turned to Hasan. "There is more, sir, that you must know … my brother should hear, too, being the eldest, he has that right." Jakup gave a brief bow, started to leave. "Jakup, you have heard so much … if your father agrees, you should stay for this too."

Arif gave a quick nod to Jakup, the three young men sat down, their eyes never leaving the distraught Shamsi.

"Brother, I assume that your Nusé has told you nothing of what happened after we left Police Headquarters?"

"Nothing," Skender confirmed, frowning.

Shamsi wiped his brow, pushed his hat back off his forehead and took a deep breath. "We were upset, angry…." His eyes flew, briefly to his father as he heard the oath. "Emin held himself in check, took your nusé's arm and we started for home … I stayed a pace or two behind them, could not bring myself even to walk beside her. We reached the main square…." He stopped, looked round at the serious faces watching him closely. "She looked up at the obelisk … it infuriated me. I gave her a push towards it…" his eyes faltered under Skender's "…she almost tripped, but Emin had hold of her arm and righted her. I pulled her to face me, spoke harshly and louder than…." He stopped Skender as he saw him start to rise. "There is more yet, brother…."

"You push my wife, shout at her, are harsh with her, and you tell me there is still more?"

"Steady, Djali." Babush put his arm on Skender's urging him back to the rug. "Let us hear all of this."

Hasan's eyes never left his son's face. "Yes, let us hear all of this," he agreed grimly.

Shamsi stood silent for a moment, then with a great effort forced himself to look directly at Skender. "I took hold of her shoulders, shook her, hard, just as a dog shakes a rabbit…."

Aslan grabbed Skender. "Skender, no, I beg of you … leave him to my father."

Hasan was already on his feet, across the room before Skender could have stood, the slap across the mouth sent Shamsi reeling. "How dare you raise your hand against your brother's wife … how dare you even raise your voice to her…." He went closer to his son. "I should throw you from this house … I should beat…."

"Migje Hasan, please." Emin stood, took a single step toward Hasan and Shamsi, but stopped immediately as he saw his father signal him stop. "Please listen … there were extenuating circumstances…."

"Nothing excuses his conduct. Nothing!" Hasan roared.

Aslan let go of Skender as he quietly said, "Let us hear him out Migje."

Slowly Hasan turned away from Shamsi, returned to his seat beside his brothers, gave a brief nod to Emin, as he sat beside Arif.

"I agree with you, Migje, there is no excuse for letting anger carry us beyond the bounds of acceptable conduct, but what we had just heard had shaken us to our marrow." Emin turned to Skender. "We had just heard that your Nusé was a Communist, was connected with the very people we have feared and hated all our lives … we lost all sense, were choked with bitterness and anger. And we were worried for your safety, brother. We did not know who Mihajlovich was, but I knew he had some importance. She had sat chatting with him, laughing … everything she did only incensed us more, confirmed what we had just heard. We were blinded with anger. I wanted to wring her neck like a chicken, beat her black and blue…."

"But you did not touch her?" Arif's voice was ominously quiet. "Not even a finger?"

"No, father," Emin sighed. "I do not really believe that Shamsi would have lost control had she not raised her hand against him…."

"What? She raised her hand against my son?" Hasan demanded in astonishment.

Emin's eyes flashed briefly to Skender before he answered his uncle. "Yes, sir … she shouted back at him, put both her hands on his chest and pushed with all her strength." Skender dragged in a long breath, fighting to control his sadness. Emin turned to him, "None of our girls would dare such a thing, not even at home, let alone in a public place. I parted them, held on to her arm while I told her to quiet herself. For one moment I thought she was going to strike out at me too, but she calmed herself." Skender lowered his head, unable to stop the anger and pain from showing. "I released her, and she sat on the wall surrounding the obelisk until Shamsi and I were ready to leave." Emin turned to Babush. "That is all of it, sir."

Shamsi stepped forward. "One last thing, I refused to escort her home, was ready to leave her there, unattended, but Emin insisted, reminded me that we had given our word…."

"Emin was right," Skender interrupted him, "Thank you." Emin inclined his head as Skender turned back to Shamsi. "Remember this, by discrediting or demeaning one who carries our name, you discredit yourself. I can understand the great emotional strain you carried. Control is not always easy. A moment ago, I would have…." He took a ragged breath. "Thank God Aslan stopped me. Now the anger has passed. But not the sadness." The room was silent, each with their thoughts.

"Babush, I have no more questions for them."

"You may both leave." Babush saw Emin hesitate. "Something else?" he demanded suspiciously.

"A question for Skender, with your permission." Babush nodded. "Brother, you were not shocked or surprised when you heard that your nusé had pushed Shamsi?"

"No." He saw them exchange surprised glances. "Had that been one of our own girls instead of Gillian, what would her reaction have been? She would be shocked, furious with you for treating her that way. Her anger would be quiet, but last long. That is not Gillian's way…" his smile was forced, "…you escaped lightly. Had that happened in a more private place she'd have fought like a wild cat. Her anger is hot, erupts as a volcano, but subsides just as quickly. For her it is over, finished … she will never mention it again."

"You may leave now." Babush turned to his brothers as the young men bowed to them, before preparing to leave, said softly, "She is not so different from our girls, will take no abuse … her anger takes a different form."

Arif nodded, "Yes, that is true." *But thank God it is not I who has the handling of this volcano!*

Skender stopped Emin and Shamsi just as they reached the door. "One more thing … which of you addressed the officer as comrade?"

"I," Emin replied, surprised at the question.

Skender nodded, "Yes, I thought possibly it was you, Emin." He waved his hand, dismissing them, turned back to the others as the door closed. "Gillian had never heard anyone use that term before. She was worried, thought it indicated some sympathy with the authorities…." He waited until the burst of laughter had died. "I think we have come full circle, have we not?"

"You had to ask who had used the word … did she not tell you it was my brother?"

"No, Jakup … she did not say it was anyone in my family, but I guessed." Skender's smile was strained. "I am tempted to call Emin here, tell him." He looked from Aslan to Jakup. "It would be such a shock to our very correct young man to know that this outsider … whom he watches so carefully … thought there was a flaw in him." He stood. "Shall we go? Join the others? With your permission, Babush?" Aslan and Jakup stood, they all bowed briefly, left, closing the door softly.

Hasan sighed, "I apologize for my son's behavior, brother. I shall deal with him later."

"Be easy with him, Hasan," Arif advised.

"He is too hot-tempered." Hasan's voice was loudly angry.

Babush and Arif exchanged amused glances. "Yes … he reminds me constantly of a young brother." Arif took out his pipe as he spoke, looked thoughtfully at Hasan. "The brother is not so young now, but still has difficulty…." Their eyes met, slowly the anger melted from Hasan's and he smiled as he accepted the proffered tobacco.

Babush smoothed his moustache with a sigh, "Mihajlovich would have enjoyed this evening if he could have heard. His seed of doubt and suspicion almost took root in this family."

Arif nodded slowly. "One word … just one … and he built upon it so cleverly that all of us, you included, were ready to condemn her."

Babush nodded, "I know. God forgive me for that."

Hasan slowly lit his pipe, "Her character is strong, brother. She did not run to Skender about my son's behavior. A word from her at the wrong time and irreparable damage could have been done to our family." He sighed, shook his head, "Can you imagine if she had deliberately fanned Skender's natural anger?"

There was a silence as each realized the rift that could have been caused. Arif pulled deeply on his pipe. "We were so concerned that Skender had not waited, married one of our own girls, that we overlooked the obvious, a tree can grow just as straight and true in foreign soil as in Kosov's."

"Yes, my daughter did well … I am proud of her. She handled herself with dignity both here and at Police Headquarters."

A smile curved Babush's lips, he started to laugh softly. "What was it she said? 'I'd have scratched his bloody eyes out.'" They all chuckled. "Not much dignity in that, but I like it."

Hasan nodded, gave a brief smile. "She has spirit, that one."

"Skender chose well. Why did we worry? We should have known that he would not take less than he is himself. He has always been strong, proud … too proud if anything. The pot found its lid, brother."

Babush smiled agreement with Arif. "Yes, I agree … they are right for each other." He sighed as he pushed back his hat and rubbed at his forehead.

"Then why are you worried? What worries you with these two?" Arif demanded.

"Nothing with them." There was a deep sigh, "Mihajlovich worries me. He is clever, too clever. Skender's greatest weakness is his feeling for his nusé. If Mihajlovich should find that tender spot, he will probe it till it bleeds."

"There is nothing to be done … we can only wait. I pray Skender will be ready for them when they come for him." Arif's voice was sad, but firm.

Babush nodded, pulled deeply on his pipe a few times. His eyes went to Hasan, he watched his youngest brother with compassion. "Do not let Shamsi's outburst eat at your heart … let us be finished with this thing, bury it here and now."

"I cannot. When I think of how close…."

"Then do not think on it. Remember only the good that came from it … a veil has been lifted from our eyes. Now we know the quality of nusé we have in our hands.

Babush stood, "Come…let us join our children."

Skender's breathing was steady, even. Slowly Gillian edged herself from his encircling arm and slid off the mattress. She slipped on her robe, went to the window bench and sat down, curling her legs beneath her so that her toes could tuck under the warm robe.

Her eyes went to the sleeping figure. *How is it possible for him to sleep so soundly knowing what is hanging over his head? He was so calm … 'within the next two or three days the police will come, take me in for questioning … there is nothing to worry about.' Not true, not true, she had wanted to cry, there is something to worry about. I have seen the serious faces, the concern of your father and uncles.*

What will they do to you, Skender? What horrors did they put you through in the past, my love? Do you really believe I know nothing of how you have suffered? You have never spoken of it, never mentioned whatever the terror was, but I knew there was something….

She shivered, remembering the nights she had lain quietly beside him listened to his cries, felt the sudden uncontrollable quivering of his body.

She put her head down onto her knees, tears falling silently. *And all I could do for you, my love, was hold you close … and all I can do now is be the way you want me to be … and I will … I promise. There will be no tears, no fear … at least none that you shall see.*

Chapter 25

Emin hesitated as he reached toward the gate, he stood still for a moment, then resolutely let his hand meet the rough wood. A groan came as it closed behind him, he half-turned, gave a rueful smile. *My feelings exactly!*

He glanced up at the sitting room window as he passed beneath it. *I hope I catch Skender alone, that Babush is resting....* He hesitated again at the foot of the steps to the house. *What if his Nusé is with him ... she is the last one I wish to see.* He sighed deeply as he climbed the steps. *I must take that chance, cannot delay this apology any longer.* He bent to remove his shoes at the entry hall, laid his coat on a bench, then opened the door to the hallway. He passed the women's guest room quietly, his eyes briefly glancing in that direction, then stopped in front of the sitting room door, checked that his cummerbund was smooth and flat, took a deep breath, and reached for the doorknob.

Gillian lay on her stomach on the floor, she picked up a black ten and laid it on a red jack, frowned at the two red nines laid out in front of her. *Which one shall I use?* She put her head on one side considering, humming softly as she looked at the game of patience spread on the rug. *I must be very careful ... this is probably going to be my major decision for the whole day!*

She turned her head lazily, expecting Skender, as she heard the door open. Both stared at each other. Gillian's heart sank as she realized her predicament. *How on earth can I stand up for him when I am in this position? Crawl onto my knees ... roll over? Either way, my skirt will ride up....* She dropped her eyes from his. "Mirëmëngjes, Emin."

"Mirëmëngjes." Self-conscious at finding the person he sought most to avoid, he stood looking down at her, oblivious to her problem.

What can I do? How can I make him turn away from me, give me a chance to get up? Gillian pointed. "Please close the door."

He hesitated, slightly annoyed at her order, then inclined his head and moved toward the door. Gillian was on her feet, hastily smoothing her dress as he turned back, he almost smiled. "That was clumsy of me ... I should have realized your difficulty, I'm sorry." Their eyes met for a second … both looked quickly away. "Skender, is he home?"

"Yes, he is with Babush, talking to Nona and Drita." Emin nodded that he understood. "Will you sit down?" She moved her hand, sighed as she realized that she still held the cards. *Whenever Emin is near, I am clumsy, make mistakes … was I correct in inviting him to sit? Perhaps that is his right, and it is I who should wait on his invitation….*

"Thank you." Emin slowly sat down, re-adjusted his hat, and smoothed his cummerbund unnecessarily, he looked up as Gillian remained standing. "Ulu, Nusé."

She hesitated, slowly sat opposite him, she saw his eyes go to the cards still in her hand, quickly laid them on the rug beside her. She glanced surreptitiously at the clock, color flooding her face as she saw that he watched her. "Skender should be here…" She stopped immediately as she realized that he, too, was speaking.

"I am here to see Skender…." Emin inclined his head as she gestured for him to continue. "I am here to see Skender, but as I have found myself with you, Nusé, I will take the opportunity of apologizing…." Emin stopped, glanced around. He stood as his eyes lit on the dictionary. Gillian stood as soon as he did, Emin looked at her in surprise, signaled for her to sit. "It is not necessary for you to stand again, not when we are alone, Nusé." He walked to the window bench, picked up their line of communication and flicked quickly through the pages as he sat down again.

"Sorry?" Gillian read the word he was pointing to, Emin nodded, flipped the pages again. "Angry?" Gillian looked at him, puzzled.

Emin gave her a brief smile. "This is ridiculous … let me sit beside you. Our conversation will take forever otherwise." He moved to sit beside her, looked directly at her and spoke slowly and clearly. "When Shamsi and I took you to Police Headquarters to register…?" Gillian nodded. "We both misunderstood, were angry and…" he stopped as he realized that he had lost her, opened the dictionary. Both heads bent together over the pages as he looked up the key words. Still speaking quietly, he continued, "… we misunderstood, were angry and shocked … that is why I am here … to apologize to Skender and to you for my inexcusable…."

"There is no need." Gillian closed the dictionary, smiled diffidently as she held out her hand. "Friends?"

Emin stared at her in amazement. *I thought you would take full advantage of this opportunity, would squeeze me dry.* His eyes crinkled at the corners as he smiled back at her. "Yes, Nusé, friends." Their handshake was firm, their eyes met, self-consciously they laughed, both a little embarrassed with each other. "So, Nusé, you are from England?"

"Yes, London...." She turned her head as the door opened. Emin came immediately to his feet, bowed.

"Emin ... please sit down." Skender glanced quickly at Gillian. "Is everything alright?"

She smiled up at him. "Everything's just fine ... would you and Emin care for some coffee? Nona and Drita are still with Babush I suppose but I think I can make it."

"Yes, we would ... don't rush. He will need to be alone with me for a little while." She nodded. Emin stood silently as Gillian left the room. Skender sat down. "Sit down, Emin ... I have missed your company these past couple of days."

"I have missed being with you more, brother." He hesitated, then went on determinedly. "I have come to ask your forgiveness for my part...."

Skender glanced up at him. "Is that why you have stayed away, denied me your company?"

"The thought that I had offended you, caused you sorrow, has eaten at me. I feel nothing but shame for my distrust of your Nusé, this reflecting doubt on you, on your judgment."

There was a long pause before Skender said quietly, "First, please sit down." Still, Emin hesitated. "Please?" He waited until Emin was seated. "Distrust breeds, feeds upon itself, Emin, growing as a cancer, consuming everything in its path. You have never breathed a drop of air that has not had that poison within it, have had a steady diet of lies and suspicion fed to you. I can understand your reaction, your feelings ... had I been in your shoes, I would probably have felt the same." Skender leaned towards Emin as Emin's eyes lifted to his. "I want this thing finished between us ... buried forever, here and now. I am proud of you, Emin, in spite of all outside pressures, you hold true to our ways, conduct yourself with dignity and honor. The slate is clean between us ... there is nothing to feel shamed about." He extended his hand.

Emin swallowed hard as he gripped Skender's hand. "Thank you, brother." He hesitated. "My father says there has been nothing from the police or Udba."

"That is true ... but I am glad you raised the subject. When they come for me..." Skender held up his hand, stopping Emin's quick denial. "They will come ... we all know that ... when, is what we do not know. When they come for me, I would like you and Jakup to watch upon Gillian for me. She has never been confronted with this situation before ... I am not sure how she will react to it."

"You have my word, brother. You think that your Nusé will be...." He stopped.

"Frightened? Why do you hesitate to say that word? Isn't it a normal reaction to what is about to happen?" He frowned, rubbed at his lip. "I almost hope so ... but it could be anger." He glanced up at Emin. "And that would be more dangerous than fear. Keep her home. Do not let her try to see me … or Mihajlovich."

"Mihajlovich?" Emin asked, startled.

Skender nodded. "I don't think she realizes…." He sighed. "Of course she doesn't realize! She has never had to handle anyone as clever and sadistic as his type. My worry is that she will go to him, ask for his help…." He frowned, continued grimly. "That would play right into his hands. Make sure that she stays here in this house. If they should keep me…" there was a ghost of a smile, "…shall we say … too long?" He shook his head, again stopping Emin's hot denial. "Do not seek to reassure me, Emin, I know these people, have first-hand experience of them and their ways. If I do not return home after a reasonable time, take her to Belgrade, put her on plane to England. Get her out of here and to safety … before Mihajlovich's eyes turn to her. Can I depend on you for that?"

Emin's voice was sadly quiet as he answered, "Yes, brother … they will have to take my life before they touch a finger of hers."

"Thank you." Skender turned as Gillian opened the door, carefully balancing a tray. "My mind will rest easy knowing she is in your hands. Now let us enjoy our coffee." He watched as Gillian awkwardly swung the jesva, gave a quick smile. "We do not have his coffee in America … it is the first time she has made it. Are you prepared to try?"

Emin half-smiled. "We will face the danger together, brother." He gave a startled look as Skender spoke to Gillian. "You did not tell her my words?"

Skender laughed. "No, if I had, you would most certainly be in danger! By the way, Shamsi was here about an hour before you came." Emin's eyes went to Gillian. Skender shook his head. "No, he did not see Gillian, spoke only to me."

Gillian glanced up as she heard her name, wondered briefly what Skender had said to Emin, then carefully poured the coffee into the two cups. She picked one up, started to pass it to Emin.

"Me first, Jill."

"Sorry, I always forget." Gillian handed the coffee to Skender.

He smiled as he accepted the cup. "It would embarrass our friend, and he has had enough of that for one day."

"Thank you, Nusé." Emin sipped on the coffee. Gillian's eyes went lazily to the cards, she almost sighed. "She must be bored … perhaps, if you are agreeable, Skender, she would like to see the University?"

Skender felt a quick stab of pleasure. "I am sure she would … thank you for offering. This coffee is good, do you not think so?"

Emin grinned, showed him the empty cup. "If you will excuse me, I have class today." He stood as he received Skender's nod. "Thank God that we have cleared the air between us … these two days stretched interminably for me."

"And for me. We have so little time to be together. It is a pity to waste even a moment. I will see you tonight, then?"

"Yes, Skender … it will give me great pleasure to have you and your Nusé in our home." He glanced down, saw Gillian hesitating between the two nines. "You do not know how to play the game…." He winked at Skender, took the one she had chosen from her hand and returned it. "This one … use this one," he said impatiently as he picked up the other and placed it on the black ten.

"Don't!" Furiously, she glared up at him, slowly smiled back as she saw his grin.

Emin turned to Skender, bowed. "Until tonight, brother. Nusé, I will see you tonight. Use the nine I chose … always listen to the advice of your brother." The door closed softly behind him.

Chapter 26

"One more bite, Gillian, just one," Skender laughingly coaxed, as he held the pastry near her mouth, catching the dripping honey on a napkin.

Gillian bit her lip. "I'm ready to pop, but…." She grinned, took a bite of the paper-thin dough soaked with honey and bursting with walnuts, quickly licked the sweetness as it dripped down her lip.

"Like a cat with cream!" Adnan laughed, pointing to her.

"And the rest for me." Jakup reached and took the last piece of baklava and put it in his own mouth amid derisive hoots from his cousins. Shamsi sat a little apart, silent, only a slight smile came as he met Skender's eyes.

Arif gave a special smile to Ilyria, nodded his approval for the excellent meal she and her mother had prepared. "Skender, your Nusé is fond of sweets … she had better learn to make these before she leaves here."

"I agree, Migje, and there is none better to learn from than Ilyria … she is the best pastry cook in Kosov."

Ilyria flushed with pleasure at the praise, her eyes met Emin's. He smiled, raised his eyebrows at her and mouthed, "Sometimes." She laughed, quickly put her hand over her mouth.

"Please?" Arif quietly called for their attention, held out his hands, palms up. Babush glanced at Gillian, smiled approvingly as he saw she had anticipated what was expected of her and was ready without having to be told. The chattering and laughter stopped, all followed Arif's lead, sat quietly until he had given thanks for the meal.

Gillian hesitated only a moment as she saw Ilyria and Drita bring the water for the men to wash their hands, while Nurije and Meliha started to clear the dishes from the table. She stood, picked up one of the large round pans and started toward the door.

Adnan stopped her, said seriously, "On your head, Nusé," pointing that she should carry the pan on top of her head.

"Adnan!" Nurije protested, shook her head at the hesitant Gillian. "He is teasing, do not listen." Gently she urged Gillian out the door.

He turned, laughing, to Skender. "I think she would have done it if my sister had not intervened."

The kitchen was full, the young girls quickly got to work on washing the dishes, clustered on the floor, talking and laughing, while the women busied themselves with preparing the coffee. Gillian carefully rinsed the dish, pouring the hot clean water from the kettle as the others did, she grinned at Nurije as she realized that she was telling how Adnan had tried to make her carry the pan on her head.

"Which of you will serve the men?" Teza called.

A unanimous chorus answered, "Skender's Nusé and Meliha."

Nona smilingly beckoned Gillian, handed her one of the huge brass trays. It was heavy, the jezves full, the coffee richly dark. Gillian took a good grip of the tray, breathed in deeply, appreciatively, as the aromatic coffee teased her nostrils. Teza handed another tray to Meliha, Gillian followed her out of the kitchen up the steps to the house.

They set the trays down on the rug beside the fire, Gillian glanced quickly around. "I'll pour, you serve," she told Meliha firmly, not wanting to have to decide who was first in importance, who should be served first. *And I'd never be able to balance a full cup of coffee on three fingers!* Hesitantly she took hold of the long brass handle, took a deep breath, and lifted it from the tray.

Adnan smiled as he saw her, came swiftly and knelt beside her, put his hand over hers. "I will help you … you must swing the jesva, Gillian, that is good." He helped her fill three of the small cups. "And now again … coffee has to swing, round and round…." He looked up, eyes full of mischief, let go of Gillian's hand and covered Meliha's ears. "Like a belly dancer swings … round and round…" he said softly to his brothers and cousins. He released Meliha as Gillian glanced up at the burst of laughter. Hasan, unable to keep a straight face, shook his finger at his son. "The truth, father, I spoke only the truth." Adnan's face was a study of innocence.

Meliha glanced nervously towards Shamsi. Jakup leaned toward her, smiled gently, "Do not worry, Nusé, it was not you Adnan was teasing. It was Skender's nusé because she cannot use the jesva properly." She smiled uncertainly at him, picked up the coffee and went toward Babush.

"May I ask how my young brother knows of these things?" Aslan asked with a wicked grin at Skender.

"Hearsay only, brother, hearsay only," Adnan assured him with a straight face.

The cup rattled as Meliha picked it up and made her way across the room. Jakup silently called his father's attention to the young girl. Arif nodded. "I think that is enough. Let us have some music. Shamsi, please?"

Gillian carefully finished pouring the last two cups of coffee, Meliha waited until her husband was seated again before she went to serve him. The music started as she took the last cup to Besim.

"Meliha," Emin beckoned her to him, "Uje, please." She bowed, went quickly to the hall, returning with a glass of water. He accepted it, dismissed her with a smile, but made no attempt to drink.

Meliha moved quietly around the room, picking up the empty cups. Emin gave her a brief shake of his head as she asked if he had finished with the water, removed his hat and stood. "Nusé … for you." He inclined his head to Gillian.

"Jill, Emin is going to perform one of our national dances … for you." Skender smiled as he saw her eyes light with pleasure. "He is very good … was in a troupe that toured for a year, performing all over Yugoslavia and some of the other Eastern Bloc countries too.

She watched, gasped as he placed the full glass of water on his head. He stood lightly poised, waiting for the music. Suddenly he moved, spinning quickly, effortlessly round and round the room, his feet doing the fast and intricate steps without faltering, the glass as steady as if it were fastened to his head. Skender smiled as he saw Gillian's rapt attention. Emin stopped in front of her, slowly came to a half sitting position, eyes level with hers.

Her eyes went to the glass, firmly nestled among the dark wavy hair, he swayed from side to side, arms extended, fingers snapping out the rhythm. Gradually he lowered his arms until his fingertips touched the floor in front of her, stretched his body backwards to its full length, balancing on the tip of his toes and his fingers, and still his body kept time to the music. Gillian gasped, jumped back as he made a sudden move, doing a complete turn, he laughed as he saw her. "You will not get wet, Nusé, I promise … unless I wish it!" The water tossed waves from one side of the glass to the other but none spilt. Her eyes shone with admiration as she looked down at him.

"Jill, you must put something in the glass for him."

Eyes sparkling, fascinated with his movements, she answered absently, "I don't have anything."

Skender sighed heavily, "Then I am afraid…." He sighed again, shook his head sadly. Gillian's eyes never left Emin, she missed the quick grins and smothered laughs.

Emin did one more complete turn, grinned at her as he faced her again. "Then you are forfeit, Nusé, must take my place."

Quickly she turned to Skender. "What did he say?"

"If you have nothing to give him, you must take his place." Shocked saucer-wide eyes stared from Emin to Skender, back to Emin again.

Emin laughed. "Watch carefully now." He did another complete turn, came swiftly, effortlessly to his feet. "Did you see how it is done?" His voice was very serious as he asked her, took the glass from his head and took a drink of water.

Carefully he smoothed her hair, asked solicitously, "Do you wish to stand before I put this on your head?"

Skender turned his head, unable to stop his laughter as Jakup pulled the reluctant Gillian to her feet, he turned her to face Emin, signaled to Besim to hand him an empty glass. The men exchanged quick amused glances as they saw her horrified expression, Skender ignored her pleading look, watched seriously as Emin took one more drink from the glass, showed Gillian that, for her, it was only half full, then lifted it over her head. Quickly, quietly, Jakup slipped a few coins into the empty glass in his hand, checked that it had the right weight, passed that to Emin and accepted the one with water while Emin kept Gillian's attention by making much fuss over getting her hair smooth and flat.

She stood silently, holding her breath as Emin carefully lowered the glass with the coins onto her head, nodded to Besim to start the music. "Dance, Nusé, but be careful … the water is quite cold." Skender repeated the warning, trying not to let the laughter spill into his voice.

Gillian's eyes swiveled as she felt a cold blast of air, saw Nona in the doorway before she let her eyes come front again. Nona shook her finger scoldingly at Skender as she saw their game, quickly the rest of the women and girls sat down, grinning at each other as they realized that Gillian was willing to join in the fun.

Slowly, keeping her head absolutely straight, Gillian started to walk toward Skender. Emin sat down, gave a quick amused smile to his immediate neighbor. "What is the matter, Shamsi? You have made your peace with Skender. Why so sad?"

He sighed, eyes on Gillian. "Her. I still have not … I avoid her, have done so all evening and that is not right." He gave a rueful smile to Emin. "It is obvious that you have already apologized to her … now I must swallow my pride."

"No, she will not make you eat dust. I expected her to squeeze me dry, take pleasure in making me humble myself … she was not that way." He looked reflectively at Gillian as she moved carefully, slowly across the room. "She could have made trouble for us, Shamsi, but she held her tongue. When I went to see Skender this morning and found her instead…." He turned with a smile to Shamsi. "Go to her … she is generous, will make it easy for you."

Both of them watched as Gillian reached Skender, stood directly in front of him. "Dance with me." Smilingly he shook his head. "Dance with me or get wet," she threatened with a smile.

"You were not the one to yell at her, shake her…."

"Agreed, but I think she will make it as smooth for you as she did for me. Excuse me." Emin stood, moved silently across the room until he stood behind Gillian, he put both hands near her shoulders, then quickly grabbed her and gave her a jerk. Gillian gasped, stood stiffly, waiting for the cold water to run down her face, her back. Everyone rocked with laughter as they saw her surprise when small coins cascaded around her. Her mouth was still half-open as she turned, saw Emin, standing, hands on hips, behind her. He smiled at her, eyes sparkling. Slowly she smiled back at him, then bent and picked up the money scattered around.

"Is this yours, Emin?" He shook his head, pointed to Jakup who laughingly held out his hand for the money, she let the coins chink together in her hand as she shook her head, then put them into her pocket. "Payment, Jakup, for entertaining you!"

"Good, Nusé … do not let these young men get away with their tricks," Hasan called to her as Skender translated and the laughter had quieted.

Emin stopped Gillian as she started to sit next to Skender. "Now I am going to teach you one of our dances from Prishtine, this other was…" he shrugged, "…a show, a performance, but now you are going to learn some of the dances we do just for our own pleasure … are you ready to learn?"

Skender quickly translated.

She looked directly at Emin. "Yes."

His lips twitched. "Speak Albanian, Nusé. Po." Jakup turned to start the record as Emin reached into his pocket, took out a scarlet handkerchief and shook it free of its folds, he took hold of her hand. "Nusé…" he waited until she looked up at him, "forget that you are being watched … concentrate on the music and me…" he grinned as he saw her nervousness, "…and enjoy yourself. We will not ship you to Siberia if you cannot follow the steps!"

She listened to Skender's translation, laughed, nodded, "I'll try."

Slowly Emin started to dance, dipping and swaying to the rhythm, his feet doing the intricate steps carefully so she could follow him. She was awkward, clumsy, it seemed impossible for her to catch the movement. Emin continued, speaking quietly, the words unintelligible to her, but encouraging. She moved her right foot, brought the left into the correct position, dipped rose as the beat did, swayed, moved into the next step and then … suddenly … she was one with the music, the feel of the dance, the mood caught her and she followed Emin easily. He pushed her away from him into a spin, flicked the handkerchief at her and she caught it, so that he could pull her back to him. As fingers touched, he gave hers a slight squeeze. Pleasure ran through her as she saw his nod of approval.

Skender and Emin's eyes met. *How happy he is tonight!* Gratitude welled in him. *And I have helped give him that joy by teaching her this dance.* The music slowed, Emin released the handkerchief that tied the two of them together, pointing that she should choose another to join them.

Babush smiled at his brothers. Hasan winked back at him, sure that now she would ask Skender. Skender saw their surprise, their quick nods of approval as Gillian slowly walked to the opposite side of the room stood in front of the young man and flicked the handkerchief to him as Emin had shown her.

Good girl, Jill … you have made me feel ten feet tall.

"Will you dance with me, Shamsi?" Her cheeks were flushed more than from just the exertion of the dance as she met his eyes. He stared at her for a moment, inclined his head and slowly stood. He reached for the corner of the handkerchief Gillian held.

They looked at each other for a long moment. "The music is ready, Nusé … shall we begin?" He smiled down at her. "I think now is good time for you and I to start from the beginning." He gave a gentle pull on the handkerchief, leading her back to the center of the room and the waiting Emin. He gave a brief smile to his cousin, said softly as the music started to swell, "You were right … she made it easy."

Emin held out his hand to Gillian, gave her a warm approving smile. "This is faster, Nusé, but basically the same, it is telling of spring, of the joy in being alive, and the beauty of Kosov as life bursts forth full and glorious, after the long sleep of winter. Are you ready?"

She nodded. "Yo."

Emin laughed loudly. "Make up your mind, Nusé, your head says yes, and your mouth no. Which is it?" He took the handkerchief, flicked it so she could catch it, laughed softly at her. "Po is the word you need, Nusé."

The dance started, Skender moved swiftly, quietly to sit beside Babush. "You are happy, Djali?" he asked with a quick smile. Skender smiled back at him. "Yes … it is there for all to see. I am glad. I have waited many years, prayed many years, to see that peaceful contentment on your face. God has been good. He has let me see and hold my son again … has given me a daughter to be proud and happy with. Have a full and happy life together, Djali." He turned back to watch the dance, accepted the pouch of tobacco Hasan offered him and carefully filled his pipe.

The music came slowly to an end. Shamsi took her hand, led her back to Skender. "I return your Nusé for a few minutes, brother." He smiled at Gillian. "Rest, then we shall try another."

"Don't I get an opportunity to dance with my wife?" Skender asked in mock dismay.

"Yes, Skender. You may show us some rock and roll with her," Besim called. Excitement rippled through the young people as they urged him to agree.

Skender laughed. "We do not have the music here … all the records are at Migje Hasan's house."

"Not all. Some … er … happened to come with me," Adnan said diffidently, looking quickly towards Arif. Arif didn't look up or turn towards his nephew, winked at his brothers. Adnan took a step nearer his uncle. "Sir, some of the American records … they came with me tonight."

Arif nodded. "All are welcome in this house, if they come in peace."

Adnan looked helplessly at Besim, turned hopefully towards Jakup, whispered, "He is your father … does that mean yes or no?"

Jakup shrugged, almost laughed as he whispered back, "It could mean either!"

Adnan's eyes went to Skender. "Brother, will you show us some American dancing?"

Skender waited for Arif's decision. "If Migje Arif is agreeable, I am willing. Do not expect too much of me, I am an amateur, but everyone assures me Gillian is good at this ... you had better watch her, not me!" He turned and explained to Gillian what was happening. "And I have told them that I am not very good at this kind of dancing."

"Oh, I don't know," her eyes flirted with him, "when they play the slow, smoochy ones, there's none better than you!"

His laugh was loud. "How lucky for me that you do not speak the language ... you would get me into all kinds of trouble." He let his fingers touch hers, said softly, "Thank you, Jill."

She glanced at him in surprise. "For what?"

"For giving Shamsi a bridge to cross, making it easy for him to become one with the family again."

She wrinkled her nose at him, Adnan's frantic signals caught her attention. He held up some of the American records, lifted his arms, silently asking "Which one?" She shook her head at both, he picked up another and she gave a quick grin and nodded.

Skender glanced towards Arif, wondering if he was aware of what was happening behind him, he gave a slow smile to Skender, "I was aware of your tricks since you and Aslan took your first steps, Djali."

Skender and Aslan glanced at each other and laughed. "You knew all the time Midge?" Skender asked in disbelief. Arif gave a brief nod Asslyn and Skender stared at each other then at him, "And all this time, we thought…."

Arif scowled. "I would have had to have been blind and deaf not to have known of all your adventures." The scowl became a smile. "Skender, do you remember the time I threatened to put you down the well, keep you there for a week?" He laughed as he turned to Babush. "You remember, don't you?"

"One two, three o'clock, four o'clock, rock…."

Adnan came swiftly to Gillian as *Rock Around the Clock* blared forth. "Come, Gillian, show me." He pulled her to her feet, almost turned away before he remembered Skender. He turned back, bowed, his face flushed with embarrassment. "With your permission, brother?"

Skender laughed, slapped him on the shoulder. "Of course, go ahead."

"…five, six, seven o'clock, eight o'clock rock…."

The ring seemed shriller, louder, more demanding at night. The sergeant sighed as he lifted the phone, "Counter guard."

"Mihajlovich here."

"Yes, Comrade Colonel?"

Mihajlovich smiled, almost seeing the sergeant leap to attention. "Pick up Skender Berisha.

"Immediately, Comrade Colonel."

"No. Not immediately. Tomorrow. Late afternoon."

"He will be here, Comrade Colonel. Shall I deliver him to your office?"

"No." Mihajlovich's finger ran down the detailed information in the thick, bulky file on his desk. His finger stopped, traveled across the page as he found what he wanted. "No. Put him in one of the Interrogation Rooms…" his voice was slow, reflective, as he continued, "let us say…" he glanced down again at the file. "…yes, number four."

"Four? Comrade Colonel…" the sergeant's tone was diffident, "we never use those rooms now. They are the old…."

"Exactly," Mihajlovich said decisively. "Number four." The sergeant shrugged. The pool of yellow light vanished as Mihajlovich switched off his desk lamp and closed the file. He stood. "I am going home now. Goodnight."

"Goodnight, Comrade Colonel." He waited until he heard the phone replaced at the other end, then put his own back on the cradle. His hand moved from the phone to the order sheets, he pulled one toward him, glanced at the date on the calendar in front of him and dated the order sheet for the following day.

"Sixteen hundred hours, detain Skender Berisha. Interrogation Room 4."

He underlined the figure, pushed a call button on the side of his desk, and then continued writing.

"Direct orders of Colonel Mihajlovich, D.D. Udba."

He glanced up as his subordinate approached. "Here," he initialed the order sheet, handed it to him, "Mihajlovich wants Berisha."

Chapter 27

The guard's thumb cocked towards the door, "Get in."

Skender's eyes lifted – 'Interrogation Room 4' – A sick dizziness swept over him for a moment.

"Do you need me to help you in?" Skender turned to the smirking guard, he suppressed a sigh and walked in. The door slammed behind him. He stood stiffly, his breathing shallow and uneven.

Slowly he let his eyes travel round the small room. The wooden desk was clear except for a telephone. He took a few steps towards it, stood looking down at it. *Why does it look so evil? An ordinary telephone, yet it looks like some ugly black insect waiting to pounce....*

His hand held the back of the wooden chair as his eyes went to the opposite side of the desk. *The officer will sit there, in the padded leather chair, slowly rocking back and forth as he asks his questions ... and I will sit here....* The wood bit into his hand as he gripped harder ... *answering him until....* He swallowed the saliva that had collected in his mouth, reluctantly turned. Beads of sweat stood damply on his forehead as he stared at the belts hanging behind the door He shuddered, forced himself to look away, his eyes lifted to the right-hand wall as he sat down. Four-thirty. He took a handkerchief from his pocket and wiped his forehead.

A door slammed, he came quickly to his feet, turned to face it. The room remained empty except for himself. The belts drew his eyes again, slowly they moved from the new, heavier ones on the left to the lighter, worn ones on the right. He closed his eyes. *Oh God, help me, give me strength ... it was hard to take as a boy, but now...?*

He swallowed, groped for the chair, hearing again the sound of the strap cutting the air, the sharp sickening slap as leather met flesh... *Not that way, that way all is lost even before they begin. Let them know that fear eats at me and they have control....* He put his head into his hands, ashamed.

You will always be afraid of them, Skender, but don't let fear latch on to you, don't let it make you its prisoner ... the only way we can handle their terror, and our fear, is to fight it, push it away....

He raised his head, took a long deep breath as he unbuttoned his coat, *I still draw on your strength, Sabri. Stay close, I think I shall need your help.*

The minute hand of the clock moved slowly, towards the next numeral, dragged itself past and started its long climb to the next.

"Sir, Migje Hasan is coming immediately and I have sent Besim to my father with the news."

Babush nodded his thanks. "Drita?"

"Crying, but calm." Emin glanced around the room, asked uncertainly, "Nona?"

"She has control, has gone to rest." Babush sighed, "Emin, have you seen our Nusé? She left this room only seconds after they took my son … I have not seen her since."

Emin paled. *Mihajlovich! I had forgotten Skender's warning.* "I will find her, sir … rest. Migje Hasan will be with you in moments." He forced himself to walk at a normal pace from the room, closed the door quietly, then hurried to the women's guest room. Panic clawed at him as he saw the emptiness, *Surely she would not have gone immediately? Where else might she be?* He frowningly stared at the rug. *The kitchen!* The nalle slipped as he rushed to put them on, he swore softly as he bent and retrieved them from underneath the bench. He took the steps two at a time, swiftly opened the door. The gentle hiss of the near-boiling kettle pierced the still silence, the red glow of the burning logs gave dull light to the near dark room. Fear gripped at his stomach. *God in Heaven, she must have gone … there is nowhere else….*

"Excuse me," he sighed with relief as he turned to face her, "excuse me, please."

"Nusé, where were you?" His eyes searched her white face, then dropped to the basket of food in her hands. "The storage shed? Why? What were you doing in there?" He stood aside and let her pass by him.

Gillian set the basket down onto the floor, walked to the flour bin and picked up the dictionary. She walked steadily back to the center of the room, sat down, and without a word asked him to sit beside her. "I must get help for Skender." He looked down at the words, gave her a brief nod. She flicked through the pages. "Will you come with me to Belgrade?" She watched his face, saw the confusion. "Skender is an American…." Her hands shook as she rushed to find the words she needed. "The Embassy will act as soon as they know that he has been arrested."

Emin waited quietly for the last word. "No, Nusé, not arrested…" he took the dictionary, "taken for questioning."

Angrily she turned on him as she read the word. "Is there a difference?" Her eyes filled, she blinked rapidly.

Gently Emin took hold of her hand. "Yes." If he had been arrested.... He sighed.

"Will you come with me? I am going to the American Embassy first, and then the British."

Emin worriedly shook his head. "I don't know ... perhaps." He rubbed at his moustache, frowning. "I will have to get permission, but there should not be any difficulty." He looked at her questioningly. "The American Embassy, yes ... but why the British?"

She pointed to her wedding band before she picked up the dictionary. "He is married to me ... they might help us ... and two squeaky wheels make more noise than one." He smiled briefly at her. "The train leaves at eleven-fifteen tonight. If he is not back in this house, I shall be on it ... oh damn!" She flung the dictionary from her. "It takes so long just to...." She turned from Emin, quickly covered her mouth with her hand.

"Hush now." Emin leaned forward and picked it up, Gillian looked down at the words as he started to speak. "We cannot go tonight. I have no permit and cannot get one until tomorrow. And we must talk first with Babush and my father ... they will decide if we should go or not." He offered her the dictionary, looked suspiciously at her as she made no attempt to answer him. *You would not try to go by yourself, would you? No. It would be impossible for you to remember the way to the station, and it is too far without transportation....* The squeak of the gate reached him, he half stood, listening carefully. "Nusé, Migje Hasan is coming ... I am going to greet him, take him to Babush." She ignored the proffered dictionary; he laid it beside her on the rug. "Continue to be brave ... you have done so well."

She heard the door click to as he left, she sighed deeply as she reached and pulled one of the large round pans from the pile beside the kitchen stove. *No, Emin, I will not wait. Time could make all the difference to Skender's well-being.* Absently she started to mix some of the rice with the meat. *The station was quite a way from here. There were some taxis outside the big hotel on the main street ... will they be there at night?* She picked up one of the soft yellow peppers, started to stuff the meat mixture into it. *If not, I must allow plenty of time to walk. Walk? A woman? At night? And alone? Here that would cause too much attention.* She sat still shoulders drooping despondently. *How ... Yes!* Emin's coat had caught her eye. *Yes! It will be too long, but that is all to the good, with my slacks and flat shoes ...* She laid the filled pepper into the pan, picked up another, brushing a curl from her forehead as she did so. *My hair!* Panic shot through her. How can I disguise that? Slowly she stuffed the pepper with meat and rice. *If I pin it all up on top of my head ... use one of their hats ... yes, it would not pass close inspection.* Her eyes went to the window ... *but it is already dusk ... by the time I leave it will be dark.*

Leave? How am I going to get out of this house? They would never let me go by myself.... She laid the pepper next to the other, picked up another. *I will plead a headache; say I am going to bed....* Hysterical laughter bubbled in her throat, she dropped the pepper, put her hand over her mouth, fighting for control. *I sound like some second-rate Hollywood movie….* She stood up, went and poured herself a glass of water, slowly she returned to the fire and sat down. *Oh, Skender please be home and safe … let all these dramatics be a waste of time, something that we can laugh about together.* Her throat tightened, quickly she took another gulp of water. *But if you are not here by nine o'clock, I am leaving this house … I cannot sit back and do nothing when right now….* She bit hard on her knuckles. *Oh God, look after him … don't let them hurt him again.* The great tearing sobs could not be controlled. Quickly she reached and pulled one of the towels hanging above her head, pushed it tight against her mouth so none should hear.

A door slammed. Skender did not move, used, now, to the irregularly repeated noise. His eyes looked at the clock, Five-twenty. *How much longer will they leave me sitting here? What is their purpose in this long wait?* He smiled grimly as he answered himself … *To shake your nerve even more … and not only your nerves, but those of your family too. Poor Nona … so upset, crying as if her heart was broken.* He sighed deeply. *God forgive me for bringing my mother so much pain. So much heartache. Drita … so terrified she had no control on her legs … a blessing that Emin was there … picked her up and carried her from the room. Jill….* He closed his eyes for a moment. *Only the stiffness of her body gave away her fear.* He frowned. *What was Babush trying to tell me? 'Your greatest weakness could also be your greatest strength….'* He rubbed at his lip as he concentrated. *'Remember, Djali, tender skin bruises and bleeds easily. Cover and protect the tenderness … let the probing finger push elsewhere…' Jill! That was his concern. Yes, Babush, you are right. They would be able to reach me through her….* He sighed, glanced up at the clock. The minute hand started again on its long climb upward.

Babush finished washing his hands, hung the towel over Gillian's arm and watched as she moved on toward Arif. He sat down at the low table, placing the cloth over his knees, then looked slowly from Arif to Hasan, then at his nephews. "My new daughter's heart is crying, and yet she has prepared a meal for us. Even though worry for my son fills our stomachs, we will eat this meal, for she has prepared it with love, and with love and gratitude for her consideration of us, we will accept it." He glanced at the clock. "He has been in their hands a little over an hour and a half. Let us pray that within the next hour, he will be returned to our hands unharmed."

"Skender Berisha?"

He stood up. "That is correct." He half-turned, looked toward the door, the man left the doorway, leaving the door open as he walked towards Skender.

His eyes ran over Skender, coldly, calculatingly, as he sat down in the leather chair. Skender heard the soft sound of the door closing, resisted the impulse to turn and see who else was in the room. "You may sit down … before you do, remove your coat."

Slowly Skender took off his coat. He glanced backwards as it was roughly taken from him. The guard, heavy set, his uniform straining across his chest, searched his pockets. Skender's eyes passed him, went to the other side of his chair. *Two of them, just as before … one to hold you, while the other….* His palms were damp as he turned back to face his interrogator.

"Sit down. I am Colonel Mihajlovich."

Yes, of course. I should have guessed.

Mihajlovich opened his briefcase, took out two files, dropped them onto the desk, deliberately letting the slimmer one slide to the opposite edge of the table. Skender's eyes automatically dropped to the top right-hand corner of the buff folder. Mihajlovich gave his victim time to read the name: "Berisha, Gillian, female", then gathered it to him with the other.

Magnetized, Skender's eyes followed the folder. *A file on Jill? Why?*

"Your papers, please" A satisfied smile played about Mihajlovich's mouth as he held out his hand.

Skender dragged his eyes from the folder, "I'm sorry. What did you say?"

"Your papers … please."

Would they dare stretch their hands that far? Skender took the slim green passport from his jacket pocket.

"Not that. Your identity card."

They have no claim on her … surely would not risk an international incident…. He saw Mihajlovich watching him, pulled himself together. "I do not have one. In America we do not have to carry such a thing. Here is my passport." He proffered the soft green book.

Mihajlovich's eyes were glued on Skender, he ignored the passport. "But you were born here, in Kosovo … is that not so?"

She was born In England…. He licked his lips, "Yes."

Mihajlovich extended his hand a little farther toward Skender, "Then … your identity card, please."

They can have no claim on her, none. "I do not have one."

"Really? Where might it be?"

"I have never had one."

Satisfaction gleamed in Mihajlovich's eyes.

Skender realized his mistake immediately. *Must concentrate, not let my mind wander … that is what he wants.*

"Mmm…. Would you explain to me how you left this country?" Mihajlovich sat very still, eyes never leaving Skender. "Without an identity card, there is no way you would be given a passport, so how did you cross the border? Could it be that you left here illegally?"

He gave a small sigh, sat forward and leaned across the desk. "You do not answer. Should I assume that I am correct? That you left this country without permission? Without the necessary papers?"

He reached, poured himself some water, sat sipping at it. "Well?" He took several more sips of the water, "I am waiting, Berisha." He put the glass of water down, "I suggest you answer." It was said too quietly.

Skender heard the threat, took a deep breath, "I am an American citizen; I am here as a visitor. Here is my passport."

Mihajlovich ignored the offered passport, slowly sat back in his chair. "We do not acknowledge a change of citizenship. Did you know that?" He looked beyond Skender, gave a small nod. Skender stiffened as he heard the gentle swish-swish as the leathers knocked against each other, waited for the heavy hand to fall on his shoulder. Mihajlovich saw the anticipated reaction, his voice came softly to Skender. "Not yet, Berisha, not yet. Do not be too anxious. We have plenty of time for that. You see you are ours … we can do with you as we please, when we please."

"You have no reason…." Skender stopped angrily, biting back the rest.

Mihajlovich gave a knowing smile. "I do not need a reason. I am surprised that you forgot that, even if it was just for a moment." The smile vanished. "I need no reason … can take you apart piece by piece if I wish."

Skender gritted his teeth, made sure his voice was firm and steady. "I am an American citizen. If any … harm … should come to me, you will answer to the government of the United States."

Laughter burst from Mihajlovich. "Don't be naïve, Berisha. Do you really believe that?" He leaned across the desk "The Russians forced down an American jet, put the pilot … one of their own officers … on trial as a spy, and confiscated a highly developed plane, and do you know what your precious United States did? Made an 'official complaint'."

Mihajlovich laughed softly. "Now tell me, do you really believe that they will bother with you? A refugee?" He helped himself to a cigarette, reached for his lighter, watching Skender through the flame. He took a long draw as he snapped the lighter closed, sat back, lazily rocking the chair, watching Skender. "Your silences are more eloquent than your answers." He laid the cigarette down, "But, should the United States choose to make an 'official complaint' about you…" he almost smiled, "I am sure my government will oblige them with an 'official apology'."

Despair swept over Skender. *Every word he said is true. I must keep my faith in my American citizenship. Must. Without that I am nothing … putty in his hand.*

Mihajlovich pulled the slim file towards him, opened it. "Gillian Berisha…" he glanced up, "she is your wife?"

Skender breathed deeply, forcing himself to calmness. "Yes, she is."

"She is British?"

"Yes."

"But you met her in America?"

"Yes."

"And you were married there?"

"Yes."

"I find it strange that you, of all people, would marry a Western girl." He looked up, met Skender's eyes. "Why did you?" He continued to watch Skender, as there was no reply. "Your family strongly objected, yet you insisted. Why?"

He must have copies of every letter I've ever written to Babush.

Mihajlovich demanded sharply, "Why?! Who is she? What is her importance to the British? Why are they so interested in her welfare?"

"I was not aware that she had any importance to them … other than that she is a citizen of that country, and automatically carries their protection … wherever she goes."

Mihajlovich's eyes narrowed, "Very good, Berisha. As a matter of fact, exceptionally good. You came as close as you dared to telling me to leave her alone. Now…" Carefully he removed some ash from his cigarette, "…there is a stamp in her passport, her Embassy has requested full assistance from us for her … why? Who is she and what importance does she have for them?"

Skender gave a small shrug. "All I know is that she registered with her Embassy in Belgrade. The British authorities know where she is, why she is here … and when she should leave."

Mihajlovich's eyes flicked immediately to Skender. "She may leave any time. Now. Within the hour if she wishes. You, on the other hand…." He held out his hand, "Passport."

Skender passed it to him, watching as he thumbed through the pages.

Mihajlovich looked up with an unpleasant smile, "I see that you do not have this, er, 'protection'. Your American friends are, perhaps, not quite as interested in your welfare as the British appear to be in your wife's?" He tossed the passport to one side, "This is useless. Not worth the paper it is written on. You were born here, Berisha … until you die you are ours. And any children you may have … we claim them, too."

Never! I will never let you lay hands on any child of mine.

Mihajlovich had returned to the file, he sat quietly reading. "Have you ever been to England?"

"No."

"I have. I studied there, but perhaps Jill has…" he stopped, gave an embarrassed cough, "perhaps your wife has already told you that?"

He asked if I called myself Jill. I said no, but…. "I did not give you permission to use my wife's name."

"I'm sorry, a mistake." Embarrassment dripped from him, he put down his cigarette, picked it up again and made much of stubbing it out. Skender steadily watched him. "Your wife is a delightful young lady, so friendly." A smile hovered about Mihajlovich's mouth, he sighed slightly, "But I thought it prudent not to accept her invitation to have coffee…."

Your poison drops on barren ground, Mihajlovich … I know it all.

"…although I would have enjoyed reminiscing on England," Mihajlovich smiled knowingly as he saw the knuckles whitely showing on Skender's hand, glanced up. "I understand you are planning a trip to Prizren?" Skender gave a stiff nod. "Be sure you ask for a permit before leaving Pristina. You are liable to immediate arrest if you leave without one."

He gloated silently as he saw Skender's surprised confusion. "You should go to the coast. Our beaches are unsurpassable, and swimming is Jill's favorite…" he bit off the words, held his breath as his eyes flew to Skender's, "I'm sorry."

'Cover, protect … let the probing finger push elsewhere.'

Skender let Mihajlovich see his anger, deliberately misled him, letting him think he had succeeded in his ploy. "How did you come by that information? Was it she that told you? And did she give you permission to use that name for her?" he asked icily.

Mihajlovich glanced down at the desk with a sigh, then looked directly and frankly at Skender. "Do not be too harsh with her…" his voice was compassionate, "try not to compare her with your own girls. Her standards are so … different shall we say … and I was careless. I should not have let it slip, especially to you, that we conversed so freely together. Let it pass. Do not let your hand fall on her shoulders."

"How I handle my wife is my concern, not yours."

"Yes, of course." Mihajlovich rubbed at his forehead, murmured to himself, "Where were we before…" he looked down at the file, then continued, "you have never seen London, then?"

"As I have never been in England, that would have been somewhat difficult."

"Yes. Yes of course. You would like it…." He was intent on reading the file. "That is if you ever have the opportunity to see it." Skender watched him closely, not sure if a threat was intended or not. "I enjoyed myself there. It is a fascinating city … a mixture of old and new…."

"I am sure it is. When you were forced to leave it, return here, it must have broken your heart." Skender interrupted softly in English. Mihajlovich started. Skender saw that he had caught him off guard, took swift advantage and continued again in English, "You are an educated man … you have lived and studied in the country which is the Mother of Freedom. How can you stand this control? You are as a bug under a microscope, studied and watched…."

"Shut your mouth." The command came rapidly in English. Mihajlovich's eyes went swiftly to the two guards, they stared stolidly ahead. "I could have every inch of skin off your back for less than you've said."

Skender smiled to himself as he saw his nervousness, *My turn now, Mihajlovich, my turn.* He spoke again in English. "Didn't you ever consider making your home in a free country? Asking for asylum…."

"Shut your mouth! Or I'll shut it for you." Mihajlovich was on his feet, leaning across the desk toward Skender before he had finished speaking.

The guards moved immediately, each grabbing a shoulder. "The thought must have passed through your mind…." Skender flinched, took a quick indrawn breath, as the iron fingers dug into his muscles. "I don't have to go back … I can stay…."

"One more word, Berisha, and they'll carry you home." Mihajlovich towered over him, face full of rage.

Skender glanced up at him, knew it was no idle threat, the anger was controlled, but barely so.

Slowly Mihajlovich turned from him, walked back to his own side of the desk.

"Get ready, dog … I will be tickling your back in seconds now," was whispered into Skender's left ear as Mihajlovich walked away from them. He kept his eyes down, gritted his teeth. The guard's fingers moved, searching.

Skender gasped, doubled over as pain shot down his left arm as the searching fingers found the nerve. *But I found a tender spot too, didn't I Mihajlovich?*

"Comrade?" Eager anticipation was in the one word. The grip on his shoulder slackened a little as the guard leaned forward.

Mihajlovich took a handkerchief from his pocket dabbed at his mouth, his back still toward them.

You realize that you've made a mistake, don't you, Mihajlovich? Listening – and answering – in a foreign tongue? What if your superior should hear of it? Within hours you will be called before him, and he will demand…. The probing fingers found the nerve again, he gritted his teeth, dropped his eyes to the floor. *…demand an explanation.*

"Colonel Mihajlovich?" Mihajlovich turned slowly toward the guard. "Shall I get the belt, Comrade?"

Flickering fingers of fear ran through Skender as the angry eyes turned on him. He forced himself to look steadily back.

The guards exchanged puzzled, silent questions, as no order was issued. The heavy one leaned toward Mihajlovich, asked again, "Comrade, shall I get the belt?"

The clock grated noisily in the silent room, the guards glanced at each other, then back to Mihajlovich.

Skender gasped but would not let his eyes drop from Mihajlovich's as more pressure was put on his left shoulder.

"Let him go." The guards gaped at each other, then turned and stared at Mihajlovich. "Damn you, I said let him go."

Skender's left shoulder was held a shade longer, the fingers gave one more dig. He took a long shuddering breath as he felt himself released.

Mihajlovich waited until both guards stood again in their assigned positions behind Skender's chair. He sat down, pulled the chair in to the desk. His eyes lifted to the heavy guard, "Next time I give you my order, carry it out immediately, without question, without delay."

"Comrade Colonel, I did."

"Immediately! Unless you wish me to teach you the meaning of obedience."

The guard paled, stood stiffly. "Yes, Colonel Mihajlovich."

Mihajlovich's eyes ran over Skender as he pulled the heavy, bulky file towards him, pushing the lighter one to one side. "Your wife did not complete the Visitor Form, but we will leave it for now." He opened the thicker file, a veiled threat in his voice as he continued, "I know exactly where to find her if I should need her … don't I Berisha?"

Panic stirred in Skender. "Ask your questions. I will answer for her."

"Thank you, but no." The cold, angry eyes looked directly at Skender. "I prefer to question her myself."

Skender's hands tightened on the arms of the chair. *Harm her in any way, Mihajlovich, and you're dead … if not by my hand, by one of my brothers.* "She has already reported here … you saw her yourself. Why didn't you have her complete the form then?"

The smile was slow, unpleasant. "Then there would have been no reason for me to recall her, would there?"

Skender licked at his lips. "And what if I refuse to let her come?"

There was a soft laugh from Mihajlovich, "I will take her." With or without your permission." He laughed again, "And I will take you too, if I wish." He sat back in the chair, a sarcastic smile on his mouth. "Well, Berisha, are you still so sure of yourself? Or have I convinced you that you are in my hands? That this…" he picked up the passport with distaste, holding it with just one finger and his thumb, then dropped it with disgust onto the desk, "…is useless here?"

Skender took deep steadying breaths, forcing himself to sit quietly and not answer, not grab at the passport.

"What was your purpose in coming to Pristina?"

"To visit my family."

"How noble! Did they recognize you after…" Mihajlovich glanced down at the file, "…seventeen years?" He picked up the slim gold pen, sat watching Skender. "What political group are you attached to?"

"None."

"You do not vote in America?"

"I did not say that. I said that I belong to no political organization."

"Not even the Free Albanian Government in Exile?" Mihajlovich snapped.

"No."

"I do not believe you." Mihajlovich's eyes were fixed on Skender. "With the approval and support of the Berisha family, they could attract many to their cause."

Skender met his eyes, "I am not interested in causes. I want to live my life in peace and tranquility."

"You have changed, then, since last we had you in our hands?"

"No. My desire was the same then. The times and circumstances did not allow it."

"Nonsense. A signature, a commitment, and you would have been left in peace." Skender briefly shook his head. "Freedom and peace for all nations…."

"Enough! Even after all these years my craw is still full of your promises. I …

Mihajlovich was half-way to his feet, "Don't interrupt me again. Ever." He waited for Skender's acknowledgement, then returned to his seat.

I heard it … all of it … over and over. I rejected it as a boy, I reject it even more as a man. Skender continued silently to himself as Mihajlovich looked down at the open file.

Mihajlovich turned a page of the file then looked up at Skender, "You do admit that you have committed a crime against the State?"

"I admit nothing. I have done nothing wrong. My only 'crime' was to refuse to join the Communist Party."

"You escaped."

"From certain death." Skender leaned forward, "Your people murdered well over eighteen hundred Albanian youths on that march, Mihajlovich. Even your own government has admitted it." Slowly he sat back in his chair. "What is it that you accuse me of? Seeking life rather than death?"

"You left this country illegally … do you deny that?"

"No. There was no other way to leave at that time."

Mihajlovich's eyes scanned the file. "Sabri Mali … did he escape with you?"

Hatred flashed in Skender. "No."

Mihajlovich's eyes narrowed, "Then where is he?"

"Dead. Shot. At Tivari."

"Are you sure of his death?"

Hurt and anger seethed in Skender, "Yes, I'm sure."

Mihajlovich heard the anger as he marked the file, "Jusuf Gashi?"

"Drowned. Pushed by a guard into Lake Skodra." He held onto his anger as Mihajlovich's eyes questioned him. "You do not live long in the icy waters of Lake Skodra."

The pen moved on the paper, "And his brother, Hamdi?"

"Frozen, his body probably still lies in stiffness in the Albanian Alps, along with the rest of them."

The mark was made again, "Morat Deva?"

Morat. Pain stabbed through Skender. He closed his eyes for a moment, hearing the cry reverberating around the mountains. His voice was barely audible as he answered, "Beaten until he couldn't walk then thrown into a ravine and left to die." His eyes lifted to Mihajlovich as Mihajlovich marked the file. "Is that enough? Do you want to hear about the rest? There are a lot more names…." Skender sighed deeply, "They are all dead, all of my friends … close your damned files and let them rest in peace."

Mihajlovich turned a page. "They had a choice. They did not have to die."

Control snapped at the matter-of-fact tone. He leapt at Mihajlovich, hands outstretched reaching for his neck, "What choice, damn you?"

Mihajlovich sat perfectly still, watching coolly as the two guards hauled him from the desk. Skender felt his arms pulled up and back, saw for an instant the gleam of hatred as the guard doubled his fist. The punch to his stomach was hard, swift, and powerful. He groaned as he doubled over, was swiftly jerked upright again. He tried not to stiffen as the fist smashed at him again.

The guard took advantage of his closeness as he doubled over in pain, whispered close in his ear, "Now he will give you to me. I promise the belt will fall hard on you, and I shall enjoy every stroke I lay across your back." He pulled his fist away, glanced up at his companion. "Let him go." Skender slid to the floor. "Hold him there." The heavy boot was pushed against his back, pinning him to the floor.

Mihajlovich glanced down at him, then watched as the guard went to the rack and carefully chose one of the belts. He casually took out a cigarette and lit it.

The guard sauntered back, flicking the leather as he came toward them. He stood over Skender, made the strap crack loudly, he grinned as he saw Skender's eyes close. "Get his shirt off." The second guard lifted his foot from Skender, bent toward him.

"I did not order that."

The guard straightened immediately as Mihajlovich's voice came softly to him. He gave an apprehensively glance toward his companion, then came to attention facing Mihajlovich.

Mihajlovich turned from him to the heavy guard with the strap. "Did I give you an order?" he asked mildly.

The heavy jowls trembled as he looked from Skender to Mihajlovich. "But Comrade Colonel, he grabbed at you, threatened you…."

"Did I give an order?" Panic-stricken eyes gaped back at him. "What kind of conceit is there in you to make you think you can interpret my wishes?"

"Colonel Mihajlovich, I'm sorry…."

"Yes," Mihajlovich's smile was cruel, "and I promise you will be even sorrier." His eyes turned back to the other guard. "Get him from the floor …

put him on the chair." He stood up. "Don't stand there you fat fool … help him."

He walked around to the opposite side of the desk, watched as they righted the chair, waited patiently until they had Skender on it. "That was a stupid move, Berisha, not worthy of you." He sat on the edge of the desk, folded his arms. "Lift his head … I want to see his face." Coolly he looked down into Skender's pain-filled eyes. "You have been in our hands many times, have never acted so foolishly before. You know what will happen now." He picked up the belt with the toe of his shoe, tossed it toward the guard. "Why did you act so stupidly?"

"Emotion … cannot … always … be controlled." Skender's breathing was shallow, ragged.

"Wrong, Berisha. It can. Everything can be controlled." Mihajlovich watched Skender closely, "I will make the statement again, they, and you, had a choice."

Skender pushed his hands against the chair, trying to straighten up as the pain started to recede. Mihajlovich's hand moved briefly, ordering the guard to release his hold on Skender's hair. "I tell you we had no choice."

"You did, join the Party, live under its protection. Or exist outside of it."

"I will tell you what our choice was." His breathing came in short, sharp breaths, "Join the Party. Spy on your family and friends, report everything they said and did … list everyone who visited your home and how long they stayed." He had to pause, to let his breathing become less strained, then continued, "or be brutally beaten, night after night. That was the decision we had to make at sixteen … seventeen." Carefully he eased himself into a more comfortable position.

"I cannot see why there was any difficulty. The Party comes first. In everything."

"Yes, of course, the Party." Skender sighed, "Always the party. They tell you where to live, what to say, how to think…."

"Correct. You are guided always."

"Guided?" Skender laugh was bitter. "There is a different word I would use to…."

"Careful." Mihajlovich warned. "So far I have been lenient with you … my patience will not stretch much farther."

He glanced at the belt in the guard's hand. *I don't think so. When he was a boy, he tasted that strap every day, sometimes twice a day … The entry was always the same, 'No response'.*

He walked back to his seat. "You asked me to close my files … that is what I want. I do not like loose ends. We have no way of knowing who is dead and who lives. You can provide that information."

Skender gave a short derisive laugh. "How can I know that? There were three thousand, taken from all over Kosov. Some lay in my arms and died and I didn't even know what name they carried or where they came from. In the situation we were in, you did not bother with the social amenities." He sighed, staring past Mihajlovich, lost to his immediate surroundings. "There was one, I still regret that I did not know his name. He was only thirteen … a child still, but he fought hard for life." His eyes turned briefly to Mihajlovich. "Most of us came to accept the idea of death, some even welcomed it, held out their arms to it. Death was a welcome visitor, bringing release from the misery we were in … but not that boy, life was his goal, to return to his home his ambition. I still think of him. What was his name? From which part of Kosov did he spring? What mother still stops, holds her breath, as she hears a footstep approach?" His eyes closed, he sighed. "She waits in vain, poor woman … not many escaped the slaughter of Tivari."

There was a long pause. Mihajlovich sat frowning at the desk. "The government was young, mistakes were made. We printed an official apology."

"Yes." Skender's eyes raised to look directly at him. "Yes, you did. That must help. When a father misses and needs his son, he can read your apology. And the mothers? When their arms ache to hold that to which they gave life, they can hold your printed apology close to their hearts."

Mihajlovich dropped the pen onto the desk, straightened the papers in the files, then looked directly at Skender. "Will you help me complete our records? As much as you are able?"

Skender sighed, *That is all it means to you isn't it? All those needlessly wasted lives are nothing to you.* "I will help you by telling you those that are dead. The living … not a word will you have from me." He hesitated, "There is one request…" Mihajlovich raised his eyebrows in query, "…that you inform the families concerned, let them know that they should accept. Waiting, hoping, is more painful than knowing."

"Agreed. I will have the list of names made ready; you will put a mark against those that are known to be dead."

He picked up the passport, tossed it toward Skender. "You may keep this until tomorrow…"

Until tomorrow? What is he talking about?

"…you will need it for identification. If you should be stopped and have no identification, you are subject to immediate arrest. In the meantime, I will issue you with an Identity Card."

"An Identity Card? Why should I need such a thing?"

Mihajlovich ignored the interruption. "Pick it up tomorrow night, when you check in."

Skender's stomach somersaulted, "When I do … what?"

Mihajlovich's eyes flashed briefly to Skender. "Check in. What was your check-in time before? Six o'clock?" His finger moved quickly over the page until he found the information. "Yes, six o'clock, that is correct. I will give you the same time. It will help you to remember." He looked up, gave Skender a cool, sarcastic smile. "After all, we do not want to have to send someone to fetch you … do we?"

Skender's hand shook slightly as he reached for the passport. "Why do I have to check in? For what reason?"

"Ask the officer on duty for your Identity Card … it will be ready by tomorrow night."

Skender swallowed, licked at his lips. "I asked why I had to check in, why I need an Identity Card."

"Hang that thing up." Mihajlovich watched as the guard went to the belt rack, then turned to Skender. "Perhaps I will discuss that with you tomorrow night, or the night after, or whenever I have the time and inclination." He stood up. "That is all. Goodnight." He stopped as he approached the guard standing stiffly to attention beside the door. "He may leave. I will sign his release on the way out. And as for you…" he let his eyes run over the man, "…I will speak to your sergeant on my way out. Report to him when you are finished here."

"Colonel Mihajlovich, I meant no harm. Please, let it pass. I will be more careful in future."

Mihajlovich laughed softly. "Yes, I know you will. One correction from me is always enough. The order stands. Goodnight."

The guard opened the door for him, "Goodnight Comrade Colonel."

Skender stood up as he heard the door close. His coat lay on the floor. He fought the pain as he bent to pick it up. His eyes went briefly to the guard standing beside the door, holding it closed, glaring at him, took a long breath then walked purposefully toward him.

The second guard looked nervously from his companion to Skender. Skender hesitated, then continued to move toward the door. He was almost abreast of the heavy guard when he deliberately leaned against the door. Skender stopped.

The guard raised his hand, held for a moment, then smacked it across the belts, making them swing violently. "You cheated me tonight," he whispered, putting his face close to Skender's, "and made trouble for me with Mihajlovich. But tomorrow night…" there was an evilness to his smile that made Skender shiver, "…I hope he gives you to me."

Skender stood stiffly silent, trying not to breathe the sour tobacco breath, not allowing himself to answer or look at the swinging belts. The second guard moved slightly, sent his companion a warning glance.

After a long moment, he moved from the door, taking his hand from the handle. Skender reached for the handle. "Tomorrow night, Berisha. Six o'clock. I'll be waiting," was whispered in his ear.

Skender gritted his teeth, walked through the doorway and turned down the long corridor toward the entry hall.

The other guard straightened the leather chair. "What was wrong with Mihajlovich tonight?"

Angrily, the fat one kicked the door closed. "How the hell do I know?"

"He has skinned many a back for less than this one did." He watched the guard straightening the belts, stopping their swinging. "But it is you I am sorry for … Mihajlovich is well-known for his disciplinarian action." He deliberately looked long and hard at the belts. "Don't be. Feel sorry for that bastard." His hand lovingly caressed the belt he was straightening. "If I ever get my hands on him…." He turned, "Are you ready?" His companion swiftly checked that the room was in order, nodded and together they left, walking the long corridor in silence.

The sergeant finished the form, passed it to Skender to sign. "Make sure you are here tomorrow night, Berisha." He took the signed form, initialed the signature as he continued, "Or do I need to send someone for you?"

Skender gave a brief shake of his head. "It is not necessary. I shall be here."

"And so shall I." The tone was threatening. Both Skender and the sergeant turned. Skender dropped his eyes, turned away from the hatred in the guard's face.

The sergeant gave a jerk of his head, "Get to my office."

"Is that all? May I leave now?' After receiving a nod, Skender put on his coat, walked toward the heavy door. He drank deeply, gratefully, of the cold, crisp air. A shadowy figure joined him almost immediately. "Jakup! You don't know how happy I am to find you waiting for me."

Jakup gripped Skender's hand, "Almost as happy as I, brother, at seeing you on this side of their door. Are you alright?" he asked as Besim joined them.

Skender gave a brief nod, "Thank you, yes."

"Go ahead of us Besim … let them know that Skender has been released. Tell Babush all is well."

"Immediately." Besim gave a quick nod to each, turned and was gone, the darkness swallowing him quickly.

They were moving slowly away from the grey stone building. "Jakup, how is Gillian?"

"As a rock, brother. Nona is calm. Drita is sleeping the sleep of exhaustion. And Babush, as always, firm and steady. Hasan and my father are with him, also Aslan and Emin." As he was speaking, his eyes searched Skender's face, saw the strain. He took hold of his arm. "Let us hurry, it is cold." He urged him to walk quicker, slowed immediately as he saw that it was an effort for Skender to move at a faster pace. *What did they do to you?*

Skender stopped. His voice shook, "I have to go back, Jakup. Tomorrow. Six o'clock."

Jakup could feel Skender's body shaking, even through the heavy coat. Fear ran through Jakup. He closed his eyes briefly, gritted his teeth, "Put it from you,

Skender, do not dwell on it. Your nusé is waiting for you. Let your mind rest with her."

"Come…" he urged gently, "home, now, brother. You need warmth and gentleness, and it is waiting for you in abundance."

"Home," Skender repeated softly on a sigh.

Jakup took his arm, together they started to walk, pulling slowly but steadily away from the long streams of yellow light that came from the windows of Police Headquarters.

Chapter 28

"I am glad to see you home, Djali." Babush's hand shook as he lit his pipe.

"Thank you, Babush. I am happy to be here." Skender put his arm around Nona as she came to him. "Hush now," he comforted her, "I am here, safe, and in your arms … what more could any mother ask?" Gently he wiped her tears, inclined his head to his uncles. "Thank you for coming, helping…" He included Aslan and Emin with a quick glance in their direction as he put his arm around Drita's shoulders. "Still crying, little sister? You will wash all dust from the earth." His eyes searched the room as he spoke, met Babush's.

"Downstairs, Djali, preparing a meal for you and Jakup." Babush answered the unspoken question. "Enough now, wife, let your son go to his Nusé. Go to her, Skender. She is as anxious as we and needs to see you."

Arif waited until he had left the room, turned to Jakup. "Well?"

"He moves slowly, sir, sometimes with difficulty … something happened, but he has said nothing. When I asked if he was alright, his answer…."

"His answer was 'yes'," Babush interrupted with a sigh, "but then it always was, even after they'd…" He stopped, pulled deeply on his pipe.

Hasan looked long and hard at Besim. "What is talked of here is for your ears only … your mouth is sealed. You understand that?"

Besim's face flushed. "Yes, sir."

Aslan waited until his father had turned back to Babush and Arif, leaned toward his brother and spoke quietly to him, "Our father thinks highly of you … at seventeen I would have been ordered from the room before they spoke of such things." The boyish grin flashed at him. "When you are rested, take the news to our family."

Besim rose immediately. "I have rested enough, will leave now, Aslan." He turned to Babush, bowed. "Sir, with your permission I will let my mother and brothers know that Skender is home." He gave a quick smile to Arif. "And then to your home, Migje."

Arif nodded. "Thank you, Besim … and thank you for your services this evening."

"I need no thanks, Migje. My reward was in bringing the news that Skender was safe." He turned toward Hasan, was given permission to leave, and nodded his good- byes to his brother and cousins, he gave an encouraging grin to Drita and turned to Nona.

She stopped his bow, pulled him to her, holding him close for a moment, and then ushered him on his way.

The door opened again before it was completely closed. "Goodnight, Besim."

"Goodnight, Skender."

Aslan, Jakup and Emin rose immediately. "Nona, would you and Drita help Gillian, please?" Skender held the door open, waiting for them to leave. Babush watched as Skender sat down, saw how carefully he lowered himself to the rug. Skender waited until his cousins had settled themselves again, looked round the half circle of faces, his eyes dropped to the rug, and he sat for a long moment, statue-still, staring at the intricate pattern. He raised his head, his voice even and steady as he started to speak. "I should not be here, sitting with my loved ones like this … my own actions, and no one else's, should have denied me this privilege." He saw the startled looks, hesitated, and then continued. "I lost all control, behaved like a fool. I showed more sense, more judgment, as a teenager."

He took a breath, looked directly at Babush. "Sir, I almost got my hands on Mihajlovich." Shocked eyes stared at him, he lifted his hands, sat looking at them, his voice barely audible as he continued, "These were inches from his neck … had I reached him, I would have throttled him." None moved, none spoke. Skender's hands dropped to his lap. "What is beyond all explanation, all understanding, is that I am here in one piece after such stupidity." Babush raised his hand, silencing Arif before he spoke. "The guard had the leather in his hand…" Skender's eyes closed for a moment, "I expected to be turned to jelly … thrashed beyond recognition." He sat silent, staring into the fire.

"What happened?" Arif demanded.

Skender's eyes pulled from the fire, lifted to his uncle. "Mihajlovich stopped him." He saw the disbelief, repeated quietly, "Mihajlovich stopped him."

"Why? Why would he do such a thing? It is not his nature to be gentle. His reputation arrived in Kosov long before he, Djali. The Croatians heaved such a sigh of relief it rocked the world when he was sent from them … and we have been groaning under his heel ever since. Why this sudden consideration of you?"

"I have no answer, Babush."

Hasan sighed, pushed his hat to the back of his head. "What caused your lack of control, Skender?"

Skender's eyes turned to his father. "I understood your warning, Babush, and you were right … Mihajlovich tried to reach me through Gillian. I let him think that he had succeeded. What I was not prepared for, what came as a shock, was that he would bring up the march, question me on it. What made me lose control?" He sighed. "I don't know, cannot remember what spark set me afire. Perhaps the one word repeated over and over, dead, dead, dead. Or was it his casualness? His complete lack of caring for all those lost lives? It did not matter to him. Sabri was a name, a number, a 'loose end'. It was nothing to him that his life had been taken as casually as one snuffs a candle … Morat's slow, lonely death, his agony…."

"Enough, Skender." Babush saw his son's distress. "It will not help to go through the painful memories again."

"I went through them again, Babush, it was not Mihajlovich I saw as he asked each name. I saw my friends, saw their pain, their suffering … and relived my own." Angrily his fist banged the rug. "His only concern was his damned files … 'Tell me those that are dead, let me make my mark.'" His hand shook as he ran his fingers through his hair. "Seventeen years ago someone selected a file, made a mark, and we were ripped from our homes, our families. Mihajlovich wanted to complete the act, wanted to make his mark, close their files, forever."

Babush laid his hand on Skender's arm, waited until he had calmed himself. "That explains your actions. What I cannot understand are his. You were in his hands, at his mercy, and he let you go … almost unhurt." Skender's eyes flew to his father as he heard the last words. "I am not blind to the way you move, the care you take in lowering yourself to the rug. He has hurt you, Djali. What happened?"

There was a long pause before the answer came. "A fist to the stomach, repeated once."

Babush had to lean forward to catch the words. "And you are ashamed. Why?" Babush watched Skender closely. "Only a fool would not be angry when he is abused, but shame? Come, Skender, you did not allow yourself this self-indulgence as a boy … why now?"

Angry eyes lifted to Babush. "It is harder now. As a boy, I was conditioned to accept their authority."

"No. You were not. Good sense and judgment ruled you. Has living in a free society pushed that out of you?"

"Brother, please?" Hasan protested quietly. Aslan kept his eyes firmly on the ground as Emin and Jakup exchanged uncomfortable glances.

"Well, Skender?" He turned slightly away from his father. "Djali, listen to me, You cannot be responsible for the sadistic action of others. We do not think less of you because your body is vulnerable; but let then touch your mind, my son, and then you are crippled more than if they had taken both legs. Let them touch your soul … you are dead."

Red tongues licked at the logs, sap hissed and spat as it was sucked from the wood and consumed. Skender dragged his eyes from the fire, looked directly at Babush. "I have to go back … tomorrow night … at six o'clock." Babush's hand gripped the cushion on which he sat as he continued to puff steadily at his pipe.

"There is one guard…." Skender gritted his teeth. "If Mihajlovich gives me to him…." A shudder ran through him, his hand wiped at his face. "I don't know if I have enough strength." He stopped; hands gripped tightly together in his lap.

Babush's worry showed as he watched him. "You were not thinking of running, Skender."

Skender shook his head, took a long steadying breath. "No, sir. That thought had not entered my head."

"Good," Babush let out a sigh of relief. "Good. Your answer was as I expected."

Arif glanced toward the door, gave a warning signal. The young men rose as Nona followed Drita and Gillian into the room. Gillian knelt on the floor, smoothing the tablecloth free of wrinkles on the low table. Skender watched her as he washed his hands.

"Skender…" he handed the towel back to Drita as he turned to Arif, "be proud of her, it was she who cooked tonight, she prepared for all of us. That was not easy … a strange kitchen, plus the burden of worry that she carried … and yet the meal was served to us correctly and at our usual time."

"I am proud of her, Migje, but your approval is an added bonus." He sat at the table, laid the cloth over his knees. "Have you eaten, my love?"

"Yes, thank you." She smiled back as Jakup smiled at her before joining Skender. "With Nona and Drita." She accepted the round pan from Nona, placed it centrally on the table.

"I am going to tell my mother and sister to leave us … you will go with them." He saw her hesitation. "My uncles will not leave until they have answers to their questions. I want it finished as soon as possible. Want them to go home and leave me in peace." She gave a half-sigh, nodded, and stood. Skender turned to his mother. "We will let Emin attend us, Nona … perhaps you ladies have work elsewhere?"

Skender broke a piece of bread, handed it to Jakup. Jakup sat quietly waiting until Skender had asked the blessing.

Hasan watched Skender as he half-heartedly pushed at the food in front of him. *He is near breaking, needs rest….*

Skender dropped the bread onto the dish, giving up his pretense of eating. "Why was Mihajlovich so lenient with me, Babush? Why does he want me back there tomorrow night?"

"I have no answer, Skender. I wish I had. Arif? Hasan? Have you any thoughts?" He turned to the young men as his brothers shook their heads. "Aslan? Jakup? Emin?"

Skender felt exhaustion flow over him in a wave and he covered his face with his hand, letting his eyes close.

Jakup cut a piece of the soft white cheese. "Did he give you any clue, Skender? Hint at all as to what he was after?"

He let his hand drop to his lap as he forced his eyes open. "No. Nothing."

"May I?" Emin received a nod from Babush. "Is it possible that Mihajlovich does not know how far he can go with you, brother? You are an American now, carry American papers, has he ever met this situation before? If not, he must seek guidance from higher authority before he dare lay hands on you."

"A good point, Emin, but he told me that my citizenship is not recognized by this government."

"He may have said that, but did he mean it, or was it a bluff?" Aslan asked quickly.

"We are clutching at straws, guessing and outguessing each other. We have no way of knowing what is in Mihajlovich's mind. This guessing is not helping Skender. What he needs is rest, not the sound of our voices drumming against his ears." Hasan turned to Skender. "If you wish, we can talk more tomorrow, but what you need now is a good night's sleep." Hasan stood, motioned for Jakup to stay where he was. "Sit still, Jakup … finish your meal."

"Thank you, Migje Hasan, but I am finished." He inclined his head to Hasan as he stood.

"Emin, I am ready to leave." Hasan picked up his pipe as he continued, "Ask our nusé to come and bid us goodnight and let my wife and daughter know we are leaving for home."

"Migje." Emin bowed, started toward the door.

"Bring our coats, too." Arif stretched as he got to his feet, "Jakup, you will stay here tonight … if my brother should need me…."

"Yes, father, I will let you know immediately."

Arif nodded, turned to Skender. "Hasan was right, you need rest. Try to put tomorrow from your mind … Mihajlovich is playing with you, tormenting you as a cat torments a mouse. Do not give him satisfaction."

"Yes, sir."

Arif gave Skender a quizzical look, smiled briefly. "'Yes, sir' … how easy to say … how easy for me to give you advice." He put his arm across Skender's shoulders. "It is not so easy to carry through though, is it, Djali?" He turned as the door opened, accepted his coat from Drita. "Be careful tomorrow. Do not let the cat pin you, stay far from his claws." He glanced at Gillian. "Tell your Nusé I enjoyed her meal."

"Migje Arif wishes me to tell you he enjoyed your dinner." He let his fingers touch Gillian's, felt hers curl about his. "I wish they'd hurry with their good-byes, leave."

"You look tired."

"I am … tired to death." He saw that the family was almost ready to leave. "Migje Arif, Migje Hasan, I will walk you to the gate."

"It is not necessary, Skender … stay and rest."

"Thank you, Migje Hasan, but no." He gave an extra squeeze before releasing Gillian's hand. "I will escort you to the gate … that is my duty and I shall do it."

Jakup looked closely at Emin. "Isn't that my coat?"

Emin gave a sheepish grin. "I could not find mine." He gave a sideways glance to Arif, "Do not tell him … he will chew me all the way home." He saw Jakup's annoyance, moved toward the door, murmured, "Father is ready … I must not delay him."

Arif pulled on his shoes at the entry hall, glanced up at Drita. "Ilyria will be here tomorrow to help you. I will send her with Emin before noon."

Color flooded her face. "It is not necessary, Migje."

He stood, patted her cheek. "Yes it is … you are over-tired and need some help. Natën e mirë, brother." He extended his hand to Babush.

"Natën e mirë, Arif." He shook hands with his younger brother. "Natën e mirë, Hasan." Father and daughter stood close together watching as their guests departed. They gave a last wave, turned and walked together to the sitting room.

Drita took the tray, loaded with dishes, from Gillian. "Stay, Nusé, rest. You have worked hard enough. These will take but a moment." Gillian stood uncertainly holding one side of the tray, not sure if she had understood Drita.

"Nusé…" Gillian turned toward Nona, "Ulu ketu, Nusé." She patted the rug beside her, smiling a welcome. "Come, next to Nona." She patted the rug again. Gillian sat down beside her, gave a smile to Babush.

"Wait, Drita, I will come with you and keep you company." Jakup bowed to Babush and Nona, held the door open for Drita, then followed her from the room.

"You are happy with your new daughter, aren't you, wife?"

"I am more than happy with her, she pleases my son, and if he is happy…" She smiled at Babush. "But it has gone deeper than that … I feel for her as if she were my own."

Babush nodded as he placed a log on the fire, pushed it down, making sure it sat firmly on the near burnt logs beneath. "Ahh, Skender, you are back. Come, sit down and warm yourself."

He ignored the invitation, went straight to Gillian and pulled her to her feet. "What is the meaning of this?" Babush and Nona stared at him as they saw and heard his anger.

Babush's eyes dropped to the paper Skender had thrust into Gillian's hand. "What is the matter, Skender?"

"One moment, Babush." His eyes never left her face. "I am waiting for an explanation."

"There is nothing to explain. Surely it is obvious from what I had written? I planned on going to the American Embassy." She looked up at him, puzzled at his anger. "I abandoned the plan as soon as you returned home … forgot all about it until this moment."

He took hold of her shoulders, gave her a quick hard shake.

"Skender?" Nona's protest came softly, pleadingly, as Gillian angrily shrugged away from him.

Skender's eyes went briefly to his mother before he turned again to Gillian. "Did I tell you to remain in this house? That on no account were you to move unless accompanied by one of my cousins?"

"Yes, but…."

"But you chose to ignore my orders, is that it?"

"Skender, what is the matter? You left this room happy and proud of her, return in anger … what caused the change? I would like an explanation…."

Skender held out his hand. Without a word, Gillian handed the paper to him and sat down. "I did not tell you to sit."

Her eyes flashed, "I do not need your permission!"

Skender glared angrily at her as he handed the paper to Babush. "It is addressed to you … she has tried to write in Albanian. The language is poor but understandable. As you can see, she planned on taking the train to Belgrade…."

A sob burst from Nona. "Why was she running from us? Was she frightened? Did she want her own mother, her own family?"

"No, wife, she was not running from us." Babush looked worriedly toward Gillian. "This is serious, Skender. Did she plan on going alone?"

"Were you going alone?"

"Yes." She saw his anger, started to explain, "Emin said…."

"Emin?" Babush's eyes raised immediately to Skender's as he heard the name. "Emin knew of this? Impossible! He would never permit himself to be included in something of this nature without permission from his father, or myself or both of us."

"Did Emin know and approve of this plan of yours?"

She hesitated, wondering if she should even answer. "I asked him to go with me … he said he would have to wait until tomorrow so that he could get a permit and talk it over with…." Her eyes slid to Babush.

"I think I understood," Babush stopped Skender as he started to translate. "So what made her decide to act against Emin's wishes?"

"Emin's wishes? I am not concerned with Emin's wishes! She deliberately ignored my orders."

Babush suppressed a sigh, "Yes, Skender, I am aware that you are upset at that, but let us discover the reason." He frowned. "In any case, there is no way for her to reach the station."

"How did you plan on getting to the station? We are a long way from there, or had you forgotten that?"

"No, I had not forgotten." Her anger paralleled his. "There are taxis at the hotel…."

"Not at night."

Gillian glared angrily at him. "I had thought of that, planned on walking."

His smile was sarcastic. "Oh, really? How far did you expect to go? A woman walking alone, especially after dark, would soon bring many eyes in her direction. One of our friends or neighbors would have seen you and returned you to us before you reached the end of this street."

She looked coolly at him. "I had thought of that and had made plans to avoid that very thing."

"Plans? What plans?"

"I will show you." She stood, walked, straight and tall, from the room.

Skender let out a long sigh as the door closed on her. "I went to our room for a sweater after I had taken our family to the gate. The note was laying on top of a pile of clothing…." He glanced toward the door. "She says she made plans to walk to the station." He gave a grim smile as he heard Nona's sudden indrawn breath. "Do not worry, Nona, she would not have left this street without…."

The light snapped off. "Now, in the dark, do you really think you would know that I am not a male?" Her silhouette showed sharply black against the glowing logs, the white hat, tipped at a rakish angle, gave her a jaunty air.

Nona smothered her cry as her husband gripped her arm.

"She looks like a young boy." Babush's voice was softly shocked. "God Almighty, if they had caught her…." He smoothed his moustache, roughly smoothed it again.

"Put the light on. I said put the damn light on." Skender's eyes met Babush's as light flooded the room.

"Well? Would I pass as a male or not?" She stood proudly, head held high, daring Skender to deny it.

"They would have beaten her to a pulp … would never have believed…." Fear surfaced, Skender reached her in one long stride, grabbed her and shook her hard, sending the white hat flying from her head. "Do you realize the danger of such subterfuge? Have you any idea of what they would have done to you?"

"Done to me? What are you talking about? What danger?" Angrily she pulled free of him. "If you are trying to scare me…."

"I am trying to make you understand what a dangerous thing you had in mind. What do you think the police would have done if they had caught you dressed in this way?" She shrugged. "Don't be so flippant! It is not only your own life you are endangering but mine and all of my family." Skender saw her anger start to give way to uncertainty, he continued in a quieter voice, "This is not a free country. It is a police state … you would have been stopped for identification, either in town, or, if you had managed to walk that far, at the station. What do you think would have happened then?"

"I … I don't know. I had not thought of that."

"You would have been taken to Police Headquarters. As soon as the officer realized that you were not what you appeared to be, that you were camouflaged…."

"Camouflaged?" She laughed nervously. "You mean disguised, I suppose. I was not going to be disguised."

"Weren't you? What else would you call it? Or more importantly, what would they call it?" Mutinous eyes glared at him. "The officer would immediately jump to the conclusion that you were connected with the Underground. You would be given to two of the guards, the officer's orders would be quite clear … 'find out why she is dressed this way and who she is going to see or coming from seeing.' Their method for extracting information is not pleasant, first they would search you…" Her eyes flew to his. "Yes, the men. They do not bother with the niceties of women guards for women prisoners. I am sure I do not need to tell you that they would take full advantage of that situation."

Nona and Babush exchanged concerned looks. "Why is Skender so angry with her?" Nona whispered. Babush shook his head on a sigh, held his finger to his lips.

Gillian half-turned from Skender. Angrily he reached and took hold of her chin, making her look at him. "My cousins told me of one guard who couldn't keep his eyes off you when you went to register. He embarrassed you, didn't he?" He saw the fright in her eyes, hesitated a moment, then went on determinedly. "What if you had been put into his hands? How would you have felt?" Her eyes filled, she tried to pull free of him, but he tightened his grip, holding her still, his voice quietly angry. "He would have been all over you, and you would have been helpless, completely in his hands … he would have done as he pleased with you."

"Stop it. Stop it. I would never have allowed…."

"You could not have stopped it."

"Yes, yes, I could…" her voice rose, "I would have asked for … whatever his name is."

"Mihajlovich?" She nodded, tipped her head arrogantly at him. "You little fool … do you really believe that he would have helped you? Why? Because he spent two years in England? Do not be taken in by the veneer of sophistication, the smooth manner and elegant dress … he is a viper and would use any means … any … to make you tell them what they wished to know."

She laughed nervously. "I would have told him that I was going to the station … what was so wrong with that?"

"Nothing. In a normal situation, a free society. But you are here. The very fact that you are married to me makes them suspicious of you, and the stamp in your passport has increased that suspicion. Mihajlovich would not have helped you. He would have instructed them in the best methods to make you speak. He would have stood and watched them humiliate you in the worst possible way, he would have ordered you beaten until you could not move, you would have looked like a piece of raw meat before he stopped." Her terrified eyes stared back at him. "And if I had still been in his grasp, he would have made me watch all of it."

"I don't believe you." Her voice was a whisper.

"Don't you? Do you want more? Had you still refused to speak … and you would because there was nothing to tell them, you acted in innocence, but they would not believe you. They would have tied you to a chair, made you watch while they went to work on me…."

"Stop it." She covered her ears with her hands, turned from him.

He pulled her hands away, made her face him. "Could you have taken that, Jill? Even if you had been able to withstand the searching hands, the beatings, and all the other degradations they would put you through, could you have watched…."

"I won't listen. I won't." Her breath came in short hard sobs as she exerted all her strength, pulled free of him and ran from the room.

Nona followed her immediately.

Babush smoothed his moustache. "Was it necessary to be so rough with her?"

"Yes, Babush, it was."

Babush opened his pouch of tobacco, eyes never leaving Skender. "Why?"

"She was told not to leave this house unless accompanied … she chose to ignore that order."

"Did you explain to her why she was to stay put, not move?"

"No." Angrily Skender glared at Babush. "Do you give a reason to your wife when you give her an order?"

"No." Babush took the pipe from his mouth. "Your mother was raised to give her husband instant and unquestioning obedience, and from the first day she set foot in this house, I have demanded that obedience. Have you ever asked it of this girl before?" His sigh was deep, "No … I thought not."

"You infer that I acted wrongly. Do you expect me to believe that if your wife had behaved in this manner you would have let it pass?"

"No, I would not let it pass. But my action would not have been as yours. I would not have taken thirty minutes to explain to my wife. I would not have terrified her as you did yours. I do not know what words you used, but I recognize fear. And I would not be sitting opposite my father if she had run from me."

He tapped his pipe against the stove, knocking out the ashes. "Had it been my wife who had directly disobeyed me, she'd have felt my hand across her mouth … and, under these particular circumstances, before the sting had left her face, she would have been in my arms, receiving the love and comfort she so desperately needs. By now my inner turmoil would be smoothed by her gentleness. Only the cold grey fingers of dawn would have taken her sweetness from my arms and my bed."

He filled his pipe, pushing the tobacco down into the bowl with his thumb. "Which would be the easier to forget and forgive? Your anger and harsh words, or my one stinging slap?" He took a piece of the wood from the fire and lit his pipe, the tobacco glowing redly as he pulled in a long breath. He leaned forward, pushed the wood back into the fire and put his hand across Skender's back. Compassion filled him as he saw the bowed head. "Skender, Djali-eim, we have all been through great stress tonight. Apart from you, she suffered more than any other. We could all speak of our fears and worry, but she? She was locked into silence, had to stand alone on a strange island. Her fear for you must have been great to undertake such an elaborate plan."

Babush sighed softly as there was no response. "There is something you should know, something I wish you to know. This house had come to a standstill. Your mother and sister were in bed, sick with fear and worry for you. At one time the thought passed through my mind that I should offer my brothers and nephews some refreshment, but…" he shrugged, "…who was to prepare for them if I offered? Hardly had the thought left my mind when the door opened and she came in with the table, set it down and brought the jug of water for us to wash. I thought I would explode from pride and joy … her very clumsiness made the act more precious to me than if she had been born here and was the most accomplished nusé in Kosov. This was not routine for her. It was not something she was born to. She was not so steeped in our customs that to prepare and serve a meal in our style came as naturally as drawing breath. If it was not routine, what was it that called forth that kindness? Love, Djali. Not the love she has for you as her husband, but the love and tenderness a woman carries for family, children. And that, Skender, is what I was hoping to find in her. When she first set foot in this house, I welcomed her as your wife. I embrace her now as my daughter."

"I am glad you are happy with her."

Babush sighed, lifted his hands in exasperation. "But you are not?"

"Correct. I am not." The cold blast of air drew their eyes to the door.

"How is our Nusé, wife?"

Nona's eyes went to Skender. "There is no comfort I can give her. Djali, will you go to her?"

"No. I shall stay in this room. Bring me a blanket and pillow."

Babush stopped Nona, beckoned her to sit down. "You will sleep in your own room, Skender, not here. The rest is in your own hands. Lay with her … or alone. She is yours, and you do with her as you please. It is not our way to interfere between husband and wife, but while you are under my roof you will not have separate rooms. Is that understood?" Skender gave a brief nod. "Natën e mirë, Skender."

"Natën e mirë, sir." Skender stood as his father did, waited until the old man had left the room before he asked, "Is she still crying?"

"No, Skender. Her sadness is too deep for tears." Nona came to him, put her arms around him. "Go to her, Djali … comfort her and let her comfort you."

"I cannot." He touched the worn cheek gently. "Go to bed, Nona, you need rest."

"You need it more. I would sleep more soundly if I had taken my son to his room?" Skender shook his head moved slightly away from his mother. "Please?"

He turned his back to her. "No."

Nona's eyes filled, "I cannot remember when I last asked anything of you, Djali. I do ask this."

Skender turned to her. "You have never asked anything of me, Nona." He reached for her hand. "Your gentle persuasion carries more weight than my father's orders … if that is all it takes to bring peace to your heart, you may take me to my door."

He stood waiting as she checked that the fire was safe to leave for the night. Together they walked across the hall.

"Skender…" he stopped as his hand stretched toward the door of his room, "she is still young … be gentle."

He bent, kissed her cheek. "Natën e mirë, Nona."

Chapter 29

"Come in." Mihajlovich looked up from his desk to the guard. "Have you searched him?"

"Yes, Comrade Colonel" The guard handed over the bulky file.

Mihajlovich laid the file on his desk, leaned back in his chair, Skender stood silent and still as his eyes ran over him. "How long have you had him in interrogation?"

"A little over an hour, Colonel."

Mihajlovich nodded, eyes never leaving Skender. "I wish to speak to you privately, Berisha … will you give me your word that there will be no trouble if I dismiss the guard?"

"You have my word."

Mihajlovich didn't move, sat watching Skender, a slight frown on his face, "I want more than your word, give me your Besa."

Skender hesitated. It was an Albanian pledge, a vow, not given lightly, and was never broken. Briefly, he wondered how Mihajlovich knew of it. His eyes lifted, and he looked directly at Mihajlovich, "You have my Besa."

Mihajlovich turned to the guard, "Wait outside. Sit down." His hand offered Skender his choice of one of the two chairs on the opposite side of his desk.

Softness cradled him. His body luxuriated in the supple leather while his mind rejected the extreme styling. The parquet flooring gleamed dully, the dark wood emphasizing the creaminess of the wool rug, while the glorious tea color of the teak desk balanced the two extremes to perfection. The walls were cream, the trim wood, stained to match the flooring, burnt orange drapes gave warmth to the room while the barred window denied it.

Mihajlovich's arm rested on a red leather blotter, gold tooled, he let the slim gold pen gently tap the desk as he read the letter in front of him. His hand moved, leaving a black flourish on the close-typed page, the die-stamped blood red emblem of flames enclosed by laurel leaves reaching for a star the only color on the starkly white paper.

His eyes lifted to Skender as he laid the signed letter in the basket on the side of his desk, and he sat studying him. "It is out of character with the rest of the room, isn't it?"

Skender started slightly, unaware that Mihajlovich had been watching him.

Mihajlovich turned, looked at the huge portrait on the wall behind. "It is a good likeness … it catches the magnetism of the man. I was happy enough to have our leader's portrait, but the frame is not to my liking. It is too heavy, too ornate." He turned back to Skender. "Do you like the office?"

"No. It is too modern, too sleek, for my taste."

"Still clinging to the old style, the old ways, Berisha? May I assume, then, that this…" his hand casually indicated the portrait, "…is to your taste?" He gave a soft laugh "The frame, eh, not the content?" Mihajlovich reached and pulled the heavy file in front of him. "Did the officer give you your Identity Card?"

"Yes."

"And then he questioned you?"

Skender's laugh was short, bitter, "You already know that. Why bother…."

"I am the one that asks the questions, Berisha," Mihajlovich's interruption was sharp. "You are here to answer. Can you remember my question, or shall I repeat it?"

"I remember. He wanted to know where I crossed the border, at what time of day, which month and how…."

"He also wanted names and addresses of those that helped you. Am I right?" There was a long silence then very softly he repeated, "Am I right?"

"Yes."

"Did you give him that information?"

Skender sat silent, lips tight together.

Mihajlovich walked round the desk, stood looking down at Skender. "When you refused to answer, did he use force?"

Skender swallowed. "No."

"No." Mihajlovich watched Skender closely. "And that did not surprise you? Under normal interrogation procedures, you would be unable to move by now … your face would be laying in your own vomit because you were in too much pain to lift your head. Am I right?" He saw the clenched hands, the stiffness of Skender's body, leaned forward and insisted softly, "Am I right?"

"Yes, damn you, yes."

"Good." Mihajlovich pushed the basket away, sat on the corner of the desk. "Then by now you must realize that it was my order that saved your skin … that you are in my hands."

Skender's eyes lifted to Mihajlovich, "What is it that you want from me?" he asked quietly. "There is some reason for your restraint. What is it?"

Mihajlovich's eyes never left Skender, "I want you to join us."

Startled, Skender stared at him. "What did you say?"

"I want you to join us … work for me. Well?"

Skender dazedly wiped at his forehead, shook his head in bewilderment. "I cannot believe what my ears tell me you are saying."

"You would work directly under me, be responsible to no other but me, and, of course, my superiors." He opened the box on his desk and took out a cigarette, as he closed the lid he glanced at Skender. "Your answer?"

"This is madness. How can you even think of asking me such a thing? You have my file…."

"Yes. And I've read it. From beginning to end."

"Then you know beyond any doubt that I have never had any sympathy with your doctrine. I have suffered much at your hands … lost home, family and country because I was not prepared to…." He rubbed at his forehead, raised bewildered eyes to Mihajlovich. "How can you even think of asking?"

Mihajlovich lit his cigarette, blew out a long breath of smoke. "I have given it careful consideration. Before you refuse, I suggest you do likewise."

"I have no knowledge that will be useful to you, know no secrets. My occupation is interesting to me, but of no value to this government, or any other."

"You are confused, Berisha. I did not ask for information … I asked you to work for me." He frowned as he saw the brief shake of Skender's head. "Why not listen before refusing?"

"No. I am not interested. In a week I will be leaving…."

"Will you?" The very quietness of his voice was ominous. "That is up to me. It is not your decision."

"You have no reason…."

"Enough!" Mihajlovich's hand banged the desk. "I need no reason … we cleared that point last night. If I want you here, here you shall stay."

"You cannot hold me against my will … you have no right…."

"Wrong, Berisha! I can hold you. I have the right, can do as I please with you." He stood up, stood over Skender. "Remember who you are, and where you are. Now…" he leaned close to Skender, "do you wish to repeat your statement?" He straightened. "No, of course not … you know beyond any doubt that my words are true."

He walked to the barred window, stood looking down into the street below. "You have a choice, Berisha. The same one that was put to you before, join the Party, live under its protection … or exist outside of it." He turned to face the room. "Have you matured enough to know which path to follow?"

"What is it that makes you hound me? Is there some information you want to suck from me? Something important that I have forgotten over the years?"

Mihajlovich laughed. "No … if it was that it would not be I who would bother with you. I have experts to wring locked secrets from reticent throats. But enough of that." His hand dismissed it.

"Last night you spoke of the March. How many died? What are their names?" He gave an impatient snort as the silence stretched, "It is impossible for me to obtain this information. But you have it." He deliberately took his time to take a cigarette and light it, forcing himself to curb his anger. He blew out a long stream of smoke, quietly continued, "Will you help me? As much as you are able?"

Skender sat silent and still, not looking at him.

Mihajlovich's fist banged on the desk "I want…" he picked up his cigarette, made himself speak quietly, "I want the records correct, finalized."

Skender sighed, "That is all that it means to you, isn't it?" After a while he raised his head and looked directly at Mihajlovich. "The dead, yes; but not a word will you have from me of those that survived."

Mihajlovich gave an ironic smile, "If I wanted, I could make you talk. But…" he inclined his head, "agreed. I will have the list of names made ready. You will put a mark against each name."

Skender hesitated, "You will honor my request?

Mihajlovich raised his eyebrows in enquiry.

"That the families are informed of their loved one's death?"

Mihajlovich almost laughed, then with a wave of his hand said, "Done."

He pushed back from his desk. "Which is the fastest growing industry in Yugoslavia?" He paused, then continued, "Tourism."

He left the window, walked to his chair, and sat down. "During the fifties, we had a trickle … the ever-inquisitive Germans who bravely entered a Communist country and a few daring English souls. But our fame spread rapidly. Our beaches, the crystal-clear water of the Adriatic, and the grandeur of our mountains, the peaceful beauty of our lakes, are attracting more and more tourists. The trickle turned into a stream, the stream into a river, a river of foreign currency, currency we need to build our economy. So far, this river has followed the banks designated by our Department of Tourism, but now there is a surge of interest in historical buildings. Architecture has become fashionable, and archaeological remains…."

"Come to the point, Colonel Mihajlovich. What does all this have to do with me?"

There was a long silence. Mihajlovich half stood, his voice was soft with threat as he said, "Do not interrupt me again. Understood?" He waited.

Skender gave a brief inclination of his head.

"Our government approves this easy way of accruing foreign currency … it wants the river to grow." Mihajlovich continued as if there'd been no interruption as he resumed his seat, "We want Americans to come, want and need their dollars, and their easy way of spending." He laughed softly as he saw Skender's bewilderment. "Tourists, especially Americans, do not go where there is unrest. Budapest still suffers from their rising in fifty-six … tourism is dead there. The Kosovo area, with its fermenting dissidents, could dam our river. The government would not like that. Their eyes, cloudy with unhappiness and disappointment, would turn to Kosovo … and me. I will never permit that. You can help destroy the dam and keep the river flowing."

"I?" Skender forced a laugh. "What do you expect me to do? Be a guide? Take these tourists where they are supposed to go, make sure they do not stray from the designated path, that they see only what they are supposed to see?"

"No." There was a trace of anger in Mihajlovich's voice. "There are many who can do such elementary work. I would not trouble myself with you for such a mundane task." He took another cigarette, pushed the box toward Skender, leaving the lid open. "I want your name. Your influence in this city, this whole area."

"I have no influence here." Skender spoke slowly as he reached and took a cigarette. "I have been away too long for that."

Mihajlovich covertly watched Skender as he lit his cigarette. "You truly are not interested in politics, are you? I find that hard to believe, but I see for myself. Your name carries much weight here. In fact, you are quite a celebrity. The Underground radio carries news of your return twice a day." He laughed softly as he saw Skender's shocked astonishment, checked his watch. "A pity … we have missed their evening broadcast, otherwise I would have let you hear for yourself. Do you begin to see now why I want you?"

"No. I am at a loss to see how I am supposed to help…."

"You have become a hero, a symbol, to these people. After we took you from the school, how many years passed before your parents heard from you? How long was it before you dared to let them know that their son was still alive?"

Skender licked at his lips, "Two years, almost three."

"Your father never openly admitted it, but in his heart he thought you dead, never expected to see you again … am I right?"

Skender gave a hard swallow, "Yes."

"Yes. And all in Kosovo thought the same. The oldest son of the Berisha family had gone. They looked to your cousin, but he is not you, does not have your flair, your personality. He is a quieter, more reticent person, and could not fill your shoes. If he could, he would have been mine by now."

Skender smiled, shook his head. "You could not break Aslan … he is too straight."

"If a tree stands too straight, does not bend in a strong wind, it breaks." After a moment Mihajlovich continued, "But enough of that, let us return to the question of you, the returned hero. If the hero returns to the place of his birth, openly forgives our government for…" his hands raised questioningly, "…let us say an 'error of judgment', shall we, and then allies himself with the Party, renouncing the West and its so-called freedom, what reaction will we have from the populace? Especially the agitators, the trouble-makers?"

"They will think I have gone mad, lost all sense. Or…" Skender looked directly at Mihajlovich, "…that somehow I have been forced."

"I do not think so. We could not bring the boy to his knees … why should they think we were successful with the man? No, they will assume, and rightly so, that having experienced both lifestyles, you prefer ours. Old men will whisper as they sip their coffee … young men will question and debate as they down their sljivovica. Both will reach the same conclusion, the one we wish them to come to, that life in the Western World is not all milk and honey as they believe."

"In that they would be right. It is not paradise, life can still be difficult, there is always a rock to stub your toe, a hill to be struggled up."

Mihajlovich's voice was softly seductive as he spoke, "I can give you a smooth path, Berisha, with no hills and little difficulty."

"You cannot give me freedom."

"I can give you power … power and respect."

"Respect? I think you have the wrong word. Is not fear a better choice?"

"Does it matter?" Mihajlovich looked directly at Skender, a sarcastic smile hovering on his mouth. "The end result is the same, walk down any street and others will stand aside to let you pass."

Mihajlovich picked up the phone as it rang. "Excuse me." His voice was quietly authoritative as he outlined his orders.

Skender suppressed a sigh. Mihajlovich carried his command easily, dominated all his subordinates without raising his voice.

Mihajlovich returned the phone to its cradle. "You have listened to my reasons for wanting you, the benefits I would accrue, now let me tell you yours if you join us. The work is not hard … the money more than generous. You could live very comfortably on the income you would receive. The benefits are extensive, both for you and your family. A car would be made available to you, and a house provided."

He curbed his anger as he saw Skender give a brief shake of his head. "What is your preference? If you wish, we will build you a house to American specifications … you have lived there a long time perhaps you have become accustomed to their buttons and switches. Or, maybe there is a house here in Pristina that makes you catch your breath? One that you have admired since childhood … if so, say … it is yours."

"And the family that lives there … what of them? Skender asked sarcastically.

"They will be moved." Mihajlovich leaned confidentially toward Skender. "You do not realize to what extent your authority would reach. Power is sweet, Berisha. I am offering you a jar of honey, dip in … taste … savor … enjoy."

"Freedom is sweeter to me than any honey you can offer."

"Is it? I have experienced both, but you have not. I dare you to try mine, once you have tasted the sweetness of power, you will not give it up easily." He watched with increasing confidence as Skender frowningly studied the rug. "You do not have to decide immediately … think about it." He hesitated, then continued, "One other thing…." He waited until Skender looked up at him. "How do you feel about your wife?"

"That is my business, concerns no one else."

"If you decide to join us, it will concern me, she is an outsider. Your family do not approve of her and her presence here will affect all that come into contact with you. Let her go … send her home."

"What are you talking about? This is not some girl I took from a street corner. She is my wife, we are married."

"Forget the marriage. Cancel it. Why do you laugh?"

"Wedding vows are recognized worldwide, Colonel Mihajlovich. Even in Communist states."

"Agreed. But in your culture, under your accepted ways, you could be rid of her easily … today, even, if you wished." Skender's eyes questioned him. "Have you forgotten your own customs?" He gave a soft laugh, "There is no child, Berisha … she has not given you a child. You can divorce her. Am I right?"

Slowly Skender reached and took another cigarette.

"You have been married to her long enough … the initial excitement has worn off by now. Send her home."

"No."

"You have pleasured yourself with her for two years…" the softly seductive voice paused for a moment, "it is time to seek new pastures, new pleasures, and they are here, waiting for you. You can find your own excitement, or…" he smiled, "your father would be delighted to find you a bride, a shy innocent from one of the leading families, whose pleasure will be in pleasing you … she will do your bidding before you even ask … she will bring even more honor to your house."

Mihajlovich sat back in his chair, a quiet satisfaction seeping through him as there was no response, no denial, from Skender.

Eventually Skender's eyes lifted from the floor. "You would let her go? Let her return to England?"

"If you are working for us, I would not want her here, her presence would cause too many complications." He watched Skender closely as he took a long draw on the cigarette before stubbing it out.

"If I refuse to join you…" Skender noticed a nerve twitch in Mihajlovich's cheek, "what happens to her then … would you still let her go?"

Mihajlovich dismissed the question with an impatient gesture. "It is you that has my interest, not this girl whom you have tied yourself to."

"Would you let her go?"

Mihajlovich leaned across the desk toward Skender, "Concern yourself with your own skin, Berisha. I would prefer to have you standing one pace behind me as my assistant, but if not … I will have you at my feet, nerves stretched, body quivering."

His eyes dropped to Skender's hands; his smile was confident as he saw their tight grip on the leather arms. He laid back in his chair, completely relaxed. "I was taught that anticipation of the strap is what terrifies … that for some, the waiting is harder to take than the beating. Waiting, watching the preparation, seeing the guard fingering the leather, selecting…."

"I could reach you, tear you apart before the guard could answer your call. Do you realize that?" Skender was on the edge of the seat, body taut.

"Yes. But you will not." He smiled as he idly fiddled with his pen. "I have your word."

"You are bringing me close to breaking it."

Mihajlovich laughed softly, "No, you will not. You gave more than your word … you gave me your Besa. An Albanian would die before he would break that. Death would be more acceptable than the dishonor of breaking a Besa. I am safer with you now, at this moment, that with my own mother." He sat forward, leaned across the desk to Skender. "That is your weakness, Berisha, you do not snatch at opportunity, you let it slip away because you gave your word."

"That is our strength."

Mihajlovich shrugged, "If you choose to think so. I will give you three days to consider my proposals. Why don't you go to Prizren? You can relax, enjoy yourself, and it will give you time to think carefully of my offer." He pulled a form toward him. "I will have a travel permit made available to you; you will also need one for your wife. Are there any others you wish to accompany you?"

Puzzlement spilled into Skender's voice. "Some of my cousins might like to join us."

Mihajlovich nodded, added some writing to the paper, then held out the form to Skender. "I have approved yours, your wife's, and four others of your choosing." He stood, walked toward the door, beckoning Skender to follow him. "I will expect you in three days' time with your decision." The guard clicked to attention as the door opened. "Escort him downstairs … he is free to go."

He watched as Berisha started to follow the guard, "Berisha!" It was sharp, a command. Skender stopped, turned back toward Mihajlovich. "Much hangs on your decision … consider all the points I raised. Be very careful. The offer will not be made again. Goodnight."

Skender turned, without a word, followed the guard.

Mihajlovich watched for a moment, then closed the door and returned to his desk. "Mihajlovich here, report to my office." He replaced the phone, slowly sat back in his chair, staring up at the ceiling. He checked his watch, pulled some of the papers in front of him and started to read as the respectful knock came.

"Come in." He kept the officer waiting until he had signed the letter, looked up as he tossed it into the basket. "Has Berisha gone?"

"Yes, Colonel Mihajlovich … I signed him out and he left immediately."

"I have issued a permit for him to travel to Prizren. I assume he will go tomorrow, possibly the day after. Inform them that he is coming and that I want him watched, watched carefully but discreetly."

He glanced up, "On second thought, I suggest Udba handle this, they have more experience in these matters than the local police." The officer nodded. "I have put a proposition to him, if he accepts, we will benefit greatly. However, if he decides to refuse…?" Frowningly he let his pen tap the desk. "He is under great pressure … Prizren is very near the border, and he knows he is out of my sight." He looked up with a confident smile. "He would not let such an opportunity pass, will grasp it with both hands."

The officer smiled back, "And then you will have him, Colonel."

"Yes." Mihajlovich picked up the bulky file, snapped it closed. "Yes, then I will have him." He laughed softly as he handed the file to his officer. "Whichever way he jumps, he is mine." He gave a satisfied smile and nodded, as his hand reached toward his desk lamp. "Yes. The Berisha myth is about to be broken, Comrade."

The pool of light vanished as he snapped of the desk lamp. "Goodnight."

"Goodnight, Colonel Mihajlovich."

Chapter 30

The car slid to a stop. Gillian's eyes lifted and in a disinterested way she watched as people crossed the street. Skender's voice was a soft background to the chatter of a drill as roadwork went on close to their car, Aslan answered him and they laughed together, quietly, companionably. She curled herself closer into the corner, her feeling of isolation and loneliness emphasized by their togetherness. Aslan half-turned, gave her a warm smile, his mouth moving.

"Aslan is asking if you are comfortable, warm enough, Gillian."

"Yes. Thank you." Aslan turned back to the front as they started to inch forward. *I have never seen Aslan in Western dress before … somehow it makes him look even more like Skender … I don't want that. Before I resented Skender wearing the white hat, resented him looking like them … why do I feel that way?* She sighed. *Perhaps because Skender and I are….* She bit her lip. *Two nights of shallow sleep, each clinging to the edge of the mattress, a no-man's land of sheet separating us … two feet of whiteness keeping us apart more than the thousand miles between us when I was in England … a day and a half of politeness, the politeness of strangers….*

The town slipped past the window as she gazed out. The streets were busy. Horse-drawn carts, a few precariously loaded donkeys, cars and trucks fought for the right of way. Horns blared, voices called unintelligible messages where there were no horns. Cyclists whizzed in and out, leg power moving them faster than the mechanical monsters invented for their speed. Aslan turned and spoke to her again.

"Aslan said that it is market day today and that is why there is so much traffic and confusion. He apologizes if you are bored by our delay." Gillian forced a smile. "Can't you answer … make some comment?" Skender's exasperated tone irritated her.

"What would you like me to do? Jump up and down and clap my hands? Or perhaps burst into frustrated tears?" She turned away, blinking rapidly, and stared out of the window.

Aslan concentrated on the street ahead as he heard their sharpness with each other, the silence stretched and he issued unnecessary instructions. "Just follow the road, brother … it passes the Mill, then there is a wide bend. Keep straight on until we reach the crossroads."

"I know, Aslan." Skender's voice was quiet. "I remember the road."

The car picked up speed as they drew away from the confusion in the center of town, the busy shopping area gave way to a main thoroughfare. Quiet streets wound away from the busyness, wanting to provide a more serene and peaceful setting for their residents. Children threw and caught balls, high-pitched voices issuing ignored orders. Gillian let her eyes follow, smiling softly, as one girl ran down the main road, a loaf of bread clutched under one arm, her other hand whipping her imaginary horse to greater effort as she raced to keep abreast of their car.

The car slowed abruptly, came to a standstill. Gillian studied the big rambling building, the dark grey stones turned to silver from the dust and wintry sun.

Aslan glanced at Skender, saw the tight grip of his hands on the wheel. "Are you alright?"

"Yes." His hands relaxed. "That was where your father tried to give me the bread." Aslan followed the direction of Skender's eyes. "A moment later he was on the ground, his head bleeding … I thought him dead." Slowly they started to move forward as Skender gave pressure to the accelerator.

Aslan looked at him uncertainly. "Perhaps Prizren is not a good choice, Skender … you do realize that it is the same road? There is no other way, you must use this path?"

'You have a choice, Berisha … have you matured enough to know which path to follow?'

He felt Aslan's eyes on him. "I know, Aslan … I will be more careful in future."

"I wish I had a permit to drive, then you could rest…." He looked worriedly at Skender; the car glided to a stop at the 'Halt' sign.

Gillian looked up at the signposts – Prizren 75 km – in the opposite direction – Mitrovic 30 km. She slid down on the seat to get a clear view of the other pointing fingers. Vuciterin 15 km. She craned her neck to see the one pointing in the direction from which they had come – Podiev 25 km – and in larger letters above that – Pristina 7 km. Pristina? *That was the pronunciation whatever-his-name used, and yet Skender and all his family say Pristine … why?*

The way was clear for them, they started to move forward, turning right. Skender slowed after only a short time, pulled over to the far right and sat staring at the field on his left. "Our first rest was here…" Aslan leaned forward, trying to catch the low words, "the ground was hard, dry, from the long summer … we stayed the night, they lit fires. It was the first time I had ever seen any guards from Nis. Their smartness terrified me." His eyes moved to the right of the field. "The officer, arrogant, sure of himself … a forerunner of Mihajlovich and his like. Our spirits were still high then…."

'Thank you for coming to this great reunion….'

Skender smiled, hearing the big Mitrovic man's voice, seeing his mocking bow to the table with the bowls of thin watery soup. "That night we were disgusted with the food … later, as hunger clawed at our bellies, our memories turned it into a feast." He sighed, saw Aslan's concern, and put his hand on his shoulder. "I crossed the border here, Aslan … left carefree youth behind…."

"There was never any carefree youth for you, Skender … you never had that joy."

"Perhaps not." His eyes went again to the field. "But here, for a moment, there was a sad sweetness. It was here that I realized that I was part of a larger family than just the Berishas, that there was a brotherhood extending beyond family, beyond Prishtine even." His eyes scanned the muddy field, his voice little more than a breath as he continued, "Almost three thousand … each one ready to help and support those weaker than themselves. We were one family … we breathed and thought as one."

He turned the key, put the car into gear.

The flat stretching plains were left behind, small hills asserted themselves, forerunners of the great Alps that were to come. Gillian pushed herself up into a sitting position and began to take an interest in the countryside.

"Not far now, Skender … fifteen minutes and we will be in the center of Prizren." Skender gave a brief nod, his eyes not moving from the long black ribbon ahead of him.

Four blasts, Oh God, let there be four blasts … I can't run any more … must rest….

"Luan and Adnan hope to leave less than an hour behind us. Luan already has the cases in his car and will pick up Emin and Besim directly from their classes…." Aslan saw that Skender was not listening, left the sentence hanging, leaving him to his thoughts.

Run, run … push your legs. There is no rest….

Skender's hand lifted, wiped at his forehead.

The whistle's mouth screamed … one blast? What is the order for one blast … can't think … walk, yes … walk….

Aslan watched him worriedly, saw the beads of perspiration on his face and slowly opened the window a little.

'Have you seen Morat or Sabri, Skender?'

Skender's mouth formed the word 'No' as his head gave a brief shake.

'What are they shooting at, Jakup?' He waited until the guard passed them,

'I don't believe you … I don't believe….'

The whistle screeched its order, 'March'.

Skender's foot pressed down on the accelerator.

'Run.' He felt Jakup's hand pushing him,' I can't … not anymore….'.

'Yes, you can, you must. Run, Skender, run … run or be shot.'

Aslan watched as the needle started to climb, he turned, checked the back window, making sure that there were no police cars in the immediate vicinity. His eyes swiveled back to Gillian as he saw her concern, and he gave a reassuring nod before he faced front again. The needle swung on, past the central point, the red marker erratically jumping. The shuddering car was held firmly steady, Skender's eyes never wavering from the black tarmac stretching ahead.

'Halt!'

Brakes jammed on, the car careened dangerously from side to side before coming to a screaming stop, dust enveloping it as the tires hit the soft shoulder.

So thirsty … my legs … won't support me….

He opened the car door, staggered across the road breath coming in short rasping gasps as he reached the opposite side.

Why don't they open the gate? Weak … so weak….

Must stay on my feet … push away the ugly blackness.

Stand. Stand on your feet.

'Three hours without rest is much harder than two, isn't it?'

The shiny black boots were at eye level, the officer's riding crop started to hit at them. Tap. Tap. Tap. Tap-tap-tap.

Tappity-tap-tappity-tap … 'It is the erratic, the uneven that tires … comrades. The officer nodded to the guard and he opened the gate….

Gillian let out a cry, fumbled with the car door as Skender opened the gate, took three steps and fell to his knees.

"No." Aslan grabbed at her, held her fast. "No, Nusé. This he must do by himself … he was alone when he faced this fear, he must be alone when he puts it behind him."

She stared at him, not understanding why he stopped her, why he didn't go to him himself.

"You cannot help him, not now, not yet." He looked over her head toward Skender. "He must be alone, alone as he was then."

He did not feel the mud, the seeping coldness. His lips were dry, throat parched, his hand moved as of its own accord, rubbing itself in the wet grass. He lifted his hand, sucked at his fingers…. *No, the ground was hard, dry … but there was moisture, I remember the dampness. Yes! The blessed evening dew was on the grass … I rubbed my hand…. No, I fell, spread-eagled and sucked the grass with my mouth, pulling the moisture from it … pressed my body to the damp earth, letting her cool my heat….*

'You must stand, walk around…."

He turned quickly, only the trees and grass were with him. "Where are you now, old man?" he whispered, "I need you as much now as I did then … perhaps more than I did then."

'If you needed, needed her badly enough, Almighty God would make sure she came to you.'

"No, not my mother … she cannot help me at this time. There is no one, old man, no one … the decision has to be mine, there is no one to turn to for help." A sick wave of despair swept over him. *I have never been this alone before … there was always someone to turn to, someone to slap me on the back, make me laugh at my fear … or face it.* "Mihajlovich has me tied more securely than we tie a sheep before slitting its throat…."

'You have a choice … one pace behind me, or at my feet….'

His eyes lifted to the great Alps in the distance. "There is one other choice, Mihajlovich," his voice was barely a whisper. "One that you forgot … there is Mother Albania. She is there, just a blink of an eye away from me … she holds out her arms, accepts her long lost sons into her bosom….

Her bosom drips blood, brighter, redder, than any you've ever experienced….

He turned his back to the crying wind, but the insistent whine still blew about his ears.

More Communist than any other country, save China – supporting Stalin and Mao extremists … cut off from the world, no voice is heard outside of that country. It sits in brooding silence, not even a whisper comes, not even a letter, loved ones die … their relatives never know, never hear.

"Can it be worse than what I am offered now?" he shouted back. "Would the Albanian Communists persecute me more than Mihajlovich? I am one of them, born of their stock…."

There is not parentage, no belonging, under Communism. You are what they want you to be….

'One pace behind me or at my feet….

"The trap has been well set, Mihajlovich … Communism is my bread whichever way I go." His eyes lifted to the great guardians of Albania. "But there I would be with my own nationality, could use my own language, stand proudly with head held high when I answer, 'I am a Kosovar.' What lies beyond that grey giant is unknown, terrifyingly unknown, but I know my fate if I return to you. It is not death I fear … it is living in your shadow, being kept alive … barely alive … to suffer the agonies that only you and your kind know how to inflict.

'I want you to join us.'

"Never! Bring that shame on my father's house? Tread on the graves of my friends, smear their memory and let their deaths have been for naught? No, never that."

His eyes lifted again to the great Alps. "Would you accept this Kosovar? Let him live in peace, raise his family?" *Jill … could I ask that of her? Ask her to give up that much for me?* "No." His head dropped to his hands. "Whichever way I go, I lose her. Mihajlovich wants her out of the way … even had I been able to accept his offer, he would insist that I send her home. And if I kept her with me and refused his offer? How much could she take? How many times would she be able to accept the battered piece of humanity he would drop at her feet? How long before Mihajlovich realized how I feel about her and used her to pressure me?"

His voice was a whisper, "Well old man, do you have a solution for me?" His head lifted; his eyes searched the vast emptiness. "What is it to be?" His head dropped to his chest as a long deep sigh escaped. "What shall I do?"

'The answer lies inside yourself, Skender Berisha.'

The voice was quietly clear. He looked up, the field stretched, empty, yawning its way to the hills, the wind cut cruelly, making the grass bow before its force. He shivered, the cold wetness of his knees made itself felt. "Inside myself there is only confusion … confusion and a fierce anger that it is permitted … no, not permitted, encouraged … to threaten and bully as Mihajlovich does. He can do whatever he will without restraint, can maim and cripple, and we have no redress, can do nothing." He looked around, waiting for an answer. "The West does not hear, does not want to hear our cries, closes its eyes to our tears." His sigh was long, full of sadness.

"What of my own situation? Does my new country, which I love so dearly, know, or care, where I am? My enemies know. They care … they know my every move, my every breath." Despair filled him; he sank a little lower onto the damp grass and let it run its course.

He walked slowly back to the car, got in and sat staring out of the window.

"Skender?" He ignored Gillian's tentative enquiry.

"Will we ever live without fear, Aslan? Will we ever be able to pursue our daily lives without looking over our shoulder?"

Aslan answer was quiet, "I do not know Skender. Perhaps not you or I, but I hope for my son."

"Do you, Aslan? Do you hope for freedom for your son, as your father hoped for you, and as his father hoped for him?" Skender put his hand out and turned the key, his voice bitter. "Keep your dreams … reality stares me in the face, and I cannot share them."

The car pulled onto the road and started again for Prizren.

Chapter 31

Prizren, Kosov

Gillian gave a wry grin as she glanced round the hotel room. *Twin beds. At least we won't have to worry about touching each other tonight.* "Which bed would you like?" she asked, her voice coolly indifferent.

"This one, closest to the door." Skender dropped their case on the floor, laid himself on the bed and closed his eyes.

Slowly Gillian sank to the other bed, watching him. *I remember a time in Carmel … we were given a twin-bedded room there. We only used one.* She laid back, her eyes staring at the dull expanse of white ceiling. *Where are we going, you and I, Skender? I want to stop this silliness between us, but I can't … you have put up a wall between us, and I cannot reach you. I am on a roller coaster, flying through space, scared but unable to get off….* Her eyes turned to the other bed. *All I can do is wait, ride the ride to its conclusion … will we end safely on the ground, clinging to each other?*

Gillian sipped at her coffee. It had been an uncomfortable dinner. Aslan had kept up a steady conversation in an attempt to disguise the strained relationship of Skender and Gillian, but all were aware of it.

"I am tired. Will you excuse us tonight?" Skender stood up, turned to Gillian and asked briefly, "Are you ready?"

"Yes." The cup rattled as it touched the saucer. "Natën e mirë." Her smile was forced, travelled no farther than her mouth, the young men murmured their good-nights, inclined their heads to Skender.

Adnan shivered dramatically as they left the room. "The north wind is not as cold as those two tonight … what has happened between them?" He looked expectantly from Aslan to Emin, sighed, as there was no answer, "Skender has not been himself since he returned to Police Headquarters. He has been morose and…."

"That is enough," Aslan interrupted firmly. "It is not your place to criticize him."

"It is true," Adnan retorted hotly. "He is not as he was. Besim, haven't you noticed it?" he demanded, turning to his younger brother. Besim wriggled uncomfortably, glanced under his lashes at Aslan but made no comment. "He has not mentioned what transpired at Headquarters, not even to our fathers. Hasan was commenting to Arif…." He stopped abruptly, eyes dropping to the table.

Aslan leaned toward him. "You heard our father speaking to Arif? How? Where were you?"

Adnan glanced at Aslan, licked at his lips, then muttered, "I was in the barn, taking care of the cow…." He hesitated as he saw Aslan's eyes narrow. "They were taking their leave of each other…."

"And you stayed quiet did not cough or call attention to yourself?" Aslan's voice was coldly angry. "You are excused, Adnan. Goodnight."

Emin continued to study the movements of the solitary waiter as Adnan left the room. Besim finished smoothing the immaculate cloth, cleared his throat and stood. "With your permission, brother?" Aslan gave a brief nod and he hurried from the dining room.

"I am sorry that you were exposed to that … Adnan is not an easy one to guide and is inclined to…." Aslan frowned, then looked directly at Emin. "Has Arif spoken to you of Skender?"

"Yes. He asked that I be ready if he should need someone to lean on. My father is disturbed at Skender's silence. He told me that Skender has confided to no one, not even Babush." He hesitated, then continued quietly, "My father is also concerned at the coolness between him and his nusé."

Aslan nodded, "My father feels the same. He is convinced than Mihajlovich has put a great weight on Skender's shoulders. But that does not explain the situation with him and his nusé. What has gone wrong between them?"

"Thank God Luan was not here tonight. At least we kept it within family, but he will not visit with his friends all day tomorrow, and then what? Even a blind man would see the way they are with each other." He sighed, glanced morosely round the near empty dining room, "There is no excitement here tonight and my mood is not to go looking for it. Shall we have an early night?"

Aslan nodded. They stood, wound their way slowly out of the dining room and up the stairs. Both glanced toward Skender's door as they passed, their eyes met. "We both want the same thing for him, Emin … let us pray that his heart will find peace tonight."

Skender took the windbreaker after only a moment's hesitation between that and his overcoat. He zipped it halfway closed and started toward the door. He stopped as his hand touched the handle, turned back and walked to the bed nearest to the window.

He stood looking down at her. *I was wrong in bringing you to Kosov....* Gillian moved restlessly, a long, drawn-out sigh escaping as she adjusted her position.

Skender's eyes lifted to the window and the sleeping town stretching beyond, waiting until she was quiet again. He bent, let his lips linger against her hair. *Sleep soundly, my love ... let sleep take those dark shadows from your eyes, shadows put there by me and my problems.* His lips moved, gently he kissed her forehead. *I love you, Jill. Remember that in the difficult days ahead. Think of the happy times and forget these past two days.*

The door clicked to almost noiselessly behind him. He tried it, made sure it was fast, turned abruptly and hurried down the carpeted stairway.

The desk clerk looked up sleepily, resenting the interruption of his rest at such an early hour, grunted as the rubber trim on the heavy glass doors flip-flopped a message that the guest had gone. His extra chin joined the other two against his chest and his eyes dropped closed.

It was cold, the coldest, quietest time when the world waits for the birth of a new day. Fog swirled on the damply glistening cobbles hurrying to catch the clouds that cloaked the mountains before day came and destroyed the ethereal beauty.

Skender felt only the dampness of the mist and pulled the zipper on his jacket to its full length, digging his hands deep into his pockets. The hushed stillness caught the sound of his footsteps and sent them back to him twice as loud as when he gave them to the cobblestones.

He crossed one of the small stone bridges, stopping after he had passed the highest point of the hump to look at the fast-flowing river. "Why are you rushing? You have all day to reach your destination ... you have a lifetime."

He turned left as he came from the bridge, following the smaller path beside the noisy waters. "I am not sure why I am going," he answered quietly. "The only thing that is clear to me is that I have to go ... now ... and that I must go alone."

The Alps pierced the horizon and then were cloaked again at the discretion of the wind. Only Mount Shari remained constant, a bride shyly emerging from her veil of clouds. A thin spiral of smoke climbed to join the swirling vapor as Skender passed a small farm, the ochre and white of the buildings melting and reappearing with a dreamlike quality, his footsteps, softer now that he had left the cobblestones, disturbed no one, not even a dog barked. The smoke comforted him, reassuring him that there were others abroad as well as he.

A soft plodding sound intermingling with the harshness of metal against tarmac stopped him abruptly, his skin tingling a warning; he cursed softly as he strained to see, while his intellect reminded him of the advantage of not being seen too clearly.

Ears flicked as the horse saw him. He was old and took his time, a pale ghost pulling a caravan of older ancestry than himself, its paint, once gaudy, clung desperately to the wood, which sought to discard it. The Romany held the reins loosely, his dark burgundy coat creasing awkwardly as he hunched close to the caravan, seeking to escape the cold wetness surrounding him. His dark eyes looked without curiosity at Skender, and the black drooping moustache moved as he sent a Romany order to his horse. There was no acknowledgement by either as they passed each other.

Almost the same place….

Skender watched as the mist swallowed the caravan.

This is all the money we have, will you sell the coat?

A true Romany would never deny someone whose need is greater than his own….

Skender's eyes searched the mists, not a sound broke the eerie stillness. "Did I see it, or…?" He sighed, let his eyes search the whiteness once more, then turned and started to walk at a brisk pace towards the veiled lady awaiting him.

The red and white stripes of the sentry box warned him that he was close to the border. He stopped, moved cautiously to the grassy bank, flattening himself against it. He let his eyes accustom themselves to the distance. *Two guards, probably one more in the sentry box … my guess would be three altogether.*

A small dirt path led away from the road and he looked at it curiously, then edged toward it and began to climb steadily. The path was narrow, a track really, and followed the curve of the hill while continuing to lead toward the top of the ridge. He stopped abruptly, staring unbelievingly at another path coming from the opposite direction, that joined the one he was on. He peered into the thickness, trying to see where it led. *I cannot tell … but, coming from the direction it does, there is only one place it could lead….*

He squinted, trying to see, but the mists swirled too thickly. Puzzled, he turned and started to climb again. "Why? Why would there be a path? Who would use it? For what purpose?" The trail continued to climb, steeper now, the path lost for a moment in the mist, then reappearing, beckoning him on.

A rocky ledge offered a natural resting place, and he sank down gratefully, his breathing deep and uneven. He leaned back against the high stone, feeling his tiredness. His head found a pocket in the rock, and he sat quietly, listening to his muscles scream their protest at the unexpected exertion while he watched the clouds veiling and unveiling the great mountain in front of him.

"What is it that you want of me? Your voice called and I came." The clouds shrouded Shari in milky whiteness. His voice was louder as he continued, "Speak! Do not play the shy virgin with me. I have traveled your face, clawed my way across your belly, and slept in your frosty embrace…." His voice trailed away as she loomed, suddenly, majestically, over him, pushing away the cloudy film.

"You do not frighten me, great giant. I am as insignificant as an ant beside you. You could swallow me in a flash, and yet you hold no terror for me. Why is that?"

He sat still and silent as the clouds covered her.

"My friends sleep in your cold arms … would they speak to me if I came to you? Or, wraith-like, appear to me and lead me into your cold heart to join them?

"No. Not they. They would not raise a finger to harm me." He smiled, pointed his finger at Shari, "Go, Skender, drink deeply of life … take hold of it and shake it, take all of it, the pain and the sorrow, the happiness and the joy.' That would be their message."

The pain and the sorrow, the pain … and the sorrow.

"And I am not through with it, not yet." He realized he was shouting and quieted himself. "I am not through with the pain or the sorrow … there is still more to live through. And, God forgive me, I do not think I have the strength."

His clenched fist pounded the rocky seat. "I am tired of bitterness. Why didn't you take me when you took the others? Answer me! Why spare me?"

The mists seemed to thicken and he strained forward.

"My destiny?" His mocking laugh echoed back to him. "My destiny is misery. Everything I love or care about is stripped from me. I thought that you had finished with me, that you would let me wrap myself in my cloth of happiness." He let out a long sigh as he dropped back against the rocks, his voice low as he asked, "Why do you demand more of me? Haven't I given enough?"

There were many deaths … you asked for life.
Your soul cried for freedom … you tasted it.
Your heart yearned for love … it was given you.
Your arms ached to hold dear ones once again … even that was granted.

He sat silent; head bent. "Forgive me," he whispered, "I had forgotten."

He sat very still, then with a great effort, raised his eyes. "What of Jill?"

Tiredness slowed his voice. "So I must send her away, send her from here?" His whisper carried lightly as the wind dropped. "Will I ever see her again? Will my arms ever hold her, know the sweetness of her again?" His tears were hot on his cheek, then, as he gave himself up to his emotion, great sobs shook him.

The clouds returned, swirling thickly around the awesome mountain. Panic caught at him. "Don't go…" he pleaded, "…stay. I need you to stay with me, just for a little while."

He lay back against the rocks, then with a faint smile, looked up and said, "They say you are a myth." He felt the tension ease out of him as she dropped her cloak over him, let out a long deep sigh. "I need to rest … just for a moment?" He smiled back at her, pulled the cloak up to his chin and let his eyes droop closed.

"What is he doing?"

"Sitting. Not moving."

The one with the hat sighed, "How much longer is he going to wait? Watch him closely … once he decides to make his move, it will take him only minutes to be in our neighbor's yard."

"My eyes will not leave him." He turned to his companion with a grin. "Mihajlovich would have my skin…."

A grunt stopped him. "Mihajlovich would have your life if you lost him." He adjusted his position so that he could rest against a rock. "Remember his orders, aim low … he wants him taken alive."

The sun was warm on his face. He opened his eyes slowly, unzipping the jacket a little as he did so. The valley was bathed in a warm golden glow, the white cap of snow on Mount Shari glistening and sparkling frosted the scene splendidly.

"I am a king up here, able to see for miles.". His arms rested on two protruding ledges, slightly lower than shoulder height. *I am a king. A king with a throne! Skanderbeg's throne!* He lifted his arm high above him. "Ho, Albanians, Sons of Eagles. Come, pay homage to Skanderbeg!" he called softly.

He lowered his arm, sat quietly, letting the golden warmth seep into him, while his eyes drank in the tranquil scene. Small farms, mostly white, dotted lush fields, doll-sized people moved, the white pants of the mountain men clearly visible against the vibrant green. He stood, stretched luxuriously, and started to walk down the dirt path until he reached the 'Y'. A movement near the border pulled him to a stop and he stood poised at the crossroads, watching.

Mihajlovich's guard grinned let the rifle lift, sighted to Skender's hip as he murmured, "Now he will make his move."

Two guards wandered to the flagpole, their uniforms dark, standing strongly against the sun. Skender watched intently, cupping his hands around his eyes. The Albanian flag, scarlet with the black emblem, broke free, fluttered in the soft breeze. His heart lifted, and he stood as tall as the mountain. And then the wind came strongly, the flag stood stiffly. There were no folds to hide the star above the double-headed eagle, it gleamed whitely.

Skender's shoulders sagged as the Communist Star became clearly visible to him. He watched the Albanian guards return to their posts, then he let his gaze return to Mount Shari. She stood in silent majesty, protecting and guarding her own.

He stood quietly, feeling the snow-cooled wind blowing across and over the top of Shari and the warmth of the sun. He stood in silent contemplation for several minutes, then lifted his head and straightened his shoulders. His hand raised in a brief salute. "Be at peace, my friends…" he called softly, "rest easy."

The dirt path was steep, and he picked his way down carefully until he reached the road. He took one last long look at Shari and then turned to the direction of Prizren.

Gillian heard the door open but did not turn, knowing it was Skender and not wanting to face him.

"Jill?"

She did not move, and he stood beside the door, watching the stiffness in her. "I cannot take this silence between us anymore, Skender." Her hands clenched in her lap as she continued to stare out of the window. "I didn't intend to bring trouble to you or your family…." Her voice shook as she felt his nearness. "Surely you know … you must know … that I would never do anything to hurt you…." She looked up at him as he came and stood in front of her. "I only wanted to help…."

His lips stopped the flow of words. "I love you; I love you," he murmured.

"I love you, too," she whispered as she helped him off with his wet jacket.

"I love the scent of you…" His hands moved through her hair and then across her shoulders as his lips moved to her neck. She loosed the belt and let her robe fall away. "…and the taste of you." His lips caressed her breasts as his hands slid the length of her. He looked deep into her eyes as he moved close to her. "Will I ever have my fill of you?" he asked as he started to caress her.

"No. Nor I of you."

"We are one, my love. We are so right for each other, belong together…." An image of Mihajlovich flashed into his mind, anger sparked and suffused his whole being. "Damn them. Damn them for interfering in our lives, our happiness."

She let out a long sigh as she felt him inside her.

He finished quickly and rolled from her.

She lay quiet, watching him, puzzled at his words and the sudden strangeness of him.

"Did I hurt you?" he asked, pushing himself up on his elbow. She shook her head. His need for reassurance was tangible as he insisted, "Are you sure?"

She smoothed his hair as she answered softly, "Could your love ever hurt me?"

"Oh Jill…." His arms closed around her and they lay close, content to hold each other.

"Why were you so angry at me?" She needed to know the reason for his long coldness.

He sighed, then after a pause he told her, "Because of something that happened when I was fifteen. I had been arrested, held for five days…." He decided not to tell her about the beatings. "In the cell next to mine, there was a girl … I never saw her, but I think she was very young … I had to listen to her pleading with them, begging them…."

Jill's wedding ring bit into her fingers as his grip tightened.

"They would laugh … I covered my ears, but still her screams reached me." He lay still, staring up at the ceiling. "And then … then there was silence." He didn't move except for some long ragged breaths before he turned to look at her. "You had put yourself so very close to danger, so very close to being in the same situation."

"Don't. It didn't happen." She pulled closer to him.

"If you had fallen into their hands…." A shudder shook him.

Gently she touched his face. "You look exhausted."

"Yes, I am. Could you sleep for a while, here, with me?"

She nodded, her smile tremulous. "I have not slept soundly since … I could not sleep…." She looked up at him, "I am used to being close to you."

"For the rest of your stay in Kosov, you shall sleep in my arms … that is a promise."

"Not just Kosov…" she nestled in close to him, "for the rest of our lives."

God help me, how am I going to tell her?

She moved her head to look up at him, as there was no reply.

He bent and kissed her. "If you are within reach of my arms, they will hold you … you will be as close to my heart as now." He reached and pulled a blanket over them both. "Sleep now, my love."

Chapter 32

"Gjelletore Te Dy Lumejvet." A wave of laughter greeted Gillian's pronunciation.

Emin shook his head as he glanced up at the lighted sign above their heads.

Adnan sighed, heavily, dramatically. "What are you doing to our language, Nusé?" He took hold of her chin, made her look at him and enunciated clearly and slowly as Besim opened the door for the Restaurant of the Two Rivers. "Try again, Gjelletore Te Dy Lumejvet." He turned to Skender. "Explain to her that Prizren is the meeting place for two rivers…."

"Later, Adnan. Inside now, we are making them lose all their heat with the door open."

Gas lamps hissed, their mantles sending out a yellow glow of warmth, welcoming and hospitable after the coldness of the night air. A young man detached himself from a small group near the door and approached them. "Good evening … please enter." His hand moved graciously toward the benches on each side of the door.

"Remove your shoes," Skender whispered to Gillian. "Put them under the seat and lay your coat on the bench."

Gillian glanced under her lashes at the young man waiting patiently for them. He wore the traditional Kosov dress, but his trousers were white, woolen and heavily decorated with black embroidery, black braiding ran the length of the outside leg and his feet were encased in soft leather slippers, the toes upturned. A striped black and white cummerbund was pulled deliberately tight, showing off his trimness while holding the rough linen shirt securely in place. His white hat defied gravity, sitting forward and to one side of his head. Gillian caught her breath as the young man gave a slight bow when Skender stood, but the curly hair won and the hat stayed firmly on his head.

"Six, plus the lady, seven?"

"Yes."

"This way, please." He led the way.

Carpets hung from ceiling to floor, the patterned intricacies of one balanced by the solid color and simpler design of the one next to it. Fat leather hammocks were scattered around low wooden tables, the center of each carried a recessed brass or copper brazier, the bases burnt black from hot coals, the edges burnished to a glorious shine. The lighting was soft, gentle, only the red-hot charcoal and a few gas lamps against the walls lighting the room. The warm aroma of good food teased their nostrils.

"It's beautiful," Gillian whispered to Skender as they settled themselves at one of the larger tables, her eyes followed the young man. "His dress is different to that worn in Prishtine."

"Yes. His is a mountaineer." Skender grinned at her. "And your admiration of him is quite obvious."

She grinned back at him. "He is rather dashing, isn't he? Even his slippers admire him." She explained as she saw his puzzled expression, "The toes turn up to look at him!"

He laughed, accepted the proffered menu. "Luan, is there something you especially recommend?"

"Everything they prepare is good, but for your Nusé…" his brow creased into a frown, "…I assume she would like something not too spicy?" He glanced up, coughed quietly when he saw Skender studying the menu. "There is one dish not on the menu, which I think she might enjoy, a fish, caught in the White River. They remove the bones, fill the cavity with pieces of lemon and herbs and cook it at the table over the hot charcoal."

"Perfect. And I will have Shish-Kebab." Skender closed the menu, turned to Aslan as he, too, laid his menu down. "How was your day, Aslan?"

"Well," his voice was low, reached only Skender, "Emin and I have checked very thoroughly … there is nothing but praise for the young man in question. The Drinis are prominent here, but also respected and well liked. I think this match would be right for Drita and that she would find happiness." Skender frowningly nodded, "Drita is special to all of us, brother … I would not recommend unless I was very sure."

"I know, Aslan … thank you." He turned to Adnan and Besim. "I'm sorry, what did you say?

Emin picked up the dictionary. "Nusé, did you like Prizren? Did you and Skender enjoy this town?"

Luan took the dictionary. "Yes, I had forgotten … this is your first sight of Prizren. How do you like this city, nestled in the arms of the great Alps?"

"Which part appealed to you the most?" Emin retrieved the dictionary, handed it to Gillian.

"The cobbled streets, the feeling of continuity … the buildings clinging like leeches to their hills, the strange biscuit color of the houses." She smiled, unable to find the words she needed and knowing it was not necessary. "The crisp invigorating air, the grandeur of the mountains ... especially the one that wears one of your hats!"

"A mountain? With a hat?" Emin questioned.

Luan's laugh was loud. "Shari! She is speaking of Shari with her mantle of snow!" He turned to Emin. "I prefer her description!"

"I, too. And she is right! The mountain is Albanian ... it is only right that it should wear one of our hats! Skender, did you hear your Nusé's description of Shari?"

Music sounded before Skender could answer. All eyes turned to the tiny stage, one of the waiters picked up a microphone. Gillian felt rather than saw the shocked glances of the cousins as the announcement came.

"Skender, I am sorry. I had no idea...." Embarrassed, Luan stopped glanced quickly at Gillian. "Had I known they would have entertainment, I would never have suggested this place."

"What do you want to do, brother?" Emin interrupted hastily as the music started again.

"Besim," Aslan's voice was quiet, but a command, as he indicated that Besim was to leave the room, "you may wait in the lobby." He ignored the pleading look, turned to Skender. "Explain to your Nusé ... tell her to go with Besim, and we will send for them when it is over."

Skender hesitated.

Emin's voice came urgently, "Didn't you hear the announcement, Skender? They are going to have entertainment!" Still, Skender hesitated. "Turkish entertainment, Skender," he emphasized the first word as his eyes flew to Gillian, then back to Skender, "Turkish!"

"I think she may stay. Why not? It is an art form ... folk dancing!" Skender saw their horror, Aslan's shock. "I remember you telling me so many times, Aslan!"

Aslan's bow was stiff. "I am sorry, I do not agree, Skender, but the decision is yours. Besim...." His hand invited the young man to leave.

"Good-bye, baby brother. Do not be too sad ... I will be most happy to tell you all about it later."

Disappointment, dismay, and anger mingled on Besim's face at Adnan's teasing.

"Aslan..." Skender leaned close, his voice low, "such disappointment ... look at his face ... let him stay. What harm can it do? He is old enough ... seventeen." He sensed the refusal about to come. "How old were you and I when we had this pleasure?" He laughed softly, "We had saved for weeks ... do you remember? She was a little fat, a little past her prime, but...." He shrugged, grin spreading as he saw Aslan trying not to laugh, then slapped his cousin across the back. "Let him stay!"

Aslan gave a brief nod to the not-breathing Besim, let his laughter come as he witnessed the quick grin of triumph sent to the still-teasing Adnan.

The gas lamps were dimmed to near extinction, only the glow of the hot coals lit the hushed, expectant room. The music slowed, stopped, and then, softly, quietly, started again. A tambourine rattled into silence. A louder, longer, rattle brought anticipation to its height. Slowly, three young women glided to the center of the miniscule stage, each dressed more brilliantly than the other. But it was the youngest that Gillian's eyes glued to.

Her emerald dimi hung low on her hips, the material almost opaque, but not quite, allowing the viewer a glimpse, a tantalizing promise of slim legs and thighs. Wide gold bands held the fullness close at her ankles, and gold coins circled her waist, chinking delicately as she swayed to the music. The ruby in her navel flashed fire as it caught the leap of a flame from one of the charcoal braziers.

Gillian did not move, let her eyes slide to Skender … he was rapt, lost in the dance, elbow propped on the table, chin resting on his hand. Jealousy gripped at her and she deliberately made her eyes circle the young men at their table. All were enthralled, intent on watching the smoothly seductive movements of the dancers.

Skender moved slightly to smilingly watch the breathless wonder of Besim, He reached into his pocket as he whispered to Aslan, took out a few bills, then put his elbow back on the table, hand pointing upwards, the bills held between two fingers. The lead dancer saw him almost immediately, he pointed the bills towards the youngest girl in green.

He has done that before … this is not the first time…. Gillian's breathing was suspended as she saw the green dimi move toward Skender.

He bent forward, talking quietly to the dancing girl, then tucked the money between her breast and the brief bolero top.

Jealousy flared again. *Was it my imagination, or did his fingers linger longer than necessary?*

The girl looked straight at Skender, red lips parting in a smile, eyes suddenly bold as she spoke.

He laughed, shook his head as he answered, "I am flattered … but no."

"Why not?" The dark eyes flashed to Gillian. "Is she with you?"

"Yes." The smile still hovered around his mouth. "She is my wife."

She smiled back at him, said softly, "She is lucky!" then moved away.

"Why did you call her here?" The question was out, spoken before she could recall it.

She felt his hand caress the back of her neck. "Your jealousy is showing … you have turned the same color as her dress!" She looked up into his laughing eyes. "I am glad you feel that way, but it is not necessary. Besim's first experience of seeing Turkish belly dancing must be exciting, never to be forgotten. Watch now, she will go to him…."

The young beauty edged toward Besim. Emin grinned, winked at Luan, asked innocently, "Are you enjoying yourself, Besim … or shall we leave?"

Aslan chuckled as Besim gave a sheepish grin but did not take his eyes from the loveliness in front of him.

She was young, vulnerable, and chaste as she danced for him, her body was liquid beauty, intangible, ethereal as she swayed to the softly haunting melody, even the coins silent, unmoving. The tambourine clamored a message, and then was stilled, as was she … as was the room.

She sighed, stretched, then sighed again. Her eyes lifted, sought, and found Besim's, and held them. Her red lips parted to a seductive smile, and this time the sigh was different. The music started. She did not falter as the tempo quickened, reached a crescendo and then slowed. Her arms lifted, carried her hair, then let it fall, a dark cloud about her shoulders, her eyes dared him outrageously as she came to her knees in front of him. Her lips parted, she laughed softly, as softly as the insistent sound of the coins about her waist, as she sat back, hair sweeping the floor. She held the position, then allowed her body to slide, slowly, to the floor.

Gillian gasped as Skender pulled her face into his chest. "What are you doing?" Her muffled indignation reached him as she struggled to be free.

"You have seen enough, the rest is not for you," he whispered, holding her firmly, eyes not leaving the girl in front of Besim.

He released her as applause came.

Coins showered onto the stage, cascading around the young girl, who stood, head bowed, hands clasped together in front of her.

"What else did she do?" she demanded.

Skender laughed softly. "She danced, my love … she danced for Besim. And every man, young and old, in this room wished she were dancing for him, and him alone."

"Did you?" She bit her lip, wished she had not asked.

Yes, for a moment. He did not speak the words, knowing that she would be hurt, would not understand that wanting the dancing girl did not touch his love or desire for her.

"Nusé, look…." Adnan saved him the necessity of answering.

For a moment, Jill, just for a moment … but I would not part with you for a dozen like her. His eyes saddened as he watched her. *I am going to have to send you away, my love … will you understand? How many months … years, perhaps … of separation stretch ahead of us? Will our love be strong enough? Or, like dry parched earth, will it crumble, fall away.*

Chapter 33

Prishtine, Kosov

The drive home had been pleasantly quiet. Prizren had risen to the occasion and decorated herself with a pale wintry sun, gilding the ochre houses and sparkling the snow on Shari for Gillian's last glimpse of the town.

Luan had led, driving at a steady, even pace, Skender followed with Aslan and Gillian. Gillian, curled onto the back seat, dozed, sat up and chatted for a while, then dozed again. When there was only her steady breathing, Aslan and Skender talked quietly, mostly about the Drini family and the various bits and pieces of information about them that Aslan and Emin had uncovered while in Prizren.

They passed the Old Mill with barely a glance from Skender. The center of Prishtine was quiet, and they drove through without delay. Aslan gave a contented sigh as they turned onto Ruga Lapit. "Home … it was a smooth journey. Are you tired?"

"No, I am quite relaxed. Luan is a good driver, easy to follow." He glanced in the driving mirror. "Wake up, sleepyhead, we are almost home." Gillian stretched, slipped into her coat as the car slowed, then stopped.

The wind was strong and cold, and she shivered as they gathered around the two cars, collecting bags from the trunks, sorting out gloves and hats.

"Emin, please take Gillian inside, she is shivering."

"So am I! Come Nusé." Emin picked up Skender's bag, took Gillian's hand. "Take care, it is very slippery."

"I will wait here for you, Emin," Luan called, watching as his friend guided Gillian away from the icy patches on the path.

"Good-bye, good-bye!" Laughter was in Skender's voice as he turned his back on his cousins. "It takes them ten minutes to say good-bye, even though they live next door to me!" He smiled at Luan, "What has amused you, Luan?"

"Not amused, just happy, Skender." Luan's chin pointed toward the now empty path. "Emin has accepted your Nusé without reservation … I am happy about that."

"As I am, Luan. Come, we will have coffee together before you go."

Luan hesitated, "I do not wish to impose on your family, Skender. Emin will be but a moment."

"I insist. I will not leave you waiting out here in the cold." Skender urged Luan through the gate, grinned as it groaned to behind them. "One day I must oil that damn thing. The kitchen will be the warmest place…" he shivered as he spoke, started down the steps, "…we will go there."

Luan stopped, started to speak, then slowly followed Skender.

Gillian and Emin were in front of the stove, the glasses of tea doing double duty, warming their hands as they sipped at the hot liquid.

Gillian smiled as she moved to the side of the stove. "Come and get warm … the fire feels good, so does the tea…." Her voice trailed off as she noted Emin's glare at Luan before he turned back to the stove.

"Nona, how are you?" Skender hugged his mother, kissed her cheek.

"Skender, welcome…." Nona stopped abruptly as she saw Luan in the doorway, her eyes flashed to Drita, then to Emin.

What's wrong? Gillian quickly took in the scene. *Of course! Drita is here….*

"Drita … why so flushed?" Skender bent and kissed his sister's cheek. "Have you been roasting your face at the fire?" Skender's teasing flamed her face more. "Well?" She shook her head, her eyes not leaving his feet. "Nona, I have asked Luan to join us for coffee. Come in Luan, if you were closer to the door you would be outside of it."

"Welcome, Luan … how are you? It is good to see you again." Nona's greeting was gracious before she suggested to Skender that he and Luan would be more comfortable in the guest room.

"No, we will stay here."

Emin glared at Luan then turned to Skender, "You will be more comfortable upstairs, brother … I will bring the coffee."

Emin is furious … doesn't Skender see?

"It is not necessary, Emin … it is warmer here and less work."

Gillian's eyes flew from Emin to Skender. *He has refused to leave the kitchen! Emin is about to blow a fuse!* "Skender, you go upstairs with Luan and Emin … I will bring the coffee."

Skender laughed. "Why is everyone so anxious to serve us upstairs … even you, Jill?"

"Skender … your sister…." Gillian muttered, sending a sidelong glance at Drita.

"Drita?" He turned to her. "Surely you are not shy with Luan, Drita? You were together often enough as children." Her eyes remained firmly down as she stood, head bent, before him. His voice dropped and he ordered, "Greet him and serve us coffee."

She bowed to Skender, then hesitantly turned to Luan, bowed, "Welcome."

"Thank you, Drita. It has been a long time since I saw you … are you well?" He smiled at her as her eyes raised to his for the first time.

She gave a brief nod; her hand offered him a seat. "Would you prefer tea or coffee?"

"Coffee, please." Luan checked that Skender had already sat down, started to take the seat offered by Drita, hesitated a moment, then moved to a different position. "My mother has missed having you come to see her, also my brothers' wives … they have wondered why you have not accompanied your mother…."

"She has been busy." Emin interrupted coldly, "We have had many guests." He turned away from Luan, "Hurry, Drita, I do not wish to delay here too long."

Water splattered, hissed, as Drita pushed the jesva too quickly over the hottest part of the fire.

She is shaking. Luan is fascinated by her, hasn't taken his eyes off her, deliberately sat there so he could watch her. Gillian was vaguely aware of Skender speaking to her and turned toward him.

"Nona asked if you enjoyed Prizren."

"What? Oh, yes, thank you." Her eyes returned to the scene by the stove. Coffee grounds spilt onto the hot ashes, sending flames leaping. *I have never seen Drita this nervous. Should I help? No, that would draw attention to her, make her even more nervous….*

"Jill, did you hear me? I am going upstairs to see Babush." She nodded absently. "Emin?"

"Yes, I have finished my tea, will pay my respects to my uncle." Emin looked directly at Luan, voice cold and angry, "I shall not be long … perhaps we could leave as soon as I return?"

"Of course, Emin, whenever you are ready." Luan stood, waited until they had closed the door, then sat down. "Can't you sit for a moment, Drita? The coffee will not prepare any faster even if you stand." She half smiled, bit at her lip. "Please?" She smoothed at her hair slowly sat down opposite him. He glanced back at Nona, then leaned forward and asked quietly, "Why haven't you visited my house with your mother?"

Drita shook her head, not answering, not looking at him.

Damn! I wish I knew what he said to her! Oops … Nona's saying something….

"Yes, thank you, Mrs. Berisha, my mother is in good health." Luan turned back to Drita. "There must be a reason for your visits to stop so abruptly. What was it?"

"You know why. It was not – proper – for you to see me."

"A glimpse in passing! Not even enough to fill my eyes…."

"And the children? They are well, too?"

He almost sighed, turned again to Nona. "Yes, Mrs. Berisha, they are all well." He turned back to Drita. "I…."

"And full of mischief, I expect?" Nona asked with a smile.

"Yes." He made himself turn again to Nona. "Full of mischief."

Nona nodded. "You will not mind, Luan, if I continue with my preparation for dinner?"

"No. Not at all." Luan waited a moment, turned again to Drita, their eyes met, held, and they laughed softly together.

I am dying of curiosity!

"I cannot believe my luck … to be invited here, to your kitchen, given an opportunity to speak to you. Drita…."

"The baby must be quite active now, Luan."

"Yes, Mrs. Berisha, I suppose it must." Luan realized his answer was a little sharp, softened his tone. "I am not too involved with my nieces and nephews, at least not when they are babies. Once they are able to walk, I take an interest, but when they are still small…."

"It will be different when you have your own, Luan." Nona smiled. "You do not believe that now, of course, but one day you will find out for yourself." Luan gave an answering smile.

Gillian watched as Drita swung the jesva, poured the coffee, waited a moment, then swung the jesva again before filling the cup. She held her breath as Drita placed the cup and saucer on the three fingers of her right hand, bowed, then offered the coffee to Luan. Disappointment surged through Gillian as she saw that he took the cup carefully without touching Drita's fingers. Drita took two steps backwards before lifting her head.

"Always so correct, Drita," Luan said softly.

She blushed furiously. "Is the coffee to your liking?"

I bet I'll know the language before we come here again….

"Thank you it is perfect." He waited until Drita sat down. "I know the reason for your absence from my mother's house…" his voice was quiet, "you were so upset when I came to Arif's and saw you there. Your visits with your mother stopped after that. Am I right?"

"Yes." Drita glanced quickly towards her mother.

Luan, too, turned to look at Nona. "But why?" he asked when he saw that she was busy with her pastry. "I saw you for a moment, spoke less than a minute, your aunt and Ilyria beside us the whole time."

"You had no right to see me, no right to speak to me. Your being at Arif's at the same time as I was not coincidence, Luan. You wished me to believe that, but I knew that it was not." Her head lifted proudly. "I am my father's daughter, carry his name, no action of mine will ever bring a shadow to his face or this house."

"My action was impetuous, regretted as soon as I saw your distress. I did not realize the position I was putting you in. I would never knowingly cause you any sorrow, Drita. There was only one thought for me … she will be there, and I could see her." He swore softly as the door opened.

"Laknor!" Skender exclaimed as he saw his mother mixing the spinach, eggs, and cheeses together. "My favorite meal. Sit down, Luan." His hand waved Luan back to the rug. "Drita, Babush would like coffee."

Drita poured a cup immediately, bowed to Luan. "Good-bye … my regards to your mother and sisters, and of course the children."

"Thank you, Drita … good-bye." He felt Emin's eyes on his back, forced himself not to turn and watch her as she left the room.

"If you have finished your coffee, Luan, I think we should leave." Emin's words were polite enough. His tone was not.

"I am finished." Luan put down the cup, stood up. He started slightly as he saw Gillian. *I had forgotten you were there. Thank God you do not know our language.* He held out his hand. "Nusé, good-bye … thank you for your company in Prizren." Their eyes met. *You do not need to know, do you? You have already guessed?*

"Good-bye, Luan."

He released Gillian's hand, went to Nona and bowed. "Mrs. Berisha, thank you for the coffee and for allowing me to warm myself."

"Come again, Luan. My love to your mother." Nona waited until he and Emin had left. "Skender, that was not wise. It was not right to bring Luan to this kitchen."

"Why not? He is family."

"No. He is the son of a friend, a dear and valued friend, but he is not family. You should not have exposed Drita to him."

"They have known each other since children, Nona."

"Yes, Djali, but until today he has not spoken to her since she left school. When I visit their house and take Drita with me, Luan's mother is most careful of Drita … she has never admitted Luan, or any of her sons, to the room where Drita is visiting. If a friend can give that respect to our daughter, then her brother should do no less."

"I am sorry, Nona, you are right. I had forgotten." His eyes glanced toward Gillian, sitting beside the stove. "I had forgotten, but she realized … did you know that she had asked me to take Luan upstairs?"

"No, but I am proud that she did."

Skender bent, kissed his mother's cheek."I am sorry. I will be more careful in future." He started to grin. "Was that the reason for Emin's anger?" Nona smiled, nodded, and he laughed softly. "Poor Luan!" Within moments he will feel the rough edge of Emin's tongue!"

Emin and Luan walked to the car in silence. Emin's hand shot out, stopping Luan as he inserted the key and started to turn it. "One moment. I think there is something for us to discuss."

Luan turned to Emin. "Well?"

"I thought I felt something … a tension, a sensation … between you and Drita." His eyes fixed on Luan's face. "I pray it was my imagination." Luan turned to the front, started to turn the key. "Damn you, answer me!"

Luan was stiff, silent, staring out of the windshield. His grip on the steering wheel relaxed and he turned with an embarrassed grin to look at Emin. "You are right … I care for her, and I am almost sure that she…. Didn't you guess? Didn't you ever suspect?" He laughed, a little embarrassed still, "I asked constantly about her, and you were always quite happy to give me news of her."

"I? Gave you news of Drita? Never!" He groaned as remembrance came, "You asked after Ilyria, my mother … the fact that you asked for Drita. To me that was all there was to it. A friend asking about my sister, and one whom he knew is as close as a sister to me." He let his head fall back against the seat. "I never thought … you were a friend asking politely about my family." He was suddenly suspicious. "Wait … she left school at sixteen. Your interest did not keep alive this long without a sight of her." He pushed himself up into a sitting position. "You have seen her before today, haven't you? Where? When? With whom?"

"Yes, I have seen her." Luan raised his hand, stopping the angry torrent of words about to come. "You forget, my friend, the Mali and the Berisha houses have been close for years. Her father and mine found each other when they took their first steps … they journeyed their school years together. Only one year separated each marriage. My father was given a son, Sabri." Emotion shook Luan's voice, then determinedly he continued, "Only one year separated the birth of Babush's son, Skender. The friendship of the two boys brought the mothers together. Another friendship sprung and branched between the two families. And then, sorrow came, binding both houses even closer together … the eldest son of each was taken … and the mothers consoled each other, dried each other's tears."

Emin gave a sympathetic grunt.

"When my parents heard that Skender lived, their joy was almost as great as…." He turned his head sideways, took a deep breath then continued, "The two mothers visit each other frequently. But you know this, you have accompanied Mrs. Berisha and Drita to my house many times…."

"And you saw her? When she was in your house?" Emin's anger had returned.

"There is always a way, Emin … you know that. My mother may close the door, but there is always a window that overlooks the path."

"You went to great trouble."

Luan smiled. "Yes, I did. And when my mother was to visit this house, I was always available to accompany her! Sometimes I think that my mother guessed the reason, but I cannot be sure. You see, there was always a chance, slim, but a chance, that I would have a moment with her, or at least a sight of her."

Emin's clenched fist pounded softly against the dashboard. "Drita … did she … was she aware … damn it! Did she give you any encouragement?"

Luan looked steadily at Emin, asked quietly, "You know her better than I. Do you need to ask?"

"No." Emin's eyes dropped from Luan's steady gaze. "No, I am ashamed that the thought entered my head."

"And me, Emin, what of me? Do you truly believe I would be interested in her if she had been that way?"

"How would I know?" Emin flashed angrily. "Other girls have sparked your interest."

"Take care," Luan warned, "do not speak of Drita and those others in the same breath. I want Drita for my wife, to carry my name and bear…." Emin's groan stopped him, "What?"

"Oh, God, what a mess."

Luan stared as Emin sighed. "Surely you did not think…?" He laughed, "Now I understand your anger. I am sorry, but I thought that you had guessed … the day we picked up Skender's Nusé, I told you, 'Someone special holds me here. My father has promised….'"

"Stop! For God's sake, stop!" Emin hesitated, not sure what to do. "Luan, my friendship for you makes me confide something that should not, in all truth, be spoken of outside of my family. While we were in Prizren…." He stopped. "You did not think it strange that I should take time from my studies, particularly at this time, so near finals? Or that Aslan asked for time off from work?"

Luan shrugged, "Skender wished to go … I assumed that you were anxious to be with him."

"Yes, that is true, but there was another matter that took Aslan and I to Prizren … a matter that needed two of the more senior members of the Berisha family. Can't you see what I am trying to tell you?" His voice dropped as Luan shook his head. "There was an enquiry for Drita. Aslan and I … it is a good family, respectable and well liked. We could not fault the young man." The silence stretched. "I'm sorry."

"I cannot, will not, accept losing her. I have waited too long." He turned the key. "I shall speak to my father immediately."

"Luan … she is practically engaged! Aslan will report to Babush tonight, or tomorrow at the latest, and then…" Emin sighed. "The intermediary will be here before the end of the week. As soon as he is given his answer, the wheels will be set in motion."

"Does Drita know?"

"Not yet. Babush wanted to be sure before telling her…." His voice trailed off wearily, "If only your father had spoken before."

"I begged him, damn it, a year ago. He refused, said Drita was too young, and that I must wait. Now … he has waited too long."

"I am sorry, Luan, so sorry. For my part, I would rather have Drita in your hands than any other."

Luan turned, looked steadily at Emin. "And Babush, what of him? Would he have accepted my father's offer? Would he have given Drita to me?"

"I cannot answer that! But everything would appear to favor you. You are here, in Prishtine. Babush would have been able to keep his daughter near him, would not have the dust of a day's journey separating them. Your house is known to him almost as well as his own. Is there a father alive that would not prefer that, than to giving his beloved into the hands of strangers?"

The car jerked forward as Luan jammed into gear. "I am going home, will speak to my father immediately. One favor, Emin?" Luan's face was grim as he guided the car between the icy ruts.

"Anything within my power."

"Keep Aslan from Babush tonight … delay as long as possible."

"Agreed." Emin watched Luan with compassion. "I wish you luck, my friend- but I fear you ride too close to the wind."

Chapter 34

Babush watched Skender over the top of his paper, his lips pursed as he returned to the news. The words made no sense to him and he gave in to his worry, folded the paper and laid it beside him as he asked, "What is the trouble, Skender?" Skender's eyes lifted to Babush's, held for a moment, then he gave a brief shake of his head. "Do not deny that something is troubling you." Babush smiled, "I have seen you sit in that position many times as a child … I always knew before you spoke that there was some prank you had to admit to."

"This is no prank, sir. I wish to God it were." Babush took out his pipe, picked up the packet of tobacco. "I do not know where to begin."

"At the beginning, Skender." Babush slowly packed his pipe, watching Skender as he did so, he reached, took a piece of wood from the fire and held it to the tobacco, pulling deeply. "Shall I start for you?" Skender's startled face turned to him. "It began two days before you went to Prizren. You wonder how I know that. Your anger at your wife was out of proportion to the cause, lasted too long. You demanded too much from Drita … even your cousins were cautious around you. And you avoided me." He examined his pipe, worked at the tobacco a little and took another spill to light it again. "That was not the behavior of my son, some problem of great magnitude weighted your shoulders. Am I right?"

"Yes." Skender's voice was low, barely audible.

"I did not approve of your trip to Prizren, I felt that it would open too many old wounds. When you returned this afternoon, I was glad that I had held my tongue, not spoken of my fears. You were in control again; you were reconciled with your Nusé. Now the weight has returned to your shoulders, you are tense and concerned. I believe your concern springs from something you need to tell me." He sat back, pulling deeply on his pipe as he waited for Skender to speak.

"Tonight I went to Police Headquarters…."

"Yes?" Babush encouraged, as there were no further words, "You checked in at six o'clock, and then…?"

Skender licked at his lips, sat straighter. "Then I saw Mihajlovich." He stood up, Babush watched him as he paced the floor. "He wanted an answer to certain demands he had made on me." He sighed, ran his hands through his hair. "Mihajlovich had given me an ultimatum two days before we left for Prizren." He stopped near to Babush, gave a sad smile. "I did not realize I was so transparent … had no idea that you had even guessed that something was wrong."

"I did not have to guess, Djali … not when you were a child, or when you were a boy. Even as you struggled to emerge to manhood, I knew when there was a problem." He smiled as his hand offered Skender a seat, continued as Skender sat down, "Why assume that it is different now?"

"Sir, Mihajlovich intends to keep me here … he will not let me leave Kosov." Babush sighed, smoothed at his moustache, "What he demanded of me sickened me, was repugnant, unthinkable. He made it very clear what would happen if I refused." His eyes lifted to Babush's face. "There is no need for me to enlarge on it, you have friends with sons who have refused to bow to their will, have witnessed their handiwork at first hand." Babush's hand shook and he took a tighter grip on his pipe. "When we went to Prizren, I was in turmoil, did not know which way to turn, and then, suddenly, I realized that there was an answer, an alternative that Mihajlovich had overlooked. Prizren is so close to the Albanian border … in a blink of an eye I could be across, out of his hands."

He took out a cigarette. "I weighed the problem of Jill … would they touch her if I left her behind? Could she accept the rigidity and poverty of Albania if I took her with me? I did not think she could. As for Mihajlovich … he would not risk an incident with her if I managed to cross the border, the danger to her was if I was caught." He lit the cigarette, took a long draw. "We both know what they would do to her to punish me."

He sat quietly smoking his cigarette. "Do you remember when I was telling you about the march, and the strange sensation I had that something, someone, was watching over me when we clawed our way across the Alps?" He picked up a log and threw it into the fire. "Migje said that it was his belief that there was a spirit in the mountains … one that guarded, protected…" he paused, eyes half-closed, "even as I laughed, I felt that presence, knew he spoke truly … there was something, something that protected me. Others, stronger, more well clothed than I, froze. Boys raised in the mountains slipped on a patch of ice and fell to their deaths. I survived. I, who had never seen a mountain before, never climbed anything higher than a hill…." He wiped his mouth with the back of his hand, sat frowning at the caves made by the fire.

"Whatever it is…" he continued quietly, "it called me again. I got up before dawn, went close to the border, as close as I could to Shari. There was a path, a track, really … and I climbed the hill. Even a seat was provided, and I sat, and I listened. I did not like what I heard. I argued…." He took a deep breath, let it go slowly. "The answer does not lie in Albania. It lies here, in Kosov, in Prishtine. I have no idea what is expected of me, where I shall end. I must leave myself open and accept my destiny. The path is not clearly marked, but a finger pointed the direction. Babush, your anger is going to be great … forgive me, there was no other way. Tonight, I agreed to Mihajlovich's demand. I shall start to work for him within the week."

Babush took his pipe from his mouth, slowly snapped it into two pieces.

Skender's eyes closed for a moment, when he opened them, Babush had not moved, still sat with a piece of pipe in each hand. He slid across the rug toward the old man. "I, too, was reviled at the idea, could not even let the thought crystallize in my mind…."

Babush's hand caught him full across the mouth. "How dare you! How dare you come to me with such news!"

"Sir…."

"Silence! Better you had never returned here than carry such tiding to my ears." Angrily Babush smoothed at his moustache. "Have you forgotten all that have gone before? The hundreds, thousands, who have stood against them, refused to smear name and flag by joining them?" His voice dropped as he leaned forward, face close to Skender's. "Have you forgotten your own friends? What were their deaths for if this is all they accomplished?"

Skender's lips were tight as he answered, "I have not forgotten."

"And what of our suffering? The fear, the heartbreak when you were dragged away? The constant terror after you escaped the march, and they searched this house night after night, harassing your mother and your sisters?

"What of your brother and the two sisters that died … died because we were refused medical aid? No medicine was allowed to enter this house. No doctor dared examine our sick. Do you know why? Do you care? I will tell you anyway. Not one of the Berisha family was a Party Member, not one of the Berisha family lowered their standards to join the Communists." He rocked back and forth on his pillow. "And now you come to me, tell me that you are joining them. Why wait this long? Why not have joined seventeen years ago? You would have spared us much suffering. I would have suffered in a different way … shame would have prevented me from leaving my house. My gate would never have opened to guests again … but at least all my children would live."

"You cannot know that. You have taught me that when your time comes, you will be taken, no matter where you are or what you do."

"A pity you have not listened closer to other things I taught. I cannot understand you, Skender. Even news of your death would have been easier to accept than this."

Skender's eyes flashed. "That was not offered. There is no value in my death … only alive can I be useful. Mihajlovich knows his trade."

"It appears he knows my son … knows him better than his father."

Skender recoiled, the angry, bitter words hurt more than the slap. He sat, head bent, for a long moment before he started to speak quietly and with control. "You have every right to be angry, but I beg you to listen before judging me…."

"Why did you not come to me for advice? Is my judgment so poor that you place no value on it?"

Skender's eyes slowly raised to his father's. "How could I come to you? How could I lay such a burden on your shoulders? What advice would you have given? 'Go to Mihajlovich, son, give his barbarians free rein over you. Let them do their worst … let them beat you senseless and then return a mindless piece of humanity to me?' No, Babush … my love, my respect for you is too great to make you pay that price. The decision had to be mine."

He swallowed, "The disgust you feel is mirrored in your eyes … their torture would have been easier to accept. I am not allowed to accept … my path is set and I must follow it." Babush did not speak, did not move. "Your face is the color of burnt wood, grey, lifeless … my heart cries that it is I that have caused you such grief, but what tears me apart, makes my heart bleed is that you have so little trust in me."

He looked directly into Babush's eyes, "Have I ever brought shame to your door? Have I ever stepped on the Berisha name? Was there ever an act of mine that caused you to drop your eyes from your neighbors?" His own eyes fell to his hands, his voice low. "Until this moment, have you ever had reason to wish that you had not fathered me?"

Babush sat poker straight. He took a long breath, releasing it slowly. "Never."

Skender moved close to his father, "Trust me, Babush. You have never withheld that trust before … I beg you to give it to me now."

"What are your plans?"

"I do not know. All I can swear to is that there will be no stain on our name or our flag."

"You have agreed to work for Mihajlovich, Skender. By agreeing to that, you have signed yourself to Communism."

Skender shook his head. "My capitulation to his demand made him overconfident. He was hard put to control his jubilation." His voice was bitter as memory filled his eyes, Babush sat quietly watching, waiting for Skender to continue. "I refused to join the Party. I told him it was impossible for me to commit myself to supporting and upholding a Party of which I knew nothing." Babush saw the clenching and unclenching of his hands. "He has suggested some books, and I am to take instruction once a week." He rubbed at his eyes, sighed, "If nothing else, it buys me a little time."

Babush watched him shrewdly. "There is still more, isn't there?" He waited a long time for the answer.

"Yes, there is more."

"Cleanse yourself of it, Skender … let us have done with this thing."

Skender stood up, walked to the window and lifted a corner of the drape. *Not even a star….* "Jill is to leave … immediately."

He dropped the drape, turned and saw the shock on Babush's face. He walked back to the fire and sat down again. "It is the only mistake that Mihajlovich has made, Babush. By releasing her, he frees me to move if the opportunity presents itself. Had he kept her here, he would have insured his control over me. I would be completely in his power."

Babush nodded, "Yes, I see that, but what was Mihajlovich's reason for letting her out of his sight?" He saw the sudden anguish, hardened himself and insisted, "Well?"

Skender took a long shuddering breath. "He wants unity in this family, with me the undisputed head. He feels that cannot be achieved with me tied to an outsider who is an embarrassment to you and the whole Berisha family."

Babush swore softly. "He squeezed you dry, didn't he, Djali?" He laid his arm across Skender's shoulders. "I have done you an injustice … I have not had need to lay hands on you since you were a young child, and now … to strike you … I hope you can find it in your heart to forgive me."

"It is past, Babush, already forgotten."

Babush's eyes fell on the snapped pipe. He picked up the two pieces and put them in his pocket. *No, Djali … not forgotten.* "When is she to go, Skender?"

"Until this evening I thought I would have her for a month, but it is not to be. Mihajlovich asked…" he licked at his lips, "…asked how soon I could be rid of her." Babush's fist pounded the rug. "I told him I would not let her go unless I was sure that her family were expecting her, would meet her at the airport. As you know, a letter to England takes three weeks. Mihajlovich laughed at the idea of waiting that long, told me to telephone her family. It was my turn to laugh. I asked if he realized how long it takes to place a call to anywhere outside of Kosov, that it would take months to get a call through to the West. 'Bring her to my office tomorrow … she can make the call from here.' I questioned bringing her tomorrow, asked if it was possible for a call to go through in one day. "Not even a day, Berisha … just minutes.'"

Babush gave a grim smile. "After you have read your books, taken your instruction, Djali, you will understand. Under Communism there are equal rights, equal opportunity for all." Skender almost smiled. "If she is to go, Skender, it is better that she go at once. The torment would be too great to have her here for weeks knowing that you are going to lose her."

"Perhaps … I cannot think that way. All I know is that I expected to have her for another month. Now, if the call goes through, we shall take the train to Belgrade tomorrow night, and she will be on the flight to England at noon the following day."

"It will be hard on you without her, Skender." Babush frowningly poked at the fire. "Do you realize what you have taken upon yourself, Djali? I am old, my friendships run deep and true. Maybe a few will turn away." He shrugged. "For the most part, they will stand this test.

He sat watching his son, seeing the strain, and sensing his despair. "But you? Your nusé will be gone. How many friends are left? Of those left, how many will still greet you once you are with Mihajlovich?"

"I don't know, sir."

"Your uncles … are they to know? Your brothers?

"No. None but you, Babush. Too many knowing creates a danger."

Babush frowningly rubbed at his moustache. "I am healthy, strong, but my age … I insist on Arif knowing. There must be one other in this family who has some idea of the truth."

"If you wish."

Babush hesitated, then, "You said 'if the opportunity presents itself….'"

"First, I must be sure – absolutely sure – that Jill is safe, that Mihajlovich cannot stretch his hands to her. Once that is accomplished…" Skender's eyes lifted to his father's. "I will be able to say nothing … one morning I shall kiss my mother and my sister good-bye as usual, will take my leave of you … when you hear that I have left this land, say your good-bye silently, let your arms reach out and hold me close … give me your blessing."

Babush's arms closed around Skender, held him tight to his chest. "Djali, Djali-eim…." He lifted his hand, wiped his tears before releasing his son. "My blessing is yours, always. Our love for you is deep in our hearts. In these difficult times ahead, draw on it, sustain yourself with that love. And when you have gone from the reach of my arms, remember this, you do not have to be in our eyes for us to see you … you do not have to be within reach for us to love you."

Emotion choked Skender. "I have not words … I did not expect such understanding, was afraid that…." He turned his head, unable to continue.

"That I would throw you from this house?" Babush shook his head, "Never, Djali. You are mine, my seed, and I claim you proudly."

"Thank you, Babush."

Babush nodded. "Have you told your Nusé she is to be returned to her home?"

"No. Not yet. I shall tell her tonight."

Babush frowningly rubbed at his moustache. "That troubles me greatly, Skender." He waited until he was sure that he had Skender's full attention. "To return a bride to her parents brings great shame to that house. Be very careful, very sure, that her father knows the reason and understands it. This Nusé whom you have given to us came as a stranger … she is now my daughter, accepted and loved by all in this family. I want no feeling of shame or dishonor to accompany her to her home."

Skender nodded, unable to speak. He stood, bowed, started to ask for permission to leave. "Babush…."

"Go and rest, Djali … I think you have need."

"Come in Berisha. Good afternoon, Mrs. Berisha, I am happy to see you again." Mihajlovich dismissed the guard, offered them a seat at his desk. "Have you enjoyed your holiday here?"

"Yes, thank you."

Skender was glad that Gillian answered coolly, looked directly at Mihajlovich.

"And now you are going home … what a pity you cannot stay longer, visit some of the beauty spots of my country."

"Yes," her chin lifted slightly, "a great pity."

Mihajlovich's eyes narrowed. *Water found its own level when Berisha found you … you are as arrogant as he.* "What is the number of your family?" He picked up the telephone, repeated the number after Gillian. Irritation showed clearly on his face, in his voice. "Since when? Very well." He opened a drawer of his desk, searched through, finally pulling a form from the inside. "It seems we have a new rule and a form is needed…." He glanced at Skender with a faint smile. "Bureaucracy extends to all government. Take this downstairs to the officer and he will process it." He signed the form, held it out to Skender. His eyebrows raised at Skender's hesitation. "Oh, come now, Berisha, she is quite safe, I assure you, and custom is hardly prevalent in this situation, is it?" He turned to Gillian. "I am sorry, Mrs. Berisha, there will be a slight delay … five minutes, no more, I am sure," he added as Skender rose, took the form from him.

Skender's hand stopped Gillian as she started to stand. "I will be but a moment … this form has to be taken downstairs." She nodded, gave a shaky smile as he left.

Mihajlovich leaned back in his chair. He had deliberately sent Berisha from the room. "I hope it is not sickness in your family that takes you away so suddenly?"

"No." Gillian did not look at him, let her eyes stay at desk level.

"Perhaps you and he have quarreled?"

Her eyes lifted, met Mihajlovich's. "You know it is not that." Her hands gripped the arms of her chair, her voice less than a whisper as she asked, "Why don't you let him go? Why keep him here?"

"My dear young lady, I am not keeping him here. Is that the reason he has given you for staying in Pristina? Why should I want him? For what reason?" He reached for a cigarette. "If you had been denied your home, your heritage, for as many years as he, and then you returned…." The lighter snapped shut. "His heart has yearned after this land, these people … do you really expect him to leave it again? He cannot deny his birthright, but you are a thorn in his eye, a reminder of a mistake. By removing you, he removes the problem."

"That is not true." Gillian was close to tears.

"Oh?" Mihajlovich leaned across the desk, his voice quiet, insistent. "You could not cope with the day-to-day life here and he knows that … never leave the house unless escorted, stand the instant he entered a room, not sit until he gave you permission. You might try, but your breeding would revolt against such servitude." He smiled as he witnessed her unwilling agreement. "And what of the work? You are a visitor now, fussed over and coddled, but if you were here permanently, that would change. The heavy, hard work would fall on your shoulders, you…." The phone's soft call cut across his words. "Mihajlovich here … yes, that is correct." His hand offered her the phone. "Your call, Mrs. Berisha."

"Hello? Mother? It's Gillian. I'm fine … I am coming home. No … he won't, just me, Mother … please? That is not true." Mihajlovich watched her closely. "I shall be arriving at London Airport the day after tomorrow, on the BEA flight." She bit at her lip, fighting tears. "I don't want to talk about it now … all I want to know is if you or Dad can meet me. Good-bye, good-bye, Mother, I will not discuss it anymore." She put the receiver back, letting go slowly.

"If you wish, you may call your husband here … to let him know that you have arrived safely." She nodded, not trusting her voice. "One phone call, Mrs. Berisha, no more. Of course, you can write to him … any letters will automatically come to my desk and I shall be happy to pass them on to him … as soon as I've read them."

"Read them?" Gillian's eyes lifted to Mihajlovich.

"Of course … all mail is subject to censor. Why does that concern you?" He smiled, "The personal, intimate parts do not interest me. You must think of me as a doctor … a doctor of letters, if you wish … examining, prodding … but in a completely impersonal way." He laughed softly as she closed her eyes and turned from him. "You are not embarrassed when you bare yourself for examination by your doctor … why be shy of me and my examination of your words?" Gillian stood up. The command was instant. "Sit down." Mihajlovich leaned across the desk to her. "Make it easy on him, keep the letters few and short. Ah, Berisha, your wife has completed her call, and I think she is ready to leave … unless you would care for some tea, Mrs. Berisha?" he asked solicitously.

Slowly she raised her head to look at him. "No. No thank you."

"Then good-bye, have a pleasant journey home. Do you have your travel permit, Berisha? Good. I will expect to see you here in a few days, then." He waited until the door closed on them, picked up the telephone. "Bring the recording immediately." His pen tapped impatiently until the officer appeared. "Play it."

He sat back, a smile hovering about his mouth as he listened. "The young lady is having a very rough time…" he continued to translate for the officer, "her mother asks if her husband will be accompanying her … her denial has brought a storm. 'I told you the marriage would not last … why isn't he coming here with you? I suppose he's having too good a time with his own girls.'" He laughed with the officer, held up his finger for quiet, "'In my opinion you'd be better off without him. You should have married some nice English boy.'" Mihajlovich switched off the machine. "Fortune smiles on us, comrade officer … I planted a worm in her heart, and now her mother has added another. I have also let her know that I shall read her letters to him…." The officer's questioning look brought a quiet laugh. "Berisha will look in vain for affection in her letters … she will be unable to write freely of her feelings, knowing that eyes other than his will read her words." He pushed the machine towards the front of his desk. "I want no other ears to hear that … destroy it." He turned a page of his diary as he dismissed the officer, picked up his pen. 'Berisha … Belgrade' was printed and underlined on the appropriate page.

Chapter 35

"Why is she leaving so suddenly?" Luan passed the second case to Emin to place beside the other already in the trunk of his car.

Emin sighed, shook his head. "I don't know, Luan … nobody seems to know except Babush." He took the small traveling bag, placed it carefully beside the cases, then closed the trunk of the car. "My father, my uncle, Aslan … all were shocked at the news." He kicked moodily at the tire. "Babush has aged overnight, Nona's tears flow unchecked, while Drita…." He stopped, looked up at Luan, "I should not even mention her to you," he softened. "Did you speak to your father?"

"Yes."

"Well?"

"If it is meant, it will happen … if it is not meant, there is nothing to be done." Emin smiled at Luan's imitation of his father's voice. "He was supposed to have visited with Babush today. Besim came with word that there was some difficulty in the family and that Babush wished to postpone their chess game until later this week." His eyes went to the gate. "How is Skender taking this, Emin?"

"As he is the instigator of her departure…" Emin bit back the angry words as he saw Luan's shock, took a deep breath, then added calmly, "…but I think…" he frowned, "she is heartbroken."

"Yes, I imagine she is," Luan said quietly as he glanced at his watch. "I do not want to disturb their good-byes, but we must leave soon."

"She had taken her leave of all but Babush and Nona when I came out … they will be here shortly."

Skender turned to Gillian, saw that she had composed herself after the emotional good-byes of his aunts, cousins, and uncles. "Now the hardest part, my love, saying good-bye to my parents and sister. Are you ready?" She nodded; his hand reached to the doorknob.

Drita rose immediately, bowed to Skender. "Sit down, Drita." His gentleness caused her tears to flow again.

"I cannot … it is too difficult for me, the hurt too deep for me to stay."

"I understand, Drita. I know how close you two have become, how much you care for her and she for you. If it is easier for you…." His hand moved, giving her permission to leave. He left the two young women together, went and sat close to Nona. He sighed as his eyes met Babush's, then he put his arm around Nona, "Please, Nona, stop your tears."

Nona watched as Drita and Gillian clung to each other. "You give me a daughter to love, and then snatch her from me. It was the same with all of my children … given for such a short time, and then…."

"Enough, wife … calm yourself." Babush smoothed his moustache as Skender tried to comfort Nona. "She and Drita have almost finished with their good-byes; she will be with us soon. Remember, it is as hard for her as it is for us." He gave Nona a smile of encouragement as he saw her put the handkerchief away and sit straighter.

The sound of the door closing quietly brought his attention to Gillian and he beckoned her to him. "Come here, daughter. Skender, you will tell her my words … be careful in the translation, I wish her to understand very well." Babush reached and took hold of Gillian's hands, gently pulled her to her knees to face him. "You have won a place deep in our hearts. Had you been born here, I could not be more pleased with you. If I had searched all of Kosov, I could not have found better for my son. You are my daughter; this is your home. My door will always be open to you."

He glanced quickly at Skender as he heard his voice tremble. "Steady, Djali, she needs your strength." He took his handkerchief and wiped Gillian's tears. "Nona and I gave much thought to what we should give you, something to remind you of us … sshh," he stopped Gillian's protest, "I know what is in your heart, know that you do not need to have material possessions to call us into your memory, but, sometimes, to be able to touch something that has been given to you by a loved one helps the pain, the loneliness." He took her hand, opened it, then closed her fingers over their gift. "May Almighty God bring you back to us soon … until that time, may He bless you and keep you forever in His care."

"Babush…." Sobs choked Gillian, Babush held out his arms, comforting her as he held her close to him. He sighed deeply. "Go to Nona, daughter." His eyes lifted to Skender as Nona gathered Gillian to her. "Djali, I would feel easier if you would allow one of your brothers to accompany you on this journey … it will be hard for you once she has gone."

"No, Babush. I wish to be alone with her for these last few hours. And, after she has gone, I shall need time to myself. Time to … accept. And to remember."

"Do not forget where you will be, Skender … tread carefully."

A sad smile flitted across Skender's face as he dragged his eyes from Nona and Gillian. "No one will harass me, sir … I am under Mihajlovich's protection now." He glanced at his watch.

Babush stood. "Come, wife, let us give them a few moments together before she leaves this house. We will wait for you downstairs, Djali."

"Thank you, Babush. Jill…." He stared in amazement as she took Babush's hand in hers, raised it to her forehead, back to her lips, and again to her forehead. Babush's eyes met and held Skender's, and he answered the unspoken question, "No, sir, I did not ask it of her."

"I thought not, Skender. It was too spontaneous, too natural, but I had to be sure." He smiled as Gillian finished the obeisance, bent and kissed her on each cheek. "Thank you, daughter."

"No…" Nona refused her hand to Gillian, pulled her close, holding her tight to her, "I do not want that from you, my child … I want you here, close to my heart." Tears mingled as cheeks touched, Babush moved toward the door and Nona released Gillian. "Come home soon, daughter. Come back to your mother." She kissed Gillian once more, then followed Babush.

Skender closed the door behind them, came to Jill and took her in his arms. "They love you, Jill, have opened their hearts to you…."

Her tears fell faster. "I feel the same for them, but … I can't say the words."

"I know," he comforted her. "Love is such a difficult word to pull from your lips, but your actions speak it. I know that you love my family, do not need to hear the words." He opened her hand, took the gold coin into his own and stood looking down at it. "They have honored you, my love … it is almost impossible to find one of these now…." His hand lifted and he fastened the chain around her neck. "For a family to part with one of their coins, the Nusé must be very special, very precious…."

"Don't make me go, Skender … let me stay here with you."

He put his fingers over her lips. "I wish that more than you, but it cannot be." He held her close, lips brushing her hair. *This is the last time these walls will witness my love for you. I will never again hold you in my own home, my own land….*

"Come, my love, it is time to go."

"Identity cards." The policeman stepped in front of them, barring them from the station entrance. Without a word, the three men handed over the small white cards. "What about her?" His eyes went briefly to Gillian.

"Give him your passport, Jill." Gillian took it from her handbag, offered it to the policeman. "She and I are the only two traveling … here is my permit." The policeman ignored the passport, took the permit, and perused it carefully, then waved them ahead as he returned their documents.

"The train is already here," Emin commented unnecessarily as they turned the corner.

The gentle breathing of the engine overrode their footsteps as they passed, they walked in silence, glancing in at the brightly lit windows of the train as their feet moved through square patches of light on the damp platform.

"Here is an empty compartment. Luan, I will take the other case from you now." Emin accepted the case from Luan, moved ahead of them to the carriage door. They watched as they saw him walk through the corridor toward the empty compartment.

Luan turned to Skender. "Skender, I will say good-bye to you … Emin will want a moment alone with you and your Nusé."

"Thank you, Luan. Jill, Luan wishes to say good-bye."

Gillian forced a smile. "Luan, thank you for your kindness to me during my stay." She held out the dictionary. "And thank you for lending me this."

Luan waited until Skender had finished translating. "I have done nothing, Nusé … it was an honor to have you here in Prishtine. Please keep the dictionary … it is a gift." He smiled down at her. "Perhaps you will have a few words of Albanian next time you visit us."

"Yes, perhaps."

Skender glanced quickly at her as he heard the shakiness in her voice, she saw his concern, took a deep breath as she held out her hand. "Thank you, Luan … good-bye."

"Good-bye, Nusé. God give you a safe journey to your home." He released her hand, shook hands with Skender. "I will await you on your return, Skender. Be careful. In Belgrade you are farther from your home than anywhere else in the world."

"I will … thank you, Luan, and good-bye." Skender stood close to Gillian, let his hand hold hers for a moment as they watched Luan until darkness swallowed him.

"Brother, I have put the cases on the rack … the travel bag, and the box of food prepared by Nona are on the seat."

"Thank you, Emin." The metallic noise drew Skender's eyes, he put his hand across Emin's back, moving him forward as the grip man passed between them and the train.

The heavy hammer swung again, bringing another ring of metal against metal. "Please, God, we are not dependent on his old ears to detect a fault!" Emin grinned as he saw Skender's smile, then suddenly was serious. "Do not go alone, Skender, let me accompany you … I have a pass…."

"No. I appreciate your offer, Emin, but no … this I must do by myself." His eyes followed the dark green uniform of the guard as he walked to the rear of the train, a green flag wrapped tight around the wooden handle swung in time to his measured step. "We had better board … it will be only moments now."

"Skender … you will be in the very heart of Yugoslavia … take care."

Skender smiled, held out his hand. "I will … good-bye, Emin."

"Good-bye, brother." Emin turned to Gillian. "Nusé?"

She blinked rapidly as she held out her hand. "Good-bye, Emin."

Emin ignored the outstretched hand, held his arms wide, with a half-sob, Gillian went to him and they held tight to each other. "I pray that you understand why you have been wrenched from our family…" his eyes met Skender's over Gillian's head, "…for I do not. Lamtumire, little sister."

"Good-bye, Emin."

His finger took the tears from her cheek as he said softly, "Speak Albanian, Nusé … lamtumire." His hug was hard as she tried but choked on the word.

The Station Master's whistle gave its warning. "Emin, quickly … we must get on the train immediately." Skender took Gillian's arm, hurried her forward as the green flag fell. "Until tomorrow, Emin." The train jolted forward as Skender swung aboard.

Skender walked the corridor, steadying himself against the sway of the train, he joined Gillian at the window of their compartment, watching as Emin walked beside them. The train gathered momentum, pulling steadily away from Emin and he stopped beneath one of the tall platform lights. Slowly he removed his white hat, held it high in a salute, arm stretched above his head.

Gillian pressed close to the window, watching the solitary figure until he was nothing … a speck under a dim light. Slowly she turned from the darkness to the brightly lit compartment. "I will never see Emin again, will I? Never see any of your family, not Babush or Nona…?" Her eyes fixed on Skender. "I will never see Drita, or Jakup, or any of them, will I, Skender?"

The train's chatter changed as they switched rails, Skender took off his coat. "Come, Jill, sit here, close to me." Slowly she sank to the seat. "It is impossible for us to foresee the future. When I was dragging myself across the Albanian Alps, I thought I had seen my parents for the last time, would never again walk the streets of Prishtine, or feel the closeness of family fold around me. For seventeen years, I dreamed and longed to return, never expecting it to happen. But it did. I have held my parents, walked the familiar streets, and felt the warmth and affection of my family reach out and encompass me. The impossible happened … it could happen again."

"No, I don't believe that. I will never see them again. And now…" her eyes lifted to Skender, "now I am wondering … will I ever see you again, Skender? Or is this good-bye for us, too?" Her face turned to the window and she sobbed quietly against the pane. Skender eased her into his arms. "I'm sorry … I tried to be brave, but…."

"I know, I understand … so many good-byes, so many tears. You are emotionally exhausted." He stroked her hair, comforting her. "It cannot end like this … not for us. Our love is too strong, too deep." He put her from him so that he could see her face. "We have overcome obstacles before … family, tradition … now there is another battle to be won. Jill, look at me … have you been happy with me?"

"Happy? These two years have been the happiest of my life … and you?"

"You do not need to ask; you know the answer. There has been a contentment, a satisfaction I had never experienced. Each day brought greater joy. Jill, our love for each other is so special … it has let us touch the stars." He held her close as she laid her face against his chest. "Since you arrived in my home, I have watched you try to please my family, have seen you win their hearts, and the love I have for you has deepened even more. How can you ask if this is good-bye, if this is the end of our love for each other?"

"Not our love, Skender … our marriage."

"Do you remember our conversation last night? I told you then that the first priority is your safety. You must be out of Mihajlovich's reach." He sighed, "And for a time I must play out his charade. But one day Mihajlovich will turn his head for a moment … when that happens, I will be gone."

"I need something more concrete than that … I cannot hold onto such a slim thread of hope, need something more definite than 'one day'."

"If I knew when, my love, this parting would not be so painful. If I could say it will be only a short separation…."

"I'm sorry. That was a stupid thing to say. I am being selfish, thinking only of myself."

"No. This is the first time you have met cruelty for the sake of it … the first time someone has deliberately tried to cause you pain and sorrow for no reason other than to see your anguish and take pleasure in it. We are used to this. It has been fed to us regularly, and we are prepared."

The brilliant overhead lights dimmed, came full strength again and were then extinguished. A soft twilight glow enveloped the compartment as the blue night-light came on. "We have talked enough … any further discussion can only take us in circles to the same conclusion. Shall we try to rest?" Skender lay back against the deeply cushioned seat, held out his arms.

Gillian curled up beside him, staring out at the darkness, seeing their dim reflections in the window. "I love you, Skender. I always will."

He pulled her close, tightened his grip as she started at the scream of the train as it entered the tunnel that straddled Kosov and Serbia.

"And I love you, Jill … do not forget that … ever."

BOOK THREE

Chapter 36

"May I have your attention, please?" Mihajlovich waited until he had complete quiet in the general office with the eyes of all upon him, "This…" he indicated Skender, "is Skender Berisha. As of today, he will be working for me as my assistant." He waited until the hum of disbelief had quietened. "As my assistant, he will be asking for your help and cooperation. It will be given to him freely and with the same promptness as it is given to me. That is all. Carry on."

Skender turned and followed Mihajlovich. The muttered, "Like hell I will", reached only his ears as they passed the heavy policeman standing beside the long counter. Skender made himself keep his eyes on Mihajlovich as if he had not heard.

Mihajlovich took the two short flights of stone steps to the first floor, turned to the left, passed a door marked, '*Stefan Mihajlovich, D.D. Udba*' and went to the door immediately next to it. Skender followed. "Good morning, Anna. I want you to meet Skender Berisha. He will be helping us in the future."

His secretary stood as soon as Mihajlovich entered the room. "Good morning, Colonel Mihajlovich." Her eyes quickly sized up Skender before she murmured a greeting.

"Good morning." Skender was surprised by her smile as he answered her, it was warm and welcoming. He glanced around the office as Mihajlovich and Anna quietly discussed telephone messages.

Rows of grey metal filing cabinets lined two walls, one topped with a single flower in a cut glass vase, its bright softness incongruous against the cold unyielding metal. Beneath the barred window stood an old mahogany desk, nothing … not even a paper clip … disturbed its polished gleam. Skender turned to look at Anna. She was thirtyish, with the flat high cheekbones typical of Slavic races. Her brown hair, already lightly streaked with grey, was wound into a tight bun, styled for neatness rather than flattery, as were the brown lace-up shoes and severely tailored suit. Her desk was as she, neat and professional, each pile of papers stood at attention in their assigned positions, while the typewriter, already filled with a half-typed sheet of letterheading, waited for her return. Skender's eyes went to the window, to the bare-branched tree that did nothing to obliterate the view of the granite obelisk in Main Square. He sighed to himself as he looked at the leather chair beside the naked desk, it was worn, soft, and offered silent promise of comfort.

Mihajlovich moved. “Berisha.”

The door leading to Mihajlovich’s private office was partly obscured by the rows of filing cabinets. Skender followed, gave a curt nod in answer to Anna’s smile as he passed by her desk. “Close the door.” Mihajlovich reached his desk and sat down. “Well, Berisha, you are now officially here.” There was a ghost of a smile, “In spite of your very obvious displeasure at that, I officially welcome you. Sit down.” He reached and took a cigarette from the box on his desk. “It will not be easy at first. There will be some … antagonism … shall we say?” His eyes reflected the flame from the lighter as he glanced at Skender, “But perhaps you were aware of that when I introduced you to the police staff?”

Skender sat down, his smile ironic. “Of course … one would have to be made of stone not to feel their hatred, their fury.” He watched as Mihajlovich drew deeply on his cigarette. “This is not going to work. Are you aware of that?”

Lazily, Mihajlovich removed the ash from his cigarette, sat studying the glowing end. “It will work. My word is law here. Whatever their feelings, they will obey me.” He looked up at Skender, the unspoken, ‘And so will you’, understood by each. “Your first duty is to go through the list of names we spoke of … I want to know those that are dead. That is as far as my interest stretches. If you wish to write to the family…” his shoulders lifted slightly, “a desk has been provided for you. For the time being Anna will handle your secretarial requirements. You will find her extremely efficient.”

“Thank you.” Skender’s sarcasm brought Mihajlovich’s eyes to him immediately.

“You could be very useful to me, Berisha. I want you, but I do not need you. Your services could simplify matters, but they are not essential to me. On the other hand, your well-being, your very life, rests in my hands. I suggest you accept these facts without further delay.” He pulled a buff folder marked, ‘Incoming Mail’, in front of him. “There is a desk waiting for you. If you choose to use it … well and good. If not….” He opened the folder, picked up the letter on top. “Six o’clock.” He started to read, sensing Skender’s indecision and ignoring it.

Mihajlovich finished reading the letter, laid it face down on his desk and picked up the second and still Skender sat opposite him. “There are two doors, Berisha … choose the one you wish to use … now.”

Slowly Skender stood and made his way across the office. He hesitated as his hand touched the door, then turned back to face Mihajlovich. “May I interrupt you for one moment?”

Mihajlovich finished reading the letter, turned it over, then raised his eyes to Skender. He forced himself to calmness, pushing his jubilation below the surface as he witnessed that Skender stood beside the inter-office door. "What is it?"

"When I was in Belgrade you arranged for a car and driver to be at my disposal … it made things much simpler and easier. Thank you."

Mihajlovich inclined his head. Slowly Skender turned back to the door. Mihajlovich sat very still, waited until the door closed behind Skender, then let out a long breath. *For a moment I thought I had lost you, Berisha.* He picked up the remainder of his cigarette, sat back in his chair and watched the smoke rise to the ceiling.

Skender sat down at the mahogany desk, sensed Anna watching him and looked over to her side of the office. "What should I call you?"

She smiled. "Colonel Mihajlovich calls me Anna."

"I am not Colonel Mihajlovich," Skender snapped.

Carefully she straightened a pile of papers, then let herself look at Skender. "Mr. Berisha, we are going to be working together; we will be in this office for seven or eight hours a day … for myself, I would prefer it to be a pleasant and harmonious relationship." There was no anger, no rebuke, just a statement of fact.

Remorse ripped at Skender. *She works for Mihajlovich, she is not responsible.* "I am sorry, you are right, of course. Please accept my apology." He forced a smile. "Can we start from the beginning again?"

Anna smiled back, handed a sheaf of papers to Skender. "Colonel Mihajlovich left these for you."

A nerve twitched in Skender's neck, his hand hesitated as he reached and accepted the papers. "He wants me to write a letter to every family that lost a son. Have you any idea how I will find the address, the name of the father?"

"That will be easy." Anna moved to one of the rows of filing cabinets. "These files are the 'open' or 'pending' ones. Unless we have definite knowledge of the person's death, we cannot close them, and they must be kept here in this office…." Skender stared at her. "But if you are able to help us, we can transfer them to the 'closed' files in the basement until such time as we can get a permit from the Head Office in Belgrade to destroy them…."

She doesn't give a damn. Skender's eyes narrowed. *You callous little bitch….*

Anna's smile was confident as she glanced over her shoulder at Skender. "As you can see, the files are really crowded … it would be wonderful if we could…."

Skender shut out her voice, made his hand move to take the pen from his jacket pocket. He laid the sheaf of papers on the desk in front of him and stared unseeingly at the neat typing. *She's a woman, though, surely….* His head lifted and he watched as she carefully closed the file drawer, locked it, and returned to her desk. *How is it possible for a woman to have no sorrow, no feeling at all for all those lost lives?* She started to type, her fingers sure, unhesitating on the keys. *Is there no pity in her, no gentleness?* He sighed, pulled the papers toward him and started to read.

The afternoon dragged by, the grey sluggishness of the day reflected Skender's mood as he continued to turn page after page of the seemingly never-ending list of names. Many were unknown, but then, suddenly, almost unexpectedly, a name would leap at him from the page. A long-forgotten face before him … a gesture, a laugh, a word, buried in the mists of memory, surfaced and seared him with pain and blind rage. He fought for control at those moments, taking deep, steadying breaths. He wanted to rip the typed page to shreds, take the few steps that separated him from Mihajlovich and destroy him and as much of the hated building with its files as he could before the police could reach and destroy him.

The last name on the page had been a friend, a neighbor's son….

'Skender, we are going to be late for class,' Adnan's grin spread as he saw Skender break the warm nut bread into two pieces as he came from the pastry shop, 'I hope my backside remembers the pleasure my stomach received when the damn teacher uses his cane….'

Skender sighed, made a mark against the name, then made his notation in the margin as he had with the previous names. 'Unable to continue because of exhaustion … shot at Shkodra'.

"Mr. Berisha, let me know if you wish to examine the files and I will unlock them for you." He was unable to answer, or even look at her, Anna, assuming that he had not understood, continued, "There are only three keys to the files. Officer Dragonovich has one, and of course Colonel Mihajlovich … and I."

Skender heard the pride in that 'And I', slowly raised his head and looked at her, wanting to shout at her, make her understand, realize what the miserable metal cabinets contained.

"Shall I unlock them for you?"

He swallowed, "No, thank you. I will not need to see them until tomorrow." His hand hurt from the grip on his pen, he worked at it, massaging life back into it, staring unseeingly at the names in order to avoid further discussion with Anna.

The coffee she brought to him late in the afternoon was good, it coincided with the reading of a name of a man who was now an active member of the Free Albanian Government in Exile. Skender smiled, *A sweetmeat to accompany the coffee.* He turned the page.

Skender Berisha, Pristina. Aged sixteen, eldest son of the Berisha family.

Cold clamminess covered his body as he read the one line that had given permission for him to be snatched from home and family.

"It is five o'clock, Mr. Berisha." Skender did not move as she put the plastic sheet over her typewriter. "Time to go home." Anna went to the door of Mihajlovich's office, knocked, opened it slightly. "Is there anything else I can do for you, Colonel Mihajlovich? Then I shall say goodnight." She smiled down at Skender as she passed beside his desk. "Goodnight, Mr. Berisha."

"Goodnight," he muttered. The silent room pressed on him, screaming 'Skender Berisha … Skender Berisha….'

Mihajlovich stood watching him noted the strain around the eyes and mouth. "Tomorrow will be easier." Skender started. "The day after that easier than tomorrow, next week…." Skender came to his feet as Mihajlovich walked towards him. "We close the office at five, unless there is something urgent, or pressure of work requires us to stay." He frowned, as Skender did not move, "I am telling you that you may leave. Your first day's work is completed." He took the paper from Skender's hand, glanced down at it, then continued, "I know that today was difficult for you, but as soon as this matter is cleared up, we can move on to other tasks of more interest and that do not affect you so closely." He laid the paper on the desk as there was no response. "Goodnight, Berisha." He turned and went toward his office.

"Goodnight," he replied automatically.

Mihajlovich about-faced immediately. "No. Not 'goodnight.' Goodnight Colonel Mihajlovich, or goodnight Comrade Colonel, but never just 'goodnight.'" He stood waiting, face tightening as the minutes dragged.

At last, Skender raised his head. "Goodnight, Colonel Mihajlovich."

Mihajlovich gave a small nod. "I will see you tomorrow." It was a statement that needed an answer.

"Yes, you will see me tomorrow." Skender opened the top drawer and laid the sheaf of papers inside. Wearily, he took his coat from the rack and shrugged into it.

He felt the cold, inquisitive and hostile eyes of the police staff follow him as he walked through the main office and out the heavy swing doors. He pulled his coat collar tight against the bitter wind, dug his hands deep into his pocket and with a deep sigh, started for home.

Chapter 37

Sleep had not left Skender completely as he rolled over and reached for Gillian. The cold emptiness shocked him into wakefulness and he lay still, looking at the undented pillow before turning on his back, staring up at the same undisturbed whiteness of the ceiling.

Where are you now, Jill? Still in your bed, warm and drowsy from sleep? Or perhaps you are already up, sipping your tea and waiting for the toast to rise like magic from the toaster? There is a time change between us now … are you ahead, or back, one hour? As if it matters…. Wearily he turned on his side to face the dead fire. *It is the distance … no, not even that … not even the barriers of nations keep us apart … our separation is the whim of one man … one man, powerful enough to change lives, or even end them, by raising an eyebrow.*

He sighed, put his arms under his head as again he rolled onto his back, the white ceiling stared solidly back at him. *The mornings were special, weren't they, Jill? A quiet time of holding each other … sometimes desire would spark, flare between us. You always needed that short sleep afterwards….* His lips curved as he remembered, *I would lay on my side watching you, a great joy in me as I witnessed your contentment….*

The indrawn breath as he sighed carried the warm yeasty smell of baking bread to his nostrils and throat and recalled him to Prishtine. He wondered idly what time it was as he glanced at the window, the sky was heavy, promising snow before the day was out, but he was unable to judge the time. Exhaustion pulled him to stay in the warm covers. Sleep had eluded him most of the night, waiting until the early hours of dawn to claim him. Now, when it was not permitted, she lay ready to accept him quickly.

Muffled voices intruded on his drowsiness, and he forced his eyes to open as he reached for the watch lying beside the bed. His eyes, limbs and mind objected as he heaved himself from the bed and made his way to the bathroom. The water was cold, icy, as it stung his face, and he groaned as he continued to splash his face and neck.

Drita stood immediately as he entered the kitchen and offered him a bowl of milk with a good-sized piece of bread, the steam still rising from its dark rich interior. "No, just coffee, Drita."

"Djali, you must eat," Nona protested. "You hardly ate last night at dinner, and now…." Babush's hand on her arm stopped her outpouring. "What meal would please you? Tell me … whatever it is I will make it for you."

"Anything you make will please me, Nona." Skender downed the last drop of coffee, stood up and kissed her. "Good-bye, Nona, and you too, Drita." He kissed Drita's cheek, then gave a brief bow to Babush.

"Skender, you asked me to invite your brothers here tonight. Are you sure that this is the right time for your news?"

"Yes, Babush, better they learn from my own lips about my – employment – than from any other. Good-bye, sir." He stooped and patted Nona's cheek as he moved to the door, "Tonight I shall eat, I promise."

Nona's eyes filled as he left the kitchen. "He only said that to comfort me, but he has no appetite, he did not eat dinner; now, this morning, just coffee…."

"His body is strong, can go without nourishment," Babush sighed as he turned from the kitchen window and accepted the bowl of milk from Drita. He dipped the still-warm bread into the hot milk and his eyes went again to the window as he waited for it to soak the milk.

My worry is not for his body … my worry is deeper than that.

He bent his head and bit into the milk-laden bread.

Chapter 38

Skender's steps slowed as he reached the long counter in the entry room of Police Headquarters. Mihajlovich had given him no instructions. He was not sure if he was supposed to go straight upstairs or report to the police sergeant.

The sergeant watched him, enjoying his uncertainty. He waited as long as he dared before speaking. "Colonel Mihajlovich left orders that you were to go straight to…" he gave a mocking bow, "to your office."

"Thank you." Skender ignored the sneer. Every man in the room was watching him as he walked through the main office area. He turned the corner, stood holding onto the balustrade, his knees like rubber. *Their hatred is more tangible than ever before….* He started to climb the stone steps. *Why?* He turned the corner to the second flight and started toward the first floor, stopped suddenly as the answer came: *Before, they were the ones in control. Could do as they pleased with me; but, now … as Mihajlovich's assistant, they must give me some semblance of respect. Even obedience. Fear and hatred … a dangerous combination.*

He glanced at the door to Mihajlovich's private office as he passed, then entered the one next to it. Anna's coat was there, some work already in her typewriter, but her chair was empty. He hung up his coat and turned toward his desk, then stared in amazement. A telephone sat on the right-hand side, beside that was a rectangular inter-office communication box, each peg carried a name of the person it contacted, a blotter covered one-third of the desk, deep red leather encasing virgin white blotting paper. Bordering it a pen and pencil holder already filled with sharpened pencils and two fountain pens, one black and one red. A leather wallet lay centrally on the blotter.

"Good morning, Berisha."

Surprise still registered on Skender's face as he replied, "Good morning, Colonel Mihajlovich."

Mihajlovich picked up the wallet. "In here are papers that you will require." He opened it, took out a card. "Your new Identity Card. You may destroy the old one." His glance flicked to Skender. "This one will prove far more useful to you." Skender's eyes questioned him. "This lists your position as my assistant.

The other…" he laughed, "just destroy it." He dropped the Identity Card onto the desk, took another card from the wallet. "This is a travel permit … you will need no other papers with this in your possession, unless you plan on leaving the Kosovo area." He laid it beside the other. "And this is your driver's license, which is to be kept clean." His eyes met Skender's. "You are a government employee, obey all laws and no speeding. This is your Medical Card. Carry it with you at all times so that you can obtain treatment if and when you should need it. And, lastly, this…" he dropped one other card onto the desk, "it is for your father … it will enable him, or any of your immediate family, to obtain the services of a physician or be admitted into a hospital."

Skender reached for the chair, letting it support him. Mihajlovich pulled keys from his jacket pocket.

"These are your car keys; you will of course use it for business, but you may also use it for your own pleasure." He saw Skender's hand shake as he accepted the keys, glanced up, Skender's pallor shocked him and his voice was uncertain as he continued, "It is parked behind this building, next to mine." He hesitated a moment, then turned and went to his office.

Skender let himself sink into the chair as he picked up the Medical Card, holding it in the palm of his hand as he stared unbelievingly at it. *It looks so insignificant, so small, and yet … permission for Babush, Nona, Drita, to have the services of a doctor. Even to go to a hospital if necessary. A piece of white cardboard….* His eyes riveted on Mihajlovich's door. *Made possible by you and I did not even….* He stood, went quickly and knocked on the door.

"Come in." Mihajlovich waited, "Yes, Berisha, what is it?"

"This…." The card still lay in the palm of his hand and he read it again before looking up. "It is impossible for me to explain its value to me, to my family. I wanted to thank you for your trouble."

"It was no trouble."

"My father lost three children through sickness. If he had been able to seek the services of a doctor…. But that is past. You have my gratitude for this, and for troubling yourself to get it for me."

"I have already told you; it was no trouble."

Skender swallowed. "Even if all you did was stretch your hand to that telephone, I thank you." Mihajlovich inclined his head. Skender hesitated, then looked directly at him. "But I think you should know that it will make no difference to the way I feel about…" his hand gestured toward Mihajlovich, and then he added lamely, "working here."

Mihajlovich hid his smile. "I did not think it would."

"Then … why?"

"Shall we say it is a gesture of goodwill? Give me your support, Berisha, let me lean on your loyalty. Put the past behind you and concentrate on the future.

Hunger need never claw at your belly again. Never again will you have to sleep on the icy ground with just the stars for a covering...."

"Never again will you have to watch your tongue or check that the doors and windows are tightly closed before you speak," Skender interrupted softly. "Never again...."

"That's enough, Berisha," Mihajlovich warned.

"...will friends disappear without trace," Skender continued as if there had been no interruption, "never again will you and yours be taken from the street and beaten for no...."

"Enough!" Mihajlovich's fist smashed onto the desk, his anger tangible.

Skender looked straight at Mihajlovich, "Tell me that Colonel Mihajlovich, and you will have my support, my loyalty."

Mihajlovich was half-way to his feet.

Skender gave a slight bow, "With your permission."

Skender stopped as he reached the door, looked down at the card in his hand, "I am tempted to hand this back, to drop it on your desk with a grandiose gesture and tell you that the price is too high, that I cannot be bought. But I shall keep it." He slipped the card into his jacket pocket, "I think my family have paid the price, over and over."

Mihajlovich's fury made it obvious that Skender should leave.

He gave a slight inclination of his head, "With your permission, Colonel Mihajlovich."

He resisted the impulse to slam the door and closed it quietly.

Chapter 39

"The dinner was very good, Drita." Drita's smile flashed to Babush as she continued to clear the dishes. With barely a movement of his finger, Babush asked Nona to stay. As the door closed on Drita, he turned to his wife, "When she has finished her work, send her to me."

Skender glanced up, aware of tension between the two and witnessed his mother's silent appeal silently denied. He laid the newspaper beside him and waited for his father's explanation as Nona left the room.

Babush took out his pipe. It was his old one, retrieved from retirement, and he packed the tobacco evenly, carefully. He took a spill from the fire and then, with a long look at Skender, said, "Adem Mali came to see me this morning." He put the flame to the pipe and drew deeply, made sure that the tobacco was alight and returned the wood to the fire. "May I ask if you knew the reason for his visit?"

"Me?" Skender was genuinely surprised at the question, and Babush saw that. "I assume he came for his usual chess game and to visit you." The grey head denied it. "Then I have no idea…" he stiffened, "unless … did it have anything to do with me?"

"No." Babush examined the glowing tobacco, "It concerns your sister."

"Drita? What possible connection can there be between the Malis and Drita?"

Skender's puzzlement satisfied Babush and he puffed on his pipe for a while, then took it from his mouth. "I assumed, as you, that Adem was making his usual social visit … he was not. He had come to ask for Drita in marriage, for Luan." Babush watched the shock, surprise, then pleasure, cross Skender's face. "The offer pleases you, Djali?"

"Yes, of course. To bind our two houses." He stopped, "But you seem to have serious doubts, Babush. Are you unhappy about this development?"

Babush smoothed his moustache, "I do not know. My oldest friend asks for my daughter … there is pride in that, knowing that someone who has such close knowledge of this house, my family, would ask for my daughter. But it complicates matters. The Drini family has asked. We have investigated them thoroughly and cannot fault their honesty, their integrity. The young man is thought of very highly in Prizren, he thinks and acts a little more modern than I, but then, that is to be expected. Drita would be happy with him … he holds enough to our ways for her to be comfortable, while embracing several of today's ideas, which would make her life easier, more pleasurable."

"The same can be said of Luan."

"I am sure it can, Djali." Babush frowned as he pushed his hat to the back of his head. "It has been many years since I saw the boy…." Skender smiled to himself. "I wish, now, that that was not so."

"The boy has gone, sir. A young man stands in his place."

Babush's eyes held Skender's, "Are you sure of that?"

"Yes. If that is the basis of your concern and worry, put it behind you. He is mature enough."

"He is Sabri's brother," Babush mused, "are you positive that affectionate memories do not cloud your judgment?"

Skender took out a cigarette and Babush's hand moved graciously, giving him permission to smoke. "I did not know who he was the first time I saw him … he was a young man who offered help when I was in need. Do you remember when I first returned home and had to register at Police Headquarters?" He took a deep draw on the cigarette as Babush nodded. "I had spent years putting those memories behind me, but as I walked through their door, the years were stripped from me. I was a boy again, terrified of them and what they could do to me. They did nothing…." His thumb snapped the cigarette into two pieces and he threw them into the fire. "But the man's stomach was not as strong as the boy's had been, held only until we had turned the corner. I was ashamed, disgusted at my weakness. And Besim, poor lad, did not know what to do. He took me to the Mali shop … I did not recognize it, was in no condition to realize that we had even entered Old Town.

"A young man ushered me into the back room. He asked no questions, sought no explanation. He pulled a blanket around me, sat me in front of the fire and insisted that I drink a glass of Slivovitz. Then he left me to myself. The Slivovitz warmed me quickly, settled my stomach … and Luan gave me what I needed most, time to quietly put my fear behind me and dress myself in control. That was not the action of a boy … a boy could not have acted as he."

"You have seen him several times since your return to Prishtine … how does he conduct himself?"

"There is no young man in Prishtine that commands higher respect. He behaves with dignity, carries himself with pride, and yet…." Skender smiled, "There is a liveliness, an enjoyment of life, that draws you to him. He is not dull." He laughed softly. "And he is a friend of Emin's … that should speak for him!"

Babush smiled. "Is he like Emin?"

"There is some similarity, but Luan has a tighter hold on himself … his temper does not flare so quickly. He accepts that life is a serious matter, but he does not let the lighter moments pass him by. He will listen to your argument, but you will not influence him with impassioned pleas unless the facts support them. He is no boy, sir … it is my opinion that he is mature enough to take a wife."

"Whoever that may be will go to a good family. Adem's house is a happy one, but…" Skender waited as Babush poked moodily at the fire, "…there is none to follow Luan, he is the youngest son … ah, come in, Drita."

"Nona said you wanted to see me, Babush?"

"Come here, daughter, there is something of great importance for me to tell you." His hand stopped Skender as he started to rise. "I would like you to stay, Djali. Drita, you have been highly honored … we have received a proposal of marriage for you. The family is from Prizren…."

Skender was watching Drita to see her happiness, was surprised to see the color drain from her face as Babush proceeded to tell her about the Drini family.

"You have never been to Prizren, Drita, but it is a delightful city with pure water and air that invigorates. What are your thoughts … do you think you could be happy there?"

Drita licked at her lips, "It … it is a long way, Babush."

Babush's smile was gentle. "Once you step past my gate, my child, any house is a long way … even if it is only next door, you would be far from me." Drita's eyes filled. "Come, sit down. This is happy news and should not bring tears. What greater happiness could a father receive than to know that his daughter holds herself with such pride, such dignity, that a family wishes to accept her into their home? What greater honor to you than that a family wish to give you their name and claim you as theirs?" He wiped her tears. "And there is yet more, another proposal has been received … two, Drita, in less than a month of each other." He tipped up her chin. "Carry your head high, child, you have brought us great honor … don't you agree Skender?"

Skender's smile was warm as Drita looked under her lashes at him. "Both families are held in high regard, one in Prizren, and the other here."

"Here? In Prishtine?" Her eyes flew from Skender to Babush, and then as Babush nodded she asked on a breath, "Which family?"

Babush leaned to the fire, knocked out his pipe and missed the stillness of her, the held breath, but Skender was aware and watched her closely as his father answered, "The Mali family. Adem Mali has asked for you for his son, Luan." Her lids closed, squeezed the last few tears from her eyes to run down to her trembling lips. "The family in Prizren has four sons … the enquiry for you is for the third son, and this pleases me. The workload would be easier for you once the younger marries. But the Mali's son is the youngest…" Babush's pursed lips pushed his moustache to his chin. Drita's eyes flew open and she saw the half shake of his head, "that would mean it would be you that carries the hardest work…."

"I would not mind that!" Babush stared at her, shocked at her outburst, that she had interrupted him. Color crept up her neck, her face, and she dropped her eyes from his. "I am sorry … it is just that … it is just that…."

"Well?" Babush demanded as the embarrassed silence stretched.

Her mouth opened, but there was no sound.

"I … it is just…."

"Prishtine is home and Prizren is far away."

Drita sent a quick look of gratitude to Skender as he rescued her.

"Is that what you mean, Drita?" His eyes warned her and she nodded.

"I understand. Well, daughter…" Babush stood, Skender and Drita rose as well. "I wished you to know that these proposals for your hand have been made." He patted her cheek. "When I have reached a decision, I will let you know."

"Babush!" Appeal was there in the one word, and he turned from the door in surprise.

"Yes, Drita, what is it?" Skender's sudden grip on her arm stopped her and she stood staring at him. "Well, child, what troubles you?"

"Please, Babush, I…." Skender's fingers pressed into her arm, stopping her.

"Drita is tired, sir, and so am I. We will say goodnight now with your permission." His hand propelled her forward. He smiled as he gave a brief bow to Babush. "We could all use the extra sleep."

Babush smiled and nodded agreement. "Of course … Natën e mirë, Djali." He gave a fond smile to Drita before kissing her cheek. "Natën e mirë, my daughter, sleep well."

"Natën e mirë, Babush." Drita closed the door after him, turned and saw that Skender had returned to the fire and sat down. "Natën e mirë, brother." She gave a bow as she spoke.

"Oh, no, little sister … not yet. Come here." He patted the rug beside him, she did not move. He insisted, "Come here." She came slowly, reluctantly, and stood in front of him. "Sit down."

She gestured toward the door. "There is work for me…." His eyes lifted to her face and with a half-sigh, she sat opposite him.

She sits like a wild thing, poised for flight. "How long have you had these feelings for Luan Mali?" Wide, terrified eyes held his for a moment, her fingers pleated and unpleated the dark blue material of her dimi. Skender watched her in silence, then asked softly, "Would you prefer me to speak to Babush, and let him question you?" He made a move to rise.

"No." The cry begged him to stay where he was as her eyes flew to him, then dropped. "No, please…."

"Then answer."

She licked nervously at her lips. "You are mistaken. I have no feelings for … him."

"I see. Then it will make no difference to you if I endorse the Drini offer." Skender started to stand.

"No, no…" her hand caught at his, urging him back to the rug, "please, brother."

His eyes were gentle on her as her fingers worked at the rug. "Drita, we could sit here all night … I, watching you making our rug bald…" Her nervous fingers stilled. "…but that will still leave many things unexplained."

Drita's voice was a whisper. "How did you know?"

"Your face, your actions, when Babush said his name." He took her hand in his as her fingers started to pluck again at the rug. "Why not tell me? When did this attraction for Luan start?" His smile was gentle and encouraged her.

"I don't know…" she said shyly, biting her lower lip and blushing slightly, "he has always been in my life. But when I was still at the gymnasium, he had already left and started University." She glanced up at Skender with a shy smile, added explainingly, "He is older than I." Skender nodded solemnly. "I had not seen him for two, perhaps three years, and then one day he happened to be passing as we were leaving the school. He saw us and stopped … to speak to Besim." Her color deepened.

"And then he said 'hello' to you."

"And Ilyria. And Nexhmije," Drita added too quickly. Skender hid his smile.

"He…" she took a deep breath, "…he happened to come by the school again … about a week later, and he walked home with us." She glanced at Skender. "So that he could talk to Besim."

Skender turned his laugh into a cough, murmured seriously, "Of course. I understand."

"Babush took me from the school soon after that…"

And while cooking and scrubbing, you dreamed about the handsome young Mali boy….

"…so, of course I did not see, or hear, anything of … Luan." Skender watched her as unwittingly she savored his name, letting it come slowly and with pleasure from her lips. "It must have been about a year later … Jakup was escorting Nona and me to visit with Mrs. Mali and the brothers' wives. As we reached their gate, Luan…" again the savoring of his name, "…was leaving. He greeted Nona and Jakup…."

And could not keep his eyes from the young loveliness who stood, half-turned from him, waiting to enter his house, but you were his mother's guest, and he could not speak to you….

Her voice trembled, "While we were having tea, Mrs. Mali told Nona that … that Luan was leaving for Dubrovnik and that he was to stay for a year, maybe two."

And so, you sipped at your tea, behaved correctly as guest should, while your heart cried.

"Drita, you have seen him since then. And it is my belief that he has seen you."

She nodded. Tears splashed onto the bright red of the rug, darkening it to burgundy. Skender had to lean forward to catch the words. "Two years ago … we were visiting … he did not know, came into his kitchen. His mother was furious…."

But before she shooed him from the kitchen, your eyes met, held for a moment….

"I did not see him again until a few months ago." The burgundy spots multiplied. "But he saw me." She covered her face as sobs shook her.

Skender frowned. "How?" He offered no consolation as the tears ran through her fingers. "I asked you how?"

"The window of their sitting room…."

Skender relaxed. "Yes, it overlooks the path." He handed her his handkerchief, smiled gently as she accepted with a quick glance at him. "You could do nothing about that."

"No, but I knew he was there, Skender. I should have told Nona so that she could stop it, but … I did not want to." Skender put his arms around her, comforting her as her body shook. "I wanted him to see me, Skender … wanted him to ask his father … I am so ashamed."

"Hush now, there is no need. Your feelings are those of any young girl trembling on the brink of womanhood." He put Drita from him, looked into her eyes. "There is no need for shame in that. The shame would have been if you had encouraged him." He smiled down at her. "Now I understand your embarrassment when I brought Luan to our kitchen … I am sorry for that. Had I realized, I would not have allowed that to happen." His smile deepened. "But Luan must have been overjoyed! I gave him his first opportunity to sit with you, speak to you."

Color spread over her face, rising in a fast flood of scarlet. "I…" her eyes crept up to Skender's chin, "…he … we spoke once before that time."

Skender stiffened. "Explain!" His sharpness frightened her, and her voice shook with nervousness.

"It was at Arif's. It was last summer. Ilyria and I work together when we are salting peppers for the winter." Her eyes crept a little higher to his. "It is not so tedious if there are two to share the work." She sighed as there was no response, no softening of his face. "I do not know who had mentioned it to Luan … perhaps Emin, maybe Besim. Luan pretended that it was chance that brought him that day, that time, to Arif's house, but…" she shrugged, shoulders drooping.

"And Luan spoke to you? At Arif's?" His teeth clenched as she nodded. "And you? You answered?" The whispered, 'yes' was scarcely from her mouth before his hands had grabbed her, pulled her roughly to her knees, she gasped as he gave her a quick, angry shake and then demanded in a tight voice, "Were you and he…" he took a deep breath, "…who else was present?"

She stared at him in disbelief, then anger caught her. She was free of his hold and on her feet, eyes flashing as she answered haughtily, "Teza and Ilyria . Why? Did you think that I would permit him to speak to me … even approach me … if I had been alone? How dare you think that of me! I am your sister, how dare you even let the thought cross your mind?"

Skender looked up at her, head held high with pride, anger stretching her to her tallest. He laughed softly, "Yes, you are … you are too much my sister, too much a Berisha." He took her hand, held tight as she tried to pull away from him. "Forgive me. I am so proud of you. So happy that you are the way you are … gentle, sweet … yet, scratch the surface and there is strength." Her hand relaxed in his and he patted the rug, pulling her gently toward it. "Sit down, Drita." She sat beside him, watched as he frowningly rubbed at his lips. "The thing now is, what to do?" he sighed and looked at her. "What are we going to do about this?"

Tears threatened again. "Whatever Babush decides, I must obey … you know that." Skender sighed his agreement as he held her close to his chest. "Would you … do you think you could suggest the Malis, endorse their offer?" She eased herself from his hold, her eyes earnestly pleading with him.

"I will do all in my power, little one, but the final decision does not rest with me."

Skender's heart went out to Drita as she gave a brief nod, while she smoothed her hair and tried to compose herself. Her lips trembled into a smile. "I am so glad that you are here, brother. Had this happened when I was alone with no one to talk to…." She plaited and unplaited the fringe of the rug. "Skender…."

"Yes?"

"What will it be like … being married to…" she pressed her lips tight together, caught the sob in her throat, "…being married to another when the one I think of…." Her body shook the tearing sobs stifled by her hands pressed tight to her mouth.

Skender held her, rocked her gently as one would a child, "Don't, Drita … please don't. Do not look ahead to sadness when it may be that happiness is within your grasp. I will do all that I can, will intercede with Babush and give my recommendation that he accepts the Mali offer."

"But if he does not listen?"

Skender sighed, looked long at her. "Then there is only one alternative … you must go to him, tell him…."

"No." The cry of pain came from her heart. "No, I could not … I could not hurt Babush. He is too dear to me for me to bring him sorrow." She sat straight.

"If he should decide on the Drini family…" she steadied her trembling lips with her fingers, "…I will obey."

Skender's fist smashed against the rug as frustration and pride fought in him. She stood, bowed to him. "Drita…." he stopped her as she moved toward the door, "Let me speak to Babush on your behalf."

She almost smiled as she shook her head. "No. There has been too much sadness in his life, and I will not add a drop more to it. If it is meant for me to go to the Drini family…" she lifted her head, "…may it be with happiness." He caught the glistening of tears before she bowed to him. "Natën e mirë, brother."

He pushed the words away, the words that wanted to come to his lips, telling her how much he cared for her, how greatly he admired her courage. "Natën e mirë, Drita, sleep well."

Chapter 40

Aslan accepted the coffee from Drita, and she moved on to Emin. He took the cup from her fingers as she bowed to him and whispered, "Do you know why Skender asked us to come?" She shook her head. "We were supposed to be here last night, but it was postponed because Aslan had to work. I have been dying of curiosity all day…." he grinned, "And still I have to wait! Are you sure you do not know?"

"I do not know." Laughter drowned her words and she leaned forward to repeat them.

Emin caught her hand, suddenly concerned. "Do you feel well, Drita? You are so pale."

"I am well." She blinked rapidly, tried to pull free of him, but he detained her, eyes searching her face. He felt her stiffness, her reluctance, and released her, but his eyes followed as she moved distractedly around the room, picking up the empty cups.

"I am sorry to be late." The younger cousins stood immediately Jakup entered the room, he gave a quick smile to Drita as she took his coat but refused her offer of coffee. "Skender, Aslan…" he bowed briefly to them and sat down at Skender's invitation, "Emin, Shamsi…."

The greetings continued, Skender let his eyes travel over them. *Aslan, reliable, steady, quiet, and gentle, almost to a fault. Jakup, considerate yet as firm as a rock, ready to let you lean on him. Shamsi, volatile, quick to anger, and as quick to forgive, a young edition of his father, Migje Hasan.*

Skender gave an answering smile as laughter bubbled from the young men at a comment from Jakup that he had not heard. His reverie continued as they returned to their conversation.

Emin … poor Emin, it is you who will be most hurt by my news … determined to stay with our customs, our traditions; yet it was always Emin who watched over Drita, saw when the workload was too heavy….

Adnan's voice rose, demanding an answer from the young men and making sure attention was brought to him. Skender smiled as he watched him. *So full of life, squeezing every drop of pleasure from each day. And, lastly, Besim … determined to step from boyhood to manhood as soon as possible … your charm, now, is in your insecurity, your youth, but in a year or two … there is Aslan's strength in you, coupled with the charm of Adnan….*

An expectant hush had settled over the room, Skender sighed. "I have asked you all to come here because there is some news that I have to impart … news that I wanted you to hear from my lips and none other."

"Does this concern your Nusé? Has she arrived in her home yet?"

"Yes, Adnan, she has arrived safely. I spoke, briefly, with her yesterday." Skender let his eyes travel the familiar faces. "As Adnan has raised the subject of Gillian, I will deal with that first, but…." He looked directly at Adnan, "Until I finish speaking, I want no further interruptions from any of you." He took a deep breath, spoke firmly and slowly. "You have all wondered, and possibly discussed among yourselves, why I sent Gillian from here … I cannot give you my reasons, but believe me, it was from necessity rather than my own wish. She is now with her family, and she will remain there…."

"You mean she will not return to…." Shamsi's eyes fell at Skender's sigh. "I'm sorry."

"She will remain with her family … she will not return to Prishtine." Startled looks were exchanged in the quiet room; and then Skender continued, "I share your sorrow at that, while sharing that sorrow, it also gives me a semblance of comfort to know that you cared…" he swallowed, "…cared for her and accepted her."

His hand shook as he took the packet of cigarettes from his pocket. Emin reached for a piece of wood from the fire and passed it to him. "Thank you. If any of you wish to smoke, please feel free." He handed the flaming wood back to Emin, pulled deeply on his cigarette. "Let us continue … the rest is difficult. It is hard for me to speak; it will be harder for you to hear. I must warn you that you will be shocked but bear in mind that sometimes an action is forced upon one, that…." He stopped, the intenseness of their concentration shaking him. He stood, walked to the window and lifted the drape, their eyes followed him, stayed on him, and after a moment he turned back to them. "There is no easy way to break this news, and so…." His hand wiped at his lips, "Yesterday I started to work for Mihajlovich."

Silence pressed on him; their eyes bored into him. A small stone dropped into a pond is swallowed immediately, but the ripples take their time, surging from the center to the outer rim. Skender watched as the force of his announcement traveled from Aslan to Besim.

A half-consumed log fell with a crack of thunder, landing in a flash of sparks, burning and consuming the rug. Tension eased as those nearest rushed to attend to it, Skender sat down on the window bench and watched, as they took longer than necessary to clean the mess.

Adnan threw a handful of hot ashes into the fire, turned to Skender with an infectious grin. "For a moment you had us believing you. It was a good joke, brother…."

"I am not joking," Skender's voice cut across him, "I am in great earnest."

Shocked eyes searched from one to the other for an answer, an explanation, before finally resting on the only one who could ask. Aslan frowned, he did not like to question Skender … but, "You have a reason, Skender? Some explanation?"

Skender's eyes met Aslan's. "No, Aslan, I am sorry, but I do not."

"Are you serious? Are you really expecting us to accept this … this…." Shamsi's explosion stopped as anger made him lose his words. "Explain yourself!"

"There is nothing to explain, Shamsi. Accept the fact that I am working for Mihajlovich … that is all there is to it."

"The hell there is! I insist … I demand…."

"Shamsi!" Aslan's voice, quiet, controlled, stopped the angry torrent. "Remember whom you address."

Shamsi wheeled on Aslan. "Whom is it I address? Skender, my brother, or Mihajlovich's puppet?" Aslan turned his head and Shamsi looked across at Skender. "Well? Tell us … are you a card-carrying Party Member now?"

Skender's knuckles gleamed whitely against the warm color of the window bench.

Emin's voice was icy, razor-sharp, "Will you repeat your statement, Skender?"

"If you wish…." He dragged in a long breath, "I am working for Mihajlovich. I am his assistant."

"Thank you." Emin gave a mocking bow. "I wished to be sure that I had heard correctly." He let his eyes move to each. "I wanted to be sure that we all had understood."

"Is there any other that knows, Skender?"

"At this moment, Jakup, Babush is telling your father, and yours, too, Aslan."

"And what am I supposed to tell my friends? Friends! Never mind friends, what explanation do I give my enemies?"

"None, Shamsi … as I give none to you. Conduct yourself with dignity, remember the name you carry…." The windows rattled in protest as Shamsi slammed the door behind him. Skender took a long shuddering breath. "As I was saying, conduct yourself with dignity, remember the name you carry…."

"It is not necessary for you to remind us that we are Berishas. I think it is you, Skender, that has forgotten." Emin stood. "I am supposed to look to you, the elder brother, for guidance. I am supposed to pattern myself…."

"That is enough, Emin. Sit down." Jakup cut across the angry words, turned to Skender, his voice quiet, "After all that this family has suffered, you can hardly expect us to accept this … announcement … without some explanation."

"I am sorry, Jakup, but that is exactly what I am asking."

"Then do not ask it of me, for I refuse." Emin, white, shaking with anger, turned to Aslan with a brief bow. "With your permission, brother, I will leave."

"It is not my place to give you that permission," Aslan answered steadily. "Skender is the older brother … ask him."

Emin's lips were tight as he glanced at Skender before turning back to Aslan. "He carries the Berisha name, but his is no brother of mine. Give me permission, or I leave without it."

Aslan glanced at his two youngest brothers as he heard their gasps, then his eyes went, for a moment, to Skender before he gave a brief nod.

Emin paused beside Skender on his way to the door, "I cared deeply about you. You have been my hero for as many years as I can remember, but you have murdered that love. Do not forget … your actions, not mine, cut it from my heart."

The quiet closing of the door was final, more shattering than the slam of Shamsi's. Skender sat stiff, willing himself to stop shaking.

Adnan and Besim exchanged uncomfortable looks, then Adnan rose. "I am sorry … I feel the same as Emin." Uncertain of whom to ask, he bowed to no one in particular, letting his request for permission to leave hang in the air.

Skender sighed wearily, "Let him go, Aslan." The door closed and then he turned to Besim, "Well, Besim, do you wish to leave?"

"I don't know." Besim silently begged for guidance from Aslan. "I don't know what to do … you are the head of this family, but…." His eyes went in desperation from Aslan to Jakup to Skender and then back to Aslan. "I do not know what action I should take, brother."

"Of course you don't, Besim. Had I been put in such a position at your age, neither would I. Go, join the others." Besim stood, hesitated, then bowed to Skender. "Thank you for your indecision, Besim … it is easier to accept than rejection." Skender's hand moved, giving Besim permission to leave.

The silence was long and heavy. Aslan realized that Skender was not prepared to make the first move. "Skender, there are just the three of us now … is there anything you wish to add?"

Skender sighed as he stood up and joined Aslan and Jakup beside the fire. "Just the three of us … the oldest son from each of the Berisha houses. My father, and yours, and yours, Jakup, have sat around this fire many times, just as we do now, discussing the problems and difficulties this family has had to face. But this time there will be no discussion, no thrashing out … there is no explanation, no reason that I can offer. What I have told you is fact … accept it."

"Skender, I cannot believe that you would go willingly to Mihajlovich … it is not your character to align yourself with them and…" Jakup hesitated, "…after all that you were put through as a boy, I find it hard to believe that he…."

The sentence hung in the air before Skender completed it for Jakup, "That he beat me into submission? No. He did not."

"Then why? What hold does he have over you? I can think of no…" his startled eyes flashed to Skender, "it is not our Nusé? She has left Yugoslavia?"

"Gillian is safe." Skender caught the sigh of relief from both of them. "This action sits on my own shoulders."

Jakup's face was serious, a deep crease between his eyes as his finger repeatedly smoothed the left side of his moustache while he stared at the rug. He leaned forward and rubbed at the blackness. "Perhaps someone could weave…." Vagueness left him and he turned to Skender. "I cannot stand beside you, Skender, not in this. I have not suffered as you, but there has been hardship, suffering … I sacrificed my life's ambition because I could not bring myself to bow to their insistence…." He stood, bowed. "I'm sorry." The door closed quietly after him.

"So, Aslan, now we are just two. What did Jakup mean, sacrificed his life's ambition?"

"All his life he dreamed of being a doctor. He had already put in four years at Medical University … the work came easily to him, he was a brilliant student. And then…" there was a pause, "he was given a choice: join the Party or…." Aslan's shoulders lifted to a shrug. "When he returned to Prishtine, he was despondent, disillusioned. It took a long time for him to get over the disappointment."

"I did not know."

"That was Jakup's request."

"Was that the reason he took up tailoring?"

"Yes. He toyed with the idea of trying for a different degree, but once their eyes fall on you … he knew it was useless. They would have allowed him to put in two, three more years of work and study, and then…."

Skender sighed deeply, let his eyes meet Aslan's. "There is nothing more I can tell you, Aslan."

"There is no need." Aslan smiled at Skender's startled expression. "Have you forgotten, brother? We grew up together. I know you as well as I know myself. You could not bring shame to this family any more than I." He stood up. "Give them time … they think their love of you is dead, but a strong tree does not fall from one blow."

"I am not so sure." Skender's eyes closed. "Their anger, their disgust was…." Emotion choked him.

"I am sure." Aslan slapped Skender on the back, pulled him into a hug and held him hard. "When, or if, you need me, I am ready." Skender nodded, unable to speak, as he returned Aslan's firm hug.

Chapter 41

"You have completed your second week with us, Berisha. So far things seem to be going well, but you must learn to handle Officer Dragonovich and his men."

Mihajlovich and Skender were about the same height, their paces evenly matched as they walked toward the Communist Party Headquarters which lay on the opposite side of the Main Square, two blocks from Old Town.

"Do not let them treat you as anything less than an officer…." Skender's lips tightened into an ironic smile. "Insist on discipline, demand smartness and prompt attention to your orders." Mihajlovich slowed, turned to Skender. "But, on the other hand, do not ride them. We are the head, the brains … but we need them, the body, to do the work. Aim for their respect, add a trace of fear to that and…" he smiled, his hand gripped into a fist, "…and then you have them, tight and secure."

He handed his briefcase to Skender. "The side pocket has come unstitched, have it repaired. I will see you in about two, maybe three, hours."

"Yes, Colonel Mihajlovich." Skender watched as Mihajlovich approached the black marble building of Udba. The guard leapt to attention, opened the door, long before it was necessary. Skender grudgingly acknowledged that Mihajlovich had what he wanted … discipline, smartness and respect with a touch of fear. He put the briefcase under his arm, making sure the gold-stamped '*Stefan Mihajlovich, D.D. Udba*' was held close to his body.

"Mirëmëngjes, Skender."

He turned. "Luan! What a surprise … what are you doing away from your store at this hour?"

Luan grinned. "My father likes to keep a close check on what I am doing. While officially he has handed over to me, he cannot quite let go." He smiled. "He worked there for many years, worried over the place for too many hours for him to retire altogether. When he comes down to the store, I make an excuse to leave so that he can poke around happily without wondering if he is insulting me!" He fell into step with Skender. "Do you have time to have tea with us?"

"I...." Skender hesitated.

"It will take but a moment ... father has the kettle over the fire always!" Skender laughed his agreement. "Good."

"We are here. Sir, look who I found."

"Skender, welcome, come in, come in. Some tea? I have the kettle heating...." Luan gave a broad wink to Skender as they followed the old man into the back room of the shop. "Please, sit." Adem Mali's hand moved graciously as he invited Skender to join him on the rug beside the stove. "How is your family?"

"Well, sir, thank you ... and yours?"

Their warmth reached out to him, bringing more comfort than the heat of the fire or the hot amber liquid on which he sipped. The cold, hard knot of loneliness in his stomach melted, washed over him, and he was hard-pressed not to let the Malis see the depth of emotion he felt at their kindness.

Luan bent toward him and refilled the delicate glass. "Thank you, Luan." His eyes followed the young man, seeing, as if for the first time, the well-proportioned build, the sudden, infectious grin that called forth an answering smile almost without one realizing. Skender smiled quietly to himself as he saw the daring tip of the white hat on the light brown hair. *You were born for that Kosovar outfit ... no wonder Drita is so enthralled with you.*

"Do I have a smudge on my nose?" Luan laughed. Skender looked up at the handsome face. "You were staring at me as if you had never seen me before!"

Skender smiled, murmured, "Perhaps I haven't." He stood. "Thank you for the tea, Luan. I must go." He turned to pick up the briefcase, cursed silently as he saw Luan's eyes linger on the gold lettering. "Good-bye, Migje Mali, my respect to your wife and family. Good-bye, Luan."

Luan walked with Skender to the door, watched from the window as he crossed the street. "Why?" he asked quietly of his father. "What possible reason could there be?" He turned to the old man. "It makes no sense! Skender Berisha? I would have staked my life, my reputation, on him." He sighed, shook his head in bewilderment and continued quietly, "When I saw him, I did not know what to do ... did not know whether to ignore him or ... did I do wrong in bringing him here, sir?"

"Skender is welcome in my home or my place of business any time," Adem Mali replied firmly as he watched Skender exit from the leather shop, minus the briefcase. "He must have some purpose, but what it is I do not know." His eyes followed Skender for a moment and then added musingly, "I doubt if he knows himself."

"There is much talk in town … the coffee shops hum with nothing else." Luan hesitated, "Emin will not even mention his name, or permit anyone else to."

"If all his brothers feel that way, Skender is badly in need of a friend."

Luan turned slowly towards his father. "Are you suggesting…?"

"I suggest nothing. I merely state a fact."

"Emin's anger would be hot … I could lose his friendship."

The old head nodded agreement. "Yes. It will take much strength to stretch a hand to Skender when all other fingers point with derision and scorn."

"I, too, would be ostracized if I were too friendly," Luan answered stiffly. "Plus, I would break a bond that has been between Emin and me for years. Are you sure you wish me to stand beside Skender when no other will even speak to him?"

"Your actions are your own." Adem Mali's eyes lifted to Luan's. "Have you the courage? Do you possess that kind of strength?"

Luan's eyes fell. "I don't know. This time I acted on impulse, but to deliberately place myself in that position, cut myself off from everyone?" He sighed, "I feel almost ashamed to say it, but my instincts tell me to keep away from Skender Berisha."

"And Drita … what of her? Has this changed your mind? Do you already regret…?"

"No. Never."

"She is Skender's sister. Be very sure. The next move must come from us … if I do not raise the subject again, it is finished. But if I ask once more, and the answer is 'yes' … then she is ours. Could you learn to love her, care for her in spite of all this?"

"I already care for her."

Adem's voice was sharp. "You cared for Drita Berisha. Can you care for Skender's sister?"

Luan's fist banged the counter. "I care for her … I already love her. Do not smile, father, in this I am serious."

"As am I, Luan, but you do not love Drita."

"I want her for my wife … that is proof enough."

"No, it is not. You are a young man whose heart has been touched by a lovely young girl. You feel desire, the longing to possess, but that is not love. There is no self in love, and yet all I hear from your lips is, 'I want, I need, I care.' Love takes time, patience to grow and mature. It needs a special kind of closeness. Are you sure that the shadow of Skender would not stand between you and your wife? I have known this girl since birth. I want no cloud of sadness on her face or in her eyes because my son sees the specter of her brother when he holds her in his arms." He picked up his coat. "Think on it carefully, we will talk more of it later."

"It is a difficult and heartbreaking problem you have given me to occupy my day."

The old man turned back from the door. "Yes, it is. But remember, if you have any doubts, it is better to cut cleanly now than to tear at your hearts for years. I will see you this evening."

Gloves flew in all directions as Luan angrily swung at them. He put his hands to his ears, then in a stride was beside the door and reached to stop the cheerful tinkling of the bell as the door closed behind his father.

Chapter 42

A satisfied smile played about Mihajlovich's mouth as he turned to the final page of the report. The burnt orange drapes lifted gently, a soft breeze moved into the room, disturbing the neat piles of papers on his desk. Without raising his eyes from his reading, he lifted the cigarette box and laid it on the papers, anchoring them to the desk.

Mihajlovich slowly closed the folder and laid it down then swiveled to face the window. The full leaf of the tree outside blocked his view of the granite obelisk, and, as in previous years, he debated whether he should order it removed. And, as in previous years, he waivered, acknowledging that without the protection of the tree, it would be a hot summer.

His hand reached, felt and found the folder, and he sat looking at the title page, 'Kosovo, A Report Prepared by Skender Berisha.' He turned to the first page, 'Part One … The Northern Territory.' He tapped it against his knee, then, decision made he stood and walked to the inter-office door.

"Anna, tell Officer Dragonovich that I want to see him at four this afternoon."

"Yes, Colonel Mihajlovich," she murmured, picking up the phone as he made his way across the office.

The large mahogany desk was gone, as was the huge leather chair. A metal table stood beneath the window, a soft pad of fiber muffled the constant and regular tap of the typewriter keys. A girl, young and pretty with long blonde hair, glanced up as she heard the footsteps, stood as she saw that it was Mihajlovich, but he waved her back to her work as he passed on his way to the door on her right.

"Don't get up," Mihajlovich stopped Skender as he started to push himself from the leather chair. "I have just finished this. "The report plopped onto the black and red ink-stained blotter. "You did a good job, Berisha, this is excellent."

"Thank you, Colonel Mihajlovich. I am working on Part Two and should have it finished for you by tomorrow." Mihajlovich nodded as he sat opposite

Skender. Skender continued, "This area is so rich in agriculture. I never realized that before."

"Of course, Kosovo can feed the whole country … it is the bread-basket of Yugoslavia." Mihajlovich looked up with a smile. "Which reminds me, have you eaten yet? Good, let us lunch together. I have to go to Party Headquarters first…." He glanced at his watch, stood and walked towards the door, calling back, "Shall we say at one? Same place?"

"One o'clock is fine." Skender waited until the door closed on Mihajlovich, then returned to his seat and pulled the typed draft in front of him. 'Part Two … Pristina, the Capital.' He turned the first page, took the pen, and started to read, 'Pristina, the Capital City of Kosovo, with a population of over 50,000….'

Chapter 43

Laughter, infectious in its innocence and joy, called Babush from his paper to the window. A smile played about his mouth as he looked down into his garden. The opening of the door made him glance backwards, and he put his finger to his lips warningly and beckoned Nona to join him.

"These three challenge the sun," he whispered. Nona stood beside him, watching as her daughter leaned forward and confided some secret to Ilyria and Nurije, their heads touched as they giggled together and then returned to their sewing. Babush caught Nona's small sigh, and he turned and sat quietly watching her, her dreamy eyes touched him and he felt a great need to know her thoughts. "Tell me," he said gently, not wanting to disturb her mood, "tell me how she feels." She dragged her eyes from the garden and he gave an encouraging nod. "Tell me."

She smiled, "Why?"

"I want to know. Please?"

Nona's eyes returned to the garden. "This is the happiest time in a girl's life, the most carefree she will ever know. There is the excitement of preparation, instead of being up to her elbows in housework. She is surrounded by softness and loveliness. Her friends and cousins flock around her. For the first time, the only time in her life, she is the important one, the one everybody fusses over. She holds the world in her hands.

"Only one other time can surpass it. The birth of her first child." The brilliant dahlias threw Drita's delicate beauty into sharp relief, Nona's eyes filled and she half-turned from Babush, but his hand against her wrist stopped her.

"Tell me," he insisted quietly. "I want to know. I want to understand how she feels, how you felt."

Surprise stopped Nona's tears and made her stare at him. She did not answer for a long time, but stood at the open window, looking down at the three young girls surrounded by the full blossoms, their laps and knees draped with material to be turned into dimis for a bride.

Babush watched her, was there a sigh or was it the breeze? Then, without permission, without asking, she sat down on the window bench beside him.

"Life for a girl is suspended at sixteen … our world narrows to serving our father, to making life as soft and as comfortable as we can for him. If we can do that, we are happy, he is the center of our world, a smile from him lights our day." She was lost in memories.

Babush watched her but said nothing; her action had already told him that at this moment she was not his wife, that she had stepped away from him.

"When you are making bread, in the quiet lonely hours of early morning, you dream. You dream of the man you will marry, of the family who will want you for their son. You dream of the day when you will be a nusé…." A smile flitted across her face. "A nusé." Her eyes closed. "Suddenly you are terrified, you are drenched in panic. What will he be like? Will he be kind, will he be … gentle?" Her hands clasped her waist, Babush watched her relive her youth.

"Fear clutches your stomach, your throat dries as you realize you will be completely in his hands, that there will be no one to turn to if…." She took a long deep breath, letting it go slowly. "And then, you remember your father. The shaking stops, the knot in your stomach slowly dissolves, and you continue the gentle rhythm of kneading the dough, secure in the knowledge that your father would not give you into just anyone's hands, that all will be carefully checked, and that he will choose wisely and well for you."

"If I had known, if I had only realized…" Babush's voice broke as he reached and took her hand in his, "I was not gentle with you…."

"Shhh." She turned to him, laid her finger against his lip.

"My father should have made me wait … when you were given to me, I was not ready for marriage."

Nona smiled, answered softly, "I think, perhaps, you were too ready." Their eyes met and they laughed quietly, a little embarrassed with each other. "We have been happy. The beginning was difficult, but then it is for many. Love and respect grew and flowered … that has been our salvation. Neither you, nor I, could have survived the heartbreak and hardships imposed on us if we had not had each other to lean on." Babush pulled her to him and they sat close, watching the girls. "This is the time she will remember when her thoughts turn to home. When the work is too heavy, the days long and dreary, or…" she hesitated only a moment, "or there is a misunderstanding between her and her husband…." Babush's arm tightened around her waist. "She will remember this time, this excitement, this happiness."

"Such a short time," Babush sighed heavily. "So short a time of happiness and then … nothing."

Nona turned to him, shocked at his bitterness and sadness. "She is to be a Nusé … marriage brings a different kind of happiness, a completeness, a fulfilling." Her eyes searched her husband's. "How can you think such a thing? She will find her joy as I found mine."

"Did you? Was there joy for you? I think I gave you pain and sorrow more than happiness." She turned her head quickly from him and he sighed, "I'm sorry … it has been many years since I have made you cry."

"My tears are for you. How can you think that there has been no happiness for me? You spoke of pain … that was not of your making. That came from outside of this house."

Babush sat in silence for a long moment, then turned her to face him. "How fortunate I was to be given such a wife. What a blessing when I got you." He dried her tears, tipped up her chin. "Thank you, Nusé."

"Nusé?" Nona's laugh was shaky. "That was long, long ago."

"Was it? Almost a lifetime … just a blink of an eye … and yet was there ever a time when I did not know you? Was there ever a time when you did not share my life?"

"Babush, Nona, look." Their eyes pulled from each other and they stretched to look down into the garden. Drita held the dimi high, then laid it against her body. "Isn't it beautiful?"

"Beautiful," Nona agreed, then turned with a proud smile to Babush. "She will be a lovely nusé … her husband will be fortunate."

"Yes, most fortunate." Slowly Babush removed Nona's scarf, her hair fell, lay heavy in his hand. "I remember when this was the same glorious color as our daughter's. When the sun caught it, it turned to ripe chestnut, the glow of the fire changed it to burnished copper … and I could hardly wait to have you to myself."

She smiled, eyes glistening with unshed tears. "That was long, long ago."

"No." He kissed her gently. "That was yesterday, Nusé, just yesterday."

Chapter 44

Anna stopped Skender after he had given instructions to his secretary and was about to leave. "Comrade Berisha, I have a message from Colonel Mihajlovich for you. He wishes to meet you at..." her eyes dropped to the written note, "...at The Crocodile instead of the hotel."

Skender frowned, "The Crocodile? Are you sure?"

Anna checked the note again. "Yes, I have never heard of the place. Have you?"

"Yes," Skender's answer was terse. "It is a Kosovar coffee house in Old Town."

"Why, that's strange ... why would Colonel Mihajlovich want to go to...." Remembrance stopped her almost in time, her eyes dropped to the note and color flooded her face. Skender watched her for a moment, then without a word, left the room.

The police sergeant stood as Skender walked into the main office, took a sheaf of papers on a clipboard from the wall and handed it to Skender. "Only a few arrests last night, Comrade."

"Thank you." Skender's eyes ran down the Daily Sheet of Arrests, paused now and again to check the reason listed for the detention. "I have an appointment with Colonel Mihajlovich ... I will deal with these after lunch."

"Yes, Comrade Berisha." The sergeant accepted the clipboard and hung it on the wall.

The heavy door was propped open, and a stream of sunlight lit a path to the street. Two policemen lolled against the building, but came to attention as they saw him approach, he nodded briefly as he passed. The air was soft, the trees full and green, a few old men sat on benches in direct line of the sun, and as he crossed the park Jill's words returned to Skender. On a sigh he nodded a greeting to an old friend of Babush's playing chess. He murmured a greeting back to Skender as he passed, while his opponent deliberately turned his back.

The deep shadows of Old Town swallowed Skender, the tall, close buildings thrust out the sun but the coolness was unwelcome this early in the year.

The warmth of spices and rich aromatic coffee welcomed him as he entered The Crocodile and he breathed deeply, appreciatively. In spite of his reluctance at being there, his taste buds salivated in anticipation and his eyes followed as a dish, held high on the shoulders of a waiter, steamed past him.

The Crocodile was crowded, and he stood at the foot of the three steps, hand on the carved rose of the balustrade, searching for a table, the pitch of conversation quieted slowly as he was seen by first one group and then the next, until there was almost silence in the busy dining room. The petals of the rose dug into his palm as his hand tightened over it.

As the quietness reached Luan and his friends, they turned to discover the reason. "Well, well, just look…." A kick under the table warned the young man next to Luan, and his eyes went swiftly from the deliverer to Luan, then to Skender, and back to Luan.

"Skender … here!" Luan's hand beckoned as he stood. "Please join us." Luan's eyes returned to his friends as he heard their gasps, then lingered on the one who had spoken and was about to stand. "I think most of you know Skender Berisha, but those of you that do not will, I am sure…" there was veiled warning, an intenseness in his look that returned the young man to his seat, "…be happy to have him join us, especially as he is such an old and valued friend of me and my family." His smile was warm as he turned. "Skender, how are you? Please permit me to introduce you to some friends."

The young men rose, introductions were made, hands were extended, some with reluctance, some with disdain, some with embarrassment.

"Will you join us?" Luan graciously moved, offering Skender his position at the head of the table.

"No, Luan, thank you. I am meeting someone."

"There is room…."

"No," Skender stopped Luan as he was about to ask his friends to close the gaps between them, "I think not." He hesitated. "I am meeting Colonel Mihajlovich."

Luan stared at him, disbelief leaving his mouth slack for a moment. "Here? That is madness," he whispered.

"Yes, I am inclined to agree with you," Skender replied grimly. Eyes dropped; heads turned away as Skender glanced around the room. "Excuse me, I must try to find a place…." He looked in vain for a waiter.

Luan took a deep shuddering breath, let it go in one fast exhale. "Let me help. I come here often and have some influence." He snapped his fingers at the boy who had deliberately turned from Skender, he came slowly, reluctantly. "A table for two…" Luan's eyes narrowed as he saw the refusal about to come, "immediately." He gave a hard swallow, "for Mr. Berisha and…." He bit at his lip, forced himself to continue. "And his guest."

There was a moment of hesitation. "We have only a small table … follow me."

Skender nodded his thanks to Luan.

Luan watched as he followed the waiter.

"I had no idea you were that friendly with him."

The sarcastic voice brought Luan's attention from watching Skender making his way to a table to the young man who had been sitting next to him. "You knew," he answered briefly, "I have made no secret of the fact that I visit him regularly."

"You had no right to expose us to him … to make us greet him, shake hands…." Luan's steady appraisal of the speaker at the opposite end of the table made his voice falter and trail off.

"If you do not approve of my conduct, you are free to leave," Luan responded coldly as his eyes traveled from one to the other. "As are all, or any, of you."

The room was suddenly electrified, all eyes fastened on the grey-suited man who walked, as if unconscious of the stir his entrance had caused, toward Skender. Skender stood motionless until Mihajlovich had sat down, then, very aware of the attention they were receiving, lowered himself to the fat hassock and offered one of the two menus to Mihajlovich.

Mihajlovich gave a brief shake of his head. "Today I am in your hands … you must choose for me." He glanced around, "Sometimes I regret that I do not know Albanian and wish that I had learned to speak…."

'I chose to learn Albanian; I speak it perfectly….'

"…more profitable to my career to study English." Mihajlovich stopped abruptly, Skender's eyes, glazed as if in death, stared past him. "What is the matter?" he demanded sharply. "Are you ill? Berisha!" The last word was sharp, a command.

Skender started, stared uncomprehendingly at Mihajlovich. The air was heavy, silent, Mihajlovich licked at his lips as he looked up to find a sea of eyes watching him. "Berisha!" He relaxed as Skender's eyes cleared. "What the hell is wrong with you? Are you ill?"

"No." Skender picked up the menu. "What type of food would you like?"

"Anything." Mihajlovich dismissed the question, glared at the sullen-faced boy who stood waiting for their order, his distaste for having to wait on them underlined by the amount of space between him and their table. "Order something, anything, before I teach this snip some manners."

There was no response, no acknowledgement of their order, only the silent acceptance of the menus from Skender's hand indicated that he had even heard. Mihajlovich watched the straight, angry back. "One day he will fall into my hands, and I will remind him of his insolence." Skender picked up the napkin, shook it free of its folds and laid it across his knees. "What was it that upset you?

You are used, now, to the stares … or is it because we are here, in your own section?"

"Why did you choose to come here?" Skender asked, grateful that Mihajlovich had provided an explanation for his behavior. "Why here, instead of the hotel?"

"It is time for you to be seen with me by these…" confidence returned in full as heads turned away from him, eyes fell before his, "these leading families of Pristina. Tonight the dinner tables will be heavy with discussion. Your name, linked with mine, will fill their stomachs before the food leaves their mouths." He looked with curiosity at the plate as it was placed before him.

Skender waited until the waiter had left. "Why have you deliberately brought me to their attention?"

"Why would you think it deliberate?" Mihajlovich lifted the fork toward his mouth.

"Your actions always have a reason."

Mihajlovich smiled, "Good – you have observed well. Now put into practice what you have learned." He wiped his mouth on his napkin. "Every year at this time I give a speech at the University. Spring brings a surge of enthusiasm for life … the youth, especially, feel this rush, this motivation. Seeds root easily … this is very good." He looked up as he felt Skender's astonishment, laughed as he saw his expression, then pointed with his fork. "The food!"

Skender grinned, "I thought, for a moment, you were referring to a different subject!"

Mihajlovich laughed, "No. And my concern is not that the youth indulge in … shall we say the pursuit of romance … but that I should capture some of their enthusiasm, their swell of energy, and direct it toward the ideals of International Brotherhood. My speech produces a crop … we are rewarded with a leap in membership, especially among the Yugoslavian students." His eyes lifted, held Skender's, "But this year…" Skender's fork stilled above his plate, Mihajlovich let his eyes wander around the dining room, "this year…" he looked up at Skender, continued softly, "tonight they will speak of you. In a few days, you will speak to them."

Skender, trembling, almost unable to breathe, just stared at him.

Mihajlovich continued, "After I have finished my lecture on the benefits of Communism, they will listen to Skender Berisha." He moved some of the food around on his plate, chose a vegetable, speared it, then looked expectantly at Skender.

Skender glanced quickly around, certain that every ear had caught Mihajlovich's words. Carefully he laid the fork down. "I would prefer not, sir, I have nothing to say."

"You will think of something." Mihajlovich pushed his plate away, leaned his elbows on the table. "If I may make a suggestion…." He waited politely for the inclination of Skender's head. "Perhaps you would like to speak of your own situation. Since you have joined me, your family, and you, have enjoyed more comfort, more security, than ever before. Am I right?"

"Yes." Skender picked up the fork, pushed some of the food around, then with a sigh, laid the fork down. "Is this an order?" He knew, even before the affirmative nod came. "I do not think I am capable of meeting this demand, Colonel Mihajlovich."

"You are. So far, whatever I have demanded of you has been accomplished. Officer Dragonovich carries out your orders…." Mihajlovich's eyebrows lifted quizzically as Skender.

Skender forced a smile, "With some reservations."

Mihajlovich smiled back. "The police obey you."

Their eyes met and they laughed together.

Instinct made Skender realize he must behave normally; he inclined his head slightly. "Yes, unless an order, already a week old, must suddenly be seen to immediately."

Mihajlovich continued to smile. "I am glad that you can be amused, that their infantile behavior no longer upsets you. In the beginning, everything was so serious, so monumental for you. Now, only occasionally do you feel … er … threatened. Only occasionally do I have to insist…." He let the rest hang, his eyes watching carefully for a sign suggesting disobedience. He allowed himself to relax as none came.

"I will look over your speech once it has been prepared."

He reached into his jacket pocket and took out a pale blue envelope. "This came for you today." He saw the nerve jump in Skender's neck as his hand reached for the letter, and pulled it back, holding it against his body. "You are still very much involved with her, aren't you?"

Skender's throat, tight with anger, the anger that came every time Mihajlovich handed him one of Jill's letters and he knew that every word, every thought, had been carefully read and digested before being passed on to him, refused to let any word pass. He swallowed as Mihajlovich passed the letter to him. "Thank you."

"Perhaps I made a mistake…." Skender's nerves jangled a warning and he glanced non-commitally at the envelope, then put it into his pocket as casually as possible, Mihajlovich was still watching Skender closely. He picked up his coffee, drained it to the end. "Perhaps I should have kept her here."

Skender wiped his mouth, threw the napkin down on the table. "I don't think so." He stood, beckoned the waiter. "Her lack of understanding of our customs, our ways, would have been irritating at least … the fact that she cannot speak the language?" He shrugged, "She would have been a nuisance to me … by now I would have lost all patience." He smiled, "You did me a service … this way I keep my pleasant memories." He tapped the pocket where the letter lay, "Even re-live them a little."

He turned. "The bill, please." Mihajlovich still had not moved and Skender was aware of his careful perusal. "Are you ready?" He forced a smile. "My superior does not approve of long lunches, you know!"

Mihajlovich nodded, "True." His thoughts returned to the letter, Skender's reaction to it, "I found you the prettiest piece of ass in Pristina for your secretary. I hope you are not letting it go to waste?"

Skender continued to pay the waiter, willing himself to remain calm.

"Well?" Mihajlovich questioned.

Skender looked straight at him, gave a small smile, a slight shrug.

A knowing smile hovered around Mihajlovich's mouth, he murmured, "Good, good."

"You had better precede me to the street, sir, unless you wish to see your assistant break a rule." Skender indicated that he intended to leave a tip.

"You intend to tip this morose individual?"

Skender inclined his head.

"Well, then…." Mihajlovich looked around the crowded room, put his hand on Skender's shoulder for a moment, then walked towards the door.

Skender paid the waiter, sighed, took a long drink of water. He gripped the table holding tight until he knew he had control, then walked toward the door.

Chapter 45

The evening stretched, dragged. Drita and Nona had gone to visit at Migje Hasan's house, and Babush and Skender had spent an hour in the garden before the coolness of the evening had driven them into the house. The nightly game of chess had become a ritual that was beginning to bore both, although neither was prepared to admit it. Skender was relieved when his father claimed the game as his.

"You were home early, Skender. I thought you had told me that you planned to work late." Babush laid the white chess pieces into the left half of the rough wooden box, he handled each piece carefully, lovingly, remembering the long hours he had spent on carving them during a particularly dismal winter.

"I had, but…" Skender watched as Babush started to place the black pieces into their section, sighed and continued, "Mihajlovich and Dragonovich were working…" his voice was low, preoccupied, '…and I cannot help but wonder why, whether there is a possibility…." He leaned forward and passed the black queen to his father.

Babush saw the deep furrow between Skender's eyes and confirmed the worry he had heard in his voice. "You may smoke, Djali, if you wish."

"What?"

Babush stopped his careful placing of the men, took out his pipe. "Shall we share a moment with each other?" he asked, holding up the pipe. He took out the pack of tobacco, carefully filling the bowl. A few strands fell into his lap, and he gathered them, each piece, and pushed them into his pipe.

"Old habits die hard, sir."

Babush laughed softly as he nodded. "For many years I smoked on an empty pipe. Now that there is plenty to fill my bowl. If I can help you, Skender, I am prepared to listen."

"Are you sure that you wish to hear?"

"A load is only half the weight if two carry it." He passed the lighter to Skender after his pipe was glowing redly. Skender lit his cigarette and sat smoking for a few moments, each draw long, deep, he stood suddenly, moved to the already closed door and leaned against it. As he straightened, he pulled against the door handle, Babush's concern grew as his son went to the partially open window and pulled it down so firmly that the frame shuddered.

Skender's face was colorless as he turned to Babush. "Mihajlovich and Dragonovich are working late tonight…" Babush nodded encouragement as he stopped, "And … all evening I have expected the sound of our gate, the heavy clatter of their boots on our path." He gave a nervous laugh before his hand wiped at his mouth.

"Boots?" Babush slowly removed his pipe from his mouth as he stared at Skender. "That means the police. But you are working for Mihajlovich … why would you expect him to send the police here?"

"To arrest me." It was said so quietly, so firmly, Babush could not question his seriousness. Skender turned from his father's shock. The sky was brilliant, streaks of orange blended, melted together, and turned to flame, finger clouds pierced into the fiery colors, leaving smudges and trails of sooty blackness, to bring a contrast so violent, so intense, that no artist would dare paint it. The red tiles of the roofs stretched to the horizon; the bright brick of day turned to insipid paleness against the majesty of color in the sky.

Skender's eyes dropped to the rows of carefully tended vegetables, each on an island of damp earth, the flowers had already folded into themselves. "May her life be as peaceful and beautiful as this garden."

Startled by his sudden change, Babush demanded sharply, "Whose?"

Still Skender stayed beside the window. "Drita's. She spends so much time, so many hours, in this garden. Her sewing is a pleasure for her to do, a pleasure for me to watch. I am glad that she is so happy, that the weather is kind and allows her to sit in the sun in our garden for her last days in the Berisha house." He turned to Babush. "I brought her some more material today. She was delighted, delirious with joy."

"You are spoiling her, she already has enough for two nusas."

"Then may she go to Luan Mali with double happiness. May the Mali family welcome her to their house with twice as much joy."

Babush's eyes closed briefly. "Amen to that, Djali." He puffed on his pipe for a while. "But we are not speaking of Drita. Your precautions against being overheard were not for her."

"No. They were not, but I pray that she will be gone from this house, that she will be at the Malis before Mihajlovich discovers…."

He opened his jacket, reached to the inside pocket, then his eyes lifted to Babush's and he took a deep breath as his hand reappeared. Between his thumb and first finger he held a small key. "Nobody knows that I have this key, nobody suspects … at least, I hope they don't." The furrow between his eyes deepened as he stared at the key. "Babush, sir, this key opens the Confidential Files of Udba." Babush's indrawn breath stopped Skender.

Babush turned and glanced quickly at the closed door. "How did you come by it?" he whispered.

"There were only three persons who had one. Now there are four: Colonel Mihajlovich, Officer Dragonovich, Anna, and…" his voice was bitter as he added, "…and Comrade Berisha."

He moved toward Babush, sat down, eyes never leaving the key as it sparked light from the overhead lamp. "Anna never lets hers out of her sight, never leaves a file open unless she is personally in the room. Mihajlovich is efficiency personified, thoroughly dependable, and his key chain is attached to him at all times." He paused, moving the key to reflect the light and flash it back and forth. "But there is one other … a sloppy, unorganized person…" he glanced towards Babush.

"Dragonovich."

Skender nodded. "Yes. Dragonovich."

"Are you telling me that the key is his?"

"No. This is a duplicate cut from his."

Babush sighed, bewilderment and confusion on his face. "Then Dragonovich must know that you have this." His hand waved toward the key still held in Skender's hand.

"No. He does not." Skender carefully put the key back into his inside pocket. "At the beginning of my time with Mihajlovich, perhaps a month or six weeks after I had started to work for him, he gave me to Dragonovich for instruction in…." He hesitated, eyes lifting to Babush, then dropping to the floor. Before continuing, he took a final long draw on his cigarette. "In interrogation."

The word hung between them. Babush was stiff, puffed with great control at his pipe, and stared solidly at the empty fireplace.

Anger raced through Skender. "That disgusts you, infuriates you, doesn't it? Believe me, they are better off with me questioning them than Mihajlovich or Dragonovich. At least with me there is no beating to accompany the questions."

"I did not accuse you, Skender."

"No, you did not, but then, nobody does … just their eyes follow…." His hand wiped at his mouth, his voice low as he added, "That is worse than when they turn their backs." Babush took a glass from the tray near him, filled it with water and in silence, offered it to Skender. "Thank you." The glass rattled against Skender's teeth and he replaced it quickly. "I'm sorry." There was an apologetic smile. "I think I am overwrought tonight."

"It was bound to come, Djali. I have watched the load grow heavier, the strain around your eyes deepen, the loneliness increase." He again offered the water to Skender, waited patiently until he had finished and returned the glass. "Now, tell me, how did you come by this key?"

"I stole it." Skender smiled as he saw his father's shock. "Or let us say instead, that I 'borrowed' it. For some reason, Dragonovich left the room … the key lay there on his desk, winking at me. I picked it up, sat there fingering it, undecided … it was into my pocket only a moment before Dragonovich returned."

"He did not miss it?"

Skender almost laughed, "On that desk? A rat could live there and he'd not know of it. That day I requested an early lunch, drove to Lipljan and had a duplicate key cut from his." Skender glanced up at Babush. "I did not dare go to any key shop in Prishtine. I drove back, slipped into Dragonovich's office, and returned his key to his desk. As far as I know, he never knew that it had gone from his office."

"There must be something of great importance in these files if all the keys are guarded so carefully, something of great magnitude to make you go to such lengths."

"Yes." Skender's voice was firm, but low, reached only the ears intended to hear. "Since the Communist takeover in 1945, a record has been kept of any, and everyone, arrested by Udba. There are no exceptions. Death is the only way to erase a name from their files. The cabinets hold the files, this key…" he tapped at his pocket, "…unlocks the cabinets."

Babush licked at his lips, roughly smoothed his moustache. "What have you done?"

"I told you of Mihajlovich's list, the one I had to go through? After I had completed my marking of those that were dead, Anna and I went through the files. They both have a fetish for neatness and wanted the files 'sifted', to use a word of Anna's." Skender rubbed at his eyes. "Whenever we came to a file of someone who had died, it was pulled and sent to the basement to await the official letter from Belgrade."

Skender saw that Babush had lost the thread, continued, "No file can be destroyed unless Belgrade has given permission. Mihajlovich must be the one who asks for that permission. Only he can write-in declaring that a certain number have died and that he wishes to destroy the files. Mihajlovich looks for that permit every day, has been expecting it for over a week."

Skender stood, walked around the room, then stopped in front of Babush. "What Mihajlovich does not know is that when permission comes, he will destroy all the current files.

He took a long drink of water. The ones sitting in locked confinement are those of dead people, or others who are far enough from this country to be safe from Udba's reach."

"God in Heaven!"

"There is not one file, no record at all, of any young man at present living in Prishtine." Babush covered his heart, trying to stop its leaping. "There were files on many we know: Luan Mali, Morat's younger brother, Mustafa, another on Chenan's two brothers, three on Shamsi's family, his brothers and his father,

Adnan's brother.... Now their files await destruction, sit quietly in the basement with a mound of others.

In the locked cabinets are files of Sabri, Morat, Chenan, and all those others that died so needlessly, so hopelessly." He gave a sad smile, "I like to think that it would please them, amuse them even, that in death they can retaliate. They are beyond Mihajlovich, he cannot touch them or hurt them...."

"He can hurt you, Skender. Have you thought of that?"

"Yes."

"And that does not terrify you?"

"Yes. When I think of it." Skender's smile was strained. "In the beginning, when I first started to exchange the files, I shook every time Mihajlovich looked or spoke to me. When a policeman walked toward me I tasted bile, and when Dragonovich's eyes lingered more than a moment on me...." There was a sudden involuntary shudder, "Now I have accepted, learned to push that fear deep down inside me."

"Is it possible that Mihajlovich will find out what you have done?"

"He cannot help but discover it. There was an unspoken rule that I am sure still exists, that when we were arrested and they asked, 'Have you ever been in our hands before?' we answered, 'No'. They always check the files of course, but it was an irritant to them that gave us a small degree of pleasure. But one day they will arrest someone whose name is familiar, someone they know they had a file for, which is now missing. Or one day, Mihajlovich will need some young men to beat and torture, and there will be none in his files to call upon." Babush's hands cupped his eyes. "When that day comes..." Skender took a deep breath and slowly Babush lowered his hands, letting them fall to his lap, "Mihajlovich will send for me."

"Perhaps not," Babush said urgently, "Perhaps he will not even think of you...."

"Do not live on false hopes, Babush. If you were in Mihajlovich's place, would you not guess?"

"Not necessarily. He does not know you have the key. It is the others he will...."

"Babush, don't ... don't torture yourself with false hopes. Anna has been with him for seven years. She would give her life for him, and he knows it." Skender smiled. "And I do not think Mihajlovich will look with suspicion at the head of his police department."

"Why not? Dragonovich has not been here long...."

"Stop this," Skender cut in angrily, "Dragonovich enjoys his work too much to bring such a suspicion to him." He swallowed, continued in a quieter tone, "When Mihajlovich ... questions ... someone, it is handled with cold contempt. There is no emotion and the beating is administered methodically. But Dragonovich..." he swallowed the collected saliva, "Dragonovich enjoys it, revels in the pain he inflicts, delights in the suffering." His hands clenched; his head dropped to rest on the clenched fists.

"And you have been made to participate, to watch this?" Babush's eyes expressed his horror.

"Only once." Skender's head lifted. "I was with Mihajlovich when his phone rang, I saw the sudden stiffening, the excitement rise in him as he spoke, 'Follow me,' he commanded. We went downstairs. Mihajlovich lead at a fast pace. I knew it was important. His energy told me that. We reached the bottom of the first flight of stairs and continued down. The old interrogation rooms on the ground floor are no longer used...." He paused, suddenly remembering that Mihajlovich had been clever enough to use the old, number four, interrogation room when he had brought Skender in for questioning, clever enough to know that old fears and terrors evoked easily in familiar surroundings.

"Mihajlovich stopped, turned as we reached one of the cells, 'Not a sound ... not a word,' he ordered. He was careful, turned the handle easily, in silence, and we slipped inside and just as silently the door closed on us. Mihajlovich leaned back against the wall, arms folded, his whole body, whole being, intent on the man who sat opposite Dragonovich, a guard on each side of him.

"Dragonovich was questioning him ... there was a moment, a flash of quiet when Dragonovich glanced toward Mihajlovich and then the questioning started again, intensified until there was barely time to draw breath between one demand and the next." Skender was shaking, and Babush watched him with concern. "'Now you will see Dragonovich at his best,' Mihajlovich whispered to me as he gave a small nod. That brief movement was what Dragonovich had been waiting for. The sense of heightened anticipation had made me wonder ... now Dragonovich's smile, the pleasurable licking of his lips as his head jerked to the leathers, gave me my answer."

Skender stared down at the clammy dampness of his palms, seemed surprised, took out his handkerchief and wiped at them. "I was shaking ... whether with anger or old fears I am not sure ... but I could not believe that Mihajlovich expected me to stay and watch. The man's head moved, followed the guard as he sauntered across the room. I witnessed his slow terror as he saw him feeling the straps, and then his eyes moved from the guard to Mihajlovich. From Mihajlovich to me. Our eyes met. I felt, tasted his fear ... and could do nothing. We still were glued eye-to-eye when Mihajlovich spoke into my ear. 'I want you to see this ... I wish you to see that our methods are efficient, and Dragonovich's enthusiasm is contagious....'"

"I wheeled on him ... 'I do not need to see ... I have felt your guards' efficiency. My back still carries the marks of their enthusiasm.' In two strides I was at the door. The guard blocked my way...." Skender sighed, wiped the perspiration from his forehead. "Mihajlovich must have ordered him to let me pass, for he moved, and I willed my fist to unwrap itself, my arm to return to my side. I think I regretted that the guard moved so quickly … I needed to hit someone."

Skender stood went and sat on the window bench. "I left the room, even left the building. I don't know where I went … Old Town, perhaps … and then … the realization that I had to return to that hated place, that if I did not walk in there freely, Mihajlovich would drag me back." His hand shook as he took a cigarette, lit it, and sat smoking.

"When Mihajlovich returned to his office, I was sitting at my desk. He never mentioned it, has never asked me to accompany him to those rooms again."

Babush pulled worriedly at his moustache, then asked quietly, "But surely you have to go to those rooms, have to use them? You told me yourself that Dragonovich has instructed you in interrogation procedure."

"Mihajlovich gave me the young boys, the first offenders … not the Yugoslavian youths of course, just the Kosovars. It breaks my heart to see them … so young, so transparent. They hold their heads high, stand tall, soldiers without a uniform, without an officer to lead them. And their bravery is strong and true, and yet so fragile. The disgust I see reflected in their eyes as they look at me tears me apart while I thank God that it is I who has the questioning of them. Dragonovich would eat them alive."

"Do they answer your questions, Djali?"

"Sometimes. I warn them, 'Answer me or he…', … there is always one guard with me, '… will take you to their officers, and things will go hard with you.'" Skender smiled, the sadness reached deep into his eyes. "As I fill out the form, they will answer hotly, 'I am not afraid.'"

"And how do you advise them then?"

"I tell them they should be, that their brave words are easy because they have never experienced a beating. As I continue to fill out the form with some trivial information that will satisfy whoever reads it, I advise them to save their courage for something important, not to be too eager to prove themselves."

"Their mothers must be thankful that their sons fell into your hands."

Skender sighed as he stood up. "I doubt it."

"Nona would have been … had you been returned to us without needing her to attend to your back, whoever it was would have had our gratitude, our thanks." Skender turned to the window, Babush sighed to himself realizing that he could not take the pain from Skender.

"When Mihajlovich discovers that his files have been tampered with, what do you think he will do?" Skender turned slowly, looked steadily at his father. "But you are working for him!"

"Babush, listen…" Skender crossed to the old man and knelt beside him, "I have made a fool of him. Mihajlovich will not be able to tolerate that. His shock will turn to anger – hot and uncontrollable for a moment – but then … he has remarkable self-control. His fury will be cold, ruthless."

"Replace the files … put them back."

Skender's head moved slowly. "No, Babush. I think I understand now. This was the reason I had to stay in Prishtine."

"Why?" There was anguish in the cry. "He will make you beg for death before he drops you at my gate. And then … will you know me? Know any of us?"

Skender held the old man close for a moment, then gently put him from him. "Think, Babush, think what this means … there are no more suspects! Mihajlovich can no longer reach into a cabinet and pick out a dozen names to bully and terrorize for no reason. He will remember a few, but not many, and those he remembers would never give him the information on why they were arrested previously. There will be no records, nothing, prior to this date. What will that do to his reputation? What will Belgrade mark on his file? He will be finished, discredited, relieved of command in Kosov. Never again will he hold such a powerful position … he will be relegated to some minor post within Serbia itself."

Babush spoke sharply. "Before that time, Skender Berisha will have been at his mercy."

"Yes," Skender answered quietly, "I know that, and I understand your fear and share it."

"He has let you roam all over Kosov preparing this report for him … why did you not try to get away then?"

Skender smiled. "You answered your own question, sir … 'all over Kosov' … but not a step farther. Babush, I must do nothing to raise his suspicion, must give no reason for him to look past my shadow."

"You cannot sit here and wait."

"I can do no other." Skender laid his hand on his father's knee. "I am not playing the hero," he smiled, "my churning stomach and shaking knees every time I see Mihajlovich near those cabinets belie any bravery or heroics."

He stretched, sat down, and as he did so, the crackling of paper reminded him of Jill's letter. He reached into his pocket, thankful that he had something to take the old man's mind off his worry at least for a short time. "Good news, Babush … a letter from Gillian. She is well and sends her love and regards to everyone." He removed the letter from the pale blue envelope and read a few excerpts from it … deliberately leaving out the fact that she had started to work. Babush's anger had been fierce, surpassing even his own, when he learned that Mihajlovich would not allow Skender to send any support money to Gillian.

"And she is excited and delighted with the news of Drita's engagement to Luan Mali…." His voice saddened. 'My only wish is that I, too, could be with you to celebrate such a joyous occasion.'" He folded the letter.

Babush sat watching him. "You miss her, Djali."

"Desperately." Skender returned the letter to his pocket. "Our plans were so simple, so ordinary … to be together, have children, become a family, perhaps, one day, buy our own house."

His fist smashed against the rug. "I wanted her to have my child, wanted to see her swell with my seed. I longed for the time when the fruit of our love for each other would be placed in my arms. I anticipated my pride when I asked for your blessing for my son, and I wondered what name you would bestow upon him."

"You speak as if you have abandoned those plans, those dreams."

"Do I? Perhaps in the cold light of day I face reality. It is at night that the dreams and longings eat at me, keep sleep at bay."

"I wish I had some comfort for you, Djali."

Skender sighed. "I am sorry to have burdened you with all this, Babush. Today was particularly difficult. While I long for news from Jill, her letters have a disturbing effect … make the longing, wanting, harder. And Mihajlovich dragged me to The Crocodile. Exhibited me as one would a well-trained bear…" he paused, "and, to finish the day, one of the young teachers at the gymnasium was caught with a book of Albanian poetry … he has been sentenced to two years' hard labor." His eyes rose to Babush. "He is very much the aesthetic teacher. He will not survive two years in that place. I pleaded with Mihajlovich, begged him to let him continue teaching, but…." His shoulders lifted, dropped despondently.

"Two years is lighter than usual, Skender."

"Yes, but not light enough for him, I fear. Originally it was three. Mihajlovich granted him one year less after my intervention, but it is not enough … he will die."

"You cannot know that … there is only One who knows that."

The sound of the gate brought them both to stiff attention.

Babush relaxed. "Your mother and sister returning home."

"Not a word of this to Nona, sir," Skender warned.

"Not even a breath, Djali, not even a breath."

Chapter 46

"Ouch!" Aslan rubbed ruefully at his head.

Skender glanced toward him, he grinned as he saw that he was unhurt. "Sorry, I had no alternative but to brake quickly … that cyclist was almost under my wheels."

Aslan continued to rub at his head. "God gave me two legs … I think, in future, I shall use them … it's safer!" He waited until Skender had manipulated the corner. "You were telling me of Gillian."

"She said to congratulate you and your Nusé, and she has sent a gift for the baby."

Aslan sighed, "I wish she could send me an uninterrupted night's sleep! The first boy was so good, so quiet, but this one…." He groaned, slid down into his seat and laid his head back. "Even my bones are tired from his crying."

Skender chuckled, "The solution is in your own hands, brother." Aslan opened one eye. "Do not compound the problem … refrain from bringing any more babies into your house!"

Aslan laughed, "The hell I will! I plan on having a dozen…" his hand moved in steps, "…each one half a head shorter than the next." They grinned at each other. "Come to dinner tonight." He saddened at Skender's brief shake of his head. "Please. I would like you to come."

"It is not a good idea."

Aslan pushed himself into a sitting position. "One word … even a look … from Shamsi or Adnan and I'll break their necks."

Skender continued to ease the car toward the curb. "We have tried it twice before … it is difficult for you and uncomfortable for me." He sighed to himself as he saw Aslan's concern. "But I will join you and your Nusé for coffee later … ask her to make me one of her custards." The car halted. "We are here, sir … your chauffeur has brought you right to your door." He laughed as he gave a half bow.

"Thank you, brother … have a good day." Skender nodded as the door slammed, Aslan's head popped back through the open window. "I will invite Jakup to join us this evening. Good-bye."

Jakup … not Jakup and Emin … just Jakup. Skender sighed, checked his mirror and moved out into the stream of traffic. *I have not seen Emin since….* He swore thoroughly as a car cut in front of him, pushed Emin from his mind and concentrated on the heavy morning traffic.

Mihajlovich's car was already parked. Skender glanced at his watch, eight-forty. *He is early this morning.* He pulled his jacket from the back seat, slipped into it, then bent to his wing mirror to make sure his tie was neat and straight.

He left the shade of the tree with reluctance, for the pavement was already hot enough to make itself felt through his shoes, the sun beat down and he quickened his pace, taking the steps to Police Headquarters in two strides. It was dim and cooler inside, but stuffy, and he thought with envy of the air-conditioned offices in San Francisco.

"Good morning, Comrade Berisha."

The unexpected greeting from Dragonovich stopped Skender.

"Good morning, Officer Dragonovich." He waited a moment, then turned toward the stairs.

"It is hot this morning."

Slowly, Skender turned back to face Dragonovich. "Yes, it is."

Amused sarcasm curled Dragonovich's lips. "It will be hotter before the day is out." Uneasiness stirred in Skender at Dragonovich's laugh. "Much, much hotter, in fact." He leaned across the counter, spoke quietly, confidentially, "Tell me, Comrade Berisha, do you like it hot? Eh?" He pushed his hat to the back of his head, laughed heartily, then made his way toward his office. All eyes were on Skender. Dragonovich opened his office door, turned back with an amused look at Skender, laughed again and closed the door.

The tension unnerved Skender, his grip on his briefcase tightened. "Get back to work," he ordered sharply, turning away from the counter.

The stairs were longer, steeper, today, his legs leaden and slow, his mind darted forward, backward, as he re-enacted the scene with Dragonovich, searching for an explanation. *Does he know? Impossible! He would have gone straight to Mihajlovich even if he only had a glimmer of suspicion. And if he had?* The second flight stretched away from him as he turned on the landing between the stairs. *Mihajlovich would have sent for me, arrested me … no. He would not. He would sit and wait for me to come to him.* He paused, breath coming unevenly. *It would give him a great deal of gratification for me to walk into his trap….* He passed the door marked, 'Colonel Mihajlovich, D.D. Udba'. *A spider, web spun, waiting for his fly….*

"Good morning, Anna."

She barely nodded. "Good morning, Comrade Berisha." The usual smile had been replaced by straight, thin lips pressed tight together.

He straightened his shoulders, took another good grip on the briefcase. "Good morning, Irena. I wish to dictate immediately." She did not answer, did not reach for her book, but glanced apprehensively at Anna. Anna turned away, busied herself with the incoming mail as Skender let his eyes follow the direction of Irena's. He turned back to Irena. "Bring your book." Again, the wary glance toward Anna, the ignoring of his order. "Anna!" Even to his ears he sounded sharp, louder than necessary, her hands stilled over the envelope she was opening, and then she looked up at him. "Is there any reason why Irena cannot take dictation now, immediately?"

"None that I know of, Comrade Berisha," she answered smoothly, then, with a pointed glance at the pile of unopened envelopes, "Is there anything else?"

Was there unnecessary emphasis on 'Comrade'? "No. Is Colonel Mihajlovich in his office?"

"Yes."

No explanation. No polite, 'Do you wish to see him?' or 'He is busy at the moment but I will advise you the minute he is free'. With a long look at her, Skender turned toward his office, his stomach nervous, mind in turmoil. His hand stretched toward the door.

"Berisha!"

Hand froze, mind raced … *Open the door, slam it behind you, shoot the bolt!* He pushed the madness away, turned. "Good morning, Colonel Mihajlovich." His eyes slid past Mihajlovich to the guard standing beside him, his scalp prickled a warning.

"I have been waiting for you."

"I am sorry." Skender stiffened as Mihajlovich pulled the key chain from his pocket. "I did not realize I was late."

Mihajlovich turned to the filing cabinet. "You are not. I was early … over-anxious, perhaps." He searched for the smallest key, inserted it into the lock at the top of the second filing cabinet, turned with a brief smile. "I have a surprise for you."

He knows. That explains Dragonovich's remarks, his damned laughter. Now I understand Anna's strangeness, Irena's reluctance…. His eyes took in the guard standing at attention between him and Mihajlovich. *And the guard! He never has a guard with him. Everything is lost. I have accomplished nothing. Nothing. The files still sit in the basement … all he has to do is transfer….*

"Do you know what the date is, Berisha?"

"The twelfth, Colonel Mihajlovich." *Was that me? Did I answer so normally?*

"The twelfth … a day I shall remember…."

The metallic sound of the drawer being opened screamed at Skender, he took a step backward, pushed against the door, as far from his enemy as he could. A gun was in his back. He licked at his lips as he realized it was the door handle. *I could open it, slip inside, lock it … what good?* He was awash with despair. *Five, ten minutes maximum, before they broke down the door and then …*

Mihajlovich was speaking as he moved toward him, the blood-red emblem of flame reaching for a star waved at Skender as the paper in Mihajlovich's hand fluttered in a breeze from the open window. Skender brought his full powers of concentration to answer Mihajlovich's accusation.

"…Three guards will help you. After the operation is completed, you will initial this form, date it, and return it to Anna. She will then make a photocopy for Belgrade and put this, the original, in our files." He leaned down to Irena's desk and affixed his signature. "I have waited a long time for this. You, too, must feel some emotion…." His hand offered the Permission for Destruction of Files form to Skender. "It is almost like a burial for your friends."

Skender's lips were dry, unable to form the words, he licked at them, held out his hand. The paper shook, rattled, and he held it close against his leg.

"Can you start immediately?"

"Start?"

An inpatient frown flitted across Mihajlovich's face. "It is unusual for me to have to repeat myself to you. The furnace is ready. All the files must be burnt. It is hotter than hell down there and will get hotter as the day progresses…."

Dragonovich! This was why he was so amused! Relief flooded over Skender.

"… start immediately?"

"Yes, sir."

Mihajlovich's eyes traveled over Skender. "I suggest you get yourself some lightweight suits, Berisha." His voice was mild, rather bored. "You're perspiring."

Perspiring? Lightweight suits! Laughter threatened to burst, engulf him, and he fought for control. "I apologize … I will see to it within the next day or two, sir."

Mihajlovich nodded, turned to the guard. "Comrade Berisha will instruct you in your duties … until he is ready, you may wait here."

The slit of an envelope, the unfolding of a letter, normal, everyday sounds of office life were music, the soft click as Mihajlovich's door closed released Skender. "I will be with you in five minutes," he told the guard, turned briskly to Irena, "bring your book." He opened his door, closed it quietly as he leaned back against it.

The trembling started in his hands, spread rapidly over his body, he made his way drunkenly to his chair, fell into it and laid his arms on the desk, letting them form a pillow for his head. *Steady … steady. Take long, deep breaths … the danger has passed….*

"Come in." The knock had been timid, and he knew it was Irena. She gave a nervous glance at him as she sat down opposite, balanced the book on her knee, pencil poised, ready. He deliberately kept her waiting. "I wish to know why you hesitated, did not obey me, when I told you to bring your book." There was another nervous glance, but no reply. "Very well. Take your things and leave … I no longer require your services." He did not know if his authority would stretch that far but knew that he must be aware of the reason behind her actions. There was a splash as a tear fell on her book. "Good-bye, Irena."

The ruled paper bubbled as the tears fell faster, he swiveled his chair to face the window.

"Anna had given me some typing to do yesterday…." He swung back to face Irena; her voice was nervous, hesitant. "I had been busy all day with your dictation, and I was angry at having to stay late. I rushed…." Filled eyes rose to Skender's, "Anna did not check it, put it straight on Colonel Mihajlovich's desk." Sobs caught her breath. "It was so badly done."

"And Anna was blamed, is that it?"

The blonde head nodded vigorously. "He was terribly, terribly angry."

"Did Anna tell Colonel Mihajlovich that it was you who was at fault?"

"No," came on a whisper. "After Colonel Mihajlovich left the office, she told me I was to re-type it immediately, that nothing was to come before that."

"And then I ordered you to take dictation, and you did not know what to do first, was that it?" Skender's eyes closed at her nod. *Dragonovich, Anna, Irena, simple explanations for all of them and their actions. An explanation, even, for the guard with Mihajlovich. My own sense of danger, guilt, fear, magnified all, made each larger than it was….*

"I am so sorry, Comrade Berisha … please do not terminate me."

"Rarely are you asked to work late … I have never known Anna ask you for help before this, and I am appalled at the way you behaved. You will apologize to Anna, and then you will go to Colonel Mihajlovich and tell him the truth." Her eyes, round with horror, rose to his as her lips formed the words, 'I can't.'

"I insist. Anna cannot shoulder blame that is due to you and your carelessness. Your actions almost caused me to … caused me great inconvenience. Do not let it happen again." He opened his briefcase. "Let us get to work … three copies, one for Colonel Mihajlovich, one on file, one for me. First draft of a speech to be presented to the University of Pristina students at a date to be decided by Colonel Mihajlovich…."

Skender handed the signed Permit to Anna. "Thank you Comrade Berisha. Colonel Mihajlovich wishes to see you."

"Let me clean up first."

She glanced up at him, smiled at the dirt-streaked face. "Yes, perhaps that would be better." There was a slight hesitation. "Let me get you something cool to drink … you look exhausted."

Skender sat down on her chair while she was gone. The basement room had been a hell that he had not minded, the heat that leapt out at them every time they opened the furnace door to add more files had singed eyebrows and hair, and each time he had welcomed it. Now he was exhausted, physically and mentally drained.

"Here you are."

The glass was frosty, he salivered as the rivulets of water ran down the cold glass, the ice cubes knocked with delicate precision against the sides of the glass. "Ice?" Where did you manage to find that?" He took a long drink. "Nectar!" She smiled, watched as he downed it to the last drop, then shook an ice cube into his mouth. "What was it?" he asked, chasing an ice cube with his tongue.

"Lemon-barley water. Colonel Mihajlovich drinks it all summer … it is very refreshing."

He pulled hard on the ice, the cold trickle a stream to his parched throat, the coldness a joy. "Where did you get ice?"

"There is a small refrigerator built into the cabinets in his office." Her eyes indicated the door to Mihajlovich's room. "He is not here, but I do not think he would mind."

"That was very kind of you, Anna." Skender stood, handed her the glass. "Thank you." Their eyes met, held for a moment, then they smiled at each other. "I had better try to clean up, make myself presentable … shall we say, ten minutes?"

Anna watched as he left, jacket slung over one shoulder, she felt Irena's eyes and turned abruptly away. "I hope you have finished his work … he will want it on his desk when he returns." Her voice had been sharper than necessary and she softened it by adding, "Colonel Mihajlovich stepped out for a moment only … we do not want to anger him again by making him wait, do we?"

A photocopy of the Permit lay on Mihajlovich's desk, Skender's signature that the work had been completed immediately underneath Mihajlovich's authorizing that the destruction of the designated files was to be undertaken.

"Come in, Berisha … I see that the work has been completed." His hand indicated the signed Permit.

"Yes, sir."

"And all the files – every one – have been burnt?"

Satisfaction filled Skender. "Yes. Every one."

Mihajlovich smiled, nodded toward the chair. "That pleases me." Skender sat down, pleasurably watching Mihajlovich's pleasure. "You did a good job, finished sooner than I anticipated."

"We did not stop, not even for a moment."

"It must have been unbearable down there?"

"Yes. It was. I have given the men permission to take a break."

"Why?"

Skender's amazement jerked his head up. "They were exhausted, needed a little time to clean up, get something to drink, some food." He glanced at his watch. "We started shortly after nine this morning, and now it is almost four…."

"They could have completed their duty hours. Another hour or so without food would not have hurt them." Skender did not answer. "Why should it bother you whether they were exhausted or not? I would not give a damn if they dropped dead at my feet. You have even less cause to worry about their health." The silence stretched. "I would like an answer."

"They are human, have feelings and emotions…."

"You would not have said so a few months ago." A small smile played about Mihajlovich's mouth as he sat back, eyes on Skender. "But then, there have been many changes in you … there is no hesitation when you enter this building, no more nervousness."

"I would prefer to drop this topic."

"Very well. First of all, congratulations on a job well done and quickly done. Now to this." He picked up the typed draft of Skender's speech. "Come, Berisha, this slop is not you. Give this speech and your audience will be asleep before the second paragraph!" He tossed the sheet of paper toward Skender. "Re-write it … put some fire – some drive – into it."

Skender inclined his head, swallowed his sigh. He was tired, his eyes heavy and sore from exposure to heat all day. He wished Mihajlovich would finish with him so that he could go to his own office and relax. "It will be on your desk tomorrow morning."

"Good." Mihajlovich stood, stretched slightly, then walked to the window. "We had a problem in town today." He leaned forward to watch someone on the street below. "The first hot weather frays tempers quicker than usual."

"What was the problem?" Even to his own ears he sounded disinterested.

"The students demonstrated at the gymnasium."

"I am not surprised. Did you expect them to sit quietly while you sent one of their teachers to almost certain death?"

"The sentence was just … he broke the law."

Skender's eyes closed, his voice was tired, listless. "It was a book of poetry, Colonel Mihajlovich, not some political masterpiece."

Mihajlovich turned from the window. "The language was Albanian. He was arrested for that, not the content. But you know that … what you do not know is that the demonstration became loud, unruly. It was necessary to send Dragonovich with a detachment of guards. There have been several arrests."

Skender had become alert at Mihajlovich's words, had pushed himself up into a straight sitting position. "The students are my responsibility, not Sergeant Dragonovich's."

"You were occupied with more important matters."

"Those arrested have been released, though?"

"No, they are in the main holding room." His hand stopped Skender as he started to stand. "You are not to sign their release."

"Why not?"

"Enthusiasm for revolt ebbs fast when young stomachs growl with hunger and throats dry like sandpaper from thirst. After a long night on a hard cement floor with no blanket, the tide will have made a complete turn. However…" he walked to the desk, sat down, "…there is one you will wish to see." He handed a typed list of names to Skender. "Half-way down." The name leapt from the page. "Your youngest cousin, correct?"

"Yes." He laid the paper down. "He has just turned seventeen."

"When he was brought in…?" Skender's impatience was obvious as Mihajlovich fiddled with the gold pen. Mihajlovich frowned. "You know as well as I that one of the guards has a grudge against you, does not care for you…."

"What have you done to him?"

"I have done nothing." He laid the pen down, sat back in his chair. "When this particular guard saw the name Berisha…" Mihajlovich's shoulders lifted, "he slapped him around a little."

The bulk of the guard was in Skender's eyes. He turned to the window, fighting for control as the slim boyishness of Besim replaced it. "Is he hurt?"

"I have suspended the guard for a couple of days, and I have decided to transfer him to some other region. There will never be peace between you and he."

"Then … how badly has he hurt the boy?"

"He will recover. No leather was used."

"That guard hardly needed it," Skender retorted in hot anger, "he is three times the size of the boy." Mihajlovich did not answer. "May I see him?"

"Of course."

"Where is he?"

"With the others." Mihajlovich waited until Skender had reached the door. "Berisha! Remember … the guard is mine. Breathe on him even…." The threat was not completed and Skender did not reply.

"Where is he?" Skender asked as he recognized one of Besim's friends. The silence stretched, their anger and disgust mirrored in their eyes. *I would have acted the same. I would have felt the same hatred; and I, too, would have refused to answer.* He sensed the watchfulness of the guard still standing at the cell door. "Where is my brother?" His voice was quiet, controlled, but authoritative. With silent contempt, one of the boys indicated the farther corner.

Someone had put a jacket under Besim's head. Skender knelt down, turned the averted face towards him. He swore softly. "He worked you over pretty well, didn't he?" His fingers were tender and light as he touched the swollen eyes, the cut lips. "Guard, bring me a bowl with cold water." He glanced up as he realized that the man had not moved, he half stood. "Do you wish me to repeat the order?" The guard hesitated, then, with a shrug, moved away.

"I did not cry out, brother." Skender had to bend his head to catch the mumbled words.

"It is of no matter…."

"He kept saying…."

Skender saw the congealed blood crack, the bright red flow start again. "It is not important…." Besim's agitation stopped Skender and he asked quietly, "Alright, what is it?"

"I did not cry out, my word, Skender." Besim's shaking hand staunched the flow of blood, the red stickiness staining, trickling down his fingers. Skender wordlessly warned him to silence as the guard reappeared, slopping the water as he moved through the cell toward Skender and Besim.

"Thank you. Put it here." The guard towered over Skender, made no attempt to leave, but stood looking down at Besim, hands on his hips. "You may go." The heavy black leather boots were ominously close to the boy's stomach, and memory brought a flood of fear. *They always choose the one most hurt, that is their way, their method.* There was a scrape as his boots moved on the cement and he altered his stance. Skender's fear leapt. "I said you may go." Still the man did not move. Skender firmly closed his lips over the pleas to be allowed to tend Besim, to cleanse the bloody face.

He glanced up, Besim was in danger, he could see it in the man's eyes, the greedy lick of his lips. "I suppose I had better clean this one up…." His voice was carefully non-committal. "Colonel Mihajlovich has expressed an interest … and I would not like to be the one to tell him that the prisoner is in no condition to answer his questions."

The guard continued to look down at Besim, then turned his attention to Skender. His lips pulled back into a grin, "Mihajlovich wants him, eh? Well, I'll wait my turn." He sauntered toward the cell door.

Skender's hands trembled as he took out a handkerchief and laid it in the water. *Jackal.* "Do not try to talk." He lifted the sopping handkerchief. "Let me tend you first. Once the congealed blood is removed it will be easier for you. Open." He guided the dripping handkerchief towards Besim's mouth. He saw that it was difficult for Besim. "That's enough … now, suck the water from the handkerchief." He gave Besim an encouraging smile, "Like your new nephew, you must be suckled. The half-smile tore at Skender, and he took longer than necessary to let the handkerchief soak in the water before turning back to face Besim and put the handkerchief in his mouth. "When your thirst is satisfied, I will wash your face." He looked around at the half-moon of boys watching, asked as he continued to soak the handkerchief and put it to Besim's mouth, "Was any other hurt?"

There was a long pause before one boy stepped forward, became the spokesman for all. "No."

"And all that were arrested are here? There are none…." He didn't want to alarm them, "…none being questioned?"

"None. We are all here. Only Besim was singled out for attention."

Skender nodded.

"Enough, thank you." Besim stopped Skender as he started to soak the handkerchief again.

"Now I will clean your face." He was careful as he wiped the cut lips, letting the water soak the hard blood before wiping it away. Skender sat back, he had done all he could. Besim's eyes, badly swollen, needed ice, but that was an impossibility.

His hands moved toward Besim's stomach, he knew where to look, what to search for even as he asked, "Where else, Besim? Abdomen?" There was a nod, he took a deep breath, asked hopefully, "His fist?"

"Yes."

"Good." *Not as much damage as a knee or a boot.* He remembered the panic, the fear, when hands had to examine the tender spot, had to push and check the extent of the damage done. "Besim, I am going to hurt you … make a fist, let your nails eat into your palms. Concentrate on that pain, that hurt…." He waited, saw Besim's hesitation, then his obedience. "Harder!" Skender's voice was sharp as his hands started to search, then, with one last check that Besim's fist was tightly closed, he pushed down.

"Aaaaahhh…."

Skender's fingers pushed, probed. "It's alright, finished, done." He sat back onto his heels, wiped his own perspiration from his brow, his lips, then wrung the handkerchief from the dark red water and wiped Besim's face. "You will hurt for a few days, but there is no damage."

"Skender, I must tell you … I had done nothing, nothing, to annoy him. We were all in line and he was checking our names, our identity cards. He swore when he saw mine, then said, 'So, you're a Berisha, eh? I would prefer the big fish, but you will do.' He ordered me from the line and took me downstairs…." Skender sat, head bent, as Besim fought to stay calm. "He took off his coat, rolled up his sleeves. 'Let's see if you are a man or a boy, shall we?' Then…" the puffed eyes looked up at Skender, "'this one is for … for your bastard brother.'" Besim's eyes dropped. "He kept on … and every time he'd say, 'Cry-out, boy cry-out. I can't make your bastard brother cry, but…."

Skender put his hand on Besim's shoulder. "Forgive me," he murmured.

"Forgive you?" Besim was puzzled.

Skender sighed, stood up. "I cannot authorize your release, not until tomorrow. Try to sleep." He turned to face the others. "It still gets very cold at night. Those who have jackets must take them off, lay them on the ground so that you have something to sleep on … the cold is more intense from the ground than the air around you. Huddle together in groups of five or six … when one starts to shiver, put him in the center and crowd him … let the heat generated by one body warm the next. Keep the groups close together."

"When will we be released?"

"I will be here tomorrow morning … the questioning is routine and then you will be allowed to leave." He let his eyes rest on each one in turn. "Remember, each of you is responsible for the other … tonight you are as one family." He bent and picked up the bowl of stained water. "Besim, take particular care. Stay well back from the bars, do not draw any attention to yourself." He held out his hand, gave an encouraging smile. "It is impossible for me to tell you how proud I am to call you brother. Until tomorrow."

He waited until the guard came, watched as he locked the cell door, and then fell into step with him as he walked back to his desk. "What time do you go off duty?" He did not want any other guard licking his lips over Besim.

"Six-thirty, Comrade."

Skender nodded. "I will be here at six. Goodnight, Comrade.

Chapter 47

"This gate has always been noisy. I have oiled it a dozen times since my return to Prishtine and still it squeaks … what do you suggest?"

The workman moved the gate forward, backward, his lips pursed and his head nodded as the gate obligingly squealed each time. "Hinges."

Exasperation closed Skender's eyes. "I know that, but why do they make that noise, and what can be done about it?"

"Bad. Need new ones."

It was the longest conversation they had had with the man and Skender grinned as his eyes met Babush's. "Fine. Then put on new hinges. Now…" he led the way back to the house, Babush following, sandwiching the workman between them, "you understand what I want done?" The workman's eyes closed briefly in answer. "I suggest we go together to purchase the stove…." Another silent agreement, "…and then I will leave the rest in your hands." The eyes agreed. Amusement and irritation blended in Skender. "The bathroom first and, after that, the kitchen." He smiled at the old fellow. "You are a man of few words, sir."

"Talk ain't necessary. Gate last?"

Skender's smile deepened. "Yes, gate last." He and Babush accompanied him up the path. "When shall we go to buy the stove?

The old fellow removed his white hat, scratched at his head while he thought, then smoothed his hair and replaced his hat. "Noon."

"Good." Skender opened the gate for him. "I will meet you today at noon. Good-bye, and thank you." The white hat nodded to both of them.

"What a character!" Skender marveled as he watched him walk up Ruga Lapit, he laughed as the grating sound came. "Even our gate has more to say than him!"

"Skender, the changes you plan are wonderful, but … not the gate."

Surprised, Skender turned. "Why not, Babush? It has driven us crazy for years … now we have an opportunity to correct it…."

"Not the gate … it is a part of us, a part of this family. As a baby, it blocked you, held you safely within this garden. It heralded the child returning from school, and its voice lifted the worry from my shoulders when you had been too long at Police Headquarters as a young boy. Its silence after you were taken was a mourning shared and felt by all. After your escape, it called to give us warning that the police were here again to search the house looking for you … it never let us down. And it welcomed my son home after so long an absence. Leave the gate; it has spoken well to us over the years, and I admit I would miss its grumpy good-bye as I leave my house, would feel a loss without its noisy welcome home."

Skender nodded, looked long at Babush. His voice shook a little as he murmured, "It shall stay as it is." He glanced at his watch. "I must hurry … good-bye, sir. I will see you tonight."

"Good-bye, Djali. Have a pleasant day." Babush watched Skender get into his car, waved, then turned and started back toward the house. The gate groaned and he turned back with a smile. "You have a good day, too, old friend."

"What is it, Dragonovich?"

Dragonovich moved with some hesitation toward Mihajlovich's desk as he heard the impatience in his voice. "I am sorry to disturb you, Colonel Mihajlovich, but it's about these travel permits…." Mihajlovich's incredulous stare stopped him, and he started to back out. "Perhaps I should not have troubled you…."

"You already have." Mihajlovich extended his hand for the papers. "Why are you bothering me with travel permits?"

Dragonovich's tobacco-stained fingers pointed, ran across the page. "Here … I thought it strange that two of the senior members of his family should wish to travel together." He relaxed as he saw he had Mihajlovich's attention. "This one, Jakup, travels quite regularly to Sarajevo in his line of work, but the other … never before."

Mihajlovich let himself lay back in his chair, eyes still on the handwritten requests. "Are there relatives there?"

"No, Colonel."

"Hmm." Mihajlovich frowningly studied the paper as if it could give him the answer. "It could be just a holiday."

"Three days, Colonel, that is all they have requested. A day to travel there, a day back … one day is all they have allowed themselves in Sarajevo."

"Yes." The contemplative tone accompanied the continued studying of the papers. "So that rules out pleasure. Then why? The elder would not take time from his work again so soon after his trip to Prizren, just to be a companion. It must be something important." The chair snapped upright as a decision was made. "Give them the permits and have Sarajevo keep an eye on them. Ask if they can find out what their interest in that area is." He paused, "Be diplomatic in your request … they will be in the Province of Bosnia, and that is outside of our jurisdiction." He handed the papers back, recognized that he had been too sharp with his officer. "Good work, Dragonovich." He nodded permission for Dragonovich to leave, his eyes followed the swagger of the man. *A pat on the head and he wags his tail. Sometimes you disgust me, but … at your job there is none better.*

He pushed the intercom button. "Berisha, I am due at Party Headquarters … is there anything you should brief me on? Good, I will enquire while I am there. By the way, we go to the University in a week. Learn your speech." He laughed. "Nerves are for fools, and you are not a fool. You will be fine, but if you feel more secure, you can carry your draft with you." He started to release the intercom button.

"Colonel Mihajlovich?"

"Yes?"

"I will need a little more time for lunch today … is that acceptable?"

"Yes, of course." He released the button, then after a moment pressed Dragonovich's. "Berisha has asked for some extra time for lunch … I would like to know why. No, I have no suspicion, but this is the first time he has asked. Coming as it does after his cousins' requests for travel permits … just check on him."

"He was buying a what?"

"A machine for washing clothes, Colonel Mihajlovich." Dragonovich waited, wanting his next announcement to have full impact. "I understand he is doing extensive renovating in his house. There are plans for the bathroom to be extended to include a shower. The kitchen is to be equipped with a gas stove." Mihajlovich's reaction warranted the work he had put in during the afternoon. "And then he has purchased the machine for washing clothes."

Frowningly, Mihajlovich rubbed at his lower lip. "That's strange."

"Are you going to question him about it, Colonel Mihajlovich?"

Mihajlovich considered for some time. "No, I don't think so. Let us wait, perhaps the answer will surface of its own accord."

The week had been busy. The gate had been carefully removed and laid on its side on their path so that the new appliances could enter more easily. Babush had brought a chair from the house and sat watching every move made by the workmen. Meantime, the sun had gone to work on Babush, and he looked tanned and well.

Nona and Drita hovered around the window, dodging out of sight when the men happened to glance up and, as soon as they left, descended to the kitchen to stare round-eyed with happiness and wonder at the new machines. Skender had wanted to remove the old black iron stove, but Nona was adamant. "It and I entered this house at almost the same moment … it stays." Drita let her hands wander with loving appreciation over the washer, marveling that such a machine could handle all kinds of laundry in so short a time, that it could 'think and decide for itself how much water was to be used.' She listened in half disbelief as Skender told her that there were also machines to wash dishes, pots and pans.

The head workman had turned out to be a jewel, speaking little, but demanding perfection from his crew. When Skender had asked if he would paint the kitchen when he was through with the plumbing and fixtures, his eyes had closed and the one word, 'Color?' had escaped from his mouth.

Now the kitchen was finished. It was clean, bright, and cheerful in palest yellow. Nurije had made new curtains for the window of a slightly deeper shade, embroidered in black and white, the 'B' for Berisha and the double-headed eagle carefully worked into the design so that only minute inspection would bring it to attention. The sheepskin rugs had been washed, stretched, and dried in the hot afternoon sun, and their black and white colors were sharp and clear on the oiled wood floor. The flour bin remained unpainted, the wood smooth and almost white from repeated scrubbing. The gas stove waited, new and virginal, against the old iron wood-burning one, which had been blackened and polished until it gleamed.

Skender stood, hands on hips, surveying it with pleasure. He smiled a welcome to Nona and Drita, put his arms around their shoulders. "Well? Do you like it?"

"'Like' is the wrong word, Skender … it is a joy, it will be a pleasure to work here."

He squeezed Nona to him. "Drita?" She bit her lip, eyes glowing, and he did not need an answer. He let them go. "I am going to join Babush … he is supervising that the gate is attached correctly. He walked the length of the path, deeply content. Babush smiled a welcome to him. "Your gate is in place again, sir. Now that the workmen are gone, your house will return to its normal calm and quiet state."

"Yes, Djali." Babush closed the gate, smiled as it gave its usual complaint. "You have done a wonderful thing. I cannot believe that there is such luxury as a heater in our bathroom. And your mother and sister are delirious with joy … I am not sure which new toy excites them most."

Skender smiled back at him, bent his knees slightly with the old man to peer into the kitchen window, their eyes met as they saw Drita filling the washer. Babush chuckled. "Not even a sock will be allowed to remain dirty!" He straightened, then put his arm around Skender's shoulders. "At this moment, I feel as if you have never been away, that it was all a dream."

"I know. Sometimes as I walk the streets of Prishtine, I ask myself, 'Was I ever gone? Was it all some strange, complicated nightmare?'" He sighed. "At others, 'Am I here? Breathing this air, feeling this earth?'" His smile was strained as he looked at Babush. "When dreams and reality start to touch, intertwine, is it the beginning of madness?"

Compassion for his son filled Babush. "It is a madness felt by all at some time in their lives, Djali … some to a lesser degree than others." He squeezed Skender's shoulder. "Enough of this! Let us see if this new-fangled stove can make coffee as well as the old one … a pouch of tobacco it cannot!"

"Done!" Skender pushed the heaviness away. "You will lose, you know."

Babush laughed as he shook his head. "I know my stove, and I know my wife … it will be a while before she admits that the new one can work as well as the old. Come, Djali." They kicked off their nalle and entered the kitchen.

Mihajlovich signaled Dragonovich to silence as the phone rang. "Mihajlovich here." He sat back, smiling. "How are you, Alex?" Then, he mouthed to Dragonovich, 'Sarajevo', before continuing with Alex, "Yes, I am very well. Everything is fine here, although I do not like it this hot so early in the year. How are you and your family? Good. And what is new in Sarajevo?" He nodded. "It is about the same here … a few agitators, a few followers…" he laughed, "…but then, Bosnia is not such a hotbed as Kosovo."

He sat listening, smiling, and nodding, agreeing sometimes, "Yes, that is correct, I did want some information on them." He stilled, listening intently, "Are you sure of that? Yes, of course. I understand that you cannot give me proof, but you feel confident … no, no, on the contrary, the news pleases me. Alex, I have not seen you for months. I plan on attending the Party Conference in Belgrade … will you be going? Yes, let us hope so. Thank you for calling. Good-bye." A knowing smile played about his lips as he replaced the phone and looked at Dragonovich. "Well, well … it seems that the two Berishas were in Sarajevo on business. That was Alexander Kulich … you know who he is?"

"Yes, Colonel Mihajlovich, Deputy Director, Head of Udba's Bosnia region."

Mihajlovich nodded. "It appears that the two young men were in Sarajevo to…" he laughed softly, "…to quietly make enquiries about a young lady. Listen to this … she is the daughter, the only daughter of one of the leading families. She has been very carefully brought up, left school early, and had a private tutor. Her education has been of the highest. It is rumored that she is exquisitely beautiful, as delicate as bone china." He smiled at Dragonovich, "And, one of the neighbors is a talker…" he sat forward, leaning across the desk to Dragonovich, "…and the talk is that there has been an enquiry for the girl's hand. From a very highly regarded and old, established family. In Pristina. For the oldest son." He laughed softly at the expression on Dragonovich's face. "Does that give you any idea, Dragonovich? Does that lead you to anyone in particular?"

"But…" Dragonovich's eyes went to the inter-office door, "he is married."

"His wife is far from here … she may as well be on the moon as where she is. And there is no child, Dragonovich. No child means he can divorce her immediately."

"Why a girl from another province? Why Bosnia? Why not Kosovo?"

Mihajlovich's shoulders lifted lazily. "I can only guess, but by taking a girl from Sarajevo, he reduces the risk of her having overheard her brothers talking of him, and of his working for me." He smiled as he rubbed at his lower lip. "She is very young … nineteen."

Dragonovich's answering smile was oily. "A tender age!"

"Yes," Mihajlovich smiled back, "very tender … easily led, easily trained."

Dragonovich frowned suddenly. "Don't you find it a little…" Mihajlovich's eyebrows rose and he wished he had kept silent. He licked at his lips as he realized that Mihajlovich was waiting for him to continue, "I was just surprised, that is all."

"Why? Please finish…" Mihajlovich's hand moved, "you were saying, 'Don't you find it a little…' …a little what?"

Dragonovich wriggled uncomfortably. "Strange."

"No, not really." The gold pen flashed in the sun as Mihajlovich's fingers twisted it. "The old man has a lot of influence on him. His only daughter is engaged to the Mali boy, and once she leaves their home, the work will fall on the mother. It is the oldest son's duty to take that load from her, to provide a younger, stronger person to handle the workload."

Dragonovich leered, "It is his duty to provide heirs, too."

Mihajlovich laughed, "Exactly!"

"Do you think he will be willing?"

"Do you think he could refuse?" Mihajlovich asked softly. He smiled as he sat back in his chair. "If the girl is as delightful as Alex suggests," he gave a slow nod, "there will be a child in less than a year of their marriage."

"This news pleased you, Colonel?"

"Yes. Yes, it does. By taking a wife…" he stopped suddenly, "that explains the re-modeling, the new stove and washer. Yes. He is planning to be married, and by accepting a girl reared in their way, with their traditions, it confirms that he is settled and prepared to stay in Kosovo. He plans to stay here, Dragonovich!" He laughed with delight. "Tomorrow we go to the University … if he can sway them, bring us an increase in membership … yes! The experiment will have proved successful." He stood up, paced the floor. "Every province will be represented at the Conference…." He wheeled to face Dragonovich, "I shall present my success to them … there is a pattern for all to follow. Our leaders will hear, and….” He stood tall, hands clenched at his sides.

Dragonovich pushed himself upright. “It will be a great day for you, Colonel Mihajlovich.”

“For us, Dragonovich, for us,” Mihajlovich corrected him. “If promotion comes to me…” he smiled as he dismissed his officer. “But let us not heat the pan when the fish is still in the sea.”

Babush stifled a yawn. “I am going to leave you two young men together … my bed calls me.”

Skender and Aslan stood as he did, gave a slight bow. “Goodnight, sir,” they murmured.

Aslan waited until the door closed on Babush and Skender had resumed his seat. “Did you write the letter to Gillian?” he asked as he sat down opposite Skender.

“No.” The answer was short, terse. Skender felt the silent rebuke. “It is not an easy thing to do.” His anger was climbing, “What the hell do you expect me to say to her? ‘Dear Jill, thank you for two good years, but please be advised that our marriage is over. I am about to become engaged to a very beauti….”

“Stop it.”

“Why? Does it offend your sensibilities, Aslan? Skender gave a mock bow. “I am sorry. Let us hope Gillian is not as sensitive.” He half-turned, almost turning his back to Aslan.

“We both know that she will be hurt.”

He swung to face Aslan. “I … Aslan, it is I who knows how deep, how painful, this wound will be for her, not you.” He picked up a pack of cigarettes lying on the floor near him, his voice quiet as he continued, “And it is I, her husband, who must take the knife, plunge it….” His hand shook as he selected a cigarette. “I am sorry … this is not a subject I can discuss calmly.”

In silence, Aslan offered his lighter and then accepted a cigarette. “Brother, forgive my insistence, but the letter must be written. You have delayed a week now. The family are waiting to make the announcement, but the letter severing your marriage must be sent before that can happen.”

“I know.” He pulled deeply on his cigarette. “I have tried … God, how I have tried … the words run in my brain, but my hand will not put them on paper.”

“You are imposing an unnecessary strain on yourself by delay. You know that the letter must be written.”

They smoked in silence for a while. “Tomorrow, Aslan.” He saw his brother’s skepticism. “You have my word.” He stubbed out the cigarette. “I hope you do not find me ungrateful … I do appreciate your efforts on my behalf."

"I have done nothing. Jakup alone deserves the credit. It was he who made the arrangements … I only confirmed them." Skender nodded. Aslan put his arm across Skender's shoulders. "She will be an asset to our family … we will be proud to accept her and have her carry our name, brother."

Skender nodded. "Jakup says she is very beautiful."

"Yes."

"And brave. It is not easy to…." His hand wiped at his lips. "I hope to God we are doing the right thing." Aslan did not answer, Skender's eyes lifted searching Aslan's. "Are you as sure as Jakup that this is right?"

"Yes."

Skender nodded. "Then if it is meant, may it be with happiness."

"Amen." Aslan stood briskly. "It is late, I must go home, Skender."

"I will take you to the gate." Skender brushed Aslan's denial away. He slipped on a pair of the nalle lying neatly together at the top of the steps, and together they walked the length of the path.

"Natën e mirë, Skender." Aslan's grip was firm, reassuring. "Do not worry … all will be well." He turned back as he was about to pass through the gate. "Tomorrow, brother," he warned.

Skender nodded. "Natën e mirë, Aslan." He closed the gate and turned toward the house. The air was soft and calm, the stars indistinct in the dark blueness of the sky. A falling star caught his attention and he paused to watch … 'You can wish on a falling star, you know.' Jill's voice was as clear as if she were standing beside him.

He sighed, climbed the steps, kicked off the nalle and left them lying haphazardly where they fell, then closed the door on the stars.

"Good morning, Anna." She smiled as she returned his greeting. "Good morning, Irena. I want a bottle of green ink, please."

"Certainly, Comrade Berisha."

Skender walked into his office, dropped the briefcase on the floor beside his desk and opened the window, he reached his hand between the bars and touched the leaf of the tree, turned his head as he heard the door open. "Yes, Irena?"

"We do not have green ink, Comrade Berisha, so I brought you a bottle of bla…."

"I want green … if there is none in stock, send to the stationers on the corner for some." She nodded, backed out of the room. He had barely sat down when the door opened again.

"Good morning, Berisha. I wanted to remind you that we go to the University today. Did you remember to bring your speech?"

Skender had risen as Mihajlovich entered the room. "Yes, sir." He hesitated. "Colonel Mihajlovich, I beg you to release me from this…."

"Show it to me." Mihajlovich sat down as Skender reluctantly took the papers from his briefcase. "My order stands, Berisha. You will give the speech." He glanced over it, confirmed it was the one he'd approved. "Have you learned it?"

Skender sighed. "Yes. But I would prefer to carry the draft."

Mihajlovich watched him for a long moment. "Still nervous? There is no need. The police will be there to quell any troublemakers." He handed the speech back to Skender, gave permission for him to sit down.

"Some group calling itself the International League of Churches or some such thing is touring the Eastern Bloc countries. They are in Bulgaria now and will enter Yugoslavia next week. They will cross the border at Skopje and stay there three days. Then they are coming here." He gave an ironic smile. "Yes, I was as shocked as you. I thought Belgrade had made a mistake and called them … it seems some fool official routed them through Pristina in error, and now it is too late to correct it. This group is hot fired to see the capital of Kosovo and its mosques. We can do no other but accept them and make them as comfortable as we can. Contact the Hotel Bozor and instruct them to have the best rooms made available. They can take their meals there, too.

"Tell Dragonovich to double his force and put down any demonstration immediately." He sighed, "I wish they weren't coming. Your knowledge of languages will come in useful. I understand we have a glorious medley of representatives from different countries, probably not one of which understands the other! What an exciting and stimulating holiday … dragging from one musty religious museum to the next."

"Do I understand that you will wish me to look after them?"

"Yes. I have no desire to meet with them, and I hardly think an official from Party Headquarters is fitting." A slight frown creased his brow as he saw that Skender had not caught his meaning. "A Party Official conducting a group from church to church, mosque to mosque?"

"There are no mosques open to drag them to, unless they just wish to admire from the outside."

"Damn! I had forgotten! Get the keys from…" his eyes lifted, "who has the keys?"

"I would not know, sir. They were locked after the Communist…." There was barely a pause, "…liberation." Mihajlovich glanced sharply at Skender, but his face was smooth and serious. "However, I do not see why we should concern ourselves as to where the keys are … this International Group can stand outside and see all there is to see."

"One or two must be unlocked. They have been told there is religious freedom here, so they must see that there is for themselves."

Skender's lips curled and he asked sarcastically, "In a warehouse sir? Or a stable?"

"Dammit! Which one is in the best condition?" Skender's shoulders lifted non-commitally. "The mill is storing flour in one," he frowningly mused, "and the blue-domed one…." He looked up at Skender, "It is the blue one that is being used as a stable, isn't it?" Skender nodded. "We would never get the smell out in time."

"The blue one was the loveliest and is the most well-known. It would take a lot of work, but perhaps…."

"See what you can do. I want at least two open before they get here."

"Yes, sir."

"Take as many men as you need. If you can't get finished in time, find out where the keys to the others are and open them. Attend to it immediately."

"Yes, Colonel Mihajlovich. One problem presents itself to my mind sir." He waited for the nod to continue, "When it is seen that the mosque is open … even after eighteen-twenty years, there will be some who will enter."

"Hmm," Mihajlovich considered, rubbing at his lower lip. "All the better! In fact, we will make a radio announcement that two of the mosques will be open to the public for … a month … and that no repercussions will be felt by those entering." He nodded, "Yes, it will give a better impression if there are people inside when this group visits. See to it. and then…" he sighed, "come in."

Papers flew as the door opened, Skender dove to retrieve them, laying his body across them to anchor them to the desk. "The window, Irena, quickly."

She glanced nervously at Mihajlovich as she passed him, put the ink on the desk and moved to the window. Their eyes watched as she reached to close it, followed as she left the room, then both smiled. "Our thoughts were quickly taken from churches and mosques," Skender said softly, his smile deepening.

Mihajlovich nodded, "It makes me happy that she pleases you … that was what I was hoping for." He gave a soft laugh as he saw Skender's astonishment. "There are others with nimbler fingers than she, but without the…." He paused, smile deepening, "Let us say, her other attributes." He stood up. "See what you can do about the mosques … I would like this church group to be favorably impressed." He strolled toward the door, called back, "We will leave for the University at two-thirty. We will take my car." The steady tap of the typewriter sounded as he opened the door and Mihajlovich glanced back at Skender, smiled, and mouthed, 'Enjoy!'

Skender laughed as he shook his head in mock despair. "Two-thirty". The door closed on him.

Skender had finished dictating and his desk was fairly clear. The bottle of ink drew his eyes repeatedly, and eventually he sighed, took out his pen, and emptied it of the black ink. He pulled the bottle towards him, opened it, and sat looking into the pool of greenness. Carefully, he filled his pen, letting it fill and empty several times so that all the black was washed out. He pressed the intercom button. "Irena, no phone calls, no disturbances for an hour." He opened the left-hand drawer and took out some blank white paper, settled himself comfortably.

'Jill, my love…'

He was very still, letting memories take him, allowing himself to relive their lives together…

When you read this, I want you to be alone, sitting in the big chair in your room that you have told me of so often. It is late spring, so your window will be open a little, curtain billowing softly. You see, I remember, I remember so much of us, of you, and that makes this letter the more difficult.
Our dreams took us, sustained us during these months, but the reality of life presses on me, and possibly on you, and it is impossible for me to continue to find fulfillment in the myth of 'one day.'
The girl is not from here. She is from another town, another Republic even, about one hundred and fifty miles distant from Prishtine. Jill, my dearest love, try to understand. Do not lay the blame for this on Babush. There was pressure from my family, but not from that source. And it was I who made the final decision.
Remember the special times, the sweetness of our marriage, and put this bitterness from you as quickly as you can. Let your mind dwell on the happiness shared, the secret things that amused us.
Sadness fills me … how much simpler to explain if I had you within sight of my eyes. So much simpler. So much harder.
There is no more to add. Shed your tears … let them wash away any anger or disappointment you may feel at me.
Good-bye, my love….
Skender

Mihajlovich folded the letter back into its original crease, pushed it into the envelope and sealed it. He turned, handed it to the guard. "Return it to the post office and let it proceed."

Chapter 48

The Great Hall of the University was crowded, the left-hand side solid with the white hats of the Kosovars, while the right had the bare heads of the Yugoslavian students. Blue-grey uniforms were everywhere, lining each wall, the guards watchful and sharp.

Skender followed Mihajlovich onto the stage, felt the hostile silence reach out to him from his own as sporadic applause was given to Mihajlovich. A lectern stood at the front of the stage, slightly off center, along one side of the stage a row of chairs, some occupied. The Dean rose and hurried forward to greet them, Mihajlovich instructed Skender to stay where he was while he met the faculty. Skender let his eyes run over the assembled students, his stomach closed in a vice grip as he saw, recognized Emin, and was ignored.

"Berisha." Mihajlovich indicated that Skender should sit with the staff while he spoke to the students. There was a pause while Mihajlovich checked the hall, two guards at the foot of the steps on each side of the stage, two on each side of the swing doors, one every five feet against the walls. Dragonovich gave an almost imperceptible nod from his vantage point at the back, and then Mihajlovich mounted the lectern.

Skender listened. It was a good speech, well written, amusing, and witty at times to relieve the boredom of facts, compelling and authoritative at others. Skender sighed, and with reluctant admiration, admitted that it was appealing and whetted the appetite, unless one had strong anti-Communist feelings, you could be swayed into joining the Party.

"Pristina has buzzed with rumors of all sizes, but none has lasted so long, or made as much noise, as the one concerning Skender Berisha." Skender started, his eyes flew to Mihajlovich. "As you can see, it is not rumor … it is fact. He is working for Udba, he is working for me." He waited for the students to quieten. Skender moved, uncomfortably aware of the stares.

"You, the youth, are the first to be officially given this information. It is you, the youth, who are important, not the old ones. Leave them to their rusty thoughts, their outmoded and outdated ideals, and join the youth of the world in their quest for freedom, for peace." Mihajlovich paused. "Step forward to tomorrow … leave yesterday behind, for it is as dry as dust. Any student wishing to join and become one of this great international brotherhood may do so now … enroll in the Party. We are waiting to welcome you."

The swing doors were fastened open, exposing the long trestle tables that lined the hall, each with two students armed with forms, pens and membership cards.

Mihajlovich approached the Dean and his staff, hand extended. "It was a pleasure to accept your invitation to speak here … the rest does not concern you and you are free to leave." Their faces registered shock at the abrupt dismissal, there had been no recognition of them at all, no acknowledgement to the students that their teachers were even present.

Mihajlovich strode to the front of the stage. The white hats were still thick and solid, a few bare heads remained on the right-hand side. "Any, other than Kosovar students, may leave." He waited, hands clasped behind his back, loosely, with no strain. He let his eyes travel leisurely over those that remained, a slight irritation pricked at him when they returned his gaze with steady eyes. "Comrade Berisha will now address you." The gasp soothed him and he turned with a smile, beckoned Skender. "Comrade Berisha." His hand offered him the floor.

Mouth, throat, were dry, legs seemed unable to support and the silence beat against his ears. He saw Mihajlovich's smile fade, his eyes narrow, and pushed himself from the chair.

"Use the lectern," Mihajlovich instructed as they passed each other.

The draft still lay on the chair, forgotten. As he reached the steps of the lectern, he remembered, and knew that he would be unable to recall the speech. He turned and made his way back, Mihajlovich's eyes on him all the way. He bent and picked up the draft. "Colonel Mihajlovich…." His appeal was coldly, silently denied. He sighed, picked up the papers and moved again toward the lectern.

He forced his feet to take the two steps, laid the draft on the sloping board. Hostile eyes watched in silence his every move; he gripped the edges so that they would not see his hands tremble and lifted his head. The big swing doors were closed again, Dragonovich nearby. With fewer students, there appeared to be more blue-greyness in the room, the blue-grey and white hats blurred, swam together …

He cleared his throat, looked down at the speech. "Colonel Mihajlovich has spoken to you at length on the benefits to be obtained from joining the Communist Party…." His voice was shaking, he could hear it, "…and there is little, in fact nothing, for me to add…."

"Then don't! Hold your tongue!"

The interruption had been yelled and unnerved him even more. He licked at his lips, wished there was some water. "Nothing for me to add to what he has told you, but he has asked me to address you, and…."

"Are you working for him? Is it the truth or not?" The shout came from a different part of the hall.

Skender took a long breath. "Yes, I would not be here if it were not."

"Better if you weren't … better for you to have died along with the others. You are a traitor…." There was a sudden movement, and the yelling student disappeared. The guards moved immediately, closing in and encircling the two who rolled on the floor, exchanging blows and obscenities.

"Separate them and bring them here," Mihajlovich ordered from the front of the stage.

The heavy boots kicked out, the soft thud as they landed on target, sounding even to those on stage. Their arms were pulled back and handcuffs applied. Skender closed his eyes for a moment, remembering how they could be tightened to bite into flesh and leave it raw and bleeding.

"Bring them here."

The students parted, making a path as the guards pushed the two forward. Skender paled as he saw it was Emin, the other was unknown to him. Their eyes met for a moment, then, very deliberately, Emin turned away.

"You brawl as two alley cats … do you consider this conduct worthy of university students? Which of you had the audacity to interrupt a member of my staff?" He waited, but there was no response from either. "Take them away."

"Colonel Mihajlovich … please?" Skender's voice was low. Mihajlovich signaled the guards to wait. "One is my brother."

Mihajlovich frowned, rubbed at his lip. "Hold them for interrogation by Comrade Berisha. No questioning, no interference until that time."

"Thank you, sir."

Mihajlovich gave a brief nod. "Are you ready to continue?"

"I don't think I can make them listen to me." Skender was ready to admit defeat.

"Insist. Raise your voice. Make them." He looked long at Skender, the repeated warningly, "Make them." He turned to the students. "Silence!" There was another long look at Skender before he returned to his chair.

Skender mounted the lectern. "I will now answer the question … yes, I am working for Comrade Mihaj…."

"What will happen to your cousin?"

"Yes! What will happen to Emin?"

"And Jusuf … what of him?"

There was pandemonium. Skender gave a helpless glance toward Mihajlovich, who sat, ankles crossed, studying the ceiling. "After I have questioned them…" he raised his voice, "…they will be released." Chortles of laughter stopped him.

He took another long breath. "They will be released, and unharmed…." Derisive hoots brought him to a standstill again, and again he turned to Mihajlovich and was still ignored.

He stood in silence; head bowed. Mihajlovich had been clever. He had managed to discredit Skender whatever the outcome. If he had been able to make them listen, they would have despised him. If not … then the dignity and respect accorded to his family were gone, the Berisha name smeared.

His head lifted, half the audience had turned their backs to him, while the rest chatted among themselves, and he stood watching them, feeling estranged and lost. He started to gather the papers together, prepared to go to Mihajlovich and admit defeat. *No! I am one of them….*

"Fellow Kosovars, listen to me." The sudden switch to Albanian electrified the room and brought immediate silence. All faced him. "We are a unique people. Descendent of the Ilyria ns, who were the first to come to this land we call Europe. Love of our land, our customs and traditions is what binds us…."

"How dare you! What do you think you are doing?" Mihajlovich was beside Skender, shaking with anger.

"Colonel Mihajlovich, unless I address them in our own language, all is lost. All was lost … now you can hear a pin drop. Order me to speak Serbo-Croatian and … you saw what happened." He saw Mihajlovich wavering. "You have read my speech, could follow on this draft if you choose."

Mihajlovich ignored the outstretched papers as he weighed and outweighed the benefits. "Continue. But be careful, Berisha, make sure it is the speech I approved." Skender gave a slight bow. Mihajlovich hesitated, then returned to the row of chairs.

"Colonel Mihajlovich has given me permission to continue in Albanian," Skender said with a slight incline of his head toward Mihajlovich, he had spoken in Serbo-Croatian, but continued in Albanian: "I have also been warned to stay with the speech approved by him." He held up the draft. The buzz of conversation had quieted to silence as Skender started to speak. He let his eyes travel over them. "There is not one among you who has not suffered at their hands … if not you, then your immediate family has someone who has felt their cruelty, screamed at their torture, gone mad under their atrocities."

"As a youth, I stood against them, openly as you do, and as did your brothers, fathers, cousins. How far have we advanced in these seventeen years? Are we even one step nearer our goal of freedom? If you can assure me that we have taken even one pace toward that dream, then I say the agony suffered, the deaths of your kinsmen, was well worth the price. You cannot give me that assurance. I, returning here after such a long absence, can see more clearly than you that we have been at a standstill."

"Your demonstrations are courageous but accomplish nothing. Your defiance of them brave, but useless." A slight cough was a thunderclap in the attentive room. He came down the steps of the lectern, smiled and gave an encouraging nod to Mihajlovich, then went to the front of the stage. "We stand alone. Accept that. If the western world hears of your demonstration, your defiance, they pause and fleetingly admire your stand against your oppressors ... and then they go about their daily lives." There was a murmur of disagreement, of disbelief."

"Look to the tragedy of Budapest in 1956 if you doubt my words. Their agony could be heard, their tears seen ... yet their cry for help went unheeded. Their hands stretched out for help and the west could see that hand, touch it, yet they were ignored. We are buried deep inside Yugoslavia, our cry is faint, our suffering not seen. How can you expect a favorable reaction from the Western world? How can you anticipate any help?"

"Do you suggest we give in? Submit?"

"Never!" Skender's answer was prompt, sure. "But do not pit soft flesh against hard metal. Do not throw away a life in a useless gesture of selfish heroism."

"What do you suggest? That we all work for Mihajlovich? Join you in service to the Party?" There was a ripple of ironic laughter.

Skender realized that Mihajlovich would have caught some of that, signaled the questioner to wait, and then turned to Mihajlovich, he spoke quietly. "I have their interest, sir ... they are asking questions. Do you wish me to continue?" Mihajlovich nodded, "Very well." He turned back to face the students and reverted to Albanian. "Yes. In fact, not only do I suggest that you become members of the Party, I insist that you must."

He held up his hands, asking for silence as the roar of anger surged through the hall. "Has any Kosovar ever been permitted to speak before this? If I were not working for Colonel Mihajlovich..." a slight acknowledgement of Mihajlovich, "...would I be allowed to address you? We do not need your demonstrations. We do not need your arrogant defiance. We need you in government, in the police, in medicine, in law." His voice was quieter as he continued, "If there was one, just one guard, who was a Kosovar, could he not protect when his own were arrested?" He paused as he heard the murmured agreement. "What if there was an officer?" He waited, letting the seed germinate.

"When your mother or father requires medical attention, they must wait until all of 'them' are attended: no matter how long the wait, no matter how great the need. What if there was one, just one, doctor who was from our own?" He saw the swift, silent agreement. "In the courts, our sentences are the heaviest; but then who defends us, who fights our battle? Would the story change if the lawyer were on of ours?"

It was as if the whole room held its breath.

"We are not permitted into any of these positions."

"You could be," Skender answered the disembodied voice, "if you join the Party." Anger swept through the hall, a few fists were raised, then shaken at him. "I understand your anger, but am I asking too much? Is it too great a sacrifice?"

"Yes!"

"Too great!"

"You ask too much!"

Skender waited patiently, let them have their say, voice their anger.

When they were quiet he continued, "I thought so too … in the beginning. I viewed it as the worst, the lowest thing, I could do; but now … the realization has come that this is the only path for us. It is a stepping-stone to free ourselves from their stranglehold. If you refuse to use that stepping-stone, you condemn yourselves and your children … and possibly their children … to the same life as your father and your grandfather. You sentence them to the same beatings, the same degradation."

"Let us examine what we give up by joining the Party – a little pride." He smiled, "We are Kosovars, so perhaps more than a little!" Their laughter included him, warmed him. "Maybe a principle or two. It does not affect our dignity as men. It does not affect the way we conduct ourselves towards our family, unless we allow it to. But, a word of warning, it does affect your friends and the way they conduct themselves towards you."

He paused and his voice shook a little as he continued, "Sometimes even family turn away. You must be prepared to accept that. You cannot whimper or whine. For if you do you become even less in their eyes. That is the loss.

Now, what do we gain? First, a small, insignificant-looking piece of cardboard to carry on our persons: a guarantee against unwarranted arrest; a guarantee against a beating. The same card frees you to travel anywhere within Kosov without the need of a permit, or the questions – the endless questions – that must be answered to get a permit! If you are sick and you flash the card, you are promptly admitted to a doctor or a hospital. A very powerful piece of cardboard, eh?"

"As a Party member, you will also be given a certificate, mounted and framed, together with a picture of our President to hang in your home. Surely there is one room in your house well suited to receive such treasures?" He held up his hand in warning as waves of laughter rippled through the students. "Enough. Take care of your reaction to my words. I am in your hands. In case you have not guessed, this was not the speech approved by Colonel Mihajlovich." He smiled, gave a half bow to Mihajlovich as he spoke his name.

"I am almost finished. There is only one course open to us … education. Suck every drop of knowledge from your professors. Devour every book within reach. Store every crumb of information in your mind. Take your studies seriously and be second-to-none in your class. Get your degree and use it. Use it for the betterment of your own life and those of our people. But, as you drag yourself from the mud of their rule, remember who you are. Remember our nationality, our heritage, our customs and traditions, and cling to those that are good. Discard any that hinder."

"Be careful…" the warning came from the front row, "someone is watching you closely."

He held up his hands asking for silence. "We are here. We intend to stay, for we have been here since Europe began. They are our neighbors. They intend to stay, for they have been here since the migration from Russia. Perhaps we could learn to be friends?"

The roar of disagreement came immediately, "No, not in our lifetime, for there has been too much hatred, too much suffering.… But is it not possible for our children to reach across this abyss let fingers, hands, touch? Is it beyond the bounds of possibility for our grandchildren to hold each other, laugh together, lay a foundation together? We have much to give each other, much to gain."

There was slow, but quiet agreement.

"Teach your children to live the life of a Kosovar: to be proud of what and who he is, to stand tall, yet be kind and tolerant. Teach him to bend, but not break, to step aside but not backward; and God willing, we will see him stand in the sunlight of freedom."

There was no sound, no movement.

"Thank you."

Applause was instant, spontaneous. He was deeply moved, emotionally stirred, and wanted to jump from the stage and join them, feel them surround him, but instinct warned him even as he considered it. He turned, bowed to Mihajlovich, and invited him to join him. He held up his hand as he did so. "One word … even an inkling of what I have said … and I am finished. If you give any value to my life, remember that we spoke of my lifestyle, the improvements possible now that I am under Colonel Mihajlovich's protection.

"And now…" he had switched to Serb-Croatian, "…I give you Colonel Mihajlovich, the man who made this possible." Skender led the applause.

Mihajlovich strode into his office, signaled Skender to follow him. He sat down, waved Skender to the chair opposite. "You were very quiet on the journey back Berisha."

"I had much to think about," he paused, "you, too, were lost in thought, sir."

Mihajlovich smiled, "I had much to think about." Their eyes met and they smiled. "We were a success, Berisha." He stood, went to a cabinet behind him and took out a bottle of Slivovitz with two glasses. He poured some into each glass, and offered one to Skender, "Shall we drink to our success?"

Skender stood, took the glass. Slowly, his eyes rose to meet Mihajlovich's, "Thank you."

Mihajlovich inclined his head, raised his glass, "Na zdravie." He waited until Skender raised his glass, repeated the toast. There was a delicate chink as the glasses touched. Mihajlovich refilled the glasses, then both sat down. Mihajlovich lay back in his chair, fingertips touching, "What a response … we have never had so many. I knew it could work…." He smiled, "I was skeptical about allowing you to address them in Albanian, but…." His smile deepened.

"If I had not … if you had not permitted it … we would have lost them. You could have forced them to remain, but you could not have forced them to listen."

"I agree. I could not have forced their membership, either, but it has been accomplished. Your speech seemed more powerful, longer than your draft."

Skender's nerves twitched a warning, but Mihajlovich still sat relaxed and quiet. He forced a smile, "Have you ever been to see a foreign film? The actors speak for four, five minutes, and the subtitle says, 'Yes.'" Mihajlovich laughed, "So it is with Albanian … it takes a long time to say little."

"I think I must learn this language." He picked up his glass, "We need another toast…." He was suddenly attentive, watchful, but Skender did not see it. "Shall we say … to your marriage?" He caught the immediate stillness.

"How did you know?"

"You mailed a letter to your wife this morning." The anger on Skender's face was there for only a moment, but it was long enough. "That irritates you, doesn't it, that I should read your letters?"

"Yes." Skender put the glass back on the desk.

"Then this marriage will not only open new doors, but close old ones that offend."

"I do not follow you."

"Letters traveling within the country are not subject to censor. When there are no letters coming or going abroad there will be no need for me to read them. The irritation to you has therefore been removed. When will the engagement be announced?"

The chair rocked as Skender moved, went to the window. "I don't know." He stood looking down into the street. "As soon as matters can be arranged. I have agreed. The rest is in the hands of my father and uncles."

"It is obvious from your actions now and your letter that you are still emotionally involved with your wife … will you tell me why you are prepared to enter into this engagement?" He reached and took a cigarette from the box, lit it and sat smoking. "Why, Berisha?"

Skender turned from the window. "It is not easy to live alone."

The ash grew long as Mihajlovich watched Skender, he laid his cigarette in the ashtray, picked up his glass, and stood, "Then … to your marriage." His eyes questioned Skender when he did not move, then slid to the glass, back again to Skender.

Skender slowly took the glass, raised it to touch Mihajlovich's, repeated quietly, "To my marriage." And both drank. Mihajlovich picked up the bottle of Slivovitz, silently asked if Skender would like another. "No, thank you."

"The girl is from Sarajevo."

"Yes."

"From a good, old established family." Skender inclined his head. "Well-educated." Skender's nod was brief. "Nineteen … and very beautiful."

"So I understand," Skender smile was twisted. "You are well-informed, Colonel Mihajlovich. Is there anything you know of this girl that, perhaps, I don't?"

Mihajlovich played with his glass, "I know all that I need to know … she has your customs, your culture. Her family is held in high regard. She will fit in well and be accepted without reservation by your family, your friends. Pristina will approve of her."

Skender's eyes lifted to Mihajlovich, "It would seem that you do, too."

"Yes," he smiled, "as a matter of fact, I do."

Skender inclined his head. There was a drop left in his glass, and he picked it up, "To the Nusé … may her life as a Berisha be long and happy."

Mihajlovich picked up the Slivovitz, poured some into his own glass, then added some to that left in Skender's. Their glassed touched, Mihajlovich's voice stopped Skender as his lips felt the glass, "And may she give much pleasure to her husband." He raised his glass a little higher, "And many children." Skender's eyes met his over the rim of his glass. Mihajlovich smiled, "Drink, Berisha." Skender took a long breath, downed the Slivovitz to the last drop.

Four hours had passed since the cell door had slammed on Emin and Jusuf. Emin sat on the floor, staring at the blankness of the walls. When he had walked into the cell, heard the sharp clang of metal and then the turn of the key, he had felt a screaming panic rise in his stomach and tear upward to his throat; it had taken all his control not to turn and throw himself against the bars and beg to be released. The constant leaping in the pit of his stomach had subsided somewhat after the first hour, but the gnawing sense of his vulnerability remained. The knowledge that he could be taken and beaten senseless on the passing whim of one of the guards had produced a terror unimaginable before. For the first time in his life, he had come face to face with deep, terrifyingly real fear.

"Do you think they will keep us all night?" Emin shook his head. Periodically, Jusuf had spoken, attempted a conversation, but Emin had not wanted to make the effort, desired only to be left alone.

He sighed, tried to push away the thoughts that had come continually to the surface of his mind. He did not want to think of Skender, did not want to acknowledge that this had been a daily experience of Skender's as a young man … the small inner voice that added 'plus the beatings', he ignored.

"How much influence does Skender have here? Is it possible that he could sign our release papers?"

"I don't know."

Jusuf sighed, turned to look up the passageway. The guard sat at his desk; Jusuf moved back out of his line of vision as he saw that he was being watched. The scraping sound of the chair startled Jusuf, and he took a step forward, being careful so that he could see without being seen. The guard had stood, was straightening his uniform, making sure that all the keys were hung in their assigned positions. "Someone must be coming…." Emin ignored the warning, Jusuf's anger suddenly surfaced over his fear, "You are not afraid, are you? Perhaps if you had seen someone…." Emin saw that he was shaking, "They had my brother for three days … he couldn't walk!"

"We have done nothing … made a slight disturbance, that was all." Emin spoke soothingly even as the tremor in his stomach started.

Their eyes followed the direction of the voices. Mihajlovich and Skender's legs came into view first as they descended the stairs. Emin stiffened as he recognized them. They stopped, stood chatting. Skender had one hand in his trouser pocket, the other held a clipboard as he smiled and nodded agreement with Mihajlovich, sometimes breaking into a soft laugh. His casual relaxation angered Emin; yet, mesmerized, he continued to watch. Mihajlovich moved, started toward the entry hall at the end of the crossing corridor as Skender's lips moved, formed words they could not hear. Mihajlovich had stopped as Skender spoke, and his laughter floated down the passageway. Emin gritted his teeth as Mihajlovich slapped Skender across the back and, still laughing, moved out of sight. Skender, still amused, turned toward the guard.

"Good evening, Comrade Berisha." Emin noted that the guard was at attention for Skender.

"Good evening, Comrade. I hear congratulations are in order." His hand extended as he smiled.

"Thank you, Comrade Berisha … yes…." The accompanying smile was proud, "A boy."

"May he have a long life." Skender turned, and together they started down the long corridor lined with cells. "None of these. The only ones I am interested in this evening are in cell fourteen. The others I will handle at the usual time tomorrow."

"Yes, Comrade." The key sounded loud, grating, as it was inserted into the lock of their cell. "On your feet! Stand at attention … Comrade Berisha is here to see you." Emin slowly stood. "Do you wish me to bring them to one of the interrogation rooms, Comrade Berisha?"

"No. I shall deal with it here. Thank you." Skender's nod dismissed the guard. He stood, reading the papers attached to the clipboard, his voice non-committal. "Disorderly conduct on government property, disturbing an official of the State, resisting arrest." He glanced up, "Do you deny any of the charges?"

Emin stood stiffly. Jusuf glanced at him, realized that he had no intention of answering, "No, sir."

"Have you ever been arrested before, Jusuf?"

"No … this is the first time."

"Under normal circumstances, you would fall under Officer Dragonovich's jurisdiction … he handles adults. However, since Emin is related to me, Colonel Mihaj…."

"We want no special consideration."

Skender's eyes lifted to Emin and he stood watching him for a moment. "If you had knowledge of Officer Dragonovich and his methods, such stupidity would not spill from your lips." He flipped back to the top page, stood writing for a moment. "I am letting you free this time. Be careful that there is no reason for us to bring you back here." He handed the form to Jusuf. "Give this to the guard. He will give you a release card which you will give to the sergeant at the entry hall."

"How well-acquainted you are with the procedure?" Emin's voice was sarcastic.

"Yes, I am, but then, I have worked for Colonel Mihajlovich for several months." Skender nodded to Jusuf. "You may go."

"Sir, I wish to apologize … what I said was unforgiveable."

Skender looked at Jusuf. "Yes, it was … especially when you are in no position to make judgments. However, emotion or anger sometimes takes us all too far. Be more tolerant in future, especially when you are unaware of the circumstances."

"Thank you, sir. Goodnight, sir. Goodnight, Emin … I will see you tomorrow." There was no response, and after a slight hesitation, Jusuf turned and left the cell.

Skender watched, made sure that the guard accepted the paper and let Jusuf proceed. He then turned to Emin, "Show me your wrists."

Surprised, Emin lifted his hands, dropped them as he realized what he had done.

"Why?"

"It is of no matter." Skender had already confirmed that the handcuffs had not been unnecessarily tight. "Now, will you tell me why you rushed to my defense when you will not even acknowledge me?"

"You carry the same name as I. I will allow no one to smear it." Emin's eyes met and held Skender's, his anger obvious.

"Yet you refuse to speak my name or permit any of your friends to do so." There was no response. "In future I suggest….

"There will be no future for you to suggest. I am leaving Prishtine."

"What do you mean?"

"I am tired of the stares, the jibes. I go to my mother's brother in Pec."

Skender frowned, "But … you are in the middle of a school year … what of your studies?" Emin stared angrily over his shoulder. "There is no University there, it is a farming community."

"Yes."

"How long will you be gone?"

"Indefinitely."

"Does your father approve this madness?"

"Madness?" Emin gave a mirthless laugh. "The whole Berisha family has gone mad. You, Jakup, Aslan…." His angry eyes dropped to Skender's, "How dare you divorce her? How dare you even consider taking another…."

"That is not your business." Skender cut him off, anger equaling Emin's.

"And why I chose to give up engineering and become a farmer is not yours. Only someone close to me … a father, or a brother … can ask why, and you, Comrade Berisha, are not my brother. We carry the same name; but no, never will I again acknowledge you as my brother."

Skender's face was white as he signed the release form. He offered it to Emin, "Give this to the guard…."

"I heard your instructions to Jusuf and can remember them."

"Very well … you may go, Emin."

Emin snatched the form from Skender. He stopped as he reached the bars, turned back, "Goodnight, *Comrade* Berisha. God willing this is the last time we will ever meet."

Skender leaned back against the wall. He was shaking and he moved into the cell out of sight of the guard.

Emin dropped the form onto the desk. "You're fortunate," the guard picked up one of the rubber stamps made sure it was covered with the purple ink, "had it been Officer Dragonovich you interrupted…" he pulled one of the release cards to him, carefully affixed the stamp, "…and then he had had the handling of you…" he filled in the date, the time and then, before adding his signature, looked up at Emin, "…you would not have moved for a week." He stared as he caught the glitter of what looked like tears.

Emin turned his head, looked back towards the cell. "I wish to God I had had the beating."

The incredulous stare of the guard followed as he walked the long passageway, then turned the corridor toward the entry hall.

Chapter 49

"Halt!" The sergeant stopped the army truck as it started to pull away. He jumped down off the back and made his way at a brisk march toward Skender who was parking his car. "We are finished here, Comrade Berisha. Did you wish to enter?"

"Yes, I must make my final inspection. We officially open the doors tomorrow at seven." His eyes lifted to the blue dome of the mosque. "Nineteen years..." he murmured, "... I wonder how many will...." He caught the sergeant's attentiveness and added, "Colonel Mihajlovich is hoping that some of the people will enter."

The sergeant's eyes were sharp, inquisitive, "Yes, Comrade. But never fear, as soon as we are rid of these foreigners, we will close them again," he grinned. "Or, bring back the horses."

Skender nodded, suppressed his sigh. "You need not wait. I will lock up when I am finished." He accepted the offered key.

"Thank you, Comrade ... then if there is nothing else I can do for you...?" Skender nodded permission for him to leave, watched as he swung up into the back of the truck, remembering one other time when he had watched the same uniform clamber in and out of the same kind of truck. The sergeant yelled the order to proceed, and the truck pulled away.

Skender walked the long gravel path, the grass on each side had been cut, the hedges trimmed and the weeds pulled. The neglect of the past years had been all but eradicated.

He hesitated as he reached the great wooden doors, then, after a quick glance around, slipped off his shoes as custom decreed when entering a mosque. The cool, dim interior welcomed him, and he moved to one side and stood back near the East wall, surveying the interior. A week ago, he had thought the task of cleaning it impossible. After the horses had been removed and the stalls torn down, the full amount of deterioration had become visible, he had almost despaired, given up without starting the monumental task.

The walls still showed signs of misuse, the wooden floors would carry the stains forever, but it was clean, the smell of carbolic not unpleasant. There was an air of serenity and peace, and he stood quietly, letting it seep into him, almost surprised that after the building had been used for the wrong purpose for so long, the feeling could be recaptured. Sunlight swept in a shaft toward him and he swung to face the door, surprise and apprehension mingling in him.

An old man, past the age of counting years, closed the door carefully behind him. His frame was bent, and he walked with difficulty, the package carried under one arm hindered him by its weight, but it was borne with great care. He moved forward until he was standing centrally in the mosque, then knelt and tenderly unwrapped the newspapers from the package. A rug, old, its colors faded and dull, unrolled itself onto the wooden floorboards. He knelt, straightened the rug, adjusted the fringes, then painfully stood. Skender came into his line of vision, and the old man started, perhaps he did not know him, perhaps it was the dimness after the bright sunlight, but he smiled, gave a slight bow, "Peace be with you, friend."

Skender returned the bow, "And to you, sir."

The old man glanced around, his lips trembled and he smoothed at his moustache to hide the emotion which moved him, "It has been so long…." His voice was a whisper as his eyes swept the mosque. There was a moment of quiet, then his hand waved toward the rug, "This pitiful offering … one time this floor was covered with rugs, beautiful … Turkish, Persian … such colors, such thickness." He sighed, shook his head, "This is the best from my house. I pray it will not offend Almighty God, for it is simple and old…." His voice trailed off, and he looked at Skender, needing reassurance.

"It is given with love sir … how can it offend?" Skender reassured him quietly. The old man nodded wistfully. "I am sorry, sir, but the mosque is not open today … tomorrow…."

"They have done their worst, desecrated a house of God, yet they could not destroy the peace." He turned toward Skender with a smile that lit his face, "You can feel it surround you, enter into your spirit even."

Skender took a breath.

"I heard you, young man, but for me, tomorrow is too far away … may I have five minutes?"

Skender bowed, "As long as you wish." He did not want to intrude on the old man. "I have to check something upstairs, please feel free…."

The steps spiraled steeply to the women's balcony. Skender sat on the topmost one. During the cleaning and restoring he had climbed the steps and walked the balcony often; but now, suddenly, he felt an intruder in that section and could not go past the top-most step. A soft thud heralded the closing of the door, and after a moment, he went with care down the worn steps.

The rug lay alone, the wooden floor stretching away from it, making it small, almost ridiculous, yet infinitely precious. He let his eyes travel the room once more. *Your former glory has gone, it can never be recaptured, but at least now you can open your arms to those who have need of you.*

He pulled the heavy door to behind him. The sun was hot on his back and head as he took the great iron key and locked the mosque.

Chapter 50

"Anna, Colonel Bora Vuksich is due here within the hour, but I want to run over to Party Headquarters before he arrives." Mihajlovich and Anna glanced at the wall clock. "Yes, I have time. Ask Dragonovich to meet me in the general office with the files I need, will you?" He took another look at the clock. "Have my car brought around … I think time will be pushing too hard for me to walk." He moved toward the door and Anna picked put the intercom phone, "By the way, have you seen Berisha?"

"No, Colonel Mihajlovich. Irena, have you?"

Irena stood, her voice was nervous as she said, "Yes, Colonel Mihajlovich. Comrade Berisha and I worked late last night."

Mihajlovich gave a knowing smile. "Did you then!?"

Innocently, Irena continued, "Yes. Comrade Berisha wanted to dictate so that it could be typed and on his desk by noon today." She colored furiously as Mihajlovich's eyes slid over her, "Was there something special you wanted Colonel Mihajlovich?"

Mihajlovich's smile deepened, "No, Irena, nothing." He turned away, "An hour, Anna … if Vuksich should arrive before I get back, make him comfortable and ply him with Slivovitz."

He whistled as he descended the stairs but stopped before entering the general office. "Thanks, Dragonovich. Anything else?" He took the file, then warned, "Only something urgent … I am in a hurry." He did not want to have to listen to Dragonovich for ten minutes.

"Good morning, Colonel Mihajlovich. Good morning, Officer Dragonovich." Skender gave a brief smile and a nod to the sergeant on duty at the desk.

Hearing Skender's voice, Mihajlovich turned from Dragonovich, "Ah, the prodigal returns! I did not see you all day yesterday Berisha."

"Your Church Tour took care of that! They are wearing me to a frazzle! Such energy! Every brick, every stone has to be examined." He gave a wry smile. "And then there is one woman who insists on photographing me with every statue, every monument!"

Mihajlovich laughed, saw that the sergeant was amused too, and said, "We have a celebrity here, sergeant … how do you feel about that?"

"I thought you were in a hurry, Colonel Mihajlovich?" Dragonovich would have liked to have added that Mihajlovich had plenty of time to gossip with Berisha yet had cut him short.

"Thank you, Dragonovich."

Skender remembered Mihajlovich's words, "Were you looking for me yesterday, Colonel Mihajlovich? Was there something special you wanted?"

"No, it was nothing. I am in a hurry. I have to go to the Party Headquarters and be back within the hour. Have you any recommendations, any requests, for this month? They have to go to Belgrade today."

Skender shook his head, then changed his mind. "An increase in salary for all Tour Guides … they deserve it!"

Mihajlovich slapped him across the back and laughed as he said, "Walk me to my car. How are these people getting along? Are they happy?"

"Bloody Kosovar!" Dragonovich murmured as he watched them leave. He became aware of his men watching him. "Get on with your work!" he growled as he strode across the room towards his own office.

"Here." One of the policemen handed his sergeant his report. His head jerked towards Dragonovich's office, "He must have hung one on last night … he's in a hell of a mood."

"Watch your tongue, Comrade!" the sergeant warned, as he privately agreed with the man. He reached for the clipboard that hung close to his desk and glanced down at the List of Arrests. Comrade Berisha would ask for it the moment he came in. He always did. There were three who would come under his jurisdiction today … by noon they would have been processed, their files completed, and allowed to leave. He waited, clipboard against his chest, as he watched the door.

"Good morning, sergeant."

"Good morning, Comrade Berisha." The sergeant continued to hold the clipboard as he peered over Skender's head. "How strange … I expected to see a halo at least, after spending so much time in church!" He grinned as Skender snatched good-naturedly at the clipboard, the sergeant released it, leaned across the counter and asked in a confidential voice, "Are there any, er…" he gave a wink, "…any pretty girls on this tour, Comrade?"

"All beautiful, sergeant." Skender's eyes ran down the list of arrests.

Some of the other policemen sauntered over and stood near their sergeant as they sensed some entertainment. The sergeant turned with a broad grin to include them as he asked, "Any rich ones who are also pretty?"

"Only three of these are for me … the remainder come under Officer Dragonovich, don't they?"

"Yes, yes. They can wait." The sergeant dismissed them impatiently, "What about these foreigners?"

Skender looked up, and a smile curved his lips as he saw the half-circle of expectancy. "Beautiful, sergeant…" his voice was extravagant, "… very wealthy, and dressed, mmmm…." His eyes closed; he kissed the tips of his fingers. He saw the nudges, the wide grins, and gave some of those standing closer to him a broad wink. "Perfect for you, sergeant, perfect … there is not one under sixty!"

The sergeant joined in the laughter, wagged his finger at Skender, as his lips threatened, "I'll get you for that, Comrade Berisha!" But his words were lost in the hoots and jeers of his comrades.

"Berisha! Leave my men alone!" The angry words carried above the merriment. There was a sudden silence as Dragonovich walked with slow deliberate steps towards them. The men melted away, finding, or inventing, something of importance that had to be attended to. Only the sergeant and Skender stood beside the counter. Dragonovich stopped, put his hands on his hips as he stood glaring at the sergeant, then, after a moment he asked, "Having fun, sergeant?"

The man did not answer, kept his head down. Skender noticed the nervous shifting around of the papers in front of him.

"No harm was intended, Comrade Dragonovich … we were just amusing ourselves at the expense of the Church Group."

"I didn't ask you, Berisha." Dragonovich still glared at his sergeant, had not taken his eyes from the man even as he spoke to Skender. "I think, sergeant, that you and I had better have a little chat later, don't you?" He waited a long moment, then turned to face Skender, leaned across the counter until his face was inches from Skender's. "Berisha…" he confided, "…you irritate like sweat dripping into my eyes … you are…."

Skender turned abruptly. "I do not have the time, Comrade Dragonovich. Sergeant, would you assign me a guard…?"

"No. You are going to listen, Berisha. Mihajlovich wants me to teach you. He wants me to teach you everything, Berisha." He took a long, shuddering breath. "God, there's something I'd like to teach you…."

Skender looked up at the threat. Dragonovich's hatred was tangible.

Skender turned away and faced the sergeant. He was surprised to see sympathy in the man's eyes. "I have less than an hour, Sergeant. I am going to the prisoners now … please assign a guard and have him join me downstairs. Comrade Dragonovich, I must ask you to excuse me … I have work to do."

"You bastard," Dragonovich muttered as Skender left, "I'll have you one day…." He fumed as he saw the sergeant dispatch one of the guards to the interrogation room usually chosen by Skender. Then a thought came. "Are there any Kosovars down there?"

"You mean under your jurisdiction, Comrade?"

Dragonovich's nod was slow, menacing. The sergeant hesitated, then answered reluctantly. "Yes. Two."

Dragonovich nodded again, then turned and surveyed the room behind him, silently pointed to one guard, looked around and selected another. He beckoned them, and without a word, they followed Dragonovich from the room.

The sergeant watched them. "Poor bastards," he murmured on a sigh.

One of his men handed him a sheaf of papers. "Who's he going to?" he asked with a toss of his head in the direction Dragonovich had taken. "Theirs, or ours?"

"Theirs. He's going to beat the shit out of them for no reason...." He controlled his anger as he saw his comrade's surprise, "Oh, forget it. I don't know what's wrong with me. It's never bothered me before when we've beat the hell out of...." He sighed. "It's Berisha. He's alright. I get along with him. He gets on with his work and he doesn't make any problems for me. Christ, half the time I forget that he's a Kosovar." He gave a sheepish grin, "It must be the heat."

The guard shook his head. "We've talked ... most of us feel the same. There's some who hate his guts, but..." his shoulders lifted, "those of us who've had to work with him...." He gave a thin smile. "Mihajlovich made a mistake, if you ask me. It was easy to hate 'em when you didn't know 'em."

The sergeant nodded his agreement and started to gather his papers together. "Well, there's nothing we can do." He straightened his shoulders and pulled his jacket straight. "Back to work Comrade. It's not our business."

Skender returned the tour group to the Bozor Hotel for their lunch, he made his excuses, and escaped in spite of their insistence that he should eat with them. He felt tired and wanted a short break from their endless questions. He looked forward to an hour, maybe even two, of silence in his comfortable chair.

"Hello, Anna ... I thought you would be at lunch."

"Colonel Mihajlovich has someone with him, so Irena went first. She has put the letters you dictated on your desk."

"Thank you. Did she finish the final part of the report on Kosovo?"

"Yes, it is also on your desk, Comrade Berisha."

He smiled his thanks. He closed the door quietly, but firmly, behind him, it felt good to be in his own office. The room was stuffy, and he opened the window a crack, then sank into his leather chair with a sigh of content. He swung to face the window so that he could look out over the tree and the street below. He would have liked to take off his jacket, but Anna had said Mihajlovich had not yet left for lunch. He smiled as he imagined Mihajlovich's horror if he came in and found his assistant in his shirtsleeves! He leaned back, putting his hands behind his head as he reminisced of the time spent with the International League of Churches Group.

They were older people, obviously used to a comfortable and easy life, they had treated him with distant kindness at first, and, after a few hours, had responded with warmth and friendship. Only one was a problem, a man from one of the South American countries who spoke no language other than his native tongue. Skender had spoken slow Italian in the vague hope that he would catch something, while one of the group screamed French at the poor man. Skender smiled to himself, wondering idly what the fellow had grasped from the two languages that neighbored his own.

"Berisha." Skender swung the chair to face the door, stood immediately, murmured, "Colonel." The man with Mihajlovich was unknown to him, about forty, with thinning hair and heavy-set. His eyes reminded Skender of a bird, sharp, darting everywhere. He disliked, distrusted him on sight. "I want you to meet an old friend, Bora Vuksich … and this, Bora, is my assistant, Skender Berisha."

"Your name again?" It was a command, even the man's voice was unpleasant.

"Berisha, Skender Berisha."

The name was noted, mentally filed and Skender knew he would never forget it.

"I have heard much about you from Colonel Mihajlovich."

Skender resisted the impulse to fidget or drop his eyes from the beady appraisal. He forced a smile, "I trust it was nothing detrimental." He glanced toward Mihajlovich, who had already sat down.

"On the contrary…." Vuksich took the other chair at Mihajlovich's invitation.

Mihajlovich turned to Vuksich, "The International Church Group arrived two days ago. Berisha took them to the mosques this morning." His hand gave permission for Skender to sit down. "How did things go today, Berisha?"

"They were very interested but asked to see more." He glanced at Vuksich not sure if he should speak freely.

"What did you tell them?"

"I avoided an answer."

Mihajlovich frowned as he considered, "This afternoon you are taking them … where?"

"Decan, to see the wall murals and the painting of the Christ figure."

"Mmm, one church cannot be stretched to fill another day plus this afternoon?" Mihajlovich mused. "Talk to me later … between us we will think of something to occupy them." He nodded permission for Skender to answer as the intercom buzzed.

"It is for you, Colonel, Party Headquarters."

"I will take the call in my office." Mihajlovich waited until Skender had replaced the phone, "Bora, stay and become better acquainted with Berisha … this is routine, and will take but a moment."

Vuksich waited until he heard the door close on Mihajlovich. "You may sit down, Berisha." The pronunciation was perfect. His eyes swept the desk. He reached forward and let his thumb run up the pile of letters awaiting Skender's appraisal and signature. "Quite a few, especially when you take into consideration that you are also looking after this tour."

Skender did not comment.

"What is that? May I see?" His finger pointed to the report. His eyes lifted as Skender made no attempt to pass it to him. "Did you hear my request?" He demanded.

"I am sorry, but I cannot allow that."

"Why not?"

"I have no idea who you are or what authority…."

Vuksich flipped open the wallet he had taken from his inside coat pocket. Skender's eyes dropped to the red and black stamped card. "As you can see, Berisha, I, too, am with Udba. Also, a Deputy Director, but one rank lower than Colonel Mihajlovich. Is that enough authorization for you?"

"I beg your pardon…" Skender, flustered, hastily passed the report, "I had no idea…."

"Your actions were correct." Vuksich cut him short as he took the report. "This says part three … were there two earlier sections?"

"Yes, sir."

Vuksich's eyes lifted immediately. "Sir?" I do not permit that salutation. Parts One and Two had approximately the same number of pages, I assume."

"Yes, Comrade … Two, perhaps a little more."

Vuksich nodded as he continued to read. He turned a page, asked casually, "Does Mihajlovich allow you to call him that?" He turned to the following page, glanced up with an amused smile. "It is of no consequence whether you answer me or not … I can always ask Stefan directly."

"Then I suggest you do that, Comrade Vuksich," Skender replied stiffly. He stood, eyes still on Vuksich as Mihajlovich re-entered the office.

"Have you had lunch yet, Berisha? Would you like to join us?"

Skender made a quick change of plans. Obviously, he was not going to get any rest here and he did not intend to sit opposite this revolting man for an hour or more. He would go home and have a quiet hour with Babush. "Thank you, no. I am expected at home." He glanced at his watch. "Unless you need me, Colonel Mihajlovich?"

Mihajlovich inclined his head, his hand offered Skender permission to leave. "I will see you tomorrow." He turned to Vuksich. "We will lunch at the Hotel ... it is quiet and pleasant there."

Skender smiled to himself. Mihajlovich had obviously forgotten that at the Hotel, there would be thirty-two excited tourists, all chattering together in a symphony of languages. He turned, gave a slight bow, "Good-bye, Comrade Vuksich. I hope that you will enjoy your lunch. Colonel Mihajlovich, until tomorrow."

Mihajlovich dropped into Skender's chair as he left the room, "Well?"

Vuksich gave a pointed glance at the pile of letters, "You work him hard." Mihajlovich smiled. "And this report is thorough and extremely well done. I tried to catch him, gave him the opportunity to speak against you...." His head shook as he dropped the report back onto the desk. "I think you have his loyalty, Stefan, but before you rely on him further, you had better be sure."

"Rumor has it that my promotion is imminent."

"Exactly. You will need him more than ever then. If I were you, I would test this Kosovar." Vuksich leaned forward as Mihajlovich hesitated, "You say he has brought a leap in membership for the Party ... that the young people listen to him? He is worth cultivating, but before you can take him deeper into our secrets, you must be certain of him."

Mihajlovich nodded, "I know. What do you suggest?"

A non-committal shrug was his only answer.

He took a cigarette, threw the packet to Vuksich and sat smoking, frowning at the ascending smoke. "There is one sure way ... send him out of Kosovo. Let him think he is beyond my reach, outside of my control." He pushed the intercom button. "Anna, where does the Church tour go to next? And when is that? Thank you." He released the button, went to the map that covered half of the wall behind Skender's desk. "On Wednesday they leave Pristina for Sarajevo, where they stay two nights." His finger traced the route.

"And then?" Vuksich could not see where Mihajlovich's finger had stopped.

He turned with a smile, "And then, my dear Bora, they are your responsibility. You did not know, were not informed?" he demanded at the start of surprise.

"Possibly. Croatia crawls with tourists at all times, as I am sure you remember. One more group is a drop in the bucket. Where are they supposed to stay, which part of Croatia is to host them?"

"Right to your own door, Bora. Zagreb! For three days." Mihajlovich's finger retraced the route from Pristina to Sarajevo and then to Zagreb. "And all that time he will be right in the center of Yugoslavia, not a border near."

"After Zagreb?"

Mihajlovich turned back to him, gave a long, slow smile, "By plane directly to Rome."

Their eyes met, the same slow smile crossed Vuksich's face, "Perfect," he said softly, "…absolutely perfect." Mihajlovich nodded agreement, "One move, even a glance in the wrong direction, and my hand will close on him…." His hand came together in a slow, tight fist. "I will squeeze the life from him the way one would squeeze the juice from a lemon."

"No, my friend. This one is mine. If he does not return to me of his own free will, then you will deliver him to me … alive and well. Do we understand each other?"

Vuksich smiled as he nodded, "Perhaps I could just … er … prick him a little?"

Mihajlovich laughed, "No. You have plenty of your own … leave this one for me."

"Agreed. You shall have him, unmarked and unscathed." He straightened the papers laying on the desk, then looked up directly at Mihajlovich. "I accept full responsibility for him only while he is in Croatia and under my jurisdiction. When he is in Bosnia…?" His shoulders lifted.

"Alex will watch him for me. In fact, I shall call him now." Mihajlovich picked up the phone. "Alex will have his eyes on him in Bosnia, and you in Croatia. Anna, get Alexander Kulich in Sarajevo for me, please." He replaced the phone, "And as added insurance, I will instruct the agent who has infiltrated this group to also watch him."

"A good thought … extra precaution is always sound."

"After this call, we will have lunch, and then I would like to show you the prison. The facilities will interest you … some of our methods for extracting information are without parallel. Excuse me." He picked up the telephone. "Mihajlovich here. Ah, Alex, this is Stefan…."

Chapter 51

"Your travel-permit." Mihajlovich handed the stamped and signed permit to Skender. "As you can see, it grants you freedom of travel anywhere within Yugoslavia." He passed over another paper. "This is authorization for transportation, meals, hotel, entertainment … produce this and there is no charge." He gave an impatient frown at Skender's ironic grin. "We are here to serve the people … it is only just that they are the ones who pay for the service."

"Of course!"

Mihajlovich's voice was sharp, "Tell me, honestly, is it any different in the democratic west?"

"No," Skender admitted on a sigh, "those who can afford to pay usually do not."

"Exactly. Authority brings its rewards in all societies. Now, if your conscience will permit, perhaps we can continue? And this. This is the most important identification you will ever receive." The card was stark white, the lettering was black, giving full information as regards his age, height, weight, coloring. In the top left-hand corner was the blood-red emblem of Udba. "As you can see, it lists you as my assistant. Use it well. It carries a lot of power." Skender almost shuddered as his fingers felt the raised surface of the die-stamped card.

Mihajlovich did not see Skender's reaction as he laid the itinerary in front of him. "When you reach Sarajevo, you will report to Captain Alexander Kulich. He is also with Udba and is in charge of the Republic of Bosnia. You will like him; he is outgoing and charming."

"May I ask why I have to report to him?"

"A courtesy, that is all. I would do the same." He almost smiled, "Remember this … never ruffle the feathers of another Udba member: even if he is one rung below you now, he could be two rungs above you in the future."

He referred again to the itinerary, "You will also report to Colonel Bora Vuksich in Zagreb. As you have already met, it will be like having an old friend to visit in a strange city." He laughed softly, "You do not like him?"

Skender's voice was non-committal, "I spoke with him for only a moment, sir … there was not enough time to form an opinion."

"There was for Bora. He found you sharp and attentive." Mihajlovich fiddled with his pen. "Be careful of him, Berisha. He is no fool, and quite ruthless…." He stopped, appalled at himself.

Skender caught himself staring, pulled his eyes from Mihajlovich and studied the typed sheet in front of him.

Mihajlovich's voice was brusque as he continued, "You will have two days in Sarajevo. The journey from there to Zagreb will be long and…."

Skender sat in quiet contemplation, making notes as necessary while his mind tossed the sudden warning, the unexplained softening of Mihajlovich toward him.

"After the walking tour of Zagreb, the group will have the afternoon free for shopping and general sightseeing on their own. You, too, will be relieved of duty. You may shop or do what you will. If you wish, you may tour the facilities at Zagreb. Police Headquarters is enormous and well worth a visit. The prison is larger than ours, but not as up to date. But it may prove of interest to you.

You will leave the hotel at nine-forty the following morning and take the group to the airport. Help them with obtaining porters for their luggage. See them safely through customs and passport control, and then…" he shrugged, "you are free."

Skender started. "Free?"

"Of course. Your duties will have been completed and you can return home."

"Home?"

"What's the matter with you today? Once you are rid of these damned tourists, take a plane to Belgrade." He sighed, leaned toward Skender, "There is no direct flight from Zagreb to Pristina, you must go via Belgrade." He gave a strange look at Skender, "Surely you did not plan on returning by road?"

"No, sir. I had not thought beyond the itinerary planned."

"It is unwise to go that far without a thought about your return journey."

Skender did not comment. After a while, Mihajlovich asked, "Any questions?"

"No, sir." Skender folded the itinerary, picked it up together with his authorization, his Udba card and permit, and put them away in his briefcase, "Everything is clear."

Mihajlovich nodded, stood as Skender did. "Then … good luck." He offered his hand. "Have a safe journey."

Their eyes met, held as they shook hands. "Thank you, Colonel Mihajlovich."

Mihajlovich watched as Skender crossed the room. Skender turned the handle of the door, started to open it, "Berisha!" His call was unnecessarily loud.

Skender turned back to face him, "Sir?"

Mihajlovich took a breath, then, as he let it go, shook his head, "Nothing," he muttered. "About a week, then."

"Yes, about a week. Good-bye, Colonel Mihajlovich." He waited a moment, expecting an answer, but Mihajlovich turned his back and went to the window. Skender closed the door quietly behind him.

Mihajlovich paced back and forth, then strode from his own office to Skender's. He was restless almost to the point of being nervous. The desk was clear except for one file, which lay centrally on the blotter. He opened it, moodily flicked through the few letters, he knew what they were, had already read them and instructed Irena to leave them for Berisha's attention.

The huge leather chair swung easily toward the map on the wall behind Skender's desk, and Mihajlovich sat frowning at the red flag that marked Sarajevo, as again he fretted over why he had almost warned Berisha, almost cancelled the whole trip, the whole fiasco.

He sighed, let the chair turn toward the window. The leaves were thick, dense, and he had to move to the extreme right or left to be able to see the granite obelisk. His hand groped, found the intercom phone, "Anna, I want that tree cut down." He gritted his teeth at her gasp. "Order it today, Anna. Do you understand?"

"Yes, Colonel Mihajlovich, it is just ... well, Colonel, without its protection, it will be extremely hot...." She pulled the phone away from her ear as the angry oath came. "Immediately, Colonel Mihajlovich." She felt Irena's eyes on her, but avoided looking up as she pushed Dragonovich's key, "Colonel Mihajlovich wants the tree removed immediately."

"What? That's madness. It'll be as hot as hell without it."

"Then you tell him," she answered, voice angry. Carefully, she replaced the phone, resisting the impulse to slam it back on its cradle.

"Why is Colonel Mihajlovich so upset?" Irena asked in a whisper with a nervous glance towards Skender's office, "And why does he spend so much time in there?"

"Get on with your work." Anna waited until the steady tap of the typewriter told her that Irena was occupied, then raised her eyes and sat looking at the door to Skender's office. She was troubled. In all the seven years she had worked for Mihajlovich, she had never known him so disoriented. He was unable to concentrate for more than a few moments, on anything. For the first time in seven years, the mail had lain on his desk, unanswered, untended. She started as the phone rang. "Colonel Mihajlovich's secretary ... yes, Captain Kulich, if you will hold for a moment, please." She pushed the buzzer for Skender's phone, waited, then pushed again. "Captain Alexander Kulich from Sarajevo for you, Colonel Mihajlovich."

"I will take it here. Alex, good morning, how are you?" Mihajlovich curbed his impatience, fought back the question, which had been at the forefront of his mind for two days, and waited until all the pleasantries were exchanged. "What about Berisha? Where is he now … what has he been up to since entering Bosnia?" It was asked. For good or ill, the answer would come.

"He crossed into Croatia an hour ago…" Mihajlovich swung back to the map, pulled the flag from Sarajevo and moved it to the border of the Republics of Bosnia and Croatia, letting it sit just inside the Croatian border, "…reported to me the following morning. He is charming, Stefan."

"Yes, there is something about him that appeals," Mihajlovich admitted. "What else?"

"The family you enquired about earlier sent the eldest son to meet Berisha … he had dinner at his fiancé's home…." Mihajlovich felt his body relax as Kulich gave him the detailed report of Skender's movements. "And last night, I invited him to join me for a meal, which…."

"You invited Berisha to have dinner?" Mihajlovich's voice was sharp with surprise, distrust.

"Yes. Is there any better time for confidences to be exchanged than after several glasses of Slivovitz and a relaxing and satisfying meal?"

Tension evaporated as Mihajlovich laughed, "Only you, Alex, would think of using pleasure to extract information."

"I offered him another pleasure, but it was refused. A pity … a lovely woman can cajole more secrets than any method I know."

"His reason?"

"'I am newly engaged; the family is also from this town and may hear….' It sounded genuine. There was not a word, not even a breath against you, Stefan … frankly, I think you are chasing moths in a dark room."

"I hope you are right, Alex. With someone of his caliber beside me, I could safely turn my back on anyone and know…" he stopped abruptly, "when do you think he will reach Zagreb?"

"It is a long journey … probably about eleven this evening." There was an amused chuckle, "Stop fretting, Stefan! I have already called Vuksich … as my eyes left Berisha, his took over."

Mihajlovich forced an answering laugh, "Is my concern that apparent? I do not want him to get away, Alex … I would prefer him beside me, but if not…."

"Vengeance will be sweet."

"Exactly. Did he suspect?"

"That he was being watched? Of course not."

"Thank you, Alex. I will not forget you for this." There was no comment, and Mihajlovich wondered briefly what payment would be expected from him for the favor. "Good-bye … I look forward to seeing you at the Conference."

"Good-bye, Stefan, it was a pleasure to help you."

Mihajlovich replaced the phone, swung toward the map, and, after a moment, moved the red flag closer to Zagreb.

Chapter 52

Zagreb, Croatia

"There is a Comrade Berisha to see you." The name was pronounced incorrectly, and a demand came for it to be repeated. The uncertain eyes of Vuksich's secretary lifted to Skender, "Berisha, Skender Berisha. You are to go in."

"Thank you." Skender made his way toward the mahogany door with the gold lettering, stopped one pace away while the professional eyes of the guard searched without touching him for any concealed weapon, then opened the door.

"Good morning, Colonel Vuksich."

"Good morning, Comrade Berisha. I am surprised to see you in Zagreb."

"I was surprised at the opportunity to come. The interpreter who was assigned to the Church Group was suddenly taken ill in Pristina and had to be admitted to a hospital."

Vuksich hid his smile.

"Colonel Mihajlovich instructed me to escort them."

"I see. How is my friend Stefan?"

"Well, thank you … he sends his warm regards."

Vuksich nodded, kept Skender standing. "You had a safe journey?"

"Yes, Colonel."

"Surely, as interpreter, you were needed on this morning's church tour?"

"The City Guide is fluent in English and German … I thought it more important to pay my respects to you, Colonel Vuksich."

Vuksich's smile was contemptuous. "There is no need for flattery."

"I did not intend it … I merely follow the orders of Colonel Mihajlovich." Skender regretted his sharpness, added, "I arrived in Zagreb late last night, and this morning I report to you. I extended the same courtesy to Comrade Kulich in Sarajevo."

"Sit down."

The French Provincial chair looked hardly strong enough to support him, he sat gingerly, allowing his weight to be taken slowly. Vuksich sat opposite, pudgy fingertips touching, watching him over the top of them. The sharp eyes did not move from Skender's face. The fingertips tapped noiselessly together. The silence pressed on Skender, stretched his nerves until he felt he had to speak, say anything, to break it.

"What are your plans for the remainder of your stay here, Berisha?"

He almost sighed his relief. "This is my first visit to Zagreb … I thought I would sightsee, stay with the group…." Skender's voice trailed away.

"Tomorrow you will take the walking tour with them, then?"

"No, Colonel Vuksich, tomorrow is Sunday, and the group tour by bus … general sightseeing … and on Monday they take the walking tour. Monday afternoon is free for general shopping."

"It is not important … I do not bother myself with minor details of every group visiting Zagreb, you understand. So … when do they leave?"

"Tuesday morning, via Alitalia Airlines for Rome."

"Good." Vuksich leaned forward, held out his hand, "Let me see your passport."

Skender's hand had moved automatically toward his inside pocket. It was too late to stop the movement, Vuksich had seen it and Skender knew it. Panic almost brought him to a standstill, but he forced his hand to continue forward to his inside coat pocket. "I do not have a passport … it was not necessary. However, Colonel Mihajlovich gave me this authorization." He took the signed permit and the authorization from his wallet, handed them to Vuksich, all the time very aware of the shape of his American passport, sure that Vuksich could see the outline of the slim green book lying next to his heart.

Vuksich did not take his eyes from Skender as he accepted the papers. "Guard!"

Skender's hand held his throat as his heart leaped for release. He smiled back at Vuksich and straightened his tie.

"You called, Comrade?"

He can see the outline of my passport, will order me searched….

"Yes. Have a car made available to take Comrade Berisha back to his hotel." The eyes lifted from the careful perusal of the papers. "Unless you wish to go to some other place?"

No sound would come, and he shook his head as he smiled his thanks.

Vuksich dismissed the guard with a nod, handed the papers back to Skender. "Before you leave, perhaps you would care to see the prison, or Police Headquarters?"

Skender considered, needing the time to make sure that when his mouth opened, sound would come out in a steady and firm stream. "Thank you, but I think not. I would like to take advantage of being with the group and having an official guide."

"As you will." Vuksich stood, extended his hand, "I hope you will enjoy yourself here in Zagreb."

He almost shuddered at the thought of taking that soft hand in his. "Thank you." There was no grip, just the clammy flesh lying within his own hand.

"If I can be of any assistance, or if you have any difficulties…."

"Thank you, Colonel Vuksich. Good-bye."

Skender closed the hotel room door, stood leaning against it for a moment, then took off his jacket and let his body slide onto the bed with a long sigh of relief. Over. It was almost over. Done with. The first hurdle, Kulich in Sarajevo, had been crossed. He lay staring up at the slowly rotating fan. It had been a pleasant evening, he had almost liked Kulich. It had taken careful concentration to remember that he was the enemy….

Not so with Vuksich. His stomach had turned to a glutinous mass of jelly at the sight of the man, while the sharp eyes alerted every nerve in his body. His face was grim as he remembered the nausea that had threatened when Vuksich had called for the guard.

His hand reached, found his jacket, and he pulled it toward him. The passport was soft and still warm from contact with his body, his fingers glided over it, around it, and then across the perforated numbers at the top.

The second hurdle has also been crossed. Now only one more lies ahead of me. He slid the passport under his body as he felt the heaviness of his eyelids. *One more … the airport. The biggest, the hardest jumps were behind him. Now there was only one minor obstacle, and then, Rome … London … Jill….*

Prishtine, Kosov

The quiet buzz barely sounded before Mihajlovich grabbed the phone. "Mihajlovich here." His breathing was difficult as Anna made the announcement. "Put him through. Bora, what is happening?" He swore to himself even as he asked. He should have waited, let Vuksich lead.

"My man called from the airport only moments ago…." Mihajlovich's grip tightened until his knuckles were white as he listened to Vuksich pat himself on the back, congratulate himself on the handling of the situation. The ingratiating voice irritated Mihajlovich to the point of explosion, but he checked himself and did not interrupt with the demand for facts.

"You were always efficient, Bora, I could always rely on you to do your best." The pause was perfect, not short enough to reassure Vuksich, not long enough to panic him, "Otherwise, I would not have recommended you for promotion to my old position." Mihajlovich deliberately reminded him, "Shall we proceed, now, to the matter in hand?"

"Berisha has passed through customs with the group. There was a slight problem, but he handled it well."

Mihajlovich smiled, Vuksich had taken the warning, "What problem?"

"Someone tried to smuggle through an undeclared item. The customs official was overzealous and confiscated it. It was becoming a little sticky…."

Mihajlovich closed his eyes, demanded with infinite patience, "What did Berisha do?"

"Flashed his Udba card."

Mihajlovich frowned, that was not Berisha's style. His stomach signaled a warning. "Watch him carefully, Bora, I want him. If he slips through your fingers…."

"Relax, Stefan, he is surrounded, could not possibly get away."

"Has he behaved himself so far?"

"He has acted as any tourist … visiting the tourist attractions, staying with the group, mostly. In fact, last night was the first time he pulled away from them." Vuksich paused, knowing how anxious Mihajlovich was, "He had dinner with one of the City Guides … he is a Croatian."

"So … he found himself a kindred spirit. It would have been interesting to know what route their conversation took."

"According to the waiter, they spoke only of generalities."

There was a soft laugh, "I think perhaps I have underestimated you, Bora. Well done."

"Thank you. My only suspicion is that he carries his case with him instead of checking it in with the JAT flight to Belgrade when he arrived at the airport."

"Does the group fly JAT or a foreign airline?"

"Foreign … Alitalia."

"Hmm, that could be touchy."

Vuksich gave a slight cough, enough to let Mihajlovich know that he had already thought of that and acted upon it. "He will be allowed to proceed as any passenger; but let him put one foot outside of the waiting lounge and we can take him. It will even be legal … he did not pass through Customs or Passport Control. If any of the passengers questions, makes waves, we will inform them that he will travel on the next flight, that it was an oversight on Berisha's part, but that International Laws must be obeyed. They will swallow the fish and go calmly on their way."

"Excellent. I could not have done better myself." Mihajlovich hesitated, still feeling the tremor of anxiety, but he bit back the additional warning, knowing it would only irritate Vuksich. "Thank you, Bora."

"The next phone call from me will be good news … either Berisha is on the flight to Belgrade or…."

The chuckle disturbed Mihajlovich, and his chair snapped upright. "He is mine, Bora. Do not forget."

The pause was long, then Vuksich answered softly, "He is in Croatia, Stefan."

Mihajlovich gritted his teeth. "I thought we had reached an understanding."

Vuksich laughed, he had retaliated, had his moment of satisfaction. "Relax! I was teasing. You shall have him." He checked the clock. "Fifteen minutes before takeoff … I will call you within the hour."

"Thank you, Bora." Mihajlovich checked his watch.

"Don't forget me, Stefan, when you are promoted."

"Oh, I won't, Bora … let me assure you of that. Good-bye." Mihajlovich replaced the phone, again looked at his watch and checked it with the wall clock. Ten twenty-five.

If Berisha was going to make a move, it would have to be done within the next five minutes.

Zagreb, Croatia

The windows of the waiting room for Alitalia Flight 502 to Rome reached from floor to ceiling, giving the waiting passengers a full view of the flight deck and the incoming and departing planes. Zagreb was a busy airport and offered plenty of entertainment for those who wished to see.

Skender sat on one of the seats overlooking the tarmac, the sleek white plane with its dark blue insignia was now quiet. The bustle of loading bags, drinks, food, was over and only a few mechanics wandered around or lounged on the steps leading to the interior of the plane. The flight crew was already aboard, except for the hostess, she stood close to the still-locked door, waiting for permission to load her passengers.

Skender studied the layout carefully. It was as if fate had smiled on him, held out a helping hand. The plane was close to the airport building so the chance of being spotted by one of the Udba agents always assigned to airports, train terminals, etc., was minimal.

He stood. The Alitalia hostess pouted prettily, her eyes flirting, as he explained that one member of his group seemed to have mislaid or lost the boarding pass. She held the important piece of card against her chin. "Where did you learn to speak Italian so well?"

Skender smiled, let his body lean against the doorjamb between them. She was Roman, her accent had told him that. "In Rome."

Her eyes dared him, "What else did you learn in Rome?"

His eyes slid over her, lingered on the accentuated waist, the well-shaped legs, then rose to look directly into hers. He gave a long, slow smile, "Many things!"

She laughed as she handed him the boarding pass, "I can see that!" She walked away, deliberately swaying on the high-heeled sandals, then half-turned to look back at him.

He smiled, mouthed, "Bella" at her as he slipped the card into his pocket and returned to his seat. He sat watching her cross the tarmac as she made her way to the plane for her final orders, an amused smile on his face. No other race flirted so outrageously, with so much daring, as the Italians. It was an art they had perfected.

"Naughty, naughty!" He looked up at the over-made-up face of Mrs. Redland. "I saw you carrying on with that girl."

"I was not 'carrying on', Mrs. Redland," Skender answered with a smile, "I was obeying an unwritten rule of Italy … acknowledging and appreciating beauty."

Her laugh rang out and he glanced around. "What did she give you? Show me!" Her hand demanded the pass. His quick check of the room was nervous. He did not need any attention brought to him by this good-natured but noisy woman from Nevada. "Come on … show!"

He took hold of the outstretched hand and gave it a squeeze. "It is her address … shhh!," he warned, glancing around at her squeal of delight, "it is a secret."

"Oh, you Europeans are so … so romantic and exciting." She shivered with delight. "So dashing, so … if only I was a young girl again!" She laughed at him, then bent down and with a slow smile and conspiratorial wink, said softly, "Look behind you."

Skender was halfway to his feet, nerves jangling. Relief left him weak as he saw he was surrounded by the Church Group, and he held onto the back of the seat.

"We wished to surprise you perhaps…." The broken English of the lady from Lyon ended in a smile as she held a slim rectangular package toward him. "Please, from us for thanking you for your help and kindness. Please." She held the package at arm's length toward him.

Skender's eyes moved from one to the other. He had not wanted this duty, Mihajlovich had thrust it on him, but the enforced close contact with these people had endeared them to him, and he had come to know and appreciate their little idiosyncrasies, their generosities. "No, you must not…."

Gold teeth flashed in a wide smile as Señor Ramirez, the South American, took the package and pushed it into Skender's hands. A torrent of words spilled from Ramirez, bringing general laughter, a medley of languages urging him to accept.

Skender pulled at the ribbon, as it undid itself, it was taken from his hands, and nods encouraged him to continue. He pulled away the paper to reveal a black leather box. He lifted the hinged lid, his breath caught, and then he let his finger slide along the engraved 'Skender Berisha' on the silver pen and pencil set nestled in scarlet velvet. He was touched beyond words, could say nothing. There was a deep emotional silence as he looked from one to the other, each feeling his emotion and reflecting it.

Mrs. Redland broke the spell, hugged him close to her ample bosom. There was laughter, handshaking, backslapping and more quick hugs. "Thank you, thank you all. You should not have been this generous…."

"Passengers for Alitalia Flight 502 to Rome, please…."

Their questioning faces looked at him as the loudspeaker announcement in Serb-Croatian interrupted. "You are to assemble at the door … it is time for you to leave."

Cards, pieces of paper with addresses scribbled, were thrust at him as he was admonished to write, to visit, if he could. He smiled and nodded, while his mind tried to cope with the next move, what it should be, when it should occur.

"This way, please." The Alitalia hostess was back, waiting.

He shepherded them toward her and the now open door. He smiled, posed beside the girl as Mrs. Redland demanded one more photograph. He was pushed closer to the girl and a close-up taken. "Yes," he assured Mrs. Redland, "if you write, I promise to answer." She gave him a hug and a pat on the cheek before leaving. "Good-bye. Good-bye…." He grinned back at the hostess as the group made their last demands on him. "It makes me happy that I was able to be of service … yes, thank you, if ever-I visit your country, I will be sure to let you know…."

Señor Ramirez was in front of him, brow creased as he held Skender's hand. He muttered something in Spanish, and then, as remembrance came, smiled, pumped Skender's hand and said with great pride, "Dovidenja, Skender!"

Skender smiled back, wished he could offer congratulations to Ramirez on his first word in Serbo-Croatian, "Dovidenja, Señor Ramirez."

His group had boarded, he moved to one side to allow the remaining passengers to embark. His eyes lingered on the plane, shimmering in the heat haze, which threatened a scorching afternoon.

"Hurry, please, it is time to board."

The voice of the hostess urging the few lingering passengers brought his eyes to the almost empty lounge. It was time. His case was conspicuous in its aloneness, and he cursed softly, wishing he had carried it with him instead of leaving it beside the chair. He sauntered toward it, moved with more speed as two men in green coveralls dropped their metal buckets with a clatter, and pulled the sopping long string mops from them. One leg moved, stretched, and as his toe connected with Skender's case, he pushed it toward him, clearing it from the dripping water of his mop. "Thank you." There was no response, no acknowledgement, and Skender picked up the case and turned.

There were very few left in the lounge as he casually walked toward the hostess. An Italian man sipped hurriedly at a cup of coffee, trying to down the precious liquid before having to board the plane. A honeymoon couple in the throes of their first argument and oblivious to anyone else in their heartbreak and anger. And, lastly, two women, schoolteachers, Skender guessed, who were already offering their boarding passes to the hostess.

Skender delayed, stared out of the window, so that the honeymoon couple would precede him. His prayer was simple, *I attempt this in Your name, but if it is not meant, grant that I am not taken alive.*

The hostess' voice had raised a decibel, "Next, please," and there was an underlying urgency as she glanced at her watch. Skender gripped the case, swallowed the nervousness, and moved toward her. "Boarding pass, signore."

He needed one more check of the outside area, deliberately let the pass slip from his fingers as he took it from his pocket. "I am sorry…." He bent to retrieve the pass: the tarmac was clear, stretching toward the plane with only three, perhaps four, mechanics lounging at the foot of the steps, and Mrs. Redland was chatting with one of them.

The Alitalia girl grinned at him as he straightened and he smiled back, apologized again. "That was clumsy of me…." He stiffened, did not release the pass to her. *Mrs. Redland? But … she had boarded first.* He saw the girl's puzzlement at his indecision. *Move! There could be any number of explanations … another photograph, anything … an opportunity like this will not be given to you again….*

Pastel-pink tipped fingers reached toward him, and he made his decision, and held out the card. A shutter flashed a picture to his mind and he wheeled. The Italian man blocked his view of the lounge. The girl laughed as the card fluttered to the floor again. "You are clumsy! Surely you did not learn that in Rome!"

He bent with her, supposedly to retrieve the pass, eyes sliding between the Italian legs across the floor to rest on the highly polished leather shoes of the cleaning men. The hostess had the pass and they rose as one. "Please proceed, signore." His ashen face alarmed her. "Are you ill? Is there any way I can help you?"

"No. There was a mistake … that is all. This pass will not be needed."

"Are you sure?" Her fingers held his shaking hand as she searched his face, suddenly afraid for him.

"Yes. Very sure." He nodded his thanks, turned away. The nerves in his body screamed at him to run, his legs shivered with anticipation as he repeated over and over, *Walk, walk, there is no hurry … you dare not, must not, let them see your fear.* The effort was unbearable as he passed the two Udba agents with their buckets. He stared woodenly ahead, avoiding the slow swinging mops, as he repeated over and over the one phrase that could save him, *Walk, walk, be casual, walk, walk....*

The passageway from International Flights to Domestic Flights was interminably long for Skender. He could feel his control slipping. His nerves jumped every time he was given more than a cursory glance by another passenger.

The line was long at the JAT counter, which carried the card 'Belgrade' above it. Instinct took him to the head of the line, and he pushed in front of the man about to be served. "One." His hand reached for his wallet.

The indignant words died on the ticket clerk's lips as he read the card thrust under his nose. "Yes, Comrade. Immediately." He turned to the complaining passenger trying to ease himself between Skender and the counter. "Shut your mouth or you will be refused a ticket." The fellow's eyes widened and he stared with awe at Skender. "This way please, Comrade ... which section of the plane would you prefer?"

"It doesn't matter. Just be sure that I have no one next to me." Skender followed the clerk, feeling the line of eyes on his back and despising himself, even as he acknowledged the necessity, for using his Udba authority.

"This row of seats will be reserved exclusively for you, Comrade." The man was anxious to please, relieved when he received Skender's nod of dismissal.

Skender sank down into the dark blue and grey upholstered seat, saw the quick, nervous glance of the hostess as the ticket clerk informed her who she had aboard. He closed his eyes, let the shivering take him. He started, half-stood, as he felt someone's nearness.

"I am sorry, Comrade, you were shivering...." Wide eyes blinked as she held the blanket toward him. He let himself relax back into his seat and she placed it around him. "Is there anything else I can fetch you?"

"Nothing. Do not disturb me until we reach Belgrade." He watched through half-closed lids as she tiptoed from him, then with a long, exhausted sigh, let them close. *Power is useful sometimes.*

Belgrade, Serbia

Skender was first off the plane. The other passengers were held back until he had descended the steps and entered the airport building. He glanced at his watch; it was pointless to hurry the connecting flight to Prishtine had left ten minutes earlier.

He hesitated, then went to the phone booths and placed a call to Udba's Headquarters in Prishtine. The connection was made almost immediately. "Good afternoon, Anna."

"Comrade Berisha!" Mihajlovich glanced up, mildly surprised at Anna's warmth as she answered. She saw him watching, covered the mouthpiece and smiled, "It is Comrade Berisha for you, Colonel Mihajlovich."

"Really!?" He moved toward Irena's phone.

She missed the sarcasm, laughed as Skender told her he felt like a grease blot. "It is hot here, too … perhaps you had better take a flight to the coast instead…." She caught Mihajlovich's raised eyebrows as he stood holding the phone, bit her lip, then said primly, "Colonel Mihajlovich is on the phone, Comrade Berisha." She pushed the appropriate button and replaced her own phone.

"Mihajlovich."

"Good afternoon, Colonel Mihajlovich … I am afraid cross winds delayed the flight from Zagreb and I missed the flight to Pristina."

"What a pity." Mihajlovich had been jubilant, full of energy since Vuksich called to advise him that Berisha was en route to Belgrade. "What do you intend to do now, then?"

"That is the reason for my call, sir … what are your instructions?" Pleasure rose inside Mihajlovich, and a smile curved his lips. "I thought the best thing would be to rent a car."

"That would mean driving all night."

"Yes, sir."

Mihajlovich rubbed at his lips. Many were killed on the roads at night. In spite of repeated warnings, the local peasantry still did not hang a light on the rear of their horse-drawn vehicles. Now that he had Berisha, he did not want to lose him to some stupid accident. "I think not. You know the difficulties of night driving, and I am sure you are tired. Take tomorrow's flight."

"But…." Mihajlovich frowned at Skender's hesitation, not able to find a cause for it. "Sir, that would mean staying overnight in Belgrade."

"So?" He laughed as the answer flashed to him. "Belgrade, the capital of Serbia, eh? Come, Berisha, no one can touch you. You are mine, and there is none who would dare to lift a finger against you." There was no response. "Rest assured that you are safe, move freely wherever you will. If you should be stopped, show your identification. That is all that will be needed."

Mihajlovich could almost feel Skender's nervousness. He continued, "We are taught to recognize fear, we can smell it. You have the authority, you carry it on your person. It should not be necessary for you to have to show it. Your bearing, your manner, should mirror that authority. Are you going to learn to dress yourself in it, speak with it, Berisha, or are you prepared to be stopped, questioned, made to prove it every time?"

Skender's voice was stiff, "I will spend the night in Belgrade, Colonel Mihajlovich, and take tomorrow's flight."

Mihajlovich relaxed. "Good. I will send a car to meet you at the airport." Mihajlovich was toying with another idea, he hesitated. To ask anyone, even a Serbian, to obey that order … he discarded it. For Berisha, it would be a monumental undertaking … and yet….

"Thank you, Colonel Mihajlovich. I will see you tomorrow afternoon. Good-bye."

"Wait a minute…." Mihajlovich sat in deep concentration. If Berisha refused, which would be understandable, he would have lost nothing, he could smooth it, make it appear that it was a suggestion, not an order. But, if Berisha obeyed him…. He swallowed his excitement, carefully phrased his words. "As you will be staying overnight in Belgrade, it will be necessary for you to pay your respects to our…" he gave slight emphasis to the word, "superior. You will, of course, find him at Udba's Head Office." He ignored the gasp, "And his name … do you have a pen handy, Berisha? … is Colonel Victor Popovic."

"Colonel Mihajlovich … you are not serious?"

Skender's fear transmitted itself to Mihajlovich, and he almost relented. "Of course I am serious! You pay your respects to two Udba Directors who have even less authority than I, and then ignore Colonel Popovic! How would that look?"

"I cannot … don't ask…."

"He is very personable … I think you will like him."

"Colonel Mihajlovich … please do not ask this. You, perhaps more than any other person, can understand how difficult this would be for me…."

Mihajlovich could hear Skender's ragged, uneven breathing. *Yes*, he agreed silently. *I do know. And that is why…. If you obey me in this, then I know that you are mine.*

"Is this an order?"

Mihajlovich did not answer, he was not going to commit himself. He was shaking with excitement, and he pulled the typing chair toward him and sat down.

"Very well."

Mihajlovich covered the mouthpiece of the phone as he let go a long sigh at Skender's words.

"Will tomorrow morning be acceptable?" Skender's voice was stiff with control.

"Of course." He had to wait a little longer, and then he could enjoy his victory.

"By the way, Berisha, I am very pleased with the way you handled this last assignment. Find yourself some little strumpet and enjoy Belgrade tonight. Until tomorrow." He replaced the phone.

He sat very still, letting his pleasure seep through him, drop down through every pore, every bone, of his being. He gave a long, contented sigh, stood, and pulled himself straight and tall. Anna's shocked face amused him. "Why so shocked, Anna? He has earned a little pleasure…." He laughed as she colored furiously and dropped her eyes to her book. "Don't tell me you have fallen for him, Anna! Tell me, do you wish you were the little Belgradian strumpet?"

"Colonel Mihajlovich!" she protested furiously. He looked at the tailored suit, the severe bun. "Bring your book, Anna," he laughed, "I think you are better suited to your present profession!"

Anna bit at her lip, surreptitiously wiped her tears as she checked that she had two well-sharpened pencils. She picked up her notebook and followed Mihajlovich. Sometimes he could be very cruel.

Chapter 53

Skender paid the taxi driver, entered the foyer of the Hotel Metropole. This was the hotel Jill had stayed at on her way to Prishtine. He took the Udba authorization from his wallet, laid it in front of the desk clerk. "A room for one. One night only."

The card worked its magic. "Yes, Comrade. I have a very nice room on the first floor." The register was placed in front of Skender the clerk picked up the pen, dipped it in the ink, and handed it to Skender. "Please register, Comrade."

Sken…. His hand stopped; the ink was green.

"Is there anything wrong, Comrade?" The man gave a nervous smile as he asked, looked from the half-written name to Skender and back again to the register.

"No." Skender finished his signature. "Tell me, why do you use green ink?"

"No reason, Comrade." The man was stuttering, his mind raced as he searched for a law forbidding it. "Shall I fetch…."

"It is not important." Skender picked up the key, leaned across the desk and confided, "Green is an untrue color, it is not a primary." Wary eyes peered at him through thick lenses. He recognized the feeling and laughed as he remembered his own reaction to Jill's words at the Post Office. "Remember, Comrade clerk, an untrue color." He sobered, added, "That is why I used green to write to my wife."

"Of course, Comrade." The clerk forced a smile, nodded vigorously.

Skender sighed. "Why agree? You don't know what the hell I'm talking about. Show me to my room."

I gambled and lost, Jill. Mihajlovich was too clever, watched me too closely. Skender lay on the bed, the room in darkness, lit only by the faint glow of a street lamp below. Dinner had been a lonely meal, eaten for the sake of eating, but without pleasure. He had taken a walk, but the close-linked arms of young couples, their soft laughter as they passed him, only increased his lonely depression, and he had returned to the hotel.

I expected to be in Rome by now, and yet … tomorrow, only a few hours away, I return to Prishtine and Mihajlovich. What then? How long before such an opportunity will present itself again?

He rolled from the bed, lifted the drape at the window, the night was soft, gentle … a night for lovers.

His eyes lingered on the bed. *Was this the room you had? Did your body warm the same sheets mine will warm? Did it leave its indentation on that bed as mine will?*

He sighed, turned back to the window. *It is of no matter. There is nothing of you in this impersonal place. Nothing of you, as there will be nothing of me….*

Chapter 54

Prishtine, Kosov

"Good morning, Anna. Anything urgent this morning?" Mihajlovich pulled the file marked 'Incoming Mail' toward him as he sat down.

"Good morning, Colonel Mihajlovich. The Belgrade office wishes to know how many will be attending the Conference."

"Two … myself and Berisha. Make room reservations for both of us." Mihajlovich waited as Anna made her notes. "And fill in an application for Berisha to attend the next session of Udba's Officer Training … I will sponsor him." She nodded as she jotted down his instructions. "Is there anything else that requires my immediate attention?"

"Officer Dragonovich is waiting to see you … he says it is important." She caught his quizzical smile and smiled back. "And there is also this letter…." She leaned across the desk, opened the file and brought Mihajlovich's attention to the top letter. "It is marked 'personal,' and is from Captain Kulich." Her finger pointed to the Sarajevo return address.

Mihajlovich picked it up, curious. "Send Dragonovich in." He turned the envelope over, checked that the sealing wax was intact, had not been tampered with then reached for the letter opener in his drawer.

"Colonel Mihajlovich, there was a call from…."

"Good morning, Officer Dragonovich." Mihajlovich interrupted the excited officer pleasantly but firmly.

Dragonovich swore beneath his breath, Mihajlovich's insistence on 'drawing room' manners as Dragonovich referred to them, always irritated him. "Good morning, Colonel Mihajlovich. Early this morning I was informed that four men attempted an illegal crossing at the border of Austria," he paused, added triumphantly, "…one of them is ours."

Mihajlovich laid down the letter, placed the paper knife beside it. "Go on."

"They were caught minutes before midnight but refused to give their names or any information. The Border Patrol transferred them to the local police." He grinned, "Now they are singing loudly!"

"They are either very daring or very stupid … it is not dark enough at this time of year to attempt a border crossing. Do we know the one from Pristina?"

"Oh, yes." Dragonovich waited until Mihajlovich looked up. "Deva. Mustafa Deva."

Mihajlovich frowned, "Deva?"

Dragonovich continued, "We have had him in our hands before."

"Yes, the name is familiar … Deva? Deva? I know that it is one of this city's leading families, but there is something else, something closer." He shook his head gave up with a sigh, "It escapes me for the moment. When are they sending him to us?"

"They're not."

"Why not?" Mihajlovich demanded sharply.

Dragonovich's teeth gritted as he reminded Mihajlovich, "The new regulation requires that any person detained in a region other than their own be sent directly to Belgrade for special interrogation."

"Damn! Stupidity!" The paper knife was pointed at Dragonovich. "It is us, you and I, who should have the interrogation of this Deva, not some pipsqueak in Belgrade who needs to practice a new technique."

"I agree, Colonel Mihajlovich. I feel as if I have been cheated, but…" Dragonovich shrugged, "they have requested that his file be forwarded so that it is available for inspection when the prisoner reaches Belgrade."

"What did we have him for?"

"I have not checked Colonel." Dragonovich's voice was sullen as he asked, "Do you wish me to honor their request, forward the file?"

Mihajlovich sighed, "Do we have a choice?" He picked up Kulich's letter, slit it open. "Yes, pull the file and make a copy for them … let me see it before forwarding it. By the way…" he stopped Dragonovich halfway to the door, "Berisha returns this morning. Tell Anna to send a car to the airport for him." Mihajlovich took the letter from its envelope as the door closed on Dragonovich, he was surprised to see that it was handwritten.

> *Stefan,*
> *I am writing to you because of a discrepancy that could be important….*

The sun beat on the back of Mihajlovich's neck, and he pushed his chair from the desk into the shadow, made a mental note to order blinds to diffuse the sun now that the protection of the tree had been removed.

> *The night Berisha dined with me, the subject of his engagement was raised, and he mentioned his fiancée lived in Sarajevo. This was in keeping with what you had told me and confirmed the rumor I had already volunteered to you from the talkative neighbor. Now, by chance, I discover that the girl is*

> *not engaged to Skender Berisha, but to one Jakup Berisha, the eldest son….*

Mihajlovich stood, face white, and re-read the last sentence.

> *I suggest you clarify this. If Berisha has deliberately misled you … and I … there must be a reason. I suggest you put a light on in the dark room.*
> *My regards,*
> *Alex*

"Colonel Mihajlovich, I cannot find … is there anything wrong, Colonel?"

"What?" Mihajlovich's eyes lifted briefly, then returned to the letter.

Dragonovich stretched, tried to see who the letter was from, "I said I cannot find the file on Mustafa Deva." There was no response. "What is wrong, Colonel Mihajlovich?"

"Nothing." Mihajlovich dragged his eyes from the letter. "What did you say about the file?"

"It is missing."

Mihajlovich pushed the problem of Berisha away. "Don't be ridiculous … how can a file be missing? It has probably been misplaced. Ask Anna to find it for you."

"I did. The Deva file is not in the drawer."

Deva…, Deva…. There was a lifting in Mihajlovich's memory, but before he could recall why the name was so familiar, the curtain dropped. He rubbed at his lip, irritated that he could not remember. "The name is so familiar … I can almost … why did we have this Morat Deva? What was the charge?"

"He took part in the demonstration…." Dragonovich stopped. "Mustafa Deva, Colonel Mihajlovich. The one who attempted the border crossing was Mustafa Deva."

Mihajlovich rubbed his temples, eyes closed as he concentrated. The name Morat Deva was sharp, clear, but the reason was out of focus. He wished Dragonovich would shut up, let him think.

"…and I thought that it was his file until I saw the name Morat. They both start with 'M'…."

"There is a Morat Deva, then?" Mihajlovich cut off Dragonovich.

"Yes."

"And we have a file on him?"

"Yes, but…."

"Bring it." Mihajlovich paced impatiently. "Ahh, good, Anna, this will clear things for me." He placed it on his desk, stood out of the hot sun. "Order blinds," he instructed Anna with a glance at the window as he opened the file.

Dragonovich's lip curled, "If you put blinds, you've defeated the purpose of chopping down the tree." Mihajlovich's steady gaze brought a nervous laugh. "But we can always look at the obelisk in the winter."

"Order blinds, Anna. Every office except Officer Dragonovich's." Mihajlovich gave a mocking bow to Dragonovich, "I would not want to deprive you of the view." He turned back to the file, was suddenly very still. "This cannot be … the last entry is April 1946." His finger followed across the page, voice soft, unbelieving as he read aloud, "Check-in time seven-fifteen, held for questioning in Interrogation Room Two, beaten repeatedly, no response." Mihajlovich turned the page, "Detained all night with regular beatings. Overlooked during rounding up of Kosovo youths for forced march…." A picture of Berisha sitting, speaking, came for an instant, he frowned, concentrating, but it was gone. "Given into the custody of guards from Nis…."

'Morat Deva.' It was his own voice, demanding an answer.

The veil lifted.

Berisha sat opposite, voice tired and heavy as he answered, 'Beaten until he couldn't walk, then thrown into a ravine and left to die.'

"Are you ill, Colonel Mihajlovich?" Anna asked with concern. She glanced to Dragonovich, as there was no reply, then leaned across the desk, gently laid her hand on Mihajlovich's arm, "Please, sit down. Is there anything I can do?"

"How did this file get left behind?" Mihajlovich's icy anger made Anna draw back. "This file was to have been destroyed. How did it return to the cabinet?"

"I have no idea, Col…." She hesitated only a moment as Mihajlovich strode from the room to her office, then followed, with Dragonovich hard on her heels. Mihajlovich seemed distraught as he fitted the appropriate key into the lock. "Let me get the file you need," she offered.

Mihajlovich ignored her. "Give me some names, Dragonovich, some names."

Mihajlovich's agitation puzzled Dragonovich. "What names, Colonel?"

"If I knew what names, fool, I would not need to ask you. Names. Names of any, any young man arrested, anyone held for questioning by Udba." Mihajlovich's impatience grew as Dragonovich frowned in concentration. "Hurry … give me anyone who has been in our hands during the past year, anyone at all who would have warranted a file."

"Shabani … Shkodra … two of them, Kadri … and, yes, Jusuf Dardha."

Mihajlovich's fingers moved frantically through the files as Dragonovich gave him the information. "None. Not one here."

"That is impossible."

"Yes," Mihajlovich agreed with Dragonovich, "Impossible … unless…." His suspicion crystallized, "Let me see Berisha's file."

"Berisha's?" Anna questioned, "Comrade Berisha's?" Mihajlovich's glare answered her and she turned, unlocked the next cabinet.

Mihajlovich's hand swept Anna's desk clear. He laid the file down, bent over it. The pages rattled as he thumbed through. "Here it is … a list of his known associates. Mali, Sabri, according to this his closest friend." The room was silent except for the faint flick of the files as Anna searched. Mihajlovich's eyes lifted, met and held Dragonovich's as she pulled the buff folder from the cabinet. "Gashi, Jusuf." In her haste to please Mihajlovich, she passed it, realized her mistake, and returned to the beginning of the file marked 'G'.

"Give it to Dragonovich. Deva, Morat, we have, of course. Try…." Each name he read brought another file, a deepening of his anger. "Lay them on the other desk," Mihajlovich instructed Dragonovich. "Now, check the date of the last entry on each one."

Dragonovich's eyes lifted in blank amazement, "Impossible."

"Read them."

"May 1946. April 1946. May 1946. March…."

"That's enough," Mihajlovich cut in, voice grim.

Dragonovich looked perplexed, "All these are outdated, old…."

Mihajlovich nodded.

"Then … where are the current files?" He glanced at Anna, silently questioned her. Her shoulders lifted as confused as Dragonovich. With some hesitation and a confirming look at the old files he asked Mihajlovich again, "Where are the current files, Colonel?"

"I'll take him apart, piece by piece" Mihajlovich's voice was soft, vicious. He gave a slow nod, "You will beg, Berisha. You will beg me to let you die."

Dragonovich looked at Anna. She shook her head, unable to answer his silent question.

Mihajlovich allowed himself a few more minutes to envisage Berisha's agony, then dragged in a long breath and turned to Anna, "Check every file. If there is one, just one, that is current, I will be very surprised."

He half-turned toward his Sergeant, "To answer your question, Dragonovich, the current ones have been burnt, totally destroyed."

Dragonovich's lips moved silently on the word, his head shook, "No." He spoke loudly, emphatically. "No. That is impossible. It was the outdated files that were burnt. You ordered it, Colonel Mihajlovich. And you put Berisha in charge…." His eyes narrowed, "Berisha." He spat the name as he looked directly at Mihajlovich. "It was Berisha … he has deliberately…."

"Yes."

"How? The cabinets are always locked … there are only three keys…."

"I have already thought of that," Mihajlovich interrupted. He turned, smiled. "Come here, Anna." Unsuspecting, thinking he needed something, she moved toward him. Her head reached just to Mihajlovich's shoulder, and he smiled down at her, then demanded softly, "Explain."

Her startled eyes flew to him. "I cannot, Colonel Mihajlovich … I have no idea how…." Her words ended in a sharp cry as Mihajlovich took her wrist, twisted it, and pulled her close.

"I want to know how Berisha got into my files, Anna." He felt for, found her little finger. Automatically, Dragonovich's hand moved, his hand muffled her scream. "Answer me, Anna." He applied more pressure and automatically Dragonovich's hand clamped tighter, silencing the agonized cry, pushing it back into her throat.

Mihajlovich held a moment longer, released some of the pressure, holding just tight enough to jangle her nerves, while allowing her to think. "It hurts, eh, Anna? Not enough to drive all thought except pain from your mind, but just sufficient to let you know that all I have to do…. Tell me, Anna, would you prefer to go with Officer Dragonovich?" Mihajlovich smiled at Dragonovich as both saw the panic replace pain. Her full eyes pleaded with him. "Do you recall the Women's Interrogation Room, Anna? You remained so cool, so calm, able to ignore the terror, the suffering … I quite admired you." He nodded to Dragonovich to release his grip on her mouth "Well, Anna, I am waiting."

"I have done nothing….

"I remember one, she was young…." He looked down at Anna. "She refused to answer. We let her bleed to death, let the life drip from her. Drop, by slow drop."

"I swear I do not know," Anna cried. "I have always locked…."

"Enough. You are tiring my patience. Answer immediately or go to Dragonovich." Her eyes slid to the blue-grey uniform, and he felt her shudder. He put his mouth close to her ear, whispered, "You have never liked him, and he knows it, has sensed how you despise him. He will enjoy hurting you." Fear was growing in her, her trembling, the shakiness of her voice told Mihajlovich that.

"I have done nothing wrong, Colonel Mihajlovich. I have never permitted Comrade Berisha to touch the files or given him my key."

"I do not believe you." She backed away from him as he released his hold on her. "You were infatuated with Berisha. You gave him the key…."

"No!" she cried on a long sob. Her own hand stifled her cry of terror as she felt the cold metal blocking her retreat, her eyes were wide, staring, as Mihajlovich bent over her. "I did not, I did not…."

"What did he promise? Marriage? Or was it just enough to have him mount you?"

She gasped, shock driving fear out for a moment, then turned her face from his. The sharp tug on her hair hurt as Mihajlovich pulled her to face him.

"So plain…." he sneered, as his eyes searched the tear-streaked face, "you had something he wanted, otherwise he would not have looked twice." The long, animal moan irritated Mihajlovich, and he jerked her upright, threw her to Dragonovich.

"Send two guards immediately." Dragonovich released the intercom button, held Anna with just one arm, "What do you want me to do with her?"

Mihajlovich let his eyes move over the distraught and disheveled Anna with slow deliberation. "Whatever pleases you. I want information. How you get it, what method, is immaterial."

"No!" The cry was wrung from deep inside Anna. She pulled free of Dragonovich, threw herself at Mihajlovich's feet, clutching his leg. "I swear, I did nothing." Her eyes were panicked as she looked up at him, her pleading intense. "Please, Colonel Mihajlovich, please…." Her grip tightened on his leg as the guards arrived at the door. "I swear I have never given my key to Berisha, never opened any file for him…."

Dragonovich's finger moved, ordering them to take her.

Her voice rose to a scream, "Seven years, Colonel Mihajlovich, seven years I have been with you…." She was sobbing, tears streaming down her face, "Seven, seven … loyal service … done nothing…."

Dragonovich's slap across the mouth ended her outpouring in a long cry.

She released her grip on Mihajlovich's leg as she felt the warm trickle of blood. Her fingers touched her mouth and then came away, she stared at the red stain in disbelief before she crumpled to the floor.

"Women's Interrogation. Hold her until I come," Dragonovich instructed the guards. He waited until they had half-carried, half-dragged the unconscious Anna from the office, then closed the door and picked up the phone.

The light click alerted Mihajlovich, and he turned from the window. "What are you doing?"

"Calling Police Headquarters in Belgrade. Berisha must be at the airport … I will have him arrested."

"Put the phone down!"

Dragonovich still held the phone as he stared at Mihajlovich.

"Put it down," Mihajlovich ordered. Slowly, the phone was put back. "Why call?" Mihajlovich smiled at Dragonovich's confusion. "Berisha suspects nothing. He will take the plane and come willingly to me. Should I permit you to place that call, though, who will have the interrogation of him?"

There was a pause, then Dragonovich muttered, "Belgrade."

"Exactly. Do you want to be deprived of him, Dragonovich? I don't. I want him. I want to take him into hell. I want to hear and see his agony, want to see him trembling on the brink of madness. I plan to take him into the shadow of death itself and then, as his hand reaches out for release from his misery, snatch him back. Back to me." His hand wiped at his mouth. "When I am through with him, he will regret that he touched even one file."

Dragonovich's eyes were caught by the files on Anna's desk, "What are we going to do about Deva? If we do not send his file, Belgrade will call, demand … will you tell them that all our records have been destroyed?"

Mihajlovich frowned. "No, not yet." He paused, he needed time, time to ensure that no blame, or as little as possible, would attach to him. "First, I want a confession from Anna that she and Berisha conspired against the State … can you do that?" Dragonovich's eyebrow rose. "Yes, of course. That was a stupid question. After that … let us wait, see what Berisha tells us."

Dragonovich's nod was slow. He knew Mihajlovich, knew that if he could shift the blame to someone else, he would. He did not intend it to be himself. "Perhaps I should work on Anna immediately. Now that she is frightened…" his shoulders lifted in a shrug, "…my work is half-done."

"Agreed." Mihajlovich moved toward his own office. The shorthand notebook at his feet stopped him and he bent, picked it from the floor, he snapped it closed and threw it onto the desk. "A pity. She was an excellent secretary."

Chapter 55

Belgrade, Serbia

The hotel clerk was quick and checked the Register for the name of his important guest before Skender had finished descending the stairs. "Good morning, Comrade Berisha. I trust you slept well?"

"Yes, thank you." Surprised, Skender realized that he had. He had slept only a short time, but it had been deep and restful. "I shall be back later to pick up my bag."

"No one will be permitted into your room, Comrade, no one," the clerk assured him.

Skender nodded his thanks, then moved toward the dining room. There were a few tables occupied, the patrons busy with their rolls and coffee. He hesitated, he wanted something lighter, more open, than this heavy, ornate room with its carvings, gilt-framed pictures and mahogany columns. The wide marble steps curved away from him to the street, an arc of grey beauty. Metropole was one of the older hotels, and still carried the influence of the Austro-Hungarian Empire.

Ulica Revolution was busy as he joined the throng of people hurrying to their desks, the salesgirls scurrying to their counters. Skender took his time and sauntered near the huge glass-paned windows of the shops, he had time to kill before his flight to Prishtine, and the offices of Udba would not open until nine o'clock. He planned to present himself there an hour later, giving them time to handle any emergencies that might have arisen during the night. One of the pavement cafés caught his attention, and he moved toward it, chose a table with an umbrella giving plenty of shade, and sat down. It was already hot, and he wished he had worn one of the new lightweight suits that he had purchased recently.

"What may I fetch for you?" Skender gaped at the man, he had spoken in English. "Coffee and rolls with some fresh butter … and, perhaps, a little jam? Yes?"

The accent was 'heavy', but otherwise … he realized the man was waiting. "Yes. Thank you, that will be perfect." He watched the black coat disappear into the back of the restaurant, idly wondering why the man had addressed him in English. He shrugged it away as he spotted the paper at the next table, reached, and picked it up. He flicked to the sports page, anxious to see how Prishtine had fared in their soccer game against Skopje. Sports held a mild interest for him, he was not as crazy as some, but soccer was his favorite, and it was his home team … his jubilation coincided with the arrival of his breakfast.

The waiter held the tray at shoulder level, his puzzlement obvious as he looked from Skender to the paper, then back to Skender, "I am sorry, I thought you were American."

The waiter had spoken Serbo-Croatian, and Skender answered in kind, "Does it make a difference?" He glanced up with a smile as he cleared a place for the tray.

There was a shrug, "You would not want this coffee." He saw that Skender had not caught his meaning. "American … weak … and with hot milk."

"I will take it." Skender waited until the tray was in front of him, then asked as he poured the coffee into his cup. "What made you think I was an American?"

The waiter balanced on the back of one of the metal chairs. Business was slow, and he felt like passing some time. "Your clothes. Your manner." His towel swatted at a fly.

"Manner?" Skender buttered a piece of the long, curling roll, added a little jam.

"Americans, English, Germans, even the Scandinavians … they are all the same, they look around, decide which table they want to sit at and…." His shoulders lifted. "Not us. We wait, ask, 'May I sit here? Is this table permissible?"

Skender laughed at the fellow's imitation of his own countrymen, "And then?" he prompted. Silver teeth flashed as the waiter laughed back at him, "You do not need to answer! You refuse, stick them back there in the corner. Or in the sun."

"Of course! It is the tourists who tip. Especially the Americans!"

Skender bit into the roll. "Don't expect too much from me! I have taken one of your better tables, but I am not one of your wealthy tourists," he teased.

The man grinned. "I know that now. Where do you work? Office? Which part of Belgrade do you live? I live in the southern district … it is close. Ten minutes on my bicycle and I am home … how about you?"

"I am not from Belgrade."

"No? Your speech is Belgradian."

Skender realized that unknowingly, his Serbo-Croatian had improved, even to the point of picking up Mihajlovich's inflections. Languages had always held a special attraction for him, and even though he had no love of the Slavic language, he felt a gratification that he spoke it well, and used the purer Belgradian dialect.

"It is hot today … I hate the heat." The man wiped at his forehead with the towel. "Why can't they let us leave these coats off, work in white shirts and black trousers? Someone told me that is how the Italian waiters dress … black trousers and white shirts." He licked at a stub of pencil as he saw Skender reach for his wallet. "All we hear is, 'Wear your coat, wear your coat….' Skender smiled as there was another imitation, supposedly of the man's superior. He handed Skender the bill, "Ten dinars, please. How can you give good service when you are hot and sweaty? Thank you. Your change. Why do we have all these rules? Why can't we decide for ourselves?" He sighed and shook his head, added morosely, "They even tell me what time to piss." Skender laughed out loud as he dropped some coins onto the table. "Thank you, thank you very much." His thanks were effusive as he pulled the table back so that Skender could pass by. "And I still think you look like an American."

Skender grinned, then answered in English, "Perhaps I am … and Americans don't use hot milk in their coffee. They use cream."

The waiter laughed, called after Skender, "I'll remember! It will bring a better tip! Dovidenja."

"Dovidenja." Skender almost asked for directions to Udba's Head Office but checked himself. He could imagine the horror, the fright, he would give the poor fellow if he asked for that place, he would wait, find a policeman….

He walked slowly, letting his eyes feast on the abundance of goods in the windows. One shop, in particular, held his attention for a long time, sausages hung from the ceiling, fat, thin, straight, curved, their skins smooth and shiny, asking for a knife to cut them and release all the glorious aroma of spices and seasonings. Great wheels of cheese, ranging from palest cream to deepest yellow, mingled with fat jars of honey, wax combs swimming in the golden amber. Garlands of dried peppers hung from invisible threads in the window, one of red, another green and another yellow, and one a rainbow of all. Apothecary jars, enormous, held ruby-red tomatoes and dark green cucumbers, both pickled in brine, while small glass containers of jams nestled among great bunches of garlic. He felt his mouth watering, even though he was not hungry.

He almost gasped as he moved to the next window. Hand-cut crystal stood on rough-hewn logs, the stark simplicity of the wood, the solidity, emphasizing the frailty and delicate beauty, the mastery of the craftsman. He remembered Jill's fascination with Belgrade, and now understood. It was a shopper's paradise.

Before retiring to his room the night before, he had walked the streets, doubling back, crossing roads on the pretext of window-gazing while checking, always checking, that he was not being followed. Now, again, it was time to check, and he stopped on the pretext of admiring a selection of leather coats. He was too close to the pane for it to form a mirror, so he stepped back a pace, apparently intent on the soft boots and shoes on the floor of the display, while his eyes scanned the street behind and in front of him.

He was not being watched. He knew it, had a deep gut feeling about it. Last night, he had lain awake for a long time, carefully considering the options open to him, road travel he had dismissed as too dangerous, private cars were suspect, and subject to long delays at the border. Rail had been his choice, he would board as Skender Berisha, Member of Udba, and, before reaching the border of Ljubljana, he would become Skender Berisha, U.S. citizen. With his Udba authorization, he would not be questioned when he boarded the train, with his U.S. passport, he would not be given a second glance at the border. It was safe and easy.

Grey despair had washed over him when he had checked the timetable available at the Metropole. The train did not leave until late morning, and took nine long hours to reach the border, which would give Mihajlovich plenty of time to know that Berisha had not returned as planned, and have all borders closed to him. The airport was dangerous. His experience at Zagreb had proved that. And yet … Jill's BEA flight had departed minutes before the one to Prishtine … it was tempting, terribly tempting. He had seesawed back and forth, deciding to take a chance, and then backing away as he realized that if he failed it would be the end of him.

The chiming of the Clock Tower pulled him back to the present, and he wound his way across the street to a policeman on the corner. "Excuse me, could you direct me to the Head Office of Udba?"

"Why?" There was an insolent sizing up of Skender, "What is it to you where they live?"

"I have an appointment…." The lips of the policeman curled in disbelief, and he half-turned away. Skender took out his wallet, reached and withdrew his Udba authorization, then added with cool deliberation, "With Comrade Director Victor Popovic."

The reaction was instant, the policeman stood poker-stiff at attention, "Pardon, Comrade, I did not realize…." The man was frightened.

Skender sighed. *Why was it necessary? What was accomplished by this constant levering of authority? He had asked a simple question. He was tired of it all, wanted to be able to approach the law with a simple 'Hi', have his question answered and go on his way with a friendly smile exchanged between them, instead of this….* "Which direction?"

"Straight ahead two streets, Comrade, then turn right. Udba will be directly in front of you." The man's eyes slid to Skender. "Would you wish for me to escort you?"

"No," Skender put his card away, then returned his wallet to his pocket, "I will find it myself." He gave a nod of dismissal, then moved off in the direction indicated.

He was going to this meeting for two reasons: to cover himself in case Mihajlovich called to check with Popovic that his assistant had presented himself as ordered; or there were complications at the airport and he could not take the

BEA flight to London and had to return to Prishtine. He strongly suspected that the latter would be the case. The largest airport in Yugoslavia, the one with the highest number of international flights, would not go unguarded.

The building was a surprise, it was modern, tall, and seemed entirely constructed of glass. He had expected something heavy, dark, and forbidding. There were two policemen, one on each side of the clear glass doors, the crease of their trousers knife-sharp, their buttons polished to reflect like mirrors. Their eyes were distrustful and curious as Skender climbed the wide steps towards the entrance.

The one on the right stepped forward, blocking the entrance, "You have business here?"

"Yes, I have an appointment with Comrade Director Popovic."

"Your papers." Skender reached for the authorization, the man checked the photograph, took a long look at Skender. "Follow me." He about wheeled, and as he did so, his comrade opened the door and allowed them to enter before letting it close. The heavy hobnailed boots thundered a halt on the marble floor as he stopped beside a desk and handed Skender's authorization to the sergeant. "This man says he has an appointment with Comrade Popovic, Comrade Sergeant." He took one pace back and stood at attention. Skender realized that he had been placed, very neatly and with great efficiency, between the policeman and the sergeant. If his papers were not in order….

"You are Skender Berisha? From Pristina, Kosovo? Under the command of Colonel Mihajlovich?"

"Yes." He stood still while his height was visually checked, his weight guessed at. The sergeant's face was as cold and expressionless as the marble on which they stood as he studied first the authorization and then Skender. The white gloves were spotless as he held out his hand. "Your Identity Card." It, too, was carefully studied. He glanced up. "You are a Kosovar?"

His stomach heaved; his whole body quivered. "Yes." The pale eyes held his for a long moment. The white-gloved hand moved, returning his papers. "Thank you."

The sergeant sat quietly watching until Skender had returned his wallet to his pocket. "Follow me, Comrade." As he stood, he dismissed the guard, then proceeded at a smart pace toward the lifts at the rear of the lobby.

As the doors closed on them, Skender's heart skipped a beat. He was deep inside Udba. He felt as if he had been swallowed alive.

The doors slid open, and he was passed to another policeman as the sergeant ordered him to be taken to Colonel Popovic. The sergeant's hand touched his cap as the doors closed. Skender wished he were with him sliding down to be disgorged onto the street.

"This way, Comrade."

Their feet moved soundlessly over the thick carpeting as they passed the closed doors of offices on each side of the hallway. The silence was disturbed as a door opened and a young woman came out, but the typewriter's sharp tap was silenced again as she closed the door. She stood aside as they passed and murmured a greeting.

"Good morning," Skender replied. The guard did not answer except with a brief nod.

"In here, Comrade." The guard opened a heavy glass door.

"May I help you, Comrade?" She was an attractive woman, not pretty, but sophisticated and well dressed.

Skender heard the quiet brush of the glass door against the carpet, and realized that the guard had gone, closing the door behind him. "Yes. I have an appointment with Comrade Director Popovic. My name is Skender Berisha." His hand reached for his wallet.

She smiled. "I will not need that … you have already received clearance. Please…." She indicated a chair, waited until he was comfortable, and then depressed a key on the telephone as she lifted the receiver. "Colonel, Mr. Berisha is here." She replaced the receiver, and said with another smile, "Colonel Popovic will see you now, Mr. Berisha. When you go in, you will present your Udba card to the Colonel." She stood, started toward the inner office.

"Thank you." Skender also stood. *No body search … no check for a weapon?* He smiled his thanks as the girl opened the door.

"Mr. Berisha, Colonel." She closed the door silently behind her.

"How very kind of you to visit us, Mr. Berisha."

He was probably fifty. His hair was iron grey and was combed straight back, it was thinning on top and made his face appear longer than it was. His complexion was sallow, as if he had started a tan and then lost it, and he was smooth shaven. He was not tall … five foot five perhaps … but he was lean and fit. His grey suit, cut to emphasize the wide shoulders and slim build, was elegant and expensive. He extended his hand, the grey eyes shrewd but welcoming as he asked, "When did you arrive in Belgrade?"

It was his voice that impressed, it was deep and melodious, and Skender felt he could listen to it forever and not tire of it. Their hands met, Popovic's grip was firm and dry.

"Late yesterday afternoon, Comrade Colonel." He took the chair indicated. "Thank you."

There was no guard. He sat, alone, with one of the most powerful men in the country. He had not kept him waiting. And he had been offered a seat immediately. Skender's fear evaporated.

"Colonel Mihajlovich extends his warmest regards and looks forward to seeing you very soon." He remembered the secretary's instructions and felt for his wallet.

Popovic smiled. "Good. I miss Stefan, but, if you will excuse me for one moment?" There was a polite pause, and then he picked up the telephone.

Skender let his eyes wander around the room, deliberately wanting to give Popovic some semblance of privacy for his call. The room was light and airy, and behind Popovic's desk, the windows reached from ceiling to floor, giving a breathtaking panorama of Belgrade. The left-hand wall held books, mostly leather-bound and gold-tooled, apparently suspended in mid-air until close inspection revealed the Perspex shelves. The opposite wall was a delicate apricot with two pictures, both, Skender was sure, Monet's framed in clear Perspex. Popovic's desk was enormous and very modern, curving and flowing, not a sharp edge or a straight line to be seen.

"Do you know the Capital well, Mr. Berisha?" The well-manicured hand reached for Skender's card.

"No, sir…." He stopped, horrified at his mistake, his eyes dropped from Popovic's steady appraisal. "I am sorry." He could kick himself for his stupidity. "No, Comrade Colonel."

Popovic smiled, a slow, lazy smile. "It is of no matter. Personally, I prefer the old greeting. It is short and smart … 'Comrade Colonel' … such a mouthful." He saw that Skender had relaxed again and looked down at the card. "You are from Pristina?"

"Yes, Comrade Colonel."

Popovic looked up, asked mildly, "So you are a Kosovar?"

Skender stiffened, "Yes, Comrade Colonel."

"Why so belligerent? I am a Serb. If you were to ask me 'Are you a Serb?' I would answer 'yes' in the same way, the same tone, as I would answer if you asked, 'Are you hungry?' or 'Are you thirsty?' Why this anger from you at such a simple question?"

"Perhaps, Comrade Colonel, because my answer to that 'simple question' could, at worst, cause me a beating, and at best strip me of my rights, or my dignity." Skender saw Popovic's eyes narrow and forced a smile. "But hopefully, for me, that is in the past … now that I am working for Colonel Mihajlovich…."

"Yes." The word was long, drawn out, as Popovic looked thoughtfully at Skender's authorization. "What classification do you have?"

"I beg your pardon?"

Popovic smiled to himself, he had his answer, but he asked again, "What classification did Stefan give you?" He had had a momentary misgiving, had wondered if Stefan's enthusiasm for this project had made him careless. "Let me put it another way, Mr. Berisha. I see that you do not follow me … can you order an arrest? Do you interrogate prisoners? Do you have access to any classified information, any files?"

The word dropped into Skender's stomach, lay there, like a rock, he took a long breath, "I interrogate the younger students, just the Kosovars, no Yugoslavs; and, yes, I can order an arrest."

"I see." It was the answer he expected. "And the files?" Skender shook his head unable to answer. Popovic smiled. "Stefan is not making full use of you … I must advise him to upgrade you." Skender gave an answering smile. "Have you had any formal training from Udba yet? I mean apart from that given by Stefan."

"No." Skender wondered what he meant. He watched as a notation was made on a pad close to Popovic's side of the desk.

"Then … would you tell me what has been your major project? The most important thing you have accomplished since you started working for Stefan?" He sat back in his chair.

Skender swallowed. The destruction of the files had been his most important undertaking He made himself concentrate, trying not to think of them, even as he wondered for a moment if Popovic was testing him. His signature had been on the Completion Form, and if he, Popovic, had seen it…. Skender dismissed the idea.

The Reports! As the answer came to him, he looked at Popovic, "Colonel Mihajlovich wanted a comprehensive report on the Kosovo area, and I have been actively engaged with that…."

"Is it completed?"

"Yes, Comrade Colonel."

"Good. No doubt Stefan will present it, or at least a part, at the Conference. How long have you worked for Udba now?"

"Seven months, Comrade Colonel."

"You have a good … no, an excellent teacher. Stefan was my protégée, now you are his … you could not be in better hands." He stretched his hand to the phone. "Would you like some coffee? Vera, some coffee, please." He had not waited for an answer.

Skender inclined his head, "Thank you."

"Please…." Popovic dismissed the thanks. "Now tell me your news … how is Kosovo?" He saw that Skender was not sure of his meaning. "Quiet? Unrest? Dissatisfied, or perhaps outright rebellion?"

Skender considered carefully. "Dissatisfied? Yes. Quiet? No. But rebellion…." He shook his head.

"A pot, getting ready to boil, eh? Tell Stefan to keep the lid tight, very tight." He beckoned the girl in, and they both watched as she poured the coffee. "And Stefan? He is well?"

Skender saw the hesitation as the girl started to leave, and realized that she, too, wanted to know. Deliberately, he picked up his coffee and took a sip, waiting until the door had closed on her before he answered, "Yes, thank you, he is very well … but a little tired."

Popovic nodded as he sipped at his coffee. "Pristina is a hotbed … it is not an easy assignment. The coffee is to your liking, Mr. Berisha?"

"Thank you, yes."

The sudden, "Do you like him?" caused Skender to almost drop his cup, and Popovic gave an amused smile as he asked again, "Stefan. Do you like him?"

Skender slowly put his cup and saucer on the desk in front of him. His mind raced. He despised everything Mihajlovich stood for, hated his cruelty, his lack of caring. He remembered the close relationship that had been gradually building, the tensions between them had lessened, were now almost non-existent. A mutual respect for the ability of each had started to form.… His voice was barely audible as he answered truthfully, "Yes, I enjoy his company."

Popovic sent silent congratulations to Mihajlovich. "So do I. He has always been a great favorite of mine. He has a good mind and is well-read, and I must admit his caustic wit amuses me … if Stefan is part of the group, there is always laughter."

We have often shared a smile at some absurdity … laughed together at the stupidity of an order … and his quick wit has left me chuckling more than once.…

Popovic watched Skender closely, decided he had let enough time elapse and continued, "And yet, give him a problem … he can go straight to the heart."

Yes, I have seen it, given grudging admiration of his handling of a difficulty … have recognized and respected his quick summing up of a problem.…

Skender's turmoil pleased Popovic. Mihajlovich had said that it would not be easy to win this one's respect and loyalty, but if they could.… Popovic let a quiet smile play about his lips, then asked, "And the work? It interests you?"

"Yes. Very much." Skender was shocked, dismayed at the truth of it. He remembered the questioning of the students, their recoil from him. "Not all of it, but mostly … yes."

"Isn't that the way in any occupation, Mr. Berisha? Some things bore, others irritate, but predominantly, you must be interested. If you are not interested in your work, you become slovenly … things begin to slide … poof. Then, not only you, but others are affected … the indifference trickles down through the chain until even the janitor senses it." He smiled as he saw Berisha's acknowledgement of the truth. "If, one morning, you find your wastebasket unemptied … look to the top! That, Mr. Berisha, is where the rot will be." There was a knock, light and sharp. "Come in." Popovic beckoned the young man in. "This is Cadet Dusan, Mr. Berisha … he is my aide. Dusan I would like to present Comrade Berisha, he has brought us greetings from Colonel Mihajlovich in Kosovo."

Skender stood. The uniform was not grey, not green, the face young and eager, with blue eyes alight with ardent enthusiasm. The high leather boots came together in a sharp click, as he saluted Skender. Skender started, he had almost offered his hand. He inclined his head in acknowledgement. "Good afternoon, Comrade Dusan."

"It is still morning, Comrade. Good morning." There was another sharp click from the boots before he turned back to Popovic.

Skender sat down, the young cadet irritated him, and he felt suddenly tired and exhausted. He pulled himself together as he realized Popovic was speaking.

"…quite a rigorous training program. In a year, he will go to Sarajevo to train under Alex Kulich … you have met Alex, I believe?" Skender inclined his head. "He was another of my protégées…."

God in Heaven, what is happening to me? Am I going mad? I liked Kulich, enjoyed my evening with him! When Popovic asked if I liked Mihajlovich … can you like someone, even if you hate their lifestyle? Is it possible to like without trust or respect?

Skender let his eyes linger on the well-groomed man sitting opposite him.

If I had met you in a neutral country, at a luncheon, I would have enjoyed conversing, chatting, with you….

"You will excuse me, Mr. Berisha? This will not take long."

Skender smiled his dismissal of the request that was not a request.

I had always thought … before meeting you, or Mihajlovich, or Kulich … that you would be obvious, that your lust for power would show. I thought of you as low, ignorant, and bestial, that no man who had any decency would want to be in the same room as you.

He trembled as he realized the truth.

That is not so … you are all charming and courteous, would enliven any gathering. And that, that is the danger … you are so easily acceptable by society….

"I have a gift for Stefan … perhaps you will be kind enough to deliver it for me?" Popovic pulled a sheet of paper toward him, and the cadet handed him his pen with a flourish, as Skender inclined his head. "Thank you."

> *Stefan,*
> *Your action, or lack of it, almost brought you a transfer to a remote Serbian village. I find it hard to envisage Stefan Mihajlovich spending his remaining days with sheepherders.*
> *Be warned, Stefan, only my friendship and regard for you permits me to overlook this refractory. Do not keep me waiting for a file again.*
> *Promotion was imminent, but obedience is what brings advancement. As it seems so important to you, I will give you this Kosovar … let us say an early 'gift' for your birthday next month, shall we?*
> *Remember, Stefan, I tolerate no disobedience. I shall not warn again. Until the Conference.*
> *Popovic*

He folded the letter twice and slid it into an envelope, addressed it simply 'Stefan', and handed it to Dusan. "Apply my seal." Both he and Skender watched as the Cadet lit a taper and let the hot scarlet wax drip onto the back of the envelope. "It is Stefan's birthday next month … this is a gift from me. It will not inconvenience you to take it?"

"No, of course not, Comrade Colonel, but…" Skender hesitated, then continued, "…I thought you knew, Colonel, that Colonel Mihajlovich plans on coming to Belgrade next week."

"Yes. I do know, but this gift is…" he smiled, included the Cadet who smiled back, then continued, "…the gift is … er … perishable. I do not think it would last another week in Belgrade." He chuckled. "No, better it goes with you. It will also save you having a taste of Stefan's temper…." He misunderstood Skender's sudden stiffening. "No, no, Mr. Berisha … he is not angry with you. He is annoyed at the system." He accepted the sealed envelope from Dusan, passed it to Skender. "Here is my letter, the accompaniment will be given to you by Dusan. Good-bye, Mr. Berisha." He stood; hand extended. "Thank you again for coming to visit us and I wish you a pleasant journey." The handshake was a little longer this time, and then, as he released Skender's hand, he instructed Dusan, "Mr. Berisha is to have every assistance … escort him to the airport and see him safely aboard."

Skender panicked, "Comrade Colonel, it is not necessary…."

"I insist … it is the very least we can do."

Skender searched for an excuse. "My bags are at the hotel…."

"We are at your disposal, Mr. Berisha. Dusan will take you wherever you please. And now, again, good-bye." It was dismissal. Polite but firm.

"Good-bye Comrade Colonel."

The secretary smiled her good-bye, and Skender inclined his head as he followed Dusan into the hall.

"Have you been long with us, Mr. Berisha?"

"No. Not long." Skender did not want to pursue that line. "I do not know this uniform…." He let the sentence hang; the young aide was eager to educate him.

"It is the Corp of the Elite … we are specially chosen. They select only the best students, the best athletes. They are very particular…."

"They?"

"Udba, of course."

"Of course." Skender's voice held a touch of irony, then his hand encouraged the man to continue.

"After selection we are sent for two years of intensive military training; and, after graduation, each Director of Udba selects an aide. Comrade Colonel Popovic chose me." It was said smugly, and he looked expectantly at Skender.

"Congratulations."

"Thank you. The remainder are distributed to various other offices throughout Yugoslavia … call the lift." The order to the guard was sandwiched between his conversation with Skender. "With Nis taking priority. I have been with Comrade Popovic for one year…" his hand invited Skender to enter, both guards held the lift doors open, "…and then, after one more year, I will be sent to Comrade Kulich." He pushed the LGF button. "I am classified D4 … and you?"

Skender's eyes were glued to the lift buttons. "What? Oh…" He had no idea but did not intend to be the same or lower than this prig cadet, "I am C … one." He saw respect and awe mingle, and wondered if he had overdone it, but he had a more serious question. "Why did you press Lower Ground Floor? Was that a mistake?"

Dusan gave a long, slow smile. "No, Comrade Berisha…" Skender noted the upgrade he had received. Or was it sarcasm? "we are going to the basement … I rarely make mistakes. Please." His hand offered Skender the right of way as the doors slid open. White gloves held them back until they were clear.

This was different. Here was the heavy, oppressive atmosphere of fear. The cement floor rang with their steps, yet you could feel the silence from the rooms on each side of the passageway. No polished wood doors with neatly lettered names here, these were iron with one small peephole at eye level.

Skender wiped his sweaty palms on his slacks as they moved ahead, fear thumped in his head, reached down, dried his throat and lay quivering in his stomach. The guard sat at an old oak desk, rows of keys framing his head. He pushed himself to his feet, hands resting on the desk as they came closer. Skender saw that they had passed the need for shiny buttons and sharp creases. The beefy hands lay close to a heavy black rubber truncheon, its well-used appearance more terrifying than if it had been new. The guard opened the drawer of his desk as they stopped, pushed a paper toward Dusan and, without looking, reached and selected a key from those behind him. He checked Dusan's signature, put the paper back into his desk, then moved to one of the cells. Not a word had been spoken.

The key rasped as it was turned. Skender swallowed. Then he heard the grate of hinges as the door was opened. He wondered when Mihajlovich had found out about the missing files…. He stood stiffly, hands clenched as he waited for the truncheon to hit … *first behind the knees, and then across the shoulders….* Memory recalled the procedure for him.

"Comrade Berisha…"

Skender jumped. *Perhaps the beating would come later. Perhaps, now, they would just order me inside. Perhaps Mihajlovich had ordered me returned to….*

"…Comrade Berisha, your 'perishable'." There was amusement in Dusan's voice.

The shaking was hardly controllable, he had to force himself to turn toward the sound of the cadet's voice. The guard stood beside the open cell, key swinging on his first finger, while the leather strap of the truncheon swayed from his little finger. The man who stood beside him held his body slack, his shoulders rounded, and his chin rested on his chest. Skender recognized the stance. The man had been beaten. To stand upright was too painful, the muscles in the stomach did not want to tighten, the skin of his back could split and bleed again if he straightened his shoulders.

"Attention." The guard's truncheon gave a light tap behind the knees. There was a smothered groan as he sagged against the cell door.

Skender's hands clenched tighter. *Now*, he willed the prisoner, *come to attention, make those screaming muscles obey or….*

"Do you need another?" The truncheon slapped constantly into the guard's left hand as he lifted it and let it drop, lifted it, and let it drop. The prisoner forced himself to stand upright, his breathing fast and ragged at the effort. "Head up." The tip of the black rubber truncheon was a breath from the man's chin. The guard smiled. "That's better. Now … face your visitors." The truncheon encouraged the man to face Skender and Dusan.

Slowly, the young man turned toward them, the light from above the cell fell onto the young face. Skender gasped, felt for the desk needing support, he shook his head, knowing it was impossible, and made his eyes focus again. "Morat," he whispered. He felt himself slipping into blackness, and made an overpowering effort to speak, he could feel his lips forming the words, knew he was calling, "Morat, oh God, is it you, Morat?", yet could not hear above the thunderous sea in his head.

"Get a chair, get a chair…." Dusan yelled as he supported Skender's inert body. "And put that bloody prisoner back in his cell." The guards beside the elevator had come running when they saw the commotion. "You, get a cold cloth, and you … find some tea, hurry, hurry. What the hell happened? Why did he faint?" He pushed Skender's head down between his knees, wondering if he should report this strangeness to Popovic. "Give me the cloth, give me the cloth…." He laid it across the back of Skender's neck, decided not to report the matter in case he was held responsible in some way. "He was trying to speak. I saw his lips move, but…." He glanced up at the duty officer. "Did you hear what he said?"

"My concern is the prisoner, not some visitor from another province."

Dusan glared at the guard. "He is Udba, C-One … he could easily make it your business." He saw that Skender was stirring. "Are you feeling better, Comrade?" The tea arrived and Dusan pushed it to Skender's mouth. "Drink … it is hot and sweet and will help." He signaled the man who was supporting Skender to release him as he saw him start to straighten himself. "What caused you to faint, Comrade? What was the reason?"

Skender pulled the damp cloth from his neck and wiped his face and hands. "Where is he?"

"Who?" It was sharp.

Skender raised his head, the young face was concerned, but the blue eyes were watchful and curious. He let his eyes close, needing time, and took long, deep breaths.

"Do you mean the prisoner?" Skender nodded. "In his cell. Why?"

Skender drank some more of the tea. The cup was thick and it was disgustingly sweet. "Why did you bring me here? Why did you want me to meet … the prisoner?"

Dusan looked surprised. "That is the perishable! Comrade Popovic's gift to Colonel Mihajlovich" He gave a short laugh. "Did you not understand?"

Skender took a long drink of the tea. "Are you telling me that I am to … to escort this prisoner to Colonel Mihajlovich?"

"Yes." Dusan was suddenly suspicious. "He is a Kosovar … do you know him? Was he the cause of your weakness?"

"No. Of course not." Skender pushed himself to his feet. "I have a tendency to claustrophobia … you understand? Each of us has some weakness." He straightened his tie, brushed at his suit, hoping that the man would swallow his excuse. He gave a disarming smile. "But I would prefer this was not mentioned…" he let his eyes rise meaningfully to the ceiling, "let it be between us, eh?"

Dusan's face lit. "Of course, Comrade. And now, would you like to see the prisoner?" He motioned to the guard without waiting for an answer.

Skender steeled himself. Common sense told him it could not be Morat, there was only one explanation….

"Here is the prisoner, Comrade." The guard pushed the young man forward. Shall I cuff him?" He pulled the handcuffs from his pocket.

"Not yet," Dusan answered, his wary eyes not leaving Skender.

Skender cleared his throat, took one step toward the boy, "What is your name?"

There was a moment of silence, then the answer came in Albanian. "You know it. Perhaps not the first, but you do know who I am related to, don't you, *Comrade* Berisha?"

The insolence would have been heard, the language would not have been understood, but the tone would. Skender picked up the white gloves lying on the desk, slapped the boy hard across the mouth with them. "I advise you to answer, not make me repeat the question again. Now, what is your name?" He spoke softly and in Serbo-Croatian, as he willed the boy to answer.

The guard took a step forward and the boy's eyes slid toward him, then he looked Skender full in the face, answered proudly, "Deva, Mustafa. I am the youngest son of Chenan Deva. My oldest brother was Morat…."

"Enough!" Skender had to stop him. "I asked for your name, not the family tree. Apply the cuffs," he ordered the guard. "I have wasted enough time here. Are you coming, Dusan?" He strode down the hall, praying that Dusan would follow with Mustafa. The two guards came to attention as he approached and held open the doors of the lift. He let out a long breath as Dusan and Mustafa joined him, and the doors slid shut.

His problem had compounded itself, now he had two more, Dusan and Mustafa.

Chapter 56

The black Mercedes, coolly comfortable with all the windows closed and the air conditioning on, purred through Belgrade. Skender and Dusan sat in the back while Mustafa was sandwiched between a guard and the 'chauffeur'. He was dressed in the traditional navy-blue uniform with peaked cap, but his stance gave away his military training.

Skender's mind darted from one mad idea to the next, and he discarded each as unworkable. Dusan, with two years' military training under his belt, would be an excellent marksman, and even if he missed, there was still the guard. And the chauffer.

Skender's eyes strayed to Mustafa, the white bloodstained shirt recalling heartbreaking memories of Morat. *But you shall not have this one, Mihajlovich. Not if I can prevent it. I had to sit, helpless, while your predecessors beat his brother to a pulp … no. You shall not have this one.*

"I cannot take him on a plane like that." Skender gestured toward Mustafa's back. Dusan did not respond. "He needs a jacket…." *Oh, dear God, those were the same words Sabri had used when he begged for a jacket for Morat….* He pushed the ghosts of Sabri and Morat away. It was Mustafa he must concentrate on now. He leaned forward and spoke to the driver, "There is a department store just ahead … stop at it." The car slowed, slid to a halt. "Wait here." He sensed the objection about to come from Dusan and laid his hand on his shoulder as he confided, "Guard this Kosovar well … Colonel Mihajlovich would be most disappointed if his 'gift' was lost, or even delayed."

He chose carefully, a jacket, indistinguishable and commonplace, and not expensive. He hesitated, added a shirt and a pair of slacks, guessing at the size. "How much?" It would leave him sadly short of cash. If Mustafa were to make a break, he, too, would need money. A thought came. "Charge it to Udba, Pristina Office, Kosovo." He showed his authorization, signed the bill, added his identity number, snatched up the bag of clothes, and left before the clerk could question it.

"Proceed," he instructed the driver as he threw the clothes into Dusan's lap and added, "The prisoner can change in my hotel room."

"That is not wise, Comrade."

Skender ignored Dusan. Mustafa must have five minutes … ten if possible … in order to clear the immediate vicinity and lose himself among the crowds.

The car rolled to the steps of the Metropole. Dusan bristled, "Comrade Berisha, I must protest … this is most unwise…."

"Are you questioning my authority, Cadet?" Skender put gentle emphasis on the last word, opened his door and ordered the guard, "Bring him." Skender had remembered Mihajlovich's advice.

"You have caused a disturbance in a tourist hotel, Comrade Berisha." Dusan stood stiff with anger.

Skender gave a tight smile, "It will give the tourists something to write on their postcards."

They had caused quite a stir as they entered the hotel, Skender had strode straight through the lobby, up the stairs to his room pausing only long enough to claim his key at the desk. He had been followed by the bloody and disheveled prisoner, still handcuffed, with the guard closely following, pistol at the ready. Dusan had paused to offer half-hearted apologies to the gaping tourists and hotel employees.

"Give him the clothes and unshackle him." He turned to Mustafa. "The bathroom is there … clean yourself up and get changed." For one moment, he thought Mustafa was going to refuse.

"Leave the door open," Dusan ordered as Mustafa entered the bathroom. As a safeguard, he placed his foot against the door and watched Mustafa's every move. Skender ignored him and moved about the room collecting his things, packing them neatly and without haste as he saw Dusan's wary glances toward him. "He could have done this at Police Headquarters."

Skender stopped, placed his hand on the telephone. "Any more questioning of me or my authority, Dusan, and it will be you who will be escorted back to Headquarters … do we understand each other?"

Dusan's eyes slid away and he gave a sidelong glance toward the guard.

Mustafa's slow exit from the bathroom back into the bedroom broke the tension. "Ah, that is better." Skender nodded his approval. He was irritated when Dusan immediately re-applied the handcuffs but decided to let it pass.

Dusan held out the key, "You will need this, Comrade."

"Thank you." He watched as the guard silently ordered Mustafa to sit on the floor, then Skender moved to the bathroom, closed the door, and locked it.

He took out the slim white envelope, turned it over and studied the sealing wax. There was no way of tampering with it. He started to slip it back into his jacket pocket, then stopped, he had to know what Popovic had written to Mihajlovich. He had a deep conviction that it was important. He flushed the toilet and immediately ripped open the envelope, letting the rush of water drown the sound of the tearing paper. He smoothed out the letter, the crest as blood on the white bond. Popovic's handwriting was flowery, but easily read.

Skender sat on the edge of the bath, he was shaking, even his insides trembled, as he acknowledged that Mihajlovich must now know that his files had been tampered with. He searched for a reason why Mihajlovich had not had him arrested, with the resources at his disposal, he could easily have had him arrested the moment he set foot in Udba this morning. *Think, damn you, think. Think like Mihajlovich. Now, what reason would I have (as Mihajlovich) to leave Skender Berisha running around free…?*

He re-read the letter, at the same time turning on the tap, letting the water run as a precaution against the guard or Dusan becoming suspicious of the time he had spent in the bathroom. The answer leapt at him, *Of course! Mihajlovich would want me for himself. Would not deny himself the pleasure of seeing me dragged through hell and back. If he had called Belgrade and had me arrested, I would be Popovic's prisoner.*

He caught his breath as another reason asserted itself, *If Popovic had me, Mihajlovich would be in danger. I have no reason to be silent, would let my tongue wag freely. Mihajlovich will go to great lengths to keep Popovic ignorant that all the files have been destroyed.* Skender turned off the tap. *Yes, Mihajlovich cannot, dare not, let me speak to Popovic … he must have me in Prishtine so that he can have his pleasure at my agony and so that he can cover himself, lay the blame on someone else's shoulders….* He slid the letter into the envelope and slipped it into his pocket.

"Are you ready to leave now, Comrade Berisha?" Dusan rose from his position on the edge of the bed as Skender opened the door of the bathroom.

Skender looked at the telephone. He would be better off in the hell-hole he'd just left than to return to Mihajlovich. He wondered if, by going to Popovic and confessing everything, he would be able to divert his anger. His hand reached toward the phone … at least, this way, he would be able to bring Mihajlovich down with him. The black instrument felt cold to his touch. There was a smothered groan as Mustafa shifted his position.

'This gift is perishable … I do not think it would last another week in Belgrade.'

Skender did not move, he could not sentence Mustafa to certain death. "Yes, Dusan, let's go. He left the bag for the cadet to carry.

Prishtine, Kosov

Mihajlovich stood by the window, his eyes searching the sky as if he expected to see the plane appear. He had sent his own car with a sergeant and one guard to the airport to pick up Berisha, he had told them nothing.

He had toyed with the idea of going himself, had wanted to confront Berisha at the earliest opportunity, but the pleasure he would receive at having Berisha walk in to him willing and unsuspecting was too great to be ignored.

There was a knock. "Come in." Mihajlovich did not move, knowing it was Dragonovich. "Not long, now."

Dragonovich checked the clock. "He will be in our basement in less than an hour."

Mihajlovich nodded, "Yes. I know." He half-turned. "Anna?"

"She has confessed … it is being typed now. However…" Dragonovich hesitated, not sure if he should bother to mention the rest, but already Mihajlovich's eyes were alert, inquisitive, "she had never been with Berisha. Or any other."

Mihajlovich shrugged, "It is of no matter. It is Berisha I want. And intend to have." He turned back to face the window, his voice softly vicious as he murmured, "Take your last look at daylight, Berisha. Enjoy the sun and the breeze on your face for the last time. Your eyes, and your mind … that is what I intend to have." He gave a nod of satisfaction, picked up the Berisha file, "Your eyes, and your mind."

Belgrade, Serbia

The office of the Airport Director was hot, stuffy, and crowded. Skender sat opposite the nervous Director, with Dusan on his right. Mustafa had been ordered to sit on the floor, and the guard stood close by, his pistol now in his holster, but the flap open and ready. The chauffeur stood beside the door, alert and almost at attention. A middle-aged woman who had been introduced as the Director's secretary sat on the edge of her typing chair, her eyes wide and frightened, making no attempt to finish her work.

"How much longer?" Skender demanded. He was irritable and nervous. There had been no opportunity for Mustafa, or himself, to make an escape, all five had been together since their departure from the Hotel Metropole.

The Director shuffled his papers, "Fifteen, or perhaps, twenty-five minutes, Comrade."

"In other words, the plane will not arrive for another half-hour … why don't you say so, instead of trying to placate me with twenty-five minutes." Skender stood up, "Your plane, Comrade Director, is going to be an hour late … why is that?"

The Director gave a nervous laugh. "It is not my plane, Comrade, and the flight does not originate in Belgrade; therefore, I cannot be held responsible…." He broke off as Skender turned his back and went to the windows, then appealed to Dusan. "It is not my fault; you cannot blame me…."

Dusan's fingers snapped, ordering the man to silence. He was hot and tired and could not care less who was blamed for the delay, he gave a malevolent glare at Skender's back. He had not even had sense enough to order lunch for them. He had come to the rather glum conclusion that Udba would not be so pleasant once he was sent from Head Office into the field.

Skender leaned his forehead against the window. It looked out over the whole runway, and he let his glance roam over the planes arriving and waiting to depart. He had had to sit and listen to the announcement that the BEA flight to London was now boarding passengers, he had watched the happy holidaymakers climbing the metal steps, entering the white bird that should have been carrying him to freedom. He had continued to watch as it taxied the runway, gathered speed, and lifted. The sun had silvered it to beauty as it climbed, and then dark despair had washed over him. It was then that he had made his decision. He would not return to Mihajlovich, he would wait until the last moment, and then, as they neared the steps of the plane, he would run. He prayed that the shots would kill him. A quick death would be a blessing, a release that Mihajlovich would not permit him. Mihajlovich would inflict pain so excruciating that it would jelly his mind. And then he would return him to Babush, a living reminder for others who might think to defy him. As for Mustafa, he would warn him that there would be a disturbance and advise him to try and make a break then. There was nothing more he could do.

"Which airline is this?"

The Director moved toward the window, nervously fiddling with his tie, "Which, Comrade? The blue?" Skender gave a brief nod. "Greek, Comrade." His finger pointed. "That, the red and white, is Russian, and the other, next to it, Swiss … the one coming in…" he picked up a pair of binoculars from the window-sill, "Scandinavian."

"Wonderful! Every nationality here but our own!" Skender said sourly. He saw Dusan look at his watch. "I have told you it is not necessary to wait." It had been his only hope. If Dusan and the guard left, there might be a chance.

"Comrade Popovic's instructions were explicit, Comrade Berisha … I am to devote myself to your comfort until your departure."

Skender gave a slight bow, turned back to the window with a sigh. There was no getting rid of them.

"The Pristina flight, Comrade … arriving now." The Director was excited, and his finger shook as he pointed. "Moments, Comrade, just moments, and then you will be on your way. You have been so patient, so…."

"Shut your mouth," Skender chewed at his knuckles, then took the handcuff key from his pocket and threw it to the guard. "Unlock them." He heard Dusan's gasp and turned to him. "You do not expect me to take a handcuffed man on the plane, do you?" He sensed the objection about to come. "The flight continues from Pristina to Budva … a coastal town, Comrade Dusan, which means there will be holidaymakers aboard. Do you want our precious tourists to have something more to complain of?" He turned his back.

"Comrade."

He took the handcuffs and key without turning to the guard. A germ of an idea was beginning to grow. It was wild, reckless, crazy….

"Move." He waved the Director away from the comfortable chair and sat down, pulling open one of the drawers. "Where is your paper? I wish to write a note to Colonel Popovic." He glanced up as the secretary handed him one sheet, sarcastically said, "Thank you … I will try not to make a mistake." She hesitated, then nervously laid another piece of paper beside his hand. He swung the chair to the right, deliberately blocking Dusan's view of what he would write.

> *Colonel Popovic,*
> *The file you requested from Pristina would never have been forthcoming. If you doubt my words, request another file … the name is immaterial, any common Kosovar name will suffice … invent one, even. If a file does arrive, it will have been manufactured for your benefit. But a careful check, quietly done, by the Belgrade Office, will bring the truth.*
> *Have you never questioned why Pristina is such a hotbed (your words, Colonel) … Kosovo such a difficult autonomy to administer? One man, with the help of his Police Department, has fanned a flame of dissent into a fire of hatred and rebellion.*
> *Your trust in Mihajlovich is misplaced … your friendship smeared. Ambition and greed reach UPWARD, Colonel Popovic. I respectfully suggest you exercise caution.*

He did not want to sign it, so he put his initials. He wondered if Popovic would dismiss the letter, ignore it.

"May I have an envelope, please?" He folded the letter and slipped it inside the envelope handed to him by the secretary, then closed it, and added the name to the front. He offered it to Dusan. "Please give this to Colonel Popovic as soon as you return to Udba."

It was as Dusan's hand took the letter that he knew it would have the desired effect. Popovic would not believe it at first, but the worm of doubt would have been sown. Popovic was a shrewd and careful man, he would test Mihajlovich. Skender hoped it would be soon … the thought that Mihajlovich and Dragonovich could be removed from Prishtine was intoxicating.

"There is no seal on this, Comrade Berisha."

Skender had no seal. He gave a disarming smile. "There is no need, Comrade Dusan … I have placed it personally in your hands. Your honor is beyond question."

Dusan leapt from the chair, came to attention with the inevitable click of the boots, pride glowed from him. Skender turned away, his smile deepening. Popovic had made a mistake with this one. He was not the caliber of Mihajlovich and Kulich.

"You can board now, Comrade," the Director fussed around.

"Let everyone else board first … we shall be the last. You have reserved seats for us?" His excitement had ebbed, he wished he could call Jill … just in case his plan failed.

"Of course, Comrade, you are in the better seats."

Skender gave an ironic smile. No more first- and second-class, Communist doctrine did not permit it, now there were 'better seats'.

"They are all aboard now, Comrade." The Director reached for Skender's hand, pumping it with enthusiasm, he would be glad to see the back of them. "I wish you a pleasant journey."

"Your good-byes are premature, Comrade Director, you will escort us to the Departure Lounge." Skender spoke smoothly, then made one last effort to get rid of Dusan. "Shall we say our good-byes here, Comrade Dusan?" He extended his hand.

Dusan shook hands warmly with Skender. "As Comrades, yes, but I shall take you right to the plane." He gave a meaningful look at Mustafa. "I do not want you to have any trouble."

Skender inclined his head.

The private staircase from the Director's office took them straight to the Departure Lounge, and the airport official opened the gate without hesitation as he saw the two Udba identification cards. "Wait here until the plane departs," Skender ordered the Director.

Dusan walked beside Skender, chatting amiably about hoping to visit Pristina in the near future. Mustafa walked a pace behind, the guard beside him, pistol now drawn, and the chauffeur followed. They paused at the foot of the metal steps.

"Take the prisoner and put him in his seat," Skender ordered the chauffeur. The guard took a pace forward. "No, not you. Your uniform might cause some panic … and put that damned gun away." He glanced around as Mustafa and the chauffeur climbed the steps. There was no cover, nowhere to go, yet he felt no panic, it was as if he had stepped outside of his body, was floating, watching it all happen. The chauffeur reappeared at the top of the steps and gave a nod, letting them know that the prisoner was safely aboard the plane.

"It is time for us to say good-bye again, Comrade Berisha. I will call Colonel Mihajlovich for you the moment I return to Udba, then he will know when to expect you." Skender gave a grim smile. "Is there any message?"

Skender shook his head. "No, no message. Good-bye, Comrade Dusan." He started toward the metal steps as Dusan and the guard snapped to attention and saluted, then turned back to Dusan as a thought came to him. "Keep our secret, Comrade … not even a murmur about the … er … 'gift' for Colonel Mihajlovich from Colonel Popovic."

"Not a word, not a breath, Comrade Berisha."

Skender sighed. Dusan was wearing on the nerves. He climbed the steps, saw that the flight steward was watching with wary eyes, he had witnessed the scene at the bottom of the steps. All to the good, the more important he, Skender, appeared, the better.

"The prisoner is on the right, third aisle, Comrade." Skender gave a brief nod of dismissal, the chauffeur touched his cap respectfully, then moved out of the plane and down the steps.

"Do not close the door," Skender ordered. The steward opened his mouth to object, then closed it at Skender's supercilious smile and cold appraisal. The flash of scarlet on the card was hardly necessary.

"Mustafa," Skender sat down beside him, "Listen to me." Mustafa continued to look out of the small window, ignoring Skender. "Listen to me, dammit." Mustafa turned his head toward Skender, eyes cold and distant. "Pay close attention. There is no time for questions or repeats. I have sabotaged all of Mihajlovich's files. He has no records for any of you. Pass that along. Let all in Prishtine know." It gave him some comfort to see the incredulous stare.

"Mihajlovich has found out, and now awaits my return, but…" he gave a grim smile, "…but that is my problem. Now to yours. Police Headquarters and Udba in Prishtine are ignorant of the fact that you are on this plane. They are under the impression that you are tucked safely away in Udba's basement here in Belgrade. But Mihajlovich is expecting me, and he knows that I've betrayed him, so there will be a reception committee when this plane reaches Prishtine. Do you think the police will recognize you?"

"I don't know. Perhaps. They have had me once … no, two times."

Skender swiftly appraised the clothes. "The odds are against it. You could pass as a Serb. Do not be the first off, nor the last. Stay close to a group, a family. Be careful how you move, how you carry yourself. They must not suspect that you have been beaten. Do not think of going to any of your friends, and stay away from your family, for they will be watched. Get out of the Prishtine area as soon as you can." He gave Mustafa a handful of money, then held out his hand. "God be with you."

"And with you." It was an automatic response. And then Mustafa said wonderingly, "But I, we all, thought you were … thought you had switched sides, were now our enemy."

"I was your brother's friend … that should answer you. Good luck."

Skender stood and threaded his way back to the door and the anxious steward. He took a long breath, now was his greatest danger. He stepped out onto the metal steps in time to see the three backs rounding the corner of the airport building. Dusan had gone straight to the car. "You may order the steps removed and depart now." He felt jubilant, cocky. "Have a good flight." He clattered down, his eyes searching anxiously for the Director. He half-ran across the tarmac, his excitement melting into fear as he realized that the man had gone.

"Let me through," he ordered the official as he flashed his Udba card. He crossed to the private staircase, took the steps two at a time. He did not knock, but flung the door open, and crossed to the Director's desk in a stride. "I told you to wait," he shouted as he grabbed at the man's tie and hauled him to his feet. "Did you not hear my order?"

"Yes, Comrade, but I thought…."

"You are not paid to think!" Skender's eyes swept the tarmac, the Russian plane still stood at the bay, waiting to load, the Scandinavian next to it. The Swiss stood farther out; the mechanics were starting to pull the steps away. He released his hold on the man. "Call that plane…" his finger pointed, "and tell them to wait. They have one more passenger."

The Director followed the line of Skender's finger, his eyes bulged. "It is impossible … I cannot … it is already being made ready, the steps have gone, the door is closed…."

"Call and stop it." Skender picked up the phone, the man's hand moved, faltered. Skender pushed it closer to the man until it was under his nose. "Stop the Swiss plane, or you will be the one making a journey, Comrade Director – to my basement."

The Director's hand shook as he took the phone. He gave a nervous glance at his secretary, who sat, turned to stone, hands lying motionless on the keyboard of the typewriter.

Skender gave a cruel smile, "She will go, too," he added softly, "and your wife, your children…."

He was no longer Skender Berisha, he was Stefan Mihajlovich.

The button was pushed. "Control Tower? This is Director Radanovich. Hold the Swiss flight, there is one more passenger." Skender heard the crackle of argument. "I order you to hold that plane." The Director's nerve was returning, he covered the mouthpiece, "How can you take an International Flight? You need a passport…." The words died on his lips, his face whitened, as he glanced down and saw the American passport. His eyes lifted slowly to Skender's. "Pardon, Comrade, you must be very important to carry that." Skender looked steadily back at him and did not reply.

The Director uncovered the mouthpiece. "Taxi that plane back to the terminal and be prepared to board an Ud…."

Skender's hand shot out and covered the mouthpiece, then he put his finger to his lips.

The Director covered the mouthpiece, whispered, "I understand. Be prepared to board an American." His fingers flipped through the passport as the angry crackle sounded again. Director Radanovich smiled; he had found a reason for his actions. "The American's visa has run out. He must be deported immediately." He smiled as he returned the passport to Skender and put down the phone. "Most clever, Comrade … I was under the impression you were to take the Pristina flight."

"You were meant to think so, as was the young cadet." Skender put the passport into his inside jacket pocket. He had to be sure that they had cleared Yugoslav airspace before Udba learned of his whereabouts. "And he must continue to think so, at least for a short while."

His hand moved toward the phone, and then he glanced up at the Director as if undecided, "I can rely on your discretion…" his glance included the woman, "it is not necessary for me to have you … er … 'isolated'?"

"No, no, Comrade. Not a word from me. If anyone asks, I will tell them you are on the flight to Pristina."

Skender nodded his agreement, then glanced at the woman, who nodded vigorously. "Good, excellent." The Swiss plane was directly below the Director's window. "Then shall we go? I am most anxious to be on my way."

Chapter 57

Skender paused, dropped the pile of small envelopes into the mouth of the fat, round, scarlet pillar box. He liked them, often had an absurd notion to put his arms around one. The bell tinkled a warning as he opened the door of the tiny shop that also acted as a Sub Post Office. They amused him these little oases of officialdom, that were tucked away on side streets, and he used them more than the main Post Office in the center of town. They were always a hub of activity, local gossip was exchanged, complaints made about the weather, the government, and the bus service. Children gazed round-eyed at the assortment of sweets and chocolates before parting with their pennies.

"Morning." The middle-aged man looked up with a smile, "Won't be a jiff, mate, just want to look after me regular here." He sent a solemn wink toward Skender as he took the few pennies from a child and handed him his bag of sweets. "What'll it be, then?"

"I have to send a telegram."

The fellow pulled out one of the forms. "Shoot, mate." He scribbled on the edge of the paper to make sure the pen was working.

"Shoot?" Skender questioned.

"Yes … tell us what you want us to write."

Skender smiled. *These London expressions! The plural substituted for the singular! It was like re-learning the language.* "I think I had better write it myself … it is another language." He took the form and moved to the flat section of the counter.

"How's the missus, then?"

"Very well, thank you." Skender smiled to himself. He would never get used to his Jill being 'the missus'. He started to write.…

Babush's head lifted from his reading of the newspaper as he heard the gate. He stood and moved down the path. The pale buff envelope from the Post Office was in his hand as he returned to Nona who sat beside the last of her dahlias, the night frosts had taken most of them, but a few still blazed in glory. He sat down, "It is a telegram from Skender."

Nona watched as he ripped the envelope, her hand clasping her chest. Babush read through, then smiled up at her. "Listen…."

Two cultures have touched, blended, and made a new.

He glanced up. "Those were almost my words to him when she first entered this house." His eyes went again to the paper in his hand.

I proudly ask a blessing for my son, and respectfully ask you, Babush, for his name. Gillian and I are well and send our love.

He wiped his tears, "It is signed, 'Skender'. Well, wife, what do you say to this news?" His voice shook with emotion. Nona did not answer, she was looking at her fingers. Her lips moved, but no sound came, and he prompted, "Well, what name shall we give this child?"

She was laughing and crying as she answered him, "Choose a happy name. A Kosovar name."

A shadow crossed Babush's face, "Kosovar? The child was born in England."

Nona smiled, enjoyed her secret a moment longer, then reached and took hold of her husband's hand. Her eyes lifted to the window above their heads, "He started his life here, in this house, in that room…" she nodded as Babush's eyes questioned her, "the seed was planted here, husband. The child is a Kosovar."

Babush squeezed both her hands in his, his happiness almost too great to bear, "May his life be as long as the mountains with snow on them."

"Amen to that," she whispered. Her eyes searched her husband's, "Will we ever see him?"

Did she mean her own son, or this new child? Babush did not know. He put his arms around her, held her close to his chest, "He is a Kosovar! Could he stay away from this land?"

Author's Note

This novel began as a two-page project about someone who had a profound influence upon me. It took over my life.

For the encouragement of family and friends, thank you.

Against overwhelming adversity by those in control, The Kosovars, with great dignity, have maintained love of their country and culture. It is a story of a proud and honorable people.

Glossary of Albanian Words

The Albanian language falls under the Indo-European group of languages. The Albanian language has no sister language(s); however, there are two main Albanian dialects: the Gheg dialect spoken in the north – throughout Kosova; and the Tosk dialect, spoken in the region located south of the Shkumbin River.

Words and phrases used in Quiet Bravery are:

Babush (bä bush)	Father
Besa (bā sä)	An unbreakable pledge of honor
Djathë (dē yath)	Local cheese
Djali (dē ä lē)	Son
Laknor (läk nür)	Traditional filo dough dish
Mirëmëngjes (mir men jes)	Good Morning
Mirëmbrëma (mir em bro ma)	Good Evening
Midge (mij)	Uncle
Nona (nō nä)	Mother
Natën e mire (nä tan ä mir)	Good Night
Nusé (nü se)	Bride
Te faleminderit (tā fäl e min der it)	Thank you
Ulu këtu (ü lü ke too)	Sit Here

Also by P. A. Varley

Enemy?

A Four-Sided Triangle

All My Yesterdays

Quiet Bravery Cover Photo by P. A. Varley

Made in the USA
Middletown, DE
01 March 2023

25849161R00305